PHILIPPINE SHORT STORIES: 1941-1955

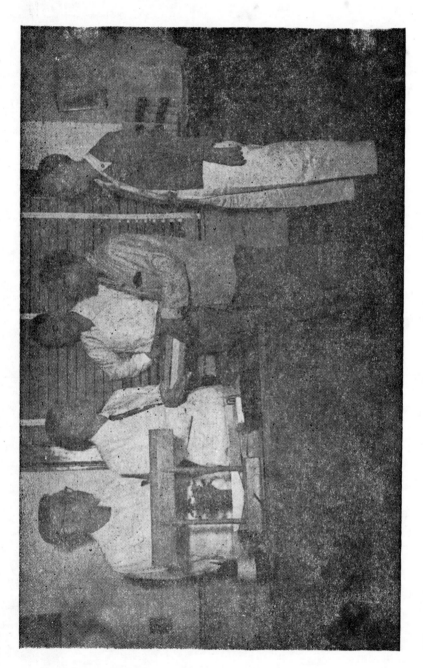

Director Eulogio B. Rodriguez of the Bureau of Public Libraries (now The National Library) receives the manuscripts of Carlos Bulosan from Aurelio Bulosan (brother) as Federico Mangahas (center), Guillermo V. Sison (extreme right), and Leopoldo Y. Yabes (extreme left) look on. (Malacañang, Manila, March 5. 1948).

PHILIPPINE SHORT STORIES 1941-1955

Part I (1941-1949)

Selected and Edited
with a Critical Introduction
by
LEOPOLDO Y. YABES

Copyright 1981 by Leopoldo Y. Yabes

ISBN 0-8248-030-0

Printed in the Philippines by the University of the Philippines Press

University of the Philippines Press
Quezon City, Philippines
1981

Copyright 1981 by Leopoldo Y. Yabes

ISBN 0–8248–0650–6

Printed in the Philippines by the University of the Philippines Press

Dedicated to

the Memory of

Manuel E. Arguilla

Antonio O. Bayot

Amador T. Daguio

Tobias Y. Enverga

Esteban Javellana

Juan Cabrero Laya

I. V. Mallari

J. Villa Panganiban

Cornelio S. Reyes

Isabelo Tupas

Jimena Austria Manalo

Carlos Bulosan

Fausto Dugenio

Salvador Faustino

Paz M. Latorena

Alfredo Elfren Litiatco

Hernando R. Ocampo

Conrado V. Pedroche

Clemente M. Roxas

Lydia Villanueva Arguilla

ARTISTS OF THE WRITTEN WORD

SOME OF WHOSE STORIES ARE VALUED

CONTRIBUTIONS TO THE ANTHOLOGIES

Philippine Short Stories: 1925–1940

Philippine Short Stories: 1941–1955

PREFACE

The present anthology, *Philippine Short Stories: 1941-1955*, is a sequel to *Philippine Short Stories: 1925-1940*, which came out in 1975. It contains stories, as in the first volume, which were originally written in English by Filipinos, and all published originally, with one exception, in Philippine periodicals during the period 1941-1955.

This collection contains more than twice as many stories as the first volume and is published in two parts. Part I contains the stories published in 1941-1949 and Part II the stories published in 1950-1955. An important story could not be included in Part I: "The Automobile Comes to Town,"* title story of a collection by Consorcio Borje, which won the main short story award in the 1941 Commonwealth Literary Contests. It was serialized in *Graphic* in 11 December 1941 – 1 January 1942. The author does not have a copy of his title story, and no person has been found to possess copies of the issues of the *Graphic* immediately before the occupation of Manila by the Japanese invasion forces.

A last minute decision excluded Estrella Alfon's significant story, "Fairy Tale for the City," from Part II. It was published in April 1955 in *This Week*, Sunday magazine of *The Manila Chronicle*, and is one of the author's most important stories. However, it became the subject of litigation in court brought against the author and the editor of the magazine, who were found guilty of publishing pornography and fined. The author did not include it in her short story collection, *Magnificence and Other Stories*, published in 1960; but it is hoped that with

---

* This long story has been listed as a novel by some critics. See Joseph Galdon, *The Philippine Novel in English* (Quezon City: Ateneo de Manila University Press, 1979), and Abdul Majid bin Nabi Baksh, *The Filipino Novel in English* (Quezon City: U.P., 1970).

the passage of time, the author will deem it wise to include it in her next volume of stories. In any serious study of Philippine literature, particularly the short story, "Fairy Tale for the City" cannot be ignored for it presents a courageous attempt at writing of things ordinary writers shy away from. It marked a milestone in the Filipino struggle for freedom of the mind and of the spirit.

The fifteen-year period covered by this anthology constitutes a most critical era in the history of the nation—war and Japanese occupation, restoration of the Commonwealth government in Manila, proclamation of independence, birth of the Republic, euphoria and disenchantment. The stories deal with various aspects of Philippine life all over the land—in Luzon, the Visayas, and Mindanao. Many of the stories deal with the war and enemy occupation—a few published in the Japanese-controlled press during the occupation, but more than nine-tenths after the war when the Japanese forces had been driven out.

In an effort to focus attention on life during and as a result of war and enemy occupation, the war stories may not be of an evenly high quality, since many of the pieces were written at very close range and therefore without the aesthetic distance desirable for artistic composition. More of the better written stories about the war and Japanese occupation were published after 1955, but they were not included here because they are beyond the time range of this anthology.

Like the anthology covering the period 1925-1940, the present is a combined historico-critical anthology. It is historical in the sense that the stories were arranged according to the date of original publication, and it is critical in the sense that the critical values were considered in the selection of pieces. Part I covers the immediate pre-war, war-time, liberation, and post-war years—1941-1949—a decade of unprecedented strife in the life of the nation. Part II covers the second half of the decade following the proclamation of independence and the establishment of the Republic (1950-1955), when there was tremendous effort at recovery from paralysis and struggle for survival and greater integrity.

An interesting feature of this anthology, which is not found in that covering the period 1925-1940, is the presence of stories set in foreign lands with Filipinos as main characters. This reflects the widening of the horizons of Filipino experience. Of course there are now more stories than in the first volume, with a Philippine setting with Filipinos and foreigners interacting as characters. This clearly means the increased interaction between Filipinos and other peoples as a result of war, independence, and international relations.

It is also interesting to note that the biggest number of selections included in this anthology were originally published in the pages of three periodicals which were later to be closed down by the martial law administration, namely: *Philippines Free Press, Sunday Times Magazine* and *This Week* (Sunday magazine of *The Manila Chronicle*). These three publications contributed greatly to the development of Philippine literature before the Martial Law Era.

Written exclusively by Filipinos, the stories reflect the ability of the Filipino writer in the use of a foreign language as a literary medium, after four decades from the introduction of English into the school system in 1901. It is claimed by competent critics that by 1955, the achievement in the Filipino short story in English had been more distinguished than the achievement in the Filipino short story in Spanish, in Tagalog, or in any other native language. It is further claimed that the present collection is more truly national than any similar anthology that could be collected of stories originally written in Pilipino or in any other native language or in Spanish. This collection has a wider geographical, ethnic, or social range than any other anthology.

This volume then could be an answer to those who believe that to be nationalistic one must write in Pilipino. It has been pointed out, correctly, that nationalism is in what a writer writes, not in what language he writes it.

Gotten out in two parts for a total of some 1,400 pages, this work definitely is, in the history of Philippine publishing, the most important collection of modern short stories ever gathered together between the covers of a book. The University of the Philippines Press therefore should be congratulated for undertaking a job the significance of which may be appreciated properly only with the passing of the years. No publisher whose interests are mainly commercial, may have the courage to undertake this kind of publication, which may not give any satisfactory material return for investment.

Thanks are due particularly to Professor Luis Beltran, acting director of the Press; to Mr. Renato L. Correa, chief of the editorial section, and to Ms. Nelia Lopez-Gahol and Ms. Maribel P. Lasala, editorial assistants; to Mrs. Pilar E. Tongson, chief of promotion section; to Ms. Lourdes Miralles, chief of production section; to Mr. Luis Manalo, chief, bindery section; and to Mr. Venancio Caguimbal, letter-press section supervisor. As editor of publications of the College of Arts and Sciences and the Graduate School over the years, I have worked with the personnel of the U.P. Press and am deeply thankful for their cooperation.

LEOPOLDO Y. YABES

Quezon City
12 June 1981

TABLE OF CONTENTS

THE PHILIPPINE SHORT STORY IN AN AGE OF TURBULENCE: 1941-1955

LEOPOLDO Y. YABES

The Historical Situation

During the Presidential and Legislative elections and inauguration of the Commonwealth of the Philippines toward the later part of 1935, war clouds were already gathering thick over East Asia and Europe. Militarist Japan had seized Manchuria from China and under the name Manchukuo set it up as a puppet state (1931-1945); Mussolini had established a predatory fascist regime in Italy which was making war on Emperor Haile Selassie of Abyssinia/Ethiopia; and Hitler had just seized power from a wobbly Weimar Republic. In 1936 Francisco Franco and his phalangists rose up in arms against the Spanish Republican government; and in 1937 Japan launched its armed adventure into the eastern hinterlands of the China mainland. In 1938 Hitler's armies drove into the Sudetenland, thus dismembering Czechoslovakia; and in 1939 came the invasion and partition of Poland between Nazi Germany and the Soviet Union after Hitler and Stalin had entered into a non-aggression pact. This was the immediate beginning of World War II.

All of these events were reported faithfully in the local press from international and other news services. But except for the threat posed by the presence of the followers of Franco among the Spanish community in Manila as well as of scattered propagandists and partisans of Japan, the local population as a whole was complacent. General Douglas MacArthur and Major Dwight Eisenhower had been asked by Commonwealth President Manuel L. Quezon to train a citizen army for the defense of the Philippines against a possible external aggression.

Until the end of the ten-year period of transition toward independence in July 1946, the defense of the country was still the responsibility of the colonial master.

It was not until the lightning conquest of the Low Countries and France in the spring of 1940 by Hitler's juggernaut and the subsequent moves by Japanese forces in French Indo-China and Thailand that the Filipinos became really worried. After the conquest of France, events happened fast. The United States decided to help the United Kingdom by arming the convoys that plied between the beleaguered island kingdom and the North American continent. Against the expectation of most people, the real explosion that brought the Philippines into the vortex of war was the Japanese attack on Pearl Harbor on December 8, 1941 and simultaneous raids on selected targets in the Philippines. In less than a month after Pearl Harbor, Manila was occupied by the invasion forces, and the agony of Bataan and Corregidor followed in the next four months and of the Death March to Capas in April and May.

Then came the three-year enemy occupation (1942-1945), which has been extensively written up in history and social science books. The Japanese Military Administration established the Philippine Executive Commission to replace the Commonwealth government, whose heads, President Quezon and Vice-President Osmeña, were given protection in Corregidor and later were invited to Washington, D.C., before the enemy's final assault on Bataan. Then came persistent propaganda of the Greater East Asia Co-Prosperity Sphere, one of whose fruits was the establishment of the Japanese-sponsored Philippine Republic in October 1943. The Allied counter-offensive, which began late in 1942, reached the Philippines in October 1944, and with the aid of the guerrillas reconquered the Philippines in less than a year. The Commonwealth government was restored in Malacañan in February 1945, with Osmeña as President, Quezon having died in the United States in August 1944. The Battle of Manila lasted almost a month and reduced most of the city to rubble and ashes, making Manila the worst devastated city in Asia, second only to Warsaw in Europe. Except for the church and monastery of San Agustin, which were not seriously damaged, the whole of the Walled City was almost thoroughly destroyed. The country also suffered widespread destruction in the wake of the liberation, as it had suffered during the Japanese invasion and the guerrilla campaigns.

Although down, the Filipino people reaffirmed their desire for independence on the scheduled date, July 4, 1946, on which date United States President Harry S. Truman issued a proclamation recognizing the independence of the Philippines.

The foreign invader was driven out, and the independence lost in 1899 was regained, but the turbulent years were to continue beyond the decade after independence. War and enemy occupation had been a blight on the life of the nation, and the struggle for freedom was still to continue for quite a while to come—even onto these days.

What was sad for many thinking Filipinos to contemplate was the fact that while the United States had emerged from World War II as the supreme military and economic power on this planet, the Philippines, which had remained a loyal ally throughout the war, was reeling in economic morass and confronted with internal dissension. Although it was one of the original members of the United Nations Organization which signed the United Nations Charter even before it became independent, it was not represented in the ceremonies marking the official surrender of Japan to the Allied Nations. For the American people the best years were the half-dozen years (1945-1950) following the end of the war, when they experienced a life of unprecedented abundance and high expectations for the future.[1] For the Filipinos, what was open for them was to strike out for themselves and make the best out of a bad situation.

The Time As Reflected in Short Fiction

After flourishing for a few years before the outbreak of the war in the Pacific, mainly as a result of the Commonwealth Literary Contests, sponsored by the Philippine Writers League and conducted by the Office of the President of the Commonwealth, the short story in English totally disappeared during the year (1942) of the battles of Bataan and Corregidor and the Death March to Capas. The year 1940 saw the publication of a volume of short stories by Manuel E. Arguilla, *How My*

[1] Joseph C. Goulden, *The Best Years: 1945-1950* (New York: Atheneum, 1976).

Brother Leon Brought Home a Wife and Other Stories,[2] which won the award in the short story. The volume included "Caps and Lower Case," a story published early that year. This story may turn out to be among the most distinguished stories by Arguilla and one of the few great short stories published before the war. That year and 1941 also saw the appearance of a young writer, Nick Joaquin, who was to win recognition in the years following as a gifted writer of fiction as well as of drama, poetry, and the essay. His "Three Generations" came out in 1940 and "After the Picnic" was published in 1941. In the literary contests for 1941, the winning work was "The Automobile Comes to Town," a collection of stories by Consorcio Borje. The title story, which was published in a weekly[3] in the week preceding the Japanese occupation of Manila, is one of the best stories written by Borje, making him an exponent of progress. A fellow writer has said Borje must also have foreseen the coming of the military jeep as an important converted civilian transport in the life of the common people.

The war and enemy occupation was a searing experience to most of the people. In the extent of the devastation wrought in the people's lives, the social convulsion that exploded around the end of the last and beginning of the present century cannot compare with the Japanese occupation of the country. There were atrocities committed by the American invasion forces against the civilian population, but maybe because they professed a common religion, Christianity, these were not as vicious or as pervasive as those suffered from the Japanese who professed Shintoism, a national religious cult which exalts the Japanese above all other peoples and glorifies war as a justifiable instrument of the national will.

Of the stories dealing with life in the few months immediately preceding the outbreak of hostilities in December 1941, two stand out preeminently for their lucidity and craftsmanship: "It Was Later Than We Thought," by Nick Joaquin and "All Over the World," by Vicente Rivera, Jr. In the first story there is just a slight hint of a war that would break out soon; as a matter of fact it ends with a diary note dated December 7, 1941. The second story begins with action as early

[2] Manila: Philippine Book Guild, 1940.
[3] *Graphic*, December 11, 18, 25, 1941—January 1, 1942.

as August 1941 and ends with the first few days of the war. People were expecting that if there were to be war at all, it would not come until the following spring, or four or five months after the actual start of war. They did not reckon with the strategy of sneak attack, which was calculated to cripple effectively the armed might of the United States so that Japan could wage a lightning campaign against the Asian colonies of the Western Powers. True enough, after knocking out the United States fleet at Pearl Harbor, Japan conquered the whole of Southeast Asia in five months, from December 8, 1941 to the fall of Corregidor on May 6, 1942. The Filipinos were much too stunned by the swiftness of the Japanese victories to realize that their freedom was to be completely curtailed for the next three years.

In "It Was Later Than We Thought" the action takes place in both Manila and Laguna. The narrative is related mainly in diaries, sermons, editorials, speeches, reports clipped from newspapers and magazines, all skillfully put together. It deals with activities in a middle class family: among its members and with the community. It ranges from a long drawn-out quarrel between an estranged strong-willed couple, to the problem of getting married within those parlous times, to the case of the youngest member who had been drafted for military training. Projected into the scene is a member of the family who has just joined the clergy and been assigned to the local parish. Not of much help to the family, he may be of better help to the parishioners. There is only a remote foreshadowing of the coming holocaust through the air-raid practices; such exercises had been programmed for sometime by the Civil Emergency Administration. But as the title itself hints, the events were happening much faster than the people's own prognostications, because the time-table agreed upon in Berlin, Rome and Tokyo so dictated.

"All Over the World" records the experience of a sensitive young newspaperman who also was a college student during the few months before the outbreak of the Pacific War. It includes his meeting and striking up of friendship with an orphan girl of eleven who was actually much more mature than her eleven years because of the peculiar experience she had gone through. They lived in a low sprawling old tenement house on Magallanes Street in the ancient walled city, he with three male cousins and she with her uncle who was the janitor of the building. Common interest in books and movies brought them closer together, but the association was not to remain long because of the intervention of war. There was no opportunity to say goodbye. While the man was in the newspaper office where he had to render overtime work, the whole area of Intramuros had been ordered evacuated, and when he went back to his lodgings, the whole building was already empty, only the air-raid warden being present to keep guard. Although there was no hint of the almost complete destruction that would come upon Intramuros during the reconquest of the country much later, the desolation of the abandoned old city could presage the worst calamity.

No remarkable story about the battles of Bataan and Corregidor has come out so far, but some fine short narratives have appeared about the long dreary march to Capas and the concentration camp there as well as the stragglers that managed to escape from the march and reached their homes in the various towns and cities including Manila and suburbs. There are two fine stories about the Capas camp: Silvestre Tagarao's "The Wire Fence" and Antonio Gabila's "A Forest of Tall Trees." The first deals with the terminal illnesses as a result of the long march, in which thousands died, one case being that of a desperate prisoner who rushes the wire fence and is shot down by the guard. The second is another sad story with a flashback of a scene in Bataan showing a forest of tall trees—in his fevered mind before it conks out. A related story is Gonzalo Villa's "A Voice in Rama" which tells of how women, both educated and uneducated, rich and poor, seek the aid of a soothsayer regarding their sons and husbands who were in the battles of Bataan and Corregidor and had not as yet come home—whether they were still alive and eventually reach home or already dead. Another related story is Ligaya Victorio Reyes' "Return to Capas," which is that of a widow of a war hero who is invited to participate in the memorial services, four years later, for those who perished in Capas in 1942.

The Japanese controlled press, which was made to toe the Japanese propaganda line, stressed the necessity of an early return of peace and order in the country, particularly in the rural areas. This was part of the Japanese war effort to reduce the garrison forces in the occupied territories to the minimum so that the great bulk could be sent to the war fronts and enlarge conquered territories in Asia and the Pacific. Most of the writers in English easily discerned the ulterior motive and did not respond; but most of the writers in Tagalog fell for it and many of their literary critics after the war claim that Tagalog literature experienced a major flowering during the Japanese occupation. There were annual literary contests and actually one anthology of occupation short stories was published and highly commended. A few short story writers in English published some stories in the Japanese-controlled press, but reserved their best efforts for the post-liberation press. Some joined the underground to harass the enemy. Only a handful wrote about the war; most of them wrote about other matters. "Christmas Visit," by Ligaya Victorio Reyes and "City of Grass," by Conrado V. Pedroche touched on the war; "The Long Wind," by Narciso G. Reyes, although not directly about the war, could be read as allegoric of the war. Other stories published during the war were "Rendezvous at Banzai Bridge," by Manuel E. Arguilla, and "Evening Meal," by Hernando R. Ocampo, both charged with the tensions of war.

Four fine guerrilla stories published in the post-liberation press are Reuben R. Canoy's "Deep River," Amante Bigornia's "A Night of Dancing," T. D. Agcaoili's "Tenderness," and Edith L. Tiempo's "The Black Monkey." "Deep River" is set in Mindanao or thereabouts, "A Night of Dancing" in northern Luzon, and "The Black Monkey," in the Visayas. "Tenderness" could have happened anywhere in the country where there was electricity. Another beautiful war-time and post-war story is Aida Rivera's "Now and At the Hour." It tells of the conflicts and tensions brought about by the military occupation of Negros Island and the memories left by these in after years.

It was difficult to rehabilitate print media immediately after liberation; many of the bigger printing presses were either seriously damaged or completely knocked out. The *Tribune-La Vanguardia-Taliba* chain of newspapers had been utilized by the Japanese as propaganda organs and the owners decided to replace *The Tribune* with *The Manila Times*. The *Philippines Free Press* could not resume publication until 1946. The *Philippines Herald*, whose plant was bombed out by the Japanese early in the war, took time to resuscitate; so with

Graphic weekly, a leading unit of the pre-war Ramon Roces Publications.

In the meantime, several newssheets and periodicals sprang up during or soon after the battle of Manila, in February 1945. They were enterprises that proved to be short-lived, except one or two, because of inadequate supply of newsprint or unavailability of printing presses. There was one exception, *The Manila Chronicle,* which was founded by a group of newspapermen. The newspaper was bought and the management taken over by a rich family, and it soon grew to be one of the leading English dailies in Manila. In due course it issued a Sunday magazine supplement, *This Week.* The short-lived magazines which managed to eke out a precarious existence published fiction and poetry, some of which proved to be excellent but far between. It was not until 1947 that the Manila press became stabilized and began turning out regular creative work.

The periodicals featured stories about the liberation campaign written and published soon after the campaign—both in the cities and in the far-flung mountain fastnesses; some are mediocre, a few quite fine. Of the latter are "Massacre at Mendoza-Guazon's" by Mario P. Chanco; "February, 1945" by Salvador Faustino; "The Forest" by F. Sionil Jose; and "Problem in Living" by Cornelio S. Reyes. Peripheral to the campaign were such distinguished stories as "A Pilgrim Yankee's Progress" by Nick Joaquin; "A Stream at Dalton Pass" by Edilberto K. Tiempo; "Transition" by Silvino V. Epistola; and "Clay" by Juan T. Gatbonton.

The first two stories deal directly with the battle of Manila in February 1945, particularly in the southern districts of the city; of the senseless massacre of civilians by the Japanese troops; of the slow but bloody liberation of a city that had been almost totally razed to the ground. When at the beginning of the war, General MacArthur decided to hold a defensive action against the Japanese troops, he moved his headquarters from Manila, which he declared an open city, and proceeded to Bataan and Corregidor. During the reconquest three years later, however, the Japanese defended Manila at all cost—hence the destruction. The story "Problem in Living" by Cornelio S. Reyes, tells the story of orphaned children, all minors bereft of both parents, trying to stave off hunger, disease, and death during the battle and after.

Of course, even in those turbulent years, the writers also wrote stories remotely relating or completely unrelated to the war. And some of them were fine stories: "Home for Christmas" by Maximo Ramos, Sr.; "The Woodsman" by Consorcio Borje; "There Was a Boy Named David" by Conrado V. Pedroche; "May Day Eve" and "Guardia de Honor" by Nick Joaquin; "The Body of Love" by Teodoro M. Locsin; "The Heirs" by F. Sionil Jose; "A Time of Peace" and "Unseasonable Sun" by Vicente Rivera, Jr.; "The Pulse of the Land" by Hermel A. Nuyda; "Flowers of May" and "Divide by Two" by Francisco Arcellana; "The Fight" by T. D. Agcaoili; "The Beads" by S. V. Epistola; "Wind Over the Earth" by Gregorio C. Brillantes; "Harvest of Humble Folk" by Gilda Cordero Fernando; "And Then the Weeping" by Lina R. Espina; "The Money Maker" by Nita H. Umali.

In a postscript to a pre-war critical study on the short story which I wrote some years ago, I made mention of a critic who had made the observation that there is no sex in the Filipino love story. That might have been more applicable to the pre-war short story, for in the post-war story there is more frank, though not clinical, treatment of sex. "First Night" by Amador T. Daguio; "Tenderness" by T. D. Agcaoili; "The Wall Between Us" by F. Sionil Jose; "Cost Price" by Kerima Polotan; "Sometimes It's Not Funny" by Carlos Bulosan; "Love in the Cornhusks" by Aida Rivera; "The Theory of Spite" by Lina S. Espina; "Love" by Jimena Austria Manalo. There's even a story—"So" by Andres Cristobal Cruz—which told about the sex life of an unmarried girl. Her sexual experiences with her boy friend may not be as explicit as that described by an Arab female poet as being plowed by the man; but there can be no mistaking about the scenes described. Sex is also dealt with honestly in "Fairy Tale for the City" by Estrella D. Alfon; and also in her "Magnificence," which later, however, is generally considered perverted sex. In "Cost Price" the lovers could not consummate the act, although the girl herself had suggested the assignation, because she suddenly became aware that they could not get married on account of poverty, and she pushed him brusquely. To his further attempt to embrace her, she swung at him, hitting the face and in addition the chest and all parts of his body. All he said was, "I don't want to fight, Isabel. There's no need. We've killed everything." In anguish she realized that she had written *finis* to their relationship.

Reflecting the troubled society of the post-liberation times are three stories: Delfin Fresnosa's "The Refugees" and "Brown Girl" and Florlinda Soto's "The Serenaders." That few of such stories were published was due to the fear of writers and editors of becoming involved in the witch-hunting campaign of the local fascists. This timidity led the American writer Wallace Stegner to observe in 1951 that "there seems to be a disturbing evasion of the hard realities of Philippine life," [4] which is one way of saying that the writers were afraid to come to grips with life. In later years those who wrote of the agrarian unrest or who published literature even remotely inclined to the dissidents were actually investigated in Congress and a few were brought to court; but the plaintiffs could not obtain conviction of the defendants. So the social instability persists to these days.

The coverage of the short story writers in English extends throughout the archipelago, including all the ethno-linguistic groups and cultural minorities. There are stories about the Muslims and other cultural communities in the south and about the mountain peoples of the north. A Muslim writer, I. A. Jubaira, has written several stories about his own people, among which are: "Blue Blood of the Big Astana" and "Sheik Abu Jahar." E. A. Enriquez has written "Jamilah," a Muslim girl married to a man several years her senior, and A. S. Gabila, "Going Away, Far," a tragic love story of a Manuvu boy and girl. In the north C. Borje, A. Daguio, A. O. Flores, S. C. Hamada, and F. Sionil Jose have produced fine stories about the mountain ethnic groups. Among the memorable ones are: "The Mountain" by Borje; "Out of Darkness and the Wilderness" by Hamada; "Wedding Dance" by Daguio; "The Outcast" by Flores; and "The Godstealer" by Sionil Jose.

This fact has given rise to the claim that the Filipino short story in English is more truly national than the Filipino short story in the native Philippine languages and in Spanish. In other words it presents a more truly comprehensive picture of the life and culture of the Filipino people in its varied as-

[4] Wallace Stegner, "Renaissance in Many Tongues," *Saturday Review of Literature*, XXXIV (Aug. 4, 1951), pp. 52-53.

pects. One need not go into the stories translated from the various vernaculars; these are stories originally written in English by writers born and brought up among the various ethno-linguistic groups. These stories are as authentic as and more readily available than the stories in the vernaculars which still have to be translated to be available to the student not conversant in the native languages.

Another interesting feature in the development of the Filipino short story in English is the increase over the years in the number of stories set in foreign lands with Filipinos playing principal characters. The first important writer to write such stories was Jose Garcia Villa, in the early thirties. His "Untitled" stories were about the experience of a sensitive young Filipino in California, in New Mexico, and in New York, in his relations with American girls and boys. Then came Carlos Bulosan and Bienvenido N. Santos during the war. Bulosan produced such stories as "Sometimes It's Not Funny," "As Long As the Grass Shall Grow," and "The Story of a Letter." Santos will long be remembered for his "Scent of Apples," "The Day the Dancers Came," "The Prisoners," "The Door," and "Even Purple Hearts." Edilberto K. Tiempo wrote "Another Country" and R. Rafael Ingles "Woman in Reno." This company was later joined by Ligaya Victorio Fruto, who wrote stories about Filipino life in Hawaii.

All the above stories were set in the United States. "Transients" (1952), written by Clemente M. Roxas, was about the adventures of two young Filipino students in Europe—in Madrid, Paris, Geneva, and finally in London, where one of them fell in love with the girl who had given him company. In later years, other stories were to come from J. Capiendo Tuvera, set in Vietnam, "High Into Morning"; and from F. Sionil Jose, set in the Basque country, Spain, "The Exile," and in Hongkong and Korea, "The Refugee."

These indicate the broadening of the horizons of the Filipino experience, a reaching out from the narrow confines of insularity and parochialism.

The Achievement in the Short Story: A Resumé

Of the more important and productive pre-war short story writers, Manuel Arguilla and Alfredo Litiatco died during the enemy occupation, while three became inactive: Jose Garcia Villa, Arturo B. Rotor and Casiano T. Calalang. Estrella Alfon, T. D. Agcaoili, Consorcio Borje, Antonio O. Bayot, Fidel de Castro, N. V. M. Gonzalez, Teodoro M. Locsin, Loreto Paras Sulit, Ligaya Victorio Reyes, Conrado V. Pedroche, Maximo Ramos, Sr., Sinai C. Hamada, Bienvenido N. Santos, Delfin Fresnosa, Lazaro M. Espinosa and Salvador Faustino continued writing. The war and post-war years saw the rise of Carlos Bulosan, Nick Joaquin, D. Paulo Dizon, Ligaya Victorio Reyes, and Max Ramos, Sr. Francisco Arcellana and Narciso G. Reyes were not very productive during and after the war, but they wrote a few fine stories. Juan Cabreros Laya and Amadeo R. Dacanay were not productive of fine stories. Manuel A. Viray and Oscar de Zuñiga (both also poets) and Edilberto K. Tiempo, who began writing before the war, were inactive during the period, but became productive after the war. Tiempo and Esteban Javellana were active in the resistance movement.

Amante E. Bigornia, Mario P. Chanco, Lina R. Espina, Vicente Rivera, Jr., Ibrahim A. Jubaira, Clemente M. Roxas, Edith L. Tiempo, Alejandro R. Roces, F. Sionil Jose, Emigdio Alvarez Enriquez, Nita H. Umali, J. Capiendo Tuvera, S. V. Epistola, Kerima Polotan, Carmen Guerrero Cruz, A. Oliver Flores, Celso Carunungan, may be said to belong to the older post-war generation—those who were in senior high school or in junior college at the outbreak of the war. Those who belong to the younger post-war generation were those who went to college after the war—Buenaventura S. Medina, Jr., Gilda Cordero Fernando, Gregorio C. Brillantes, Godofredo M. Roperos, Rony V. Diaz, Andres Cristobal Cruz, Anthony Morli, Aida L. Rivera, Reuben R. Canoy, Adrian Cristobal, Pacifico N. Aprieto, Elmer A. Ordoñez, Linda Ty Casper, Wilfredo Nolledo, Jose A. Quirino. This classification of the post-war story writers should be taken only in a loose sense because they did not all start writing at the same age; some started younger, some older. Many of the post-war generation writers, particularly the younger ones, still had to write their better stories after 1955. Among these were Edith Tiempo, F. Sionil Jose, Gregorio Brillantes, Gilda Cordero Fernando, Linda Ty Casper, Kerima Polotan, Celso Carunungan, Vicente Rivera, Jr., Ibrahim Jubaira, Emigdio A. Enriquez, Aida Rivera, J. Capiendo Tuvera, A. Oliver Flores, Lina Espina.

During the fifteen-year period, among the more productive were: D. P. Dizon and C. V. Pedroche, each with more than forty published stories; C. M. Roxas, Max Ramos and Nita Umali, each with more than thirty; and E. Alfon, V. Rivera, Jr., B. N. Santos, M. A. Viray and O. de Zuñiga, with more than twenty stories each. With slightly below twenty stories were Fidel de Castro, K. Polotan, E. K. Tiempo, and J. C. Tuvera.

In quality and in significance, during the same period some of the better written stories came from the pens of Alfon, Arcellana, Borje, Bulosan, Gonzalez, Joaquin, Pedroche, Victorio-Reyes, B. N. Santos, E. K. Tiempo, and Edith Tiempo. It should be interesting to know that all these writers were born before 1920. The oldest, the late Pedroche, was born in 1909, and the youngest, Edith Tiempo, was born in 1919. Within the time range of this survey, 1941-1955, the youngest grew up from 22 to 37 years and the oldest from 32 to 47 years. All of them chose English as their medium of expression; not one of them has ever regretted making the decision.

As to ethnic grouping, Dizon, Pedroche, de Castro and Santos are Pampangueños; N. Umali, M. P. Chanco, Joaquin, Victorio-Reyes, and Zuñiga are Tagalogs; V. Rivera, C. M. Roxas, and Polotan are Bicolanos; Arcellana, Borje, Bulosan, M. Ramos, E. L. Tiempo and Tuvera are from Ilocandia; N.V.M. Gonzalez is from Romblon and Mindoro; E. K. Tiempo is from Leyte; Alfon is a Cebuana; Viray is from Pangasinan.

Some additional facts should be interesting. Santos was born in Manila of Pampango parents, married a Bicol girl, lived much of his life in Bicol about which he wrote extensively. A Pampangueño also, Dizon married into the Ilongo ethno-linguistic group. Kerima Polotan was born in Jolo, Sulu, of a Bicol father and a Boholana mother, and married an Ilocano. Roxas was a Bicolano but grew up in Baguio and went to college in Baguio and Manila. Arcellana is from Vigan, Ilocos Sur, but grew up in Tondo, Manila, and married a girl from Cavite. Edith Lopez was born in Nueva Vizcaya, migrated to Central Visayas, and married a Leyteño. Born in Pangasinan, Viray married a Tagalog girl. Born in Romblon, N.V.M. Gonzalez married an Ilocana. An Ilocano from Tarlac, Tuvera is the husband of Polotan. Carlos Bulosan was born in Pangasinan of Ilocano parents, migrated to the United States in the early thirties, lived through the difficult years of the Great Depression and World War II as an itinerant worker and writer, was able to savour a little of success and its rewards only to be struck down at 42 years by a complication arising from lung trouble. A Tagalog and a bachelor, Joaquin has written some of the more erotic stories in Philippine literature. Borje was born in Cervantes, a highland town in Ilocos which did not have a chance to see a motor-drawn vehicle until late in the American occupation.

In trying to pick out what I believe to be the more competent and significant writers of the period, I am not dismissing the other writers as of little or no consequence. Some had contributed more during the 1925-1940 period (Paz Marquez, Rotor, Villa, Calalang, Latorena, Paras, Arguilla, Daguio, Hamada) and some still had to write their better stories in the 1956-1970 period. Every writer eventually will find his own proper place in literary history. As I said in a lecture which I delivered in December 1975 as holder of the U.P. professorial chair in literature:[5]

> The function of all literature whether imaginative or non-imaginative, whether primarily aesthetic or primarily intellectual, is the recording of human experience in artistic form. Certainly it plays an important role in understanding the totality of human experience. The beauty and significance of each literary piece depend on how successful the author develops his theme, how keen his insights, how noble his thoughts, how sincere his feelings, how high his seriousness. The greatest pieces are superior in quality or in character and illumine the life of man. They may be the creation of writers belonging to a particular nation and they may treat of life of a particular nation, but their significance transcends national boundaries and become part of world literature, cherished by the whole of mankind. But even those of lower quality have their own place in the literary tradition of a nation or people. Therefore great, superior, middling, or inferior literary works have their own proper place in the literary heritage of man.

Conclusion

As reflected in the literature of short fiction, Philippine society during the period covered by our survey was a gen-

[5] L. Y. Yabes, "A Common Scientific-Humanistic Culture and the Study of Literature," *Philippine Social Sciences and Humanities Review*. XXXXI, December 1976, p. 489.

erally sick society. Having been subjected to three colonial regimes over a period of almost four centuries, Philippine society has never been completely free; it has been enslaved most of the time.

Through the centuries, ours has been an uphill struggle for survival. More particularly during the war and enemy occupation (1941-1945), we struggled against the most formidable odds for the right to exist as a people and as individual members of society. It was a traumatic experience, but we managed to survive Bataan, Corregidor, and Capas.

We have been criticized by some of our own countrymen for deciding to commemorate those events. Why then, one might also ask, commemorate the martyrdom of Rizal? Rizal's death eliminated one of the powerful critics and opponents of the Spanish Empire; but that martyrdom also marked the prelude to the end of that empire. As the poet Cecilio Apostol aptly said,[6] "Si una bala destrozo tu craneo; tu idea, en cambio, destruyo un imperio." (*"Al Heroe Nacional"*) So the fall of Bataan and Corregidor and the Capas Death March also marked the effective initial setback for Japanese tyranny in its imperial design for conquest.

These great historical events as well as the lesser ones during and after the war brought out the strengths and weaknesses in the Filipino character, as reflected in the literature of the period. And from these we should be able to draw inspiration as well as warning so that we can be properly guided in planning our future.

But there is only one conclusion derivable from this recent traumatic experience of our people, and that is, that democracy is the only sure and proper solution to our ills as individuals and as a nation; not fascist or communist totalitarianism, or constitutional authoritarianism. These are passing phenomena— even constitutional authoritarianism—for the most viable way of life is democracy, which guarantees the freedom and dignity of the human person, values which man has been fighting for through the centuries.

It was a memorable literary period, distinctive and notable in its own way, offering a rich cross-section of Philippine life.

[6] Cecilio Apostol, *Pentélicas (poesías)* (Manila: Manila Grafica, 1941), p. 48.

Reading through the short stories, particularly the more significant ones, is a tremendous experience one will not soon forget. A people that can produce such volume and quality of writing deserves to survive as a free and independent nation and to grow as a self-respecting, peace-loving, law-abiding member of the international community dedicated to the pursuit of universal human rights and fundamental freedoms.

Quezon City
November 1980

BY WAY OF ACKNOWLEDGMENT

Although proper identification of each story included in this anthology is already indicated through the by-line, the date and place of original publication, as well as the Table of Contents, in addition to the brief notes on individual authors, which acknowledgment should be deemed adequate for inclusion in the listing, nevertheless kind permission has been sought for reprinting the stories in this anthology. Most of the writers have been my friends and acquaintances and they readily gave verbal permission to reprint them, in fact were thankful for my including them. I have not been able to contact a few due mainly to difficulties under the eight-year-four-month martial rule. In their original form as published in magazines, dating from twenty-five to forty years ago, most of these short stories were not copyrighted; it was only the stories that were subsequently included in anthologies or textbooks published in book form that were covered by copyright. However, acknowledgment of indebtedness for the use of all the stories is individually made to the following:

Philippine Magazine for: "Going Away, Far," by Antonio S. Gabila; "Two Friends," by Delfin S. Fresnosa.

Graphic for: "After the Picnic," by Nick Joaquin; "Blue Blood of the Big Astana," by Ibrahim A. Jubaira.

Herald Mid-Week Magazine for: "The Next One's On Me," by T. D. Agcaoili.

Sunday Tribune Magazine for: "The Grave Diggers," by Edilberto K. Tiempo.

Pillars for: "The Evening Meal," by Hernando R. Ocampo; "The Homestead," by Maximo D. Ramos, Sr.

Philippine Review for: "Rendezvous at Banzai Bridge," by Manuel E. Arguilla; "It Was Later than We Thought," by Nick Joaquin; "A Peace Like Death" and "A Christmas Visit," by Ligaya Victorio Reyes; "City of Grass," by Conrado V. Pedroche; "Nocturne," by Veronica L.

Montes; "The Long Wind," by Narciso G. Reyes; "Home for Christmas," by Maximo D. Ramos, Sr.

The Recorder for: "Massacre at Mendoza-Guazon's," by Mario P. Chanco.

Filipino Observer for: "I'm Coming Home," by D. Paulo Dizon.
People's Magazine for: "Colonel Sampa," by Isabelo Tupas.
New Horizon for: "Woodsman," by Consorcio Borje.
The Nation for: "Sea and Land and Time," by Juan Cabreros Laya.
Philippine-American for: "I Am Thinking of Us Today," "Return to Capas," by Ligaya Victorio Reyes; "Plighted Word," by Narciso G. Reyes; "A Pilgrim Yankee's Progress," by Nick Joaquin; "Yours Faithfully," by Lydia Villanueva Arguilla; "The Wire Fence," by Silvestre L. Tagarao.

The Sunday Post Magazine for: "The Door," by Bienvenido N. Santos; "Brown Maid," by Antonio O. Bayot; "There Was a Boy Named David," by Conrado V. Pedroche.

Philippines Free Press for: "There Will be Another Christmas," by Tobias Y. Enverga; "Maker of Songs," "The G.I. and the Laundrywoman," by Stevan Javellana; "Story for Summer," by Maximo Ramos, Sr.; "May Day Eve," by Nick Joaquin; "The Body of Love," by Teodoro M. Locsin; "And Beyond, the Hills Are Green," by Antonio S. Gabila; "Unseasonable Sun," by Vicente Rivera, Jr.; "The Money Maker," by Nita H. Umali; "The Outcast," by A. Oliver Flores; "Paying a Debt," by Lazaro M. Espinosa; "The Miracle," "A Voice in Rama," by Gonzalo A. Villa; "My Father Goes to Court," "As Long as the Grass Shall Grow," by Carlos Bulosan; "Clay," by Juan T. Gatbonton; "Out of Darkness and the Wilderness," by Sinai C. Hamada; "Reverend Baker," by Mario P. Chanco; "A Stream at Dalton Pass," by Edilberto K. Tiempo; "The Pulse of the Land," by Hermel A. Nuyda; "A Harvest of Humble Folk," by Gilda Cordero Fernando; "The Doll," "Jamilah," by Emigdio A. Enriquez; "The Wing of Madness," by Francisco Arcellana; "The Living and the Dead," "A Wind Over the Earth," by Gregorio C. Brillantes; "Chambers of the Sea," by Edith L. Tiempo; "The Other Woman," "The Crowded Room," by Virgilio Samonte; "Kite in the Sky," by Julian E. Dacanay; "The Trap," by Kerima Polotan.

Sunday Times Magazine for: "The Boarding House," by D. Paulo Dizon; "Problem in Living," by Cornelio S. Reyes; "Broken Glass," by Manuel A. Viray; "Pattern," Carmen Guerrero Cruz; "The Forest," by F. Sionil Jose; "The Fight," by T. D. Agcaoili; "House for Sale," by Lazaro M. Espinosa; "Low Wall," by Estrella D. Alfon; "My Brother's Peculiar Chicken," by Alejandro R. Roces; "A Night of Dancing," "Story for an Old Man," by Amante E. Bigornia; "The Blue Skull and the Dark Palms," "Where's My Baby Now?" by N. V. M. Gonzalez; "Love," by Jimena Austria Manalo; "Deep River," by Reuben R. Canoy; "Flowers of May," by Francisco Arcellana; "The Meadows," by Conrado V. Pedroche; "Even Purple Hearts," by Bienvenido N. Santos; "Cost Price," by Kerima Polotan; "Sunset House," by Clemente M. Roxas; "First Night," by Amador T. Daguio.

This Week for: "Scent of Apples," "Accept the Homage," by Bienvenido N. Santos; "So Still the Night," by Silvestre L. Tagarao; "Sometimes It's Not Funny," by Carlos Bulosan; "Tempest," by A. Oliver Flores; "Morning Star," by N. V. M. Gonzalez; "Vines and Walls," "And then the Weeping," "The Theory of Spite," by Lina R. Espina; "The Heirs," "The Wall Between Us" by F. Sionil Jose; "Matter and Spirit," "Transients" by Clemente M. Roxas; "Tenderness" by T. D. Agcaoili; "The Mountain," by Consorcio Borje; "Children of the Ash-Covered Loam," by N. V. M. Gonzalez; "The Serenaders," by Florlinda F. Soto; "Brownie," by Pedro Padilla; "The Leader," by Adrian Cristobal; "Rebirth," by Buenaventura S. Medina, Jr.; "Time: The Present," by R. Rafael Ingles; "So," by Andres Cristobal Cruz; "Afternoon Walk," by Lazaro M. Espinosa; "Strange Country," by Estrella D. Alfon; "Silence," "The Line Between," by Antonio O. Bayot; "February, 1945," by Salvador Faustino; "Wedding Dance," by Amador T. Daguio; "Final Bud," by J. Capiendo Tuvera; "Love in the Cornhusks," by Aida L. Rivera; "The Young Man," by Gregorio C. Brillantes.

Evening News Saturday Magazine for: "A Forest of Tall Trees," by Antonio S. Gabila; "Another Country," by Edilberto K. Tiempo; "All Over the World," by Vicente Rivera, Jr.; "The Other Boarder," by A. Oliver Flores; "The Fifth Man," by Stevan Javellana; "We Filipinos Are Mild Drinkers," by Alejandro R. Roces; "The Native Vendor," by Roman A. de la Cruz; "Two in a Clearing," by Romeo C. Velasco; "Portrait of a Patriot," "Flood," by J. Capiendo Tuvera; "Receding Darkness," by Manuel A. Viray; "This Door," by Kerima Polotan; "The Black Monkey," by Edith L. Tiempo; "The Prisoners," by Bienvenido N. Santos.

New Masses for: "The Story of a Letter," by Carlos Bulosan.

The Literary Apprentice for: "Transition," "The Beads," "The Lost Ones," by Silvino V. Epistola; "A Time of Peace," by Vicente Rivera, Jr.; "Woman in Reno," by R. Rafael Ingles; "Dada" by Anthony Morli; "The Quarrel," by Andres Cristobal Cruz; "Death in a Sawmill," by Rony V. Diaz; "Night," by Pacifico N. Aprieto; "Gate," by Kerima Polotan; "Broken Disc," by Elmer A. Ordoñez.

Collegian New Review for: "Divide by Two," by Francisco Arcellana; "The Father," by Godofredo M. Roperos.

Sands and Coral for: "The Chieftest Mourner," by Aida L. Rivera; "The Witch," by Edilberto K. Tiempo.

Diliman Review for: "Now and at the Hour," by Aida L. Rivera.

Scope for: "Daughters of Time," by Edilberto K. Tiempo.

Philippine Review for: "The Morning Before Us," by Gilda Cordero Fernando.

Philippines Herald Magazine for: "Joseph's Harmonica," by D. Paulo Dizon.

—LEOPOLDO Y. YABES

Quezon City
February 16, 1981

PHILIPPINE SHORT STORIES: 1941-1955

GOING AWAY, FAR

Antonio S. Gabila

He stood almost six feet in his bare feet, a brown giant. His tight short pants, decorated with colored beads, barely reached down his knees, and his coat of the same material hardly reached his waist, as though he had outgrown them. He wore nothing under his coat, and the open front disclosed the thick, heart-shaped muscles of his chest. His bare legs were lean and lithe, and suggested the fleetness and stamina of the deer. His long hair fell over his head like a discarded bird's nest. Stripped, he could have posed for an artist's Apollo.

It took two burly soldiers to bring him in, handcuffed, and throw him in jail. Inside the cell, the prisoner rushed wildly about, a fierce forest creature, shaking the rusty bars of his cell.

"Murder," the Chief of Police said. "Double murder. Cut off their heads in their sleep. Treacherous dogs, these Mano-bos." The Chief was a short, fat man who waddled when he walked. A year later, he was out of his post—for incompetence and connivance with vice moguls.

The prisoner thumped on the concrete walls with his now free hands balled into fists, walls that gave back only dull thuds. He cried and shouted in his dialect, his tone at first furious, then desperate. In another moment, I thought he would burst into tears.

"What's he say?" the Chief of Police asked.

"He says he wants to get out," I said.

"Ha...ha...ha! That's funny...ooh...hoho! He wants to get out!" Everybody within hearing distance of the Chief echoed him.

"He also says he wants his girl back," I said.

The Chief stopped laughing, but the silly grin on his face remained. "What girl?"

"Naya."

"Who's Naya?"

"Must be his girlfriend," I said. *"Cherchez la femme,* you know."

"Nonsense," the Chief said. "You newspapermen are all alike. Romantic. This is an open and shut double murder. Most treacherous I have ever seen. Unprovoked. Two honest, hard-working settlers murdered for no reason at all. It's time these natives are taught a lesson!" The Chief's smile had gone out of his face. He was now a fanatical upholder of justice. He pounded his fist into his open palm; his voice thundered through the room.

"These natives do not kill for nothing," I said. "There must be a reason."

"Bah!" he ejaculated. "These ignorant devils have no reasoning power!" He laughed at his own wit, slapped me on the back, and went into his office two cells away. The crowd, their curiosity satiated, dispersed, leaving me alone in front of the cell.

The prisoner had given up his futile pounding on the unyielding concrete walls, his shaking of the equally unyielding iron bars, and was silent now that his cries had fallen on deaf, ununderstanding ears. He sat on the lower of two bunks set against one side of the cell, his head in his hands. I whistled to him, not knowing his name. He looked up, saw it was just another Christian, perhaps curious or maybe hostile, and sank his head back into his hands. Then I spoke in his native dialect.

"Tell me your name," I said.

He looked at me as if he could not believe his own ears.

"Even little boys have names," I said.

A light broke on his face. He stood up and almost ran to where I stood on the other side of the bars caging him in.

"Who is this who speaks my people's speech and yet is not of us?" he asked.

"One who believes that people do not slay without reason," I answered.

"Ai, but what matters is to kill with or without reason. One has killed. That is all the *sondalos* want to know." His face had fallen again, dark and sad. His eyes were veiled and without light.

"But the *sondalos* are not the law," I explained. "The law will consider whether one has killed with justice or without."

He jerked his head up and said, "Who are you that you seem to know so much?"

I tried not to smile, but his naiveté proved too strong for me. Yet it was difficult to answer his question. I did not know enough of his dialect to explain to him that I ran the local paper. What was "write" in Manobo?

"I am your friend," I said.

"Friend?" he repeated, his brow clouding. I realized a mistake. The word had gone into disrepute with the natives. So many Christians had used the word to get into the natives' confidence only to betray them afterward.

"I am not a *sondalo*," I said. "I have no land, and I don't want any."

His face cleared a little. He was a credulous young man, typical of many of his tribe before they fell foul of Christian cunning and shrewdness.

"I want to help you," I said. "If I can."

He smiled, but shook his head. He was not afraid, yet he held no hope out to himself. He must have heard of Christian justice, summary and swift when it concerns the non-Christian peoples. Murder does not hold for them the same horror that it does for the Christian. The tribesman kills because he feels he has been wronged and there is no other way to right it. He does not call it murder. It is a personal war with him.

"Are you sorry?" I asked.

He looked at me for a moment, then shifted his gaze. He shook his head of uncombed hair. "They were bad men. Very bad," he said. The thick fingers gripping the rusty bars tightened, hardened.

"Everywhere there are all kinds of men," I said. "Good and bad. Even with your people; even with mine."

He seemed not to listen. He continued gazing at a far corner, his hands solid on the bars.

"One day, they saw Naya," he said, his voice dragging in monotones as though he were telling his story to himself. "She was on her way to the village with a load of camotes and bananas. She lived on the other side of the forest." He pronounced the past tense awkwardly, as though his tongue wasn't used to it yet.

"They said they wanted to buy her load. They asked her to bring it to their house. There they showed her many things. Colored beads strung together for the neck, cloth for dresses, mirrors, and much more. They made her drink devil-water. Her head ached, she wanted to lie down, she said. She did not want to go on to the village anymore."

His hands on the bars had whitened, were without blood. His jaws were welded together, showed through his skin. His eyes were like a wild animal's, grown small and fierce. Then he relaxed, his jaws loosened, but his hands remained solid on the bars.

"Naya, she was to be my wife. We were to be married at the coming of the new moon. Her father wanted two big *agongs* and a carabao for her. I worked hard, sold many bales of *abaca* to buy them. Naya, she loved me too. But we were waiting for the new moon." He was breathing deep and fast as if he were running.

"Next day, she came to me. I was in the field, stripping abaca. She said the new moon would never come. She said she was going away, far. I told her I did not understand. I shook her until she cried. She told me all then. I could not work after that."

Quiet had fallen in the jailhouse. It was approaching noon, and the Chief of Police had gone home. Also the usual loiterers. Only two or three guards were left, and they took turns at playing checkers on the desk sergeant's table.

"That night, Naya's father came running to my house. Naya was dead. She killed herself. With a knife, she did it." He stopped telling the story to himself. He was breathing hard. His throat was dry and he swallowed continually. But he was not finished yet.

"She had said, 'There will be no new moon for us. I am going away, far,' she had said." A sob shook his body and he did not stop it in his throat. He seemed unaware of my presence, then. I waited for him to go on. I waited, silent, a long time, but he did not speak anymore. Then, slowly, as if he were too sick to move, he went back to his bunk without looking at me.

The next day, he had several visitors, relatives and friends. They milled about in front of his cell, smelling of dried herbs and betel nut and lime, which they chewed and spat out in red blobs all over the place. They regarded me with unfriendly eyes, full of suspicion.

"We don't want any *abogado*," one said in understandable Tagalog. "We have no money."

I disregarded him. But I did not push through them. I had a glimpse of the prisoner over his visitors' shoulders. He was in much improved spirits. He talked lightly and laughed loudly with them. He told them he would be back in the village with them before another moon. He asked his father, an old man with a venerable head of hair, how the farm was. A young girl who seemed to be his sister from the close resemblance to him, had brought him a basket of bananas and boiled camotes. Everybody seemed to have forgotten why he was there.

In the days that followed, I talked to several persons about the current topic of the town: the double murder. I told them the prisoner's story as he had told it to me, keeping to the facts. The Chief of Police and the Fiscal laughed; everybody saw the difficulty of supporting such a story in court without any witnesses. The trial judge was a mild man who had a phobia against all sorts of bloodshed. And this was double murder, apparently consummated in treachery! Everybody knew what the verdict would be.

The trial was held a month after. The court was packed with tense, unfriendly faces. A few natives, friends and relatives of the prisoner sat in a group in one section of the courtroom. The rest of the audience was made up of settlers and curious townsfolk. All were tense, eager, as for a spectacle.

The prisoner was brought in, handcuffed to two policemen. He had grown thin and pale from his incarceration. He did not look as strong as he had been when he was first brought to jail. But he walked into the room with his head erect, almost defiant in attitude.

The court had assigned him a counsel. Poor, neither he nor his relatives could afford to pay a lawyer. During the trial, it was evident the defense attorney could not do anything much. He called the father of the girl to the stand, and after him the prisoner's father. The prisoner's counsel handled the case half-heartedly. He was getting nothing out of it; the sooner the thing was over, the better for him. On the other hand, the Fiscal, ordinarily a modest fellow outside of the courtroom, was swelled up with self-importance and took pains to show off his store of legal knowledge. He was a little man, and he took great delight in painting the tall prisoner's character as black as he could. All the while the prisoner sat silent, not understanding what was going on about him. Sometimes he looked at the judge, sometimes at someone he knew in the audience. But most often he looked down at his manacled hands. When he was brought to the stand, he hardly knew what to say. He had not been coached how to answer, and the Fiscal's questions through an interpreter bewildered him. It was all over after that first session. When the court met again to pass judgment, there was a smaller crowd in the courtroom. They knew what sentence to expect, and they were not wrong. It was the electric chair for the killer.

When the sentence was translated to him, the prisoner remained unmoved, his eyes half-closed, his shackled hands immobile in front of him. When two guards came to take him away, he walked between them docilely, his head bowed, his body softened into an aspect of resignation.

At the door leading out of the courtroom, there was sudden commotion and the room was filled with cries of surprise and alarm as the prisoner turned upon his guards and lashed at them with his manacled hands. The two guards reeled under the attack, and the prisoner had gained the street outside before a volley from the rifles of the other guards stopped him. For a second of time he stood poised, frozen in an attitude of sprinting, while more rifles crashed about him; then his legs broke under him, and he fell into a heap as we rushed up.

He was a gory sight with blood oozing from a dozen holes in his body. The men formed a thick ring about him; the women shrieked. The District Health Officer gave a look at the prisoner, and shook his head.

"Saves the government transportation money," commented the Chief of Police.

No one said a word. Sudden death had laid a spell upon the crowd. It was only after the body had been picked up and taken away, that anyone could breathe freely again. And even then they could not say anything for some time.

Philippine Magazine
May 1941

AFTER THE PICNIC

NICK JOAQUIN

They should be walking back now, the Doctor said, if they wanted to reach the car before the rain fell. For it was going to rain, he continued, glancing up moodily—yes, it was going to rain surely, though they might see no threat of it yet in the sky.

The four of them sat sprawled on the warm grass, watching the afternoon die out on the hillside. After a day of too much food, walking, laughter and talk, they had begun to feel bored. Walking back was an anti-climax. But the Doctor was insistent; it was going to rain.

Fe Chavez, his daughter, agreed immediately and rose at once from where she sat, brushing away the blades of grass that clung to her skirt. Young Pepe Valero, who was sitting beside her, stood up also, but more reluctantly. He was very much in love with her; he had spent a whole day at her side; and now that rare day was ending and he had accomplished nothing.

He felt frustrated and desperate and very unhappy, and the look he turned on her father was anything but affectionate. "I told you how it would be, Doctor. I was for bringing the car up with us. We wouldn't be worrying now about the walking back or whether it's going to rain."

But the doctor was not listening. He was gazing intently at, waiting for the comment of, the fourth member of the party; the tall, glowing, large-bodied woman seated slightly apart from them, absorbed in the mending of the parasol on her lap. To so trivial a task she seemed to bring a very passion of toil and concentration: her head was bowed, her shoulders pressed intensely forward, winglike, about her breasts. Sweat pulsed on her upper lip and eyebrows and from the tips of her ears.

Noting the expectant silence focused upon her, she looked up. "Rain? Is it going to rain? But how fine for us if it would! Picnics always end in boredom."

The Doctor had not taken his eyes off her. "How you love excitement, Chedeng! How is it you are never tired?"

She glanced swiftly into his eyes and her lips curled. "Tired? It would take a revolution to make me tired, señor doctor!"

"Father was in the Revolution!" Fe Chavez cried out impulsively. "He was a colonel and he rode a horse. He was shot in the shoulder."

The other woman, amused, gazed at the girl and then at the father. "And were you then already wearing those mustaches, Doctor?"

A curious constraint came upon her, as soon as she had spoken, and upon the girl and the young man, and their eyes involuntarily sought the Doctor's face. And the Doctor, unflinching and unsmiling, stared back at them.

Manuel Chavez was just turned sixty—a man of much neck and shoulder, with thin hair and very small cold eyes. Above the long thin lips outrageously flourished a pair of very black, luxuriant, and much-tended mustaches, carefully curled at the ends.

With calm insolence, he stared back at them—at his daughter, who, he saw, was shocked, worried, a bit angered, and very frightened, and at her young man, that poor little boob of a Pepe, thin and fragile like all the young men these days, hands externally thrust into pockets, eyes eternally agonized and defiant, lips eternally pressed tight and sullen; and, last of all, he stared back at the woman, at this Chedeng Dacanay, this long-desired and long-resisted piano teacher, this woman of perilous contradictions, with her flesh so softly ripe and her eyes so hard, her body so languorous of build and so sharp and alert in motion....Oh yes. A woman to be wary of.

He had known that from the first time he saw her (she had, the year before, given his daughter lessons in the piano), knowing as surely at the same time that he had never before wanted a woman as much as he wanted this one.

A devil of a thing to happen. His wife had been dead for ten years. He had, after a period of unspeakable loneliness, managed to walk through those ten years peacefully enough.

He was sixty. However taut the body's muscles might still feel, his life was over. But now, this woman had come. Son-of-a-harlot—he was in for it again.

So now he stared back at her, silently swearing at her, and saw that, half-afraid and half-malicious, she was mocking him, goading him again. It was a long time before he answered.

"Yes, my dear professor. I was already very vain of my mustaches then. I was probably not more than twenty at the time—but one became a man quicker in those days."

Pepe Valero suddenly kicked at a pebble. "What nonsense, Doctor! Whiskers do not make a man!"

"Whoever said they did, boy?" retorted the Doctor.

"And the women, Doctor," interrupted Chedeng Dacanay, "were they as rapidly mature?"

"They were born so, I would say. Oh, they made very silly girls—but they knew their roles instinctively. Once married, they became a part of their men. They suffered when we suffered, they could be happy only when we were happy. That was natural. A wife was one flesh with her husband. She could have no feelings separate from his."

Chedeng made a mock gasp and turned toward the young man. "But do you hear that, Pepe? And what does that make of a woman—an extra male organ? You are a man, too, you would agree with the Doctor?"

The boy smiled at her. "It's not a question of agreement really. The Doctor lived in one world, we are living in another. A system that worked in his time will no longer work in ours."

"I can tell you why it will no longer work," broke in the Doctor, looking not at the boy, but at the woman. "Because there are no men left that can make it work."

But Pepe Valero shook his head. "The reason, Doctor, is that women have become human beings, too—not just another piece of male property—not just something to be whipped into line, like a horse when disobedient."

Chavez turned curtly to the boy. "We had no need of whips to exact obedience, my friend. It had become instinctive in our women to obey—but only because their men had made themselves worthy to be obeyed. We believed in ourselves, they believed in us. Their obedience sprang from there, a natural act of faith—because we never failed them."

Chedeng Dacanay said: "I would laugh if I did not feel like crying too. Those poor, blind, unhappy women!"

The Doctor turned to her again.

"They were not always poor: a man owed it to himself not to make his wife that. And they could not be blind: too many things to see to. And they were quite happy. Oh, they were not always giggling and pinching each other, no. Their happiness went deeper; they probably took it for granted, so much at one was it with the tempo of their lives.

"Look—money in those days was not among the things a man had to guard with his own hands. Once earned, it became his woman's. Thirty pesos or three hundred pesos, it made no difference: she received it all—down to the last centimo. In her hands reposed the fortunes of the family. And such a responsibility, my dear Profesora, does not make for poor, blind, unhappy women. Nor for stupid ones."

But the Profesora remained unimpressed. "What do you think about all this, Fe?" she asked, looking around at the girl.

Fe Chavez flushed slightly. She had been listening tensely to the talk, worried by her father's earnestness. Why should he try to justify himself to them? Or had he begun to doubt himself? Was it himself he was really trying to convince?

She said aloud, gravely: "Oh, I have never been married."

Chedeng Dacanay bit off a smile. "Well, what do you think about love?"

"I think," said Fe, her brows knitting, "that it's a very simple thing—and that you people are making a holy mess out of it. A woman loves a man—that is, she has faith in him and a respect for him. She feels herself impelled to follow him, to make his road her road, but only because she believes he knows where he is going. If she could not believe that, she could not respect him; and if she could not respect him—how could she possibly love him? Chedeng, you would surely wish to look up to the man you married, no?"

"Look up to him? Look up to him, girl? But what an idea! Certainly not! Nor to look down on him, either—except when he so deserves."

Chavez sat up and leaned forward over his drawn-up knees. "I wonder, do you know, what kind of a man you would marry."

She met his eyes gravely. "You do, Doctor? Good. First of all, then, he would not be wearing mustaches."

He inquired, equally grave: "And why is it that, if I may ask?"

"Ah, because mustaches stand for tyrannical governments. I am willing to share some part of my life with a man. I refuse to let him rule any of it all. I will not make myself the mere mimicking shadow of the most perfect man in the world." Her voice had become savage and cold, and suddenly she rose to her feet, spreading the parasol open above her. "Was that a drop of rain just now? We should be walking back really. Doctor, you are always right. It *is* going to rain."

But Manuel Chavez did not stir. He remained hunched up on the grass, his eyes lifted to the woman, the beginning of a smile on his lips.

"I may be right about the other things, too, Chedeng," he said lightly; but the face of the woman remained cold and contemptuous and at last he looked away from her and, almost sighing, stood up also.

When he spoke again his voice had lost its momentary playfulness, had reassumed the tones of command: "You three wait here while I bring up the car. There is no need for all of us to walk back. Besides the women have done enough walking for one day."

Pepe Valero sank down beside the two women who had settled back on the grass. They could still see the Doctor, walking with quick strides along the brook and down the slope, and then the belt of trees below hid him from view.

Fe Chavez looked around. "What is it, Pepe? Stop pinching my elbow."

"How about those guavas? The ones we passed, remember? Shall we go and try to get at them now?"

"Father may come back at once. He does not like to wait."

"But it won't take us long. Not a minute."

The girl turned to her companion. "Will you come, Chedeng?"

"Oh no—my shoes hurt. You two go along."

The wind was moist and colder up there, higher up the hill. They could see the clouds gathering around the surrounding slopes, obscuring the last light of the seaward falling sun. In the morning this place had been murmurous with the insect- and bird-life; now, they found it silent—a premature evening hush.

Pepe Valero took over the mood of the place for his own. He had been born irritated and into a large family, and had early worn his voice out trying to make himself heard. He was grateful for any silence. He wished the girl walking at his side could understand how he felt without his having to speak. But she was preoccupied. She was not thinking of him at all.

He moved closer beside her and pressed her hand. "Afraid the Profesora will catch your old man?"

She lifted her large troubled eyes to him. "Tell me, Pepe— do you think she loves him?"

He considered a moment. "Yes, I would say she does. And sincerely, too."

"Why is she always trying to hurt him, then? Sincerely . . . Can a woman love a man sincerely and still laugh at him?"

He could not help smiling. This girl would never see it that way, of course. And that is why I need her, he thought— that is why I need a woman like her so much. No one has ever had any faith in me. Not even the people who love me. Oh, they love me sincerely all right. That does not keep them from always laughing at me though.

He said to Fe: "Oh, with the Profesora, laughter is a kind of weapon. She has certain strong and fine ideas of what a woman should be, in relation to a man. But she is not quite sure of her own self. So, she needs a weapon. She is, as I say, a sincere and very serious woman. She is always serious—yes, all the time. She dare not be otherwise. Her laughter, her mockeries, her pranks—all these have a purpose."

"And when she twitted him about his mustaches—was she being serious then?"

"Very serious, I would say."

The girl came to a halt, her eyes flashing. "Do you see, then, why I am so afraid for him? He needs to be respected and to be honored. He cannot make everybody do that, maybe. But he does require it of the people he loves and who love him. She would never give it to him. You heard what she said. She will reserve the right to respect what she likes in him and to ridicule what she does not. She thinks his mustaches only a pompous affectation: so, they must go. But you cannot break father up like that. Either you like him wholly as he is or you do not like him at all. He is all of a piece."

Pepe Valero stood staring at the girl. After a silence, he said: "Don't you think he should be broken up?"

Her eyes widened. "Broken up? Why?"

"So you can be free."

"Free for what?"

"Free to live your own life."

But she shook her head. "I don't want anything else."

He grasped her hand. "Fe, for God's sake—wake up! Don't you realize what you've got yourself into?"

She averted her face. "Mother left him to me. I must take care of him."

"But what can you do? Don't you see he's bound to get broken up sooner or later? And what would happen to you then?"

She turned her large surprised eyes towards him.

"Whatever happens to him," she said, "happens to me."

Seated on the grass, her arms clasped around her knees, Chedeng Dacanay watched the twilight creeping slowly up the hill. Now that she was alone, her face relaxed, her stiff neck drooped. How she would have liked to fling herself on the grass! She felt herself at the point of tears—vexed and tired and dissatisfied. The only daughter in a family of cultured but ineffectual males, she had been working all her life and had a horror of such moments as this, when she must sit still and think. Her father and brothers never did anything else. She loved them and supported them even while she despised them. She did as she pleased; they stood in fear of her. She enjoyed being their bully; she would have liked to be their pet. A part of her craved for tenderness, envying those feminine women who make such docile wives; but another part of her bitterly spurned such women, was proudly independent, cynical and hard.

The unresolved conflict made her difficult for men, she well knew. They found her attractive at a sight but repellent on acquaintance. Well, what could she do? The poor fools wanted tenderness; but how could she give what she could not feel? What, indeed, she disdained to feel? They were not babies, they were grown-up men; why, then, should they hanker for nursery pap and sentiment? But when it was the other way around, when it was they who would be tender with her, she felt just as quickly disgusted. She was certainly not a baby either, she would think grimly, promptly stiffening; and the unhappy lovers, finding turned upon them the full Medusan mockery of her eyes and smile, would, in the middle of their coo-cooing and baby-talk, begin to stammer and fumble, and would prematurely depart, highly indignant for having been made to feel foolish.

She did not mourn them. She saw through most of them and felt contemptuous. And yet, for quite a number, she had to suppress a very real and biting desire. For how can you give yourself to men you cannot help despising? Probably, the poor fools thought her frigid! She knew only too well how shameless the essential woman within her was, how voluptuous. If she went clad in armour, was it not for fear of being betrayed by the little panics of the flesh?

She had especially feared that upon meeting the Doctor. No man had ever aroused her so much before, physically. It had been necessary to be doubly hostile. And she recalled, smiling, that he had responded with equal hostility. Why, she wondered, had they been so certain instantly that either one or the other must go down before they could come together at all? For there had never been any question of meeting as friends and equals. From the first, they had seen the necessity for a conflict and of the eventual surrender of one to the other.

She knew, from his early attitudes, that he had taken for granted that she, being a woman, would do the surrendering; had expected, in fact, that after a little preliminary coyness, she would do so, leaving him, she supposed, as conqueror, to exercise the rights of possession, to twist and torture and pound the soft woman and the hard woman that she was to fit into his cruel and perverse definition of a wife. Well, the gross fool knew better by now, she hoped. Her hostility had probably betrayed to him her aroused desire; and he thought that, given a chance, he could use her flesh to break her spirit. She had led him on very slyly, indeed; but—no, sir—she had never had the intention of giving him the chance.

Oh, she wanted him, yes. No question about that. She wanted him. And I will get him, too, she thought quite gaily, smiling at her own coarseness. But it is I, I who will do the possessing; not he. She gripped her knees closer to her breasts, lifting her face to the wind. It would be necessary to break him a little, of course. The man was too stiff! He needs to realize that I will not tone down my voice to his—like that little kowtowing first wife he had. He must understand that I will not confound my will with his.

And as she pondered their encounter, his image rose and towered before her. Her eyes smiled mockingly into his cold eyes. Her lips wandered over the thin line of his lips. Her fingers played with the little pointed ears that grew so flat against the skull. And she closed her eyes and flung her head back to relish him the better.

The sunlight had faded and the wind increased; and along the brook and up the slope a car crept quietly, came to a stop, and the Doctor stepped out; but the woman on the grass was lost in thought and did not see or hear. When suddenly she found him standing beside her, she started violently, in vivid and naked guilt, eyes wide open, lips parted, and the blood flaming in her face.

The Doctor saw the start, the blush, the guilt in the eyes, and the hushed cry on the lips, and he knew at once that he had surprised her when she was thinking of him. He had been very careful the whole day. He was always careful when around this woman. He suffered when away from her, but at her side he promptly became hostile. He was no fool and no saint. A paid harlot, he had found out, could, after all, take nothing away from a man except his chastity. But this woman, if you gave in to her, would not even leave you enough to hide your nakedness with, and then would taunt you for it. He had been very, very careful the whole day; but now, seeing the start, the blush, and the confessed heat in those eyes, suddenly, swiftly, all his carefulness collapsed and he was dropping down beside her, was clutching her two thin wrists in his fingers.

They could not speak; they were both breathing heavily, hoarsely, her face averted from his, her lower lip caught tight between her teeth, her bosom erect; and then, as her body began to shiver, he found his own body responding, beginning to shiver also, sweat bursting out of all his pores, the blood congesting painfully in his veins, the small hairs on his arms and at the back of his neck standing up straight. Upon the wind came faintly the sound of approaching voices.

She pulled at her wrists. "Give me my hands, Manolo. Be careful. I hear them coming."

He gripped her wrists more tightly. He could not speak at once. The words choked in his throat. "I shall be at your house tonight. You will not go out?"

For a moment, looking at her face, he thought she was going to cry or to be angry; but, when she spoke, it was in the familiar voice—pert, unmoved, and mocking. "Come whenever it pleases you. Tonight, or tomorrow, or the day after tomorrow. I shall be waiting. But you must leave your mustaches behind, señor doctor. I require that."

Abruptly, he dropped her hands and stood up; and, looking around, suprised, she saw his fingers clenching. The next moment the young people were upon them.

The Doctor turned savagely on his daughter. "Where is it you have been wandering, Fe?"

The girl gazed at him in astonishment. She saw how red the veins stood out on his forehead and in the whites of his eyes. "What is the matter, father? Do you feel unwell? Pepe and I went to gather some guavas."

"What stupidity! If you had stepped on a snake, it would have served you right!" He strode away, trembling, towards the car, and the others followed in silence.

She has been working on him again, Fe Chavez thought wearily as she hurried, almost stumbling, after her father. She was not actively bitter against the woman. Chedeng Dacanay existed in her mind along with those other things (very hot weather, an unpleasant day at the picnic, the wrong election returns) which made it imperative that her father should immediately find his slippers, that the soup should be hot and the supper to his complete liking, and that the ash-trays and the carefully folded newspapers should be found waiting beside his private arm-chair in the sala. And as she hurried after him, pale and breathless to see his body tremble so, in her mind she was already searching for his slippers, setting out the ash-trays, folding the newspapers, and running out to the kitchen to attend to the soup.

Pepe Valero was following more slowly behind her, studying her peevishly. What a queer nation women really were! I was practically weeping before this one just a moment ago, and she did no more than stroke my hair. But that old brute bites her head off, and there she goes running to apologize to him for it. He glanced at the Doctor. A brute, yes: but, really, rather a pathetic one right now. But how easy it was to hurt the man! That was one disadvantage of being but one piece throughout. Made you vulnerable. If you were built up of fragmentary selves, you could be hurt only at one place at a time. You were incapable, the truth was, of being wholly and profoundly hurt at all. Too many other selves to escape into. But with fellows like the Doctor, you could strike anywhere and be sure of hurting the whole man. That, probably, was why the slightest petulances of men like him somehow acquired an air of high tragedy. Women felt the difference, he supposed, and responded accordingly.

Not the Dacanay one though, he thought, and his heart leapt. I hope she does destroy him, he gloated, kicking at the grass as he walked. I hope she does knock him down. These guys of old order still seem to see themselves as the salt of the earth. Maybe they were once, long ago. "But if the salt lose its savor wherewith shall it be salted?" Look at that one. Thinks himself some sort of sun with the women revolving around him. Well, you've met one that won't revolve so easily, mister. You're in for a nasty hard fall, mister. Yes, you are—you damned, arrogant, old brute!

Chedeng Dacanay followed far behind, walking meditatively, her hands pressed hard against her breasts and around the handle of her open parasol. Her brows were furrowed, her eyes misted, her lips tremulous.

In the instant when she looked around and seen his fingers clenching, when she had looked up into his face and seen how she had hurt him, there had come upon her an overwhelming impulse to be tender—to take him into her arms, lay his head on her breast—to comfort, to caress, and to submit to him. In that instant she had known how deeply she loved him. She had not known this before. He had been simply the man who had most stirred her physically. The idea of love had never actually entered into her thoughts about him.

She smiled wryly, shaking her head to dislodge the mist from her lashes. So, that was what love made of you. It made you tender and it made you humble. It was easy, she reflected now, for any woman to see through a man as long as she was not in love with him. When she was, she might still see his weaknesses, but only that she might make them easier for him

to bear. If he should come to me tonight, she thought, he would
find as meek and submissive a woman as ever his first wife
was. And that must not happen, she told herself quickly, the
tears starting again in her eyes. After an infinite second, she
added: It is *not* going to happen.

She looked up at him, striding rapidly far ahead, and her
heart gave a twist. But why should the heart betray me now
whom the flesh could not? I love him, yes, as I have never
loved before. As I shall, perhaps, never never love again. But
I was thirty years building this woman that I am and, whether
I made a good or bad job of it, no one is going to change
me now. Not even he. He may come tonight—or he may not. It
doesn't matter. Not to me. I shall not be waiting, Doctor. I
shall not be there at all.

The pain was spreading from her heart, and she pressed
her hands harder against her breasts. There was a noise going
on in her ears, a maddening sound of things falling, as though
walls and pillars of stone were crumbling down upon her. She
thought: I have never suffered like this before, but I would
go through this the rest of my life rather than surrender. She
was vaguely alarmed to note how, even at such a moment,
there was a self of hers that stood apart thus, watching and
commenting, while another self was being so grievously tor-
mented.

Chavez reached the car and climbed into the driver's seat.
He pulled the door shut and glanced up at the three people
coming, and then at the clouded skies behind and above them;
and even as he looked, a cloud parted before his eyes and a
solid, square sheet of rain dropped down, the wind whirling
it into fragments as it fell. The wind and the rain were everywhere all at once, and the three people were running now, and
it seemed to the man in the car that they were really fleeing
his wrath, which had (not surprisingly) become the wrath of
the skies also.

That evening he was sitting in the dining room, listening
to the sound of the rain falling. The newspapers were spread
out before him on the table, but he had found it impossible to
read. His daughter came in, bearing a cup on a saucer, and he
looked up testily. "What is in the cup, girl?"

"Some tea for Aunt. Her head aches."

"Her head aches whenever she is not taken along. You leave that right here. Get her another if it pleases you."

But when she came back later, with some sewing that had to be done, the tea, untouched, stood cold in the cup. His chair was empty and the newspapers lay crumpled on the floor. The ash-trays were piled with cigar-butts. The sour smell of gin drifted through the room.

She found him in the sala, leaning out a window. He looked around as she entered, and asked: "Is the Valero boy coming tonight?"

"He said he would drop in after supper."

"The young boob will drown. What a beast of a rain! Will it never stop?"

"Are you going out, father?"

"I have needed a haircut for days. You said so yourself."

"But you cannot use the car. You will get wet."

He left the window and dropped listlessly into a chair. "Yes, maybe you are right."

She went out to the porch. As she sat sewing there, in the faint light that came from the window, she heard him moving about inside. His restlessness became hers and at last she gave up trying to sew, folded her hands on her lap, and leaned back on the chair, listening to the falling rain and the sound of the slippers pacing inside.

Her brows puckered. Perhaps she should go in and talk to him. But she shrank from such intimacies. A man's moods must be respected, her mother had always said. You suffered with him and you stood near enough to hear if he should call, but you stood aside. He must be allowed to battle it out with himself.

His full-moon moods, her mother had called the Doctor's periodic ill temper; and she had learned to pick a safe way through them for herself and her children, being a wise wife and a serene woman. Curious, Fe had often thought, that she should remember her mother thus—as a serene woman—for all that she had been so jumpy and nervous when alive, so very fearful of numberless things—mice and lizards, street-cars and trucks, blood and thunder-storms . . . . But under the surface frailness, she had always discerned a hard, impregnable core of serenity, the rock of a proud peace.

Since her mother died, those rushes of temper and of melancholy in her father seemed to have become chronic; the outbursts of a man increasingly ill at ease in the world, of a man stranded and lost among an alien people, with whom he had in common neither speech nor sympathies, neither ideas nor gods. There were fewer and fewer to whom he could turn to assuage his loneliness. Of the men with whom he had borne arms in two wars, worn the blue uniform, and carried the tricolor, the best-loved were long dead; and for the others that remained, he had only a vexed impatience. They were unworthy of the tradition, he said.

He kept in touch with those ones, nevertheless—from pity, maybe, and from loneliness; and would often bring them home to supper that he might have someone to talk with; frail shabby old men, proverty-stricken most of them, that needed to be led and to be fed, that looked up at you with helpless mouths and misted, childlike-beseeching eyes. Why, most of them were younger or no older than he was! They had allowed themselves to be broken, he cried. They were shamefully defeated. They had been proved and found wanting. Look at me, he thundered at them, I do not like these times any more than you do. But am I broken? Do I hide? Am I poor, old, helpless?

And when they were gone, he would turn to his daughter with as furious a torrent of talk and narrative. The past would come vividly alive for her in the storm of his words. She followed him into his youth, she sat with him upon the academic benches, she tortured with him the fine print of stubborn texts and tomes. From flag-hung balconies, flowers rained down upon her as the great annual procession of Corpus Christi advanced through the narrow streets of "this noble and ever loyal city of Manila." Her mind went drunk like his with the eloquence of Lope and Cervantes, the conceits of Gongora, the sweet ravings of the Spanish Carmelites. She rode with him to battle and found throbbing in her heart the harsh conflict of a hate that was also a love, of an anger that was also a tenderness, of a fear that was also a respect, because the proud, dark, tragic nation whom the men rose to meet as a foe, they also rose to salute as a mother. And she felt the hot hiss of the bullet, saw his shoulder explode, heard him cry out and fall from the horse, watched him writhing huddled on the ground, the bright blood streaming forth profusely, draining him of youth, soaking the grass purple, begetting a new nation . . . .

On and on he would talk, walking back and forth the whole while, dragging her along with him into the past, pouring out all the pent loneliness in him, until, finally, purged and exhausted, he dropped into a chair and fell silent, staring before him.

The downpour had slowed down at last, and the girl on the porch noticed that, inside, the sound of pacing had stopped. Looking around, she saw her father standing on the porch, not far from her side, gazing out across the garden. He glanced down at her, and she caught a smell of liquor. "It is not raining very hard now. I might as well get that haircut." She said nothing and he returned inside. She heard him in his room. When he came out again, he had his shoes and his raincoat on. She went in and fetched his hat.

"Will you come back at once, father? Pepe is coming."

"Of course. Where else would I go?" He took the hat, put it on, and finished buttoning his coat, but still he did not go. They were standing close together, avoiding each other's eyes.

Both of them were at that moment thinking of the woman, the dead wife and mother, who had so quietly, so competently woven the pattern to which they had both moved so long and which now they found fragile about them: the small, timid woman who had painfully forced herself to sit up when dying to take a last look at her husband and sons, her chin tilted high, her eyes shining with the immemorial pride of women: One man loved me and I bore him sons . . . . And they were both so conscious of her presence that the Doctor said again, "Of course, I will come back at once. Where else would I go?"

She watched him walk down the porch stairs and up the garden path and, returning to her chair, took up her sewing again; but her fingers refused to work. Pepe Valero found her, an hour later, still sitting there motionless, staring at her fingers spread open on her lap.

He slipped into a chair at her side. "You are not sewing in the dark, Fe?"

"No, I have done no sewing at all." She looked up at him. "Father is not in."

He smiled and seemed embarrassed. "Yes, I know. As a matter of fact I saw him."

She looked away quickly. "You did? Where?"

"Oh, down the street. Do you know, I was not sure at first it was your old man."

She could hear her pulses throbbing. "Why?"

"He didn't have mustaches."

He waited, but she said nothing.

"It had stopped raining then," he continued, "and I was coming down the street and I saw him standing on the corner. I was going to approach him but, as I came nearer, I saw that this man was clean-shaven. So, I thought I was mistaken and walked on. Then I stopped and took another look—and I saw I hadn't been mistaken after all."

He paused and stole a look at the girl, but her face was guarded.

"I wanted to approach him, but you know how he jumps at me, and I thought he smelled rather strongly as I passed. Well, I stood there, trying to make my mind up and wondering what he was doing there. He wasn't waiting for a cab anyway, because they kept passing by and he never stopped one. I thought we were going to stand there all night, but just as I had about resolved to go up to him, he walked away—and when I saw it was not towards here, I came away myself. You wouldn't have wanted me to follow him?"

Her eyes blazed at him. "Why should you?"

"I didn't! Why jump at me?" He stood up sulkily. "Anyway, you know very well where he has gone." He smiled vindictively. "The Profesora has won after all."

"You sound very glad, Pepe—almost exultant."

"Do I? Maybe I am!" But he was instantly conscience-stricken. "I'm sorry, Fe," he mumbled, and touched her shoulder.

She shrank from the touch; rose suddenly from the chair, away from him. The boy read the repulsion in her eyes and the furious desire came upon him to hurt her. He grasped her by the shoulders and would have shaken her roughly, when they heard rapid footsteps on the sidewalk outside. Looking around, they saw the Doctor coming along the fence, swaying slightly. He looked up towards where they stood as he opened the garden gate; and in the street light his daughter saw for the first time his new, strange, shaven face—so much smaller than she remembered, so naked-looking.

She caught her breath. She felt she should run away, hide, as from something shameful, but her legs refused to move. She could only stand fascinated, watching this unknown man wobbling up the path. Unconsciously, her hands made a gesture of warding off, of delaying his approach.

He was at the porch-steps now. As she stared helplessly, he stumbled against the bottom step, slipped, stood tottering for one horrible moment, his arms wildly flying, and collapsed. She screamed, covered her face with her hands, and fled into the house.

Pepe Valero leapt down the steps. The Doctor was sitting in the mud, looking rather surprised. The boy dragged him up to his feet. He sagged limply in the boy's arms, his head drooping, the naked drooling mouth opening and closing with each hoarse gasp of breath; and it occurred to the boy that he had often called the Doctor an old man but had never really, till now, believed him one.

The Doctor lifted his head and peered into the boy's face and, as he recognized him, something of the old contempt flared up in his eyes.

"Take your hands off!" he muttered, pulled himself away, and staggered up the steps and into the house.

Pepe had an impulse to follow; he checked it swiftly. The thing to do, he told himself, was to get out at once. As he hurried to the street gate, he could hear the Doctor shouting in the house:

"Fe, where are you? I did not go to her, Fe! I never went at all! I swear it! Do you hear me, hey? Where are you?"

Pepe reached the gate, swung it open, and strode off down the street. It was raining again. He tucked up his collar and groped in his pockets for a cigarette with shaking fingers; and as he walked, he stared blankly at the trees, the people passing by, the lighted houses and shop windows, and tried hard not to think, not to think at all. But a feeling of horror was growing upon him, and he found himself walking faster and faster.

Graphic, June 26, 1941

THE GRAVE DIGGERS

EDILBERTO K. TIEMPO

Agustin was beginning to feel the damp bite of the nine-thirty sun on the back of his neck and the creeping warmth of the hard-packed ground under his bare feet. The earth itself, the naked mounds, the garish tombs of various shapes and sizes, the pile of human bones beside the cemetery chapel all exuded a sticky heavy heat made solid by the surrounding moldy crypts, some cracked with age, lined in tiers against the concrete walls of the cemetery.

Nicolas' knobby finger drew a line between two low mounds and a rectangle around one mound. The man's helper, Agustin, thought the marked space too big. "Si Ya is a small girl."

"I know, I know," said Nicolas. "The fat Ho Ya can lie in it also, if he wants."

Nicolas drove a bamboo peg into one corner of the rectangle with the base of his palm. Agustin knew no other man in town who could drive a peg into hard ground the way Nicolas did.

"I wonder what the Chinese bury with a man." Nicolas moved to another corner to drive a second peg. "But I know what they bury with a girl. You'll find more jewels on this girl's body than you'll ever see in your lifetime. The fingers of her hands will have rings and there will be necklaces and earrings and bracelets and all kinds of jewelry. And they will be ours, *chico*. Ours."

On the opposite corner, Nicolas, a peg in his hand, looked at two men putting up a tomb about sixty meters away near the cemetery chapel. "We place her on this side, and the cement will be poured on the other side."

"Won't they know?"

"Know what?"

"That the girl will be placed to one side of the hole."

"No, not exactly on this side, chico—but nearer this side than that. Who'll know the exact spot when she's all covered?"

Nicolas bent down for his pick mattock. "This," he jabbed at the left side of the dividing line, "is where we dig tonight. That's why the big hole—makes quicker work tonight."

He hewed on the line of the rectangle. "Start in the middle, Osting."

Their picks chopped steadily on the hard earth.

"You think, 'No Kulas, nobody will know?"

"There you go again. Know what?"

"About tonight."

"Nobody will know. Nobody will ever know."

"You sure of that?"

"Sure as the quarter moon tonight. We start work when the moon sets."

"Suppose we're seen."

"You know very well in this town, nobody comes within a hundred meters of the cemetery after eight at night. The ghosts will see us, yes, but they don't talk. You don't believe in ghosts, Osting, do you?"

"Well—I don't know. I never saw one."

"Don't you believe what you can't see. When a man dies he's dead. I've been digging graves seventeen years and I've not met a ghost yet."

"Don't you believe in life after death, 'No Kulas?"

"Do you? If there's such a place as hell or heaven or purgatory—you can't drink tuba out there, can you? I like my tuba now. After you have dug so many graves you wonder what really happens." He pointed at the side of the cemetery chapel. "Look there, Osting. What do you see?"

"Nothing but bones."

"You're right. There's nothing but bones. You helped me pile them there. Where did you get them? From under this ground. We bury this Chinese girl Si Ya and after a year what do you see under this?" He thumped the earth with his mattock. "Nothing but bones. Now tell me, chico. Tell me, has anyone of those buried come back? Has anyone of them come back to tell us they've been anywhere? No, no, chico. I believe only what I see."

Nicolas stepped over to the adjacent grave, picked up a couple of leaves of the carabo growing lushly on the head section of the mound. He gave one leaf to Agustin. "See how fat and juicy it is? You don't see *carabo* as fat as that except in a cemetery. Well, *chico*," he said laughing as though at a discovery, "that's where the body goes."

Agustin crushed the downy leaf and the sap was cool in his hand. It had a tangy, secret, fertile smell. Why should people plant *carabo* on the grave when it was used to spice mongo beans? The *carabo* didn't bear flowers. Perhaps the heart-shaped leaves, thick with sap, absorb the heat of the sun and keep the head part of the grave cool.

"Why do you think they plant *carabo* here, 'No Kulas?"

"The maggots also need appetizers, *chico*."

They bent on their mattocks again, and then Nicolas spoke, "Why don't you take off your shirt, Osting? By knee deep you'll be soaked. Besides, the sun's good for you."

Agustin blew short breaths on his chest to cool himself. "It's all right. I'll wash my clothes when I get home." It was not to hide his skinny body that he had his shirt on; the real reason he didn't tell Nicolas: he did not want the penetrating earthy odor to stick to his skin.

In contrast, Nicolas' splendid torso shone like wet bronze, his breasts like cymbals. His muscles bulged unevenly around the shoulders and neck and arms from hauling lumber, bales of hemp, and sacks of rice and copra at the wharf when he was not digging graves.

"You have done this before, 'No Kulas—this thing tonight?"

"I wish I had the chance, *chico*. I know someone who had, and a nice digging he made. You wouldn't know he was a grave digger."

Nicolas spat into his hands and raised his mattock high and drove a mighty arc into the ground. "I wouldn't be unhappy if another rich Chinese girl's buried next week."

They were quiet, their picks busy again.

"Won't you—won't you feel bad after this? After this digging tonight—I don't know how I'd feel. Afterwards, I mean."

"You don't have to feel guilty. I won't. All those jewels to be buried with the girl—now tell me, where did Ho Ya get all his money? When I was a boy he had a small candle shop. In a dark, crowded cubby-hole of a room. Does he believe in the candles? That fat heathen makes them for the money. Look at him now. Ho Ya makes the soap for the town, and other towns. Ho Ya owns the biggest bakery. And where do you buy your kerosene and your *camiseta* and everything? Go to Ho Ya for a ganta of rice. Pay it on Monday—or you sweat it out in the candle shop for a day and a half instead of one. And what does Ho Ya do but sit on his fat tail and smoke his trombone of a pipe?"

Nicolas drove in his pick mattock hard, splitting the fat back of Ho Ya, so Agustin thought. The pick wrenched out a block of earth. "That's the kind of money he got for the jewels he's burying with the girl. *Chico*, we're just getting back what Ho Ya has cheated the people of this town—and that includes us."

"It's the dead, *'No* Kulas. What's buried with the girl is hers."

"What use has the dead for a pearl necklace, can you tell me? Maybe it looks pretty around a vertebra. Your wife doesn't have to wear it. I know how to get the money for *them*."

Quietly, without their knowing it, a woman, her clean but threadbare gingham dress too loose for her thin body, appeared before them. She stood on the edge of the pit and tried to hold a cough with her hand.

"Good morning, *Tio* Kulas."

The two men looked up at her as though at a ghost.

"Osting, you didn't leave me money for rice. We have no more for noon."

"Can't you go to Ho Ya—get a ganta. He's paying us for this, and for tonight also."

"But we still owe Ho Ya's store eight-seventy, Osting, and I'm ashamed."

Nicolas put his hands in his pocket, drew out a peso bill and a few coins. "Here, Sebia, take this and go to the market. I'll eat lunch with you and Osting. Now go."

Nicolas watched the woman shuffle away, and then he turned to Agustin. "Now listen to me. I didn't have to tell you about tonight, you know that. I can get all—all for myself. But your wife is my niece, her mother's dead, she's the only kin folk I have. I want her to eat good and get well."

He wrenched a chunk of earth off the mattock. "Tell me, man. Have you been giving Sebia the medicines the doctor says she should take?"

"No, not always. How can I?"

"Now tell me. Did the doctor say Sebia has a chance to get well?"

"Yes, 'No Kulas. That's what he said. Rest, no work, good food, and the medicines—she'll get well. That's what the doctor said. Six months of complete rest."

"Sebia is not getting all this, is she?"

"How can I give these to her—no matter how I try."

"You can, Osting. You can give them—rest, food, medicines, and more. After tonight. That is if you don't turn coward, you know what you will be? You'll be the murderer of my niece!"

Nicolas gripped his mattock and savagely struck the earth. He did this several times before he subsided. Pausing from his work, he leaned on the mattock and looked hard at Agustin shoveling earth out of the pit. "Osting, are you all right?"

Agustin looked puzzled.

"I said, are you all right? Do you feel well?"

"I'm all right."

"You're thin, you know. Have you been coughing yourself?"

"No."

"I'm an ignorant man, but I know your wife's sickness. It has been in her mother's family. My wife, Sebia's aunt, died of *tisis* also. What I've seen of this sickness is when one has it, others in the same house get it also. Now, *chico,* if you don't watch out, you might get it from Sebia. I know. I myself almost got it from my wife."

For three months now Agustin had been sweating at night, the way his wife did before the doctor said she had tuberculosis. He had not started coughing, but lately food didn't seem to taste so good. This and his restlessness at night he knew came from worrying. The doctor had advised him to be careful, not using the same dishes, not sleeping in the same bed, but he couldn't always follow the advice, because he didn't want to hurt his wife. He didn't tell the doctor, he wouldn't tell him about his own suspicions about his health. Nothing would come out of it; the situation would become worse because he, too, might be advised to rest. How could he?

"Now, man, this is what I've been trying to say. If you don't take advantage of my offer about tonight, it means you're decided to kill my niece and yourself. That's what it will amount to, if you decide to let me do it alone."

The two men worked steadily for a while, and then Nicolas spoke, less angrily this time. "With your share, Osting, you will not only make Sebia well again. You'll have a new start. You can handle scissors better than that shovel. You can open a barber shop of your own. Of course, you'll have to do it slowly, you know, so people won't get suspicious. As for me, I'll go to Cebu City or even Manila—and see what it's like out there. Nobody outside the town would know I was a grave digger."

Because Agustin was quiet, Nicolas went on. "A diamond ring, *chico*, would bring no less than two to three hundred pesos. Your share from just one pair of earrings will be enough to get you some equipment—scissors, clipper, razors, a mirror or two, towels, a few gowns. And there will be necklaces and bracelets and rings. You can bet your life all of Si Ya's jewelry will be buried with her. *Chico*, this is the chance of a lifetime. A thing like this won't happen again. Don't you agree with me, Osting? Don't you?"

"I agree." I should be glad for this, Agustin told himself once more. But he knew only an alternation of nagging anxiety and numbness. He was angry with himself; after all, it was for his wife, mostly. Without this money—any kind of money— his wife was going to die; and so was he, perhaps in half a year, or a year at most. What he got as a *cargador* and as grave digger with Nicolas couldn't buy him the kind of food his wife needed. He shouldn't have to think about what he felt, about the wrongness. He must just do what was to be done tonight. He would even make penance for it later, burn a candle for Si Ya to the end of his days.

"Your father," said Nicolas irrelevantly, but startling Agustin because he seemed to have an uncanny way of intruding into his mind. "Now there was a man of guts. I knew no other man with whom I'd rather share my *tuba*—or whose *tuba* I could really enjoy. You know, *chico*, if he were alive he'd jump at this opportunity I'm sharing with you. He was a man, that Tubal. Your father had nothing but he knew how to live."

That's the trouble with me, Agustin was about to say aloud. He was not his father's son. His mother had a greater hold on him, his rigid old mother five years dead. She would lash him now if she were alive. The hold of the dead was a hard one. You couldn't talk to it, it listened to no excuse. Especially a dead one like his mother. He thought of one Sunday evening

when he was fourteen—there was nothing to go with the rice
on the supper table, and his father came and handed her three
paper bills. The old man was flushed with drink, with his run
of good luck. His shock of iron-grey hair bobbed at her, coaxing
her to accept the money. She got hold of the bills and tore them,
scornfully shouting, "I have no use for money you have not
earned." A year before, she had cut off the heads of his seven
fighting cocks on discovering he had used for bets the ten-
centavo coins she had been depositing in the hollow of a bamboo
joint on the head side of their bed. It was his mother who took
care of the family; this was the reason his father was really
dead to him, although his mother had died three years earlier.

"Trouble with me, 'No Kulas, I am my mother's son."

"How well I know. But that has nothing to do with your
responsibility to your wife now. If you don't do it tonight,
you'll hold yourself responsible for her death. It's as simple as
that. Tell me, can anything be more simple than that?"

"I didn't say I wasn't going to do it. It's just that this
isn't too easy for me."

"Tell you the truth, *chico*, I can't understand you. I've been
trying to point out there's nothing wrong with this business
tonight. Look at it this way. The jewels are buried with the
girl. All right, they belong to the girl, I can even say that. The
girl's body becomes dust, and the jewels belong to the earth.
It's like knowing there's a diamond and gold mine here." He
struck the bottom of the pit with his mattock. "We know there's
a mine here. We're digging only what belongs to the earth,
not what belongs to the girl. Now tell me, *chico*, is not my
reasoning simple enough? I don't know how to make it simpler."

Instead of answering, Agustin swung his shovel to throw
out the earth that had piled. Nicolas sat in one corner of the
pit waiting. When Agustin had cleaned the pit of the loose
earth, Nicolas spoke, with patience and with almost no trace
of anger.

"All my life, Osting, it's been worse than hand-to-mouth.
When I became an orphan at nine, I started working. Stiffening
candle wicks, rows and sickening rows of them. You stiffen the
wick with tallow before it's dipped in candle molds. I did as
much as grown-ups, finished as many rows of wicks. But you
know how much Ho Ya paid me? Only half the amount others
got. Because I was only a kid. Years later, when my wife had

tisis, I often had to get rice and sugar and other things from
Ho Ya's store on credit. And for that I had to give much in
additional hours of work in his candle shop. Because I got them
on credit. That's why, *chico,* I don't feel bad about tonight. As I
said, I'm only getting back at Ho Ya for cheating me years
and years."

"By tonight, *'No* Kulas," Agustin said with hesitation, "by
tonight the body of this girl—won't the body be bloated?"

"Maybe, but what of it?"

"Won't it be hard to get the rings out of the bloated
fingers?"

"Why should it be hard? It's all so simple. Just break the
fingers, *chico.* Just break off the fingers. Then put them in your
pocket and we clean them up later. You may use your bolo but
I don't think it's necessary."

Nicolas picked up his mattock again. About an hour later
they were joined by two men cementing a tomb near the cemetery chapel.

Inggoy, the older one, squatted on the edge of the pit. He
was chewing *buyo* and betel nut. "When is the burial?"

Nicolas hardly raised his head from his work. "Ho Ya said
between four and five this afternoon. Maybe later because one
uncle of the girl is coming on the *Don Marcelino.* The boat comes
late sometimes."

Julian, Inggoy's companion, pulled out a folded tobacco leaf
from his hip pocket. Julian was a loosely-built man, about
forty-five, who somehow kept his faded khaki work clothes
clean even after hours of mixing and spattering cement. He also
managed in a mysterious way to keep the crease of his pants
after sitting on his haunches. He smoothed down the tobacco
leaf on the back of his palm and moistened it with his breath.
"Want a smoke, Kulas?"

"Can't smoke now, *chico,* but give me a little for *mascada.*
I want the part near the stem."

With the help of his thumb nail Julian cut a fifth of the leaf.
Nicolas popped it into his mouth and masticated with relish.

Julian neatly rolled the rest of the tobacco into a thin
cigar. "Ho Ya wanted us to begin work after the burial. We
told him we couldn't do it because we're still doing Lupo's tomb.
We can't finish it today. Inggoy's going home and can't help
me."

"My wife," explained Inggoy. "Any time now."

"That makes it eleven—or is it twelve? For a little man like you, *chico* . . . ! And you're still strong—strong as a two-year old bombai goat." Nicolas poked him unexpectedly in the rib and Inggoy almost fell into the pit.

Inggoy was unruffled. He dangled his legs on the edge of the pit. "Ten only because one died the other year. But this one coming is the last."

"If you can help it, but you can't," said Julian quietly.

Nicolas guffawed. And then soberly he asked, "Who'll make the tomb then?"

"We will," said Julian. "But Ompong-Miguela will pour the first layer of cement."

"We will be here for that," said Nicolas. "In fact Osting and I will be here all night."

The cement workers looked at Nicolas and Agustin.

"We're staying here all night," said Nicolas. "To keep watch. It's foolish to throw away four pesos which is just for keeping watch. Anyway, why should we be afraid?"

"These Chinese are very queer," observed Inggoy, squirting yellow-brown juice of the *buyo* and betel he was chewing at the mound of earth to his right. "I remember Bun Ting's wife. It was three years ago. I and Ompong-Miguela began mixing cement when the last Chinese women stopped yowling. You know how their women make so much of it. A lot of it was purely dishonest, but when it's getting dark even dishonest crying doesn't sound good in the cemetery. I and Ompong-Miguela worked till past nine. You know how the bones look at night, they look alive. I told myself and Ompong-Miguela I wouldn't do it again. This hurry about the cement, they don't give the dead a chance to come out for a last look at what they left behind."

Julian fumbled for a match in his shirt pocket. He lighted the tobacco roll. "I hear the Chinese bury trinkets and such with their dead. That can be the reason for the hurry."

The group was quiet.

"If what I said is true," Julian went on, "much jewelry will be buried with Si Ya. She's Ho Ya's only girl, and the youngest."

"I don't see how that's possible." Nicolas looked significantly at Agustin. "A more tight-fisted people you'll never know."

Pushing his mattock to a corner of the pit, Nicolas searched a pocket for some coins and gave sixty centavos to Inggoy. "I'm thirsty. Run to Talya's store and bring us one *dama* of *tuba*. If she has roasted fish, get twenty centavos' worth. I'll pay her when Ho Ya gives me the money."

Inggoy hurried away.

Nicolas turned to his companion. "Now, Osting, let's get to work. Stay a while, Julian."

The two men dug steadily while Julian sat on his heels, smoking his tobacco thoughtfully. At waist-deep they struck bones. They shortly uncovered a skeleton, each bone to the smallest toe in place. Nicolas picked up the skull and held it before him for sometime. "I know this fellow," he said. "This is dear old Pantaleon. I chased him once for beating up my dog. And now look at him." He tossed the skull to Julian.

"I wish," said Agustin impulsively, "you wouldn't throw around a skull like that."

"What do you want me to do? Kiss it?" Nicolas laughed. "What's the matter with you anyway?"

"Just a little respect."

"Respect? You mean it? Julian, did you hear that?" He turned to Agustin, looking at him almost angrily. "That's the more reason, *chico*, you should stop digging graves and start a barbershop."

Julian was examining the skull and did not seem to hear the two men. "How do you know it's Pantaleon?"

"See the big scratch above the left ear hole? That's from the bolo of Juan Libat. Almost chopped off Pantaleon's ear. Spent five years in jail for it." He added, "besides, I dug his grave four years ago. I remember now this is the place."

While Julian was still examining the skull, Agustin began throwing up the bones to one side of the grave. He was going to scoop up the hand bones with his shovel but paused instead to look at them, fascinated. He picked up the middle finger. The bone was light and cold and immaculately white. You will pull golden rings from cold fingers tonight. Rings from cold dead fingers. You will pull hard. Just break the fingers, said Nicolas, just break off the fingers.

Observing him staring at the bone, Julian said, "Why do you look at it like that, Osting? Haven't you seen a finger bone before?"

Nicolas looked at Agustin impatiently, and then forced a laugh. "He has not grown up yet, Julian. But he's discovering a few things. He has to grow up in a hurry, or I'll be digging a pit for him in no time."

Agustin flung the bone away.

"The government should widen the cemetery," Julian said, setting the skull beside him. "Unless your grave is cemented, you'll find yourself ejected like Pantaleon there. You don't want to be thrown out of your last bed, do you, Kulas?"

"Come to think of it, no. Though how'd I know I was thrown out for someone else? Would you know, Julian?"

"My soul wouldn't be around, but I certainly want privacy. How did you pick this place?"

"The mound had almost disappeared. Nobody to take care of it. The wife, you remember, had beri-beri and died a year ago. Her grave's near the acacia." He pointed at a tall huge tree in the southeast corner of the cemetery.

Nicolas and Agustin were throwing up the last of the bones when Inggoy came with a rattan-encased demijohn. He also had four mullets run through the body, from the caudal fin to the mouth, with bamboo spits on which they were roasted.

"Eight centavos each," Inggoy told Nicolas. "Talya wants the money tomorrow."

"I see your ears have the color of broiled lobster, Inggoy. You couldn't wait for us, could you? Bring the *dama* here, let's see what's left."

The jar was belly-shaped, a foot and a half in diameter, and had a tall neck. Nicolas tipped it from the edge of the grave and guzzled noisily like a very thirsty bull. His Adam's apple moved up and down, up and down, like a choked valve.

"Are you trying to drown yourself, Kulas?" Julian looked apprehensively at the jar.

Nicolas paused for a long breath and again wrapped his mouth around the jar's brim. When he finally released the jar, sweat starting like beads rolled down his face and armpits and along the narrow valley on his chest. He was about to give the jar to Julian but changed his mind. "There's plenty for all," and he tilted the jar's neck to his mouth once more. The *tuba* gurgled down his throat for such a long time Agustin had to stop shoveling to watch in wonder. A glass of *tuba* was enough to send his own head reeling.

Nicolas finally pushed away the demijohn and with a grunt wiped the froth from around his mouth with a hairy paw. He heaved himself out of the pit but the left foot barely touched the edge and he toppled back. "Miscalculation," he said.

He heaved himself up again, but he couldn't raise his leg high enough; losing balance he tumbled into the bottom with a thud.

Julian cackled. "You should have taken it easy," he said, nodding at the jar.

Agustin helped Nicolas up, but he brusquely shook him off. "Leave me alone. I can do it." He shuffled to one corner of the pit and planted his two palms squarely on the corner edges: slowly he hoisted himself, at the same time raising one leg to the rim; leaning to his right, he clambered up, out of the pit.

Success sobered him a little and he pushed away the memory of Julian's insulting cackle. He gave out one stick of the roasted fish to each of the three men. "Come up, Osting, we'll finish the work later."

"I'm not hungry yet," Agustin said. "I had a late breakfast."

"Osting's not happy eating with bones around," Nicolas said. "But by the time he's old enough to vote, he'll get used to it—unless he'd rather have another job." He bit off the head of the fish, crushed it with his teeth, and washed it down with another long draught. "Don't think my thirst is quenched," he said, giving the jar to Inggoy. He turned to Julian. "I can drink a whole jar, *chico*, without losing my head."

Inggoy, short and stocky, clasped the body of the demijohn and drew it up, as though blowing a savage horn, and drank from it without difficulty. When it was Julian's turn, Inggoy had to raise the jar for him. But Inggoy was half a foot shorter and couldn't regulate the flow of the *tuba;* he had tilted the jar so steeply that Julian choked with his third gulp and the wine spilled down his neck, soaking and staining his shirt.

"You should have borrowed a cup from Talya," Julian complained irritably, shaking the collar of his shirt.

"She couldn't spare anything, not even a coconut shell," Inggoy said. "Her store, it's full of thirsty men."

"You could have stopped at Amalia's on the way—or Akay's."

"I was hurrying. I'll show you how, it's very easy." Inggoy perched the demijohn on a tall mound of earth thrown out of the pit. "You crouch like this and tip the jar. See?"

He looked like a frog. As he drank he slowly stretched his right leg and then his left, in an obscene way, until he was lying on his stomach. Taking his mouth off the brim at last he looked up, grinning at Julian. "Have to find a way, Julian, and be master of the situation."

Nicolas laughed approvingly. "That's right, *chico*. You spoke like a man."

"We can't be drinking like that," said Julian. "Like animals."

"Animals, huh?" Julian's cackling laughter over his fall echoed gratingly in Nicolas' ear, and now the man was flinging insult with this insane demand. "I am like an animal, am I? You're my guest here and you say I'm an animal. You want a cup in a cemetery, Julian? Then you'll have one."

He picked up Pantaleon's skull, wiped the smooth surface on the thigh of his rolled-up denim pants, beat on the cranium's top with his palm to knock out the dirt inside. He poured in some *tuba*, shook the skull for a moment, and threw away its contents. Then he poured in *tuba* again and offered it to Julian. "Drink," he commanded.

Julian was too astounded to move or make any reply.

"I see you don't like my cup, but I'll show you."

Still in the pit, Agustin had watched every movement of Nicolas with growing horror. Would he really do it? Could he do it?

Facing the base of the skull to his mouth, Nicolas drank all of its contents. He refilled it and offered again to Julian. "Now drink." The sharpness in the command would not brook refusal.

Julian was not looking at the brimming skull but at the knotted muscles of Nicolas, who was not too drunk to crush him if he wanted. Nobody had started a fight with Nicolas without getting hurt. If he ran away—that meant talk and disgrace. He received the skull, balanced it in his hands.

For a moment Agustin thought Julian might hurl the skull at the man's face, but it might not stun him. He half-wished Julian would do it.

Julian looked at the skull and closed his eyes. His mouth fumbled for the opening, where the spinal column had joined the cranium.

Agustin saw the red wine coming out like blood from the hollow eyes and ears and nose. He looked at Nicolas fearfully. Was this the final evil gesture before despoiling the grave tonight, or was this only the beginning? He felt moth wings quivering in the pit of his stomach, but he couldn't turn away from the skull oozing red into Julian's mouth. The nose was hollow. The eyes were hollow, they seemed to glare protest. The ears weren't there....

But there will be ears tonight. In the dark you will be feeling for the ears, for the earrings. Diamonds in golden sockets clasped through tiny ear holes. You'll have to hurry, you won't unclasp them, you'll snatch off the earrings, tear the bloodless ears.

"Drink all of it!" barked Nicolas.

Julian emptied the skull and returned it to him.

Nicolas refilled the skull. "Inggoy, now it's your turn. Drink, drink to the soul of dear old Pantaleon. And I want to add," he said, placing a heavy arm on Inggoy's shoulder and looking over meaningfully at Agustin, "this is also the celebration of a great event. Let's celebrate—Pantaleon's release from eternal darkness of the grave! And of course let's celebrate, *chico*, the coming of your tenth son." Instead of giving the skull to Inggoy, he quaffed it himself.

He handed the skull to Inggoy. "Hold it while I pour. There now. There's still enough for Agustin. He has to celebrate—his becoming a man at last. There comes a time for everyone to celebrate." He winked at Agustin standing petrified in the pit.

Inggoy raised the skull, the outraged face toward him. "To you Pantaleon—and your freedom. I drink to your soul, Pantaleon. May you rest in peace." He took a long draught, and held the half-empty skull before him, contemplating it with sorrow. "Poor man. You weren't happy on this earth. Poverty and prison and sickness and all. But from the candles burned for you by your wife you should now be out of purgatory."

Tears started running down Inggoy's face when he raised the skull once more. "To my unborn son—may his fortune be better than mine." After emptying it, he cradled the skull on a loose mound of earth and lifted the demijohn. The jar gurgled out of its remaining contents, the skull brimmed, and the red wine spilled over the hollow nose, ears, eyes and mouth. "Now it's Agustin's turn." He raised the overflowing skull like a chalice and turned to the grave.

Agustin had jumped out of the pit.

"Here, Agustin. It's yours. Drink it—in remembrance of Pantaleon."

Agustin gripped the handle of the shovel. "No."

"Now man, don't be a coward. Come, drink it."

Agustin's hands were tight on the handle of the shovel as he raised it. "Force it on me and you get this." He added, "It goes for anyone. I don't know how low, how very low a man can go down."

Inggoy turned dumbly to Nicolas.

"Leave him alone, *chico*. Maybe he's not a coward. He is a fool—a huge, bungling, miserable fool. You, Inggoy, and you, Julian, look at the man's eyes, look at his face. You see a murderer there. Leave him alone. I've nothing to do with fools."

Agustin walked away.

Sunday Tribune Magazine
July 27, 1941

TWO FRIENDS

DELFIN FRESNOSA

It was mid-afternoon and the sun at its hottest. Clouds of dust rose after every passing car and even long afterwards the air still seemed to be laden with patches of greyish mist. It was seldom that a passerby hurried along the pavements, and on the whole the street was silent and dead. Even the houses seemed deserted. But farther away, the city rumbled on in its usual way, muffled and overspreading.

The Luzon Funeral Parlor was deserted except for a number of boys playing *cara y cruz* near the premises and an attendant asleep on one of the long benches. It was only a small establishment and the furnishings were meager and much-used. A number of unpainted coffins lay stacked up in a sideroom, together with electrical fixtures. Outside, near the doorway, stood parked a black-painted car. There was another car under a makeshift roof and it was much more decrepit.

Tirso was a shoe-shine boy. His hands and face were stained with shoe-polish and his clothes were black with grime. He was about thirteen, but his body was small for his age. His friend, David, was younger. He was dirtier, too, and much darker. He had kinky hair and the other boys called him "Negrito." The two were inseparable companions. They walked the streets together, each shared whatever the other had and felt lost when the other was not around. They were like brothers. But David was from the city and Tirso came from the province.

Tirso was having rotten luck in his coin-throwing. From time to time he fished out a centavo from his pocket, and almost all his earnings for the day was gone. David was not playing. He had only very little money which he had earned selling newspapers, and he was thinking of saving up enough to buy a shinebox. He had one a few weeks ago, but after a game of *cara y cruz,* he had lost everything. Now he had gone back to selling newspapers.

The telephone inside started to ring. Tirso glanced up from his play and told his friend to find out about the call. The attendant was already answering the call and, at the end, he asked again the source of the call and then he said, "All right. We'll send one right up."

The man went outside to look for the driver of the car and finally, when the driver showed up, he told him to drive the car to a certain address. The driver with one helper placed an empty coffin inside with some electric fixtures, and drove away. The attendant went back to resume his interrupted nap and David rejoined the other boys. He told his friend about the phone call.

"I think I'll be able to sell some more papers," he said after some time.

"All right. I'll meet you there," Tirso said.

"When are you going?"

"Maybe a little later. I can pick up some more customers."

"Then we'll meet each other there tonight."

"All right."

David tried to sell some more newspapers at an important intersection of the Meralco street-car line, but there were many other newsboys there. He ran after each passing tramcar shouting the afternoon editions, pushing copies at the faces of some passersby, argued with some of the other boys. Before long he was sweating and he felt tired. Business was not good. There was not enough important news and customers were scarce. There were still many papers left unsold, and feeling the money in his pocket, he calculated he'd not be able to make more than twenty centavos.

Night fell and the stream of home-bent people thinned. The city was aglow with many lights, neon-lights blinking in many colors and plain electric bulbs stolidly burning. The roar of traffic diminished.

The newsboys continued to peddle their papers. David wanted to sell every copy he had gotten from the nearby news-stand, but the prospects were not bright any more. From time to time he brought back to mind the address he'd heard the attendant in the funeral parlor repeat to the driver, and he wondered whether Tirso was already there. The night was still early and maybe he could wait a while longer. The lighted clock atop a drug-store showed it was barely past seven.

Sometime later David returned the papers he had not been able to sell. He decided it was about time to meet his friend. The many streets of the district were familiar to him. He had already left the broader and more brilliantly-lighted streets behind and now he had come to the poorer quarter. The houses were small and ill-kept and large patches of shadow hid him for long stretches of time.

The house which death had visited was in the interior of a block of houses. David noted the many lights burning and the hum of activity. He had to grope his way through a long, tortuous alleyway, which, in places, oozed and reeked with filth and refuse. Then finally he came into the yard and there were many people there. A number of children were playing about in a corner of the yard and David found his friend among them.

It was an old decrepit house, and the living room could barely accommodate all the people who had come. The mother of the dead child sat by the head of the coffin and her eyes were big and red with weeping. She was an ill-kept, middle-aged woman, big with child. She had already a large number of children, most of them still very young, and they played about on the crowded floor. The other people in the house were mostly relatives and neighbors.

Downstairs, in the yard, many people were playing cards. At one table some women were playing *quajo* and at another, a mixed group was playing *entre-siete*. The father of the dead child superintended the goings-on downstairs. He attended to the needs of those who had come to mourn with them, brought cigarettes and *buyo* and betel-nut, looked after the can of boiling water over an improvised hearth in a corner of the yard, greeted newcomers. He worked in a lumber mill and most of his co-workers had come to the house.

From time to time more people arrived. They talked and smoked and sometimes watched those who were playing cards. There were still many unaccommodated, but it was not long before a neighbor brought in the paraphernalia for playing *casuy*. People dragged along a few more tables and they were promptly occupied. Pretty soon they were rapt in the game.

There was the pleasant smell of coffee escaping from the can over the improvised hearth. Cups and glasses and saucers tinkled in the kitchen and some of them were brought down. A woman passed around the coffee together with *aglipay, tajada,* and crackers. Even the children playing in the yard were included in the hand-out. Tirso and David had each a glass of coffee and they grabbed a handful of *tajada* from the paper bag the woman extended to them. Some of these they put in their pockets. After a while they had another helping. They felt ravenous because they had only very little to eat at noon and that morning they had scarcely eaten anything.

Tirso had lost all his money and now he was reluctant to ask a few centavos from his friend. The only thing left to him was his shine-box, and he didn't quite like to part with that. Anyway he was fed up with gambling for the present. He mingled with the other children, but he did not join in the fun. He merely looked on and he appeared sad and forlorn. It was better when his friend came, but he was still sad and moody. David asked him what was the matter, but he merely replied he was feeling all right except for a slight headache.

The night deepened. The neighboring houses had all become silent and dark. Even the noise in the house of mourning had abated somewhat. Up in the house, a group of singers enlivened the drowsy guests. The electric lights burned on brightly and the dead child lay pale inside the coffin.

Downstairs the card games went on. David had put down two centavos on a card and he listened intently to the woman who was calling out the numbers. His friend stood beside him, hoping that they'd win. But presently an elderly woman sang out, *"Casuy,"* and she got all the money. David put down another two centavos. But still he didn't win and he cursed his ill luck. He turned away with his friend and went up into the house. There were more eatables on a big plate and the two boys got some and settled down in a corner. They listened to the songs and kept their mouths busy at the same time.

David fell asleep. He was very tired and now he had something to fill up the ever-present ache in his stomach, so, despite the noise and the crowd, he managed to drop off to sleep. His friend sat beside him. Tirso's eyes were a little red and teary and he seemed very sleepy, too. From time to time he put a cracker in his mouth, sometimes he'd vary this by drinking a

glass of water or a little sarsaparilla. At intervals he lighted
a cigarette and blew out the smoke contentedly. He wanted,
too, to get some sleep, but the ache in his head persisted. The
pain even seemed to have increased and his temples throbbed
and his hands and feet were cold and clammy. He felt chilled.

The hours dragged on wearily. Some of the people had
already left and those who were still around were either in
the yard playing cards or up in the house watching the dead.
Even the singers had stopped sometime ago and they looked
sheepish and bedraggled. The cocks in the neighborhood had
already crowed twice and the night had grown more chilly and
quiet. Dawn was still far off and there was hardly anything
to do to relieve the monotony.

The two friends left shortly before dawn. David was still
somewhat foggy with sleep and he could hardly understand
why the other seemed in a hurry to get away. Their pockets
were filled to overflowing with *tajada* and *aglipay*, which would
last them some time. It was not so long ago they had to depend
for days on end from whatever they could secure visiting houses
where there was someone dead. They could easily locate such
houses because they hung around the funeral parlors a great
deal.

"What's the matter?" asked David.

"My head is burning hot. Feel my forehead."

"Yes. Are you ill?"

"It seems my head's going to split open."

"Then why did we have to go out so early?"

"Maybe the night air would do me good, I was thinking."

They walked about in the deserted streets, the houses
looming tall and dark, the street-lights shining foggily in the
dark night. After a while David's drowsiness had worn off and
he began to like the cold night air and the silence. Then a little
later he noticed that his friend was lagging. Tirso's head hung
low and he had thrust his hands deep into his pockets.

"You're much worse than you think," David said. "Where
do we go from here? Give me your box and I'll carry it for you."

"We can go to *Mang* Lorenzo's house."

"That's right. You can stay there for a while."

Mang Lorenzo lived in a ramshackle hut by the seashore.
He and his aged wife eked out a meager living by going about
the city begging for alms. He was a very kind man and some-

times his hut housed a number of homeless boys. Tirso and David sometimes visited him and often met him and his wife in the streets. He was blind, and his wife invariably went with him; he sang in a thin reedy voice, accompanying himself on a cracked guitar, and she begged for alms.

The boys found the aged couple still in the house, but they had already eaten their breakfast because they were going to Quiapo that morning. *Mang* Lorenzo bade them cook their own breakfast, but David said they were not feeling hungry, maybe later. David then told him that his friend was not feeling very well, and the old couple were quite upset. The aged woman spread a mat on the floor and told Tirso to lie down. They bustled about the sick boy like a couple of fond parents.

Tirso's condition grew worse. When *Mang* Lorenzo and his wife came home that night they immediately called for an *herbolario*. Tirso raved and tossed about and his fever was still mounting. The other boy constantly sat by his side. He had bought food for his friend with the last of his savings, but Tirso hardly touched what he gave him. David seemed to have grown dumb with worry and fear.

The next day the aged couple did not go out to beg. They sat with David, watching the sick boy. Tirso's fever had not diminished, but he did not rave or toss very much. He could hardly recognize those around him any more. He could barely talk either. It seemed as if he were already far away.

Philippine Magazine
August 1941

BLUE BLOOD OF THE BIG ASTANA

IBRAHIM A. JUBAIRA

Although the heart may care no more, the mind can always recall. The mind can always recall, for there are always things to remember: languid days of depressed boyhood; shared happy days under the glare of the sun; concealed love and mocking fate; etc. So I suppose you remember too.

Remember? A little over a year after I was orphaned, my aunt decided to turn me over to your father, the Datu. In those days, datus were supposed to take charge of the poor and the helpless. Therefore, my aunt only did right in placing me under the wing of your father. Furthermore she was so poor, that by doing that, she not only relieved herself of the burden of poverty but also safe-guarded my well-being.

But I could not bear the thought of even a moment's separation from my aunt. She had been like a mother to me, and would always be.

"Please, Babo," I pleaded. "Try to feed me a little more. Let me grow big with you, and I will build you a house. I will repay you some day. Let me do something to help, but please, Babo, don't send me away..." I really cried.

Babo placed a soothing hand on my shoulder. Just like the hand of Mother. I felt a bit comforted, but presently I cried some more. The effect of her hand was so stirring.

"Listen to me. Stop crying—oh, now, do stop. You see, we can't go on like this," Babo said. "My matweaving can't clothe and feed both you and me. It's really hard, son, it's really hard. You have to go. But I will be seeing you every week. You can have everything you want in the Datu's house."

I tried to look at Babo through my tears. But soon, the thought of having everything I wanted took hold of my child's mind. I ceased crying.

"Say you will go," Babo coaxed me. I assented finally. I was only five then—very tractable.

Babo bathed me in the afternoon. I did not flinch and shiver, for the sea was comfortably warm and exhilarating. She cleaned my fingernails meticulously. Then she cupped a handful of sand, spread it over my back, and rubbed my grimy body, particularly the back of my ears. She poured fresh water over me afterwards. How clean I became! But my clothes were frayed....

Babo instructed me before we left for your big house: I must not forget to kiss your father's feet, and to withdraw when and as ordered without turning my back; I must not look at your father full in the eyes; I must not talk too much; I must always talk in the third person; I must not . . . Ah, Babo, those were too many to remember.

Babo tried to be patient with me. She tested me over and over again on those royal, traditional ways. And one thing more: I had to say "Pateyk" for yes, and "Teyk" for what, or for answering a call.

"Oh, Babo, why do I have to say all those things? Why really do I have..."

"Come along, son; come along."

We started that same afternoon. The breeze was cool as it blew against my face. We did not get tired because we talked on the way. She told me so many things. She said you of the big house had blue blood.

"Not red like ours, Babo?"

Babo said no, not red like ours.

"And the Datu has a daughter of my age, Babo?"

Babo said yes—you. And I might be allowed to play with you, the Datu's daughter, if I worked hard and behaved well.

I asked Babo, too, if I might be allowed to prick your skin to see if you had blue blood, in truth. But Babo did not answer me any more. She just told me to keep quiet. There, I became so talkative again.

Was that really your house? My, it was so big! Babo chided me. "We don't call it a house," she said. "We call it *astana*, the house of the Datu." So I just said oh, and kept quiet. Why did not Babo tell me that before?

Babo suddenly stopped in her tracks. Was I really very clean? Oh, oh, look at my hare-lip. She cleaned my hare-lip, wiping away with her *tapis* the sticky mucus of the faintest conceivable green flowing from my nose. Poi! Now it was better. Although I could not feel any sort of improvement in my deformity itself. I merely felt cleaner.

Was I truly the boy about whom Babo was talking? You were laughing, young pretty Blue Blood. Happy perhaps that I was. Or was it the amusement brought about by my hare-lip that had made you laugh? I dared not ask you. I feared that should you come to dislike me, you'd subject me to unpleasant treatment. Hence, I laughed with you, and you were pleased.

Babo told me to kiss your right hand. Why not your feet? Oh, you were a child yet. I could wait until you had grown up.

But you withdrew your hand at once. I think my hare-lip gave it a ticklish sensation. However, I was so intoxicated by the momentary sweetness the action brought me that I decided inwardly to kiss your hand every day. No, no, it was not love. It was only an impish sort of liking. Imagine the pride that was mine to be thus in close heady contact with one of the blue blood . . . .

"Welcome, little orphan!" Was it for me? Really for me? I looked at Babo. Of course it was for me! We were generously bidden in. Thanks to your father's kindness. And thanks to your laughing at me, too.

I kissed the feet of your Appah, your old, honorable resting-the-whole-day father. He was not tickled by my hare-lip as you were. He did not laugh at me. In fact, he evinced compassion towards me. And so did your *Amboh,* your kind mother. "Sit down, sit down; don't be ashamed."

But there you were plying Babo with your heartless questions: Why was I like that? What had happened to me?

To satisfy you, pretty Blue Blood, little inquisitive One, Babo had to explain: Well, Mother had slid in the vinta in her sixth month with the child that was me. Result: my hare-lip. "Poor Jaafar," your Appah said. I was about to cry, but seeing you looking at me, I felt so ashamed that I held back the tears. I could not help being sentimental, you see. I think my being bereft of parents in youth had much to do with it all.

"Do you think you will be happy to stay with us? Will you not yearn any more for your Babo?"

"Pateyk, I will be happy," I said. Then the thought of my not yearning any more for Babo made me wince. But Babo nodded at me reassuringly.

"Pateyk, I will not yearn any more for...for Babo."

And Babo went before the interview was through. She had to cover five miles before evening came. Still I did not cry, as you may have expected I would, for—have I not said it?—I was ashamed to weep in your presence.

That was how I came to stay with you, remember? Babo came to see me every week as she had promised. And you—all of you—had a lot of things to tell her. That I was a good worker—oh, beyond question, your _Appah_ and _Amboh_ told Babo. And you, outspoken little Blue Blood, joined the flattering chorus. But my place of sleep always reeked of urine, you added, laughing. That drew a rallying admonition from Babo, and a downright promise from me not to wet my mat again.

Yes, Babo came to see me, to advise me every week, for two consecutive years—that is, until death took her away, leaving no one in the world but a nephew with a hare-lip.

Remember? I was your favorite and you wanted to play with me always. I learned why after a time, it delighted you to gaze at my hare-lip. Sometimes, when we went out wading to the sea, you would pause and look at me. I would look at you, too, wondering. Finally, you would be seized by a fit of laughter. I would chime in, not realizing I was making fun of myself. Then you would pinch me painfully to make me cry. Oh, you wanted to experiment with me. You could not tell, you said, whether I cried or laughed: the working of my lips was just the same in either to your gleaming eyes. And I did not flush with shame even if you said so. For after all, had not my mother slid in the vinta?

That was your way. And I wanted to pay you back in my own way. I wanted to prick your skin and see if you really had blue blood. But there was something about you that warned against a deformed orphan's intrusion. All I could do, then, was to feel foolishly proud, cry and laugh with you—for you— just to gratify the teasing imperious blue blood in you. Yet, I had my way too.

Remember? I was apparently so willing to do anything for you. I would climb for young coconuts for you. You would be amazed by the ease and agility with which I made my way up the coconut tree, yet fear that I would fall. You would implore me to come down at once, quick. "No." You would throw pebbles at me if I thus refused to come down. No, I still would not. Your pebbles could not reach me—you were not strong enough. You would then threaten to report me to your Appah. "Go ahead." How I liked being at the top! And sing there as I looked at you who were below. You were so helpless. In a spasm of anger, you would curse me, wishing my death. Well, let me die. I would climb the coconut trees in heaven. And my ghost would return to deliver . . .to deliver young celestial coconuts to you. Then you would run home, helpless. I would shout, "Dayang-Dayang, I am coming down!" Then you would come back. You see? A servant, an orphan, could also command the fair and proud Blue Blood to come or go.

Then we would pick up little shells, and search for sea-cucumbers; or dive for sea-urchins. Or run along the long stretch of white, glaring sand, I behind you—admiring your soft, nimble feet and your flying hair. Then we would stop, panting, laughing.

After resting for a while, we would run again to the sea and wage war against the crashing waves. I would rub your silky back after we had finished bathing in the sea. I would get fresh water in a clean coconut shell, and rinse your soft, ebon hair. Your hair flowed down smoothly, gleaming in the afternoon sun. Oh, it was beautiful. Then I would trim your fingernails carefully. Sometimes you would jerk with pain. Whereupon I would beg you to whip me. Just so you could differentiate between my crying and my laughing. And even the pain you gave me partook of sweetness.

That was my way. My only way to show how grateful I was for the things I had not tasted before: your companionship; shelter and food in your big *astana*. So your parents said I would make a good servant, indeed. And you, too, thought I would.

Your parents sent you to a Mohammedan school when you were seven. I was not sent to study with you, but it made no difference to me. For after all, was not my work carrying your red Koran on top of my head four times a day? And you were happy, because I could entertain you. Because someone could be a water-carrier for you. One of the requirements then was to carry water every time you showed up in your Mohammedan class. "Oh, why? Excuse the stammering of my hare-lip, but I really wished to know." Your Goro, your Mohammedan teacher, looked deep into me as if to search my whole system. Stupid. Did I not know our hearts could easily grasp the subject matter, like the soft, incessant flow of water? Hearts, hearts. Not brains. But I just kept silent. After all, I was not there to ask impertinent questions. Shame, shame on my hare-lip asking such a question, I chided myself silently.

That was how I played the part of an *Epang-Epang*, of a servant-escort, to you. And I became more spirited every day, trudging behind you. I was like a faithful, loving dog following its mistress with light steps and a singing heart. Because you, ahead of me, were something of an inspiration I could trail indefatigably, even to the ends of the world . . . .

The dreary monotone of your Koran-chanting lasted three years. You were so slow, your Goro said. At times, she wanted to whip you. But did she not know you were the Datu's daughter? Why, she would be flogged herself. But whipping an orphaned servant and clipping his split lips with two pieces of wood were evidently permissible. So, your Goro found me a convenient substitute for you. How I groaned with pain under her lashings! But how your Goro laughed; the wooden clips failed to keep my hare-lip closed. They always slipped. And the class, too, roared with laughter—you leading.

But back there in your spacious *astana,* you were already being tutored for maidenhood. I was older than you by one Ramadan. I often wondered why you grew so fast, while I remained a lunatic dwarf. Maybe the poor care I received in early boyhood had much to do with my hampered growth. However, I was happy, in a way, that I did not catch up with you. For I had a hunch you would not continue to avail yourself of my help in certain intimate tasks—such as scrubbing your back when you took your bath—had I grown as fast as you.

There I was in my bed at night, alone, intoxicated with passion and emotions closely resembling those of a full-grown man's. I thought of you secretly, unashamedly, lustfully: a full-grown Dayang-Dayang reclining in her bed at the farthest end of her inner apartment; breasts heaving softly like breeze-kissed waters; cheeks of the faintest red brushing against a soft pillow; eyes gazing dreamily into immensity—warm, searching, expressive; supple buttocks and pliant arms; soft, ebon hair that rippled....

Dayang-Dayang, could you have forgiven a deformed orphan-servant had he gone mad, and lost respect and dread towards your Appah? Could you have pardoned his rabid temerity had he leaped out of his bed, rushed into your room, seized you in his arms, and tickled your face with his hare-lip? I should like to confess that for at least a moment, yearning, starved, athirst...no, no, I cannot say it. We were of such contrasting patterns. Even the lovely way you looked—the big *astana* you lived in—the blood you had....Not even the fingers of Allah perhaps could weave our fabrics into equality. I had to content myself with the privilege of gazing frequently at your peerless loveliness. An ugly servant must not go beyond his little border.

But things did not remain as they were. A young datu from Bonbon came back to ask for your hand. Your Appah was only too glad to welcome him. There was nothing better, he said, than marriage between two people of the same blue blood. Besides, he was growing old. He had no son to take his place some day. Well, the young datu was certainly fit to take in due time the royal torch your Appah had been carrying for years. But I—I felt differently, of course. I wanted....No, I could not have a hand in your marital arrangements. What was I, after all?

Certainly your Appah was right. The young datu was handsome. And rich, too. He had a large tract of land planted with fruit trees, coconut trees, and abaca plants. And you were glad, too. Not because he was rich—for you were rich yourself. I thought I knew why: the young datu could rub your soft back better than I whenever you took your bath. His hands were not as callous as mine....However, I did not talk to you about it. Of course.

Your Appah ordered his subjects to build two additional wings to your *astana*. Your *astana* was already big, but it had to be enlarged as hundreds of people would be coming to witness your royal wedding.

The people sweated profusely. There was a great deal of hammering, cutting, and lifting as they set up posts. Plenty of eating and jabbering. And chewing of betel nuts and native seasoned tobacco. And emitting of red saliva afterwards. In just one day, the additional wings were finished.

Then came your big wedding. People had crowded your *astana* early in the day to help in the religious slaughtering of cows and goats. To aid, too, in the voracious consumption of your wedding feast. Some more people came as evening drew near. Those who could not be accommodated upstairs had to stay below.

Torches fashioned out of dried coconut leaves blazed in the night. Half-clad natives kindled them over the cooking fire. Some pounded rice for cakes. And their brown glossy bodies sweated profusely.

Out in the *astana* yard, the young datu's subjects danced in great circles. Village swains danced with grace, now swaying sensuously their shapely hips, now twisting their pliant arms. Their feet moved deftly and almost imperceptibly.

Male dancers would crouch low, with a wooden spear, a *kris,* or a *barong* in one hand, and a wooden shield in the other. They simulated bloody warfare by dashing through the circle of other dancers and clashing against each other. Native flutes, drums, *gabangs, agongs,* and *kulintangs* contributed much to the musical gayety of the night. Dance. Sing in delight. Music. Noise. Laughter. Music swelled out into the world like a heart full of blood, vibrant, palpitating. But it was my heart that swelled with pain. The people would cheer: "Long live the Dayang-Dayang and the Datu, MURAMURAAN!" at every inter-mission. And I would cheer, too—mechanically before I knew. I would be missing you so. . . .

People rushed and elbowed their way up into your *astana* as the young datu was led to you. Being small, I succeeded in squeezing in near enough to catch a full view of you. You, Dayang-Dayang. Your moon-shaped face was meticulously pow-dered with pulverized rice. Your hair was skewered up tower-ingly at the center of your head, and studded with glittering gold hair-pins. Your tight, gleamingly black dress was covered with a flimsy mantle of the faintest conceivable pink. Gold buttons embellished your wedding garments. You sat rigidly on a mattress, with native embroidered pillows piled carefully at the back. Candle-light mellowed your face so beautifully you were like a goddess perceived in dreams. You looked steadily down.

The moment arrived. The turbaned *pandita*, talking in a voice of silk, led the young datu to you, while maidens kept chanting songs from behind. The *pandita* grasped the datu's forefinger, and made it touch thrice the space between your eyebrows. And every time that was done, my breast heaved and my lips worked.

Remember? You were about to cry, Dayang-Dayang. For, as the people said, you would soon be separated from your parents. Your husband would soon take you to Bonbon, and you would live there like a countrywoman. But as you unexpectedly caught a glimpse of me, you smiled at once, a little. And I knew why: my hare-lip amused you again. I smiled back at you, and withdrew at once. I withdrew at once because I could not bear further seeing you sitting beside the young datu, and knowing fully well that I who had sweated, labored, and served you like a dog....No, no, shame on me to think of all that at all. For was it not but a servant's duty?

But I escaped that night, pretty Blue Blood. Where to? Anywhere. That was exactly seven years ago. And those years did wonderful things for me. I am no longer a lunatic dwarf, although my hare-lip remains as it has always been.

Too, I had amassed a little fortune after years of sweating. I could have taken two or three wives, but I had not yet found anyone resembling you lovely Blue Blood. So single I remained.

And Allah's Wheel of Time kept on turning, kept on turning. And lo, one day your husband was transported to San Ramon Penal Farm, Zamboanga. He had raised his hand against the Christian government. He had wished to establish his own government. He wanted to show his petty power by refusing to pay land taxes, on the ground that the lands he had were by legitimate inheritance his own absolutely. He did not understand that the little amount he should give in the form of taxes would be utilized to protect him and his people from swindlers. He did not discern that he was in fact a part of the Christian government himself. Consequently his subjects lost their lives fighting for a wrong cause. Your Appah, too, was drawn into the mess, and perished with the others. His possessions were confiscated. And your Amboh died of a broken heart. Your husband, to save his life, had to surrender. His lands, too, were confiscated. Only a little portion was left for you to cultivate and live on.

And remember? I went one day to Bonbon on business. And I saw you on your bit of land with your children. At first, I could not believe it was you. Then you looked long deep into me. Soon the familiar eyes of Blue Blood of years ago arrested the faculties of the erstwhile servant. And you could not believe your eyes either. You could not recognize me at once. But when you saw my hare-lip smiling at you, rather hesitantly, you knew me at last. And I was so glad you did.

"Oh, Jaafar," you gasped, dropping your *janap*, your primitive trowel, instinctively. And you thought I was no longer living, you said. Curse, curse. It was still your frank, outspoken way. It was like you to be able to jest even when sorrow was on the verge of removing the last vestiges of your loveliness. You could somehow conceal your pain and grief beneath banter and laughter. And I was glad of that, too.

Well, I was about to tell you that the Jaafar you saw now was a very different—a much improved—Jaafar. Indeed. But instead: "Oh, Dayang-Dayang," I mumbled, distressed to have seen you working. You who had been reared in ease and luxury. However, I tried very much not to show traces of understanding your deplorable situation.

One of your sons came running and asked who I was. Well, I was, I was....

"Your old servant," I said promptly. Your son said oh, and kept quiet, returning at last to resume his work. Work, work, Eting. Work, son. Bundle the firewood and take it to the kitchen. Don't mind your old servant. He won't turn young again. Poor little datu, working so hard. Poor pretty Blue Blood, also working hard.

We kept strangely silent for a long time. And then: By the way, where was I living now? In Kanagi. My business here in Bonbon today? To see Panglima Hussin about the cows he intended to sell, Dayang-Dayang. Cows? Was I a landsman already? Well, if the pretty Blue Blood could live like a country-woman, why not a man like your old servant? You see, luck was against me in sea-roving activities, so I had to turn to buying and selling cattle. Oh, you said. And then you laughed. And I laughed with you. My laughter was dry. Or was it yours? However, you asked what was the matter. Oh, nothing. Really nothing serious. But you see....And you seemed to understand as I stood there in front of you, leaning against a mango tree, doing nothing but stare and stare at you.

I observed that your present self was only the ragged reminder, the mere ghost, of the Blue Blood of the big *astana*. Your resources of vitality and loveliness and strength seemed to have been drained out of your old arresting self, poured into the little farm you were working in. Of course I did not expect you to be as lovely as you had been. But you should have retained at least a fair portion of it—of the old days. Not blurred eyes encircled by dark rings; not dull, dry hair; not a sunburned complexion; not wrinkled, callous hand; not....

You seemed to understand more and more. Why was I looking at you like that? Was it because I had not seen you for so long? Or was it something else? Oh, Dayang-Dayang, was not the terrible change in you the old servant's concern? You suddenly turned your eyes away from me. You picked up your *janap* and began troubling the soft earth. It seemed you could not utter another word without breaking into tears. You turned your back toward me because you hated having me see you in tears.

And I tried to make out why: seeing me now revived old memories. Seeing me, talking with me, poking fun at me, was seeing, talking, and joking as in the old days at the vivacious *astana*. And you sobbed as I was thinking thus. I knew you sobbed, because your shoulders shook. But I tried to appear as though I was not aware of your controlled weeping. I hated myself for coming to you and making you cry. So...

"May I go now, Dayang-Dayang " I said softly, trying hard to hold back my own tears. You did not say yes. And you did not say no, either. But the nodding of your head was enough to make me understand and go. Go where? Was there a place to go to? Of course. There were many places to go to. Only, there was seldom a place to which one would like to return.

But something transfixed me in my tracks after walking a mile or so. There was something of an impulse that strove to drive me back to you, making me forget Panglima Hussin's cattle. Every instinct told me it was right for me to go back to you and do something—perhaps beg you to remember your old Jaafar's hare-lip, just so you could smile and be happy again. I wanted to rush back and wipe away the tears from your eyes with my headdress. I wanted to get fresh water and rinse your dry, ruffled hair, that it might be restored to flowing smoothness and glorious luster. I wanted to trim your fingernails, stroke your callous hand. I yearned to tell you that the land and the cattle I owned were all yours. And above all, I burned to whirl back to you and beg you and your children to come home with me. Although the simple house I lived in was not as big as your *astana* at Patikul, it would at least be a happy, temporary haven while you waited for your husband's release.

That urge to go back to you, Dayang-Dayang, was strong. But I did not go back for a sudden qualm seized me: I had no blue blood. I had only a hare-lip. Not even the fingers of Allah perhaps could weave us, even now, into equality.

Graphic
August 28, 1941

THE NEXT ONE'S ON ME

T. D. AGCAOILI

One early evening, while waiting for a taxi on the Escolta, I saw Marcos Santa Romana swiftly crossing the street towards the sidewalk where I was standing. I hailed him and when he recognized me, he took my hand and said, "Well, well, look at that, I've been thinking of you only this morning, and now here you are."

"Thanks to the rain," I said, for it was raining.

I was nothing much to Santa Romana, except as a publicity man for a couple of his pictures before I finally had an altercation with the all-knowing Big Boss of his movie company a few months ago, after which I returned to legitimate newspaper work.

That's why, curiously, I asked him, "Now, what would you be thinking of me for?"

"You're still a reporter, aren't you?" he asked.

There were people listening. "No," I replied, slightly irked, "I'm now an editorial staff member."

"Of the same paper?"

"Of the same paper," I said.

"That's good," he said. "That's very good." He looked at the street, at the rain. "You're not intending to go home this early, are you?"

"Taking for granted that I do, do you think I could?" I answered rather brusquely.

"Still tough, aren't you?" he said, laughing softly. He led me around the corner, on the sidewalk of the street that crossed Escolta. "Do reporters drink?" he asked.

"Editors do," I said. "Guide me to it."

And that's how I found myself drinking at the bar just off the Escolta, with Marcos Santa Romana sitting at the table opposite me.

In the well-lighted barroom, I looked at Marcos directly for the first time in two or three months. He was still the same fashionably dressed man he always had been—an orchid on his lapel, matching tie and handkerchief, correct color harmony of shirt, suit and socks, and expensive shoes that were none the worse for the rain.

If you read the movie magazines, you would know that Marcos is a be-moustached Spanish mestizo, well on his late thirties and baldish on the temples. He is a personable middle-aged man, and his look of prosperity does not suffer a whit by the natural way he holds a cigar to his mouth.

As we waited for our drinks, Marcos lit a cigar. He offered me one matter-of-factly, and matter-of-factly I told him I only smoke cigarettes.

"You want me to do something for you," I said, taking a cigarette from my case. "Come out with it."

"You've heard of my case, of course," he said.

"Of course," I said, lighting my cigarette. "Your wife is perfectly right in suing you for maintenance and support. Your children and their schooling, you know."

"Oh, I'm already taking care of that," he said. "You don't know my newest case. My wife is now charging me with adultery."

"You mean that she won the first case?"

"Yes," he said. The waiter came with our glasses of beer. "I am *obligated* to maintain her and my children. I don't mind the children, I love them, and I will always be glad to support them. But the idea of giving my wife money every month while she runs around with another man is...." He was at a loss for the correct word. "... *repugnante*," he said in Spanish. "... what you call disgusting."

"She won her first case," I said, "and now she has another one against you? What a woman!"

"Yes, what a woman!" he said, "a very bad woman. She has always been."

I lifted my glass from the table. Marcos took his in his hand too. And I toasted, "Here's wishing success to your next picture."

"Wait," he said. And changing my toast, he said, "Here's to us, better. My pictures will always take care of themselves. Let us wish ourselves well instead."

The toast seemed reasonable, and so we drank.

"Failures develop from carelessness," he said, wiping his mouth with a napkin. "I was careless in the way I first dealt with my wife," he explained, "that's why our marriage failed.

"I should not have loved her the way I did. There are women who are good to their men when they know that their men care for them only slightly. The worst thing a man could do if he had a woman like this would be to show he cared for her very much; for then she takes advantage of his affection and changes him from a lover to a slave. This was the kind of woman my wife Anna was, and the kind of lover I was to her.

"Now, as you know, I have many girl-friends to run around with. You know how some women are with directors!"

He shook the ashes from his cigar, and downed his glass of beer.

"The next one is on me," I said.

"Don't be foolish," he said, "I invited you. Besides," he added, "I prefer buying you drinks, all the drinks, all the drinks you want, to paying maintenance money to my wife!"

"I've been separated from her now for ten years. And she never tried until now to sue me. Ten years ago, I never made as much money as I do now. I was not badly off either. But she is dirty, always has been. And, to think of it, I loved her very much. It is sad."

The waiter brought our drinks and a saucer of peanuts.

"It is a sad thing that I loved her. I showed her that I loved her very much; and instead of appreciating my feelings, she took advantage of them. When I had money, I gave every centavo to her, and she was satisfied. When I had no money, she cursed me. You know how it was to work in the movies ten, fifteen years ago. Pay was so little, and directors were not paid on monthly basis, but on picture basis. You get paid this much for a picture, and do not get anything until you start on another. That's why sometimes, I could not bring money to her every month. To solve this situation, I had what you call a side-line.

"I am deft with my hands, you think I don't know manual labor, don't you? Well, I can write movie stories, direct pictures and even compose music; and I can also make beautiful wooden cabinets and picture frames.

"I canvassed my friends for orders of picture frames and cabinets, and this way I managed to make a living for the periods between my making moving pictures."

Marcos, as I told you, is a Spanish mestizo, and he is not very fluent in English. But that night, his volubility more than made up for his lack of fluency.

"It was at this time that I came to know the duplicity of Anna, when I was making cabinets. There was a friend she met, a foreigner, Mexican. He had very limited funds and no relatives in the Philippines to go to, so I offered him the hospitality of my home. I told him he could take his breakfast, lunch and supper at home, and that we could even take care of his laundry. But he must find a place to sleep in for it would not·look good if he slept with us also. Well, Diaz the Mexican, ate with us and had his laundry included with ours. I trusted him, considering that he owed me a favor; and I never had any bad thoughts of him in my mind until the afternoon I came home to find a cigarette butt in our bathroom. I knew Anna never smoked, and I didn't smoke cigarettes either. I wondered about the cigarette butt being in the bathroom, as Diaz was not supposed to take a bath too in our house.

"So the next day, I made it a point to come home unexpectedly and who do you think I found?"

He lifted his glass of beer to his lips and gulped the whole drink without furnishing the answer to his question. I finished my drink also, and called the waiter for another round. "And bring me a tuna sandwich," I said. "Won't you have a sandwich too?" I asked Marcos.

"I'll have a tuna sandwich too," he told the waiter. The waiter left to fill our orders, and Marcos turned·to me again. "That was the time when I wished I were dead. That's how I felt. That's the worst feeling of loneliness a man can feel, when he wishes he were dead. You love a woman very much, you love her alone, and then you find her with another man. You love her and she is your wife. Diaz was a very big man, but that time, I felt I could kill him with my bare hands. Perhaps he knew my powers too, or rather he sensed them, and he ran out of the room, and out of the house before I could get hold of him. Then, left alone with my wife, I turned my fury upon her. I removed my belt and lashed her with it. She was naked, and I lashed her body until she was crying and I was also crying. When I saw her crying, and I saw the welts on her body, I loved her and hated her at the same time. I was all mixed up, and I turned the belt on myself. I lashed her with the leather; I lashed myself with the buckle. Then I was exhausted and sobbing bitterly, and Anna came to me and asked for forgiveness. I took her in my arms and asked for her forgiveness. I'll never do it again, she promised me, and I believed her. It is easy to believe when one loves.

"And I loved her very much, and was very willing to forget the incident. Diaz, I learned later, quickly booked passage for his country; and I thought that was the end of the affair. That affair was really ended," he said, "but another one like it happened."

The waiter brought a new round of beer and our tuna sandwiches. "I like tuna sandwiches. I like tuna sandwiches," Marcos said.

"Have you tried tuna salad?" I asked, biting into my sandwich.

"Yes, I often order it," he said, also biting into his sandwich.

"Tuna sandwich is good with beer," I said, drinking my beer.

"Swell combination," he continued, also drinking his beer.

"What happened after the Diaz affair?" I asked.

"There were petty troubles, of course," he said, "as could be expected from any married couple."

He relit the cigar he had forgotten to smoke. Then he resumed:

"Do you know Reyes, the cameraman?" I nodded, and he said: "He has started working only recently. For some time he could not find work in any movie company. I was responsible for that. He was able to work again only after he came to me practically on his knees and crying, begged me to pity him and let the producers know that he, Reyes, can have again my permission to work.

"Reyes used to be one of my best friends. I treated him like a brother, like a member of the family. He often had his dinner at home, and I always had him shoot my pictures. I taught him many things about camera angles, and we worked together as a team.

"But one noontime, I arrived home unexpectedly and found him at home when he was supposed not to be there. I asked him what he wanted and he replied that he was looking for me. Well, now that I'm here, what do you want? I asked him and he stammered, answering me inaudibly. We were in the sala, and I went into my wife's room without waiting for Reyes to speak more clearly.

"I found Anna in her room, dressing. I tricked her into admitting she had an affair with my friend and I rushed out into the sala to find Reyes already gone. I looked out of the window, and saw the rear of a taxi cab turning around the corner.

"I did not lay my hand on my wife this time. Our two children were home, playing quietly in their room, and I did not want them to see me hurting their mother. I just went out of the house after leaving some money on top of her dressing table.

"I was feeling so bitter and lonely as I stayed away from her for three weeks. I finished the picture I was currently making, allowing Reyes to photograph it. I never said a word of reproach to Reyes, no statement referring to my wife. On the last day of shooting, I eventually called him aside and told him I was not going to use him as cameraman for my next picture. I never cared for a next picture, and although my last picture was successful and producers wanted me to direct other productions, I turned down the offers. I had no desire to work. Inside of me was bitterness. My mind was disturbed. I had no desire to live.

"This was the time I attempted to commit suicide. Now seeing me the way I am, you would never think it was in me to think of suicide, would you? Well, I'm different now. I no longer love my wife. I have been able to live without her for more than ten years now, and I'm happy. There are two kinds of women in this world, bad women and good women. It is when a man loves a bad woman that he is better dead than alive.

"It was when I realized I was married to a bad woman that I understood that life was useless for me. I loved her so much, and she was so bad! With no work to bind me and only bitterness to guide me, I tried to commit suicide. I swam from Fort San Antonio Abad one night, and headed for Cavite. I expected that I would never reach Cavite. I thought that halfway, I would have an attack of cramps and just drown. It was a moonlit night. With only my trunks, I swam out to sea. The sea was very cold and calm."

He paused to eat another layer of his sandwich and drained it down his throat with beer.

He set down his empty glass and continued: "As you see, I did not die. I lost consciousness, but a U.S. navy patrol boat rescued me. They wanted to know if I had wanted to kill myself, and before answering their questions, I thought twice. Now that my attempt was foiled, I felt ashamed to make any sort of admittance. So I lied, and said that I must have swam unknowingly far out to sea until I got washed to where the patrol launch found me. Then they asked where I lived, and I told them. In the morning a navy jitney brought me back to Manila.

"Anna made no fuss about my return, but when the American sailors were gone, and we were alone, she said one word to me; she said, *Fool!*

"However, she nursed me until I was well again and I was not worried about money because when I left the last time, I left a sum that I expected to last her some months.

"But when I was up and moving, she said, You cannot just be lying around here and let me support you. You must go out again and find work. And don't think that you can come back into the house until you bring me some money.

"Well, I found work, grabbed one of the offers made me by some producers. And before starting the filming, I made an advance withdrawal against my pay and with some of the money bought a coat, a handbag and some costume jewelry for Anna. The rest of the money I placed in the bag. I wanted to surprise her. So I hurried home. It was evening, and as I knocked at the door, I expected Anna to answer it. Instead, it was Mary, one of my daughters. Where is Mamma? I asked Mary, and she said that Mamma was out. Mary looked at the packages I had under my arms and I felt ashamed upon realizing that I didn't have anything for her or her younger sister, Ester.

"I was thinking up some way to make it up with them when I heard a car stop in front of the house. I went to the door and met Anna, for it was Anna who arrived in the car. But she was not alone. Driving the car, and coming down from

it, was Merced, a friend of hers whom I had never approved
of. Merced was one of those girls men talked about in snicker-
ing whispers. However, since I was returning home with good
news, I didn't want to spoil the evening by showing my disapproval of Merced.

"So, I pretended not to be aware of her, and just greeted
Anna warmly, offering her the packages. But she casually
took the packages and laid them carelessly on a nearby sofa.
Oh you're back, she said, and then turned smilingly to Merced
who was now coming in at the door as casually as if it were
her own house.

"My temper was now aroused, fed by faggots of suspicions gradually forming in my mind. Apparently, Anna did
not care if I was home or not. Apparently, she and Merced
were what you call thick as thieves. I didn't like the look of
things. But also, I wanted to be patient. So I said, there right
in front of Merced, I said to Anna, Honey, let's you and I
step out tonight. Look into those packages, I have many things
for you.

"Anna looked at me as if seeing me for the first time,
and said, Merced and I are going some place tonight. I had
looked forward the whole day to a dinner and dance with Anna
tonight. And now, she was telling me she could not go out
with me because of some place she and Merced were going to.
I was now aroused. And I said, Oh, so you are going out
together tonight, are you? I used a certain term to describe
what I thought they were. When I said the term, Anna swiftly
flew at me. It was so quick, so sudden, I was taken unaware.
She scratched my face, and pushed me towards the door. I
tried to argue with her, all kinds of words coming out of me,
possibly not intelligibly; but she would not listen. My last
glance before the door closed on me was Ester's and Mary's
faces—my children's faces distorted with pain."

He called the waiter and ordered another round of drinks.

"Children are always the sufferers when a home is broken,"
I said.

"Yes, but I think they can adapt themselves quickest to
the new situation, better than the fathers," Marcos said. "In
my case, I could never reconcile myself with the thought of
losing my home with Anna. I loved her so much that I could
condone almost anything she did.

"But there was one thing she did which finally destroyed all love I had for her. It was the least thing you or anybody would expect to kill a man's love, for it does not really seem even half as terrible as when you see your wife in another man's arms. But, strangely, it was the thing that eventually killed my affections for Anna. It was this way.

"The nights after that incident when I was forced out of the house, I never failed to go under the house, and through a hole of the floor, spoke to Anna and begged her to let me in, and to forgive me. I even went to the extent of telling her that she could do anything she desired, just as long as she would let me come home again. I cried under the house, and let her hear I was crying. I threatened to attempt suicide again, but she would not let me in. I heard the children beg her to let me in, but she would not listen. She said only one thing to me, stop annoying me or I'll send for the police. I said, Pity me, Anna darling, I love you only, and I cannot live without you. I will be slave for you, and give you everything. I will make myself the best in my profession, only you must love me too, and let me in.

"But she had a heart of stone. She was bad, a bad woman, and there was nothing I could do about that. On the eighth night I had been going under the house to beg her to let me in, she suddenly shouted for all the neighbors to hear, There's a burglar under my house! Help, there's a burglar under my house! She knew I was the one under the house, as I had been there already an hour long, begging her to forgive me, humbling myself as much as any man could ever humble himself.

"When I heard her shouting, and I heard the answering furor from the neighbors, I became alarmed. From alarm, I felt humiliation. This was the first time perhaps that I actually saw myself as I was: the humblest, and the cheapest, man. And when I ran away from under the house and saw people with clubs looking for me in the shadows, I felt dirty all over, I suddenly felt very dirty and with this feeling was anger. Then even the dirty feeling was gone, and there was only anger. Anger and a feeling that was very satisfying at that time. The feeling of hate.

"I never hated her when I saw her in the arms of Diaz, nor when I was convinced that she was no better than her

friend Merced; but when she knowingly made me up as a burglar, my love for her died. I hated her then, and I hate her now.

"As you know, I have succeeded in becoming the best director of the Philippine movies," he said, "and yet . . ."

"You're sure of that, aren't you?" I interrupted him.

"Why," he said, looking me in the eye, "do you doubt it?"

"I don't," I said, soberly.

"I have succeeded to become the best director, and the
highest paid man in the industry, yet it seems that I'm forever
cursed with the love that I bear for that worthless woman some
ten years ago," he said.

"Why do you say that?" I asked.

"Because sometime after that evening I was hunted like a
common thief, that evening my love for Anna died, I met another woman. Her name is Lina, and she's a good woman.

"Now with this new case I have with Anna, I must leave
the home I shared with Lina, and not see the son she gave me,
for the home and the son and Lina are the three things that
Anna can use to win her case against me; yet they are also
the only things dear to me."

His cigar was cold, had been for a time, and he lit it again.

"What can I do for you?" I said, remembering his request
earlier in the evening.

He looked long at me, and then at the glowing tip of his
cigar. Presently, he said, "You can buy the next round."

"All right," I said, "the next one's on me." And I shouted
to the waiter for another round of beer.

Outside, it was still raining.

Herald Mid-Week Magazine
September 17, 1941

RENDEZVOUS AT BANZAI BRIDGE

MANUEL E. ARGUILLA

In the club I could not forget him.

"*Kampai*," said Sakuda-san.

"*Kampai*," said Nanding.

"*Kampai*," said I

Lourdes, the plump Bicolana waitress, filled our emptied beer mugs. She leaned across the table to fill mine from the tall tawny bottle and down the low front of her black dress I could see clear to her belly.

But I could not forget the man I had met earlier that evening on Banzai Bridge.

He wore a ragged straw hat that threw a shadow on the upper half of his thin strange face. But the shadow was not dark enough to hide the bright gleam that flashed at me, like a knife blade from his eyes. He leaned with his back against the stone parapet of the bridge, hands in his pockets, a thin nondescript figure from the distance of a few paces. But as I came abreast of him, he had sent me that strange, disturbing look.

Perhaps it was all my imagining. At nine o'clock in the evening, Banzai Bridge is about deserted of pedestrians. I was quite alone, as a matter of fact, when I crossed it that evening on my way to meet Sakuda-san and Nanding. A calesa or two rattled past me, drawn by panting, patient ponies. Then just before I came to the top of the bridge, I saw a man.

I saw him, noted the way he leaned against the stone parapet of the bridge, automatically put him down in my mind as one of the thousands of jobless men in the City and took no further thought of him.

Then I came abreast of him and our eyes met and from under the shadow of his hat had come that questioning glance.

In the club I could not forget him.

I said, "*Kampai.*"

And Sakuda-san grimaced, pointed a finger at me and said, "You, very good drinker."

I said, "*Kampai.*" And Lourdes filled our beer mugs again and I got up and went to the men's toilet room and Nanding said, "We are at a disadvantage. His kidneys work overtime."

And all the time I was thinking of the man on Banzai Bridge.

Should I have stopped and talked to him? My heart quickened at the thought. He was no ordinary loiterer, of that I had felt certain, after the odd look he had given me. A thief, perhaps? Waiting for some hapless woman pedestrian? I pictured him standing there, looking deceptively harmless, quite forlorn. The woman walks up to him all unsuspecting, even pitying him a little perhaps, and perhaps just a bit apprehensive. Then the sudden leap and snatch, the silent frantic struggle in the first moment of surprise on the part of the woman, then her frightened and enraged shouts as the man flees with his booty.

No, it was better that I had left him where he was. What could I have said to him?

Then a thought entered my head. But I dismissed it almost immediately afterwards as being too fantastic. It had occurred to me that maybe the man was a guerrilla agent and that he was there on Banzai Bridge waiting for someone. That explained the sharp, questioning look he had given me, I thought. Perhaps he had expected me to murmur a password and then he would have murmured back its complement, but I had walked past him silently without even a backward glance. It was all too absurd and fantastic and I shook my head and grinned at my own foolish thoughts.

"Ah, the beer is getting you," Nanding said.

"Not beer," I said. "I am an Ilocano and was suckled on *basi*. Besides, beer flows out of me fast as it flows in."

"Our kidneys are not so good," said Nanding, pointing to Sakuda-san and then to himself. "That's where you beat us with beer. But with whisky, I guarantee to put you under the table."

So Sakuda-san motioned to Lourdes and she skipped to his side and leaned close to him and Sakuda-san said, "Three whisky-sodas."

I said, "Whisky-water for me."

When the order arrived, I looked under the table and I said, "Sakuda-san, where are you?"

Sakuda-san said, "Under the *taberoo*," laughing in his jolly, infectious way. And we drank our highballs slowly, not *kampai*, which means dry your cup, or in other words bottoms up.

And all the time I thought of the man on Banzai Bridge. I began to wonder what he was: Tagalog, Ilocano, Visayan, or Pampango? And his name? Juan, Pedro, Silvestre, Jose? This is all very silly, I told myself. Why should I bother my head over the fellow? A feeling of annoyance began to creep upon me. I drank my whisky-water and felt more and more annoyed. In a little while more, and I was sure that I thoroughly disliked the man on Banzai Bridge. What did he mean by giving me that queer look as I had passed him by? And why did I not stop and challenge him to explain? I was annoyed with myself and for that reason became more annoyed with the strange man. If he were anywhere near at hand then, I would have picked a fight with him. I even thought of getting up and leaving my companions and going back to Banzai Bridge to see if the man was still there and if he was still there to have it out with him one way or the other.

"What's eating you?" Nanding said. "Don't tell me the whisky is getting you."

"Whisky on beer, never fear," I said, repeating the old limerick; "but beer on whisky is damned risky."

"Say that again, prease," said Sakuda-san.

So I said it again and he repeated it after me and it made him very happy. I felt happy to see him so happy. For a time I forgot the man on Banzai Bridge. A year ago, I thought, who would have imagined that I would now be sitting here with Sakuda-san, drinking with him in this jolly fashion, feeling absurdly glad to be able to add to his sum of happiness with an old limerick! Such is life, I sighed and found myself in the middle of a hiccough. My God, the whisky was going to my head!

I caught Lourdes' hand and got up to dance. The band was playing *I'm Getting Sentimental Over You*. Lourdes hummed the tune as we danced and when she was not humming it, she told me of her little son whose father she did not know. We danced several pieces and I began to perspire and my perspiration smelled of beer and whisky and I wondered what Lourdes thought of it and I tried to draw away from her as we danced, but she clung close to me and hummed the tune the orchestra was playing.

When I brought Lourdes back to the table, Nanding danced with her; Sakuda-san was dancing with another girl. I was left alone and my thoughts went back to the man on Banzai Bridge. I remembered that he had on a *maong* shirt, patched at the elbows; his pants were either much-faded khaki or long un-washed white drill. He wore dirty canvas shoes and there was an upright buri sack at his feet. I remembered all these details about the man although I did not recall having tried to notice them particularly when I passed him by earlier that evening. Remembering him now with all these details added to the picture of him in my mind, my thoughts about him underwent another change.

He began to appear as an object more to be pitied than feared or disliked. Sympathy for him welled up in my heart; I longed to put my arm around his shoulders and comfort him. For I became convinced that he had suffered much, had under-gone privations beyond my imagining. I saw him leaning there against the cold stone parapet of Banzai Bridge seeking a ray of hope from another man's look and, remembering how I had walked past him silent and unmoved, even somewhat suspicious, I was filled with remorse. Perhaps he was at the end of his tether, in the last ultimate tussle with unfeeling circumstance and he was about ready to give up the struggle. How much would another man's understanding and sympathy have meant to him at that time!

That glance he had sent me was not the furtive glare of a suspicious character but the anguished look of a soul in tor-ment....Perhaps the man had gone there to make a final end to all his troubles, to make his peace with this world in the turbid bosom of the Pasig. Perhaps even now he had taken the fateful leap and somewhere in the Bay his bloated corpse would be found floating the following day; my thoughts were getting hysterical—

"Don't tell me you are weeping into your whisky," came the voice of Nanding.

Across the table, I saw Sakuda-san looking at his wrist watch.

"Sakuda-san," I said, disregarding Nanding, "mighty drinker."

"You," Sakuda-san said, waving his hand toward me, "ver' good drinker."

I heard Nanding say, with a snigger, "If we had more time, I guarantee to put both of you under the table."

We left the club and Nanding took a street car to his home in Maypajo. I walked with Sakuda-san to his hotel. The streets were deserted; they smelled of horse manure. A tricycle came up to us and there was a girl inside and the man pedalling it said, *"Konban wa,"* and the girl sat inside silent and waiting.

"Live bait," I said, turning to Sakuda-san.

"You know what we call like him?" he said, waving away the man and his passenger; "we call them *konban wa* boys."

"I like that," I said. *"Konban wa* boys; it's good."

When we got to his hotel, Sakuda-san invited me to his room for one more highball; just one more, prease.

In the room it was hot. Sakuda-san removed his coat, his shirt and his tie and sat on his bed in his undershirt.

"Last August," he said, "I went up to Baguio ne? Ugh! It was ver' cold. Always raining. Ver' wet everything. We stayed in the hotel all the time and drank whisky to keep warm ne?"

"But I like Philippines ver' much," he went on. "With the Philippines already I feel like brothers."

He thumped his breast and said, intensely serious, "Inside here, deep inside, inside—I feel like that."

When I left, he walked with me down to the hotel lobby. He urged me to take a tricycle—several were waiting at the hotel entrance. But I told him not to bother; I'd walk. My home was just across Banzai Bridge. The moment I had said that I remembered the man I had met on the bridge earlier that evening.

What in the name of heaven was the man doing there really? I asked myself, walking fast for it was nearing curfew time.

Then I reached the foot of Banzai Bridge and to my startled surprise I saw the man leaning against the stone parapet in exactly the same posture that he had when I first saw him that evening. I was as powerless to stop my legs from carrying me towards him as to sort out my whirling thoughts....

When I was only a few steps from him, the man deliberately turned around and threw the upper half of his body over the stone parapet. The damned fool is going to his death! The thought leaped to my brain.

"Stop!" I yelled. I plunged forward and grabbed his legs. He tried to kick but I held him and put him back to his feet. Then he turned upon me.

"Are you a fool?" he asked.

And indeed I felt like one as he calmly turned around again and began pulling at a line that he held in his hands. Wordlessly, I stood by his side while he pulled in the line and finally brought up a crab trap baited with a piece of meat. There was a crab caught in the trap and he shook it into the buri sack at his feet. And all I could think of at that moment was, "This is what comes of too much *kampai!*"

Philippine Review
April 1943

IT WAS LATER THAN WE THOUGHT

NICK JOAQUIN

From Tony Banzon, in Laguna, to his wife, Chayong, in Manila

Oct. 20, 1941

I have never pretended to understand you, or females in general. You say your dreams have all gone wrong, that I satisfy you no longer, that our life together has become a "mere plaything." You do admit that I can still give you a "purely physical satisfaction" that, however, is becoming "less and less important with the years." And you further assure me that the "last creature of mine" had nothing to do with your packing off. Which makes my feeling very, very sorry about that business quite irrelevant, does it not? Or maybe you're just mystifying me as usual? Hell, darling, my old bean is not very quick; you've proved that often enough; must you go this far?

One of your sex once found out she was living in a doll's house and promptly walked out of it. It simply isn't possible you've walked out of mine for so inane a reason. In the first place, in ten whole years, you haven't stayed long enough inside these walls to make a doll's house out of them, let alone a man's. Now look, I'm not kicking; I never did, did I? and I never will. I made a deal with you when we married: hands off your "career," and all that. You can't say I haven't kept it. You've always done pretty much as you pleased. Boy, did you have me awed? All those "drives" and "movements" and "activities!" Now, it seems they're not enough; they don't satisfy; something's still rotten in the state of Rumania.

Well, it's not a toy-house you're itching to walk out of now: it's a toy-world. A big gaudy doll's world. And you built it yourself. You females have a genius for turning everything you touch into mere toys and dolls. I myself don't consider anything in this world of more importance than toys and dolls.

Only, I have the good sense to stay out, and you females haven't. You want to eat your cake and have it too: is that sense? You want to commute between two worlds and use us males for ponies: is that kind? I'm very sorry if your dreams have all busted; but dammit, darling, why use me for a stalking horse?

From Doña Ada Cabrera, in Manila, to her son Bitoy, at Camp X

Oct. 23, 1941

...I send with this the books and magazines you asked for. I have also enclosed your two sweaters and a can of Mentholatum. They say it is chilly up there. Does your nose clog at night? Remember to rub your chest and back with the menthol before retiring. Always sleep in a sweater and away from drafts. And stop reading so much.

Since my last letter, your father has quit his bed and we were able to celebrate his birthday in a small way. You were much missed. Last night we had another blackout. I was not so nervous as the last time. Besides, there were no whistles. Your sister Chayong is here. For a vacation, she says. But I suspect that she and Antonio have been fighting again. There is much excitement over the elections. They hold meetings every night at the plaza and are so noisy I cannot sleep.

Of course, you have heard by now that your brother Noe has been appointed parish priest. It is a great honor for our family. Everyone here likes him. You can imagine how I tremble with joy whenever I receive the Sacrament from my own son's hands.

And you, my youngest: do you commend yourself to God at every step? I rejoice that you hear mass daily. Do not begrudge the hour or two you must rise up earlier. Do it, I beg you, if not for the peace of being, then for mine.

From Lulu Cabrera's Diary

Oct. 19, 1941

Father's birthday. Chayong and I chipped in for a box of cigars; Angel gave a book of Spanish poems; Noe, a devotional. Special chicken-spread this evening: Mother's offering. She's in his black-list too. He's hurt she should be on our side. He's become even more silent since this illness. At table tonight, his eyes kept getting fixed on one or the other of us. Probably thought us a queer batch of sons and daughters for God to have given him, poor dear. Trouble is: he's a gentleman, and none of us could be. We're this ugly and vulgar world he hates so much, and here it is, eating right at table with him! Mother kept remembering only Bitoy absent....

Oct. 22, 1941

Hear I'll be promoted to section manager, which means twice as many shekels, come payday. Chayong at store this morning, "just looking around." Told me she couldn't imagine what I liked so much in being a salesgirl. And how could I bear to stay put in one place all day? Now, when *she* was my age....

Found Johnny waiting at closing time. Said he wouldn't have me going alone on a blackout night because everyone felt queer then. Carried a copy of the last *Merchandizer* with him; shocked at my column. Asked if I thought up all those things myself. Told him no: they'd all been thought up before; I just unthought them all out again as far as they'd go. Which seemed to relieve him. At all theaters we passed, queues and queues of people. Seeking sanctuary, we learned, from impending blackout.

Supper long over when I got home. Mother very nervous as usual; Father locked up in his room; Chayong wandering listlessly around; Angel at window—hand in pockets. When lights went out, Mom started moaning; Chayong and I finally got her into bed.

Heard Angel knocking at Father's door to see if he was all right; Father shouting: "Leave me alone, I implore you. Only leave me alone."

Oct. 24, 1941

Chayong still furious with Angel for having taken her and me to hear those women candidates, last night. She claims he did it to mock her. Angel amused. Asked if I was, too. Told him no: it was coarse without being funny....

From a column in a Manila paper

Oct. 26, 1941

About the watchtower in Samar that suddenly crumbled down the other day: we were wondering if the occurrence was without significance. We're not entirely blind to the tremendousness of certain trifles, you know, and in the collapse of this antiquated tower, built in Spanish times, in the Spanish manner, and for purposes peculiar to that dispensation, we seem to read a moral of happy pertinence to us—in these vexatious days, especially, when, challenged and threatened on all sides, runs the one way of life that's dependable. We'd just like to point out what a pity it is the builders of that tower didn't first sit down to reckon, following a famous injunction. And if they had only used American cement as well as some of that good old American engineering genius, their tower might still be lording it over the Samar coastline.

From Chayong Banzon, in Manila, to her husband Tony, in Laguna

Oct. 26, 1941

...It's a great deal to ask, but if you know how, will you please be serious now? Because my "packing off" this time is serious. I want to think us out of this mess, Tony, and I can't over there. With you beside me, giving me those creeps, I'd never be able to find out how much I am your wife and how much only another of your women. My grandmothers would know. I don't. That's how great a mess our marriage is.

No, I'm not concerned about culpability. Maybe it's your fault, maybe mine, maybe not ours at all. We picked a ghastly age to be married in, Tony-boy; an age where "nothing is clear, nothing defined—not the relation of man to God, nor of man to society, nor of man to woman. Wherefore: in the streets, a war of classes; in the home, a war of the sexes; and within the flesh, a soul that is its own battleground and its own fierce foe." Know where I picked *that* up? In a confessional. Noe's. (I must tell you that our little skirted brother is fast becoming a personage. The ladies of the great world have quite taken him up and his confessional is now as fashionable as any at San Ignacio.)

I've laid our case before him and his advice is (surprise!) babies. He's shocked I haven't sprouted anything after ten years. But I've told him I didn't think a baby would be any solution. It might have been, earlier. Now, it would be only one more nuisance to divide us. He was pretty bitter at me; said I was worse than a harlot; harlots, at least, did it for a living. And he's right too, Tony, I *am* worse than a harlot. That much, anyway, I can blame you. You've made me so that I can't even hear what Holy Church is saying. My soul's deaf, dumb and blind. I'm just body, and that body's not even mine; it's yours. I could never let it bear a baby. It would be a sacrilege....

From a sermon by Father Noe Cabrera on the feast of Christ the King

...Progress! you cry. Progress and more progress! But what is progress? I ask you. It is like the tides, you answer. We are caught in the tides! We must move! *Ah, caught in the tides.* No expression could be more apt. The tides do move. They come and go. Relentlessly. Leaving upon the shore dead weeds, dung, rubbish, shipwrecks and corpses. This is their end. And what is their principle? Is it not the carcass of a star? A whirled heap of dead rock and sand? A very graveyard of a planet?

As with the tides, so with man's principalities: they come and go. How runs the old cry? *"Put not your trust in princes!"* So man has cried and will cry again, being tough of head but flexible of neck. So has he bewailed himself in all ages, bewildered and uprooted, confused and afraid?

Why? Has God abandoned us utterly to the tempest? Was it God scattered us among the tides? Above this madness of waters, this eternal flux of salt waters, does no Rock rise unconfounded: unmoved, unmoving and unmovable; for ever assailed and for ever victorious?

From Angel Cabrera, in Manila, to his brother Bitoy, at Camp X

Oct. 27, 1941

...Why come agonizing to me? If it's advice you want, I don't stock it: try Mother. If it's solace you need, I never touch it; try Noe. I could shame your terrors by invoking that one about cowards dying continually, the brave only once. But they've made death your occupation and prime purpose: what wonder that it should obsess you so? that you should cling so desperately to this life and its pitiful pleasures? You want so little, "just books, converse and music; a tranquil room of one's own; a girl's love." Unfortunately, it's been decided you can't have any of those things unless you die for them first. Your betters have so made it necessary. It's your honor and great privilege to quench with your blood what they've set on fire. You mustn't fail them.

As for your troubles in getting acclimatized up there, I think it stupid of you to have aroused the pack to your differentness. You're a round peg they're hacking at to fit a square hole. Submit, brother, submit. Or they'll hack you to pieces. Talk as they talk, dress as they dress, walk as they walk. In short, be the complete cad and hypocrite. When in Rome, put on wolf's clothing. It's easier than hiding. Easier on the hide too.

You might amuse yourself by pondering what those who sacrifice you will say when you're dead. I can tell you. First, they'll say that when the hour of need came you showed yourself a true exponent of the breed: you were as a lamb led to the slaughter. They'll say that the truth or falsity of the cause you perished for isn't what matters; what matters is that you *did* perish. They'll say that in proving you knew how to die you proved *their* fitness not to. And they'll say that in reality you're not dead at all; that you're more alive than anyone living; that you will always be alive—for ever and ever—in their hearts, and in the books, converse and music, tranquil rooms and love affairs you've made possible for them, and the hearts of the generations *they'll* make possible, never you fear.

From Angel Cabrera's Journal

Oct. 28, 1941

...Showed Noe "watch-tower article." Who found it serious reflection on supposed thinking practised today. With that kind of reasoning, you can prove anything. Church of San Agustin has stood for three centuries: therefore...Heacock's building collapsed in a year: therefore....Told him article important as indication of gross narrowness, incredible provincialism these people are bred in. Taught to walk in a certain manner, they can no longer imagine other gait possible. Those not in their files are reactionaries, fifth columnists, Charlie McCarthies. *They* are the real McCoy. Yet if tomorrow there arose a need to walk in reverse manner, these people will walk reverse. And immediately. And with greatest ease. And for reasons just as numerous, just as profound. Proud moreover they've grown "older and wiser." When fact is they've only changed their mind. Or (more accurately) have had it changed for them.

Noe thoughtful: asked why I persisted in ranging heart against mind. Told him Intellect has proved itself traitor ever. And liar, cheat, opportunist, Pharisee, seducer. Heart and blood have yet to be proved wrong. Which proves me manichean, says Noe. Answered yes, unfortunately, because today we have heart and mind to divide, but originally heart was supreme, being to man what instinct is to beasts. Beasts can mate openly, cleanly, because there's no mind in them to pervert sex into loathsome hysterical egoistic self-assertion. Look at Chayong and Tony, tearing each other with their minds and bodies, being heartless. As with sex, so has mind perverted all of man's other properties, functions, till today he's most corrupt, most misplaced ingredient of creation. Noe asking, did I propose to go back to beasts? Answered no: home to them rather, before upstart mind destroyed us utterly....

From Tony Banzon, in Laguna, to his wife Chayong, in Manila
                                                        Oct. 31, 1941

...Suppose I just say it's all my fault and ask to be forgiven: will that make everything okay? Or what must I promise to do, be, give or permit to have this all over with? Maybe our marriage is not such a mess as we think. Maybe we haven't even begun to live it. If so far you haven't been more than a fancy woman of mine, I can argue that I, too, have been no more than a sort of gigolo of yours. I haven't been your husband yet, have I? You wouldn't give me the chance.

Darling, let's really begin this time. Noe is right; we need a baby. It's hard, I know, to think of me as a *pater*, but while at college I did some acting they all thought pretty good. Funny, isn't it? Most people marry to become parents. I don't think you or I have ever considered the proposition. The world needed our "services" too much. We couldn't jeopardize our "liberty." And besides we wanted "only each other." Not even that much really; only so much of each other as wouldn't interfere with the "drives" and "movements" and "activities."

Don't you think we've been unselfish long enough? Come back and let's start being selfish and married, huh? I'm so tired of having to smile and smirk when people ask where you are and when you're coming back. And darling, I do miss you so. They had a blackout once and I didn't even notice. Every night has been a blackout night since you went away, and will be, siren, till you sound the all-clear....

From a sermon of Father Noe Cabrera on the
Feast of All Saints

...Of the devout that crowd this church on Tuesdays to venerate St. Anthony of Padua I have tested many, asking of them whether St. Anthony be Spanish, German or Italian. No one could tell me. Nor could the lovers of even so recent as popular a saint as the Little Flower say to what nation on earth she belonged. Yet the same people could readily inform me that Bonaparte was French, Washington American, and Garibaldi Italian. I do not chide the faithful on their ignorance. I don't dare call it ignorance even. Rather do I believe that in *ignoring* this particular fact about the saints the popular heart obeys an instinct wiser than all theology, exposing the said fact for what it is: an accident, and therefore unimportant, and the more transmuted the man, the less shackled to the accident. The Paduan thaumaturgus has traveled widely and is still traveling; at the service everywhere of all men, lettered or unlettered. But Washington remains on Mt. Vernon, and in the ruffles of the eighteenth century....

Consider this Faith we profess: among us it is attacked as "Western"; the Romans abhorred it as "African"; the Russians refused it as "European"; and the Europeans disdain it as "Oriental." How elusive is the Christ-Child! He has long ceased to be merely of Bethlehem; He is also now the Holy Child of Prague; the Holy Child of Timbuctoo, the Holy Child of Tondo, Cebu and Pandacan. He is of nowhere in particular and everywhere in general.

And this, also, is the chief glory of those heroes we honor today, these forerunners of a new, universal race: the race of Christmen. Like Christ, like Christianity itself, these men and women have defeated mere geography, dissolving the barriers of Time, Race, Color and Language. If they were ever the citizens of any state, it was the City of God. If they are the patriots of any country, it is the Kingdom of Heaven....

From Angel Cabrera's impressions of an
Election Rally in Manila

Nov. 4, 1941

Peanut vendors, ice-cream vendors, pickpockets, stray dogs, the citizenry..."Finally, I would have you bear in mind that the destiny of the Younger Set has been entrusted into her hands. Fellow-countrymen, I now give you the one and only Miss Vanitas, Manila's own Heart-Throb. . . ." A platform that's four planks roped together, installed with a loudspeaker, curtained with unwashed flags...huge, blinding luminous

bulbs...an eight-piece band playing boogie-woogie music...
Popcorn- peanuts- pepsin! Ice-cream! Genoowine avocado ice-cream..."Allow me, therefore, to explain in detail my three-year plan as well as my program of thirty-two points in which I have endeavored to meet the manifold problems of our age and to remedy the evils that afflict us as a nation...." Babies wail; are fed; the shawled mothers squatting down the grass... a pitiful expectancy in the air: hope springing eternal...
Popcorn- peanuts- pepsin! Ice-cream! Genoowine ube ice-cream!
..."Nor do I heed the taunts of my other rival who claims I will bring my entire family into the government if elected. My reply is that I, at least, will be contented with just my immediate family, but she would not. She will also bring her aunts, uncles, grandmothers, grandfathers, and grandchildren. Maybe even her boyfriends!"....A general weariness, drowsiness ...ears that ring from the blare and thunder of the loud-speaker...but start applause and everyone applauds...raise a cheer and everyone cheers...*Popcorn- peanuts- pepsin! Ice-cream! Genoowine caramel ice-cream!*...at nooks and corners, pools of urine eddying round piles of ordure...."You have seen her, you have heard her now. The one and only Miss Vanitas! My countrymen, have we the heart to let her down? Shall we not altogether pledge to vote Vanitas for Efficient-Up-to-the-Minute-Government and Dynamic National Uplift?"

*From Chayong Banzon, in Manila, to her husband
Tony, in Laguna*

Nov. 8, 1941

...Why be so sarcastic? You know very well why we never had a baby. You were going to have all those nasty little pleasures you wanted and no brat around to break in on the fun. You say I've never given you the chance to be a husband. That's unfair, and a lie. I tried to in the beginning and how you shook in your pants! Cuddling and petting and playing the whore was okay, but each time I approached you seriously, each time I tried to make you feel some responsibility, each time I tried to break past that hide of yours and into whatever heart or brains you possessed—you shrank away; you laughed and called me a girl-scout; you ravished me into silence.

It takes a man to be a husband, Tony-boy, and being a man's a fulltime job. Proving yourself one in bed isn't enough:

people don't spend all their lives between sheets. You have to get yourself respected in quite a number of other places.

Break your shell, Tony; break your shell and come out to this world from which, so far, you "have had the good sense to stay out." I never made a doll out of you. I found you the lone toy-dweller of the lone toy-house in a lone toy-world and I stayed as long as I could stand it. But it's not safe any longer—this china-universe of yours. There's going to be an earthquake soon and I don't care to be smothered under your fragments, or the fragments of your house, or the fragments of your world....

From an editorial in a Manila paper

Nov. 11, 1941

Never has there been a period of history so crucial as the present, nor so momentous. Similarly we may speak of the election set for today. In all humility we can declare that the eyes of the world are gathered upon us as we march to the polls. It is therefore our duty to think clearly, to cast a sincere vote, and to avoid all muddleheadedness....

The new "block-voting" will present difficulties the voter should carefully study. The voter should first decide whether to vote a "straight" party ticket or not. Should he decide to do so, then he need only write the name of any of the three parties mentioned on the ballot. Should he decide to vote "straight" but happens to be in a district declared a "free zone," then he shall write the name of the party on the space reserved for that purpose and on the space reserved for the representative write the name of his candidate. If he wishes to vote "straight," excepting only for the representative (his choice for this being either the "rebel" or opposition candidate), then he must fill the ballot as if he were voting "independent." To vote "independent" the voter must leave the space for the party unfilled and instead write the names of his candidates on the blank space reserved for the purpose on the left side of the ballot....

*From Chayong Banzon's impressions of a Literary
Conference in Manila*

Nov. 12, 1941

Art, culture, the world of ideas...Plenty of other things in this world besides love...more important too, more thrilling....*Haven't you read the "Bell" yet? Boy, it's a "must!" The first mystical proletarian novel I'd call it....Oh, gosh, I've*

*seen the "Wind" four times myself. What a gauginian handling
of color....*"The word *utilitarianism* sounds gross to the ears
of pure artists. Besides, the word *function* suggests another one,
form, presupposing an independent existence for each"....
Probably thinks I just sit around moping...he should see me
now...how exciting all these are...how did I ever stand
those awful cats' clubs....*The new Hemingway? I experienced
it like a death, comrade. A death and a birth....And that
marvelous last scene of Scarlett's on the stairway. Wow!
Truly Euripidean....*"Poetry is the Art of the Word—the Art,
in fact, of the *individual* word. Poetry may have *nothing to say,*
in which case the *Art of saying it* becomes the *whole* Art"....
Wonder what he's doing now....* "Every night's a blackout
night"*...complete with sirens I'll bet...." Proletarian Art
is an Art of definite hope and growth. Proletarian Art is re-
volutionary. Proletarian Art is, by its very nature and function,
realistic. Proletarian Art is wisely conservative."...Wonder
who it is this time...probably that vile dancer again....
*How Hemingway can involve you, eh? I couldn't tell where I was
—one the chair or on the page...No, by golly, the "Wind" is
Art. It is to our day what Vergil's epic was to the Augustans.
The intellection in it, kiddo—the intellection....*That most harlot of harlots...talking of me, laughing at me...I'll kill
her...."That Art, then, that *fails* to defend the democratic
way of life is *invalid* Art, is a *prostitution* of *Art,* and by being
itself *doomed* may *doom* Art....I'll kill both of them....Oh,
how can he do this to me....how dare he do this to me....
Oh, Tony, Tony....

From Angel Cabrera's Journal

Nov. 12, 1941

...Art: still possible today? World's best artist couldn't
paint flood he was drowning in. Primary requirement is some
point of vantage. Where shall that be found today? In Church
perhaps; but then artist knowingly cuts himself off from that
portion of audience that's heathen. His work's bound to suffer
by that much. Yet Church's viewpoint most universal available
today. Only one, moreover.

Marlowe's Come live with me and be my love: if equivalent
of that song were written today it would be denounced as es-
capist, ignored as irrelevant. Quite rightly too. Because even if

a super-Shakespeare did the writing he couldn't make it ring true today. Nothing so proves utter degradation into which we have fallen.

Yet times in which Marlowe wrote neither sweet nor gentle. Injustice above; misery below; wars in fields; plagues in towns; filth everywhere. But there was also certain feeling among men those things (wars, governments, pestilences) were irrelevant. What was relevant was the saving of a man's soul, the winning of a maid's heart. In sordid heap of corruption that was Medieval Paris Villon could and did sing of Helen, Thais, snows of past years. At agreed intervals (e.g., Christmastide, Paschaltide) wars stopped short, enemies gathered under one roof. And in every fury of battle could often be found some minstrels improvising songs that said no more than that grass was green and skies blue and women's hearts mostly untrue. And (what's the point) he could make his song ring pertinent. Because wars were irrelevant, love was not. And still available was some peak in Darien from which to exorcise ocean.

Today no such eminences permitted to stand. World has turned upside down. It's war that's relevant, love that's not. We may sing of killing, we mustn't sing of wooing. The first is last, the last is first. No wonder our art belongs to Dada....

From Father Noe Cabrera, in Manila, to his
brother Bitoy, at Camp X

Nov. 15, 1941

... What if your faith seems to fail you now? What if you seem to hear a hollow ring in the formulas of religion? What if you find it hard to accept the solace of a promised heaven? Do not torment yourself too much. You are not culpable. It is not your faith that is little: it is the faithlessness of the world that is great. For, modern notions notwithstanding, religion can be no one man's private affair. What the rest of the world believes—or fails to—conditions his capacity for either affirmation or denial. In an age of faith, everyone is devout, even the most depraved; in an age of heresy, everyone is a heretic, even the most orthodox; and in an age of unbelief, everyone is a skeptic, even the saints.

How else are we to sustain devotion in an age like ours, and at a time like this, save with labor and difficulty? If eight of the ten men needed to row a boat be slackers, the conscien-

tious pair at the job will find it hard going, and the rougher
the sea, the harder the going. Doubt if you must, then; pity
yourself if you must, but keep rowing. So few are on the job
the defection of a single one imperils us all. Remember: a couple
of good men might have saved Sodom. For it is not ourselves
alone we have to get across. We are responsible for the slackers
too. Are we not all on the same boat?

From Tony Banzon, in Laguna, to his wife
Chayong, in Manila

Nov. 17, 1941

...If my roof's unsafe you have every right, certainly,
to look to your safety. I would no more stop you than I would
those creatures that desert ships about to sink. Which reminds
me: if you find my scrawl scrawlier than usual one reason is
that I'm scrawling this in moonlight and on a boat.

Yes, darling, we're on the lake, and it's full moon, and
all these blots and blemishes are the lanzones and boiled chest-
nuts we're eating. The other half of the "we" is (surprise)
Eden Rios. Yes, siree, it's good old Eden again and she's all
the other reasons for the scrawliness.

No, she didn't pick me up this time; I was man enough to
do it myself, right after I got your last letter. I went to ask her
if she's as good as ever, and she said she was, which is a lie.
She's very, very bad. And couldn't have been better. Or so
I thought then. But she keeps improving every day. Getting
worse, I mean.

Being a discreet girl, she's never voluntarily mentioned your
name, but you know how I am. I've cried our whole history
upon her bosom. She declares herself not surprised, after what
she's had to bear from me. She says her sympathies are all with
you and begs to be allowed to send you her love....

From Lulu Cabrera's Diary

Nov. 19, 1941

...Eva de Leon called up at store; wanted me for a
"blackout party" she's throwing tomorrow. Managed to wriggle
myself off but only on promise I'd show up at another dance
they're giving for the soldiery. Told her I couldn't take a step
nowadays without bumping into them. Did I have to bump
against them on dancefloors too?

Came home to find Chayong in bed. Headache, she says. Eyes very swollen. Must have wept oceans. Found out (from mother) she had a letter from Tony this morning and the headache afterwards....

Nov. 20, 1941

...Found Johnny waiting at closing time. Said to him: Don't tell me there's another "blackout?" Was feeling very tired and blue; quickly consented. We had supper at the Silver Heron; few lights carefully shaded; made that most respectable place look rather bawdy. Afterwards we went walking down the boulevard. Total darkness by then. Could guess what Johnny was up to, step by step. As we walked, from darkness came whispers, giggles, hushed rustlings. Could feel that "blackout mood" in the air. We sat down on the grass and Johnny started maneuvering. Didn't let him get anywhere. Told him his plan of battle perfect except for his choice of horse; that blackouts didn't work that way with me; that in fact he couldn't have chosen a worse time. Asked me why I persisted in refusing to marry him. Told him I couldn't, not because I didn't like him but because I didn't like the world.

It's true, too. Tonight only made me more sure. Maybe what I feel for Johnny is what they call love. I'm sure, anyway, I like him as much as I'll allow myself to like anyone at all. Which isn't much. And can't be more. Not so long as they have blackouts....

Came home past ten. Mother much worried. Chayong still in bed and really sick. High fever. Weeps openly and continuously I don't think I'll be able to sleep tonight.

Nov. 21, 1941

Was right. Didn't sleep a wink last night. Have never, never suffered like this. All day today. Noe here for supper. Afterwards, got him and Angel out on the porch. Told them about Johnny. Noe says there's no ideal time for marriage; it's always been a difficult and momentous thing to do. Angel said yes, if you did it *consciously;* but people didn't; it was something that just happened to them and then babies started coming. He said the trouble with me is I won't do it except consciously. Noe said: That's the one proper way to do it. Angel laughed and said if people ever *really* stopped to consider the vast crime they perpetuated by marrying and furnishing this world with fresh victims....Noe asked, was that how I felt about it? Answered yes, that I couldn't think of having a baby in a blacked-out world. He said, how about all those women that had the courage to become mothers in times no better than the present? Angel said courage had nothing to do with it: what Noe meant was Nature. I told them that if there was any nature in me I'd take care it didn't betray as it's always betrayed my kind. I told them that by marrying and having babies I consented, I said yes to this world I'd been born into and of which I heartily disapproved. Angel said it was saying yes, not to this world, but to the world older than this one of air-raids and blackouts. Noe said: no, it was saying yes to something older than all worlds, than all stars; it was saying yes to the God who authored creation and found it good.

We didn't get any further. Mother was calling for me. Chayong had turned delirious....

From Tony Banzon, in Laguna,
to his wife Chayong, in Manila

Nov. 21, 1941

LETTER MERE MOMENTS INSANITY FORGIVE FORGET WILL DO ANY PENANCE YOU NAME PLEASE ANSWER AT ONCE LOVE YOU MADLY.

Nov. 23, 1941

...and in the heat of that fury, seeing how, having offered to abase myself, you merely injured and insulted me, I did what we two have done all our life together: hurt myself to hurt you; spited myself to spite you; disgraced myself to disgrace you. And yet, don't these shameful devices but prove again that solidarity of being which is ours by marriage? If, so far, we have misused it to our suffering and shame, can't we wield it as effectively to our happiness and honor? Please answer me.

Nov. 28, 1941

...Why do you persist in silence? I have never felt so impotent. I have sinned against my love; there ought to be something I can do now; something simple, something direct, something *inevitable*. My grandfathers would know. I don't. That's how great a mess I am. I can only sit here and burn.

Just a line, darling; or a few words; or a single word even— but answer me, darling, answer me....

Dec. 2, 1941

...You're a foul, vengeful, hard-hearted, stinking little
whore, and I could wring your neck with pleasure. Words are
wasted on you. Go to hell and be damned. I don't care. Or—no—I
do care. I do care to have you damned, as you've damned me;
to have you in hell, as you have me. And be sure that where
I am will be twice hell for you. And vice-versa.

From Lulu Cabrera's impressions to a
"Red, White and Blue Ball"

Dec. 5, 1941

Khaki among rainbows...smelling of starch, iodine, tobacco, chewing gum,...*O sweet and lovely Lady be good! O
Lady be good*...on the other hand: Paris perfumes, deodo-
rants, face-creams, chewing gum....The smooth blonde giant
who was sure the garden would be more int'restin' than the
dancefloor...."How long have you been over here? How'd
you like it?"...*Ay-ay, ay-ay, have you ever been in the tro-
pics*....Balloons, lanterns, flags, colored lights...Boogie woo-
gie, rhumba, boogie-woogie, conga, waltz, boogiewoogie....
The jolly little red-head who was a complete gallery of tattoo-
art he "wouldn't mind throwing open for me" in private....
"How long since you arrived? Getting to like the place?....
Iowa, Kansas, Chicago, New Hampshire....*Some folks go for
the eight-beat rhythm*....The sulky brown-haired lad who
doubted if "the natives" were gentlemen: they could exist without blondes..."Been long over here? How are you liking it,
When and where do you think the War will start?"...*Aurora*
came from *Rio de Janeiro*...."I had an impression you guys
went around eternally comparing two cigarettes of unequal
sizes"....*Fools rush in where angels fear to tread*...."How
long have you been around? Liking the place?"....Talk, laughter, giddiness, heat, nausea....*The music goes round and
round*....

From a sermon by Father Noe Cabrera during the
novena to the Immaculate Concepcion

Dec. 7, 1941

...Christ did not say His kingdom would not be *on* this
world. He did make it plain it would not be *of* this world, as
politicians love to remind themselves. And they are quite right.
Christ's kingdom is not of *their* world.

Not so uncomprehending have been the great saints and poets. One of these latter stoutly sang that he "would not cease from mental strife, nor would the sword rest in his hand, till he had built Jerusalem in his own green and pleasant land."

The Building of Jerusalem! Is not this the task to which we are called and to which we should be dedicated? The ground on which we must build: it is defiled: we must make it holy. The air in which we must build: it is shackled: we must set it free. Why are there today so many refugees in the towers of ivory? Is it not because we have made a vast sty of the earth? And why are there among us so many sitters upon fences? Is it not because we have cluttered the world with fences?

So must we travail to bring forth Heaven's empire upon earth even as *She* travailed the feast of whose conception we celebrate tomorrow; from whose flesh was hewn the Corner-Stone upon which we are to build; and like whose flesh, even the New Jerusalem must arise: *out of all our imperfection, yet itself perfection....*

From Angel Cabrera's Journal

Dec. 7, 1941

...Might as well have been born in Babel. Would have felt perfectly at home there among dynamic progressive people who thought nothing of annexing heaven. Wonder how they felt when curse fell upon them. Didn't know it for a curse, of course. Probably thought it one more "blessing of progress": that less and less people could understand each other. Probably went about proclaiming it "freedom of speech" and an article of Babelian faith. Which it is. How long before first inspired prophet arose, extolling beauties of his own babbling and declaring his soul translatable in no other? How soon before they found reasons for canonizing as progressive the fact (fruit of curse) that fewer and fewer men agreed, and on fewer and fewer things?

Tower, of course, had to be abandoned. Oh, be sure they found good reasons for that too. It was unsuitable to the landscape; it was an antiquated undertaking; they'd only been hoodwinked to the building of it. Now, being free, older, wiser, they would construct something really advanced and appropriate; something "truly native," "truly Babelian," in keeping with their new-found tongues.

And not a soul in all that roaring whirlpool of confusion—not a soul in all that vile welter of lust, lies, greed and pride and corruption—not a soul in all the damned miles of Babel-town to realize that it was cursed, cursed, cursed, and cursed...

From Tony Banzon, in Laguna, to his wife Chayong, in Manila
                                                    Dec. 7, 1941

...How was I to know that you were ill? But even before I did, I had already begun to realize how this sitting down and waiting for an answer is sheer cowardice and but furnishes you with more proofs of my unmanliness. And I also see now that the obvious, the direct, the inevitable thing to have done was to have taken the first train to the city and flung myself at your feet. Which I never thought to do; subconsciously recoiling as usual from any decisive act whatsoever, and subconsciously aware that to go forth thus could mean a going forth from "the shell," and that to face you thus were to face the world. Which, fully realizing (and having taken a deep breath), I now resolve to do.

But not this week, darling, because, some monstrous ass having thought I'd make an air-raid warden, there are all sorts of dances and tea-parties I am to go to. Besides, you'll have to allow me a few days (of course!) in which to pace back and forth murmuring to go or not to go or to go or not to go or to go or not to?

From Lulu Cabrera's column in the December 1941 Merchandiser. *Rehearsal*

We thrilled to see this Babel city of ours go very, very still when the alarms went wailing for that air-raid drill. The halted cabs and peoples and horses reminded us of the sleeping palace in the fairy-tale, and we found ourselves wishing some such enchantment might befall us, might strike us all rigid and asleep, and, thus enchanted, bear safely through this hour, across these days, out of these times—on, on, and on—till the last shot be fired the last patriot—fallen—and we, among our cobwebs, may safely hear at last the footfall in hallway, the royal "O" of a princely surprise, the lifted curtains, the kiss....

But would it be any use, we wonder. Fairy-tales are most realistic, and this one ends on a true note: the cook resumes his boxing of the kitchen-boy's ears. And (of course) the politicians resumed their politicking, the ministers resumed their ministering, the soldiers resumed their soldiering, and everybody resumed preparations for the next one.

USAFFEET

We've just received a letter from our soldier-boy and it was all about his feet, his feet, his feet. He says they're killing him. This rather surprised us who have always vaguely believed armies traveled on their tummies. Anyway, we've dutifully written to cheer him up, saying phooey and shame on him: shouldn't he be willing to do for his country what most smokers would do for a Camel; and didn't he know that these are the times that try men's soles; and that no wonder his feet hurt; he was always kicking.

After we'd mailed our letter, we thought it merely just to punish our own dogs, and resolved to walk them all the way home. Halfway through, however, we realized how silly we were acting, and promptly hailed a cab. . . .

Advice to Girls in These Parlous Times

Eat, drink, and don't marry. Keep your powder (and lipstick) dry. Burn your candle at both ends and keep *him* flying. For tomorrow we're all going to put our legs in one casket. . . .

Philippine Review
July 1943

A PEACE LIKE DEATH

LIGAYA VICTORIO REYES

The road lay white and stark under the lead-gray skies. On both sides, round trees filled the sight, then vanished swiftly, their fat branches waving languid goodbyes. Rita, leaning out of the bus window, saw first one tree vanish, then another. They're going so fast, she thought, they won't tarry long enough to register in my mind. When I come back, can I recognize any of these trees? I can usually recall a tree by the shape of its branches or the snarl of its limbs. But these trees have no individuality apart from each other. Probably planted by the government from identical seedlings.

The road went unhindered for miles, no vehicles of any kind spotting its smoothness. Far to the left, a solitary farmer led his carabao among dim furrows of young green. Huts jutted out of the horizon, brown moles against a face of flatness, their holes of windows not more than light specks in the distance. Every once in a while, threads of smoke would lift from the earth to join the greater grayness of the skies—flimsy threads bridging the indeterminate distance between immensities.

Rita leant out of the window, hypnotized by the stillness. She did not know that there was a life like this, a life so unchanging it was like dreamless sleep. If she closed her eyes for a little while, she could identify herself with the landscape, be any of these specks discernible afar, unmoving, unfeeling, unheeding. She could forget that she was on this jerky yellow bus with the merciless seats and the hard back rests, forget this rushing that was life, hurrying her where she had no desire to be. It would be nice to die like this, she thought, to float from unconsciousness to unconsciousness in this gentle, seemingly endless stillness.

At the thought of death, she closed her eyes quickly. One does not think of death. One savors the idea merely. In the midst of life, one feels it subconsciously, neither thinking one thing or the other about it. One does not think of death as a losing of the heartbeat, a stiffening of the limbs. It is, rather, a sort of drifting, a cutting free from physical ties and surfaces of feelings, an idle journeying through a void where impressions gather only to be rejected. One does not think of the harshness of what one has known as death: none of the flowers and the candles and the bitter, unendurable causes. None of the pain and the struggle, the desperate clinging to the things that are associated with living: the people and places, the light, the shadow, the smells and sounds, even the memories that one cannot drive into limbos dark enough, that creep upon one, tempering one's present thoughts and activities, intensely overwhelming.

The hypnosis was ended. Rita felt the floods of living breaking the dam reared for a brief moment by the stillness. Now she was again tired limbs and more tired mind. Now she remembered why she was on this bus, why she was crouching far out of the touch of other passengers, leaning close to the window in intense self-protection. She wanted none of the lighthearted joshing, the careless touch of another who would smile friendlily and speak, breaking the silence. She had not looked at anyone since she had gotten on the bus, and her neighbor's face was a blur that her sight avoided. Far behind her she could hear a buzz of conversation, rising and falling with the movement of the bus, a quiet buzzing that had no character either of gaiety or enthusiasm, simply a formal drift of sound, as though those who were responsible for it cared not whether they spoke or kept silent.

The bus changed its speed. Rita could feel the giant heart beneath her feet whirring more sluggishly. Houses began to appear by the sides of the road. Ugly houses first, with broken nipa eaves overhanging blank, uninspiring interiors. Small children with staring eyes and gaping mouths began to dot the flimsy gates—drab, unsmiling children, foretellers of the drabness within. Then the houses changed character. Now they were bigger and more solid. Bright, unsuitable curtains fluttered against the vacant faces of windows. Every now and then, a girl's face would break the expanse of blankness, looking at the passing bus with careless curiosity. The gates grew more sturdy, the children within them better dressed. The bus was passing a town.

Rita drew a little away from the window of the bus, withdrawing her gaze simultaneously from the sights that were now more variedly inviting. She had no wish to watch this life that flowed on both sides of the road. She was not interested by the movements which went with the noon-day tide, movements of living so common and yet so individual. People were essentially different yet essentially the same, their samenesses and differences predictable and unpredictable.

They had so many arguments about people, she and Cesar. Cesar maintained that people were there to accomplish some perfect design, to live and to struggle for some end known or unknown to them, to fight and to die, if need be, for this obscure end. She had jeered that there was nothing obscure about the ends for which people worked: to eat, to sleep, to eat again, as comfortably as they could. And Cesar had said that that was just it. People must eat and sleep, like humans. She had laughed, thinking of the humanity falling upon its food daily, tumbling upon its mat nightly, sinking over more prosaically into the grave destined for it. So many did not care, she had argued, how humanly they lived as long as they were alive. They did not dream of a greater life, of a better time when there would be forks and spoons bridging the narrow gap between hunger and appeasement, when there would be soft beds for backs instead of hard bamboo floors. So long as backs could recline in peace, their owners did not bother to long for anything better.

And Cesar had gotten angry and at the same time distressed that she could think so contemptuously about people, that she could so draw herself away from them, an individual watching a passing herd, uncaring, untouched by whatever fatigue, hunger or pain was discernible from the distance she maintained. She had laughed at his anger and his distress. "I cannot cure the world's ills," she had said, "I am no female Messiah." "And why aren't you?" he had demanded passionately. "Because you would not risk the merest portion of your damned self-content. You don't even want to feel."

The bus slid to a halt. There was the surge of voices, insistent whining voices. Messes in green leaves were thrust close to her face. The sweetish smell of bananas not so recently cooked rose sickeningly above the other odors. From within the bus, passengers fought to be heard, haggling mock-desperately. Rita saw one oily package after another change hands. Coins clinked upon outstretched palms as passengers and vendors did business together. She alone sat withdrawn in her corner, shaking her head emphatically as someone, more determined than the rest, shook a glass filled with yellow liquid near her face. She felt the fine spray dash softly against her cheek, and more annoyed now than ever, she stared down at the vendor who slunk away to seek a more promising customer.

The driver's voice rose loud and welcome at last above the din, warning travelers and vendors alike of his intention to proceed on the journey. Rita sighed deeply with relief, shifted to a more comfortable position, and stared more expectantly ahead. There was no break in the monotony of the skies. No sun threatened to pierce the leaden gray of noon-day. The dust rose briefly as the great bus lurched into motion, and they were on their way.

The spectacle of half an hour ago was repeated, only in reverse. First the solid, pretentious houses flashed fast. Then the nipa houses, getting fewer, smaller and more shaky-looking as the trip progressed. Next came the flat expanse once more, the hypnotic vista of flat land, green and brown, of grey skies and round trees and a distant horizon. No wonder people slept during journeys. The eyes were tricked into sightlessness, the mind was lulled into dreaming by the long spell of stillness.

Rita thought of the journeys she had taken. These were so few and mostly towards the north. There was that single trip to Baguio with Cesar and other college friends. How lighthearted they had been, how full of fun. They had not had much attention for the landscape then. They were too intent on looking at each other. Every remark seemed witty, every smile meaningful. They had sung foolish songs, Cesar's voice rising above the others. He had a good baritone. The conductor had smiled indulgently, and other passengers had smiled or frowned as their ages or moods dictated. But they had not cared, not she and Cesar, for they were too delighted with the sound of their own voices to care whether others were delighted or not. As usual, Cesar had discoursed about the common *tao*, about his rights and his opportunities, or his lack of them. She had gone on singing, humoring him, not really listening.

For they had been too long in love to pretend politeness and a breathless interest in each other's bright sayings. She had always felt so superior. Even when she loved him most, she had felt more level-headed, more assured than he was. To her, his seemed a fumbling idealism, a groping for something but dimly imagined, a stumbling onto a dream which she now knew meant life to him.

She had always been so content with the conditions of her own life. On that Baguio trip, she was young and gay and carefree, and those were enough for her. Later, she had found a good job without too much trouble—her family had always been an asset. She had attaind a measure of independence and the nice things that came to a woman through it. She had Cesar's love, felt she would always have it and the things she would have through it; his grave good looks, his devotion, the queer mixture of idealism and despair that so appealed to the contentment in her. She had fallen easily into a pattern of existence that she felt would satisfy her for at least a hundred years, and she was in no hurry to end it with marriage, even to Cesar. Cesar had gotten into trouble once or twice about what she laughingly termed his ideals, but these did not bother her. He would outgrow them, she told herself. He would not be young forever, and ideals such as his survive only with youth. They could not exist in the mature quiescence of age. One, she felt, was entitled to an adolescence, no matter how long and drawn out it may seem.

Once in a while she had "ragged" him about his "preaching." Every now and then she would pretend jealousy, chide him coyly because he loved the common tao more than he loved her. She had refused to take seriously the distress in his voice, the solemn cast which would fall over his features when she was more vexingly flippant. She felt that he was acting out his role of Messiah to the limits of its satisfaction, and she was well content to let him have his fling for as long as it should last. It could be another passion, it could be another girl, she had reasoned shrewdly. And level-headed though she was, self-sufficient though she was, she could not be entirely proof against another girl. There was something about an infatuation which could leave a man slightly spent, which could spoil him entirely for life, protestations to the contrary notwithstanding. I want him whole, she had thought selfishly.

I'm his first love. I want to be his last. So she had humored him, pretending interest when she felt that he needed it, soothing him when he was more heatedly rebellious than ever, laughing away his reverence for certain things to which she felt such utter disbelief.

And now she was on this bus. This was one trip she had never planned to make. Even now she felt a shred of surprise that she should go hurrying to something she longed to forget. The minutes, the hours, the day dragged on. One moment, so fleetingly passing, seemed to her inexpressibly heavy with the weight of her feelings. It went merely to give way to another like it. There was no motive for the flight of the hours, for she was merely hurrying to an end that should have waited, for it was only the end. One hated to behold it. One went on to it because one could not help one's self, and going, must forget that it was there, implacable, a period to everything that one had held so important. She felt the veil of her self-content giving way, falling apart so slowly but surely—so strong had it seemed.

Rita stirred from where she had sat stiffly on her seat. She closed her eyes, not wishing to see any more. There was so much of this flatness. So much sameness. Green, brown, grey. They were everywhere. For interminable eternities they stretched, flat, uninspiring. Those specks that moved in the distance. Were they people? What lives did they live, of what precious importance were they to the scheme of this world that people should risk death for them? Did they realize that to certain minds they assumed a greatness beyond their own puny wills to imagine, a height, a meaning that is incomprehensible to their own stupid little minds? They lived, they desired love, they died. They complained about small things. Did they ever concede, during moments of mental distress, that there were bigger, more important things than mere birth and death? (Indeed, could anything be more important?) Were they ever scorched by the fire which those who led them sought to kindle in them? Or did they follow where they were led because it was simpler to follow than to question, easier to be part of a mob than to stand out alone, more natural to herd together than to go variously apart?

She would never know. She did not have it in herself to know. She herself would never comprehend the dreams which

filled Cesar's life, the ideals which he followed from one end
of this world to another, the clean fire which seared him and
refreshed him even when he suffered most. Now there was no
way of knowing. She would never care to find out. She would
always long for an easy, comfortable flatness, for a hypnotic
stillness that could soothe without delighting.

But the flatness was ending. Rita sighed wearily. This
was another town. Here were again the houses—nipa, wood,
concrete—marching solemnly past with their inscrutable faces
and their inscrutable lives within windows. There was a renewed bustle of conversation from the depths of the bus. The
driver, too, was thinking. There was in his voice a rise of
interest, a timbre of enthusiasm which showed his certainty
of the importance of what he was saying.

"Where did it happen?" someone inquired.

"Just two kilometers from here, in front of the church."
The driver was driving more slowly, handling the wheel with
attention which was not for the road alone. "My cousin saw it
all. He was driving a homebound bus and he stopped it there
in that little by-path when the shooting started. The place
was dark with uniforms. The socialists did not have a chance."

"And I passed by only that morning," a female voice in-
terposed. "Everything seemed quiet then."

"But it was planned long ago, was it not? One could not
stage a thing like that on the spur of the moment."

"I saw it!" This voice was sure, triumphant. "There were
men all over the ground, dead men. It reminded me of the revolution."

"How many were there?"

"I do not know. I was too terrified to count."

Rita forced herself to look ahead. They were approaching
a churchyard. So this was it. How suddenly the end could
spring upon one. She had thought it was just another town.
She thought she had the whole day to get ready, but here
it was. She fixed her eyes on the churchyard, not wishing to
stop. But she must.

"I'll get down here," she said in a strained voice, and
the man ahead of her leaned forward to tap the conductor's
shoulder. The conductor turned, noted Rita's pale face, then
blew his whistle for the driver. The passengers all leaned forward, some of them in surprised protest.

"Why are we stopping?" The woman's voice had a note of hysterical fear. "Let's hurry on! I don't want to stop here!"

Rita rose from her seat, attracting considerable attention. Amid an awed silence she alighted. She stood for a while uncertain, her back turned away from the church gate. She watched the bus go, leaving her with a memory of widened eyes and open mouths.

She turned slowly at last and faced the deserted churchyard. It did not seem possible that drama could happen there. That church looked too benevolent. That doorway could have witnessed nothing more dramatic than a wedding. One could imagine the sound of footsteps scraping against the fine gravel, footsteps going in or coming out the threshhold on missions of gentleness and peace.

There was no stirring of memory to mar the utter stillness. There was a stillness over the whole scene which was of desolation, unbreakable and permanent. No ghostly breath of drama, no echoes brutal or savage, rose above the sleeping earth. No bells tolled, no shots resounded. There was nothing, nothing at all.

Rita shifted her gaze from point to point. She looked at the distant church spire, and, closer, the noble arch of the gate. Someday, she thought, I shall forget this empty churchyard. Someday that spire won't rise behind my eyelids, searingly clear. This church will fade into the identity of a hundred other churches I have seen and soon forgotten. That smear now rising from the ground to envelop me in a bloody haze will disappear into a blind spot that could be anything but what it really is. There would not be this deathly quiet that is the peace of desolation. Later, even the name ringing over and over in my brain will be a vain sound. This scene would eventually disappear, for all things disappear in death.

Her eyes were tired with the staring. She felt a need to get away, but her feet were reluctant to move. She knew where she would go, for he had been very explicit before. "You have only to stand before the church to see where I live when I am away from you. And you can read, can't you? My sign is there as big as life."

Life. Such a frail, fleeting thing at the mercy of a tiny bullet. They should remove that sign, she thought wearily. No need for it to gather dust further. She turned back to the church, striving to dam the tide of feeling which surged within her at sight of his name. This was a dream, she thought, steadying herself. I am alone, wandering in this ghostly churchyard in a nightmare that will soon end. That grinning face is really a knot on the church door. This is not reality—this weightless desolation that seems as natural as the very breath I take. Cesar is reality. Cesar laughing, despairing, making love. Cesar worrying about the fate of the world and the misery which ruled that fate, and who, in putting down the cross, had passed on to her the pain that would haunt her all her life.

She felt the desolate peace stealing into her heart. She knew that for the rest of her days, a part of her would nevermore wake up from this dream that was so like death.

Philippine Review
August 1943

CHRISTMAS VISIT

LIGAYA VICTORIO REYES

She opened her handbag and fished out a slip of paper. She looked at this, then up at the dirty grey building which loomed before her. This is it, she thought, noting the attempt at holiday garb which the house had donned. The colored streamers above the cement path looked faded in the Christmas sunlight. Lanterns, now unlit, fluttered above the doorway, and holding up one hand, she touched the blue and white streamers which rustled beneath a particularly sad-looking star.

She went up the short flight of cement steps and walked towards the uniformed girl who sat behind the information desk.

"I have come to see Lt. Pardo," she said softly. "I have a permit to see him today."

The nurse looked at her for a brief moment, then she opened the register before her and ran a finger down one page, locating a number.

"Bed No. 15," she said, closing the book. "Upstairs. To your left."

With a murmur of gratitude, she left the nurse and went up the stairs which rose to her left. She walked carefully in the middle of the stairs, deadening her steps. At the top, stepping gently over the linoleum, she paused. She must get hold of herself. She looked at her hand, noting its slight trembling, then clenched her fist tight. She glanced about her. There was about the hall that slightly sad, slightly spent holiday air which seemed to belong to Christmas Day. The greens and the buntings, the flags and the stars, all the sad efforts to bring in the spirit of Christmas into the antiseptic severity of a hospital, now partook of the weariness of the morning after Christmas Eve. She looked at the beds lined neatly on both sides of the hall, then walked slowly down the aisle, searching for a number.

There it was—Bed No. 15. She stopped and looked long at the figure lying straight on the narrow bed, wrung by the thinness apparent beneath the sheet. Her glance swept over this figure once, then travelled swiftly up to the face now so pallid above the pillow.

"Merry Christmas, darling," she said huskily, then she laughed gently and added, "It's I, in the flesh."

There was silence from the depths of the bed, but a hand slowly emerged from beneath the sheet and lifted towards her. She reached for this hand and held it carefully. Not too tightly, she told herself, or he'll guess how much this hurts. She held this thin hand between both her own and looked down smilingly at the face on the pillow.

"Here we both are," she said, "in the flesh."

The face on the pillow lost some of its frightening paleness.

"Loida, it's really you."

"None other," she said, and, releasing the hand she pulled the white chair which stood beside the bed and sank into its iron depths. She looked closer at the face now so near her own, noting the lean sweep of jaws and the veins which showed faintly beneath the blue down of the cheeks. He had always been a handsome boy. This was the face which never gave her peace. It was in all her dreams, waking or sleeping. Those eyes, dark-rimmed and gentle now beneath those fine eyebrows. How she adored them.

"You have not looked as glamorous in years," she told him, and he smiled. "You don't look sick when you smile, my darling. Gary Cooper has nothing on you," she added, working for another smile.

His hand reached up to her arm and patted it. He always did that when he was pleased with her.

"You are so lovely," he said.

"There are still cosmetics in the market," she parried, and this time he laughed. He raised his hand and cupped her chin in it. He held her face like this for a second, then his fingers moved slowly over one cheek, seeking the dimple which showed above the lips when she smiled. She was smiling now, and he looked at her in hunger, loving her, until she felt like pushing down his hand and turning her face away. Don't do that, she begged him in her heart. I cannot stand it, you must not see me cry.

"That dimple is still there." he whispered.

"They knew how to make dimples in the old days," she countered.

He laughed again and pinched her cheeks gently. He drank in the softness of her eyes and the sweetness of her lips. Lips and eyes he had never thought to see again. That look he never expected to behold once more. He sighed softly and brought his hand down over the sheet.

"Well," she said after an interval of silence, "what does one say to heroes?"

"You're kidding me," he said, "as usual."

Thank you for the "as usual," she thought. You haven't forgotten. She bent above him and kissed him softly on the cheek. "That," she said, "is the usual on Christmas Day."

She saw the joy leap into his eyes and she looked away briefly. I can't stand it, she cried within her.

"Now," she said, and seating herself firmly back on her seat, she smoothed the sheet where his hand lay, "that's over, and we can start on the conversation which is a must in hospitals. How is your temperature? Do you feel any pain? Are you comfortable? Don't answer. I'll guess." And she closed her eyes and placed a finger beneath her chin, considering. He laughed at the picture she made and she opened her eyes a little.

"You will be gay," he said. "no matter what."

"No matter what," she repeated, "and don't you forget it."

She pulled her chair closer to the bed, and placing one hand over the dark, curling hair, smoothed this gently. She gazed at the face beneath her own, then "How are you, truly?" she asked softly.

"I'm well," he said slowly, "except that...."

She placed one finger over his lips and shook her head. "That will be all," she told him lightly. "I've heard enough of your complaints."

He laughed at her in the helpless manner that he always laughed when she was like this. "Oh, Loida, Loida," he said, and he laid her hand over his cheek, delighting in its warmth.

"Tell me about over there," she said. "You have to tell me sometime. Let it be now."

"You must have heard the stories already," he said, and a weariness crept into his voice. "About there being not enough food, and so much thirst."

"Those are old stories," she said, dismissingly. "I want to hear real blood and thunder stuff—you know, the bang bang type with lots of people biting the dust and so forth."

"Oh, that," he said, with a lift of tone. "There is plenty of that."

And he started talking. She watched him as he talked, not listening really. He talked of huge bombs which made craters as large as chapels, and people who could not be found afterwards. "Not a trace of them, not one solitary finger left to tell of a man who had once been." He spoke of men who stared at the skies, ready, when the deadly birds flew, then turned to the earth to cry when danger was past. He told of men who were so hard-boiled that they could count the pieces and guessed what they had been before. Of Christmas in the forest, with God lighted by two tiny candles, while men cowered in the foxholes and crossed themselves with their hands smeared with earth. Of a soldier weeping in a deserted evacuee camp, hugging the ruins of a crude little truck with which he had gifted his son the Christmas before. And while he talked, excitement crept into his face, strength was in his voice. For he was talking of a time when he had been alive—and whole.

She watched his face as she half listened. That face she had lain awake nights calling to mind. You'll never guess, she told him without words, how much I have hungered to hear your voice. There were mornings when she would wake up, forgetful, waiting for the sound of the telephone calling her to him. He had called her, always, first thing in the morning, "because I must be the first thought in your new day." She had lain with her eyes closed, the sunlight waiting for her first glance, timing herself. In a moment now, she had thought, the telephone will ring and he'll be there. I'll hear his voice saying good morning, quite as though he did not love me and I did not love him. Always, formally, he had said good morning, simply, without an inflection even, just establishing his presence. Then warmth would creep into his tone as she responded equally formally, and they would laugh together at the little joke that was of politeness.

She would lie there waiting, forgetting. Then suddenly she would pull herself out of bed, emptiness draining her being at the realization of his farness. He was where no telephone could reach him, playing a game that had nothing to do with love. Those eyes, those lips, the fine sweep of that brow, would rise then in her memory with overwhelming dearness, and loss would tighten within her, bidding her cry. But she would get up as though nothing had been amiss, as though she had not forgotten for one moment that there was a war on and telephones did not ring so early in the morning. She would take her shower, put herself to rights, and then to breakfast, thankful for this day that had a beginning and soon would have an end. One day less, in the dull march of days that must pass before he should come again.

It's funny, she thought, how little we know of loss. It could come upon one with the stealth of a thief. It could lie in wait so patiently, not revealing itself. One moment you were laughing at some slight joke about some stupid thing, and the next moment, loss was upon you, wringing your heart with a pain so deep it was foolish to cry. That December morning, she had answered the telephone, ready with a flippant quip about tin soldiers who did not go to war but strutted around in uniforms stolen from theatrical wardrobe departments. And there was no good morning at the end of the line. Only a voice saying that he'd be over to say goodbye because war was no longer a joke but some reality flung into their midst, working its way into their lives, mocking their dreams of being married before Christmas. No home in the suburbs, no little battered coupe—"because we don't want to look too new and honeymoonish"—no little dog as a family starter. Just a hurried goodbye and some vague hopes of seeing each other again in a month or so, because this war won't be a long one, mark his words. And all the while she had looked at him, noting the excitement which made him look so alive, not truly believing him. Not next month, she had thought dully, not the next, perhaps not ever. And because she had felt so frightened, she had thought of some joke to dispel her fears and had sent him away laughing, loving her because she was so brave. No tears, he had said, and none there had been, not while he was looking. "See you in 1943," he said, and they had both laughed.

Because 1943 seemed so far away and so many things could happen between now and then.

She had smiled when he looked back and waved that last time, then she had gone slowly to her room and unhooked the telephone. She had removed her shoes carefully and lain on the bed, not yet daring to cry. She had placed her hands over her face, wishing never to see light again. Longing for the dark which would hide the pain she felt from the glare of the day. Now I am alone, she thought, inviting the relief of tears. Now I can cry. But the tears would not come, and she had lain there, tearless, longing to die.

That was centuries ago. Now here he was, and his voice sounded the same. His face was thinner, more weary, and his hands were limp when they were not holding her own. She watched his lips moving, following his stories with one half of her mind, matching the broken pieces of her memory of him with the other. She remembered him running up the stairs, two steps at a time, swinging his tennis racket gaily up at her as she flew down to meet him. She saw him learning the conga, his legs flashing in and out of sight as he danced by the piano. She thought of one Christmas Eve, hundreds of years ago, when they had run away from a Christmas party in Baguio and watched the moon come and go above the delicate veiling of pine leaves, happy because they were alive and alone and in love.

"Now I feel like Christmas," she had said, and he had hoisted her up at arms' length in an excess of delight, laughing up at her face so close above his own. He had flung himself down like some resting god, his legs long and relaxed against the deepness of the green. He had always moved so quickly, so completely in control of his limbs was he that one could not get quite reconciled to the thought of him spending the rest of his life like this. Her eyes traveled slowly down the foot of the bed, determinedly looking at that place where the mound of flesh ceased and emptiness began. When did this happen? She asked him in her mind. Perhaps at some moment when she was feeling safe and secure, some moment when the thought of him was warm about her, making her neglectful of fear. Perhaps she was sitting safe in some movie theater looking at pictures through his eyes, carrying on a mental conversation with him to temper her loneliness. Perhaps she was in bed, dreaming of the time when fear would be something to laugh at and loss an old wives' tale.

She was brought up short by his silence. She tore her eyes away from the foot of the bed and looked at him. He was gazing at her with such pain in his eyes that she felt like covering her own.

"You were looking at something," he whispered.

"Was I?" she said, striving for lightness. "I was just wondering."

"Wondering?"

"I was wondering how good a pair of legs I can be."

He smiled sadly and shook his head.

"We'd make a beautiful pair, you and I, when we go walking together."

"Walking," he said softly, and there was that in his tone which could have said "death."

"You'd look so romantic and I'd be so proud...."

"Yeah?" he said, and for the first time bitterness was in his voice.

"Yeah," she repeated, "and no buts about it."

He laughed at that and she laughed with him. They looked at each other, laughing, because they could not cry. Because the dreams they had known were now so many ghosts come begging, and they, out of their emptiness, could give nothing. She placed one arm beneath his head and looked at him long. They looked at each other thus, speechless, the smiles still upon their lips, love like a sword between them, hurting them exquisitely. She passed her fingers through his hair, and like a child, he sighed gently and leaned his cheek against the softness of her arm. He closed his eyes luxuriating in the silence.

Nights in the dugouts and the foxholes he had thought of her. Like this, close to him, arms soft about him. He had looked at the planes threatening overhead and thought of her, wondering if she still wore the sweet blue dress that he loved on her. If she still had the same smile. He had wondered how she did her hair at the moment, if her curls were bound by a ribbon, leaving her lovely face framed in a coronet of curls, or if these curls were left to play wildly in the wind. And he could not decide how he liked her best. Laughing or serious, moving or still. All these he had thought while death was about him. For to him she was life.

He opened his eyes and looked at her, addressing her
without words. And when this happened (his hand clenched
under the blanket), I thought of you, wondering what you were
doing then, knowing in my heart what you would do if you
but knew. The thought of you was magic balm over my consciousness and I clung to it with all the strength I possessed.
I should have given up, but I had to see you once more. When
they brought me here and I heard you had come, I thought
I was going to die with joy. Life seemed nothing compared to
one look at your face. To see those eyes again, those lips in a
smile. . . .

She passed a hand over his brow then, and he closed his
eyes once more.

The days he had lain there wondering when she would
come, arguing himself about how she would look when she did.
If she would wear a blue dress or a green, a ribbon or just
some trinket in her hair. And if she still wore gaiety like some
radiant cloak about her, so plain for everyone to see, to love
and delight in. Somehow, thinking of her, he could forget that
so many things had happened, and that he could never...

He looked at her with such suffering in his eyes that she
turned her head away.

"Don't," she said softly. "It isn't kind."

She was silent, and they stayed like that, not moving, fearing to talk. There was the sound of distant church bells and
he murmured, "Somebody's getting married this Christmas
Day." Not us, he thought despairingly, no, not ever us. His face,
drained of all excitement, was tired with a deathly tiredness.
She passed her hand over a thin cheek, love weighting each
fingertip. Over and over, her mind called his name, as one would
repeat a favorite prayer.

Suddenly he opened his eyes and she smiled.

"It's still there," he said abruptly.

"Which?"

"Your face."

"But of course," she retorted.

"There's no one like you."

"None," she said, laughing. "I'm made to order."

He called her name, love like fine veiling over his face.

He repressed a sigh as she rose to go. She smoothed his hair in final gentleness, then stopped over him once more and kissed him lightly on the lips. "A merry Christmas again, darling. When you can be moved, we shall go home."

He smiled at her but said nothing.

"I'll take such good care of you that you won't be able to tell the difference between home and this hospital. You'll have to marry me soon, though, if you are to be properly left at peace. When we're married..."

"Married," he echoed, with lips that had gone white.

"Certainly, my darling," she answered softly, evading the agony in his eyes. "I have to worry about your reputation."

She picked up her bag and removed a beribboned package from within its depths. "For your gory amusement," she said. Then seeing the look in his eyes, she added, "I'll come again, very soon."

She looked back and waved gaily when she reached the top of the stairs. Then she went slowly down. She walked past the nurse at the information desk and out onto the street. She walked smartly down the street, her face serenely lifted. Round the corner, an old church rose, solid and formidable. She glanced into the cool interior, hesitated for an instant, then went in. This heavenly darkness, she breathed, as she sank into a shadowed bench. She sat straight, staring ahead of her. There was the portrait of Christmas as she had always remembered it. She looked ahead of her, studying every little thing minutely, seeking escape in the familiar, the remembered, the long beloved. Above hovered a star. She fixed her eyes on this and spoke distinctly but softly. "I'm a brave girl," she said. "Not one single tear. I'm brave, brave. I've never been so brave."

Then she slid on her knees and burying her head in her arms, sobbed long and endlessly.

Philippine Review
December 1943

THE LONG WIND

NARCISO G. REYES

It began as a breath of coldness in the air. Thick gray clouds blanketed the sky, allowing only a ghost of sunlight to seep through. By the time the sun should have risen above the east hills, there was a stillness, and the cold became perceptibly sharper. Then it began to blow, a small wind out of the southwest, out of the sea. There was as yet no rain.

By mid-morning it was half a gale. The bamboos in the backyard were whistling softly, and the dried leaves of the big mango tree in front of the house fluttered in clusters to the ground. Milio propped his hoe against the trunk of the young papaya growing near the foot of the bamboo stairs and gazed up at the ashen sky. The dark masses of clouds, like a herd of frightened carabaos, were hurrying helter-skelter to the northeast, stampeded by the wind which increased in strength every minute.

Milio whistled softly, went up the low stairs at a bound, and walked straight to the kitchen, forgetful of his muddy feet.

Sela, his wife, was sitting on the bamboo floor, peeling green papayas on the low, square *dulang* which served as dining table and ironing board. A small pretty woman she was with brown, serene eyes and a ready smile. Although she was big with child and near her time, she gave such an impression of youth and delicacy that Milio, looking at her, was painfully aware of his great, raw-boned body. He noticed with dismay that she had paused in her task and was staring at his feet and the muddy tracks they had made on the shiny floor.

"I forgot to wash," he said apologetically. "This wind..."

"I will have my house clean, wind or no wind," Sela's voice was curt, reproving. But before Milio could feel resentful, she added gently, "Is it so bad out there in the fields that you didn't finish hoeing the tomato patch?"

Milio nodded ruefully. "Whenever I lifted the hoe, I felt as though the wind would wrest it from my hands and blow it away."

Sela glanced through the window at the creaking bamboos. "It isn't so bad here in the village," she said and resumed her task. "The wind's blowing high."

Milio reached for the coils of stout wire slung on a piece of stick thrust through one of the bamboo supports of the nipa-thatched roof. "I'll string a wire or two to help the old posts." Just then *Inang* Juana, Sela's mother, came out with her *buyo* mortar. She was an old, shriveled woman of sixty, with thinning white hair and a shrill, quivering voice.

"Just like you, Milio," she said. shaking her head. "Just like you to string wires when the storm is already upon us." She turned to Sela and asked querulously, "Where on earth did you put my pestle again? I have ransacked the whole house and I can't find it. My mouth is watering so I can hardly bear it."

Without looking up, Sela answered, "It's where you left it last night, *Inang,* when you washed it in the *batalan.*" Milio had already gone down, his old pliers in one hand, the coils of wire held tightly in the other. Soon Sela heard the scrape of a ladder against the bamboo wall. A few minutes more and the dull thuds of a stake being driven into the hard earth announced that he was already rigging up the first wire.

It was very cold now. Sela laid down her knife and stood up slowly. Slowly she went to the room and put on her woolen, rose-colored *kimona*. When she sat down again to her task, she did not pick up the knife at once but sat there for a while quite still. *Inang* Juana came in from the *batalan* shivering from the cold. She saw Sela's hands and she clasped her own to her breast, exclaiming, "Merciful God! Is this the time for idle thoughts or for dreaming? If you don't finish peeling those papayas at once we won't eat this noon. The wind is blowing harder and harder and soon you won't be able to build a fire." Then a thought came to her and she asked in another tone, "What ails you, child?"

Sela lowered her eyes and said in a voice the old woman could hardly hear, "Oh, nothing *Inang*—nothing at all. A little pain...." She picked up the knife, took one of the papayas, and began peeling quickly, with deft strokes.

By now Milio had finished rigging up four lengths of wire, one to each corner of the house. He came up just as the first spatter of rain began to fall. Hurriedly he washed his feet at the *batalan,* but forgot to wipe them on the rag before entering the kitchen. This time, however, Sela did not notice it. She had built a little fire, and was trying to keep it burning, nursing it cunningly against the gusts which blew in through the chinks in the wall and below the eaves.

"Leave that fire and get a wrap, Sela," he said. "Take a few clothes, too; you might get wet on the way. I'll take you and *Inang* Juana to *Tata* Lope's house. It has stout *ipil* posts and there are no big trees near it."

"Why?" Sela had to raise her voice to be heard above the roar of the wind.

Milio pointed to the front of the house. "The upper branches of the big mango trees are cracking up; they will fall if the wind keeps up."

"The house seems steady and sturdy enough," Sela shouted, "and perhaps the storm will pass away in a few hours."

Milio shook his head impatiently. "Not this storm. And anyway we can't take any chances with you the way you are."

This silenced Sela. Without a word she left the fireplace and went back to the room. Milio looked about for pieces of rope or thin wire with which to lash the windows to the sills so they wouldn't be blown away. Inside he could hear *Inang* Juana talking to Sela in a shrill querulous tone. Milio jerked hard at the string so that some of the loose strands bit into calloused skin of his thumb and forefinger. *Inang* Juana was still grumbling when she came out with Sela close behind her. Both were wearing large black shawls which covered their heads and shoulders.

"I told you not to build the house too close to that big mango," the old woman muttered plaintively. "But you are too hard-headed, you and Sela."

The bamboo posts creaked ominously as a gust more violent than the others before it hit the house squarely. There was a rending sound and a moment later a mango branch as big as a man's leg crashed on the front yard fence. Milio stuck the bits of twine he was holding into his pocket. "Let's go down," he said. "I'll take the two of you to *Tata* Lope's house and tie the other windows later."

The rain falling in big scattered drops stung their faces. They had a spell of terror as they passed by the big mango. The wind howled and tore at the great tree, pushing against it with such force and fury that all except the biggest of its branches were bent back, and it seemed as though the huge trunk itself might topple over.

Tata Lope himself opened the door to them. He was a big, handsome old man with a booming jovial voice and eyes that seemed always to be laughing at some secret joke. Now he looked very solemn, subdued and strangely shrunken. His broad shoulders were hunched; he held his hands wedged tightly between his thighs as though the cold were too much for him. When he had closed the door again, he sank to the floor on his haunches and, with shaky fingers, tied a big colored handkerchief round his head. Now and then he shivered like a wet rooster.

"The wind's strong...," he said in a quavering voice. "Like in '34 when our house was blown down and I was nearly killed by the falling roof. I thought it was the end of me."

From the kitchen came *Nana* Tinay's hearty voice. "Make yourselves at home, *Ka* Juana, Sela; I'll be through with the cooking in a minute."

"It's good Milio brought you over," she added when Sela had put down her bundle and come to the kitchen to help. "That old mango tree is too close to your house, and with the wind blowing from the southwest, there's no telling what may happen." Sela nodded, remembering how the wind had torn and pushed at the big tree while they passed by.

It was almost noon, but from the leaden sky and the slate-colored air it might have been very early morning. The five people in the house ate their midday meal quickly, with little appetite. The cold had become more intense; the wind mounted steadily in fury. *Tata* Lope shrank deeper into himself and ate no more than two or three mouthfuls of the steaming rice, washed down by a bowl of soup which he gulped scalding hot.

At three o'clock it was so dark in the house that Milio had to light the kerosene lamp. The rain still held back, but the worst of the storm was upon them. Already a dozen houses had been blown down, and now and then they could hear the crash of a tree falling across the road. People began to pass by in groups, carrying bundles in which they had hurriedly packed a few clothes and perhaps a blanket or two. Food they did not bring so as not to give offense to their hosts. Huddled together, their heads bowed before the wind, they struggled up the road to the big houses near the village church. Children clung tightly to their fathers' arms; mothers pressed their babies to their breasts, shielding the little ones with their bodies from the cold and lashing wind.

Someone stopped at the gate and shouted *Tata* Lope's name. It was *Lelong* Imo, Sela's grandfather, a grizzled veteran of the revolution who feared nothing on earth.

"Is Sela there?" he wanted to know. He had been to Sela's house and found no one there. *Nana* Tinay answered him. "Sela is here," she shouted back, adding solicitously, "Do come up, *Tatang*. It's cold out there and it's starting to rain in earnest. Come up and drink a cup of coffee with us."

She had indeed managed to cook a pot of coffee. She filled a big earthen bowl with the black, steaming liquid and handed it to *Lelong* Imo. "Drink first, *Tatang*," she said. "It's only coffee," she added apologetically. "We ran out of sugar."

Have you ever seen me drink coffee with sugar?" *Lelong* Imo demanded. "Sugared coffee is for women and children."

He took a sip and almost spat it out. "It's still boiling," he spluttered. "Do you have any grudge against me, Tinay, that you should try to scald my tongue?"

"Give it to me," *Tata* Lope pleaded in a small, piteous voice. He took the hot bowl in his trembling hands and drank the coffee in great hungry gulps.

"Why, you drained it!" *Lelong* Imo exclaimed in wonder.

"It's cold, cold...," *Tata* Lope complained, shivering in his corner.

The rain was now falling in gray sheets, making a sharp, throbbing noise upon the wooden walls and the galvanized iron roof. Night came swiftly and shrouded the village in icy darkness. No one except *Lelong* Imo had any relish for supper. Even *Nana* Tinay became less voluble and assured; she lapsed now and then into thoughtful silence. *Tata* Lope left his plate untouched, content with drinking bowl after bowl of hot coffee. Sela did not sit down to eat at all. As she stopped to squat on the bamboo floor, she had a flash of dizziness, and she pressed her hands to her sides. "I have a headache," she said. "I'll eat later." And walking slowly, heavily, she went to the sala, spread a mat beside *Nana* Tinay's big *camagon* chest, and lay down.

There she lay quiet and pale all through that long night. For a time the rain fell in such heavy torrents that it seemed as though the wind had scooped up the sea and were pouring it in such great cascades upon the earth. Then, suddenly, the rain stopped and there was only the wind, tearing through the trees and beating upon the houses with a thousand angry arms and fingers.

Lelong Imo lay down in the corner and was soon asleep. *Tata* Lope wrapped a thick blanket about his shoulders and shivered against the damp wall, his big, frightened eyes fixed upon the creaking roof. *Nana* Tinay and *Inang* Juana lay unsleeping beside Sela, ready to get up and attend to her needs at the first sign that she was in pain. *Nana* Tinay was a midwife.

Milio could not lie down at all. He could not bear the sight of Sela lying there pale and wide-eyed and waiting silently for her time. After supper, with the rain still pouring, he went back to the house, tied fast the windows, and covered with jute sacks Sela's *aparador*, *Inang* Juana's *tampipi*, and the heavy rectangular narra chest in which they kept their most valuable possessions. Then he went under the house to see how the chickens were faring. In one of the nests, there was a hen with a new brood of chicks. He put up pieces of wood behind it so that the sprays blown through the bamboo fence might not wet the nest.

The carabao sheds stood in the corner of the backyard about fifty yards from the house. Milio groped his way through the litter of fallen branches that covered the yard. As he approached the smaller of the two sheds, the yearling which *Lelong* Imo had given him lowed softly. Milio's heart went out to the little beast. He stroked its head gently and rubbed its back and sides vigorously. It was wet. Gratefully it snuggled close to Milio, and rubbed its cold nose against his bare legs. Milio took it to the other shed and made a bed of dry straw for it in a corner. The sheds were in a sheltered spot; the carabaos were safe enough. Yet Milio lingered for a while, testing the supports, feeling for leaks in the roof. An urge to do things moved him.

On his way back to *Tata* Lope's house he was nearly hit by a falling branch. The storm was in full fury now. Milio thought

he could feel the big mango in his front yard shaking; it was
as though the wind would wrench the great tree—trunk, branches, roots, and all—clean out of the earth. As he crossed the
narrow road, the rain stung his face and arms with the force
of clay pellets shot through a blow-gun. Lightning flashed in
quick succession, and Milio saw how the wind bent the tall
bamboos in *Tata* Lope's backyard so that their tips almost
touched the roof-tops. Some had been snapped like twigs; others
had been split lengthwise, and the wind, blowing through the
slits, made a wild, piercing, desolate sound, the most mournful
sound Milio had ever heard.

All night that strange wind blew with hardly a lull or a
moment's let-up. The rain fell again and stopped and fell again.
The wind blew on, endless and inexorable, with a sustained,
terrifying fury.

"It's not so strong as the storm in '34 or '37," *Nana* Tinay
remarked.

"Perhaps not," grumbled *Inang* Juana, "but it's longer,
much longer. We'll surely lose the season's crop."

Tata Lope tried to say something, but the words stuck in
his throat; after coughing two or three times, he gave up.

Sela lay silent and very still, with such an expression of
serene, patient waiting on her pretty face that Milio could
hardly bear to look at her.

Towards morning she began to moan softly. *Nana* Tinay
spread three more mats and half a dozen large jute sacks around
her to keep out the cold, damp air seeping in through the slits.
Then she took out two big blankets and fashioned a makeshift
screen.

"Boil some water in the big pot, *Ka* Juana," she called out.
"Pour a little oil on the firewood to make it kindle quickly."

"Is there anything I can do?" Milio asked.

"Yes," said *Nana* Tinay. "Keep out of our way."

Milio went to the kitchen to heat the coffee. There he would
at least have a fire to tend, and the storm to listen to and think
about.

How long would it last, he wondered. The great wind had
been blowing for a day and a night, yes there was no percep-
tible ebbing of its strength, no sign that it might soon spend
itself. It stamped and snorted like a herd of maddened bulls;
it roared like a hundred locomotives coming on at full speed,

and all the time its long icy fingers clawed and tugged at every exposed thing, and the force of it was as even, as steady and relentless as the pull of a tide. Now and then there would be a brief lull and Milio would listen to the wailing of the bamboos and find himself trying to catch the sound of Sela's voice.

Morning came, sunless and gray as the soil in Milio's rice paddies. As soon as it was light, Milio went out to feed the chickens and give the carabaos straw and fresh water. They would have to do without the grass until the storm was over. He did the chores as quickly as he could, pausing only to pat the yearling's head and rub its fuzzy neck with rough tenderness. The little beast lowed contentedly and strained at its leash as though it would follow Milio out into the howling wind.

It was raining again. Milio went back to the house dripping wet. He went straight to the kitchen and poured himself a bowl of coffee. *Lelong* Imo was standing before the stove, heating some herbs over the embers. He sensed Milio's anxiety and said kindly, "Not yet. She's having a hard time, but she'll pull through." Milio put down the bowl abruptly, spilling some of the coffee. He thought he could hear, above the din of the storm, Sela moaning in that quiet, patient way of hers....

He was glad when Beting, *Tata* Isko's twelve-year-old son, came to him with word that the yearling had broken loose and fallen into a ditch in the adjoining yard. Here at least was something a man could do. He took a coil of rope from under the house and followed the boy.

It was hard work getting the yearling out. The ditch was not very deep but the poor beast had been frightened and could not be coaxed to climb up the steep, slippery side after it had been roped. Milio had to get into the ditch himself and half-push, half-carry the yearling up, struggling meanwhile to keep his own foothold in the treacherous muck. He climbed up panting and covered with mud.

After taking the yearling to its stall and giving it a bath and a brisk rubbing with dry straw, there was nothing to do but go to *Tata* Lope's house. Milio headed for the well in the backyard to wash his arms and legs before going up. He never got there. At the foot of the front stairs he was stopped by the cry of a new-born child. He ran upstairs and nearly knocked *Nana* Tinay down in his hurry to get to the sala.

"What's the matter with you?" *Nana* Tinay scolded. "Didn't I tell you to keep out of my way?" Then, taking pity on him, she added, "You may go in now. It's a boy."

"How's Sela?" Milio asked.

"By the grace of God." she said solemnly, "she's all right."

Milio saw that Sela was indeed all right, pale and spent but with her pretty eyes as calm, clear, and full of life as ever. Milio looked at the child and saw that it was red-faced and had only tiny slits for eyes. It was crying lustily and he concluded immediately that it was hungry.

Only then did he feel his own hunger. He had not eaten anything since the night before. And he had been out in the storm since dawn, doing everything he could think of or lay his hands on. He went to the *batalan* and washed his arms and legs, slapping his thighs sharply three or four times. Then he sat down before the pot of cold rice in the kitchen, took a handful of dried shrimps from the cupboard, and ate a hearty meal.

After eating he went inside the room and lay down on the bare floor. The strain and fatigue of the past thirty-six hours weighed upon him like a load. He stretched his arms, yawned, and was soon fast asleep.

He slept all afternoon and far into the night. When he woke up, the storm had nearly spent itself. There was a succession of fierce gusts, each more violent than the former. Then, gradually, the wind thinned to a confused flurry. The rain stopped altogether. By morning there was hardly a breath of wind.

"What a storm!" exclaimed *Lelong* Imo. "It's the longest I can remember."

"I thought it would never stop," said *Tata* Lope, finding his voice at last.

"The mangoes will not bear fruit this season," mourned *Inang* Juana. "After such a wind the rice will be good only for the fodder." She wrung her hands. "A whole season's labor gone to waste . . ."

Nana Tinay smiled. "We should be thankful we were spared from harm," she said cheerfully.

After breakfast Milio went out and saw, with a sinking heart, how true were *Inang* Juana's words. Half the village had been destroyed by the storm. All around were fallen trees and houses. The leaves that had not been torn off the mango and santol trees had been withered to dull shades of red, orange, and purple, as though they had been scorched by fire.

"It's because the wind blew from the sea," explained *Tata* Isko. "It was a salty wind."

The rice had been flattened in the paddies except for patches of green here and there in sheltered places; but the tips of the lush stalks which remained standing had been buffeted so long by the wind that they had dried to a length of four or five inches, so that from the distance the fields, with the withered foliage of the mango and santol orchards in the background, looked like an autumn scene splashed with gray and faded purple and strongly suggestive of decay and death. It was as if a great stream of fire had passed over the village, leaving ruin and desolation in its wake.

Milio walked listlessly through the fields, stooping now and then to touch the fallen rice stalks. He felt like cursing the storm that brought such misfortune upon him. Then he remembered Sela and suddenly it didn't seem to matter so much. After all, the trees would send forth leaves and bear fruit again, and other crops could be planted. He thought of his little son and decided he would continue hoeing the tomato patch. Yes, he would do it that very day, as soon as he had gathered some herbs for Sela and put his house in order.

Philippine Review
June 1944

CITY OF GRASS

CONRADO V. PEDROCHE

Every afternoon on my way home from the office I pass by the City of Grass. I call it the City of Grass: a huddle of several cogon-roofed huts which sprang from the ruins of big buildings scorched down during the war just in front of the railroad station at the bend of the road to town. It began from one or two tables and a provisional shed made of two worn-out blankets sewn together and hoisted on four sturdy sticks.

This was the nucleus around which the City of Grass grew. Three *beto-beto* bankers and several crap shooters set their squat-legged tables on the sidewalk and the rattling noise of the dotted cubes attracted the people. *Viajeros* flocked around to stake a peso or two while waiting for trains that always came late and already overloaded. This was the beginning of the City of Grass.

An enterprising Chinaman built a row of narrow rooms and called it a Lodging House. He put up a sign-board done in black letters on a rusty piece of burnt corrugated iron sheet. There in the dark moist-smelling rooms, the *viajeros* found rest for the night after a day of much haggling and heat. The city had definitely started on its way towards existence. When I saw the building I knew at once that a city was bound to grow around it.

Right the very next morning bamboo posts were erected on both sides of the Lodging House. The posts stood awry and naked under the sun for some time but soon the builders—they were not really carpenters—came and steadied the posts and built enclosures of sawali around them and roofed them with cogon grass. These were the *carenderias*—the pioneer eating places where the flies, said a wag, were thicker than the soup—the large green flies which would describe silly triangles of sound if disturbed from their rich repast of mango and banana

peelings. The rats and the cockroaches were not slow to follow
and they too were as bold as the flies and the men that lived
in the backrooms of the cogon shacks—bold and shameless and
unafraid, for they seemed to realize that life was starting in
a new direction and to pioneer one must be all these—fearless
and brave and with few scruples.

Other shacks sprang in quick succession from all sides and
in all known shapes and sizes, for this was only a makeshift
city and no provisions were being made against future winds
and rains. The minds of those who built the huts were primarily occupied with only one thing and that was the providing
of space and shade against the fierce glare of the sun for the
better transaction of business.

But as though fearful of those who preferred to live outside
the city of lawlessness, the shacks grew huddled together not
for warmth, to be sure, but for protection and economy, for the
wall of one hut could as well be utilized as one side of a new
and adjacent one and what little jutting roof from this could
just be added to with a few meters wide of cogon which in
past years could be had almost for the asking but was a costly
thing now like most of other commodities.

This then is the City of Grass—a strange and vital city—
and the dwellers of this city are men and flies and cockroaches.
And life here is pathetic and warped and base but at times
it is beautiful and tender though very often it is ugly and un-
compromising.

Here you see the half-wit Chinaman naked but for a
tattered underwear, standing against a post and dozing the
whole day long, flies torturing the raw sores of his bare fat
back. Awake, there is only one thing he can think of: food.
And since this is not so easy to get in this struggling city
without a thick wad of bills, you will sometimes see him looking
for it in the garbage cans, in competition with the flies and
the dogs.

And children must forever be children. For very often you
would see them tormenting the idiot with blowguns, raining
mongo at his fly-infested sores. And the poor man would slap
his back, thinking of mosquitoes, close his eyes and begin dozing
anew. And his dreams? Who shall say what his dreams are?
Maybe he dreams of his boyhood by the shore of the Yangtze
or maybe of a distant and fancy country of his imagination.

Everything is sold in this City and the price the vendors ask for some of the goods they sell is as unreasonable as the shapes of their stores and as fantastic as the dreams of the Chinese idiot. And here not a few middle-aged prostitutes display their decaying teeth at passersby in the hope that they might find one more man willing to forget a day of loss with them. But sometimes a young girl with dark eyes full of tenderness would smile at you and bare her white teeth and you forget the weight of years upon your shoulders and return home healed of all the weariness.

The city is filled with the noise of commerce and this noise is compounded of all known sounds in the world: it is musical at times with sharp undertones of wheedling cajolery; sometimes it is raspy with impatience and sometimes it leaps over all barriers of resistance with loud and persistent importuning. Chicken feed, chico...no dice... or shoot... slightly used... pick up...roll the dice. The noise of the city is laughter of scurrilous girls over some juicy piece of anecdote, the whimpering of a child with sore eyes, the voice of anger rising, of man chasing thief. And through it all: the buzzing of the flies and the noiseless scurrying of rats.

And here the young man sits brooding over the past which to him is mad man's dream. He has come back from the front and returned to his home and found it in ashes. Now he sits in a corner of the City of Grass and broods over the past. He thinks again of the guns and falling men. How can he forget the putrefaction and ruin? The war has destroyed him but the destruction was incomplete. He saw death and now returns a dead man alive. He is here now and he should want to speak of death quietly and without bitterness but his thoughts are a muddled riot of incoherence and are without organization and clearness.

Walking around the city he feels meaningless though alive; the sound of commerce is as maddening as the sound of guns to his ears. He feels homesick for the front. He is in the field again, young, embittered, charging madly against the incomprehensible enemy he could not see, hopelessly caught in the noise and the horror and the voiceless protest of the dying. He had wanted to fall with his comrades, to fall and never rise again. But he rose each time he fell and now he is here—dead but alive and quietly walking the earth again.

If I don't die, he had prayed, please, God, let me have a new beginning in order that I may grow new roots for my being—a chance to remake the world and live among uncrazed men. He did not say it this way. He said it more beautifully because he could not form the words nor untangle the knot of his harassed thoughts. Give me time, he prayed, time to see the living truth of my existence upon the earth and realize its loveliness.

But now he is back and the men, though uncrazed, are strange beings who understand nothing but the language of the market place: *Bigatin tayo, chico*...genuine...chicken feed ...shoot...no dice. Money, money-money now, not the bullets. It is terrible and maddening. God, says the young man, I wish I were dead among my comrades in the field, and never rose again.

Here, too, lives the shoe-shine boy with the bedridden sister. Every evening when the boy returns from work he counts his money by the light of a dim oil-lamp and his sister looks lovingly at him. In the evening when she coughs he stands and gives her water to drink and rubs his hand over her fevered brow. Here lives Gutot, the one-legged ladder boy who went to Manila to have his harelip sewed and met disaster on the way. He sits on a stool and offers cigarettes to passersby. Here are the beggars: lousy and unshaven and leaning on staffs. An old woman with white hair cropped close and quite naked to the waist walks with uneven gait, lurching forward here and there with a pitiful whining. Here squats a blind one with a hole for a nose, his hat on his lap. He sings an unearthly tune with all the nasal intonation of a priest suffering from a cold. Another roams the city on a box with four wheels and a large cross in front to ward off the devil. He sits on the box and propels himself with mittened hands. He is not legless but his lower limbs had been atrophied since birth and would not grow.

These are the dregs—the unwashed people who yet must live. They, too, have their rights to existence, to life and to light. And here are the quacks—the vendors of "genuine goods" —of imitation tablets masquerading in the name of the real medicine. Here, says the wag, you can buy "sul-*patay*-sol" and "quaknine" tablets cheap but on your own responsibility and at your own sweet risk. These people, too, have their rights to live. And they live in this democratic City of Grass—with the rats and the flies and the roaches.

And soon the first rains began to fall and the city was a soaked city—a city of wet grass. Leaks in the roofs were hurriedly patched up with all kinds of patching materials: wooden boards, plain cardboards, tin, canvas, and even banana leaves. And children, huddled in corners, slept as soundly as ever as though they were sleeping in palaces under thick warm blankets. But the menfolk and the womenfolk passed the nights scheming, plotting and planning for the morrow's business, and going on as usual with their dark preoccupation.

People continued to eat in *carenderias*, business picked up more than ever and the flies buzzed on as before. While the rats, afraid of the rains, remained in their holes in hunger, waiting for the night and the dark. The house lizards grew fat on so many insects that flew in, seeking shelter from the rain. And the Chinese idiot grew stouter, though hungry, because of beri-beri while the sores of his back developed into ulcers. You would see him now, his hair dripping with rain, his tattered trousers clinging wetly upon his hairless thighs, leaning against the post, dozing as always, the rain pattering against his bare back and the children pestering him with their blowguns and mongo bullets.

And then one evening the end comes for the City of Grass. The moon, shining balefully through a rift in the heavy clouds, casts a sinister radiance over the huddled roofs. It had stopped raining since two days previous and in the afternoon the sun shone so fiercely the heat was unbearable. The grass roofs, soaked with nine days of rain, dried almost instantly. Grass, soaked grass, when drying, exudes a terrible warmth that could suffocate. Along the street are puddles shining like monstrous eyes in the moonlight and in the distance the frogs are croaking a scherzo of many moods.

Inside one of the huts a young girl's sides are being torn asunder with the pain of childbirth. This is the prize she must pay for a dark night of laughter and deep passions. She is brave now, for this thing she is delivering to the world, she knows is a part of her, of her youth and her dreams. The girl feels suddenly released as of some terrible torture. She is quiet and pale. She opens her eyes to see the cause of all her fears and joys; the little child does not move. It is voiceless in the night.

Somewhere from within an inner room of the Chinese lodging house, a strange one-string instrument makes a weird monotone, a torturing kind of sound that resembles the thin whisper of mosquitoes before they sink their poisoned stings into the blood. On and on and on it goes in the stillness of the night—an unconquerable and maddening monotone.

In a corner *carenderia* three belated diners are seated around a table over a bowl of *pansit*. They are silent but for the sound of noodles being sucked into their mouths. Once in a while the fat fellow in shorts will bend and slap his legs. The mosquitoes are biting. But he does this without complaining. He bends and slaps his legs and goes on with his *pansit*.

Now the tall one is talking. Let us hurry, *pare*, it is getting late. You are afraid? asks the third man who is eating with his hat on. You are afraid of this, Ponso? Leave him to me, *pare*.

He is armed, says the fat one, slapping his legs again.

Yes, says the first, I am afraid. Who is not afraid of a gun?

I am not, says the third one.

Suddenly, from outside, in the moonlight, a gun is fired; a flash, another flash, and still another. Two of the three men topple over and are dead. The blood flows fast and dark. The fat one crawls under the table and runs out through the back door. A police siren rings sharp in the night. The unknown assailant slinks in the shadows and disappears towards the dike. The Chinaman's music suddenly stops. The insistent monotone is ended.

And then a flame rises quickly from one end of the City of Grass. The flame at first is a thin tongue licking the roofs of the city. And then it is no longer a tongue. It is a horned monster lapping at the sky. All sounds are stilled as the people watch the thing taking on shape; the shape is gorgeous in the moonlight. It is like a huge unearthly flower growing as by magic in intensity and dimension every second.

In the moonlight the City of Grass kneels slowly beneath the monstrous flower and against the lurid light are dark sil-

houettes of people running here and there like helpless puppets
in the hands of a terrible and flaming god.

Philippine Review
August 1944

NOCTURNE

VERONICA L. MONTES

It was customary of the young mistress of the big stucco residence which was lording it over with the distinctive Spanish style a broad garden luxuriant with petunias, China aster and roses, in the city's southern residential section, to sit after dinner in the sofa on the open west-side veranda, with lights turned off, and then rest in the quiet solitude and contemplate the evening world. This had been her ordinary pleasant routine long before her marriage four years previously to Vic, a successful business executive and sportsman in his early thirties, a junior partner of a growing banking and financing organization. She got that habit from her parents who led a sort of Arcadian life in their sugar cane plantation home in the Visayas; and her marriage, instead of breaking that habit, effected on the contrary a subtle attaching of her husband to her idea of an after-dinner preoccupation. She set her reading after lunch, and, occasionally, in bed before retiring, but the early evening hours were, as a matter of conduct, spent quietly in the pleasant semi-darkness of the porch.

As usual, that evening after dinner, the mistress, Remy, was couched deep in the sofa on the west-side porch, mentally drawing the scene from her propitious position which had a good command of the district. Lying before her was a poor neighborhood of ill-assorted houses and tenement-dwellings of the middle class and factory worker folk, strikingly drab at daytime; but after sunset, the gloom dotted by stars and low-power electric lights kindly camouflaged much of its run-down condition, and the composite silhouette of the surrounding low houses against a starry sky would even strike the beholder with a sense of poetic elevation. The stucco residence offered a remarkable contrast to the neighborhood; and in fact, situated at the edge of the opulent conservative section, it stood as a steadfast symbol of high-class living endeavoring to penetrate a poor frontier to lend it a touch of glamor. The west-side garden of the residence was the demarcation line of the shabby and the splendid. From the picket fence guarding a blooming bed of flowers, ran an area of unkempt narrow lots strewn with rusty tin cans, and junk of all sorts carelessly abandoned by children, and clustering houses long impaired by neglect and consistent change of occupants who were existing shiftlessly like leaves in the winds of circumstance.

From the porch Remy was descrying some of these new drifts of circumstance in the neighborhood. They were a family of six who had moved just two days before into the bare bamboo house patched clumsily with pieces of board here and there, just across the garden. She had a talk with three of the little neighbors as they played outside her garden fence that afternoon. She had been tending the plants then, and the three children, the eldest a girl, and appearing to be barely six, all in the meager clothing of their class, had approached her garden. The youngest, wearing a red cap, had been pressing his cheeks against the fence, so that his nose was forced through a space of the pales, in order to watch her at work more closely. She had walked to the tots, greeted them candidly, but they had at first regarded her with some fear and childish shyness that had, however, vanished presently when she had made several overtures and profession of friendship through words and smiles.

Now that evening she could see through the open window of the bamboo house the children playing on the floor in the electric light. She could see them well, because the house was low and she was practically looking down at it. Intently, she watched them wrestle with lusty abandon that seemed to shake the whole frame of their dwelling, and letting off peals of laughter or gladsome shrieks which she could distinctly hear. The mother of the children entered in that happy family picture framed by the window, like a madonna holding what appeared to be the youngest member of the family. The mother, only in white cotton chemise, was feeding the infant on her breast; then she seated herself on a wooden stool and watched her children play. The father of the family appeared also in the scene. He was robust, mild-faced, was wearing short khaki pants and undershirt. He stayed only momentarily. After giving the infant in the mother's arms a loving pinch in the cheek, and a kiss on the forehead, the father skipped nimbly to avoid stepping on the others on the floor, and disappeared into the next room.

Remy drank the felicitous beauty of the domestic scene. She was in no way addicted to eavesdropping of a despicable sort, and if she was spying now into the house of the neighbors, it was because such indulgence, she knew, did not in any way involve a question of normal or social deportment. Furthermore, the picture of the happy children in the next house was intensely appealing. Children are always irresistible, command a universal interest, and, at play or asleep, crying or laughing, in silk or rags, there is about them an abiding attribute which enraptures everyone, and it is verily this abiding attraction which enraptured Remy and instilled in her a deep consciousness of an inviolable right which transcends morally, under certain circumstances, the privacy of a home.

Her sensitive affection for children brought to her that evening an even harder realization of the bare melancholy world in which she lived. She had been married four years, and had almost all of the things a woman could ask for—wealth, devoted husband, social position, charm, and a big beautiful house, but hardly a home. It had servants, a car, and the best appointments and equipment, but a sense of incompleteness came repeatedly to her, oftentimes during moments of leisurely meditation, to vex her, a vexation from which she would attempt to seek an escape through some undefinable affectionate consecration to children of other people. And yet such consecration would somehow make her all the more keenly aware of her loneliness, and the escape she would be seeking meant alas! only dragging herself more into the austere moments of sighs and longings.

If she had a child, she wouldn't perhaps be sitting on that porch, brooding as she did, and passing the solitary hours in some momentary solace that the evening could offer. She would undoubtedly prattle with the child, laugh in happy abandon as they played with small woodblocks of attractive colors, construct a miniature castle out of some dovetailing wood pieces, or wound a toy train and play to their hearts' content, speaking a language and behaving in a manner that bring together an oldster and an infant into a sweet communion. Or she would

be reading a big primer of big red and blue and green pictures
to her baby, or perhaps coaching it with the first piano lessons.
But the Fates had been against that. Since the first year of
her marriage, when she had realized that no child was coming,
she had prayed ardently, had gone on a pilgrimage to Obando
and made several offerings to the patron saint, San Pascual
Bailon, like so many other unblessed wives; and the year previous, on the advice of an old family doctor, she had gone with
her husband on a world trip, hoping that a change of atmosphere
and new environments and the experiences of travel would work
up for her, as they had to many other wives known to the family
doctor, some chances of motherhood. But she still had to wait
and hope. Of evenings, when the weather was fine, and she
was not out to a movie, or had no callers, she would be out
sitting on that porch to look at the familiar city sights at night,
and sigh deep familiar longings.

Vic, who had been attending to some private mail, came to
join her. Pulling a cushioned chair, he seated himself beside
her, and, placing his hand fondly on her shoulder, asked with
his usual opener: "Well, what have you been musing about.
Dreamer?"

"I am not musing," she said softly as she took his hand
in hers. "I have just been watching our new neighbors play
over there on the floor. They moved in only the other day.
Look, they have been wrestling for the last half hour and they
are hardly tired out."

Vic looked across the garden and noted at once the particular sight she had indicated. The evening panorama was a
remarkable mixture of views which are quite an absolute part
of that kind of vicinity stretching before them. At one corner
was a combination of *sari-sari* store and coffee joint operated
by a Chinaman; farther away was a small shop where swarthy
laborers stayed overtime at night with always some gadgets
or iron-pieces to fix or hammer; and to the other side, under a
small house, was an improvised bar dispensing *tuba* and moon-
shine to groups from round the neighborhood, usually consisting
of gossips, loafers, stevedores, and small-paid white-collar job-
holders. In between were homes, just plain houses or weather-
beaten *accesorias*, all with wide-open doors and windows in
the early evening, showing out their lights, but in the gamut
of these lights Vic made out easily the one house that Remy

meant, and he was instantly attracted by the children on the floor. Somewhere in the direction of the workshop a waltz was issuing fullblast from a radio set and wafted with the shrill song of a girl lulling a baby to sleep, and from the *tuba* stand some hearty wild laughter of the drunken men would burst forth occasionally, accompanied by familiar curses and oaths. However, the merry voices of the new neighbors at play came above all the other sounds.

"That's my namesake holding Sluggo above her head," she said.

"Sluggo," Vic said. "What a curious name!"

"It's a pet name from a comic strip character," she explained. "The real name is Jose."

"How fast you know our neighobrs," declared her husband. But he did not mean to chide her.

"I met them this afternoon," she said. "They came to the fence while I was trimming the roses. They don't seem to be of the common run of alley children, though they are just as poorly dressed, and they don't have the impudence of street urchins. In fact I had a rather difficult task trying to get them to talk, and their language is rather decent, I judged."

"They are robust," Vic said.

Now, Remedios, the namesake of the mistress of the rich home, had hurled Sluggo on his feet on the floor, and he fell on his back with a thud, but taking the hard game playfully as it should be. Then Remedios pinned him down by the shoulders as the third and smallest in the group, who was still wearing his red cap, quickly sat on Sluggo to simulate an equestrian atop an overturned mount. Sluggo wriggled mightily to free himself from Remedios' hold and the weight of the other—the horseman—and in this unrestrained muddle, some hand had taken hold of Sluggo's sleeveless cotton shirt, ripping it in front, almost half-way down from the neck. Upon being suddenly aware of this fact, the three almost simultaneously desisted with a snap from their struggling and stood up facing their mother, somewhat electrified in breathless fearful anticipation of a verdict.

What the children had expected did not happen. The mother who was holding the infant did only as much as reproach all the three by a sedate waving of a forefinger and speaking in a low voice which the couple on the veranda of the rich house divined to be only a mild chastisement. It was apparent that the attitude of the mother produced in the children a reaction akin to one coming after a tense expectation of a bomb explosion which had turned out to be only a small firecracker burst.

"Look," Remy said to her husband, "the woman is not angry. She told Remedios to get something."

The eldest child disappeared from the scene and reappeared a few moments later giving what presently appeared to the couple watching from the dark porch to be a threaded needle with which she sewed up the ripped shirt of Sluggo. She had lain the infant on the floor where it kept on jerking contentedly on its back as the elder ones crowded around to play and fondled it, finally keeping it from the view of the couple across the garden.

"How happy they are," Remy said softly, quite half-meditating as she cuddled closer to her husband. There was a tone of wistfulness in her remark. She was speaking of a happiness which she, despite her fortunate position, had been sadly incapable of owning. Nearly always when she had wanted something, she could invariably attain it almost in a flash by means of the great magical power which opulence had endowed her family, and she was aware that there was a limit to the power of that magic. That awareness made her a lonely woman. All those four years she had been living in hopes and prayer. The sharing by her husband of such loneliness and hopes could not give her anything beyond the grace of a temporary solace. Strange, it seemed, that although it pained her deeper the more she saw mothers with children, she would not dare insulate herself from such interest in mothers and children; it was like reaching out vainly for some enchantment, and failure to attain it intensifies hope rather than prompts bewailment. That was partly why, of evenings, she liked to get out to the porch and live in a world of dreams and loneliness.

Later, as they sat there on the veranda, they heard a distant church clock chime the hour of ten. The evening scene had changed. In many homes of the district spreading before their ken, the lights had been either shut from the outside or turned off. In the house of the new neighbors, Remy saw the father of the family appear in the intimate living picture framed by the window.

He talked to the children who tugged gleefully at his feet. Then the man reached for the electric bulb and switched off the light. Everything was dark in that room now, and Remy and her husband could only hear the children pleading excitedly for a few more minutes of fun. But even the poor had regulation hours for their children. The small shrill voices shifted to the rear room and became indistinct, and in the next few minutes the house was hushed.

Silence took its turn for the evening. There was still some intermittent hammering in the workshop, and in the *tuba* stand spirited conversation would rise to a pitch, and then, farther out on the main driveway, cars were still whizzing along, but the late hour had subdued the noises somehow, and on the whole, ten o'clock p.m. in that neighborhood was relatively quiet and tame. The stucco residence which was on the rim of both the fashionable section of big residential houses and of the drab, meager place of low-earning residents, was inevitably wrapped up in the usual evening repose.

Darkness employs itself in many imponderable manifestations; it sharpens the senses, and it has a mysterious glow that illumines thought and spirit. Oftentimes men see better in the dark. This was more or less the circumstance in which Remy and Vic found themselves, seeing distinctly in their mind's eye the even more beautiful picture of their neighbor than what the electric light revealed; they saw the wealth and luxury of the poor of which they themselves, for all their happy material possessions, had been destitute. Both sat on the porch, silent but keenly conscious of the longing and restlessness they were sharing. Often the thought kept recurring to Remy of how, back in the days shortly before their marriage, she and Vic had one day come to talk seriously of children, had made plans for their schooling, their bringing up in exclusive colleges; of children who would perpetuate and uphold the family name and tradition, and inherit the fortune and take care of it frugally and wisely. And as the fruitless years of her married life advanced, she recalled more bitterly those dreams and the more she felt her loneliness.

Vic put his arm around her and hugged her softly. "It isn't utterly hopeless, dear," he said, sensing intimately her thoughts and feelings.

In the dark he could discern her looking closely into his face, and he felt the warmth of her cheeks, the emotions of her dreamy eyes, and understood the unspoken language of her small apologetic mouth. She also placed her arm around him, and, still looking into his eyes, she shook her head slowly. Then he pressed his cheek unto hers, warmly and lovingly, and then their lips met tenderly. Between kisses she managed to say in a low, steady voice, "It isn't utterly hopeless." And he could feel her heart beat against his. When they had disengaged from the embrace, Remy prepared to rise, and he rose too, and they went into their rooms.

The light had turned on first in Vic's room, and then in Remy's. Remy had changed into her silk nightgown and was sitting on the edge of her bed, her dainty feet toying at the sandals. Then she reached out for a volume of Hemingway's on top of her escritoire, thumbed dryly a few pages, and decided she could not do any reading. Almost dispiritedly she rose, put the book back to its place, and switched the light off. Sitting again on the edge of her bed in the dark, she noticed from the bright beam falling at a sharp angle on the linoleum in the hall, which she could see through the half-open door of her room, that the light was still on in Vic's bedroom. Her ears faintly caught him whistling a strain of a familiar nocturne, his favorite music it was, and she picked up a bit the tune in a hum. Then she inhaled deeply a few times, and stretched herself on the bed, her head upon her hands on the pillow, and her eyes wide open. She could see etched against the dark background of the room, some mental images of children playing and laughing—Remedios, her namesake, Sluggo, and the little one with the red cap, and the mother suckling the infant.

Then almost instinctively she noticed the light in Vic's room snap out, and in a moment she heard him in his slippers crossing the hall, and in the next instant, tapping gently at her door.

"Yes, dear," she called.

Vic came in his white silk pajamas and deep-green lounging robe, which she easily detected in the dark with the aid of the pale light of the sky through the window. He sat on the edge of her bed, while she remained lying on her back, her hands under her head. Vic bent to kiss her lips.

"Lonesome?" he asked.

"A little." she murmured.

"You feel too much the little neighbors," he said.

"I was thinking of them," she said, "and also of what you said about it not being utterly hopeless."

"You also said it. You feel the same about it," he said.

"Yes."

"Are you glad, then?"

"Glad," she said, "and hopeful."

"I am hopeful too. We are young yet. Rather silly of me to say that but I can't help it. We are young and strong." He paused. And they listened to the deep silences, which are the children of the night. And they were, like the night, filled with hope.

Philippine Review
September 1944

EVENING MEAL

HERNANDO R. OCAMPO

It was nearly nine o'clock in the evening when I arrived home, and the electric light in the veranda was on because Father had company. The light in the veranda consumed much electricity because it was a big bulb and we never used it except when there was company. Our veranda was big and spacious and the floor was shiny.

I was at the foot of the stairs when I heard Father's last words, "...I signed the check and dismissed the idiot!" After which, one of the visitors laughed boisterously, saying: "Ah, Don Paco...that's a good one..." Francisco was the name of my father, and his friends called him Don Paco, sometimes Señor Paco, but Mother used to call him only Paco, or Papa.

"Good evening," I greeted the visitors when I reached the threshold. "Good evening, Father," I greeted my father, and the three of them (Father and his two visitors) returned my greetings with a slight bow.

"You join us," one of the visitors, who was the president of our Neighborhood Association, said as he offered the glass he was holding. The glass contained calamansi-ade. I know, because that was the only thing we could offer visitors these days.

"Please do," the other visitor said. I did not know who this man was, but he was older than our neighborhood association president, and he was fat and big around the waist. He had a certain prosperous look about him—more so, because he sat near Father who was thin and pale. Father was not sick, though. He was merely getting old.

I thanked them and asked to be excused and I went directly to my room. In my room while undressing I thought of what we would have for dinner because I was very hungry. It was already past nine, and I had not taken any merienda downtown.

Feeling the acidic gnawing in my stomach, I even thought that the family had already finished supping.

We always supped not later than eight in the evening. I should have gone home earlier and eaten with the family but coming from the office at five-thirty, I took in a late stageshow with an officemate. The show was lousy and the theatre was a veritable hot-house, but the darn thing set me back by four pesos. Tomorrow I'd have to borrow at least ten pesos from my younger brother for pocket money.

After changing into my pajamas, I hurried to the dining room. I found the dining room dark so I pushed the electric button and, with the light on, found the table set for the whole family. Mother's favorite blue-and-white plates and her silver were laid nicely on the white linen tablecloth. "So they are eating here," I said to myself, referring to the visitors, of course. It was because we never used Mother's favorite plates and silver for ordinary days. We used the ordinary white *china* and the nickle-plated forks and spoons unless there was company. Mother was very careful with her favorite set of silver, but somehow two spoons and one fork were lost, and since then Mother refused to set them on the table except on special occasions.

My sister came in from the kitchen. "When do we eat?" I asked her. Sister was younger than I but older than Nestor, our younger brother. "When do we eat?" I said again when she did not answer my first question. "I am starved."

"Why—what time is it now?" Sister asked in response, with an obvious effort to put a smile on her face and to make her voice sound nice.

"It is already past nine," I said, "and I'm starving. When do we eat?"

Sister did not answer. She left me in the dining room without answering my question, but once outside, she shouted: "Put that light out!"

I was angry. But I did not say anything. I put the light out and left the dining room feeling angry and hungry. I went to the sala and found Mother mending something. "Good evening, Mother," I said, "have you not eaten yet?"

Mother laid aside what she was mending and breathed deeply, looking very tired. She peered at me through her gold-rimmed spectacles, and I looked at her and saw her lips moving imperceptibly. I knew she was about to say something, but instead of doing so, she merely swallowed and chewed her toothless gums, her cheeks curling in and out of the hollows, her fragile chin moving up and down in a very funny way. Mother is also getting old, I thought. She always looked tired and sleepy.

I took the chair opposite Mother and lit a cigarette. For a while we looked at each other silently and listened to the occasional burst of laughter coming from the veranda. The fat man's laughter—it was rolling and joyful and rose above that of Father's and the NA president—was especially contagious, and I could not help laughing inwardly with them in spite of Mother's grave face. I did not know what they were laughing about, but just the same I laughed with them with the fat man's laughter.

But I could not forget my hunger. I puffed my cigarette and asked: "Where are the children?" By *children* I meant Diding, Enchong and Cion—my two brothers and sister aged eleven, nine and seven respectively.

"In their room—sleeping probably," Mother said softly.

"Have they..." I began, remembering my hunger, but swallowed and said instead, "Who is that fat man?"—because the fat man was suddenly laughing his rolling laughter again.

"I don't know," Mother said. "Perhaps another—what do you call them?—buy-and-sell men?"

"Ah," I said.

And for a while Mother and I were silent. Father and his visitors were also silent. After a while Sister came in and said, "Come with me." I followed Sister and when we reached the dining room, she said, "What time is it now?"

"Nearly nine-thirty, perhaps," I said.

Sister fidgeted restlessly around. Presently she went to the cupboard in the corner of the dining room, pulled its door open, closed it, and came back to me, her face clouded by a frown. "Don't you have any money?" she said.

"Nothing," I said, "except fifty centavos." After a brief pause, I asked, "Why—what do we have in there?" indicating the cupboard.

"Fried dried fish and tomatoes," Sister said.

By and by my younger brother Nestor arrived in the dining room. He was still in his street clothes when he came into the dining room. Always he did not bother to undress first in his room before eating because he was very hungry when he arrived home. He worked for a stage-show company and he arrived home some minutes before ten and he was always hungry, too hungry to bother about undressing first when he arrived home.

"Why? Have you not eaten yet?" Nestor asked when he saw the table set.

I looked at Sister and she looked at me. Then I said, "Not yet..." I paused, then continued: "Do—do you have..."

Then we heard the visitors taking their leave, and Father in his turn was insisting that they stay for supper.

"They are leaving now," I said, when we heard the visitors saying, "next time...thank you" again and again. And then I saw Sister's face. It was suddenly cleared of the frown that she had been vainly trying to hide a while ago.

The three of us went to the sala and saw Father leading the visitors toward the stairs. They talked some more upon reaching the threshold, and we thought they'd never end their conversation. At last they shook hands, said "good nights" and "good-byes" and "next times" and "come agains," before the visitors finally left.

Father came into the sala and his face looked tired, but he smiled and said jovially, "Now, we can eat! Wake up the children and let us eat!"

Mother looked at Father strangely and Father kissed Mother a loud smacking kiss full in the mouth, and Mother tried to hide her embarrassment by saying, "Now...now...Papa" (she called him Papa during tender moments) and we could not help laughing at Mother's discomfiture.

Sister woke up the children, and they came out of their room rubbing their eyes, looking at Father and Mother.

"To the dining room—all of you." Father said, his voice somewhat exaggeratedly happy and buoyant, while he led the way with Mother's hand tucked in the crook of his right arm.

In the dining room, at the head of the table where Mother's blue-and-white dishes and shining silver were laid attractively on the white linen tablecloth, Father sat and said: "Bring out the pork-chops...bring out the fried eggs...bring out the puchero..." His face was all smiles, and although there were deep wrinkles on his forehead and the sides of his mouth, he looked actually younger. "It is too bad those two fellows left without eating. They wouldn't know how good a dinner they are missing. Com'on...bring out the pork-chops...bring out the fried eggs...bring out the puchero...I'm famished."

"Eggs...eggs...," the children chorused joyously, anticipatingly while Sister placed the big platter of white rice in the middle of the table. "Eggs...eggs...," the children shouted again.

"Eggs...yes, eggs," Father said softly, and I saw the smile slowly vanishing from his face.

A period of silence followed. Then Sister said, "Yes, eggs," and she smiled, and Father smiled again, and all of us smiled, except Mother.

Sister went to the cupboard and brought back to the table a big white platter and a blue-glass salad-bowl. "Yes, eggs, and pork-chops and puchero, too."

Father smiled, and Nestor and I smiled also until we saw Mother and the children staring at the platter containing the fried dried fish and at the salad-bowl containing the sliced tomatoes, and all of us, even Father and Sister, ceased smiling. We went on eating silently...

Pillars
September 1944

THE HOMESTEAD

MAXIMO RAMOS

The war caught us, Didi and me, in Mindanao. Returning to Luzon was out of the question, and yet our savings were fast playing out. The provincial capital where we had been teachers for several years was a tourist spot in the interior of Mindanao. It had never been self-sufficient in food, and now starvation was in evidence everywhere. Prices went up until we had nothing left but a few hundred pesos hidden in the lining of one of Didi's old dresses.

"We have to leave this town," I finally said.

"I suggest Lala," she replied with an enthusiasm I hadn't expected in her. "Now we can develop our homestead. After all we once had dreams of having a productive land down South."

"Your aim is worth its weight in rice," said Greg Villanea, who owned the twenty-four-hectare lot north of mine, when I proposed to him that he go with us to live in Lala and help produce food. "Still, I doubt whether outlawry has become any less popular among the Moros there lately. Outlaws have roamed the Lala jungles for years and years, you know."

"Before the war it used to take us half a day to go to Lala on a fast bus," said Tuazon, the civil engineer to whom belonged the rights to the homestead south of my lot. "There are no buses now; the best you can take is a carabao-cart. I'm afraid my wife and I won't be able to stand the isolation in Lala, especially these days."

"Besides," said Valdez, owner of another adjoining lot, "malaria won't leave the jungle just because we town-dwellers now find it necessary to go and live there. No. I'm not prepared to add my old crate to those of my tenants who have died of the fever."

"The crocodiles and thirty-foot pythons in Lala," added the wife of Jose Aquino, another Lala neighbor, "are ignorant of the times, and they must still be there."

However, Didi and I proceeded with our plans. We procured strong mosquito nets, bought plenty of quinine, collected seeds, and stocked up provisions to last us at least a year. We completed our preparations with two carabaos, a pair of goats, some chickens, and the most essential farm tools. In a couple of weeks we were ready to start for the homestead.

The trip took us the better part of three days in an old cart over the motor road now deeply buried in cogon and tiger-grass. We were travel-worn when we arrived at Lala, and at once difficulties confronted us.

I had imprudently taken Didi and all our gear to Lala without making a preliminary visit. I was now dismayed to find that the tenants whom I had expected to be still living in the clearing not only had quitted the place but had torn down and taken with them the hut which I had built shortly before the war. Thick weeds now covered the former patches of maize and rice, and seedlings from the great trees of the jungle had started to grow all over the place.

I went to work at once, however. Under a broad-leaved *catmon* tree, I put up a lean-to. The rafters were of yearling saplings and the roof of banana leaves. After we had eaten our hastily prepared meal it was fairly dark. Didi and I crept under a double mosquito bar and I slept like a log.

Waking up next morning I found everything dripping wet and Didi complaining of a headache. The weird jungle sounds had been so strange to her that she had not slept a wink, and the rain that came at about midnight had not added to her comfort. But that first morning in the jungle was sunny, and the place was in its brightest colors. Cockatoos of gorgeous plumage were about with a lively flutter of wings. From a tree-top, flying squirrels glided playfully on furry leathern wings down to the foot of the next tree, clambered awkwardly up that, and sailed gracefully down to the foot of another tree—all entirely unmindful of our presence. Wild pigeons cooed half awake. half asleep in the cool depths of the woods, accented by the call of a gecko hanging upside down beside its hole in some old tree-trunk.

"What does the jungle look like inside?" Didi asked.

"Come and I'll show you." I led her through the second-growth belt into the jungle proper.

Delightedly she would point to an occasional orchid, a flash of flaming loveliness in the perpetual twilight among the trees. "What's that?" she stopped suddenly and gripped my arm as a rending cry came from a large *tucang calao* tree rooted down in the mold of centuries. "It must be a large beast."

"It's only a bird," I reassured her, as once more the call broke forth.

"Bird or beast, it must be very big, making such an awful sound."

I persuaded her to go with me to the foot of the tree and pointed upward. "There he is," I said. "A hornbill."

"What a big fellow! Almost a meter long! And what's he doing with that large banana in his mouth?"

"That's no banana, silly. It's his beak!" I said, but she would not believe me until the bird hopped down to a lower branch and the ponderous scarlet bill stood in clear contrast to its glossy black feathers. "The hornbill is one of the most beautiful birds in the Philippine forest, and certainly the noisiest. There are a number of other birds here similarly pretty," I added, trying to win her over to the beauties of the jungle.

We were not wholly alone here, we soon found. Scattered in the wide stretches of virgin forests were other clearings, nearly all of them still tenanted by Christian settlers. They came to us, these new neighbors of ours, at first singly, then in groups.

Moro strangers also dropped in on various shallow pretexts. We had previously learned that Moro outlaws robbed and murdered for people's money and firearms and we took care to show them that we had no money and that I had surrendered my gun to the authorities before we left the provincial capital. Then gradually we became friends with them, too. They knew how to reciprocate good acts. For the little quinine, salt, and sugar that Didi sometimes gave them, they would bring us venison and fresh-water fish, besides taro, yams, yautia, and camotes, both to eat and to plant in our clearing.

"Just tell us when you are ready to put up your house and we shall do it together," said our neighbors. Before the month was out a modest little house stood in my clearing. The rafters and joists were of young trees, the posts of black *camagon*, and the roof was thatched cogon grass. The flooring was made of black and shiny slats from trunks of the *palma-brava*. After we moved in and Didi had given it the woman's touch, our new home was as *cozy* as ever a young couple could desire.

By paying some of our new friends a reasonable wage I had soon planted two hectares of the clearing to maize and choice varieties of rice. These quickly struck root and began reaching in emerald luxuriance for the sun. Beans of different kinds—winged, string, hyacinth—tomatoes, eggplants, sponge cucumber, even pechay and lettuce and cabbage, now flourished lushly in the fecund loam. I also planted two long rows of papayas and pineapples and shortly they had broad, dark-green leaves ready to produce fruit. On both banks of the small stream which flowed through the middle of the clearing I planted avocados, breadfruit, custard apple, *santol*. Later, working for variety, I was also to put in jackfruit, hog plum, *lanzones*, mangosteen, *durian*, and oranges.

It was pleasant to feel the safe isolation of our jungle home, and to listen to the rain falling softly on the thatched roof.

We had brought with us a pullet and a cockerel, and I built a roosting place for them under the floor joists. In a few weeks the hen started to lay and soon the cheep-cheep of chicks following their mother in the yard was added to the sounds of the jungle. Shortly I found it necessary to build a separate chicken house.

The goats multiplied, too, and every morning we now had milk for ourselves and to share with our neighbors.

Didi took fancy of a young Moro boy named Mangorsi whom she taught how to read and write. He was well built, had high cheek bones, full lips, and a massive jaw, but his black eyes twinkled brightly under thick eyebrows. He was intelligent and very dependable. His knowledge of the jungle was wonderful. We succeeded in inducing Mangorsi to live with us, and with him he brought a fine game dog which he named Puga. After a short hunt with Puga over the deer-runs that he was so familiar with, he would return home with a large spotted deer across his shoulder. (He still had the Moro's deep-seated prejudice against pork and he never went near a wild pig.)

Our neighbors did suffer from malaria, though their cases were generally mild, and our quinine stock was soon exhausted by them. But a little precaution against the bite of anopheles mosquitoes was all we needed to keep off the fever. We made it a strict point never to come out of our mosquito bars after ten at night, and malaria never otherwise bothered us. Our friends were later to adopt our system, which led to the eradication of the fever from the locality.

In a little over two months my first crop of maize was in ear, and soon it ripened. Two months later the rice, too, was ready to reap, a rich brown stand in the jungle green. The barn that Mangorsi and I had put up proved too small for the first harvest; we had to store the excess rice in one corner of the house and the corn we hung from the rafters and joists. All this was more than we could use; with the extra grain I hired Moro workers, who cleared two more hectares of the virgin forest. This was planted with additional rice and maize and it, too, became a waving field of emerald among the black cinders of the clearing.

At this point other things began to happen. One morning, while Mangorsi and I were at work on an extension of the barn in anticipation of a big harvest, we heard a painful yelp from Puga, Mangorsi's dog. The cry proceeded from the river, and hurrying there, we saw the dog in the last stages of its fight with a large mud-colored crocodile. We could do nothing but pelt the monster with stones, which could not have affected it anymore than verbal pleas to release its prey. In a few moments the scaly saurian submerged with Puga and made for its dark, vine-concealed cave on the bank of the jungle belonging to the Aquinos.

We went down to the brink of the water where Mangorsi often took the goats and carabaos to water. There we saw the footprints of Puga, and we knew then that while the crocodile lay beneath the surface, waiting patiently for prey behind some reed cover with only its protruding eyes and snout above the water, the unsuspecting dog came down to drink. There must have been a sudden rush, and then the painful yelp that we heard as the crocodile clamped its jaws shut on the muzzle of the poor dog, and finally the latter's futile struggle as the crocodile made inexorably for midstream.

At night I had often seen the eyes of crocodiles glow grimly on the bank at the mouth of the cave, but I had made it a point not to tell Didi or Mangorsi for fear of unnecessarily scaring them. Although we were somewhat in the interior, ten kilometers above the labyrinthine nipa and mangrove swamps that is the natural home of crocodiles, the densely forested banks here were ideal stalking grounds. I had hoped for the day when the place would be finally cleared so that the monsters would return downstream.

After that the crocodiles attacked the goats till our source of milk had evaporated down to the original pair. Even one of the carabaos lost the tip of its nose when a crocodile seized hold of it with its teeth while it was getting a drink in the stream. Finally we had to water the animals at our open well up in the clearing, giving the monsters a wide berth.

Not long after the loss of Puga we had just eaten supper when there was a sudden flurry in the chicken-house. Looking out, I sensed a disagreeable smell that made me take down the spear. I lighted a torch and Mangorsi accompanied me to the chicken-house, out of which the fowls had in the meantime flown blindly in all directions. When we had gotten near, Mangorsi pointed to the foot of the bananas. There, looking at us with baleful slit-eyes, was a python as thick in the middle as my thigh. Keeping at a safe distance, I let go the spear, but my aim was wide and the python glided indifferently back to the jungle, the undulations of its sinuous body graceful to see even in its overawing size and shape.

"Mrs. Aquino was not wrong. The jungle is a terrible den of monsters," said Didi. She had stood at the window, imploring us to come up to leave the python alone. Her face was dripping with cold sweat and there was a disturbing light in her eyes.

Following that she had protracted nightmares about giant snakes, crocodiles, and dragons. Cold perspiration would break forth on her forehead at the hoot of a grass-owl or the shriek of a nocturnal bird. I had to kill the gecko that had come to live in the barn, even though Didi herself had credited it with the abundance of our harvests: its sudden series of calls would send her into convulsions of fright.

A week passed, two weeks, and steadily her nerves were going to pieces. "We have to return to town before the isolation blows you up," I said finally.

"No, we can't quit," she replied. "Only give me time to adapt myself to Lala."

But her nervousness grew worse every day. "We shall not wait for the harvest," I said. "We better leave at once." And I began to prepare for our return to the provincial capital.

The next day Tuazon and his wife stumbled into our clearing complaining about the long journey and showing the scratches they had received on the way. It was very evident from their looks that want of food had badly affected them, while on their part they expressed surprise at our health. "You folks seem to have taken to the jungle very well. You actually look more healthy than when you left us," they said.

"I see you are finally coming out to live with us," I replied. "What about the others?"

"We just dropped in," said Tuazon, "to say goodbye. I am looking into the possibility of leaving my homestead to you, Gat. We have to return to Luzon. Can't stand life here any longer."

I winced. Tuazon being a road-construction engineer, he had had much contact with the jungle and I had hoped that among our neighbors he should be the first to join us. And now he was planning to go home.

Still, I showed them the place. With delight I saw the appreciative look in their eyes as we went among my young cultivated trees proudly pointing their branches at the sun. I took them around my patches of lushly growing rice and maize, the new clearing with its first crop coming up fast, and my fine vegetable plots, the plants broad of leaf and thick of stem.

But I did not show them the stream with the crocodiles' cave.

I gathered beans, leafy *pechay* and cabbages. I told Mangorsi to kill the fat hen and I roasted early maturing maize which we ate steaming and fragrant from the cob after we returned from the fields. Hearing about our guests, our neighbors came with baskets of *dalag* and *hito* trapped in the rivers, avocados, *madang*, bananas, coconuts, pineapples, and papayas.

"It is for you," they said, modestly offering their gifts as a sign of friendly greeting to the Tuazons.

"You know, Didi, I never gormandized like this even before the war," said Tuazon at table, as he took a fourth helping of the avocado-and-papaya-and-pineapple fruit salad.

"Be careful, my dear. Sulfathiazole is a hundred pesos per tablet now," bantered his wife, at the same time taking an additional slab of the venison that Didi had roasted over coals from a special kind of wood.

"Then this will be definitely the last," he said to her, taking a big slice of wild pig meat dripping with fragrant fat.

"Please do take some more," said Didi and I. We were overflowing with genuine hospitality. It especially did my heart good to see Didi, poor girl, so changed by a visit from old friends. If they would only come to join us permanently, I thought.

"Deliver us from temptation! After slenderizing for almost a year, we'll get sick following this debauch," said Tuazon. Finally he applied himself to the *tuba* which had always been dear to his merry heart. He had a standing boast that no amount of coconut-sap wine ever floored him.

With an eye on strategy Didi and I filled the better part of the bullcart with produce from the clearing, both mine and my neighbors', and from the jungle. There were strings of dried venison and pork, fruits of different kinds, chickens, vegetables, camote, yams, taro, cassava, young ears of maize for roasting or boiling, even rice, shelled corn, and dried fish. "Share this with the Valdezes, the Aquinos, and the Villaneas," we said.

"And persuade them to come with you next time," added Didi.

"How shall we carry home so much food, and our gizzards already overloaded?" said the couple as Mangorsi drove them to the road, where their own cart was waiting for them.

"Do come again soon!" shouted Didi after them.

As we turned to go back to our clearing, I saw tears in her eyes.

"Cheer up!" I said. "Didn't you see they forgot all about leaving their homestead to us?"

Days passed, and Didi's gloom returned. It did not help her nerves when a civet-cat stole on velvet feet into the chicken house and made off with the fattest mother hen. Then the python followed with another night raid that laid waste our poultry. Too, the mating season of the crocodiles had set in, and Didi would shake with fear at nights to hear the bull crocs roaring gutturally in the jungle.

After harvesting the rice and corn, I made no move to till the soil again, and Mangorsi asked me why.

"I am sorry, Mangorsi," I said. "The three of us alone cannot conquer this jungle. It will break us; it is breaking Didi already."

The boy looked at me uncomprehendingly, intelligent as he was.

"How would you like to return to the town with us? I should hate to part with such a trustworthy boy as you. We have to leave the homestead shortly, Mangorsi."

Tears came in the young Moro's eyes then. "I—I want to come with you. But, you see, the jungle is my home."

Next morning I was having a bad dream about my clearing being invaded by monkeys, crocodiles, and pythons which crushed and trampled down the plants and devoured the fowls and domestic animals. Suddenly I was awakened by Didi.

"Get up, get up, you sleepy-head!" she said excitedly. "Don't you hear?"

I listened, my thoughts still lingering on the dream-monsters. Then I jumped up and danced Didi around the room. It was the ringing sound of many axes from the homesteads of the Tuazons, the Villaneas, the Valdezes, even the Aquinos.

Pillars
October 1944

HOME FOR CHRISTMAS

MAXIMO RAMOS

Along about the middle of 1943 Gat mailed a letter to Maul, the capital of the province. Addressed jointly to Aquino, Valdez, and Villanea, three men who owned the homesteads adjacent to his own, the letter urged them to come and join him in Lala. For effect Gat pointed to the hunger and misery which his friends and their families were putting up with in Maul, contrasting this with the quiet abundance and the cool contentment to be had in the homestead.

The answer to this letter came in September. Gat's friends replied that they knew how necessary it was for them to leave Maul, but the lack of transportation and the perils attendant to travel over the road to Lala made it impossible for them to join him. They sounded light-hearted about it, but Gat felt that a little more prodding would make them pack up. Moreover, Christmas was nearing and he counted on a happy reunion in the homestead with his comrades in arms.

Promptly Gat went to mail a rush order with the wheelwright at Maul for an extra-large wagon, the need for which he had long felt in marketing his ever-increasing farm yield. Another letter he sent to Aquino, inclosing a money order. He asked Aquino to buy him a strong Indian bull. "Hitch the bull to the wagon," he continued, "and dump your family, the Villaneas, and the Valdezes into it. Then hightail it to Lala and be here for Christmas. Come to Lala and be done with the dog's life."

That letter got them. That, at any rate, added to the effect produced by the cart-load of grain, poultry, game, and other foodstuffs from the homestead which Gat had sent them earlier in the year. Now Aquino went into a huddle with the other two men. They paid the wheelwright an additional amount to finish the wagon as quickly as he could and to make it roomy enough to hold their three families and the belongings which they had to take to the jungle with them.

Aquino went to purchase the finest bull in the Pantar ranch on the following day. Their houses were rented out and their unessential gear disposed of; their wives busied themselves with buying mosquito nets, household medicine, soap, matches, thread, and such things which they felt would be hard to get in the jungle. The men also bought themselves ploughs and other tools in opening up the land.

"This is a lot of Christmas presents for the highway robbers," remarked Borja, a cynical neighbor.

"We hope part of it will go through," they replied cheerfully.

In a few weeks they were ready to leave for the homestead. The men rigged up a specially tall covering for the wagon and then loaded the vehicle with their families and their wares.

"On this day," observed Aquino's wife as the wagon crossed the steel bridge which was going to start them on the long, uncertain road to Lala, "big things began for this part of the world."

"I hadn't realized that," replied Mrs. Valdez. "December— the start of the Greater East Asia War, and now—our setting out for new worlds to conquer."

"So many things have happened since," said Aquino.

"Things like eternally rising prices and eternally falling avoirdupois," said Villanea, exhibiting his loose waistband.

"What are temporary difficulties like those to freedom and dignity and honor?" said Mrs. Valdez.

The late-risen moon was a silver ship spilling cool silver over the dawn world. The silver wagon followed the silver road which wound on and out of the silver hills. The mountain wind flowed like a thin, cool liquid, and on silver wings a night bird flitted over silver fields of fern and broom grass.

As day broke, they passed Pantar. The Indian bull lowed cavernously to its haunts that it was leaving forever. From a high-topped Moro house among the banana trees a rooster sent out spurt after spurt of belligerency. The morning breeze swept over the river, breathing health and trailing the scent of unmowed grass.

The wagon stopped at a spring by the road, and soon a fire was roaring under a large kettle. Breakfast consisted of rice gruel—the kind of preparation which had been their break-fast, lunch, and supper in Maul for months and months. Valdez and Aquino disappeared in a clearing by the road, and shortly returned with a handful of string beans and some eggplants; hurriedly boiled with salt, these formed a welcome addition to the meal. Breakfast was over in a little while, and soon the bull was trotting down the pebbled road again.

Lunch consisted of the unfailing rice gruel, plus some paddy snails which the menfolk had picked up in the ricefields. Travel was resumed promptly after the noon meal, so that by nightfall the group pulled up in a barrio of Momungan. They parked by a house which was Aquino's favorite stopping place before the war. They found it locked up, but learned from the neighbors that the owner had evacuated months before to his homestead in Dalipuga; so they moved on to an empty nipa shack. Momungan, a mere eighteen kilometers from Maul, was not over-abundant with cereals. But already here, rice cost one-third less than what it did in the capital. They procured six gantas of rice and six more of corn, and they bought chickens and pork, which the women dressed and salted to keep against hard days ahead.

After they had been in Momungan two days the women and children had sufficiently recovered from the sore muscles and aching joints which the jolting wagon had given them. Early at dawn on the following day the group took to the road again.

The going was easier now, though the road went deeper and deeper into tiger-grass and cogon. The travelers made Buro-on before dusk on the same day. Buro-on was but thirty eight kilometers below Maul; yet what a difference that made! Here they could have fine fresh sea-fish for the ridiculously low price of ₱10 a kilo, as against ₱200 in Maul. One never realized till then what a little matter of transportation could mean.

They purchased a goodly store of fish, which they dried at the beach and stored away. They spent the whole of three days in this delightful fishing village, feasting on boiled barra-cuda and bonito, roasted pampano and mullet, oysters, and crabs with meat as firm as copra. The men climbed the coconut palms that stood on the shore drooping with unpicked fruit; before they resumed their journey, they loaded the wagon with a hundred young nuts which they felt would be needed farther down the way where safe drinking water would be hard to get.

From Buro-on the road went parallel to the shore, undulating southwestward in the direction of Pangil Bay and Zamboanga. To their right was the blue sweep of the inland sea; on the left the shaggy mountains were like gigantic cattle coming down to water. A hot day's travel brought the party to Kausuagan, now a village of charred ruins where the once cultivated land had been taken over by weeds. Gallinules and watercocks, coots and moorhens now nested in marshy paddies where rice and corn used to be grown; miserable shacks were scattered about.

"When we wake up tomorrow," said Villanea, "I'm afraid we shall be minus some of our things."

"I don't like the looks of the place myself, but it's more risky to keep to the road at night," said Aquino.

"And my poor old bones must have rest from the endless rattling in the wagon," said Villanea's wife.

Valdez went to hide the bull and the wagon behind a thick screen of bushes and piled fresh fodder before the animal. Then he took out a trusty chain which he had brought along for the purpose. Passing one end of the chain around the neck of the bull, he secured it with a stout padlock. The other end he fastened to the axle of the wagon with another lock. "If that can't save our transport," he said, "only God or a battleship can."

After sunset the men made a strategic dispersal of their gear and provisions, hiding these under bushes and camouflaging them with mallows, capers, and ferns. A filling dinner of boiled rice from Momungan and boiled crabs from Buro-on was then had by all, and after that they promptly retired into a small deserted hut.

"Now," Aquino held an erect finger before the children, "the robbers must not know there are decent folks here. The boy or girl who makes a noise tonight will walk tomorrow with his Pa, instead of riding in the wagon."

"And during the rest of the journey he will drink canal water instead of refreshing coconut water," added Mrs. Valdez.

Not a single sound came from the hut at night. But when day broke and the men went to retrieve the things they had hidden, they found that every single item had been spirited away. Seeing the smoke of culinary activity in the evening, the thieves must have sneaked down and observed the proceedings from well-concealed vantage points, then made off with their loot during the night. However, the wagon, the bull, and the cooking utensils were safe. Without wasting tears over their loss, they picked camote leaves growing wild in the deserted patches, boiled them and called this breakfast, then resumed their journey in haste.

They made Kolambugan, twenty-five kilometers farther on, before five in the afternoon. This once prosperous town which had grown around a British lumberyard had been burned down in the early days of the war, and it, too, was now a ghost town. At this point the group paused to do some figuring. They had gone seventy kilometers in nine days, stop-overs included. It was a hundred and ten kilometers from Maul to Lala. Take seventy kilometers from one hundred and ten, and it left them only forty more.

"At the rate we've been going, we should be in Lala in five or six days," said Valdez.

"Today is December—say, what's today?" asked Mrs. Aquino.

No one knew, and a recapitulation of the journey had to be made. After summing up the days during which they had travelled from one point to another, and adding to that the days they had spent at each stopping place, they figured that today was December 16.

"December 16. Six days from today," concluded Mrs. Aquino with a bright glint in her eye.

"Hurrah!" shouted all five children together. "Christmas in the homestead!"

"If God permits," cautioned Villanea and his wife.

"If God doesn't permit, we'll still have an allowance of three days," came the defiant answer from Romeo, Valdez's son.

"Junior!" warned the boy's mother.

An inquiry at Kolambugan revealed that Mr. Echiverri, ex-supervising teacher at Kolambugan, had retired to his farm, a kilometer behind the town. Thither they were led, and before long they were knocking at the gate of a comfortable farm-house. Mr. Echiverri was some sort of a village grandee hereabouts. He was well-respected even by the lawless elements and lived in this seclusion without molestation from anyone. He now met the weary travelers with a cordial welcome.

"Rest at least two days with us," said he. "You deserve a month's rest after traveling so hard."

"Plenty of time to get to Lala for Christmas," said his wife.

When the two days with the Echiverri's were over, travel was resumed. Not, however, before their host had restocked the wagon with enough provisions to last them till the end of the year. There was rice, corn, cassava, taro, and squash, beside sugar, salt, venison, and dried fish. But perhaps even more important than this, Mr. Echiverri gave them a note, meant for the bad eggs on the road, requesting that the bearers be spared from annoyance on their way to Lala. The note was written in the Moro and Visayan tongues and both in Arabic and Roman characters.

"That should give you safe conduct as far as Tubod, at least," he said.

The letter worked like magic. Along the stretch of wild, rarely traveled road, beyond Kolambugan, armed ruffians fell upon the travelers no less than half a dozen times only to spare them after reading Mr. Echiverri's note. The trip to Tubod took them the better part of three days, however; the rains in the preceding monsoon season had wrought havoc on the newly constructed dirt-road, making travel over it extremely difficult. Many a time the human cargo had to alight to allow the men to lift the wagon over obstructions. It was December 21 when they finally got to Tubod. They had four days in which to make Lala, or eighteen kilometers farther on, over the most uncertain part of the way, and where Echiverri's magic note had no more potency.

At ten in the morning, before they had gone two kilometers beyond Tubod a score of heavily armed toughs with long, ragged beards and evil looks stopped the wagon. For all the men's unkempt appearance, their tight coats were of rayon fabric, of expensive weave though badly in want of soap. They had diamond rings on their fingers, and their woolen trousers tapered down to an anticlimax of bare feet and spread toes. Their chieftain was a small mean-looking man with agile movements. He was heavily convoyed by *buyo*-chewing men with rifles on their shoulders and revolvers and *kampilans* on their waists. With a rasping voice he ordered the men, women, and children out of the wagon. The three citified men had no chance. They each had a dull bolo, to be sure, but it would have been

stupid to match these against the armory of the seasoned highway pirates seven times their own number.

On being shown Echiverri's letter, the bandit leader tore
it up. There was no choice but to leave everything and proceed
to Lala on foot. Valdez, however, would not let go of the wagon
and the bull. "These do not belong to us," he said in broken
Moro. "Take everything that is ours, but please leave us the
wagon and the bull."

Without a word the chieftain hit him across the face. Cut
to the quick, Valdez would have retaliated with a vicious hay-
maker at the pint-sized rascal, but Aquino and Villanea had the
quickness of getting hold of him before he could further com-
plicate matters.

"Eighteen kilometers to walk to Lala, without provisions
and with these five kids on our hands!" said Mrs. Villanea
dolefully.

"That's a lot of time," said Romeo. "Eighteen over six are
three. Even if we go only three kilometers a day we shall be in
the homestead in time for Christmas."

"If God permits," snapped Mrs. Villanea.

But it was eighteen kilometers of miserable roads walled
in on both sides by thick jungle. It was just as well that the
bull was spared the agony of pulling the loaded wagon over
that path. And when they began to look for food, food for nine
hungry mouths in this desolate wilderness, and when they
found any edibles, to prepare it for their meals—then even
Romeo became disheartened.

They spent most of each day looking for bamboo shoots,
tops of edible fern, wild beans, plantains and snails. When they
had secured enough grub, they cooked it in pots improvised from
green bamboo joints, over fire which they kindled by rubbing
two sticks together. They had also to boil water to drink,
carrying it along with them in jars made of bamboo tubes.
On the day they were despoiled of their means of transportation
and their remaining belongings, they made less than two kilometers. The second day they did three kilometers, thanks to a
cloudy sky and to their good luck in obtaining food easily. But
on the third day the women and children were too exhausted to
walk, and they were unable to gain a meter of ground. The
men, however, made use of the enforced delay by gathering

enough bamboo shoots and plantains to last the party three days.

"Almost fourteen kilometers more to Lala, the land of boiled corn and fragrant rice and roast duck," said Aquino that night.

"Tomorrow is December 22," added his wife. "We've averaged but a kilometer a day."

"A kilometer a day keeps the duck sure away," quipped Valdez.

But the others were too sleepy to laugh, and soon they were snoring at each other under the tree which served as their roof.

By four o'clock the following morning breakfast was over. They began walking at a brisk pace, determined to make up for lost time. The men helped the youngsters by occasionally carrying them on their shoulders. By lunchtime they had passed four kilometer posts. A short rest followed their noon meal, then they walked on again. Before the party encamped for the night, three kilometers more had been done.

"Not a bad day's work," said Aquino. "Seven kilometers today. It leaves us less than that many more to do in two days."

"Fat chance we have to make it. I'm run ragged," said Mrs. Villanea.

"And look at my blisters and bruises!" Mrs. Valdez broke down.

"And the thorns in my soles!" joined Rose, her ten-year-old daughter.

"That Gat! I'd like to claw him for luring us into this miserable trap of a trail," said Mrs. Aquino.

"Keep a stiff upper lip now," said her husband. "Gat doesn't know the road is this bad. He has not seen it for at least a year, for he markets his products at the post-office town northwest of Lala, from where mail is sent by boat through Iligan to Maul."

The next day was December 23. It rained almost all morning, and they could not start till after lunch. They walked in the mud for two kilometers, then retired to a deserted grass hovel by the road, rain-soaked and travel-worn.

"We can still get there by tomorrow evening, can't we, Pa?" inquired Romeo appealingly. "If God permits?"

"And if Rose thinks about the thorns less and shakes her legs more," replied the lad's father.

But the weather took a turn for the worse on the morning before Christmas. The wind tore off the branches of the trees, lightning zigzagged over the jungle, while the roaring thunder shook the world. But on they walked in the raging storm. It was the final lap of a very trying journey, and even Mrs. Villanea was determined to get the trip done that day. Lunchtime found them passing Kilometer Post 106. They paused to eat their remaining stock of bamboo shoots boiled with camote leaves; then off they went again.

Finally came what the three men had agreed to keep as a pleasant surprise for the women and kids. At Kilometer Post 108 they walked onto a first-class asphalt road, wide and even and glossy-black in the rain.

"Don't tell me we're about to reach Manila," said Mrs. Valdez.

"It's only the road from Gat's door to Baroy," said her husband.

"Baroy?"

"The market town where Gat and Tuazon sell their farm produce. This road goes past the homestead."

Before twilight the children were excitedly making guesses whether the next clearing would not be *the* homestead at last.

"I hear Moro gongs!" Rose soon announced. "I bet that's a folk dance in some Christmas celebration."

"I can smell roast duck and venison already," seconded Romeo.

"And the fragrance of boiled young corn," said little Nita, her imagination getting the better of her.

"Ah," sighed Villanea at last. "It has been a difficult journey, this!"

"We've been on the road seventeen days since December 8," put in his wife. "What difficulties we have met!"

"Don't let's be a killjoy now. We have arrived," said Aquino.

"There go children's voices singing 'Silent Night,' " said Rose.

"Say, men," said Valdez," I propose that we enter the scene singing *We Three Kings of the Orient Are*. I alone present unto Gat and his wife three gifts: namely—and here he pointed to his shivering daughter Rose and to Romeo—"cold, and dirt, and Frankenstein."

But neither of his two children heard his kidding. Both had joined the others in a full-throated chorus, singing "Hark, the Herald Angels Sing!" Their voices had lost all trace of weariness and carried clear through the storm and the jungle shadows to the cheerful warmth of the hearth in the homestead.

Philippine Review
December 1944

I'M COMING HOME

D. PAULO DIZON

He stood in the middle of what used to be a street, his own street, the street of his early manhood, amidst heaps of debris, lost in a pensive state of reminiscing. Here was our house, he thought, and there was Mr. Red's to the left, and to the right was *Aling* Atang's, the money-lender, the cheat, and in front of our house was Paciencia's, another money-minded hag, the wife of a browbeaten man who should have been a painter by profession instead of a broker. Thinking of it, the bitterness of the past was born again in him. No use raking up the rottenness of it all over again, he said to himself. But just the same he could not help remembering the neighbors and himself and the people he had known there, the ones he loved and the ones that displeased him both. It should all be buried under these jumbled heaps, all the unpleasantness, and here they are coming back on us again, like rain within myself.

Ruins, ruins, he thought, you are ruining my heart.

He shifted his weight from one leg to the other. He had intended to go away from this neighborhood of ruins, but somehow something held him back. She used to come home late at night, he thought, and I'd be standing there on the porch waiting for her, worrying myself to death, anxious to meet her, and then she would come home hugging a big bundle of things in her strong arms for supper and she would make many excuses and I'd kiss her good evening. It should have been myself going out and staying out late at work and she waiting at the porch worrying herself to death. But it was different. I did not work at all. I did not earn at all. She said it was all right, dear. She said dear, imagine that. And of course it was all right with her, her doing the earning instead of me. I don't want you to work under these bullies, she had told me. It was very sweet of her. Oh, she was a sweet girl. Eding was. Eding, he said, half-aloud.

I love you. I am thinking of you. It is twilight and I am thinking of you. And he remembered her letter. She had given him a letter before he left for him to read as soon as he reached the city, and not before that, and he had promised. She mentioned something about the twilight in her letter. She said: Please think of me too. In that way we are together at twilight, if only in our thoughts.

All right, baby, he thought. How are you getting along there? Iloilo is a nice place, isn't it? Let's skip the weather. There is no time talking about the weather. I love you and I am thinking of you and I am talking to you. If you have not forgotten to do what you have said in your letter, well, we are together in our thoughts. It is twilight, baby.

It was getting dark and he was alone in the neighborhood of ruins. He made a shift to go, and again something seemed to hold him back. But this time he really moved. He walked in his usual slow way, thinking while he walked, dreaming, along the desolate street.

Someday I shall write about them, he said to himself, thinking of the neighbors again. He had grown to love the neighborhood, and he felt he was missing the old neighbors, too, with all their pettiness and common stupidity. They never understood me, he thought.

At the street corner he saw a young woman standing, hugging her loneliness, and her face was marred with cheap facial paints. When she saw him coming she became restless. He noticed that. Oh no, he said. I am in love with a girl somewhere in this world. The woman made as if to attract him, but he pretended not to see her. He almost ran, and for the first time in many years he walked hurriedly. I will be faithful to her. Yes, sir, I will. Nothing in the world can wipe out my faith in her. I shall keep myself clean for her.

He remembered her letter again.

Now he was back in the heart of the city. Nothing, he said to himself. He wondered what he was thinking of, he wondered what made him utter in his mind the word nothing. He was hungry and the whole swirling city seemed ready to get itself fed with the sweet soul-satisfying bread of supper. He watched for sometime the swarming crowd hustling homeward. Everybody has a place to go home to. Go home at night and eat supper and sleep in the cozy pleasantness of home, no matter how humble. He was about to hum the tune about the home being sweet and there being nothing like it, but he restrained himself. There was a sentimental lump in his throat.

Home, he said to himself. Home? He tried to laugh. Laugh it off, fellow, he told himself. You're not the only one. Everybody else is homeless. What is home? Nothing. Look at that young buck there on the other sidewalk drowning his loneliness, his homelessness. Home, I never heard of you, he said. But no matter what he thought or said to himself, he could not quite convince himself there was no such thing as home. He wished, after all to be with her, at no matter what place he could call home. Eding, he thought, it is evening in the city. I am coming home to you, in my heart I'll be home. That's the only home for me, baby.

The Filipino Observer
October 10, 1945

COLONEL SAMPA

ISABELO TUPAS

"Now it can be told and I am going to tell it," declared Sampakuta with a grim sweep of his amputated arm that was concealed under a poncho. His elite audience burst into a laugh that was both a challenge and reproof for Sampakuta was known as a teller of tall tales. He repeated them so often with new details that his friends took his statements as good-humored lies. And it was unbelievable that he chose to repeat the performance in Miss Rosie's parlor.

"Will it be about your arm again?"

"No," he answered with an emphatic jerk of the head not unlike that of a soldier when he salutes his officer. Sampakuta, by the way, served as a kind of constabulary agent in Lanao in the good old days when the constables and the Moros enjoyed chasing each other. According to him, it was there that he earned his famous nickname, Sampakuta, assaulter of "cotas" or Moro palisades. He did not lose his left hand in those dangerous assaults. It was as a "gurami" that he lost it, and at this instance he meant to tell the truth before his doubting friends. That explained his severe answer that made them look at him with no little surprise. The arm however was not the all-important thing in his purpose. It becomes only the excuse of this evening's affair.

"Well, won't you come in?" invited Rosie who came forward with a lamp which she set down on a center table adorned with a burnished 105 mm. shell filled with tuberoses. Her invitation was charmingly casual. The fragrance of the white lily-like flowers was reminiscent of the years when Rosie and he were young. Sampakuta, however, preferred to remain where he was, standing just out of the bamboo awning. He did not remove his poncho either, the obvious reason being the evening

shower. So thin and fine it was that it enveloped his overseas
cap with a gentle aura so Rosie thought.

"Now then, how is how?" asked the Mayor. That's the
greeting that used to make Sampakuta gush out with his tales.
His friends laughed coaxingly. It did not catch as usual. No,
Sampakuta was not there to brag of his exploits. He was there
with an impelling purpose; and he must realize it promptly, so
promptly that he became confused. For among the violent things
he wanted to tell there should be woven delicate sentiments
which only Rosie and the gentle shower and the tuberoses
should comprehend. There was his reputation and his honor
as a "gurami" to vindicate. There was his worth as a man to
prove. As a bachelor of forty-five odd years, there was his
future to settle that evening, or Rosie would remain only a
dream. This one time in his checkered life he winced before a
group of four persons: the Mayor, the treasurer, the chief of
police, who took him for granted and the woman who could not
bring her exacting mind to accept his very long standing proposal.

"Where have you been these many months? The first jeeps
had been here three months ago," Rosie spoke with a hint of
resentment.

"Thank you," Sampakuta said absentmindedly; but that
woke him up. "I came to visit you, Miss Rosie, and to renew
acquaintances with...." He nodded politely to the men who
nudged one another. That was the last straw that broke the
camel's back. Sampakuta stepped forward.

"I came home to correct certain impressions...here!"

"Fine!" the three men said quite embarrassed.

Rosie felt some queer sensations. This man proposed to
her many years ago; she could not remember what year it was.
She was a girl of seventeen; he was twenty-five: a dashing
constable—but then constables were doubtful characters, full
of humbug. Now he was forty-five and she must be....Well,
he was before her now and the gentle shower put an aura
around his cap. That shower fell nearly every evening lately and
made the grass on the plaza send up green shoots to greet the
spring. This evening might also be spring to her judging by
the vague stirring in her breast.

"We are sure happy to listen to you again," said the men
rather condescendingly.

Sampakuta faced them. "You remember Colonel Akli? The memory of that gallant man, may God keep him, gave us the strength, fortitude and confidence to carry on till D-day."

"But you did not serve under him?" the Mayor said accusingly.

"I did not. Colonel Akli had his command in the hills. I had my own on the water, stretching from the Pasig to Punta with headquarters on Talim."

"But that belonged to Colonel Sampa," interrupted the Mayor, certain that Sampakuta was not a genuine "gurami."

"Wait, Mr. Mayor; not so quick. I commanded an outfit on the Lake. I had eight hundred surface craft of various categories: bamboo rafts, cascos, paraus, lambatan, armadahan, and logs, plain logs—each serving its particular purpose in the fleet that shuttled to and fro, manned by six thousand men, bringing food from Laguna to Rizal, orders and arms from Rizal to Laguna, and secret information from nowhere that must get over there somehow."

"What force you had!"

Sampakuta ignored the acid remark. "While we were known as legitimate fishermen, merchants, fish-dealers, and evacuees, we constituted a combat unit. Rescuing ship-wrecked evacuees and American aviators who fell on the lake and guiding them to safety was a part of our business. Our main duty, however, was to intercept enemy supply and communication wherever they might be on the Lake. We crisscrossed it day and night without regard to time and weather, checking the zones and the routes. On the side we kept Colonel Akli supplied with arms, ammunitions, men and food. My outfit was the life line and the communication line...and the front line whenever we caught up with Japanese tugs. Then our guns started rattling. The Japs fought like mad dogs. We fought like devils. We simply swarmed upon them from all directions shutting all their means of escape except the bottom of the Lake; and the Japs who took that were damn fools not knowing that my men worked in the water like sharks. It churned as if some sea monsters were engaged in a life and death struggle; then before long the water was streaked with crimson."

"Terrible!"

"Yes, and that was our style of combat. We fought violently and expected to die peacefully. After the affray the men scrambled to their boats bringing the heads of the enemy which they tossed on the pile of coconuts; and as they sat on the gunwale drinking coconut water, gleaming breasts rose and fell heavily at every draught. While they enjoyed the repast, our telegraph system began to work in relays until the "fish-dealers" came around to get the day's haul."

"You had a telegraph?" The men were very condescending.

"Yes, but it may sound primitive to you. We did not have the speed of motorized units or wires. Unless there was wind we literally crawled; but not our telegraph communication. The more dead the wind is, the faster it works. The conchshell, of which every sea-dog was familiar, was our telegraph. A long, high, thin note like the whistling of the wind in the bamboo-brakes meant ATTENTION! The low, bass boom coming in measured rhythm with the surge of the breakers meant SPEED-RUSH-FIGHT! When relayed concentrically from one vessel to another, the message spread from its source to the distant beaches and hidden coves before you finished a cigarette. An alarm, a signal for rescue, attack or reinforcement could be broadcasted in this manner. Reports were written in code and relayed by couriers, five kilometers apart. One such report read as follows:

Dropped nets at banks 3.

Hauled 7 crates of "hito." All salted.

No snails.

Decoded, it reads thus:

Engagement at zone 3.

Encountered 7 Japs. All killed.

No casualty.

"Marvelous! ingenious!"

Sampakuta knew his time-table. Surprise was his tactic. So he pressed on his attack: "The movement of the vessels was at turtle's pace when the wind was dead. But when it's up and on a rampage, countless sails blossomed and billowed; outriggers splashed and the shuttle-shaped prows sliced the water, sending up sprays that glittered in the sunlight. Coming from their stations to rush on enemy tug-boat, the armada was like the mass flight of giant sea-gulls skimming over the water in pursuit of their prey."

"Beautiful! I have crossed the Lake more than once and I know the thrill of flight on the water," Rosie exclaimed, feeling positive in her thirty-seven years of maidenhood that she was still young.

"That much was really beautiful, even if the mission of your armada was gruesome," said the Mayor. "We had similar experiences in Colonel Akli's but not as violent...and we did not have the eyes and sentiment that saw the grandeur and the beauty of a combat unit in action."

"Was there money on the merchant-side of your operation?"

"There was death, no money, Mr. Treasurer. And when it came, as once it did, spitting bullets from a Japanese plane that swooped and swooped upon us, we lost our minds. We had no means of escape. How I wished the water grew trees to serve as cover! And we could not dig a foxhole in the Lake. You could jump in it and see the light no more. I did jump! God alone knows how I came to see the light again—but minus this...."

Sampakuta suddenly threw off his poncho and emerged from it raising his left arm whose extremity was a flat stump at the wrist. But his audience did not see this proof of his sacrifice. They saw the glory of his deeds in his shining uniform with silver eagles on the collar. The men stood up and shook Sampakuta's hand warmly. The Chief of Police executed a military salute.

"So you are the Colonel...the Colonel Sampa...we heard so much about whose identity we knew just now."

The men were sincerely apologetic. Rosie alone stood her ground. Her intuition had forewarned her to wait and see....

Sampakuta bowed. Yes, he was the famous Sampa . . . assaulter of Japanese tugs.

"Now, Miss Rosie, will you pass 'Don Pedro'?" the Mayor said turning to the lady. But Miss Rosie had hurried behind the counter and brought forth a short Japanese sword. Holding it in her hands, her chin up and with a wistful smile on her lips, she showed the weapon to the man that gave it to her three years ago as a token of his honest suit which she did not mind seriously. And now her heart, rising to the call of spring, knew why he had returned.

People's Magazine
October 25, 1945

MASSACRE AT MENDOZA-GUAZON'S

MARIO P. CHANCO

The Quiogues are a familiar name to old city residents. Through decades marked by constant change they have managed to weather fair times and foul. They have gone through depressions, calamities brought by acts of God and the creatures of His making, with nothing more marked than a passive complaint against today's high cost of living and the unflagging conviction that God does look after His own.

Like millions of their countrymen, they have felt the breath of war. The Quiogues are a trifle more fortunate than many, and Mr. Quiogue himself will tell you that he still does not know how he and his little flock escaped the February conflagration.

There have been contentions favorable and otherwise, on the power of prayer, of an abiding hope that God knows what is best and will bend events to conform to a well-arranged plan. But in February, people who prayed died just as quickly and as violently as those who resigned themselves. To prostrate yourself on your knees and exhort the Almighty to protect family and self against the inferno which sought to destroy you appears to be the stock-in-trade of people who have made a full-time profession of religion. No doubt it has helped, but who can deny the cynic who has seen with his own eyes how both the bad and the good fell on their knees with anguished prayers and often ludicrous promises for a better future life if spared, and then were struck down ignobly by pagan pieces of steel?

The week preceding the American reoccupation of Manila, Mr. Quiogue tightened the reins about his two sons. Joe and Angeling were teen-age youngsters, full of the zest of living, restless and with the brimming energy of youth. They had both been in high school at the outbreak of the war. They resumed studying a few months under the Japanese regime, but Mr. Quiogue promptly hauled them out when the incongruity of the situation one day struck him as being not too funny.

"Go around and enjoy yourselves," he told his sons. "I'd much rather see you walk the streets than listen to that fop about Greater East Asia."

The boys fell to playing with a will; they had a large circle of friends known among themselves as the Wartoms. Despite food shortage, their fond parents watched them burn out energy on the basketball court, on impromptu jam sessions at some neighbor's yard.

"You're only young once," Mr. Quiogue told his wife when she reproved him gently for allowing his sons such an abundance of privileges, unheard of in their times. "In my old age, when I see my sons grown with their own families, I will have the satisfaction of knowing that they were able to enjoy what little I was able to give them."

But the boys did not always play. In the family funeral parlor at Herran Street they found time to help in the business, learn the ropes of a long and treasured profession. Joe sat down at the office table, answered telephone calls and talked to friends when business was slack. Angeling lounged about, running errands and otherwise making himself useful.

The boys were dear to Mr. Quiogue, dear as only a father and family man can ever hope to love his flesh and blood; so when the Japanese began clamping down on civilian activities in Paco, he lost no time warning his boys. He had seen Japanese trucks pull up before a group of males and without ado proceed to haul them off elsewhere either as guerrilla suspects or as laborers on Japanese defense projects in the city.

"Stay in the house," he told them. "It is not advisable to loiter in the streets nowadays. When the Americans come back you can have all the fun you want."

The Wartoms and the Quiogues lived within hailing distance of each other, so it did not hamper their activities. Instead of going around, they met at Mr. Quiogue's house on Pasaje Eduque, the narrow side street beside the Bellevue Theater, and there they wove the dreams that youthful dreams are made of.

Following the American entry on the north side, the peace and quiet of the last few weeks became as vague and as nebulous

as the plans they had made for after the war. Daily, the thunder
of artillery duels and exploding charges rocked Pasaje Eduque
and its environs. Even the most optimistic tightened his lips
and fell silent. What few people ventured out into the deserted
streets were furtive, slinking, fearful of what lay in store. At
every street corner there stood a Japanese sentry, ready to
shoot at the slightest provocation. The brash and the adven-
turous stayed home. Save for women, hardly a male creature
wandered about as south Manila prepared for its long siege.

On Thursday evening, February the 8th, the explosions
grew louder, the rifle and machine gun fire became more pronounced.

"Target practice," Mr. Quiogue said bravely. Days before,
there were rumors about the Americans having entered the
north but as far as the people of South Manila were concerned,
they might very well have been in the heart of China. After
three long years of waiting and hearing all sorts of crazy stories
a rumor like that just about killed the last threads of hope
a man could be reasonably expected to cling to. If the Americans
were there, well and good. Let them come before it was too late.

Friday morning, February 9. The skies were black and
orange gold from the smoke of the greatest holocaust yet to
hit Manila. Through the desolation, the artillery barrage rose
heavier, heavier, till finally, the shells began bracketing civilian
homes and enemy gun emplacements alike.

At 9 o'clock that morning, a quartet of shells whirred overhead and landed on a string of tenement houses not far from
the Quiogue home. Loud cries rose; and then the wind, rising
evilly above the turmoil, fanned the flames which sprung up.
Another shell landed short against the concrete wall of the
Eduque mansion, right in front of the doorway where Mr.
Quiogue and his brood stood crouched. If the wall had not been
there, or had been a little lower, the postlude of this story
might have been written differently. It is possible the men who
stood behind the guns were tired. Killing, after all, can become
monotonously mechanical.

Midway through the roar of crashing shells, a squad of
Japanese marines went trooping up the narrow Pasaje. They
paused before closed doors, smashed rifle butts against but-
tressed windows, called out imperiously for the terrified in-
habitants to open. Swiftly, they corralled the men and boys,

herded them with others who sat bleakly under the guns of other guards close to the main street.

Mrs. Quiogue, anticipating such a move, had ordered the house doors left open. While securing the other men, the Japs merely peeped in, saw Joe, Jr. and his mother huddled together in a corner. Angeling was upstairs, preparing his things.

On the way back they went in just the same and took out all three men. The family dog, resentful at the intrusion, snapped at the leg of a stolid marine. The marine drew back, coldly furious, and fired his rifle. Unsatisfied, he unhooked his bayonet and thrust it repeatedly through the still pulsating body, until the last breath had left it. Through a haze of tears Mrs. Quiogue looked on. The marine glared at her, shoved the father and his sons outside and joined the rest there.

Out through the mined, debris-strewn streets the party went, bound for the Japanese flower garden on Singalong street, where several hundred other men and boys forced out of their homes on the surrounding streets of Colorado, Kansas, Singalong and Herran were gathered. They sat on the cratered grounds, their faces in varying degrees of despair, a study running the gamut of all human emotions, awaiting the fates that confronted them.

As Mr. Quiogue and his sons sat down, a whispered hush went up and down the doomed ranks.

"Maria Luisa...," they heard. Turning, Mr. Quiogue saw a trim feminine figure in black silk slacks running up and down the pavement. He asked a weary old man who she was.

"Maria Luisa Ri...," the man said. "A Japanese spy."

She was pointing to the men, and the Japanese with her promptly pulled out the luckless selectees to another side, where lengths of rope awaited.

Voices rose from the stunned multitude.

"Maria Luisa, what are you doing to your countrymen?"

"Maria Luisa, we have done nothing...."

"Maria Luisa...."

She looked past the men haughtily.

"Only the guerrillas are being taken," she announced. Then she went on to point out almost all of the gathering.

Overhead, the sun was at its zenith but the atmosphere resembled twilight. Clouds of smoke and flame were shooting skyward all over the city. Hot cinders fell on their bare, up-turned faces. South toward the Paco railroad station, the grey pall was even thicker. Through and above all these the whine of shells probing out Jap defenses came to their ears.

The leader of the squad arose and bade the manacled civilians rise after him. The other guards deployed themselves about the men. They stumbled through the streets to the tower-ing Mendoza-Guazon apartments.

At the corner, the leader paused. Then he jabbered a few words in Japanese and the marines began herding the men inside, on the ground and second floors. How many hundreds ultimately were sandwiched within those narrow confines will never be known. Mr. Quiogue estimates the number between 500 to 600. It is possible that there may have been slightly more, or slightly less, but in the heat and confusion of battle, estimates are deceptive.

The building had already began to burn by then. From the second story, where flames began licking out of the windows and other rooms exposed to the thermal updraft, cries of agony rose as maddened civilians began hurling their flaming bodies on the cold pavement below. Waiting marines pumped bullets into them, mercifully ending their misery. A few jumped out of the backway, crawled through red-hot iron sheets and twisted railings to escape later into American lines.

But many were not as fortunate.

Mr. Quiogue gathered his two sons about him. They had been pushed to the ground floor, where despite the approach-ing flames, it was not too bad yet. The Japanese hurled grenades, fired their .25 rifles, trained their light Nambus, on the scream-ing, frenzied mass. Hemmed in on the extreme northeast end, the bullets fortunately escaped the trio. A section of the wall gave in as more shells began plopping within the area. Mo-mentarily confused, the Japanese scooted for cover, giving the men between the scarred walls a temporary respite.

"Now," Mr. Quiogue said as he saw a few stout hearts break out and run unscathed toward the street. Their clothes drenched with blood from wounded and dead companions, they rushed pell mell, and then paused as a Japanese stood up from behind his shelter and hurled a grenade in their general direction.

It hit a man not ten feet behind them squarely on the stomach. Joe looked back with horror, saw the intestines trailing out. Yet the man kept running.

They sprinted across the vital street corner, followed by several others, and then white smoke suddenly billowed in front of Joe. He clutched at his left eye, mumbled, "I'm hit," and kept on. Mr. Quiogue had not seen him; Angeling was pressed against him as they dashed back to the Pasaje. All of a sudden he felt wetness on his trouser leg. He thought he had been hit but when he looked at his younger son's pants he saw a jagged hole where a piece of shrapnel had embedded itself.

"It is nothing," Angeling protested as his now enraged father tried to carry him. "I will be all right."

They reached the Pasaje without further mishap, to find the house still standing. With what neighbors remained they tried to get what shelter was afforded. Shells and bullets were hitting all around, but miraculously none of the family was hit again. Neighbors edged in around them, bundling their children and personal effects together, later only to fall silently.

They kept on praying.

Toward afternoon, a neighboring house caught fire. In a few minutes their own house followed. Blackened with soot, cinders and mud—it had rained a short time in the morning—they hopped about smoking timbers, past fresh corpses of people they had known. In this way, they passed the evening.

The following day saw a repetition of the previous events. Bands of marines crouched in the ruins of other burned buildings, shooting at stragglers who dared venture into the streets. Toward afternoon, as the Eduque mansion caught fire, the howling of the dog woke up the master. Mandy Eduque, 23, but eight months married, stood undecidedly as he listened. At length, unable to hear the dog any longer, he left the Quiogues, amid the loud cries of his beautiful wife who insisted on coming with him.

"I'll be back shortly," he called cheerily.

That was the last thing he said. Five minutes later, they heard a rifle crackle spitefully from the top of the Bellevue Theater. Mandy crumpled on the browned grass of his once palatial mansion, a bullet through his back.

Sunday morning. The barrage grew fiercer as the retreating Japanese pointed their guns toward the oncoming Americans south of Paco bridge. The Quiogues and their neighbors huddled fearfully in crude shelters while shells from both sides whined over their heads.

Prayer had become almost mechanical. Everybody was resigned to death. Elvira, Mandy's young wife, was sobbing quietly. Around them, the stench of decomposing bodies rose to assail their nostrils. Mr. Quiogue had spent a considerable portion of his life attending to the dead but there was never a carnival that approached the carnage of the last few days. Tending his young son's wound, he wondered how it was possible to go through such fearful murder and still retain one's sanity. There was no food, no water. There were uncooked staples but no one felt like eating. Even the young seemed to have lost natural capacity for absorbing nourishment.

Monday, February 12. Shortly before noon, a shell burst a few feet away and wiped out another family. The boy servant, clutching at Mrs. Quiogue, staggered uncertainly and fell. There was a small hole on his right forehead; Mr. Quiogue thought it was but a flesh wound, but the shrapnel had buried deep into the youthful brain.

Two hours later, loud talking was heard from the ruins of the Eduque mansion.

"Americans," Angeling yelled, then subsided as his father admonished him.

A helmeted face peered slowly over the concrete wall.

"Americans!" Angeling cried again, and Mr. Quiogue almost hit him.

"That's a Japanese," he whispered. "My God, do you want us all to be killed?".

Minutes later four burly figures hurtled over the wall. This time, the recognition was mutual.

They were dirty, splashed with mud, and several weeks' growths of beard rendered their faces almost unrecognizable.

But they were Americans.

"Quiet," the leader said, then grinned and made the V-sign. "Where are they?"

Mr. Quiogue stood up, oblivious of the firing around him, and pointed. He begun to do a number of crazy things.

"Camel," Joe said reverently, holding the cigarette which one of the soldiers had given him. He refused a light and put it back in his pocket. Then he took out his pocketbook, gave out his entire wad of Jap war notes.

"For souvenir," he said simply.

The Recorder
November 1945

SEA AND LAND AND TIME

JUAN CABREROS LAYA

Glancing up from a game of checkers, they noticed the Pantranco bus and the dust it snorted in its wake. The bus snorted again, then stopped. In the silence only the conductor's shoes crunching on the gravel could be heard.

A few looked speculatively at the quiet, dark man. He had a big trunk, which he and the chauffeur were trying to pull out of the rear of the bus. They grunted over it as they let the brass corners fall with a bang to the ground. It was an old, black trunk. The other pieces of baggage were all durable but old. There was a portable phonograph and two old leather suitcases. It needed a carretela to load all that baggage in. They remarked the bell-shaped pants, years out of fashion. They saw the dark suit that enclosed a broiling human being just come from abroad. They snickered. More heads put themselves together and snickered.

"Another great lover. God, can't we ever be rid of them?"

"Never mind this one. He looks mild."

The man avoided the eyes of the people covertly watching him. He was not a very big man. There was nothing outstanding in his features except perhaps a little scar on the tip of his nose and still another one seaming his cheeks diagonally and of course the small lower lip that imperceptibly merged with his chin.

But the afternoon was well crowded with the people who had come to hear Mr. Bartolome read the mail. They now crowded forward so as to exchange gossips with the genial harelipped conductor and get a closer look at the new arrival.

It was then that the young girl who sat selling peanuts near the wall stood up and stared. She sat down again, then stood up and stared at the man as though she had seen an apparition.

"*Manong* Berto!" she whispered awed.

Perhaps the man's brain was attuned to even the slightest sound of his own name, just as the eyes may in one glance distinguish one's name in a sea of print. He turned around, glad to be greeted at least by someone. His face lighted up.

"Nena!" he said. He came quite close to her, his face beaming and homesick. "My, but you have grown!"

Before he could reach her, he stopped to stare at the basket of peanuts she was selling. He looked at her questioningly.

"I am not Nena, *Manong*. I am Lydia."

"Lydia? The—the little girl?"

"I look like my *Manang* Nena. *Manang* Nena is in Manila now."

"You have grown big!"

"Yes. It has been nine years since you went away."

Lydia cracked her joints.

"Yes. It seems only yesterday. And your *Manang* Laura?"

"She—she is all right."

It must have been then that someone detached himself from the crowd of onlookers and made a dash toward the south, exciting news at his heels. Then there was running and scurrying about, and the slow life of Guisit Sur hummed as the people waited for the carretela to come jogging along with a load of leather things and a big trunk and a man whom they would watch through the cracks in the windows and from behind fences as he passed by on his way home—where he expected his wife to go down the ladder and greet him.

The carretela came jogging down the street. It jolted on stones which smoked with dust when they were jostled out of place.

Lydia was in the carretela, too. She did not look happy. *Manong* Berto was a jolly man now, greeting people as he recognized them. He often stopped the carretela in order to shake hands and exchange greetings with old acquaintances. In fact, before they had gone one block from the school building, he had to jump down because *Nana* Paran wanted to chat with him and wished to ask him about nine years in one gulp.

And all the time Lydia was in the carretela cracking her joints, glancing neither to the left nor the right. Her brother-in-law shook hands and became excited over everybody whom he had not met for years. His shyness was almost gone. He gave details about Isto, Andring, Metring—they were doing fine, he said. Yes, everything was fine.

He was held up again in the next corner by *Manong* Turin. Boys and girls came running to see the new excitement—boys abandoning their *tangga*, girls leaving their *sikki*. Apprehensive adults approached, too, and caught each other's eyes behind his back.

They wondered why Berto never once asked about his wife Laura. Nobody mentioned her name, as though they dreaded the very sound of it. Then, at the drop of a hint about his desire to hurry home—"Sure, I'd like to be home now. You must excuse me. I'd want to be home right away. Excuse me,"—the crowd parted, drew back involuntarily from him.

"What's the matter?" he laughed in embarrassment. "You are all acting so queer. What's the matter with me, anyway?"

"None. Nothing's the matter with you, Berto," and they drew farther back, as though he had been a plague, as though they feared his slightest displeasure would blast lightning at them.

The frightened *Nana* Teriang told him that Laura was at the brook washing clothes. They could hear her wooden mallet on the stone.

"Then she does not know I'm coming home."

"Nobody knew, Berto."

"Isn't it a complete surprise, *Nanang?*"

"Yes," agreed *Nana* Teriang soullessly.

"I myself thought I could not come home. It's almost impossible to get boats now. But I was lucky, unusually lucky I got a boat at all."

Neighbors were at their windows, wondering as they looked out what was to happen next. But, patient man though Berto was, there was hardly any doubt that he came home with plans in his head.

He hung his coat on the nail and loosened his tight necktie by pulling hard at it from side to side. He picked up a broken piece of cardboard and fanned himself for an abstracted while.

Suppose he heard the children sing the scurrilous song about Laura?

"There, *Nana*," he said to *Nana* Teriang, handing her a big bag.

"That's full of things to eat—all sorts of things. Give the children some."

The children swarmed about *Nana* Teriang. The tension was broken somewhat. Every smile of his was like a benediction, so relieved and grateful were the watchful faces upon sight of it.

"What are you people staring at me for?" he laughed. Haven't you seen anybody come home from Hawaii before?"

"Oh, it's—it's just that they have not seen you for so long, Berto," said *Nana* Teriang.

Then he looked down from the landing and studied the faces that came over to see him. They were all congregated at the foot of the ladder. Some looked curiously from a distance. They looked as though excited with gossip, they had been caught in the utterance of a foul word.

"Did you say your sister is washing clothes at the brook?" he asked. "Lydia, did you say—"

"Yes, *Manong*," said Lydia.

"This late?"

"Yes, *Manong*, this late."

"Where?"

"In *Lacay* Andong's, *Manong. Lacay* Andong is the blind man."

"Yes, I know *Lacay* Andong. Everybody knows *Lacay* Andong, the blind man. I think I'll go see her there myself."

The people broke ranks. He seemed lord of all. Nobody dared restrain him. He could have been the finger of God itself. Even his hands were not angry or excited. Could it be possible he did not know? Impossible. Nena herself had written him about her sister.

He walked through the parted crowd. He carried nothing with him—only his bare hands.

Eyes followed him. Necks twisted slowly. Bodies swayed to one side as the bamboo clump hid him from view.

They followed a little way. They saw him walk as though in a casual saunter toward the secluded nook within the private yard of *Lacay* Andong.

It was now almost impossible to see anything from the road where the people made purposeless motions. There was the screen of banana grove, green throughout the year because *Lacay* Andong managed to water it even during the dry season with water baled out of the brook. The craning of necks stopped at the gate, behind the bamboo clump. People gathered, curious, waiting to hear the shriek, the choking, the....

They waited for a long time. But of course *he* knew. Everybody knew. Nena had written him asking him to come home. And Laura had of course been replying to his letters. With what lies?

No noise from the grove in *Lacay* Andong's yard. They could hear no note of explanation coming from the twilight under the big trees. Then they heard a muffled cry, but it sounded more like that of joy than of terror. Then nothing could be heard for a while.

For a long time, they waited as the sun set and the twilight blackened the leaves. They stood on one foot and then on another. They waited behind the bamboo clump. *Nana* Teriang was at home sobbing, but Lydia had dragged herself to the bamboo clump and there she waited too. Emilio tried to draw her away saying Lily wanted to talk to her, but she knew Lily was not on vacation. Luna was flexing his developing muscles.

Nana Andeng talked in whispers all the time. She said:
"He knows, I tell you. But there is a saint in his heart. He knew all the time. He was only waiting. There is a Christ in his heart, I tell you—"

At last Lydia broke forth into a sob. Emilio patted her on the shoulders, tried to calm her. She would not be comforted. Then she tore herself away from Emilio and ran toward the gate.

The spell was broken. God's awful and invisible hand was not so horrible as the visible bloody hands of a man, after all. A girl had dared it. Now there was a general scramble toward the gate. Lydia was soon over. Emilio was just going to hurdle it, too, knee poised to jump over. But he stopped. Lydia had stopped, too. For there, in the gloom under the banana grove, blocking them effectively with the earnest entreaty of a blind saint, was *Lacay* Andong. The old man was small, but he was resolute as he stretched his arms sidewise and looked as though he would block all men that poured through the gate with his very body. He was tottering but strong.

"You must go home, my children. What's there to be excited about?"

"You don't know what's happening here, *Apo*," said Emilio. "There's violence being committed—a bloody...."

The expression on the old man's face did not change. It did not even show puzzlement—only calm, quiet certainty.

"What violence, son? I see nothing."

"*See!*"

"Yes, I see nothing," repeated the blind man.

"Listen!"

Everybody listened. The silence was thick, but in it the soft sob of a woman could be heard.

"Let them be," said *Lacay* Andong. "Let them alone. They have been separated. Sea and land and time broke them apart. Now...let them be by themselves under the peaceful trees. The trees are above them. Let them be."

Emilio looked down. He withdrew his knee. Lydia came up, too. Their heads were bowed.

It was a long, long time, it seemed. The dusk began to gather, and yet nobody came out of the gloom of the brook where the bamboo trees curved above them and the trees shot up into the sky with white, stained trunks and grey thorns.

Then two quiet figures emerged from the gloom. One was the figure of a woman, and she was weeping. The other was the figure of a man, and his head was bowed. An arm was around her waist. With the other arm he held the tin basin that held the washing. They walked slowly home in the gathering dusk—the man and the woman.

The Nation
November 1945

THE WOODSMAN

CONSORCIO BORJE

In May Cleto set out down the river. Deep down on the floor of its hundred-meter-wide channel the river shuttled from one sheer wall to the other, and the brawny brown man with thick black hair crossed and recrossed it several times before noon overtook him near a spring. For dinner he had boiled rice and salted fish that his wife Mariana had packed in banana leaves. He chased the lot down with *bagoong* anchovy and tomatoes out of a bamboo joint.

When his meal had settled, he slung his *kuppit* basket pack of plate, earthen pot, and rice on his back, picked up his loaded carrying pole, and jogged on down the river bed. The sun smote the white quartz boulders blindingly. The heat, caught in the narrow gorge, engulfed him, burning his skin a dark, angry red. He would have found it impossible to walk without his automobile-tire sandals.

Sunset overtook him in a camachile forest that had grown in an abandoned channel. He stopped to cook rice, using dried twigs scattered in the sand for firewood. While the rice was cooking, he located a fresh spring near the bank, and scooped up some of its clean water. His supper consisted of rice and squashed tomato with *bagoong*.

Throwing sand on the fire he picked his way along in the gathering darkness, until he spotted a sandy hollow in the forest at a safe distance from his campfire. Carefully he swept the sand of pebbles and twigs. On it he arranged branches of the coniferous *aro-o*, with the leafy ends pointing in one direction. They made a warm, soft bed. He laid his head on his *kuppit* pack and slept, his finger tips touching his axe and bolo. An old trail of the head-hunting Bontocs ran hard by, and he slept with his senses alert to any sound not of the leaves sighing in the night wind nor of the ageless river rustling among the rocks.

Early in the morning he woke to the crying of wild roosters in the forests that crowned the river walls. He lay unstirring with a deep wonder in his eyes, while blood-red dawn mantled the east and flung across the sky a pink, blue, and green bridge. He stared up at the bridge fascinatedly. It was broadest where it bent into the bowl of the sky.

The sun was rising when he reached the deep bend where the great narra grew in a cleft of the towering east wall. For a time he stood looking up into the ugly gash, his body tense with the majesty of those giant trees that had sprung among the boulders big as the Burayoc church. Beside the small, bubbling stream of clear, cold water that ran down the break, he built his fire. While the rice cooked he searched for shrimps on the undersides of the rocks in the deep pools. He caught three big ones, besides a number of brown *palileng* the size of his thumb. He rolled his catch in salt, and roasted it on live embers, and stuck it into big balls of rice. He swallowed his food with great hungry gulps.

He spent the next few hours locating a good campsite, collecting grass and saplings, and building his hut. He built the hut under a windbreak a safe distance from the cleft where pythons dwelt. It was also hidden from all sides except the downstream one, but the water flowed in a millrace there, and beyond that millrace rose the inhospitable sandstone heights of Maasin, where neither man nor cattle ventured.

After a cooling-plunge into a pool, lunch, and a nap, Cleto ventured up the steep course of the stream in the cleft. There, in the sylvan dusk that at times terrified this big man, he cut his way in the underbrush, sizing up the boles of the narra trees and marking with his bolo those that would make good lumber and yet were small enough to drag down to the river.

At times he came across droppings of deer and wild pig. He knew he would not do without fresh meat in this place.

It was not a kilometer to the very top of the gully, and the way was so matted with wild bamboo, and so obstructed by pools, waterfalls, and immense boulders, that it was dusk before he could get back to his hut.

In the day there was work to do for felling the trees, lopping off their tops and branches, cutting them into sections.

At night there was the suspension of motion that was half sleep, half wakefulness, his muscles at rest, but his every sense alert to any break in the sound of river and forest that was not part of the pulse of earth and open sky. And then the miracle of dawn, accompanied by the madrigal of birds, and work again. At a spot in the gully where there was no detour, he bent a young tree with snare attached, over a spoor of wild pigs. On his third night he heard a terrified squealing. Lighting his way with a pine knot that had been washed up on the bank in a previous year's flood, he made his way up the ravine and found a half-grown pig caught in the bamboo noose and hanging in the air.

The meat he salted and dried, and the bones he boiled with ginger roots and wild pepper leaves and wild cabbage, and he had a feast of them.

After two weeks he had a dozen logs painstakingly squared with his ax, to show for his labors. Each log was three meters long and averaged more than a foot square. Kirbas, one of his brothers-in-law, should be arriving in one more week with the carabaos; waiting for him, Cleto felled more trees for the posts of his projected house. He cleaned them and carried them one by one down to the beach.

He was nearing his hut one noon with the last post on his shoulder, when he stopped dead in his tracks. There, unmistakable in the sand, were footprints. He stood tense for several moments, his huge chest heaving, his nostrils dilating, his eyes scanning the river bed and the far side of the gorge.

The mild sun lay upon the tawny landscape. Velvet shadows lay in the hollows, on the undersides of trees. A light haze overspread the sky. In a tree over his hut several crows quarreled over a piece of dried meat they had stolen from his hut. Otherwise his belongings in the hut were undisturbed.

He put the log down and examined the footprints. He decided, after some thought, that they were those of one man who had approached within a few feet of his hut, circled undecidedly for a few moments, then backtracked. He followed the tracks around the windbreak, up the river, across the ford. In the distance, through the lambent heat haze, he could see the downstream end of the thorn tree forest where he had spent that first night. He was sure now that the lone visitor had come from the forest, and near that forest ran the old warpath of the Bontocs.

He cooked rice, roasted a piece of meat on the embers, pared his last tomato, mixed meat and tomato with *bagoong* and ate, making balls of rice with his big fingers. He had no time to spare now. He could not wait for Kirbas with the carabaos to drag the logs upstream. In the back of his head he knew his mysterious visitor had returned to his village—possibly Mainit—to round up a head-hunting party. Mainit was two days' journey away, going uphill. The party should be back in about three days.

Or, the prowler might have had a party ready in the forest, and he had merely been scouting.

But Cleto knew the practice of these people, and he doubted the latter possibility. They always went in a bunch, attacked in a bunch, it was true, but he preferred to think danger was not so near at hand. Such big people as they, among the strongest men Cleto had ever known, they should have been the match of anyone in man-to-man combat; but no, they would not attack a group of equal strength. They pounced upon a straggler, man, woman, or child, their eight or ten to their victim's one. They attacked treacherously. They hit a man with their deadly head-axe from the back.

A moment's reflection while eating convinced Cleto that a head-hunting party would return to raid his camp. He had heard that several years ago an escaped Mainit convict was killed by a policeman from Malideg, a village some 20 kilometers down the river. Now, this Mainit's son had grown to manhood; it was time he carried out the law of his people. He would take the lower jaw and the fingers of his father's slayer. Similar trophies removed from any of the slayer's relatives would also do. In practice the avenger did not look meticulously into the blood relationship; any unfortunate he encountered near the marked community satisfied the tribal law.

It was highly possible that the strange visit had something to do with this case. It could not have been chance prowling only. The obvious haste of the man (the size of the footprints indicated that sex) leaving his camp was strong cause for suspicion. The smoke of his campfire had been seen, and someone had come to investigate.

Cleto had no time to lose. Carrying the logs down to shallow water, he lashed them together into a raft, placed his clothing, pot, *kuppit*, tools, sandals, rice and dried meat on it, himself sprang on it, and poled the contraption into the main current of the river. Slowly the raft began to move with the water, gathering speed as it reached the rapids. Then, despite Cleto's best efforts, it swung around and made the rapids broadside, bumping over the submerged tops of rocks, dipping into the foaming water, and shooting almost upended in a churning millrace between two huge boulders.

Finally the unwieldy craft made the still waters below the rapids, and Cleto had to pole with all his might in order to get enough movement to reach the next rapids. And so on. The process was repeated over and over.

Late in the dark night the occasional barking of dogs to his right told him that he had reached Malideg. He beached the raft on the nearest sand bar and contrived to get it on dry land. He could now see, in the distance, the glimmer of a light or two. Arming himself with a stick with which to beat off the dogs, he picked his way carefully among the boulders on the riverside and then followed a lane cut deep into the side of a hill by countless walking feet and torrential monsoons.

Something jumped up suddenly in his path as he was about to step on it. In the starlight he had thought it was a rock. It was a dog, and it began snapping and barking furiously at him. The other village curs took up the warning; with a pack of dogs snarling at his heels, he came at last to the cluster of bamboo-and-cogon grass huts squatting on the brow of the hill.

Some men were sitting in the middle of the road, their home-made cigars glowing in the dark.

"Where is your *concejal*—headman?" he asked.

"Why?"

"There are Bontocs up the river."

Thirty men left Malideg early the following morning for the camp of Cleto up the river. The *concejal* carried a double-barreled shotgun. The rest abristled with bolos and spears.

After three hours' brisk walking they came within sight of the camp. They saw smoke rising where the hut should have been, but the hut was no longer there. It had been burned to the ground. The fireplace of three stones was uprooted and strewn about with savage ferocity. The sand around the ruins was tracked up. The departing footsteps paralleled the route taken by Cleto's visitor of the previous day.

And Cleto had first thought to give the raiders three days' time to return! Going back to Malideg, Cleto's companions helped salvage the lumber left behind in his flight.

At the appointed time Cleto's brother-in-law Kirbas arrived with the bandsaw, the sledges, and the carabaos. At Malideg they sawed the logs into boards, lashed the boards on the sledges, and took the overland trail home that followed the tops of the rolling hills west of the river divide. It took several trips to take home all the boards and the bigger pieces intended for post, beams, bracers, and rafters.

In three more months Cleto's house was built. All the neighbors enthusiastically lent a hand building it, but Cleto of course did the biggest lick of work. The house was his. It stood in the middle of its yards, surrounded by its new fence. Its unpainted hardwood frame walls took a high polish from the planes. Along *Calle* Quinto Gobernador it was agreed that the house did justice to Cleto's and Mariana's four-poster bed, which was the only bed in all Burayoc.

He had gone into the woods, faced the unknown, had a brush with death, but now his house stood on four strong posts. It's good for a man to have a home.

New Horizon
December 1945

YOURS FAITHFULLY

LYDIA V. ARGUILLA

I stood on the corner and stuck out my left thumb. A jeep with two first lieutenants in it pulled up to the curb.

"Which way are you going, please?" I smiled my best bumming-a-ride-smile.

"The way you're going, sweetheart."

The boy who wasn't driving moved into the back seat and I climbed in front. It was April of 1945. Baguio had not fallen. Nor Ipo Dam. Nor Cagayan Valley. American soldiers smiled at every Filipino. The novelty of the V-sign and greeting of "Victory, Joe!" had not yet worn off.

"My name's Oren," said the boy at the wheel.

"And mine's Harry. What's yours?" I told them.

"How about a date, honey? We're a couple of strangers in this town. We don't know anybody. And we like to dance."

A couple of Americans. We waited for them three years. Friends. Even if I just met them. It isn't done in this country, but it would be now.

I turned to Harry because I liked Oren better. "Are you coming along too?"

"Why, sure. If you can get me a girl that looks like Ann Sheridan."

"I'll try my best, Harry." I didn't like him very much.

"You mean we get a date?" asked Oren.

"Sure. You asked for it. Here's where I get off. Thank you very much, boys. See you what time?"

There was to be boating, picture-taking, dinner, and dance.

The boat was out of order. So we drove out to the Chinese cemetery and took pictures. I wonder how many snapshots went back to the States of GI's in the Philippines against a background of Chinese pagodas?

Rose is half-American—brown eyes, chestnut brown hair, very fair skin, and if she didn't look exactly like Ann Sheridan still she was attractive in her own right and I knew Harry would like her. But in her great desire to be friendly and with her limited vocabulary of American slang she gave the impression of being fresh. She and Harry started off well enough but pretty soon Harry's teasing began to get under her skin. She didn't like it when he tried to put his arm around her for a picture. Generally Filipino men don't put their arms around a girl unless she is a relative, wife or sweetheart. I'd known enough Americans before the war and seen enough American movies to understand that an American boy's arm around a girl's shoulder could mean simple friendliness, but I must admit even to myself that Harry was just a wee bit more familiar than friendly.

Unless a girl is stupid she knows when a man has that just-another-girl attitude toward her and no self-respecting girl anywhere in the world would feel flattered by it. It was catching too. In a little while the way Oren said "sweetheart" or "honey" made me feel like a gun moll. The way it's said, not what's said counts. I felt very sad. I regretted having accepted the invitation.

At the restaurant where we were to have dinner, I decided to lay the cards on the table. "Look, fellows, before you order anything I want a few things straightened out. We came out with you because you're Americans. You came all the way across the ocean to liberate our country. Tomorrow or the next day you may not be here. You said you wanted to dance. So do we. We can help you to a nice, clean, good time. But if you expect kissing and petting thrown in you won't get it. We don't go in for that sort of thing."

"You got us wrong, honey."

"It depends on you what kind of evening you want. It's still early. The sun hasn't set. You have time enough to find yourselves some other dates. We can stop here now and decide not to go on together the rest of the evening."

"Sweetheart, if we wanted loose girls we could have them any time. But we like you. We don't want any other date. Please go on with us to the dance."

It was Oren who spoke. I looked at Harry. I didn't like his smile. "It's not being uppity. But we can't help being what

we are. We don't want you to expect something you won't get
and then feel gypped when you don't get it. If you want a different evening from the one we can share with you, that's your
business. Only, leave us out of it."

"Don't get us wrong, honey. We like you just as you are.
Okay? Now that we're all straightened out, do we go on with
the evening?"

"How about you, Rose?"

"It's all right. I'm going on."

We got a good table—right where everybody coming in
stumbled into you. Danced. "For a guy who likes to dance, I
dance awful," Oren said. "I've been dancing for years and
never improved."

"I like to make people mad," said Harry, "the trouble was,
that you girls didn't understand us American boys at all. We
meant no harm."

"I didn't like your language," Rose laughed.

"That's better, honey, now we're friends. What didn't you
like?"

"Your language. You said 'hell' something."

"I meant no harm, honest, I didn't. You said you were out
with a colonel last night. And I said, 'what are you doing now
with a mere lieutenant? That's a come-down. Least you could
have gotten was a major.' And then you sat away and pretended to be peeved. And so I moved farther away to the edge
of the jeep and I said, 'if she wants colonels, to hell with her.'
I was just kidding."

"In front of a lady you just met, hell is no word to use
without begging her pardon."

Harry laughed, "Maybe you're right at that."

"Fine," I exclaimed, "can this be the dawn of understanding?"

"Don't try fancy words on us, honey. We're low-brow
Americans. All we talk is slang."

"I like slang. Teach us the latest. We're three years behind. Waiter, can we have paper and pencil, please?"

"You're cooking with gas."

"What's that?"

"It means you're all right. You're cooking on the front
burner. Boy, oh Boy! Look who's coming this way. She could
eat hay out of a bottle."

"Why?"

"Strictly from hunger. It means she's ugly."

"That's not kind."

"But true."

I laughed in spite of myself.

"This ice-cream is no good. We're eating it because we can't get anything better. This ice-cream is strictly from hunger."

"Look, honey, there's a Casanova over there."

"A what?"

"A Casanova. He doesn't bring a girl. He comes alone here and thinks every girl will swoon into his arms. Look, he's heading for prey. He'll cut in. I hate his guts. Do you know what a Casanova is?"

"In history he was a famous lover."

"Ha, ha. That's right."

Oren said, "I tell you she's smart."

"And you're condescending," I said.

"What's that? Oh! I didn't mean to be. Sorry."

Harry laughed.

"Wasn't what?"

"Condescending."

"Why were you sorry, then?"

More laughter.

"Seriously, honey. I like you. You're a nice girl. I'll marry you and take you to the States."

"Oh, you big snowman!"

"That's no snow-job. Wish I didn't teach you that expression. Can't you tell the difference between a snow-job and the real thing?"

"Sure I can."

"I love you. You're clean and decent. You believe me, don't you?"

"If you believe yourself, sure."

"I mean it, honey."

"Yes, you met me this afternoon."

"But I've been looking for you three years. I've never met anyone like you."

"There's nobody like me. That's a nice tackle. But you're not scoring any points. *How'm I doing, Harry?*"

"You're on the ball, sister. You're on the beam."

"Thank you. What's the matter, Oren? Isn't my slanguage beautiful? What are you moping about? Straighten out and fly right?"

"Oh, my aching back," moaned Oren.

"Who started all this anyway?"

"I had a good time, honey. Honest, I did. The dance and everything. Thanks. Only, I'm sorry about the first part of the date. You'll forgive us, won't you? We drank a little bit before coming out to get you. We weren't sure you'd keep your date. Won't you see me again? I like to talk to you. Soft music. Less crowd. Not rah-rah like tonight. Maybe I made a bad first impression. But I'm really nice. Give me a chance to prove it." He smiled, a smile you'd call disarming.

"The evening was most educational. And I enjoyed the dance too. Good night."

"Do I see you again?"

"Yes."

II

Lovely, quiet evening. Candlelight. Red tablecloth. A girl at the piano.

"It seems unbelievable that you and I should be talking here like this, you a Filipino and I an American. Never in my wildest dreams did I ever imagine myself in Manila, sitting at this table, at this moment, with you. Three years ago I was in college. Working my way. Making good money too. I won't have trouble about a job when I get back. My job's waiting for me."

"Is it a job you like to do?"

"Yes. Metals. I work hard and play hard. My parents were poor. And honest. For a while just before the war I went wild like many college boys. I seldom drink, but when I do I take too much. On one of my drinking sprees I woke up to find myself married."

"Did it turn out all right?"

"No. We both decided we'd made a mistake, and got a divorce. Whew! That put the fear of God in me. I let her divorce me. Ever since I've sobered down a bit. This war has aged me as it has other boys like me. And yet when I see the ruins of your city around me I feel that what we've gone through

in the Solomons, in New Guinea, and in the landing and fighting here are nothing in comparison. Else, why should I, a
stranger, have felt a spasm of grief come over me when I first
saw Manila from the air?"

"Why grief?"

"It was, too. I felt like crying. Wasn't that strange? I'd
never been before. Down in New Guinea where we had nothing
to see and nowhere to go but jungle we read up on Manila and
drew programs for sight-seeing here—just to help pass the
time you know—but at the back of our minds we did expect to do
as we planned. I knew about your Walled City, the Jai-Alai and
the nightclubs....And then to come at last and find nothing
but heaps of rubble. I tell you that was when I came nearest,
I think, to feeling as you do about your city."

"Thank you. You don't know what it means to have you
talk the way you do."

"You don't know what it means to have you sit there and
listen. In the army...but there I go again. I'll sound like
griping. And maybe I am."

"Go on. In the Army..."

"In the Army you get lost among so many others. You all
dress alike, day in and day out, eat identical food, form lines.
Your entity, your personality, is merged into the mass. You
become part of an operation, a strategy, or you're just waiting.
You, for yourself, don't matter. If you die, there's always someone to replace you. You're a government issue, just like your
clothes, shoes, rations, one detail in a gigantic effort to preserve
a so-called way of life. And you don't always see where you
are heading for. In your little sphere within the Army, and
because you're just one of millions and not a general, you see
all the little irritations, pettinesses of rank, privilege, army
politics. You wonder sometimes, lying in your bunk in the
dark, 'God, why am I here? How did I get here?'

"Do you mind if I hold your hand? I just thought: Here
I am. The war is not over. Outside is a city in ruins. But
here within the glow of many candles (I am glad there is no
electricity yet and we have to use candles), in here is peace and
quiet talk and friendship.

"That is a lovely piece. White Christmas. Shall we dance?"

"The girl plays beautifully. I can only guess. But that song
must make so many boys homesick when they hear it."

"I know what you mean. Have you ever seen snow?"

"Only in pictures."

"Oh, you must see and feel snow. I'd be happy to teach you to make snowballs and build a snowman and skate...."

"I'm sure you would," I laughed, "and that is no snow-job either."

Oren threw his head back and laughed. "Let's not have any slang lessons, huh?"

We stopped briefly on the floor. Other dancers turned to look at us. Laughing we walked back to our table. "I must have made an awful impression on you that evening. Tell me, didn't I though?"

"Yes and no. Or I woudn't be here with you," I answered.

"You haven't talked much about yourself. Where did you live? What did you do before the war? You don't look like a War Sufferer. But could anybody have lived three years in enemy-occupied territory and not suffered?"

"I used to live near the sea, one street removed from Dewey Boulevard. I had everything my heart could wish for— the man I loved, a comfortable home, books, orchids and the porch, friends dropping in every now and then. Everything is gone—as though a giant bulldozer had passed over my life and reduced every wall and post to rubble."

"I'm sorry."

"I won't shrug my shoulders even to cheer you up. I have depressed you, I know. For me, it was the end of a happy life. I could die now and not really care. And it wouldn't be dramatics either. In normal times, personal calamities like mine stand out. But my fate is that of millions. To tell it to you is to repeat a story that you have heard and will hear over and over again in this country. And yet simply because it's not isolated does not make tragedy any easier to bear for each individual."

"I'd be a very poor friend if I lumped you and your story with millions. Before I came out here the Philippines to me was just some group of islands in the Pacific that America was honor bound to redeem from the clutches of the Japanese. Filipinos were people who were natives of the Philippines. But if I were back in Ohio now and a typhoon were in Manila and I heard about it, I wouldn't just feel vaguely sorry for the mass of anonymous sufferers. Before I ever came out here, yes. But not now. Now I'd think of you. I'd think of actual Filipinos I had come to know. And my sympathy would be very active, very real."

"They're closing up now, Oren."

"Oh, I hadn't noticed."

"How soft and cool the night is!"

"Shall we take a spin?"

"I think not, Oren. I've got to get to work tomorrow morning."

"On such a beautiful evening, you have to mention the ugly word work. But just as you say, lady, just as you say."

"Well, here we are. *We have returned.*"

"So we have."

"Don't go in yet just this minute. Listen! Can you hear that? What's that sound?"

"Do you mean the frogs croaking?"

"Is that what it is?"

"Have you never heard frogs croak?"

"Listen. They've got a band leader!"

"Sure enough."

"They've stopped! All of a sudden. Now why did they do that? Do you ever wonder about such things?"

"Yes."

"You're crazy, then. So am I."

"Thank you."

"Honey...."

"Don't. Don't spoil it all. It's been so perfect."

"I'm sorry."

"Good night."

"Good night."

Dear Oren—it was a lovely evening. You made it so. And it wasn't a dream, though in a way it was. And as dreams end so does this one—at its loveliest and best.

An hour of beauty and trust and friendliness in a world of disillusionment and ugliness and pain—surely it is something worth keeping and remembering so.

God bless you and keep you for more gracious days of peace, of permanent affections, of safe and measured living.

God keep of you for that interrupted college education, home, family and friends and white Christmases.

God grant you a soft spot in your heart always for my country—you and all the other Americans who came over to help us get back from the invader what is our own.

Yours faithfully....

Philippine-American
November 1945

I AM THINKING OF US TODAY

LIGAYA VICTORIO REYES

I am thinking of you today because it is Christmas, the time of year when one remembers those with whom one has been happy. Outside, the ruins of Manila lie bleaching in the sun, skeletons of a city desecrated and forsaken. From afar comes the blare of an army radio, making the dream of a white Christmas a nightmare of noise for homesick GI's still sweating it out in the camp you have left. There is no leisurely ring of horses' hoofs striking the asphalt, no spattered red of potted poinsettias, no lofty warmth of flame trees sturdy by the roadside. There is only the roar and sputter and grind of huge wheels against dirt, the drift of billowing smoke upon seared grass.

There is no Christmas tree in our *barong-barong*. Neither is there a miniature representation of Bethlehem, nor gifts wrapped in green and red and twinkling with silver ribbon. But the obi that you sent me from Japan is laid on the one good table, a flesh of brilliance to defy the gloom. I look at it now, and the thought of you is a glow like the gold that weaves through its pattern—sunlight through lattice-work. And I remember that today it is Christmas, even if the trappings are of decay and the setting is desolation.

You meant to spend Christmas with me, but the plans of men and women do not count for a centavo against the will of the Army. You have been gone these many centuries—it is hard to believe it was just a month ago. For so many things have happened. I now have a job which gives me security to wipe off the fear of last year's hunger. I have been given a dress that looks prewar. The prices are still up, but there is talk of their going down, and this once we hope that where there is smoke there will be fire. Manila is coming more firmly to life— a bit too hysterical, a bit too gaudy, but life nevertheless.

Because it is Christmas, let me be sentimental and recall the fun we have had. Remember the day we spent by the seaside? We watched the ships come in, loaded with the stuff that life is made of. You said that very soon there would be rice and meat and even sugar to put some flesh in cheeks that starvation had made haggard. You looked at my arms which were just filling out, silent about the scars that covered bayonet wounds. You passed your hand over my hair, murmuring that the edges, burnt when our home took fire, were softer to the touch. Tenderness is food and drink when one has known cruelty, senseless though it may be, and I could have kissed your hand because you had it then for me.

I remember the jeep rides we have taken, your hand holding my shoulder against a particularly rough bounce, our laughter superior and amused at the jibes pedestrians flung at me. I remember the dancing we had done, myself in my one good dress and in a pair of pretty shoes a cousin had given me after I left the refugee camp. The music was sweet, the floor was good, and I forgot that my mother lies buried in some strange backyard and that my brother is still missing. I wore an orchid in my hair and I was in love, and the past buried itself deeper in my heart.

And I remember that once, centuries ago, you actually asked me to marry you. I wonder if you understand why I didn't, then. I have told you I love you, and love can be sufficient excuse for marriage. But love is not all in wartime, or immediately after peace. There is no normalcy, even in the heart. There is still the hangover of combat fear, of starvation and insecurity, of death. Man is lonely, woman is despairing, and in both is an eagerness to make the most of the moment which each fears is but passing.

But marriage is not a passing moment. Not for me—nor for you.

Marriage has never been easy, but it is more difficult under circumstances like ours. I know we speak a common language. Our feelings are alike. Your sight and mine are focused on the same appreciation of beauty. Our laughter rings the same, and we know the same respect for the right of people to live the way they believe. Your skin has been browned by three years overseas. My complexion has been paled by months in a hospital. My cheek comes to rest against the funny curve under your chin and my heart is only a little distance from yours when we dance. But your past is different from mine, your future promises to be. You have seen both the East and the West—you can make comparisons. But what I know of your country is what I read in magazines and what I see in the movies. My knowledge of your people is limited by contact with people like you—fighting men who are geared to friendliness or hatred by the machinery of war. I suspect that life in America is not all chromium and streamlining, not fur coat and satin, that beneath the power and the wealth lies misery and want and despair. And that beneath the fine talk and the admiring smile are curiosity and even veiled hostility. But these are still suspicions. I don't dare find out if they are true.

The things we remember are different. We must be sure that the things we look forward to are the same. Even the colors of our Christmases are different. Yours are white, mine are green. Christmas to you must mean snow on the ground, and a huge Christmas tree with glittering parcels to contain the spirit it represents. These things mean Christmas to me: a new dress for Mass, kissing the hands of our elders in simple greeting, coins clinking in beaded purses, the pleasant reek of green oranges, the mouth-watering vapor of *lechon*. We have no Santa Claus. We know just whom to thank for Christmas cheer. Christmas, they say, is the same the world over. But would you recognize Christmas if the wrappings were different? I want to be sure that you can.

Lately, we have welcomed Christmas trees into our salas and piled bright parcels of foreign gifts about them. But we still have our shiny coins, we still go about kissing the hands of our elders, we still consider hearing Mass the most elevated way of observing Christmas. For we are westernized just so far and no farther. We are Malayans, and Malayans we shall remain while our skins remain brown and our country floats on the face of an ocean near the sun of morning. We shall feel proud in so remaining as long as we remember that there is pride in being what you are no matter what you might hope to be, and that pride in so being is lasting panacea against prejudice, a shining shield against the small-minded contempt and ignorance which varies in cruelty of expression according to the amount of pigment in people's skins.

You say you are different. I must be certain that you are. When you look at our peasants and our nipa shacks, do you remember that in your own country you also have peasants and shacks? Or do you believe that we have a monopoly of them? When you gaze at our slums and our scum, do you think of your glittering mansions and your dazzling debutantes? Do you remember that this is a country ravaged by war and that possibly beneath the muck and ruck, there is decency and the gentleness of peace? The looting and the thieving, the cheapness and the mire—have you ever wondered just how much misery and want they cover? Dearest Keith, I'm not apologizing. But how many among us remember that war is a cancer that eats deep into the soul of man, and the stench can be the odor of martyrdom?

And I must be certain that between us there is no prejudice. That to you I am a woman desirable and not just intriguing, because I possess the qualities that you find desirable in woman. I don't want to be just part of the strangeness that is war—the strange sights and tastes and feelings that are thrust upon a fighting man, and which in peacetime must fade into the shadowiness of dream. We must know what love between a man like you and a woman like me must survive in peacetime. The companionship that we know must be something apart from the loneliness that is such a curse in wartime. The dovetailing of tastes, the similarity and dovetailing the basis for a rich life together should be made to stand the test of time.

We must be certain that passion is not a brief candle which burns at both ends and rests against the precarious edge of youth's vanishing moment. Passion should be a steady glow that cannot consume itself, and which, towards the end, must simmer down into a mellow warmth that will ease the cold of the years' dying, a mere breath, but scented with the memory of delight it had served to deepen.

Of these we cannot be certain while the poison of war lingers in your mind, while peace is still so strange a dream in your heart. You must go back to the world which four years ago you have left, and in the embrace of the things which to you, have stood for security and peace, try and decide if the look in a woman's eyes, the yearning in her arms, the flame of love in her heart now reflected in yours make for a strength that can combat whatever bewilderment and pain a marriage like this can bring.

I have said all these to you before, but I put them now on record because I have to convince myself that I am right. Because today, being Christmas, I feel so lost and alone without you by my side. And because despair is in my heart. I may be right, but I also want to be happy. Sometimes I wonder if the future is worth all the pain of the present. Because I still have youth, I am still wondering if respect and love like ours can combat the serpents of pettiness and cruelty which man, being man, has nourished in his bosom. The casual cruel word, the glance askance, the discrimination and ostracism—will they be matters for deep despair or instrument for a closer drawing together? I do not know—I cannot know now. I only know that I love you, even if this love is not reckless enough to snatch at the happiness of the present and let tomorrow take care of its pain.

You keep saying that you love me, that you will come back for me. Much though I love you I beg you to take your time about it. Make certain that I fit into the life which you will build for yourself. Make your own adjustments, then you can help me make mine. In the meantime, this being Christmas, I send you my love. Wrapped though it is in banana leaves and tied with abaca twine, it is still of the height and depth and strength that make it the perfect Christmas gift.

Philippine-American
December 1945

PLIGHTED WORD

Narciso G. Reyes

Having said what had to be said, Damian stood up and crushed the lighted end of his cigar in the bamboo ash tray. Sima sat quite still, hardly discernible in the darkness of the sala. The silence between them deepened, became a live and palpable presence.

"It's for Flora's own good," Damian said, as though the silence had spoken and he was giving answer. "Marcos is a good man. Flora will be happy with him."

Sima nodded as if she understood perfectly.

"Come," said Damian, leading the way to the kitchen. "Supper will get cold."

Without a word Sima stood up and followed him.

I understand, she thought, as she watched Damian and Flora eat their meal of rice and broiled fish. I know, I know.

It was plain enough. This man, Marcos, had seen Flora and he would know no rest until she had become his wife. He was rich in his own right, and he was the nephew and heir of Don Luis, who owned half the province and two or three towns in the next one. It was like a novel or a movie come true.

On Sunday, a week from now, emissaries would come to ask formally for Flora's hand. Damian would be surprised; he would protest Flora's unworthiness and otherwise dilly-dally according to ancient custom. But in the end he would be prevailed upon, albeit reluctantly, to give his consent. A date would be set, and the marriage would be as good as consummated.

It would be, Damian had said, for Flora's own good. For her and hers, thought Sima, as she went through the motion of eating.

There was a big, lush farm near the creek. Damian had often stopped there, and watched, and walked the length and breadth of it, and picked up the rich turned earth, seeming

to weigh it in his rough, strong hands. Marcos would put him
in charge, or perhaps give it to him outright. At long last he
would own land, and the things that go with being an owner
of land.

And Flora? Sima choked on a half-chewed morsel of fish.
She coughed violently and tears came to her eyes. Wiping them
with the sleeves of her *camisa* she left the table and groped her
way back to the sala.

After eating, Damian put on his hat, lighted another of
his home-made cigars and went out. The neighborhood association was having a meeting. As vice-president, he had to be
present. Flora's brother, Pastor, had gone ahead to remind the
members and prepare the meeting-place. Mother and daughter
were left alone in the house.

Now this silent woman, who in twenty years of married
life had not once raised her voice against her husband, and
who had not said a word when her daughter was given a chosen
mate by him, began to talk. Quietly, she told Flora all that
Damian had told her. Then gravely, she said:

"The word is all-important—the plighted word. Your father's word, once given, cannot be broken. Better death than
dishonor, as the saying goes. The poor have only one word;
they cannot afford the luxury of duplicity.

"On Sunday, Marcos' mother will come and perhaps also
his uncle, Don Luis himself. Your father will give his word—
on Sunday. That is a week from now. Seven days. After Sunday
your first duty, as a good daughter, will be to obey your father's
desire in this matter, to see to it that his promise is fulfilled.
After Sunday, after your father has given his word, the thing
is settled. No one else's wishes should matter...."

Flora sighed and for a while she was silent, thinking. She
tried to see her mother's eyes. "Perhaps," she said softly, "no
one else's wishes can matter, even now. Seven days is a short
time. The hills are far. Danger lurks along the roads. Who can
go to the hills and back in seven days?"

Sima leaned back and her talk took on a relaxed, medita-
tive tone. "One hears all sorts of rumors these days," she said.
"Christmas is only two weeks away. There is a story that the
men in the hills are coming down to spend Christmas with their
families. They have left their camps, it is said, and are now

in the outlying villages, waiting for a chance to slip through
the guards. San Anton, they say, is full of these men, and
some of them are headed this way. San Anton is not so far
from here. Two days' leisurely trip. Three, allowing for un-
foreseen delays."

"Not everyone can wander about."

"They weave beautiful piña cloth in San Anton. I am
thinking of sending Pastor there to buy me a new *camisa* to
wear on Christmas Day."

"When is *Ka* Pastor going?"

"I'll talk to him when he comes home tonight. He can
leave early tomorrow morning."

"I'll be up before sunrise to prepare his meal...."

Pastor left before dawn, before his father had awakened.
He borrowed his friend Mente's bicycle, intending to ride to
Maliwag and from there cut across the fields on foot to San
Anton. He had an uncle in Maliwag with whom he could leave
the bike. San Anton was a well-known guerilla outpost. The
main approaches to the village were closely guarded by Japanese and Constabulary troops.

He rode at a brisk pace. His instructions were clear. He
was to look for piña cloth with color and design becoming a
woman of forty, letting it be known that it was intended for
a *camisa* to be worn on Christmas Day—or, perhaps, at a
wedding which might soon be held. Then he was to go to Guadalupe's house and give her a message from Flora.

Guadalupe was Tonio's cousin and Flora's closest friend
and confidant. The message was: "*After Sunday, let Tonio consider me as one dead. Let him forget me utterly and live his
life as though he had never known me.*"

If Tonio was in San Anton with his men, as rumor had it,
he would be staying in Guadalupe's house. If he was anywhere
within call, Guadalupe would find a way to reach him. If he
was out of touch with Guadalupe, the news that a marriage
was being arranged in Maytubig might yet fetch him.

Seven days. Pastor leaned forward like a racer and squeezed
a little more speed out of Mente's bicycle. His father would miss
him today. He had started hoeing the vegetable patch and Damian wanted it finished before the clods became too hard.
Pastor spat on the road. If the old tyrant wanted the work

done, let him do it himself. Let him work the big farm near
the creek, too, if he can get it. Pastor thought of Marcos and
Don Luis, and anger caught at his throat and made breathing
difficult. Damned sons of a bitch. Wealthy, good-for-nothing
leeches who thought they could buy anything they fancied.
Pastor put his weight on the pedals until the wheels hummed
and the cold air bit into his face.

Sima had her answers ready, but Damian was not deceived.
"I know Tonio is in San Anton," he said, cutting short
her explanation of Pastor's absence. "I know, too, that he cannot come to Maytubig. If he does...." Damian shrugged his
shoulders. "You know how the Japs punish bandits."

"Tonio a bandit?"

"He calls himself a guerrilla. What's the difference? He
takes rice from the farmers, eggs and chickens from the poul-
terers, money from everybody, hogs from the raisers of live-
stock."

"He has to live, like us."

"Why doesn't he work like us? Why can't he keep the
peace like Pastor who was his brother-in-arms?"

As always when her heart cried out in protest, Sima was
silent. She was proud of her son who had fought in Bataan,
but she was prouder yet of that other one who had never stopped
fighting.

She remembered the last time she had seen him. He was
in rags and had a wound in his left shoulder, but he walked
with his head high and his fearless eyes shining. It was the
12th of April, three days after the fall of Bataan. In the confusion of the surrender, he had escaped and was on his way
to the Sierra Madre foothills. He had passed by, he said, to
give them news of Pastor whom he had seen among the prisoners of war.

"Aren't you going to surrender?" Damian asked him.

He had smiled and shaken his head. "The air in the towns
does not agree with me," he said. "I'll stay in the hills for
a while."

In another tone he had added, glancing at Flora: "God
willing, I shall come back. Soon, I hope."

And he had gone, taking with him, Sima felt, part of themselves and of the things they wished to be....

Pastor had come home without mishap and now it was a matter of waiting. He had bought the cloth his mother wanted, and delivered Flora's message to Guadalupe. Tonio had gone to Sta. Monica on a mission, but would be back in San Anton Friday morning. Friday to Sunday was three days. Three days, Guadalupe had remarked, was a long time.

It was Wednesday afternoon when Pastor returned. He had expected to be scolded, and was surprised when his father greeted him civilly, almost cordially, as though nothing had happened. There was a curious gleam in the old man's cunning eyes. "He's happy," Flora had explained. "Don Luis sent for him this morning. They had a long talk and after lunch they went to the town hall together."

"I don't like it," said Pastor.

On Thursday, something happened. A large contingent of Jap troops, reinforced by three companies of the constabulary, raided San Anton. The village was razed to the ground; all the men captured were killed on the spot. That night, the neighboring villages were zoned.

Damian himself brought the news when he came home to lunch. It was terrible, he said. The whole countryside between San Anton and Maytubig was swarming with Japs. Even the fields were alive with them. A man could not even hope to get to Maliwag without a special pass; the cordon was that tight. There was talk that the zoning had been extended to Sta. Monica. . . .

Sima and Pastor listened, pale and tight-lipped, to the tale of horror.

"How long will it last?" Flora said and could not help asking.

Damian looked at her until she lowered her eyes. "A week or two," he said. "Certainly not sooner than Sunday. . . ."

Three days, Guadalupe had said, was a long time. Flora and Sima couldn't find enough things to do in the house that long, terror-charged Friday. Pastor had a better time. He was out in the fields, where a man could expend his strength and tire himself out. In the evening he came home hungry and silent, ate a meal of cold rice and fish, and went to sleep without saying a word.

Damian, however, was in fine spirits. He had gone fishing in the creek by the big farm that afternoon. He brought home a string of mudfish, the biggest of which was just a bit smaller than Flora's forearm. Damian dressed it himself and roasted it over the embers, whistling as he worked. His mind was on the future.

"What a farm," he said softly, to no one in particular. "Most fertile land in Bulacan and right by the creek, too, with its swarms of fish. It has never been fully exploited yet it has the biggest yield, per hectare, in the whole province. Half the year it lies idle, a pasture for stray carabaos....Easy to double or triple its yield...a good strong fence...a mango orchard back of the house...."

He had never been more genial. He insisted that Sima eat the choicest morsels of fish and deprecated Flora's lack of appetite.

"When I was your age," he said, "I could eat a whole pig all by himself. How old are you, Flora?"

"I shall be nineteen on Christmas Eve."

"A good age to get married. Not too young, not too old."

"I—I'm not so desirous of getting married."

Damian pushed back his empty plate, making a little clatter on the table.

"Don Luis himself is coming on Sunday evening," he said, addressing Sima. "Kill the suckling pig and the fattest of the chickens."

He stood up, lighted a cigar, and went to bed.

The night passed somehow and it was Saturday, and Sunday was only a day off. After breakfast, Sima called Pastor aside. "What's the news?" she asked. "Can people go through now to Sta. Monica or San Anton?"

Pastor shook his head.

"Be on the lookout for anyone coming from town," she begged. "You might hear something new."

"I'll go to town myself."

"Your father might get angry."

Pastor looked deep into his mother's eyes. "I don't care," he said quietly. "From now on I'll go to town whenever I want to go to town."

"Be quick, son."

Pastor nodded. "I'll borrow Mente's bicycle."

He came back late in the afternoon, depressed and grim. There had been a fight near Sta. Monica the day before. Tonio's party had been waylaid by a battalion of Japs. Tonio had been wounded but had got away. Pastor had the story from a girl who had been there at the time and who had later been allowed to pass through the lines on the strength of a pass issued by the provincial commander.

"But he is wounded!" cried Flora.

"He is not the kind to let a wound keep him from doing what he wants to do."

"He has a night and a day to do it," said Sima. "After Sunday night, it won't matter whether he comes or not."

Tonio did not come that night, nor did he show up the next day. At sundown, Sima gave him up. Don Luis would be coming at supper time. After Damian had given his word, the betrothal would be a public compact which neither party could break without incurring lasting disgrace.

"Resign yourself, my child," she said. "Perhaps it's God's will that this should happen."

"I wish I were dead," said Flora.

"Don't say such things, child. Who knows? Perhaps it's for the best."

"I wish I had never been born."

"Hush, Flora, hush...."

"Death would be sweeter."

"Will you dishonor your own father, child? Will you bring disgrace upon us all?"

Flora was silent. Burying her face in her mother's lap, she wept like a child.

Don Luis came at the appointed time. The formalities were punctiliously observed. The seals and guarantees of custom and convention were ceremoniously impressed upon the betrothal. When Tonio finally came, the thing was done.

For Tonio did come. He came alone. He came on foot, limping from a saber wound in his right thigh. He reached Damian's farm a little after midnight.

He stood at the gate and Flora, who had fallen into numbed slumber, stirred and opened her eyes as though her name had been called.

He pushed the gate open and limped across the yard. Flora was wide awake now and acutely aware of the night and its strange sounds. Her mother lay beside her in the room. Her brother Pastor slept in the sala; her father lay, snoring, near the door to the kitchen. Flora turned over on her belly and listened to the noises outside.

The house was built high. The lower part was unfenced and Tonio had no difficulty getting under the room where Flora lay. He knew she would be there, awake and waiting. He stood quite still to ease his heart and he raised his face and called her name.

"Flora," he said softly and Flora, listening, heard music and felt again the quick wild rush of wonder his voice had evoked, that first time, when he had looked boldly into her eyes and seen his own image there, transfigured in the clear, luminous depths. Again it was harvest time and they were alone, for a moment, at the foot of old Polonio's haystack, and he was saying, "I shall wait for you here tonight, Flora," in a voice of honey and fire.

Tonio called her name a second time and Flora, her face pressed against her pillow, knew again the feel of straw in her hair and the taste of fragrant *anis* in her mouth. Tonio's strength was a cloak about her and the ache in his voice was in her heart also. Time moved to a new pitch and measure; from another world dogs barked and a cock crowed, the scented air was of a new country.

A third time Tonio called her and now Flora, weeping silently upon her pillow, knew what it was to be alone, and what it meant to have part of her claimed by things and places she knew only by name: patriotism and a beach called Lingayen, democracy and a peninsula named Bataan, freedom and strange hills and ranges in central Luzon's unmapped sierras. She knew, then, that she would never be whole again until the war was over and the last soldier safely come home.

There was silence and now Tonio said, "Goodbye, Flora," and it was as though he spoke also to air and space, and Flora was aware of the stars shining in the darkness and again the world was a little ball in the hollow of her palm, just as it was when Tonio had asked her to be his wife.

He waited a moment, conscious of the distance to the gate, his weight on his wounded leg to see if he could thrust it in the deepening silence. He flexed it a little and was satisfied and he moved out and walked straight across the yard and shut the gate behind him.

Philippine-American
January 1946

A PILGRIM YANKEE'S PROGRESS

NICK JOAQUIN

The uneasy lunch came to an end. The Camachos had felt it would never be over: they would eternally sit there, spooning food to their mouths while pondering what on earth to start talking about next. Actually—Edong Camacho informed his wife—the meal had lasted a bare forty minutes.

They had a moment to themselves now, the American guest having been shown to his room. They could breathe again.

Pepang Camacho said: "I could see those forty minutes were as funny for him as they were painful for us. What I fail to see is why, why."

She and her mother were doing the dishes; Edong stood in the kitchen doorway, strapping on his watch.

He said: "We probably are being penalized for something some other people did. He may have been sold rotten liquor or rotten women. He holds that against us."

"These Americans!" exclaimed Doña Concha. "Must they be such great innocents, even in their vices?"

"Tell us, mother," said Pepang, "how was he when he arrived? I was at the market," she explained to her husband. "Oh, Ed, do you think he may have been offended because we were not here to receive him?"

"More likely, the door offended him," said Doña Concha. "He was eyeing it with little affection when I opened it to him."

"Whatever did they do to him? I feel so mean! Was I nice during lunch, Ed? Did I show I resented his not being pleasant?"

"Did you?"

"—resent the way he behaved? No. I was too busy keeping the talk going round. And most of the time I just felt baffled .... Oh, come and get me out of this apron. My fingers won't work. Look, they're trembling.... How about this afternoon?"

"I have to be at the office after all."

"You won't be able to take him to where this uncle of his is buried?"

"I was going to let you do it instead. But he has upset you enough already. Stop squirming, will you? How have you knotted yourself into this thing?"

"Oh, nonsense. Of course, I'll take him."

"Of course, you will not. Look at the way you are now."

"But, Ed, that's one reason we asked him to come down, no? One of us will have to take him to the place. Oh, don't worry about me. I want to make it up to him, whatever was done to him that's so nasty. Mother, will you come along, too?"

"He would only regard me as the crowning insult, I fear. And he appears offended enough. Besides, how would my grey hairs look in a 'jeep'? No, no; we will humor the boy. Since the American does not believe in the duenna, we will not afflict him with one."

"Is that ours coming down now?" asked Edong.

The three of them stood still and listened. Noting how the footsteps lagged coming down the stairs, they glanced at one another.

Then: "Hurry, mother; hurry, Ed," whispered Pepang. "It will not be nice for him to come down and not find us around."

Doña Concha Galang, widow of Moreno, was a girl of fifteen when she first saw Americans. This was on an April morning in the first year of this century, and she and her mother and sisters were on a small boat going down the Pasig. They were coming back to the City after almost a year in Laguna, where they had "evacuated." During the trip they had craned their necks and peered from bank to bank, hoping (though with no little terror) to catch sight of the strange and awful men from across the sea, the new lords now of the land.

The Galang house in Paco stood on the riverbank; its imposing azotea opened on a broad tiled stairway that swept right down to the water. As the boat approached, the Galang women marvelled to see a brilliant gathering sporting on their azotea. All the primary colors were moving about on it, and up and down the steps. Then, the boat having glided nearer, they gasped collectively. For those masses of color, they now saw, were shawls and blouses and skirts; were, in fact, their very own shawls, their very own blouses, their very own skirts. And the creatures moving in those clothes—the monstrously huge men, fiery red of face and golden of hair, with cigars dangling from their mouths and big boots sticking out from under the delicately swelling rainbow skirts that hardly reached to their knees—those gorgeously colored and gorgeously appareled giants were, indubitably, the strangers they had so craved a terrified glimpse of.

Doña Concha was never quite to recover from the shock of that first encounter. All her life, she could not look on an American without catching her breath and warning herself not to stare; in her mind, she was busy rigging him up in the drooping laces and the vivid balloon skirts of her girlhood.

She had been delighted, however, when her son-in-law Edong announced that he had found the GI grandson of old Mr. Newman and had invited the boy down for the week-end. Old Andrew Newman was one of the few persons on earth of whom Doña Concha stood in awe; he was an old-timer who had come over early in American times to establish the firm in which her father and, afterwards, her husband had been manager. Edong, too, would have been in line for that very desirable position if the firm had not been dissolved just before the war. But old Newman was still alive, over there in America, and had already expressed an intention of abandoning retirement and returning to business. It might pay, Edong had remarked, to be as nice as possible to his grandson.

But what if the grandson will *not* let us? wondered Doña Concha, watching late that afternoon, her daughter and the American drive away in the jeep. For young Newman had clearly come in a spirit of gay malice, as one comes to enjoy a highly unsuccessful pageant put on by one's foes. He had better not push Pepang too far though, thought Doña Concha, turning away from the window.

The drinks were still set out on the parlor-table. She poured herself a cup, took a long sip, pulled up an armchair and sank down in it, groaning with relief. And as she sipped the liquor she fell to pondering what made Americans so big. One would think old Newman huge enough, but his grandson was tremendous. A pity they did not keep their figures. Narrow-waisted now, and wide-shouldered; the skin with the fire-glow; the hair a dull gold; the eyes like fresh violets; the thin straight line of the lips locking up the jaw into a triangle the austere nose soared away from—young Newman looked very much like his grandfather, before age, drink and success had polished the curls off his dome, multiplied his chins, and inflated his waist-line. A nice looking boy really: the grandson. The nastiness was probably only his delightful way with strangers.

But delightful or not, mused Doña Concha, closing her eyes and leaning back in the chair, he had better be careful about Pepang. And who knew? He might do Pepang good. And Edong too. Might shock them both back to life. Oh, they had been such a gay and active couple. Too gay and active, she had felt once. In the fighting to liberate the City they had lost everything— their home and their two small boys....

When Doña Concha opened her eyes again she was still holding the empty cup but she was not thinking of Pepang and Edong. She was thinking about the American. Not young New-man in particular; simply *the* American. He had been given her room, she remembered, and her clothes were in there. Before she quite realized why, she was hurrying up the stairs. Her heart pounded as she opened the door of the room; and it occurred to her, fleetingly, that all over the world where Americans were the women were surely up to some similar snooping.

Once inside the room, however, she felt disappointed. No-thing had happened here, everything was in its place. The late afternoon sunshine bristled in through the curtains. At the foot of the bed stood Newman's bag and pair of slippers. She opened a couple of the drawers of her bureau: within lay her clothes undisturbed.

She began to feel foolish, but still frightened too, the room being so quiet. She tiptoed to the door, paused there a moment and holding her breath took a quick last look around the room. She was the young Concha for a moment, going down the Pasig on the small boat, and craving (with desperate terror) to see an American.

At about that time, Pepang Camacho was standing before one of the gravestones of that old walled cemetery just outside the City where, since Spanish times, white foreigners of the Protestant faiths have been buried.

The inscription on the gravestone proclaimed it sacred to the memory of Sergeant John Emmet Newman of the United

States Army; born on May 4, 1877, in Temperance, New Hampshire; killed in action on December 2, 1899, in the Philippines.

Pepang glanced up at the American soldier standing at her side. The cool, dim graveyard, more orchard than graveyard now, roofed over almost entirely by its trees, seemed to have subdued the rancor in him. He was polite now and looked deathly tired. She had begun to like him.

She said: "It was not here he was first buried. He died out in the province. When your grandfather came over he had the remains transferred here."

"I know," murmured Newman, staring down at the gravestones. Then, as if to bring himself to, he gave his head a shake, dug his hands into his pockets and brought out matches and a rather crumpled cigarette. And as he lighted it, speaking into his cupped hands, he mumbled:

"He rests, he is quiet, he sleeps in a strange land...."

Pepang leaned forward.

"I beg your pardon?"

"Oh, nothing. You know what? I've long dreamed of coming here, of making a sort of pilgrimage to this place."

"Was he that real to you? Most grand-relatives aren't, don't you find?"

"This great-uncle and a certain unspeakable great-great-grandfather of mine, I have found much too real," boomed the American, suddenly and unexpectedly grinning down at her.

Now what? wondered Pepang, grinning back at him, though she couldn't for the life of her say what all the grinning was about; she thought the conversation solemn enough.

"Too real," sighed the American, sucking at his cigarette. "And you know another thing? They were both over here."

"The unspeakable great-great-grandfather too?"

"Him and me and this one. The three of us. One for all and all for one. I'm the third circumnavigator. Oh, grandfather Andrew was here too but he never left home. He doesn't count. Just me and my great-uncle and my great-great-grandfather."

Pepang began to feel all this was too much for her and decided to sit down. Young Newman promptly dropped down on the grass, too.

"I'm not kidding," he went on. "Ever heard of the Clippers? The ones from New England, I mean. The ships. Loveliest that ever hit the water. Well, my great-great-grandfather—he was captain of one of those. He was around these parts lots of times. Ceylon and Madagascar and the Indies. Came here to Manila to buy a cigar and stayed so long to smoke it the Spics had to call out the army to chase him away. Boy, was he mad! Told them he'd come back with a cannon and blow their walls down on them. He'd have done it too, you bet. Only he got mixed up in some other trouble down in Borneo. Went there to get the cannon and picked up the local princess for good measure. The natives chased him clear back to Salem harbor."

"Quite a character, wasn't he?" commented Pepang.

"Oh, he was a good guy. Only he didn't like New England."

"Funny way of showing his feelings."

"This one didn't either."

"Your great-uncle? Was he a character too?"

"Oh, no. He was the romantic sort. Oh, I am too. But I try not to show it."

"What was he romantic about?"

"Don't laugh. The East."

"And so he ran away on a Clipper ship and sailed off to the Orient...."

"Uh-uh. No more Clipper ships for him. Those days were over. The unspeakable captains were long dead. Ceylon and Madagascar and the Indies—they weren't even names to Americans anymore. Nothing was left of the old days except a few shawls and fans and carved idols rotting away in the attics."

"So, what did your uncle do?"

"Well, he'd go up there to the attic when he was a kid and bury his face in all that sweet-smelling stuff, whispering the names of the strange places they'd come from and trying to imagine the Puritans among the islands and bazars and temples of the East. They wouldn't fit in somehow. And then he'd go down and out to the porch and look up Main street and he'd see the Methodist church and Mr. Higgin's General Store and Ed's poolroom and a saloon, and then he'd look down Main Street and see the Baptist Church and Mr. Pelter's General Store and Kelly's poolroom and another saloon and then he'd run to his room and write down in his diary how lonely he was and practically dying of suffocation...."

"The poor kid....But I don't understand. Your grandfathers didn't need a map to tell them where Ceylon was. Or

Manila. But for their grandchildren those places weren't even names!"

"Say, when the war with Spain jolted us out of Main Street we had an idea Manila was some sort of canned goods!"

"But have you people no memories?"

"We were too busy," replied the American, somewhat dryly. "We had a huge continent to tackle and a great many other things to do besides remembering what Manila was."

"But to have forgotten at all!"

"Oh, we Americans have a genius for forgetting. Especially things that don't pay anymore. It'll be harder now, I suppose. The world has become so small. But for our primitives, it wasn't only easy, it was required. Those old Yankees weren't going to let the world upset them: they liked themselves too much as they were. The East was only a market, was only where they bought and sold and let out steam. They took care not to become a part of anything they saw. That was easy too. Their Puritan flesh was their armor. They suffered no sea-change. Or we might have been spared the reformers and the realtors. Venice became what it was because the East came to the Adriatic. But the Indies gathered at Salem harbor and Salem remained—Salem. Boston sailed to India, and came back—Boston."

And all the Bostonians will be going back Bostonians this time too, mused Pepang.

She said aloud: "You make America sound like a sort of nunnery."

"America is a sort of nunnery."

She could not help laughing at that, and the American was presently laughing with her.

He said: "You mean because we don't behave like nuns?"

She shook her head, giggling. "But, then, I don't know how Americans behave when there isn't a war around. How do they?"

"Well, we—we *behave.*"

"Boston back as Boston, eh?"

"Exactly. And that's what worried this great-uncle of mine. He thought there was something wrong about how we were built. That we didn't have pores or something. Jesus, was he glad when the War with Spain finally—"

"That comic-opera war?"

"Oh, he knew it was comic-opera all right. But for a million boys like him, it was an escape at last, a release from the boredom and the tyranny of the small towns. You should read his letters. Coming over, he could hardly sleep, he was so excited. He was sailing east at last. He'd sit around the deck watching the skies and he thought the stars looked larger and that there were more of them."

"Took a war to make him really see them, didn't it?"

"Him and a million other boys. And he thought the war might do more. Might help America become a part of the world instead of being a world to itself. That all those astonished American boys that sailed out to discover the Orient afresh might discover it for good, and that the blood they spilled here might help fix the Orient in the American imagination."

"And he was wrong?"

"Completely. He came here, he fought here, he died here, and some thirty years afterwards Manila was again an unknown quantity for Americans. Though, of course, they were quite sure it *wasn't* canned goods."

"How about now? Would you remember now?"

"No helping it that I can see. We went the hard way to discover the world and America is wherever we've made ourselves part of the earth. You can't look along Main Street now without seeing Tarawa at one end and Anzio at the other."

"You never thought, did you," smiled Pepang, "that the pilgrimage you dreamed of making to this grave would turn out so grim and so expensive?"

"Expensive is right," chuckled the American, looking rueful, "though I guess every pilgrimage is, to be worth making." And turning towards the gravestone, leaning forward and clasping his knees in his arms: "Oh, it was quite a voyage, his and mine, from that attic where the shawls and fans are. I used to go up there myself. I'd bury my face in the silks, too, and roll the strange names around on my tongue. Now, when I go home, the names won't be strange any more; they'll be American. I suppose that's what the War was about."

Rather an American assumption, thought Pepang. But she was not at all annoyed. She was sure now she liked this boy. Not only liked him, respected him. But it was getting late. And her companion seemed to have gone off into a trance, staring at the gravestone. He looks cute, really. All those blonde curls.

But my behind is sore from all this sitting. And why ever didn't I think to bring a coat? Oh, no—not the navy blue one with the fur, Josie. Not that one ever again. It's perished. Burned. . . .

And instantly, she was seeing—and hearing—their house explode into flames. That first explosion, like all the world splitting apart. . . .The minor explosions afterwards, so rapidly continuous she heard them as one roar. . . . And then, from among the flames—the loudest, clearest, keenest of all—the sound of her children's voices, the sound of her children screaming in vain. . . .

Pepang abruptly rose to her feet and the American, startled, glanced up. For a moment she could only stare back at him, biting her lips.

Then: "It's late isn't it?" she said quietly. "Shall we be going?"

The American stood up and side by side they walked slowly across the graveyard.

I'm fake, Pepang was telling herself. I'm just acting. No one can suffer like this and live. I must be making up the pain. It was alright to feel guilty once but you can't go on feeling guilty forever or you start enjoying feeling guilty. I must stop it, stop it. God doesn't let your children die a horrible death just because you played mah-jong for three years.

"Anything the matter?" inquired the American.

She smiled up and shook her head. "I was just having a little talk with myself," she said.

"Gave yourself a spanking, didn't you?"

"Why yes. How ever did you know?"

"Oh, I could see you were pretty disappointed," replied the American. Pepang stopped short and stared at him.

"Disappointed! What do you mean?"

"Oh, come now. I'm a disappointment, ain't I? I did none of the things you expected me to do, didn't I? I snatched no kisses, made no passes. You've been waiting all afternoon for me to love you up. Now, you're bawling yourself out because I didn't, aren't you?"

Pepang Camacho felt herself go rigid, her hands arrested at her breast, the blood burning slowly up to her lifted face. All the world had suddenly become so quiet she could hear her heart beating.

When the seventh extremely loaded bus refused to stop for him, Edong decided to walk home. It was dusk by then and getting chilly. He rolled down his shirt sleeves and turned up the collar. Impossible to hurry through those teeming sidewalks. The pavement was intermittent; the street, plowed rubble. And how limply the City sprawled under the night; propped up with sticks and tin-sheets; gaudy with fresh paint; festooned with colored lights; and screaming hysterically.

But his flesh thrilled, his eyes blurred to see all these people—crowding home, or to the shows and night clubs, or just ambling around; the soldiers and sailors bumping past in twos and threes, linked arm in arm and roaring out a song—or boozing in the bars, or packed in front of shop-windows, or dancing boisterously in the cabarets, or seated comatose on the curb; while the army cars thundered down the streets, the MP's waving and whistling, and the shrill street-boys combed through the crowd hawking eggs, cigarettes, beer, combs, watches, K-rations, Vick's, pomade, GI clothes, fountain pens, mentholatum, matches, magazines, and all of post-war Manila's confusion of newspapers.

He loved it all—all the people and the noise they made. He felt exultant. Be happy! he cried to them in his heart. We have come through! We are alive! We *live!*

Oh, nothing should mar, nothing spoil this fresh beginning, this new life, he thought, bumping now against a pavement-stall. For this was a new life, wasn't it? Not just a taking up where we left off when the Japs came?

The shameful and shameless greed, frivolity, and hardheartedness of the war years—people turned their eyes away from all that now, piously shuddering. Shocking, they agreed. But what could you expect? The War was to blame. The War and the Japs. Everything—and everybody—had been so good before. But you know what war does to people, tch, tch. And so it's always because the war this and the war that; because the Japs this and the Japs that.

Oh, willfully blind, blind, blind!

As if the war had brought up anything new. As if the war had taught us anything we weren't past masters in. As if the war hadn't merely swollen to insanity the feverish, ferocious, fear-haunted, hate-breeding, money-worship, food-worship, comfort-worship, and pleasure-worship of the years before the war;

the criminal greeds and cynical grafts that fester when the spirit rots. The war had merely bloated what corruption was already there.

I should know, he thought grimly, turning now into his own street. I was at all the wrong shrines, wasn't I? And seeing Newman's jeep parked at the curb, he thought of Pepang, of their marriage, of all the bitter brawls before the war, when they would come home in the small hours dead-tired, drunk and savagely disgusted with everything. They had become practically strangers to each other during the war years; himself off all day to all the big buy-and-sell sprees where the big money you made vanished quicker than you could count it, herself off to all the big mah-jong sprees where the big money you won melted faster than you could stack it.

And going up the garden path, he thought of their children, their two boys, dead among the debris of that world. We made a wrong start, he thought, Pepang and I, and our children paid for it. An overwhelming sense of guilt had brought them together again, kept them together now. Not a very healthy emotion, maybe. But we can start from there, can't we? Had already started, rather, he amended, going up the porchstairs. For they were living very carefully now. Keeping away from the old crowd, renouncing the old frivolities. Not stepping out except to early Mass daily; and in the evenings, to take the air, the two of them, hand in hand and not talking much. Himself in denim pants, now, walking home from a small steady job; Pepang washing dishes and not wearing her nails like before. . . . Oh, God in heaven, keep us trying! he prayed as he reached the doorknob. But the door opened and Doña Concha came out and closed the door behind her.

"Has something happened, mother?" he asked, startled by the look on her face.

"Nothing. Except our American is leaving."

"Oh, why?"

"I know nothing. Pepang came home alone. Something wrong with the jeep, she told me. The American just arrived. How he frightened me, Eduardo. *'I'm getting the hell out of here!'* he shouted at me when I opened the door to him. Then he stormed upstairs to get his clothes."

They heard the American coming down the stairs and lowered their voices.

"What does Pepang say?" asked Edong.

"To let him go at once and with no fuss. She does not intend to be present."

They heard the American inside put down his bag and strike a match.

"You need not see him either," said Doña Concha, worried. "I will say you have not arrived."

But her son-in-law had already pushed the door and entered.

Young Newman, freshly capped and uniformed, was standing at the foot of the stairs, lighting a cigarette. He did not look up as Edong approached.

"Leaving, Newman? Weren't you staying for the weekend?"

"Hi there, chap. No, I'm afraid I can't. One or two things I forgot about. Sorry."

He picked up his bag.

"But must you go at once? You haven't had supper, have you?"

"Skip it. I'm not hungry."

"Okay, Newman, I won't press you. But drop in again soon, will you? The house is yours anytime you're in town. Of course, you write your grandfather?"

"Sometimes," replied the American, smiling at his cigarette.

"Well, give him my best wishes. Do you think he'll be coming back here soon?"

"I don't know," said the American, still pondering his cigarette, his eyes hooded. "I don't know really. I'm not even sure he's coming back at all. But look here, guy, you shouldn't have gone through all this trouble of being so nice to me just so I'd be sure to mention your name next time I wrote him."

Edong's face went blank.

"Because," continued the American, looking up, his voice curt, his eyes frosty, "I don't write my grandfather very often anyway, and the next time I do I'll be extra careful *not* to mention your name."

He flung the cigarette to the floor, trod on it, and moved to the door.

"That was pretty low, though," he added, pausing at the door, his hand on the knob, "throwing your wife at me like that. You don't want the job that bad, do you?"

He opened the door and stepped out.

Doña Concha, who was standing at the top of the porch-stairs, looking out at the street, wheeled around.

"And you, señora," said the American, pausing to doff his cap, "you had no objections to having your daughter thus employed. Yours is a delightful family! How I regret I must leave so soon." When she turned her back on him, he cocked an eyebrow, shrugged, and pulled on his cap. He said: "Adios, señora, and next time don't pick a New England Yankee. They've got the damnedest nose for a rat."

He strode down the porchstairs and up the garden-path, hopped into the jeep and drove away.

Doña Concha hurried inside. Edong was still standing at the foot of the stairs. She started to say something nasty, changed her mind on seeing his face and walked off to the kitchen.

Pepang was sitting on a stool beside the sink, peeling pota-toes.

"Has he gone?" she asked as her mother entered.

Doña Concha was feeling furious but she noticed just the same that, since arriving, her daughter had brushed and rolled up her hair and that her lips and eyebrows were crisply and vividly defined.

"Perhaps," began the old woman, "you are now in the mood, Josefa, to explain what the devil that man was so of-fended about?"

"About nothing that is true," replied her daughter, dropping the last peeled potato into a bowl on the sink. Smiling smugly to herself, she laid down the knife and began gathering in a heap the peelings on her lap. "You see, mother," she began, but seeing her husband enter she sprang up, scattering the peelings to the floor, ran to him and twined her arms around his neck. "Ed, darling," she whispered, brushing her lips along his cheek, "let's step out tonight."

"Step out? Where?"

"Anywhere. Night club or something."

"But what on earth for?"

She burst into laughter.

"Oh, Ed, Ed! We *have* changed!" And tweaking his nose: "Imagine you asking such a question! I want to go dancing, darling. Boy, do I feel like painting the town this red!" she cried, flaunting her fingernails before his eyes.

Within a month, Pepang and Edong Camacho were looking, talking, and behaving so much like their old prewar selves that one might wonder, as Doña Concha found herself *almost* wondering, if there had really been a war to interrupt them. It was presently even harder to recall the interlude of spiritual nakedness, of tears and heart-searching, when they had desired to hide themselves, inarticulate for once, and avoiding each other's eyes. Doña Concha could only conclude that the times discouraged normality. One had to be either in sackcloth and ashes, or painting the town red. And the lives of the many people who were soon infesting the house at all hours seemed to her a continual and violent propulsion between the extremes, equally hysterical, of penitence and whoopee. She could now ruefully recall having once hoped young Newman might shock Pepang and Edong back to life: he had proved too effective. And he had done something else. He had made Doña Concha feel old.

Upon being explained his behavior, she had felt incredulous; then amused; then, rather touched; and finally, old.

That a total stranger should expect to be welcomed and loved strictly for himself alone—that was incredible. And funny. But, apparently, young Newman had so expected, and had held out against them from the first, suspecting beforehand that their welcome of him was not disinterested. But what welcome, what affection in this world is entirely disinterested? The most immolated nun still thinks of heaven when she thinks of God. Was this the *absurdum* of Yanqui innocence? Certainly the rest of the world had long learned to take for granted that no prayer is pure piety, no kiss pure affection, no alms pure benevolence, and that even the noblest act of sacrifice is selfish somewhere.

Edong did say—and all of them did hope, being "realists"—that "it might pay to be as nice as possible to old Newman's grandson." But that was not the sole reason, not even a principal one. They had tried to be as nice as possible chiefly because he was the grandson of an old friend of the family; and because he was a stranger in the land; and because he was an American; and because he was a soldier in the army that had liberated them and they wished to express their gratitude; and because they had become thoughtful through suffering and were feeling profoundly human for the first time in their lives.

That was not enough, of course. She had had experience of innocence and knew how stubbornly it refuses to bargain, to compromise, or (when the rest of us wink and bear it) to be cheated of a grain. And in her heart she knew it to be right. Impossible, yes, its dream of perfect charity; impossible the people who measured reality by the dream. Impossible but not mistaken; though the reality of human relationships be a shameful traffic in profits. The 'realists' took what they could get; the dreamers, demanding the true measure of nothing, usually got nothing. That was better than the spoiled commodity the 'realists' always ended up with—the dropped crumbs of love that so quickly became ashes in the mouth.... To be loved for oneself—that was what the speechlessness of babies demanded of the grown-up heart. And surely she had seen everything when a big full-grown man demanded to be accepted as one accepts a child.

All this made Doña Concha feel—for the first time in her sixty years—old.

Not as old, however, as her son-in-law often felt now.

Edong Camacho had found easy the abrupt emotional about-face. It had only proved something he was always forgetting and learning afresh: that it was Pepang who set the pace of their lives and that he could stay sincere in a certain emotion only as long as she chose to share it with him. The moment she refused to feel guilty anymore, the weight of the past vanished. Since there was no more past, you could do as you pleased. To do as you pleased, you had to know as many clever people as possible. To know as many clever people as possible, you had to be a "live wire." And a "live wire" does not plod away at a small steady job with so many opportunities around to make big money the quick way.

And yet, while acting the "live wire" for all he was worth, he felt old. Though the past no longer weighed on his shoulders it was still around somewhere—outside, peering in at windows; or lurking in corners and in the pauses of talk; or, in the morning, when you first opened your eyes, leaning over you, staring and swiftly disappearing. And when people said how nice that they had started going around again and how brave they were and showed the right spirit not allowing what those monkeys did to ruin their lives but getting right up again to business as usual and not moping at home with the blinds down and that private grief is rather selfish at times like these, don't you think —or when he heard them say that yes, those were Pepang and

Edong Camacho who lost both their children; and yes, they took it rather hard at first, shut themselves up in at her mother's house and wouldn't see anybody and we all thought they would go mad; and yes, thank God, they're back to normal now and have learned to be plucky about what happened like all of us and looking very much like their old selves, don't you think?— he felt violently nauseated and had to dig his fists into his pockets to keep from bashing their faces.

For these people meant by grief, mere vindictiveness; by courage, callousness; by business as usual, dirty business; and it was now they had gone mad, Pepang and himself, who recently were so sane and healthy, or anyway, had had a chance to be really sane and healthy but had thrown the chance away and now were indeed "back to normal."

And he understood now the cold shock of guilt and shame that had paralyzed him on hearing young Newman's words of contempt and accusation. Hearing those words and knowing them to be false; knowing Newman to be wrong, to have misunderstood, and that they had welcomed him because they felt it their duty and not because they had an axe to grind; knowing his conscience clear and his intentions innocent he had yet known, at the same moment, with the same sureness, and with a paralyzing immediacy of guilt and shame, that the American spoke right and that somehow, in some deep and obscure manner—simply by existing, perhaps; simply by being the sort of people they were—they had injured, they had insulted young Newman.

He did not tell Pepang this. He was afraid she would laugh and not understand. He was wrong. Pepang would have completely understood. And she would not have laughed. For this was how she had felt herself that afternoon in the graveyard. But where Edong had been paralyzed cold, she had felt stung alive, blazing.

Besides, she was the sort of person who, on being accused of anything nasty, justly or not, promptly and gaily goes forth to provide the accusation with all the grounds it needed. If she was the scheming harlot the American thought her, then she was also a big hypocrite. The American had been wrong in his assumptions. But by the time she had finished making herself over to prove those assumptions correct she could no longer determine whether she had ever been sincere in her period of penitence.

Anyway, she had ceased to care. She had often been described as shallow, as liking only shallow people; an appraisal that succeeded in worrying her in other days. Not now; not anymore. This first experience with a "deep one" was enough. She would never again care to go below. Now, as before, she would deal with people only on the surface, giving of herself and asking of them only the self we wear at parties, take to the movies, and generally offer to the public, because it is worthless, easy to please, impossible to insult, and completely superficial.

She was especially cautious with Americans, though the post-Newman varieties relieved her mind by being precisely what they looked like: desperately tired and homesick boys wanting to be amused. Still, she was taking no chances, and with even the most apparently inarticulate prepared herself against the possibility of a chasm exploding suddenly wide open where his grin had stood before. Newman and herself were quits now, she would think at such moments, for as she feared, in each American, a lurking Newman, so he must have feared, in each Filipino, even before that dismal week end, the Camachos lurking in ambush. And, she would mentally hoot, I bet he now keeps his wallet in an iron pouch—along with his virginity!

Which is unjust.

Newman's increased mail home, mostly because of the Camachos, can prove that their effect on him was not so elementary; was, possibly, as racking as his effect on them.

There were (he wrote, in a letter to his mother) *no signs they felt revolted by what they were doing. They were perfectly at ease. If I hadn't been so mean as to spoil their game, they would probably have patted themselves on the back afterwards for having been so hospitable and at the same time so provident.*

And yet I keep feeling I was wrong somewhere. Maybe their ideas about honesty are not the same as ours, and how judge them at all in that case? Or maybe it's just because I'm an American. You can't imagine, Mom, how hard it is for Americans over here to get themselves taken for human beings. We're not just Tom, Dick and Harry to them. We're the richest nation in the world. We're Packards, and Hollywood, and Camel cigarettes, and Harvard, and B-29's, and Sunkist oranges, and the Empire State Building. But we're not people. We're the happy hunting ground. We're the dollar-sign made flesh. And they can't think of us except in terms of the profits we mean to them. Maybe they're not really mercenary. But our being this rich and this lavish makes them so. We're afflicted with something like that curse on Midas: we corrupt what we touch.

Look how far I've traveled again from the Camachos. Trouble is whenever I start on that family I find myself digging up everything I ever thought and everything that ever happened to me as if to justify how I acted. I feel there was something about them I missed. I was too busy at the time playing detective and looking sardonic. But I surely figured them wrong somewhere because now when I try to put them together the way they should go if I was right, the pieces don't fit. It worries me. . . .

Newman had evidently gone on worrying: a month later he was writing his mother again on the subject.

I can't sleep (he wrote). *I keep seeing that girl's face, and her husband's. I can't begin to imagine the enormity of what I did, supposing I was wrong. And something tells me I was. Those people did want to be nice. And simply because they were nice people. They wanted to like me, wanted me to like them. And I brushed off their attempts at friendship. I flung their hospitality in their faces. I messed up everything with all my damnable suspicions, dratted cuss that I am. And it's such a hopeless circle, Mom. First, you botch all relations with other people by being so difficult and wary, then you worry yourself to death wondering if you hurt somebody. Yes, I know, I wouldn't have all those Puritan ancestors if I didn't worry. But remember how I boasted it would be me riding them and not them riding me? I was so confident, wasn't I? I could make fun of all the Yankee Marco Polos that went everywhere, saw nothing, and understood less. I laughed at you when you told me about your running away to New York and Art, and then to Paris and more Art, and finally giving up and coming back to Temperance, New Hampshire, because anyway that was where you had always been. Well, it's your turn to laugh now, Mom. I'm coming home on the same boat myself. I never left home, either. And me telling that girl about the attic and how when I came home the things there wouldn't be strange anymore. No wonder she called me batty. But now that we're back to those*

people, what do I do about them? For either I do something—
and quick—or I burst. No use warning me to think it over
some more. I'll have to see them again soon. And crawl....

So, about four months after his first encounter with the
Camachos, Doña Concha burst into her daughter's room and
announced that "the American" had come back.

"Which one?" asked Pepang. She was sitting on the bed
in her chemise, polishing her nails, and she went right on polishing them.

"Which one?" echoed Doña Concha blankly. "Why, the
first one of course. The Newman. Old Andrew's grandson."

"Newman!" And her husband coming in from the bathroom at the moment, rubbing his hair in a towel: "Do you hear
that, Ed? Young Newman has come back.... Where is he,
mother? What did he say?"

"I have not yet talked with him. He is waiting downstairs.
The maid let him in and told me. But I saw him arrive. I was
in my room looking out the window."

"My God!" moaned Edong, collapsing on a chair. "But why
has he come again?"

Doña Concha threw him and her daughter a scornful glance.
She said: "The man has, of course, come to apologize."

"*Apologize!*" gasped Pepang and Edong together.

"Naturally," said Doña Concha, "having realized his offense. He brings flowers and a box. Of candy, perhaps. Oh, the
boy shows himself of a good heart. He is not above confessing
an error and begging for pardon."

"But he must not do any such thing!" cried Pepang, rising,
trembling slightly, brush in hand.

"Oh, God, no!" groaned Edong, rising too, and flinging the
towel away.

"But why not?" demanded Doña Concha. "Why not, if he
wants to, if he feels a need for it? It would make him feel
good."

"Only for the moment," said Pepang bitterly, dropping the
brush on the bed and pressing her palms against her cheeks.
"Afterwards, he would feel ashamed. Ashamed and disgusted.
It would make him hate us more."

"But this is your own heart that you let speak for him!"
taunted her mother. "You assume too much, Josefa, that the man

would react as you would. But perhaps he possesses a conscience. Perhaps he understands the dignity of penitence and of the desire to be forgiven. And you yourself, a few months ago, when you were still in your senses, even you would have understood such a desire; you would have respected it; you would not have babbled all this about hate and shame and disgust."

Pepang listened, quite still, her palms pressed against her cheeks, her eyelids faintly flickering. Then, she looked at her husband. Edong was standing still too, staring at his feet. She knew he could feel her looking at him but would not lift his eyes. She smiled—her smug, crafty smile—picked up the brush, sat down on the bed, and, briskly resuming the polishing of her nails, said:

"Listen, mother; you too, Ed. Why all this holy solemnity? This boy, when he first came here, had a very unpleasant time. Through no fault of ours, yes. But still he suffered. We are all agreed, I suppose, that he is to suffer no further unpleasantness in this house if we can prevent it. And whatever you say, mother, having to apologize is a highly unpleasant business. Just because we bear him a grudge is no—"

"I bear him *no* grudge!" interrupted her mother.

"Very well, you bear him no grudge. All of us bear him no grudge. Then, why make him go through such a painful comedy at all?"

"Certain formalities," promptly answered her mother, "are established and must be respected. Oh, we made a grave mistake the first time in not standing fast by convention. You went out alone with him and what conclusion did he draw? Now, we must stand rigid. He is in Rome, he must do as the Romans."

"We are to butcher him then," smiled Pepang, "to provide Rome a holiday? I thought you bore him no grudge, mother! No, no. The tactful, the truly polite thing to do is to ignore what happened previously and—"

"You do not cancel the past," broke in her mother, "simply by ignoring it."

"Perhaps not. But, anyway, we can pretend to ourselves that we are meeting him for the—"

"If he is not to apologize to me," again interrupted Doña Concha, "I will not see him."

Rising, to put an end to all this nonsense, and crossing to her dressing table, Pepang said, firmly: "He is not to apologize to anybody and you need not see him, mother."

"I *refuse* to see him!" the old woman corrected her, sweeping furiously out of the room.

"And now to get dressed," breathed Pepang, springing to action: and as she hurried into her frock: "Whatever are you waiting for, Ed? That boy has been sweating it out, you know, while we blabbed....Come on, get up; you're sitting on my stockings. And will you please omit the misery from your face? You're not going to be difficult, too, are you?"

"I only want to know," said her husband, rising reluctantly, "how we are to act towards him if he is not to apologize."

Pepang groaned.

"We act," she patiently explained, as she pulled on the stockings, "exactly as if he were any other American. You should know the routine by now. Only, we talk louder, funnier, and we hog the conversation. Give him as few openings as possible. Especially when it looks as if he wanted to bring up what happened. That's absolutely taboo. So, clap down quick. As far as we're concerned we are seeing him for the first time. Though heaven save me from anything like that first one!... Funny how long ago it seems now. Ages, really....Oh, well, I guess it's all part of one's education. Throw me my shoes, will you?"

When Pepang came down, young Newman was sitting in the parlor, holding a bunch of flowers and a box on his lap. He stood up to greet her and she immediately asked him to sit down again; told him how nice he was looking; asked him, as she sat down beside him on the sofa, if he didn't find this sudden heat spell killing; laughingly deplored how she looked and hoped he would excuse her and said she practically lived in the bathroom these days; which reminded her of Bougainville and all those places and was it true they did nothing but take showers out in the rain and how about the women there and how awful and did he know a certain McCoy, a Jimmy McCoy of the 37th, and she began to tell him a very funny story about this guy when he was still in Brooklyn.

When Edong came in bearing a tray of drinks, Newman stood up again but they made him sit down and Edong said he didn't find it a hell of a climate and that he had the medicine for that right here and what poison did Newman prefer and Pepang laughed and hoped he wasn't on any sort of wagon and Edong passed the glasses around and declared that no wagons of any sort were allowed in the City because of the military traffic. Then they spent four minutes arguing whom to toast and Pepang said Yamashita certainly deserved toasting but Edong said the devil was going to take care of that and they finally just tossed down the drinks without toasting anybody and Edong filled the glasses again and lighted cigarettes for everybody while Pepang resumed her story about Jimmy McCoy and somehow managed to get Newman to rid his lap of the embarrassingly conspicuous box and flowers without mentioning them.

Before this combined onslaught of the Camachos, Newman at first seemed rather startled; then, increasingly mystified. He strove, now and then, to break through the barrage, but the Camachos were vigilant on all sides, blocking him in. He seemed to give up finally; his wondering face went blank. When, after a while, the blankness twisted itself into the sardonic expression he had worn with such relish the first time, Pepang, honestly surprised (she had not expected to produce this particular effect) stumbled for a moment and floundered about in her talk. Why should she worry? It was a relief rather. And she signalled Edong that the point of greatest danger was past: they could relax.

Edong promptly slumped in his chair, glass in hand, and grinned savagely. Each time his eyes chanced to meet the American's, his belly heaved and water sourly swelled in his mouth.

When Newman finally rose to leave, Edong noticed that he did not offer to shake hands, and thought: I'll be damned if I got up. He contented himself with merely bobbing his head and grinning. But the box and the flowers still lay on the sofa and Newman seemed unable to go without disposing them. Pepang solved that one by picking up the flowers herself.

"For me? How nice of you, Joe. They're lovely. What's in the box?"

"Candy," replied Newman; and as they moved to the door: "But why Joe? You know my name."

"All Americans are Joe to me," drawled Pepang as they stepped out to the porch.

"Don't you try to distinguish?"

"Uh-uh. I stopped trying, long ago.... Well, goodbye again—Joe. Take extra good care of yourself. You're going home, you know. No more boozing, no more late hours. Have a pleasant voyage. And try not to think evil of us."

The American hesitated on the porchstairs.

"I did, you know, the first time," he finally blurted out.

Pepang felt her heart lose a beat but managed to say at once, lightly: "And now you've found out you were mistaken?"

"I've found out," said the American, looking her in the eye, "that I was *not* mistaken after all."

And that, mused Pepang when the jeep had driven away, is what I get for being so damn considerate.

She marched into the house, dumped the flowers in one chair and herself on another, and asked Edong to pour her a stiff one.

"That was the cruelest thing I ever did," he moaned as he handed her the glass.

She said: *"Please.* Nobody found it a picnic," and gulped down the drink.

"Your mother was right," pursued Edong, looking miserable. "We should have let him apologize."

"Okay, *okay!* We were wrong again. But we were only trying to spare him a lousy time, weren't we? What's wrong about that, I'd like to know."

"Us!" cried Edong savagely. *"Ourselves! What we are!"*

"Oh, you make me sick. You and your eternal breastbeating."

"We weren't trying to save *him* a lousy time. We were trying to save ourselves a lousy time. We knew we would have suffered like hell to have him apologize to us. And why, sweetheart, why? Because we know we're worthless; because we know we're corrupt, because we know we're—"

"I do not!" snapped Pepang. "Will you stop howling nonsense?"

"What do you want me to do? Sing the praises of what we are? Extol my cowardice? Extol your bitchiness?"

"You can *stop* screaming, that's *what* you can do!" screamed Pepang, rising and hurling the glass in his face.

And Doña Concha, upstairs in her room saying her beads, jumped up to hear the screams and the glass breaking. It has happened at last, she told herself. This was the couple's first fight since their resumption of the normal life. She had felt it coming a long time. And the American who had marked off one phase in their lives now marked the end of another. The period of readjustment was over. Pepang and Edong were now completely back to normal.

And if to be mad was now to be normal, thought Doña Concha, sitting down and resuming her beads, then it was futile indeed to preach moderation, and too late for moderate cures. The pattern of society, mutilated by war as it was, had better be pulled loose altogether. How now invoke the ties that bind men when all human intercourse was an infection? A plague was abroad and a plague calls for quarantine. Herded together, men rotted each other; apart, their own loneliness might heal and purify them. It was time again, thought Doña Concha, for the cell of the ascetic and the cave of the anchorite. Time again for harsh hermits to lead the populace out of the cities and to disperse them among the wastes of the desert. Thus had the world saved itself once from the violence of its own disgust with itself. Disciplined and rejuvenated by solitude, tears, fasting, silence and wrestlings with devils, it had emerged to discover, with awkward awe and astonishment, the green of the leaves and the joy of human companionship. Had emerged to discover and to adore Salvation as a Woman (whether virgin or mother) and, enthroned in her arms, Deity as a Child. How long before the world would be fit again to make that discovery? wondered Doña Concha, hearing another glass break, downstairs and Pepang shrieking. It would take a long time, she feared, considering that the world had fallen so low there were no more women these days. No more women and no more children, grimly concluded Doña Concha, rising and going off to fetch ammonia and mercurochrome.

As for the young Newman, one would have thought this final encounter would mean something really final. But, with a New England Yankee, one apparently never touches bottom. For, in the last letter he was to write his mother before embarking, and in the middle of such an important announcement as the precise date on which he expected to arrive in Temperance, New Hampshire, he was to jolt that former Paris expatriate by abruptly breaking off and resuming on the Camachos.

You never know (he wrote) *just what you expect people to do at a certain moment until the moment occurs and they don't do it. I think it funny now to have brought along candy and flowers but only because I have realized that, after how I acted the other time, if I ever dared show up again they would naturally (if they were really innocent) and promptly have done certain things—like slapping my face, breaking my neck, and throwing me out of the window. When they came down instead with grins a mile wide and started trying to get me all hot and confused by giving me the 50-caliber-talk-stuff and winking at each other all the time—why, I started smelling that rat again, all the way from Denmark....*

It's a strange thing alright, to be an American. But maybe it's just as strange and difficult to be other people. Trouble is we Americans act as if we owned a patent on strangeness. We do any number of things that must annoy and flabbergast other people and we do them as if it were our duty to annoy and flabbergast others. But we don't like to find other people's actions annoying or flabbergasting in any way. We take for granted that anybody that's civilized at all and smart acts like an American. It will surely take a █ *of time, goodwill and labor before no people are strange to* █ *er people and nobody's a foreigner anywhere. We Americ* █ *s don't exactly hasten the process by being so awe-struck b* █ *the strangeness of us.*

You will gather from all this that my mind's not yet at ease about the Camachos. It isn't. I still think I was wrong somewhere, that there was some vital item I missed. I feel now they were struggling to reach over to where I was but had to grope and grope because, as usual, I had sullenly turned off the lights too soon. And yes, Mom, it worries me....

Philippine-American
March 1946

THE STORY OF A LETTER

CARLOS BULOSAN

When my brother Berto was thirteen he ran away from home and went to Manila. We did not hear from him until eight years later, and he was by that time working in a little town in California. He wrote a letter in English, but we could not read it. Father carried it in his pocket all summer, hoping the priest in our village would read it for him.

The summer ended gloriously and our work on the farm was done. We gathered firewood and cut grass on the hillsides for our animals. The heavy rains came when we were patching up the walls of our house. Father and I wore palm overcoats and worked in the mud, rubbing vinegar on our foreheads and throwing it around us to keep the lightning away. The rains ceased suddenly, but the muddy water came down from the mountains and flooded the river.

We made a bamboo raft and floated slowly along on the water. Father sat in the center of the raft and took the letter from his pocket. He looked at it for a long time, as though he were committing it to memory. When we reached the village church it was midnight, but there were many people in the yard. We tied our raft to the riverbank and dried our clothes on the grass.

A woman came and told us that the priest had died of over-eating at a wedding. Father took our clothes off the grass and we put them on. We untied our raft and rowed against the slow currents back to our house. Father was compelled to carry the letter for another year, waiting for a time when my brother Nicasio would come home from school. He was the only one in our family who could read and write.

When the students returned from the cities, Father and I went to town with a sack of peanuts. We stood under the arbor tree in the station and watched every bus that stopped. We

heated a pile of dry sand with burning stones and roasted peanuts. At night we sat in the coffee shop and talked with the
loafers and gamblers. Then the last student arrived, but my
brother Nicasio was not with them. We gave up waiting and
went back to the village.

When the summer came again we plowed the land and
planted corn. Then we were informed that my brother Nicasio
had gone to America. Father was greatly disappointed. He took
the letter of my brother Berto from his pocket and locked it
in a small box. We put our minds on our work and after two
years the letter was forgotten.

Toward the end of my ninth year, a tubercular young man
appeared in our village. He wanted to start a school for the
children and the men were enthusiastic. The drummer went
around the village and announced the good news. The farmers
gathered in a vacant lot not far from the cemetery and started
building a schoolhouse. They shouted at one another with joy
and laughed aloud. The wind carried their laughter through
the village.

I saw them at night lifting the grass roof on their shoulders. I ran across the fields and stood by the well, watching
them place the rafters on the long bamboo posts. The men
were stripped to the waist and their cotton trousers were rolled
up to their thighs. The women came with their earthen jars
and hauled drinking water, pausing in the clear moonlight to
watch the men with secret joy.

Then the schoolhouse was finished. I heard the bell ring
joyfully in the village. I ran to the window and saw boys and
girls going to school. I saw Father on our carabao, riding off
toward our house. I took my straw hat off the wall and rushed
to the gate.

Father bent down and reached for my hands. I sat behind
him on the bare back of the animal. The children shouted and
slapped their bellies. When we reached the schoolyard the carabao stopped without warning. Father fell to the ground and
rolled into the well, screaming aloud when he touched the
water. I grabbed the animal's tail and hung on to it till it rolled
on its back in the dust.

I rushed to the well and lowered the wooden bucket. I tied
the rope to the post and shouted for help. Father climbed
slowly up the rope to the mouth of the well. The bigger boys

came down and helped me pull Father out. He stood in the sun and shook the water off his body. He told me to go into the schoolhouse with the other children.

We waited for the teacher to come. Father followed me inside and sat on a bench behind me. When the teacher arrived we stood as one person and waited for him to be seated. Father came to my bench and sat quietly for a long time. The teacher started talking in our dialect, but he talked so fast we could hardly understand him.

When he had distributed some little Spanish books, Father got up and asked what language we would learn. The teacher told us that it was Spanish. Father asked him if he knew English. He said he knew only Spanish and our dialect. Father took my hand and we went out of the schoolhouse. We rode the carabao back to our house.

Father was disappointed. He had been carrying my brother's letter for almost three years now. It was still unread. The suspense was hurting him and me, too. He wanted me to learn English so that I would be able to read it to him. It was the only letter he had received in all the years that I had known him, except some letters that came from the government asking him to pay his taxes.

When the rain ceased, a strong typhoon came from the North and swept away the schoolhouse. The teacher gave up teaching and married a village girl. Then he took up farming and after two years his wife gave birth to twins. The men in the village never built a schoolhouse again.

I grew up suddenly and the desire to see other places grew. It moved me like a flood. It was impossible to walk a kilometer away from our house without wanting to run away to the city. I tried to run away a few times but whenever I reached the town, the farm always called me back. I could not leave Father because he was getting old.

Then our farm was taken away from us. I decided to go to town for a while and live with Mother and my two little sisters. Father remained in the village. He came to town once with a sack of wild tomatoes and bananas. But the village called him back again.

I left our town and travelled to other places. I went to Baguio in the northern part of the Philippines and worked in the marketplace posing naked for American tourists who seemed

to enjoy the shameless nudity of the natives. An American
woman, who claimed that she had come from Texas, took me
to Manila.

She was a romantic painter. When we arrived in the capital
she rented a nice large house where the sun was always shining.
There were no children of my age. There were men and women
who never smiled. They spoke through their noses. The painter
from Texas asked me to undress every morning; she worked
industriously. I had never dreamed of making a living by
exposing my body to a stranger. That experience made me roar
with laughter for many years.

One time, while I was still in the woman's house, I remembered the wide ditch near our house in the village where the
young girls used to take a bath in the nude. A cousin of mine
stole the girls' clothes and then screamed behind the bushes.
The girls ran about with their hands between their legs. I
thought of this incident when I felt shy, hiding my body with
my hands from the woman painter. When I had saved a little
money I took a boat for America.

I forgot my village for a while. Then I went to a hospital
and lay in bed for two years. I started to read books with
hunger. My reading was started by a nurse who thought I had
come from China. I lied to her without thinking of it, but I told
a good lie. I had no opportunity to learn when I was outside
in the world but the security and warmth of the hospital gave
it to me. I languished in bed for two years with great pleasure.
I was no longer afraid to live in a strange world and among
strange peoples.

Then at the end of the first year, I remembered the letter
of my brother Berto. I crept out of bed and went to the bathroom. I wrote a letter to Father asking him to send the letter
to me for translation. I wanted to translate it, so that it would
be easy for him to find a man in our village to read it to him.

The letter arrived six months later. I translated it into
our dialect and sent it back with the original. I was now better.
The doctors told me that I could go out of the hospital. I used
to stand by the window for hours asking myself why I had
forgotten to laugh in America. I was afraid to go out into the
world. I had been confined too long. I had forgotten what it was
like on the outside.

I had been brought to the convalescent ward when the civil war in Spain started some three years before. Now, after the peasants' and workers' government was crushed, I was physically ready to go out into the world and start a new life. There was some indignation against fascism in all civilized lands. To most of us, however, it was the end of a great cause.

I stood at the gate of the hospital, hesitating. Finally, I closed my eyes and walked into the city. I wandered all over Los Angeles for some time, looking for my brothers. They had been separated from me since childhood. We had had, separately and together, a bitter fight for existence. I had heard that my brother Nicasio was in Santa Barbara, where he was attending college. Berto, who never stayed in one place for more than three months at a time, was rumored to be in Bakersfield waiting for the grape season.

I packed my suitcase and took a bus to Santa Barbara. I did not find my brother there. I went to Bakersfield and wandered in the streets asking for my brother. I went to Chinatown and stood in line for the free chop-suey that was served in the gambling houses to the loafers and gamblers. I could not find my brother in either town. I went to the vineyards looking for him. I was convinced that he was not in that valley. I took a bus for Seattle.

The hiring halls were full of men waiting to be shipped to the canneries in Alaska. I went to the dancehalls and poolrooms. But I could not find my brothers. I took the last boat to Alaska and worked there for three months. I wanted to save money so that I could have something to spend when I returned to the mainland.

When I came back to the West Coast, I took a bus to Portland. Beyond Tacoma, near the district where the Indians used to force the hop pickers into marriage, I looked out the window and saw my brother Berto in a beer tavern. I knew it was my brother although I had not seen him for many years. There was something in the way he had turned his head toward the bus that made me think I was right. I stopped at the next town and took another bus back to Tacoma. But he was already gone.

I took another bus and went to California. I stopped in Delano. The grape season was in full swing. There were many workers in town. I stood in the poolrooms and watched the players. I went to a beer place and sat in a booth. I ordered several bottles and thought long and hard of my life in America.

Toward midnight a man in a big overcoat came in and sat beside me. I asked him to drink beer with me without looking at his face. We started drinking together and then suddenly, I saw a familiar face in the dirty mirror on the wall. I almost screamed. He was my brother Nicasio—but he had grown old and emaciated. We went outside and walked to my hotel.

The landlady met me with a letter from the Philippines. In my room I found that my letter to Father, when I was in the hospital, and the translation of my brother Berto's letter to him, had been returned to me. It was the strangest thing that had ever happened. I had never lived in Delano before. I had never given my forwarding address to anybody. The letter was addressed to me at a hotel I had never seen before.

It was now ten years since my brother Berto had written the letter to Father. It was eighteen years since he had run away from home. I stood in the center of my room and opened it. The note attached to it said that Father had died some years before. It was signed by the postmaster of my town.

I bent down and read the letter—the letter that had driven me away from my village and had sent me halfway around the world—read it the very day a letter came from the government telling me that my brother Berto was already serving in the Navy—and the same day that my brother Nicasio was waiting to be inducted into the Army. I held the letter in my hand, and, suddenly, I started to laugh—choking with tears at the mystery and wonder of it all.

"*Dear Father* (my brother wrote):

America is a great country. Tall buildings. Wide good land. The people walking. But I feel sad. I am writing you this hour of my sentimental.

Your son,
Berto"

RETURN TO CAPAS

Ligaya Victorio Reyes

You draw your mourning cape more closely about you, embarrassed by all the attention. You gently, unobtrusively spread your rouge more evenly upon your cheeks. You bite your lips which are parching in the wind then carefully rub the corner of your handkerchief to the edges of your front teeth to remove possible lipstick smears. You keep your eyes bright, your smile fixed. You show that there is no real need for all the understanding, the pitying glances which are cast in your direction. You show that even if you are the widow of a hero, you, yourself, are still alive. And even if you are now on the way to the memorial services in Capas, the cross does not rise from atop your head, no sod reposes on the length of you, no green growth pushes upwards from your dead flesh—pushing upwards to life you never thought of living, you with your once living clay.

And you shudder at the thought that what was once part of you was doing just that in Capas. Being repose and sod and growth, and marked by a cross. And you think, what a waste of usefulness. For Rene was an engineer-architect, and could be so useful now. He knew how to draw growth on paper. The growth of buildings and the life which went on within them. The growth of fulfillment and security, and just plain contentment. He could draw a curve, and that was a shelf for books. A triangle, and that was a kitchen where life eddied in small, satisfying streams. And a careful, perfect circle that was a room where friends met for laughter and for silence. He could dream up buildings and make the dreams come true. He knew just where a peg could be driven in to hold the dream together, where a rod was bent to anchor it to earth.

You watch such substantial, once realized dreams in ghastly procession past the train window, broken into a pile of rubble here, a broken pillar there, a series of shell-riddled steps, and you think again: here is work for builders like Rene. Who could look at a demolished building and dream up another to stand in its place. Something better, more solid, to live a longer year. He could accept the challenge of need even as he accepted the bitterness of loss.

You cannot help but wonder what he would say now if he could see the panels of rusty tin that stood where he had fitted slabs of smooth masonite to hold the reflection of fluorescent lamps ("the newest, darling. Perfect for your eyes"), the carefully selected stained glass panes ("squares of light and shadow, honey"), the beautiful tiles on the walls ("to echo my baritone, when I sing in the bath"), the ornamental boxes to hold the roots of cascading green.

There is only silence to your wondering. So you think of something else. Of carabaos wallowing in cool mud, of trees bent by forgotten winds, of people who were always gaping at trains. And you listen to the murmur of reminiscence behind you as an old voice talks of sons now at rest in Capas. And you try to ignore the sound of quiet weeping in one corner. You think impatiently, this is no time for tears. Impatiently, even if you know that tears are there for all time, awaiting the summons, filling throat and heart because your eyes deny them passage. And you think, this is foolish. Grief has grown up in four years—it is too old to cry.

So you think again of something else. Of Bataan, because that is the obvious thing to think about now that you must return to Capas. Of the Death March, because it never failed to hurt. And you must be hurt, because you were not there to drag one swollen foot after another, to push your starved belly forward, to retch your empty bowels out. You were not there to taste the dust, to feel the butt of a gun upon your back, the heaviness of a boot against your thigh. You did not know the feel of hands weaker than yours clinging desperately and the limpness of flesh that through suffering had become one with yours. You were not there to mull over defeat so bitter because your faith in victory had been so great. You were not there at all. How could you be? You lay in bed for days, unwilling to eat, unwilling to live, because what you at last knew was hope lay upon you dead.

And you think: this is stupid. Why go back to the beginning of Capas? Why remember the long wait, to end at last with a note that made a mockery of all the stealth and the sacrifice because it was not legible? As what note written by a dying hand could be? Why go back to the beginning of despair? And you ask, what for am I on this train? Why this pilgrimage to Capas? What is there to see but a cross to mark a length of earth? He is not there. He could never be. He is beside you now, part of the coolness of wind rushing past the train window, part of the sound of wheels grating against rails, part of the growth in varying shades of green flitting beneath you. He is above—in the changing shape of cloud, the peeping bit of blue, even the length of telephone wires cutting across the skies. He is movement and light and sound wherever you may go.

He is throb of your heart and thought in your brain. The slow and quiet growth of pain, the swiftness of memory, the transient joy of forgetting. He is the sense of security you now enjoy, the unshackling and the freedom. He is the discontent and the content you share, the heights to which you can aspire, the source and the expression of what to you stands for democracy. He is that touch of immortality in you which you have transmitted to your children and which, in turn, your children's children must immortalize if man must be as the gods.

He is not in Capas. He is wherever you are.

And yet you know why to Capas you must return. Because loss must have a place and pain a memorial. And Capas is where both victory and defeat wear nothing but a cross.

Philippine-American
June 1946

THE WIRE FENCE

Silvestre L. Tagarao

All day long I watched the wire fence. Each day for one full month I had watched the wire fence that stood between us and freedom.

The wire fence was not high. It reached up to my chin only. It was not intricate, either. There must have been six strands of wire for the entire height of the fence. The posts were no bigger than my arm. Once I thought I could go near one of them in the night and break it with my hands. Another time I thought I could get near the wires and push two of them wide enough apart to let me through.

But even as I thought this plan over, I knew I could not do it. If I tried it, I would be within easy firing distance of a watchtower just outside the fence. There were many of these watchtowers, and there were well-armed guards in each.

The wire fence surrounded the entire camp. It was a big camp and we were all concentrated there. Every morning I would come out of the shack which we occupied, just to look at the wire fence running all around the camp, and I always saw the many watchtowers standing outside at one-hundred-meter intervals. And the more I looked, the more I felt that the fence was not very high.

But even if I could get over the fence, there would still be a wide, wide field, a waste land covered with cogon grass. Beyond this field there would be a mountain, but even the mountain looked like a mound of waste land: bald, treeless. There might be a good chance of hiding in the cogon growth and then reaching the mountain but there would be nowhere to get food. So each day, for one whole month, I watched the wire fence, saw the watchtowers, saw the wide field and the mountain beyond, and did nothing.

"I think I will die here," I told Felix.

"We are really not very strong any more," he said.

Felix was my new friend. So many of them had already passed away. The last to go was Dolfo. Dolfo had been very talkative his last night. He had been very funny, too. He talked about food, the best food he had ever tasted in his whole life. He made me very hungry that night. But I could not make him stop. He was very happy and I wanted him to stay happy. It was hard to see anybody getting happy there. So I let him talk and talk until he fell asleep. In the morning I tried to wake him up. He was already cold and stiff.

And then Felix came. He was thin and yellowish. He smiled feebly as he sat down beside me.

"Malaria," he said.

"Same here," I said.

Felix did not talk much. He just looked at me and I looked at him, and that was how we passed the day. Every day, though, we saw each other getting thinner and thinner, weaker and weaker. There was very little food in that hospital, if any at all.

It was already very cold at night. There was nothing to lie on. The floor was of bamboo slats. The wind passed through the spaces, and the night was unbearably cold. Felix would press his back against my back, and I would press my back against his back, and we would feel all right. Then, when he would have an attack of malaria, I would press closer to him and I would feel very warm and I liked the warmth. And when I would have my attack, he would press very close to me, and he would feel very warm and he liked the warmth very much.

Whenever morning came, we would be up again and wait and wait and there would be no food. As we waited, flies, big and blue, would swarm on those too sick and near dead to move.... Then they would fly around again....

So I would come out of the shack that was called the hospital and watch the wire fence. Felix would watch it with me. But we did not talk much. We just did not want to look the other way. I tried looking the other way once and it was not good. When I did, I first saw several rows of darkened bodies lying there under the sun. Then, beyond that, where the road was, you could see an endless train of dead bodies being moved to the cemetery. The bodies were borne on bamboo poles and most of them were naked. So Felix and I just watched the wire fence each day, feeling that after another day there would be no more morning, and we would be among the nameless.

Once there was food. I saw it and told Felix and so he saw it, too. It was a small calf and it was moving slowly between the shacks and all eyes followed it hungrily. Its journey ended at the kitchen, and then somebody tied it to a post, raised a piece of hard wood, and delivered the blow. The small thing went down on its knees, gave a little cry, and then lay on the ground. We just looked on, knowing that only the sight of it was meant for us, the reality of its meat and its liver and its heart and its tongue going to the reality of a group of officers who lorded it over our part of the camp.

We never saw the calf again, but we did see the hide, and then somebody started getting his piece of the hide, and soon there was Felix getting his own piece of the hide and then myself getting my own piece of the hide. Then, holding our pieces of the hide, we did not know what to do with them until we saw somebody throw his piece into a mound of burning human waste and debris, and so Felix and I also threw our pieces there and waited. The fire burned the hair off and smoothened and blackened the hide, and then it was stiff and it smelled good. We held our respective pieces before our respective noses and smelled and smelled, the smelling of it alone making us feel as if we were really eating the reality of its meat which had gone to the reality of the officers there with us. Then we went back to the shack, and everybody there was envying us, coming closer to us and smelling the good smell of the burnt hide with us.

I put my piece in my mouth and started to chew. The others watched. Felix also put his piece in his mouth and started to chew. They watched. Then we were chewing in earnest, but the hide was so hard and stiff and tough my teeth could not bite into it. But we went on chewing and making faces, and they all watched us, asking if it was good, and all I could say was good, very good. And we went on chewing, and they kept on watching, and they thought it was good, really good.

I kept on chewing and then I got up and looked around madly and spat my piece out and picked it up and threw it away. I was shouting still and saying things, ugly things, but there was nobody listening any more. Everybody weakly got to his feet and desperately made a scramble for the piece I had thrown away. They pushed and struck and bit and kicked one another. And then it was in somebody else's hand and the struggle stopped. The one who got it wiped the dirt off, raised it proudly and dropped it into his mouth and, looking around, started to chew contentedly, yes, contentedly.

I stayed in the hospital a full month. There was no medicine, hardly any food. When I rose in the morning now, I did not look around any more. It was not good to. Just try to remember seeing a human skeleton, I mean a real human skeleton—all bones and nothing else. Then cover this with skin, just skin and nothing more. Give it a pair of eyes so that it does not look dead. Look at it again and see if you can keep on looking....

We were packed in there at night and there never was a moment of silence. All you could hear were voices, men's voices, crying and moaning like sick children calling for their mothers, always their mothers. In the morning those who had cried loudest in the night were dead. So I would get up and Felix would get up with me and we would go outside the shack and watch the wire fence and the field and the mountain beyond.

At noon there would be a bird flying in the sky and our eyes would follow the bird, for in this way we would not be looking at those dead bodies stiff and naked there alongside our shack being counted and numbered.

"When there is so much death around," Felix said, "you pretty nearly feel dead yourself."

That morning the fellow lying beside me died. Felix and I were picked to take him out so the body could be numbered. I held the body by the arms. Felix was at a loss where to hold him. The poor man had died of dysentery and was covered with filth, and Felix did not know where to hold him. Finally he tried to pick him up by a small bit of the pants that looked cleaner than the rest. But the body had gotten so thin and bony and small that when we had lifted it and were carrying it outside, it slipped out of the pants and fell with a thud on the ground. Then Felix seized the legs, and we carried him hurriedly outside and laid him beside the other dead bodies, and then Felix rubbed his hands on the ground and then asked me not to go back to the shack for a while but stay with him watching the wire fence, looking at it in futility, seeing the distance and the blue sky and the barren clouds and thinking that soon we, too, would die. There was no bird flying then. There was no motion beyond the fence. Felix was crying passionately. "It's a pity we had to drop him," he said. Then he shook me cruelly. "If I go ahead of you," he said, "will you see that I don't drop that way?"

I did not look at him. I only watched the wire fence, seeing how deathly still it was, seeing how deathly quiet the wide field beyond was, seeing how deathly blue the sky was, and I knew it was useless, useless to ask for anything in that place where everything was dead and quiet and still. It was useless to ask for anything when death was all you could talk to. But I nodded my head and kept on looking at the wire fence, knowing how futile it was, knowing that I would not, ever, feel the grass growing beyond it.

There came a day, one whole day, when I did not watch the wire fence. I did not know where I looked then, but I just looked, not really knowing or seeing where I looked; I only opened my eyes and thought that somehow it was coming, that to all of us it was a certainty and we could not escape it, and so I looked and looked, not really knowing or seeing what it was all about.

Felix was very talkative that night. Must it always be so before the unending silence? He talked and talked. About his mother. His brothers and sisters. A little kid who was most dear to him. That dear little face that was always before him. Oh, how he loved them all. Oh, God, but how could they ever know how much he loved them. It was there. All of it there. The way he said it. The way he gasped it. Oh, God!...And then he went to sleep. In the middle of the night he edged close, very close, to me. He placed his arms around me and said, "It is cold, very cold." And I said, "Yes, very cold," and edged very close to him and then we fell back to sleep, and soon it was morning, and everybody was awake, but Felix was still breathing heavily and snoring a bit. I watched him and I did not touch him. It would be best for him to keep on sleeping. There was no food anyway.

Then Felix was up. It was unusual. He did not rise slowly. He fairly jumped up and he was looking at me straight in the eye and then he seized me and laughed.

"Didn't you see her?" he asked.

"Who?" I asked.

He laughed. "My mother—didn't you see my mother?"

"No."

"But she came here," he said. "Why didn't you see her?"

"She came?"

"Yes. And you saw her. She came and she was very lovely and gentle and kind. She was very good to all of us here. But she was kindest to you and to me, and we both liked her, and you told her you liked her very much."

I looked at him. "Let's go out and watch the wire fence," I said.

"No, not yet. Didn't you really see my mother when she came? She was lovely and gentle and good to all of us. She came riding in a beautiful automobile. And before she left she gave us biscuits and many other things to eat. She said that she would be coming again. And you were very happy and you thanked her very much."

I wanted to cry. "Come on, let's go out, Felix," I said.

"Now you want to go out because you don't want to give them back to me."

"Give which back to you?"

"The biscuits."

"The biscuits?"

"Yes, give me back the biscuits."

"What biscuits?"

"The ones I gave you."

"I don't have them."

"But I gave them to you to keep for us."

He looked at me steadily, then cried, "Because you ate them! You ate them. I gave them to you to keep for the two of us, and you ate them all and gave me nothing. How nice of you to do that!"

"God!" I said. Felix cried and cried and I could not do anything.

"You ate them!—all of them! And now what will I eat?" He was trembling as he shouted. He was breathing hard.

"Felix...."

"You are no good!" he shouted and ran out of the shack.

I stood up. "Where are you going?" I called after him.

"To my mother," he shouted back.

But before his voice reached me, there was an interval. By the sound of his voice, I knew where he was going. There was no time to get him back. I held my breath and waited.

I came out of the shack only when I heard it. It came repeatedly, deafeningly, and then there was silence....

I saw his body hanging limp on the wire fence. He must have been going through it when the guard in the tower saw him. His body was left hanging there for a whole day, and so, for one whole day, I did not look at the wire fence but just stayed by the shack, looking and knowing and seeing that everything was futile, that the field was wide and barren and the mountain was far and barren and the sky was still and dead blue, and there was a big bird soaring and twisting up there, soaring and twisting, mockingly, mockingly, and I knew that all day long the next day I would again watch the wire fence, and I would just look at it, keep on looking at it all day long for how many more days I hated to think, knowing that it would always stand mutely there, between us and freedom....

Philippine-American
June 1946

THE DOOR

BIENVENIDO N. SANTOS

Oh, the stories I can tell you, if you but have the time to listen, but you are going away. Everybody is going some place. They are all in a hurry, they will not listen to me. And those who will tarry here forever, they have no ears for my stories, because they have seen them happen everywhere, and they don't want them told, they are a commonplace, they say, they should be hushed and forgotten. We have had happy moments which, truly, had not quite lasted but there will be other such moments. So my friends will not listen, because my tales are sad, because they do not have the heart.

But you will listen to me, Ben, even if you, too, are going away. Because I saw the look in your eyes as you turned around to gaze at Nanoy and shared his loneliness, you could have suffered in your heart as we that loved him had suffered. So I walked beside you and held your hand, and deep in my heart I felt, Ben will understand my stories, to him I shall tell them.

I

In our apartment, there were four of us. I was happy with my friends, because everybody spoke my language, our language, I feel so happy using now with you. We spoke in English only when we cursed, it came in so nicely. Or when another countryman dropped in for a chat, and he kept talking in English, then the other boys talked, too. They talked very well, and all I would say was, "Yes," or "Hell, that's a fact," in an attempt to cover up my terrible ignorance which my rough trembling hands so often exposed.

There were other boys and Filipino families in the apartment building. I knew Delfin because I often met him near the stair landing. His room was just across the way, at the foot of the staircase. Here he lived with Mildred, his blonde American wife and her two little daughters, Anne and Esther, by a previous marriage.

I was very fond of the two little girls because they were so pretty and little and they had such curly golden hair. Soon they were calling me Uncle. Often I brought them candy bars and they would rush to meet me near the main door of the apartment building. I put my arms round their wet sticky necks and gave them what I had remembered to buy. Mildred would scold them sometimes, saying nasty things. She would come out of the door wearing a silk negligee and she would run after them in the hall as they squealed and cried and ran away from her. "You spoil their appetites," Mildred would tell me, and I would answer in English, of course. "It don't matter none, really," I said. Delfin would sometimes be around watching the chase. All he would do was smile stupidly and look on. He never invited me to his apartment. Often I would stand near the open door and talk with the little girls. That was all.

One day I heard the boys in our apartment talking about Delfin. I was surprised at the things they said about him. Dick, Noli, and Sev seldom agreed on many things, but they were one in their condemnation of Delfin. It wouldn't have been for meanness. My friends were not angels, but they led such busy lives that they had no time to sprout wings or grow horns. It must be true then, the things they said.

"You don't know him yet, Ambo," said Dick, "but wait till you do, and then you would be saying the same things that you hear us saying now." Dick had finished law school, working days and studying at night. He was very gentle by nature, and wouldn't be talking of another man this way if it was not a fact that Delfin was everything they said about him.

"He's a disgrace to our people," said loud-mouthed Noli, for whom everything was country and politics. He had a shrill voice and wanted to be a Senator in the Philippines. He was intensely nationalistic. Everything a Filipino did in America was a reflection on our country and our people.

"Delfin's a damn fool," was Sev's private opinion. Sev drove a taxi. He was neat and effeminate in his ways. His taxi was adorned with pictures of the Lady of Lourdes, of all sizes.

There were also pictures of MacArthur and the American and Filipino flags intertwined as if in lovingness.

It seemed that it was common knowledge that Mildred ran around with other boys. She would take them to her apartment, and Delfin would leave quietly and walk the streets. If he was not home and came later, and he would find the door locked from the inside, he knew that he had come at the wrong time again. He would wait outside the apartment building, till a strange man came out, and he would try the door again with his key. Often he slept elsewhere, especially on winter nights when walking up and down the streets or loafing in badly heated hamburger joints made him sick—a shooting pain through the meat of his legs or through the stoop of his back. He would go to our apartment. He would knock at our door at the most unholy hours of the night and say, "May I sleep here tonight?"

The boys would let him in the living room, show him the couch and throw him a blanket. Dick and Sev would pretend to be very sleepy, for they hated to see him that way, as though the thing were happening to them, too. But if Noli was awake, he would shout from his room, "Is that you again, Del? God, you're not a man. You must have been castrated in childhood. Why don't you leave that woman? Why do you make a goddamn fool of yourself? She's beautiful. All right. Aren't there others as willing, less shameless? Man, where's your sense of honor? We're ashamed of you! If you don't listen to us, why come here at all? You insult us with your presence. You contaminate us with your...with your...filth!"

Delfin would pull the blanket over him, as if to shut off the words a little and the light from the street lamp below. Then he would be quiet as though fast asleep.

Once when Delfin came to our apartment, the boys told him stories of men who defended their honor.

Sev said, "Have you heard of the Filipino in St. Louis who caught his wife with another man? He chased the man through the streets. The man was naked and held a pillow close to his breast as if that protected him. He was so scared. Then the Filipino went back to his wife and slashed her throat." Sev made a slashing motion with his hands across his throat, then a choking sound. It was picturesque. It was gruesome.

"And after he had slashed her throat," Sev continued, "he cut off her nipples. Then he gave himself up, carrying the nipples in his hands, staining the sergeant's blotter with blood. He's now in an insane asylum."

Dick had the kindness of heart to change the subject. Meanwhile Delfin hadn't said a word in his defense, but he clung to every word of the story-teller, and he swallowed a little near the end. Then when everybody was quiet, he said, "I don't think I can kill Mildred. I don't think I can live without her." His sincerity touched us all. For the first time I saw Noli look at him without contempt, but with pity, with a little kindness.

I was coming home late after midnight in October when I found Delfin sitting on the stone steps of our apartment building, his head against the stone pillar.

"You frightened me," I said as soon as I was sure that it was he. Delfin had a young face. He was tall and very dark. His teeth sparkled whitely when he smiled. And he was smiling now.

"Did you have a good time?" he asked, and without waiting for a reply, he added, "Sit down a while with me. It's too warm inside."

"You're not staying here all night, are you?" I asked, sitting down on the cold stone steps.

"Oh, no," he said, looking in the direction of their apartment.

"You got a visitor?" I tried with difficulty to make my question sound matter-of-fact.

His answer was a slight nod of the head.

"Man," I said, "You're crazy."

"I know," he said softly.

This would go on. I would be saying a lot of things that wouldn't mean anything to him. So I asked after Anne and Esther. Were they all right? Of course, they were all right. What did the little ones know? God, why did they have to know? God, why did I stay there, sitting down on the cold stone steps, sharing these crazy hours of waiting with a man like Delfin? A terrible anger was welling up inside me: all I wanted to do was try to understand.

"Let's go upstairs to our apartment," I said. "It's getting chilly out here."

"No," he said. "Noli's just come up. He told me not to go to your apartment tonight or else he would throw me out."

"That would serve you right," I said, clenching my fist, getting all of Noli's anger in me.

"Hell!" I cried impulsively, jumping to my feet. "Let's go to your apartment. We'll bust the door and take the...out of both of them."

"No," said Delfin, "you'll wake up the little girls."

I stared at him for a while, spitting at the pavement at my feet. Then I sat down again and laughed softly. What had got into me? What business did I have straightening, so to say, the back-hanging collar of this cuckold of a man, countryman or no countryman?

"Oh, well," I said after a while, "I guess you know best."

"No," he admitted. "I'm all wrong. I'm all sick inside of me, worse than leprosy."

"You know," I said, "there are many nice girls at the Club."

"I know."

"Some of them a lot better looking than Mildred. And a million times nicer."

"How do you know?"

"I don't. But I know Mildred."

"I love Mildred."

"Love, my God! What do you know of love? It's a curse; it's a disease that has got into you."

"I know. I know. I told you it's worse than leprosy. But sometimes I tell myself it's love. We called it love in the beginning. We have moments of beauty together, Mildred and I, and I find this nowhere else. No other woman could give it to me. I cannot live without her, I tell you. I can't...I can't."

He held his head in his hands and he was quiet. I sat there, looking at him, and thinking: Lord, the things Filipinos do in this country. The things we say. The things that happen to us. What keeps us living on like this from day to day, from loveless kiss to loveless kiss, from venomed touch to venomed touch. Thrill of the gaming table, what keeps us alive, thrill of a woman's arms, sight of her body, sharp fleeting moments of dying...they are the blessed ones like Nanoy, though it took him too long to die.

Busy with these thoughts, I had not noticed a man leave the building. Now only his back was visible in the street light beyond. His steps were brisk and fast as though already late.

"Was that the man?" I asked.

"I don't know," Delfin answered. "I don't know any one of them."

Then we stood up, and together we walked through the hallway, pausing in front of his apartment. The door was closed still. Delfin placed his hand upon it, and it opened quietly to his touch.

"Goodnight," he said, his teeth sparkling in a happy smile.

I went up to my room, groping in the dark. Someone had turned off the stairway light again. Now I would have to fumble for the lock on our door, or maybe it would yield to my touch like magic.

II

It was not often during these many years in America that I could look forward to a Christmas with honest joy. Christmas to me was just another day. It meant more people spending money, bigger tips, and the spoken words, "Merry Christmas." It meant that there would be more boys at the club, more little men at the races. It meant silly talks in corners, at lonely tables in Filipino restaurants: "Last night I dreamed I was back home in the Philippines and it was Christmas. Sister was a grown up lady. She was wearing an afternoon dress I had bought at Hecht's. She was lovely, like my memory of Mother when I was a child. There was a whole platter full of rice cakes, *suman* wrapped in yellow leaves. The air was full of the smell of roasting pigs. And many little children came to me and kissed my hand. In each of their palms I placed a new silver dollar—I had a bagful from Riggs National Bank—you should have seen the glitter of the silver under the lamplight; you should have seen the glitter in the children's eyes."

Sometimes Christmas meant walking up and down the icy streets, looking for a restaurant, and finding none, for most of them are closed on Christmas Day. Because most people should be home on Christmas instead of walking up and down the streets, with icy winds blowing from the river, their steps swinging to the music of Christmas carols, sung everywhere, loudest in the crowded streets above the din of hurried steps turned towards home; megaphones blaring forth joy to the world, the Lord is come. But, please, Lord, let me find a place where I could eat. I'm so hungry.

But I looked forward to that Christmas with honest joy. For the first time in many years, I had a Christmas gift for someone, for two little blonde girls who called me Uncle.

Once I had fever and I kept to my room. Every time the boys came from work, the first thing they said, invariably, was, "Anne and Esther want to know how you are."

On the third day, the two little girls came to my room crying. "Mom would not let us see you," they said. "But now she's away. Get well quick, Uncle," they pleaded.

Anne put her little soft hands on my forehead. "Do you have a headache?" she asked.

"A little," I said truthfully. She passed her fingers across my forehead, lightly, gently.

Little Esther said, "I'll rub your legs."

"Don't," I said, "that will tickle me." And we three laughed.

After a while, I said. "You'd better go now." And they kissed me goodbye. When they had gone, I turned to the wall and closed my eyes.

And one day, shortly before Christmas, the two little girls came up to me, crying, "Uncle, Uncle, we've a Christmas tree!"

They opened the door of their apartment wide enough for us to see across the hall in a corner: a pretty, lighted Christmas tree.

The next day I got busy asking friends what I could give for Christmas to two little girls. There were a number of suggestions. Different persons told me different things. I spent the next few days, walking through F Street, between 7th and 14th Streets, looking for an apt gift for each child. And I was happy within me. For the first time in many years, there was a glow in my heart. Christmas felt truly like Christmas, and the songs in the streets, and the carols in the air, and the little tinkling bell in the hand of the Salvation Army man or woman now freezing in the cold—all had meaning.

As soon as I had their gifts packed nicely, one for Anne and the other for Esther, I attached a little print card decorated with holly on each, and wrote, "Merry Christmas." My hand didn't seem heavy and my heart was light; there was no hesitancy, no sluggishness in the movement of my hand as I wrote on each, "Love, Uncle," as though my hand for such things need not have to tremble, since there was nothing to hide, and something deep to say, which I was just saying, after these many years, love to you, to anyone, this time to two little girls with windblown curls and the prettiest freckled noses you ever saw.

I gave the two little packages to Mildred. She stood by the open door and received them from me. "For their stockings," I said.

"Anne and Esther have also something for you," Mildred said.

And I stood at the open door wondering what it was that tugged at my heart, like the singing of many happy voices that have not had voice nor music for a long, long time.

On Christmas eve I went down after dinner and the little girls were there awaiting me. I stood by the open door while their hands held mine, pulling me into the room.

"Where's Del?" I asked.

"He's working tonight." said Mildred. She stood in the hall, slim and attractive in a red housecoat. She was combing back her yellow curls. "I've just had a bath," she said as though to apologize. She exuded soap and orange blossoms.

"Merry Christmas," I said as I allowed myself to be pulled in by the two eager girls.

"Nice Christmas tree," I said.

"The winkers don't work," said Mildred. She showed me a box of winkers that she said she had been trying to use.

I fixed the socket and the wire ends, and turned on the juice, but they wouldn't work. I sat on the rug and fixed the wiring. Then Esther went to the door and came back, saying, "I've closed the door. Uncle is staying with us tonight." Anne was also saying something else. Mildred had turned on the radio and there was loud singing. I heard Esther's words, but I didn't bother to weigh their meaning. Mildred watched me as I worked, and she, too, knelt playfully on the rug and puttered around the Christmas tree. The little girls were dancing about and singing.

Soon I turned on the juice again and the winkers came on and went off in a glorious moment that seemed success, and the two little girls gave out a cry of happiness. It was short-lived, because the winkers didn't come on any more, and I was beginning to get embarrassed about my inability to do anything about them.

"We shouldn't have put them on too early," Mildred explained, and in a resigned voice, added, "They're really no good though. The other lights will do."

"But we like the winkers, Mom," the girls cried. And they urged me to keep on trying.

So I spent several minutes more, tinkering with the wire ends. I was getting hot round the neck, so I said, "Mind if I take this off?" and I removed my jacket, and the girls ran away with it to their room.

"Be careful!" Mildred shouted after them. She turned to me and asked, "Isn't there anything important in your pockets?"

"No," I said without looking up from my work.

Well, by the time the winkers were good and working, it was nearly bedtime for the little ones. The whoop of delight with which they announced my success was not as loud nor as vociferous as their first, though protracted, yell of delight earlier in the night.

Anne gave a Christmas poem about a silent house without noise, and without a mouse, but she kept yawning and forgetting the lines, we had to clap our hands before she was through. Then Esther sang "Silent Night" and Mildred and Anne joined her; and I kept humming, too, and it seemed, I had always known the melody without having been aware of it.

"Now you'll go to bed like good girls," said Mildred. "And Santa Claus will fill your stockings with gifts."

"Yes, Mom," they said sleepily as they pulled me to their bedroom. It was a pretty bedroom, done up in blue and red. There was a bed where they slept side by side. Over the wall that looked like fireplace, they had hung two empty stockings.

"That's mine," said Esther.

"This is mine," said Anne.

Mildred pulled Esther to her and started dressing her for the night.

"Help me," said Anne, getting up on a chair. And I helped her, a little awkwardly at first.

"Thank you," said Anne, putting her arms around me impulsively, and nearly falling off the chair. Then she kissed me hard on the cheek, saying, "Goodnight, Uncle."

"Goodnight," said Esther, pulling me down to her. And she kissed me on the cheek, less fervently, sleepily.

"It's beyond their sleeping time," said Mildred, as she turned off the light and closed the door after us.

"I have my jacket there," I said.

"It's all right," said Mildred. "What about a midnight snack?"

I turned the radio low as Mildred got busy in the kitchen.

"What would you have?" she asked.

"Anything," I said, going to the kitchen. "I'm not really hungry."

"The kitchen is a mess," she apologized. Then she added, "Del should be here by now. It's past midnight. I wonder what's detaining him?"

Mildred placed a couple of sandwiches before me and a bottle of cold milk. She sat at the other end of the table with a glass of milk.

"Spending Christmas with the boys, I suppose?" she said.

"Maybe," I said, not really having any plans.

"Did you know Del quite well before you came to America? He talks a great deal about you. It seems, you people knew each other quite well."

"Yes," I said, lying deliberately. When we talked of boys we liked to our American friends, we always said we knew each other in the Philippines; and we talked about our families as though we had deep ties of association and kinship. Mostly it was just talk. Perhaps it gave us strength to talk like that. We didn't want to appear the homeless waifs that we were. We didn't wish to be known as the forgotten children of long lost mothers and fathers, as grown up men without childhood, bastards of an indifferent country.

"Yes," I repeated. "We knew each other very well," adding another deliberate lie. "His family was well known in our province. His father was tall and dark like him, and deeply loved by all. Del's father was noble."

"And his Mother?" Mildred asked. "He talked of her more often."

"She was a sweet lady. She was loving and religious. She was faithful."

"Do you want another glass of milk?" Mildred asked.

"No, thanks," I said, "I'd better be going. Must be past midnight now."

"I'll get your jacket," she said.

When she came out of the girls' bedroom, she had the jacket in her hands.

"Let me help you," she said.

"No thanks," I said, taking the jacket gently from her hand, and folding it. "I'm just going up like this."

"Well, it's Christmas Day," Mildred said, giving me her hand. "Merry Christmas, Ambo."

"Thanks," I said. "Merry Christmas also." I let go off her hand quickly. Mine were trembling so.

"Anne and Esther make me very happy," I said. It was a great truth that I had to say.

"They love you very much," Mildred said, undoing the bar. "I never bolt this door except..."

As the door opened, we saw Delfin sitting on the stairway, his head in his hands. Now he looked up at the sound of the opening door, and when he saw me, he stared hard and long. Then he looked away and bit his lips.

"How long have you been sitting there?" Mildred asked him. "Come on in."

Delfin had not moved. He was looking at me still with deep upbraiding eyes.

"Merry Christmas, Del." I said, trying to be casual. What else could I tell him, what could I say? Did I not sit up with him on a night in autumn, while the door to this apartment remained bolted from the inside?

Now he had hidden his head in his hands, and when he looked at me again, his face was contorted as in pain. I wanted to give him my hand, but it lay heavy on my side, my trembling fingers clawing at the folds of my woolen jacket. With great effort, he stood up in answer to Mildred's now insistent bidding, and as he came to my side, a great sadness was on his face, no longer pain and tears stood in his bloodshot eyes. In a vague whisper, he said, in the dialect, "Why you also, Ambo?"

Then he went in, and the door closed upon them.

Instead of going up to my room as I had intended, I put on my jacket and went outside. It was a cold night; an icy breeze was blowing. But I walked on and on. Then the bells of St. Mary's on Fourth Street began pealing loudly, but the spirit of Christmas had already gone out of me, all the songs,

all the music, all the singing gladness within me, all memory
of ringing bells.

Sunday Post Magazine
June 2, 1946

BROWN MAID

ANTONIO O. BAYOT

"Why, hello!" exclaimed Mrs. Orosco as she spotted Patria Perez in the same jeepney with her, and tried to squeeze her corpulent buttocks between two slim men on the bench which could only sit four persons but already sat five.

"Halo," Patria answered back with an inane smile, as she fanned herself with her perfumed handkerchief, and then covered her nose to keep from smelling the gasoline fumes that steamed out of the motor in front.

Their exchange of greetings was momentarily drowned by the ten-year-old conductress' shouts of "España! Rotonda! España!" After the usual last minute rush of late passengers to fill the jeepney to overflowing and the traffic cop's insistent whistle hissing them away, the jeepney finally wormed itself out of the congested corner and in no time was racing bumpily along the spacious, airy avenues leading to Quezon City.

Meanwhile the two women lost no time in appraising each other from head to feet. Patria Perez dismissed the object of her scrutiny with that usual sense of superiority she had always felt for Mrs. Orosco's stout aspirations towards pulchritude, but Mrs. Orosco felt neither superior nor inferior to her friend.

Patria Perez had been lovely, and statuesque, she was thinking; and how, even after getting married, divorced and eventually widowed through the battle of Manila, she could still hold her own against any debutante in town. She had been that rarity among debutantes: a combination of pure Filipino stock with all that travel and opulence could add to give it an Occidental polish. And one could see how unhappy she was for having to ride with the common herd in this jeepney. One could feel it would not be long before she would again ride in a limousine, when things permitted.

"Are you still living at Kamuning?" Mrs. Orosco asked her, as they turned the Rotonda and she put a hair back in place.

Patria nodded with another inane smile, patting her head as the wind attacked the jeepney from all sides. Somebody beside Patria now jumped out, and Mrs. Orosco grabbed this chance to sit next to her.

"I saw your housemaid the other day," she whispered as soon as she had settled herself. "She was with an American GI. She looked so different! Her hair was done up in rolls, she had make-up on, and she walked arm in arm with the soldier—"

"That must have been Larry."

"You mean, Larry the GI you told me about the last time we met?"

Patria nodded quickly and turned her face away, as if concentrating on the bumpy road.

"But I thought—" Mrs. Orosco did not continue. She remembered how enthusiastic Patria had been as she talked about the fair godlike corporal who had become such a steady visitor at her house, enjoying all the comforts of home that she could give him within conventional limits. "He's so uninhibited, so pleasure-loving, so strong and different! And he comes from a well-to-do family," Patria had described him to Mrs. Orosco. Surely Patria must have wanted him for herself when she could talk like that! And yet—

"Can't you find me a housemaid?" Patria was pleading. "Someone who does not have GI fever and is really a servant."

"My dear! You know how hard it is to find servants these days! Ever since the Jap occupation the servant class have turned into barmaids and now with the GI's it's even worse. There are not enough women to entertain these soldiers."

"I hope those GI's return to the States soon and let us live our old life again." Patria's voice was terse. "They only leave broken hearts behind them."

"Did Larry marry your maid?"

"Yes, yes!" Patria replied irritably. "They had a mixed marriage last month. He is now in the civil service. She's going to have a baby, he told me yesterday. Naty wants to go to his hometown in the States but Larry is too wise to do that. He knows she'll never be happy there."

This outburst of fallacious information put a stop to Mrs. Orosco's inquisitiveness for a while, but it was not because she was satisfied. She simply felt that if she kept trying to feed her curiosity Patria's mounting anger might snap. She must be angry at the way things had turned out! But Mrs. Orosco would not have been a woman if she had left the whole thing at that. With a funny feeling inside as she saw that she would soon have to get off the jeepney and leave Patria behind, Mrs. Orosco again broke the awkward silence.

"They're going to have nice children," she remarked. "Remember, I told you that Naty looked like a carbon copy of Maria Montes? These Ilocanas have good features. Stella Johnson is an Ilocano mestiza—her father was an American veteran, no?—and look how lovely she is!"

"American boys will love anything," Patria murmured sullenly. "When they come here they don't know right from wrong—their sense of values is all mixed up. It didn't take me long to find him out."

Sour grapes! Mrs. Orosco told herself with malicious delight.

"Why, what did you find out?" After all, Larry may have turned out to be a disappointment, not all that he claimed to be.

"He never had any family, well-to-do or otherwise. He was an orphan since childhood. He was only a factory worker in the States when war came. No wonder, when I really talked as I have always been accustomed to talk I'd notice a vacant look in his eyes, as if he could not understand my language. And I thought I could learn a lot from him!"

"I suppose he found Naty more his type."

"He remembered his place, you mean. She gives him a sense of superiority, something indispensable to masculine egoism, while I guess I couldn't help making him feel like my chauffer or something. She is so much more illiterate than he, so he can teach her the little he knows."

"He knew you taught for charity once, didn't he?"

"I never got to tell him. They'll be happy," she added with a sniff, "especially Larry. He's already gone completely native, and seems to have forgotten all about his countrymen. I don't know which it was, if he never liked white girls, or the white girls never liked him. I'll never know now. I've done my duty by marrying them off. Now I can look after myself."

"Who's your current boyfriend? Another American?"

"No! A captain in the Philippine Army. He used to be a lawyer before the war."

"That's perfect for you," Mrs. Orosco exclaimed happily. "A factory worker could hardly make a good husband for a society girl."

"I never thought of Larry as my husband!" Patria turned on her. "He was only useful while food was so scarce and he could bring me canned stuff from his camp. Besides, his jeep was always at my disposal. My kitchen was overflowing with canned foods. When I found out it was illegal, I told him to stop it. I guess he noticed how indifferent I became then. From that time on he seemed to pay attention to Naty, helping her in her housework, can you imagine?—and bringing her candy and things from the snack bar. They must have discovered each other then, and found out they had so much in common. She took it all, and I guess he took a lot from her in return. These soldiers from nowhere are lucky to find a good woman like my housemaid. He was just as eager to settle down as she was to become her own mistress, instead of a servant."

"Oh, those girls are easy. They can't resist the flattery of a white man making love to them."

"All I can say is, water seeks its own level," Patria declared, with a tone of finality, and with those words she turned her face away again, as if Mrs. Orosco did not exist. At the next corner Mrs. Orosco got off, and as she said goodbye to Patria with a big smile and started to walk hurriedly towards her chalet, she was thinking what a juicy tidbit of gossip she had for her friends this afternoon at their weekly mahjong session. Patria Perez, the glamorous, haughty Patria, jilted for another girl, who was her housemaid! Trust these GI's for upsetting the local women's set of values....

Sunday Post Magazine
October 20, 1946

THERE WAS A BOY NAMED DAVID

CONRADO V. PEDROCHE

There was a boy named David. He was born in Victoria but the wonder of it is that he could have been born somewhere else, may be in Samar or perhaps in Pampanga or even in Mindanao, had not a man in Bulacan looked out of the window one fine sunshiny morning and fallen in love with a woman who was passing by. And this is as tender a love story as ever was told. The woman was passing by at the moment and she was riding a cart and she was on her way from Manila to Tarlac. It was an open cart, gayly decorated— for there was a fiesta in Tondo—and the carabao was panting and snorting through the difficult road and the woman was shrieking and laughing at every bump.

Because the man who looked out of the window saw her and fell in love with her instantly—maybe he heard the laughter and the shriek and maybe later he saw the laughing eyes and the sad little chin—because the man lost his heart to her then, he followed her to the ends of the world and that was the beginning of David but David did not know it for David came only after his mother was born of the man and the woman who met somewhere in Bulacan in the days when the railroads had not yet come to being.

At about the same time, somewhere in Pangasinan, an old woman was talking to her young son just turned to manhood: Go, she said, and see the world. To the young man, the world was a wide open space of about a few hundred kilometers square and the next day he was on his way to see it. He arrived in Tarlac a week later and settled in town. He, too, was the beginning of David, on David's father's side. The young man prospered and married and one of their sons was the father of David and this man married the daughter of the man from Bulacan. There were David's parents but David knew of this only after many, many more years.

When David was ten his mother told him about the man who looked out of the window and the woman who was passing by and his father told him about the man who walked all his way from Pangasinan and settled in town. To David, listening, these people were remote and mysterious. He did not see his grandparents for they all died before he was born. They were remote and far away as though they were people in a dream. But later he began to think of them as human beings and the mystery of their meeting began to fill the boy with wondering.

Suppose, he would think, the man from Bulacan did not look out of the window that moment or looked out of a window facing the yard instead, and suppose the man from Pangasinan took another direction and settled down in another place? Where would David be now? Possibly he would be another boy in another town or another land. The wonder was unceasing.

From bearing eleven children, David's mother could not recover. Not many women could. Whenever David looked at his mother he would think of the woman in the cart, because his mother had the woman's sad chin and the woman's laughing eyes. The little sad chin was, to him, the symbol of short life because his mother died young. David knew his first heartache when his mother died. She was a loving mother. When she died, David realized for the first time that he had a heart. He peeped out of the window and through his tears he saw that the world was sad and old. It seemed to him then that all loveliness was dead and the only sound he could hear was the beating of his heart.

David's mother was tall and thin but her heart was warm with love. David's mother called him many affectionate names. One of these names was Ding. It sounded like the tinkle of the little bell in the dilapidated church belfry. Sometimes when she called him Ding he would be startled like a bird from his play or from his thoughts for the name sounded so much like the bell and whenever he heard the bell he would think of the dimly lighted church altar and the bearded gods standing there and he would feel afraid all of a sudden. But she would smile at him and call him to her side and wrap her arms around his shoulders and he would feel her heart beating against his cheeks.

Forever after, David would feel this warm heart beating against him whenever he thought of his mother and her small sad chin.

David's father was the town treasurer. Every election there was a change of mayorship and the mayor did not have sufficient time to win the love of the people completely. But David's father was the treasurer for almost twenty years and the people came to love him. To them he was a symbol of honor and integrity. They trusted him with their money and their secrets. The history of the little town was David's father's personal history. David was proud of him but one day he found him slightly drunk and reeking with the smell of gin. David would not have minded this so much but when his father came home he scolded his mother and said many ugly words to her. David cried in his heart for a long time.

David thought that his father was a rich man because one morning when David visited him in his office he saw him counting bundles of paper bills. Once David asked him for one of them and his father smiled at him over his *ante-ojos* and kept on counting his money without saying a word and once in a while he would moisten his fingers with his tongue and resume counting the money. David raised himself up on the window and peered through the bars and he kept counting to himself but very soon he got lost somewhere near one hundred and he gave up.

David's father was also an artisan. He loved to fashion things out of boar's tusks and deer's horns—small objects of art such as cigarette holders and pipes, tiny birds and nameless little animals which David had never seen before. He loved to do this on Sundays and David would watch him pecking away with a thin sharp blade on his clattered worktable. David's father likewise carved many beautiful objects of wood and clay. This seemed to make the old man happy. He was a sad man but his sadness was only in his face. In his heart his father was happy for his life was simple and rich and human.

When David's father slept he snored aloud. He would say before he went to sleep, David, I'll give you a penny for every five gray hairs you pull out from my head while I sleep. And David would squat before his father's form and begin the weary but interesting job of pulling white hair from his father's head with the aid of a grain of palay while his father snored away. There were not many white hairs on David's father's head then, but David now remembers his father the day he lay dead in his coffin. His nose was shiny with the clammy sweat of death and his hair was very white.

David's brother was a maker of masks. With clay he would fashion the face of a laughing clown or maybe of a long-nosed, sharp-toothed monster. And after the clay had dried up he would paste soft wet newspaper over it. Layer after layer. And when it was thick enough he would let it dry up and afterwards paint a goggle around the eyes or maybe a ridiculous mustache over the lips. David's brother wanted to be a sculptor—he is now a doctor of medicine. When David told him about this in later years he smiled at him and made faces which David thought looked like the masks which he used to make.

One other brother—Carlos—was a musician. He played beautiful music with a violin and he could draw figures on paper and etch tiny objects on chalk with a scalpel. David would find these things wrapped up in cotton and kept in little boxes. Once brother Carlos did one—a figure of a woman—in blue chalk. It was beautiful and frail but when it was finished it fell on the floor and was broken. David tried to piece it together again but it was no longer as lovely as before. Brother Carlos would have been an engineer but he died young. When he died, David's mother kept the violin but the rats soon made their home inside it and later, David remembers, he tried to play with it but the strings made a queer squeaking sound which reminded him of the rats.

David remembers his first poultry shed. His father built it for him out of the frame of an old *caballarisa*. He began with three hens and a rooster. He loved to fondle the rooster and the hens which he pampered with too much feed. The chicks were David's first loves. So smooth, so light, so lovely to behold. But one day the mother hen fought him with many a muffled but furious bonging of her terrible wings and claws because she could not understand David's tender affection when he tried to hold one chick and stroke its fine delicate feathers with his fingers. Thinking of this now, David asks: Or

did the hen understand this affection and was merely jealous
of it?

Also he remembers the crazy woman in the presidencia.
For many days David went to see her. She was silent for a
long time. Then one day she began to sing and her voice was
sweet and soft and it was filled with all the sadness in her
heart and the dark night of her soul. Then suddenly her voice
rose high and piercing, soared high and shrill and mad and
the song was demented and nameless. There were tears now in
her eyes and she began to rip her clothes to tatters and very
soon she was all naked before David. David saw her nakedness,
stared in wonder at her body for a moment, and then he fled
screaming away.

David went down the house one early morning before his
mother was up and met a man under the guava trees in the
backyard. The morning was cool and sharp, or was it only the
fear in the heart of the little boy? David remembers now that
he had taken a bath before he went down the house in accord-
ance with the old man's instruction. The secret ritual under
the trees held no mysterious significance to the little David
then. But now David knows that it marked the beginning—
for him—of his first consciousness of the shapes of things—
their color and smell, and the textures of new thoughts and
feelings.

The man knew nothing of surgery but for a consideration
and with one careless slash from a gleaming blade he severed
David, completely and forever, from his childhood. For two
weeks after that David suffered because not even the young
shoots of guava leaves could have saved him from tetanus
had not his brother—the maker of masks who was now a
doctor—taken him to a drugstore. Then the mystery of medicine began to work its wonders on the wound of David's body
and in three days' time he was healed. And forever after, David was to be no longer a boy except in moments of remembering.

The days that followed after were filled with wonder for
David. First he waited for his voice to change. He waited for
a long time—for years in fact—but he did not seem to notice
any change at all. Then one morning his sister said to him:

Don't shout at me so, your voice is as big as a cow's! Then he knew that it had come at last.

David was a five-year-old youngster shouting his childish defiance at the world in Victoria, Tarlac, when his wife was born in Mexico, Pampanga. He wonders now what forces had conspired to bring them together years and years later: if he did not do this or that or something else, would he have met the girl who was destined to be his wife? He thinks that if he did not wake up one morning, for example, and see the dawn in the hills and then and there determined to write poetry, he would not have met her, because, you see, he wrote a poem about the sunrise right the very next morning and this poem he showed to his brother who shook his head and said: No, my dear brother, you should not write poetry. You should take the civil service examination and join the government service. Come with me to San Fernando and I shall give you training in arithmetic. So David gave up poetry and joined his brother in San Fernando and then there was a storm and David saw the world uprooting itself and shaking violently in anger at the winds which were shouting from the treetops. And after the storm he met the girl who was to be the mother of his children—as tempestuous a trio of boys as ever was born into the world.

David wonders now very often on the mystery of things upon the earth. And the wonder is ceaseless. How else could he have explained it? The meeting was not accidental. Things do not just happen like that. He thinks again of the man who looked out of the window in Bulacan. And of him who walked all the way from Pangasinan. No, surely not. David knows just as clearly as simply as he knows that a trillion other quivers starting from the sun and the light hundreds and hundreds of years ago have joined to make that glint on his wife's dark hair as she bends now to kiss him while he writes.

Sunday Post Magazine
October 20, 1946

THERE WILL BE ANOTHER CHRISTMAS

TOBIAS Y. ENVERGA

As Isidoro neared the town he heard the pealing of church bells cutting clear through the mist of the morning. He had come a long way from barrio Silangan. There were muddy puddles along the brown trail, for the December rain had come to cool the earth and nourish the young, tender stalks of green palay. Occasionally, Isidoro jumped over clumps of thorny *makahiya* plants that crawled timidly along the way. He could have enjoyed sitting on fallen brown coconuts scattered beneath the groves, but he had no time to waste pulling off the tiny *makahiya* thorns that had stuck into his bare little feet. He was hurrying to town. And the church bells were pealing loud and long, full and melodious.

A flush of shyness crept inside him. He realized that he was already eleven years old—too old to ask for a Christmas gift from his godfather. It had been different many years ago, when he used to clamber on his godfather's neck; pinch his flat, but bulky nose; and threaten not to release his hold unless that man gave him a new centavo coin. But now he was already big.

It was good that he had brought with him his fat, brown hen. That would be for his godfather. Isidoro had not seen him since the previous Christmas. He fancied that he would first give the chicken, kneel for the blessings, and then ask for the toy gun promised him many years ago. Of course that would be embarrassing—asking for a Christmas gift. But simple minds were keen at knowing the age-mellowed principle of give and take. At home in the barrio, his mother had reminded him of that. She said, "Isidoro, big boys do not ask for Christmas gifts without giving something in return." And he had answered brightly, "Why, mother—I have a fat hen for my godfather."

Now he was passing a narrow path with tall cogon bushes growing profusely on both sides. He kept to the middle of the path because little cakes of soft, brown mud clung annoyingly on the cogon leaves. He knew that a carabao, fresh from its mud bath, had passed by a while ago; and because the path was narrow, the cogon leaves had scraped the broad sides of the huge beast. This clinging mud he triumphantly evaded.

He crossed a rice paddy. He stepped onto the trunk of a coconut tree that served as a dike; and a small frog jumped from the grasses onto his knee. He squirmed. The hen wriggled its legs and cackled questioningly as he precariously tried to maintain his balance.

He looked at the striped polo shirt and the short, faded blue pants he was wearing. They were not soiled. The exposed parts of his body were deep brown. His skin had been burned in the ricefields during the hot days, and now it was peeling off. At first he had been glad that his burned skin was changing. But then he found out that as the skin peeled off, it looked like tiny, white scales of dried fish.

He was perspiring although the wind was cool; and when he felt the wind blowing on his face, he pulled the buri hat firmly over his head, almost covering his big, black eyes. He touched his flat nose and his big ears and found them cool. He rubbed them vigorously with his fingers until they were warm. His haircut worried him. He had insisted on wearing long hair so he could part it in the middle and pour coconut oil on it as his friend, Marcial, used to do. He had instructed the barrio barber, Mako, to cut off only the edges. But his uncle Polon had come and had sternly insisted on the close cut. He was afraid of his uncle Polon.

His godfather had promised to give him a good Christmas gift this year. "Next Christmas," his godfather had said, "I shall give you a toy gun. At peacetime." And now it was 1945, and peacetime. Isidoro knew that. His teacher in Silangan barrio school had told him so.

He remembered the time when his godfather had first promised him a toy gun for a Christmas gift. Let me see, it was 1945-44-43-42-41, yes 1941. He was seven years old then. His playmate, Andong, had pointed a toy gun at his stomach, and he had cried. He had wanted to get even with Andong ever since; and, when he asked his godfather for a toy gun, his godfather had said, "Next Christmas, Isidoro, you shall have one."

But then, two days before Christmas that year, the airplanes had come and dropped glittering bombs over the town. He remembered clearly how his mother had paled and run off with him into the hills. And when he saw his godfather one month after that Christmas, his godfather said, "Sorry, Isidoro. There is a war going on. Do you know? The war has started. I had a toy gun ready for you but my house was burned and your toy gun went with it. I shall give you one when peacetime comes. Next Christmas, maybe."

The Christmas of 1942 came and Isidoro asked his godfather to bless him. And his godfather said, "I cannot even feed you with rice cakes, Isidoro. Too bad. There is no sugar—and no rice. I shall give you a toy gun when peacetime comes. Next Christmas, maybe."

And so on through the Christmases up to the year 1944. His godfather would always helplessly wave his already calloused and thinning hands and say, "At peacetime, my boy—next Christmas, maybe."

Isidoro crossed a shallow stream. He washed his feet and legs before stepping onto the stony street for now he was in town. Some boys shouted at their play and the fat, brown hen he was carrying gave a sudden jerk, freed its wings, and flapped them vigorously. He held the hen up by the legs and it wriggled and peered into his face with a puzzled look. Isidoro tucked the hen again under his arm and smoothed its shiny, brown feathers.

People from the church were streaming out and big bells pealed cheerfully and incessantly. Isidoro wondered at the ringing of the bells. The full metallic clang burst with joy. A whiff of rice cake odor reached his nostrils and for a moment he thought it was the smell of Christmas. The smell of peace. He felt like a big, strong man.

He looked around and saw the town still a shambles. There was the improvised church with a nipa roof. That ground over there, on the other side, was where the school building had been. There were only a few Christmas lanterns, he thought. Not like many years ago when there had been many Christmas trees and big, red stars hanging at the windows.

He turned to the left and there was his godfather's house. Before the war, his godfather had owned a big store and he had lived in a big house. Now, in place of the big house stood his tiny bamboo and nipa hut with rusty, burnt galvanized iron clumsily patched here and there.

And that was his godfather. He could see him sitting by the window smoking a cigarette. His godfather's long face was wearing an ugly scowl. It was unusual. UnChristmas-like. Isidoro had known him to be young and tall and cheerful. Now he had grown old and his closely-cropped hair was beginning to run gray.

His godfather sighted him as he entered the gate of the bamboo fence and Isidoro's face lighted into broad smile. He ascended the three-step bamboo ladder and found his godfather barefooted and wearing only a pair of green drawers and green undershirt. His godfather was alone in his house; for his wife, Inang Asiang, was still in the church and the children were visiting their relatives. Isidoro knelt awkwardly and grabbed his godfather's right hand which was holding a half-smoked, slovenly-wrapped, homemade cigarette. His godfather transferred the cigarette into his left hand and allowed Isidoro to kiss his right. "Merry Christmas, *Ninong*," Isidoro said. And his godfather patted him on the back and said, "Merry Christmas, my boy."

Before Isidoro knew it, he was already asking for the toy gun. He forgot to give first the fat hen as he had previously planned, and felt ashamed. He looked at his godfather's face. It was tired-looking and sad. Then timidly, Isidoro said. "Here is a chicken for you, Ninong. I raised this myself in barrio Silangan."

His godfather unwound the *buri* cord that tied the already swollen feet. "Thank you, Isidoro," he simply said. He led his godson to the kitchen and tied the hen quietly to a bamboo leg of the stove. The hen could not stand for its feet were numb. Isidoro looked at the stove and saw nothing but the last ember dying.

His godfather threw the cigarette butt away, and sat on the creaky floor by the nipa wall, and spat between the stripped bamboo flooring. Isidoro squatted near him. Then slowly, a scowl appeared on his godfather's face, and he looked like an ailing man with the mark of bitter experience on his knotty brow. And the man said, "My boy, people say it is peacetime—but still, everything is too heavy for me. I cannot find work. You understand? I want to work but there is no work. And there is no peace."

Isidoro somehow felt in the quiver of the voice that there was something big at stake in his godfather's life. But his boyish heart could not understand how work, or the lack of it, could make and unmake Christmas, could make and unmake peace. He could not comprehend the harsh and exacting relation between work and existence itself.

The godfather raised his head and leaned on the nipa wall while thoughts about unChristmas-like realities reverberated in his brain.

The boy was about to say something he knew not, understood not, but then the two—godfather and godson—heard the merry voices of young boys and girls who had just arrived from the old town church. The gladsome and excited voices greeted one another with the Season's joy. The incessant reverberation of church bells grew louder, choked the ears of Isidoro and his godfather, and drove away whatever fears had petrified their lives.

They looked around and saw the big fat hen stand and cackle wonderingly. The hen's cackle, proud and full and throaty, was warm and reassuring.

Isidoro's face brightened and his eyes told the man that they must carry on. His godfather smiled at him like a sick child who had become strong at the sight of the playmate. "I shall give you a gift, my boy," his godfather said. "Next Christmas. Without fail."

And Isidoro was happy because he had faith in his godfather and in the pealing of church bells.

Philippines Free Press
December 14, 1946

FOREST OF TALL TREES

ANTONIO S. GABILA

To the end, he remembered Bataan. But not as a monument to the courage of his race, not as a graveyard of hopes and dreams.....That came later, for others, years later, the bright shining words, the bugle-sounds, the flag-waving, as though all that could wash away the blood on rock and grass, the palsy and the unforgettable hurt.

Lying sick in Capas, he thought of Bataan. But always it was as a forest, a wide forest, of tall trees. Perhaps because the trees in Bataan were a symbol, and symbols do not die. Or perhaps because Capas and Bataan were two worlds. One, a world of the living—dying suddenly. The other, a world of the dying—dying slowly.

There were no trees in Capas. Only stumps and bare branches whose leaves had long before been chewed up for food. There was no hope in Capas. Only worms and white lice and fat blue flies and rotten flesh and the deep canker of bitterness.

When he first arrived after the agony of the long march, he would stretch himself in the dust, in the sun, within the barbed-wire fence, and pick lice from his clothes and skin, and talk. There was always Caro who'd listen to him, and sometimes one or two more of their group. Talk was a release; there was escape in the sound of words shaped in the mind and given voice.

He talked of his home, his mother, his girl. And of what he would do, afterward. How he would build bridges and roads and homes; not the way he had been taught in college, but the way he wanted to build them now. Beautiful spans that would fling a bow at heaven and yet be anchored solidly to earth. Swift roads that led somewhere. White, comfortable homes that would be worlds unto themselves. Things for men and women, and their children, too. Solid things, useful things.

But all these things were designs for the morrow, patterns drawn in the dust of Capas, within the wire fence, born in the brain, with the feel of God's sun on the face, though only a few feet away from the barracks and the filth and smell of death. That was during the first month, the first few weeks, when there was some hope for the living and still a few tears for the dead and the dying.

Afterward he was among the men who stayed all day and all night in the barracks sprawling on the two tiers of floors; there was no more lying in the sun and playing with the warm dust of the compound. There was no dreaming of deeds to do tomorrow, no talk of home and girl.

There was only a staring at the ceiling, fighting off the flies and suffering the lice, and the eternal hungering for food in thought and actuality. And the chills and smells, and the noise that pain makes in the human throat. And above all else, the unutterable anger and bitterness and hopelessness that poison the blood and make a man suddenly jump up in the night and shout and cry.....

Afterward, how long afterward he would not have been able to say, he would watch the distribution of the few grains of rice and few drops of water without feeling any need or attaching any importance to the event. He would listen to the muttering of his comrades on how their former officers kept most of the food for themselves that should have gone to nourish the sick. He watched the inevitable moral disintegration of the men as they fought, without being ashamed, over a single boiled potato, the still strong against the sick. He would look on the recently dead being stripped of their rags to clothe the ragless living and then flung outside to await burial, without any emotion or protest or shock.

The days and nights were alike without promise, and thought and feeling merged sometimes into a haze through which he drifted like a dry leaf. The blue flies settled on his face and body and left tiny wet pellets that dried on him. He seldom moved, because it cost so much effort, except when the fever and the chills seized him.

Sometimes he would have fits of new strength, when he would feel strong enough to talk to Caro, who lay quiet and unspeaking beside him. Caro took ill five days after he did. Caro, who went through Bataan and the long sad trek to Capas, was always by his side. Strange that he should think of Caro.

"Caro," he said. "Caro."

He had to shake the other, and the effort left him weak.

"That's right," Caro answered weakly. "Want to know if I'm still alive."

"Don't be an ass," he said.

"Ass is right. Soon I won't even be that."

"How are you feeling?" he said.

"Haven't any," Caro said.

"Same here. Feel as though there isn't any me any more."

"Wonder who we are," Caro murmured.

"Don't know," he said. "You ask the most damnable questions."

That sort of talk. But it was getting rarer and rarer, such fits of energy cropping up in talk. Most often he would just lie quietly, midway between waking and sleeping, and once when the burial detail grabbed at him thinking he was dead, he moaned, and as from some vast distance, he heard someone laugh and say, "Not today, Josephine!"

And he wondered who Josephine was and why not today ...but somehow the thought got mixed up with the sound of waterfalls...and then he was back again in Bataan, bathing his feet in the icy waters of a mountain spring, or sitting at the foot of a tall tree, feeling the stoutness of the thick trunk seeping through his tired, frail body, or trudging through the undergrowth, looking up at the thick mass of leaves high overhead and marveling at the little pieces of blue sky caught in them....Bataan without the shrieking shells, the splintered trees, the spattered blood.

But it was not always as peaceful as that. Sometimes he would fight the battles of Bataan all over again...the hideous shriek of shells tearing through the air to blow up among trees and rocks and men, with ear-splitting thunders...the high-pitched whine of diving planes, machine guns chattering, and then the climactic bursts of bombs. And he would roll on the floor where he lay and cry....

No one minded any more. It was the usual thing, the thing expected. Sooner or later, everyone did it—the inner will giving way to the horror once lived and made part of the mind, the deep anguish breaking all bonds, the utter hopelessness given release.

At the end, it was Bataan that he remembered.

For days he lay in a coma, then he had another dream.

There was that secret pool he knew so well, far from the touch and thought of war. There stood the same gnarled old tree spreading its branches and leaves over the pool and sending its thick roots running thirstily down to the water as though to drink it dry.

He and Caro came upon it at the end of a long day's forced march on the weary retreat from Mt. Samat. But it was he who saw it first.

"God," he said, sinking tiredly under the tree and drinking in the peace and beauty of it all. "This is where I want to die."

"Well, you're not dead yet," Caro said, peeling off his clothes. "And I can still swim."

So he stood up and took off his clothes, too. For one brief moment he stood poised on a thick root over the edge of the pool, looking down at Caro who was splashing and crawling through the cool water. And then he plunged....

In the morning, they found his clothes on the floor two tiers above the aisle where his naked body lay. There was no need of stripping him, so they lifted him by the arms and legs and threw him outside. Then they went back and took Caro, who had died the same night, and dropped him beside his pal until a common grave could be dug for them and the others who had not lived through the night.

And there they lay, once more in the dust of Capas, under God's bright sun, inside the barbed-wire fence....

Evening News Saturday Magazine
January 25, 1947

MY FATHER GOES TO COURT

CARLOS BULOSAN

When I was four, I lived with my mother and brothers and sisters in a small town on the island of Luzon. Father's farm had been destroyed in 1918 by one of our sudden Philippine floods, so for several years afterward we all lived in the town, though he preferred living in the country. We had a next-door neighbor, a very rich man, whose sons and daughters seldom came out of the house. While we boys and girls played and sang in the sun, his children stayed inside and kept the windows closed. His house was so tall that his children could look in the windows of our house and watch us as we played, or slept, or ate, when there was any food in the house to eat.

Now, this rich man's servants were always frying and cooking something good, and the aroma of the food was wafted down to us from the windows of the big house. We hung about and took all the wonderful smell of the food into our beings. Sometimes, in the morning, our whole family stood outside the windows of the rich man's house and listened to the musical sizzling of thick strips of bacon or ham. I can remember one afternoon when our neighbor's servants roasted three chickens. The chickens were young and tender and the fat that dripped into the burning coals gave off an enchanting odor. We watched the servants turn the beautiful birds and inhaled the heavenly spirit that drifted out to us.

Some days the rich man appeared at a window and glowered down at us. He looked at us one by one, as though he were condemning us. We were all healthy because we went out in the sun every day and bathed in the cool water of the river that flowed from the mountains into the sea. Sometimes we wrestled with one another in the house before we went out to play.

We were always in the best of spirits and our laughter was contagious. Other neighbors who passed by our house often stopped in our yard and joined us in our laughter.

Laughter was our only wealth. Father was a laughing man. He would go in to the living room and stand in front of the tall mirror, stretching his mouth into grotesque shapes with his fingers and making faces at himself; then he would rush into the kitchen, roaring with laughter.

There was plenty to make us laugh. There was, for instance, the day one of my brothers came home and brought a small bundle under his arm, pretending that he brought something to eat, maybe a leg of lamb or something as extravagant as that, to make our mouths water. He rushed to mother and threw the bundle into her lap. We all stood around, watching mother undo the complicated strings. Suddenly a black cat leaped out of the bundle and ran wildly around the house. Mother chased my brother and beat him with her little fists, while the rest of us bent double, choking with laughter.

Another time one of my sisters suddenly started screaming in the middle of the night. Mother reached her first and tried to calm her. My sister cried and groaned. When father lifted the lamp, my sister stared at us with shame in her eyes.

"What is it?" Mother asked.

"I'm pregnant!" she cried.

"Don't be a fool!" Father shouted.

"You are only a child," Mother said.

"I'm pregnant, I tell you!" she cried.

Father knelt by my sister. He put his hand on her belly and rubbed it gently. "How do you know you are pregnant?" he asked.

"Feel it!" she cried.

We put our hands on her belly. There was something moving inside. Father was frightened. Mother was shocked. "Who's the man?" she asked.

"There's no man," my sister said.

"What is it, then?" Father asked.

Suddenly my sister opened her blouse and a bullfrog jumped out. Mother fainted, Father dropped the lamp, the oil spilled on the floor, and my sister's blanket caught fire. One of my brothers laughed so hard he rolled on the floor.

When the fire was extinguished and Mother was revived, we returned to bed and tried to sleep, but Father kept on laughing so loud we could not sleep any more. Mother got up again and lighted the oil lamp; we rolled up the mats on the floor and began dancing about and laughing with all our might. We made so much noise that all our neighbors except the rich family came into the yard and joined us in loud, genuine laughter.

It was like that for years.

As time went on, the rich man's children became thin and anemic, while we grew even more robust and full of life. Our faces were bright and rosy, but theirs were pale and sad. The rich man started to cough at night; then he coughed day and night. His wife began coughing too. Then the children started to cough one after the other. At night their coughing sounded like the barking of a herd of seals. We hung outside their windows and listened to them. We wondered what had happened to them. We knew that they were not sick from lack of nourishing food because they were still always frying something delicious to eat.

One day the rich man appeared at a window and stood there a long time. He looked at my sisters, who had grown fat with laughing, then at my brothers, whose arms and legs were like the *molave*, which is the sturdiest tree in the Philippines. He banged down the window and ran through the house, shutting all the windows.

From that day on, the windows of our neighbor's house were closed. The children did not come outdoors anymore. We could still hear the servants cooking in the kitchen, and no matter how tight the windows were shut, the aroma of the food came to us in the wind and drifted gratuitously into our house.

One morning a policeman from the *presidencia* came to our house with a sealed paper. The rich man had filed a complaint against us. Father took me with him when he went to the town clerk and asked him what it was all about. He told Father the man claimed that for years we had been stealing the spirit of his wealth and food.

When the day came for us to appear in court, Father brushed his old army uniform and borrowed a pair of shoes from one of my brothers. We were the first to arrive. Father sat on a chair in the center of the courtroom. Mother occupied a chair by the door. We children sat on a long bench by the wall. Father kept jumping up from his chair and stabbing the air with his arms, as though he were defending himself before an imaginary jury.

The rich man arrived. He had grown old and feeble; his face was scarred with deep lines. With him was his young lawyer. Spectators came in and almost filled the chairs. The judge entered the room and sat on a high chair. We stood up in a hurry and then sat down again.

After the courtroom preliminaries, the judge looked at Father. "Do you have a lawyer?" he asked.

"I don't need any lawyer, Judge," he said.

"Proceed," said the judge.

The rich man's lawyer jumped and pointed his finger at Father. "Do you or do you not agree that you have been stealing the spirit of the complainant's wealth and food?"

"I do not!" Father said.

"Do you or do you not agree that while the complainant's servants cooked and fried fat legs of lambs or young chicken breasts, you and your family hung outside your windows and inhaled the heavenly spirit of the food?"

"I agree," Father said.

"Do you or do you not agree that while the complainant and his children grew sickly and tubercular, you and your family became strong of limb and fair of complexion?"

"I agree," Father said.

"How do you account for that?"

Father got up and paced around, scratching his head thoughtfully. Then he said, "I would like to see the children of the complainant, Judge."

"Bring in the children of the complainant."

They came in shyly. The spectators covered their mouths with their hands. They were so amazed to see the children so thin and pale. The children walked silently to a bench and sat down without looking up. They stared at the floor and moved their hands uneasily.

Father could not say anything at first. He just stood by his chair and looked at them. Finally he said, "I should like to cross-examine the complainant."

"Proceed."

"Do you claim that we stole the spirit of your wealth and became a laughing family while yours became morose and sad?" Father asked.

"Yes."

"Do you claim that we stole the spirit of your food by hanging outside your windows when your servants cooked it?" Father asked.

"Yes."

"Then we are going to *pay* you right now," Father said. He walked over to where we children were sitting on the bench and took my straw hat off my lap and began filling it up with *centavo* pieces that he took out of his pockets. He went to Mother, who added a fistful of silver coins. My brothers threw in their small change.

"May I walk to the room across the hall and stay there for a few minutes, Judge?" Father asked.

"As you wish."

"Thank you," Father said. He strode into the other room with the hat in his hands. It was almost full of coins. The doors of both rooms were wide open.

"Are you ready?" Father called.

"Proceed," the judge said.

The sweet tinkle of the coins carried beautifully into the room. The spectators turned their faces toward the sound with wonder. Father came back and stood before the complainant.

"Did you hear it?" he asked.

"Hear what?" the man asked.

"The spirit of the money when I shook this hat?" he asked.

"Yes."

"Then you are paid," Father said.

The rich man opened his mouth to speak and fell to the floor without a sound. The lawyer rushed to his aid. The judge pounded his gavel.

"Case dismissed," he said.

Father strutted around the courtroom. The judge even came down from his high chair to shake hands with him. "By the way," he whispered, "I had an uncle who died laughing."

"You like to hear my family laugh, Judge?" Father asked.

"Why not?"

"Did you hear that, children?" Father said.

My sisters started it. The rest of us followed them and soon the spectators were laughing with us, holding their bellies and bending over the chairs. And the laughter of the judge was the loudest of all.

Philippines Free Press
January 26, 1947

MAKER OF SONGS

STEVAN JAVELLANA

In those days we had a name for him: Napoleon. There was little about him, really, to suggest the French caesar except for the fact that his stature was just a gauge above the diminutive. In fact he was much shorter than the man after whom we called him. As I remember now when I first saw him I was immediately struck by his slender build, his round rosy face which he constantly dabbed with a handkerchief, and his quick, sharp movements. He had a manner of walking, with full strides that was rather disproportionate to his short legs, his left arm swinging out jauntily in a wide arc while his right hand hugged a portfolio of music sheets to his outthrust breast. In those times too, I recall, he smiled often and when he laughed you wanted to laugh with him. He was a likeable fellow, pleased with himself and contented with the world.

When I first came to know him he had not yet taken a wife, and being young and flushed with his first success, he appeared to be perpetually walking on a cloud. He had just finished composing a series of kundimans that had instantly caught and held the fancy of the public. The music sheets were selling very well and he got around, radiating good fellowship and an engaging conviviality with which (he thought) a singularly successful creative artist ought to dilute his feeling of importance and greatness. Always he walked briskly like a healthy cock robin, flashing his friendly smile, with his rather large head cocked birdlike to one side as if he were listening to a strain of music—his music.

For he was a maker of songs, was this man, and he looked at all things around him with the interpretative, rainbow-colored eyes of the artist. Bright colors shimmered and glowed in the songs he made. Songs that were meant to be sung by happy folk and I suppose that people were happy those days because so many sang or hummed his songs or played them tirelessly on the piano or the sobbing guitar. The few sad songs that he made were a happy man's sad songs. Discontent had not cupped dark over his eyes nor yet grief sheathed his voice.

He was brother to all sounds and shapes and emotions. He sang the joyousness of laughter in the throat of a happy child. He sang the beauty of many women. He sang the ecstasy of love. Sometimes, as we sat on the rocks near Fort San Pedro and looked at the blue blur of Guimaras across the dark Iloilo Strait, he would gently touch my hand and whisper, "Listen!" And I would try to listen while he, rapt-eyed and grave, said, "Tis the song of the wind but it is lost now." Among many he was one who could hear the song of the wind. He had the heart, we used to think.

I was sort of a poet then, trying to catch the varying moods of weather and light and shadow, the subtle shades of feeling. I could not help but be somewhat envious of his success. Sometimes on an afternoon as we strolled he would stop all of a sudden and exclaim, "That's my music!" And from a nearby house would hobble the limping notes of his danza being picked out by inexpert fingers from the keys of a piano. He would stand there entranced because it was his music. Later I began to suspect that he did not ask me to walk with him on afternoons to capture new ideas but so that he could espy some singer of his songs. But I found out that I was wrong. Listening to his compositions being sung by others actually gave him new ideas and the inspiration to make still another song.

To annoy him, I would sometimes plead that I was busy working on something. But he had a way of persuading people. In the end I always went with him.

You might have heard some of his songs. They were sentimental songs, songs of serenade, songs of heartbreak. They told of happiness, laughter or tears.

At that time he was turning out songs with an inspired energy that was matched only by the enormous capacity of his public for his music. His simple music had everybody singing. His lilting kundimans were played on tinkly pianos everywhere. People danced to his dreamy waltzes. Bands and orchestras blared his interpretations of folk music.

Money came in and he felt big like a king. Sometimes he would stand by a rock by the sea, his short figure erect against a high wind that ruffled his long hair. He would stand there, not saying a word, motionless and small against the sea. I could imagine him flinging a haughty challenge at the waves: Look at me. I have made music. I have captured joy, love and laughter in music, grief even. I have caught in song the heart and soul and dream of man. Everybody laughs with me, cries with me. Am I not truly godlike?

Recognition came to him from Paris, France. The committee in charge of the Colonial Exposition that was being held there that year awarded him a diploma for the exhibit that he had entered. My friend, you see, had for many months been painstakingly compiling folk songs, old and new, and the reward for his work was this diploma from Paris, France.

It was a pretty thing, this diploma. Made of parchment, its face was liberally sprinkled with naked human figures in heroic or symbolistic postures, representing the arts and letters and sciences. There were also figures of ferocious-looking bulls and other animals; there were wheels and sailing vessels with billowing sails and cathedrals and fruit-bearing trees and machinery and such like. They had a sculptured look of a bas-relief. The diploma was indeed an imposing affair.

There were also words but they were French and we did not know French. Anyway, what we were most interested in was the name which was written in delicate script right in the center of the diploma. And this name, although written in French in a weblike tracery of elaborate script, was the name of our friend, the maker of songs. It was good to look at it.

For several weeks he carried around this diploma in his portfolio to show his friends and acquaintances and to anybody who might express a desire to see it. Later he had the citation translated by a sister of charity who was teaching French in one of the *colegios* for girls. The French words said that the diploma was the only one of its kind and was being awarded to my friend for the beautiful Visayan folk songs that he compiled and submitted for the exhibition.

When my friend had shown the diploma to everybody he caused it to be reproduced on the back of his music sheets. I don't know if this made any appreciable increase in the sale of his songs. Then he framed the diploma in an elaborate golden frame and hung it in the place of honor above his piano.

Not so long after his receipt of the diploma he said to me, "Don't you think that it is about time that I wrote something important?"

"Important?" I echoed. I was rather surprised because I had thought he was perfectly satisfied with his folk tunes and the encouraging way they were selling. I thought he was happy and content with his beautiful diploma won in an exposition in Paris, France.

"Yes," he said softly, and he leaned toward me as if he would confide a secret. "Yes, something really important," he repeated, his eyes shining a little. "A piano concert, for instance, with a distinctly Filipino theme. Or a symphonic poem for a full orchestra, to interpret the Filipino spirit. How about that?"

His small, high-pitched voice was eager, demanding.

"I can do it, too," he said a little breathlessly before I could answer, as if he wanted to hear the sound of his voice reassuring himself that he could do it.

"Why not?" I said because I did not want to hurt him by asking what background he had, because I did not wish to discourage him by saying that composing a piano concerto was not as simple as compiling folk music or as easy as making a song, even a happy song.

"I can do it," he repeated firmly.

Afterward I knew that he was actually working on the "really important" thing because I did not see him in his usual haunts for the next two weeks or so.

At last he showed himself again. "I have made a good start," he said, tapping with his blunt fingers on the coffee shop table. "A very fine start."

"That is nice," I said. But he was not listening to me anymore. His eyes were half-closed and dreamy and that was always a sign. Then, without another word, he picked up his bulging portfoilo and hurried out of the shop.

The next time I saw him it was plain that he was fairly bursting with important news from the way his face was wreathed with a luminous smile.

"I have great news for you," he announced. "I am getting married."

It seems a long time ago and I don't remember very clearly everything that happened on his wedding day. I still recall, though, that there was an abundance of laughter and singing. There was much singing. Maybe they thought it as a good omen to start marriage with laughter and song.

My friend, the brave maker of songs, had married a pretty young girl with a pleasant enough singing voice. He would make her the singer of his songs.

"She has the talent to become a great singer," he whispered to me. I noted the possessive pride in his voice as we stood apart in a corner of the parlor listening to her sing to the wedding guests one of his most popular kundimans. "And what is more important, she has the heart. That is why I know that she will become a great artist.

"I will send her to study. She will study voice. She has the art, she has the gift. One day she will be a great singer. She will sing my songs. Together we will be great. From now on I will make only happy songs. Having her beside me I cannot make anything but happy songs."

Shortly afterward I had to go away to study and for several years we lost track of each other. One summer I came home for a vacation and encountered him in Calle Real.

"And what are you doing these days?" I inquired after we had exchanged greetings.

"Oh, the usual thing," he said carefully, somewhat evasively.

"How many kids do you have now?" I asked.

"Three."

I should have attempted some sort of joke, something that might have been expected to be said to a friend married just four years who had already three kids. I don't know why I did not.

"Tell me," I said. "How is your wife?"

"Oh, she is fine, fine," he said quickly.

I invited him to have a drink with me but he said no; he was in a great hurry because he had an appointment. I wanted to ask him if he had been able to send his wife to school but I suppose I realized, even then, that as things were he could not possibly send her to school to become a really good singer. I wanted to ask him if he had completed his concerto or symphonic poem or whatever it was that was "really important"

but already he had walked away, his limp ancient leather portfolio tightly tucked under his arm.

I had a vague suspicion that he would have avoided meeting me had that been possible and was therefore surprised
when he called at home two days later. He had his wife with
him.

She was still very pretty and she could still smile. But her
face bore the traces of four years of child-bearing and child-
rearing. There were wrinkles at the outer corners of her eyes
and her mouth had a tired droop. She was big with child.

For a while the three of us struggled valiantly with small
talk, both of them plying me with questions regarding my stud-
ies and my life away from home. Desperately we tried to re-
capture the easy amiability of the past until I felt compelled
to ask him what new songs he had written.

"Of course you have made many new songs," I said.

He stood up, walked toward the piano, and opened it. He
ran his fingers experimentally over the keyboard. He twirled
the piano stool to the desired height and sat down. He began
playing a new song with the old and timeworn gestures and
flourishes of hands and fingers that I knew so well.

In the meantime his wife had snapped open the portfolio
and drawn out a stack of music sheets.

"These are his songs," she said in a soft voice so that we
would not disturb his playing. Tenderly she fingered the sheets
so that I could see the title of each. They were his old songs,
I could see at a glance, except for two or three new ones. Three
new songs to show for four years.

"Inday," he called over his shoulder, "will you sing a song
for our friend?"

"Yes, please," I seconded.

She gave me a quick smile and rose. She stood beside the
piano and twined her fingers before her. She assumed the stance
of a singer as he ran off the usual trills of the introduction.
And then she sang. At that moment I could have closed my
eyes and believed that I was listening to the same undis-
tinguished voice that had sung at a wedding party years ago.

The singer finished singing and I clapped my hands softly,
politely. Already he was playing the introduction to another
song and presently she was singing this second song. She also
sang the third new song.

They were not the happy songs that on his wedding day he had vowed he would make henceforth. They were not sad songs either. To my ears they were mediocre, monotonous, indifferent songs, without body, without distinctive melody, surprisingly not much unlike his earlier songs.

She had taken his place at the piano and was playing his other compositions. She played hard and loud and the piano shook.

"Well?" he said to me.

"They are nice," I lied.

"They are good songs," he asserted quietly, almost in the same voice that had affirmed that he would make something "really important" one day.

His wife had stopped playing. She stood beside his chair and she had a hand on his shoulder. "Doesn't he like any of them?" she asked wearily. Perspiration stood at the tip of her nose and on her forehead. She looked very tired. Perhaps she shouldn't be playing so vigorously in her condition.

"Now, Inday," he protested, somewhat embarrassed.

And then I realized that there was a purpose in their visit. They had come to sell some music sheets. They were peddling his songs. It had come to that.

"I like them," I said quickly. I counted ten of the sheets. "I'll get these."

"But you haven't chosen," he remonstrated.

"It doesn't matter," I said. "I know that they are good."

I glanced at him quickly. I saw that I had not deceived him. There was a deeply hurt look in his eyes, like that of a child whose first illusion had been broken.

But she had not seen it.

"I will choose for you," she said happily. "I know that they are all good but I'll choose my own favorites for you."

There was some desultory talk after that but they left shortly, the ten-peso bill that I had handed him folded safely inside her handbag. As they walked away I stood there staring after them, at the maker of songs and his wife who was to have sung his happy songs. She was leaning a little on his arm because she was heavy with child. And I thought of the piano concerto that he had hoped to compose, the happy songs that he was going to write.

That was the last time I saw them before the war. After liberation I saw him again. During those first few months after liberation, clothings were still difficult to secure and those that could be had were being sold at high prices. So that when I returned home one of the first things I did was to go to the city market, hoping to meet some American sailor or soldier who would be willing to sell a shirt, maybe, for the price of a drink.

One day near the market place I saw men and women crowding around a pushcart that was full of all sorts of relief second-hand clothing. I pushed my way through the crowd and began rummaging for a shirt among the jumble of ladies' dresses, chemises, men's pants, shorts, jackets, sweaters, pajama bottoms without matching uppers, drawers and so forth. At last I found one and looked up to inquire of the vendor the price.

The peddler was he, my old friend, the maker of songs. His hair had turned grey at the temples, and his round face had lost its boyish look forever. I remember the name that we had for him: Napoleon.

He was looking straight at me but he did not show any sign that he knew me.

"How much does this cost?" I said, holding up the shirt.

"Ten pesos," he said.

I knew that the oversized, secondhand blue shirt was hardly worth half that price but I did not haggle. I gave him the money and stepped hurriedly out of the crowd.

Philippines Free Press
August 9, 1947

STORY FOR SUMMER

MAXIMO RAMOS

Kardo ranged across the arid land, a flat rattan bag slung across his back. Away to the north and east the mountains stood purple, the outlines of the individual peaks lost in the distance.

He had gone without water during the greater part of the summer afternoon and now he was thirsty. Earlier in the day he had been to Apga, out near the San Felipe border, a place still moist enough to be September, with the rice puffing out of the ear. Lotus beds grew thick in the hollows, their broad leaves dark-green on the water. The broom grass was thick there, too, and coucals blew with full throats as if unaware that they had a whole six months to wait before the July monsoon came around again to give them cause for celebration with so much singing.

The climbing perch that he ate for lunch he had caught in Apga while bathing among the water plants. He had playfully overturned the water hyacinths hardening on the bank and had caught frogs there. Then he had cooked rice under a clump of bamboos, at the same time broiling the perch and frog-legs on a spit of reed stalk. The melting fat dripped onto the live coals and curled up in fragrance.

After his meal he had dug a shallow well where the grass grew in a thick mat. He made the water come out clear by draining the hole three or four times till the water showed limpid over the clean blue stones and washed sand. Then he knelt on the bank and immersed his mouth, drinking deeply. The water was cool and Kardo doused his face and neck with it. He sat up for a while, then lay down under a casuarina tree, and the trill of a marsh warbler on the farther bank of the brook lulled him to sleep.

And in his sleep he had a dream. It was about a girl he had never seen before, light of step and long of hair. Her laughter was pleasant to hear, and laughing now for some reason, she showed her white teeth. When he arose she turned lightly and fled, and the outline of her back and litheness of her motion were good to see. He pursued her and was at the point of overtaking her when the cavernous lowing of a bull awoke him and broke his delightful dream. Kardo rubbed his eyes, slung his rattan bag across his shoulders, and was off again.

He thought fondly of the pleasant place now because he was so thirsty. He had made one more search of the nearby fields to see if his carabao might not be right there after all, but among the herds grazing on the banks and in the hollows he did not see his animal.

And so here he was, following a footpath across an arid plateau. From where he stood he could see nothing except a large tree standing among leafless bamboos far to the north, a little down the edge of the high plain. He felt too tired to go as far as that tree today; but telling himself he must find a well somewhere and get himself a drink, he set his jaw and plodded on.

He got there and found the large tree to be a *duhat*, taller than he had thought it would be, massive of bole, its abundant black fruit hanging in juicy plumpness from sprays. On the ground were overripe fruits which had dropped of themselves. Birds from the surrounding fields had come to this lone green spot and were even now loud in chorus among the branches: starlings and orioles and numerous warblers.

Kardo could not encircle the bole of the giant tree with his arms, so he walked to a bamboo clump and cut down a dry bamboo, leaving its lateral branches for holds. He leaned the bamboo against the gnarled trunk of the *duhat*, and soon he was clinging among the topmost branches, eating of the succulent fruit as he went along.

He climbed as high as he felt it safe to go and then he stopped to look about. There was nothing he could see to south or east, but to the north, farther down the slope, a green grove stood beyond a long line of young trees. Groves of bananas and still unidentifiable trees, and a wide field of black beans, surrounded a house with a pointed roof of thatch, and there, drawing water from a well, stood a woman, he could

not say whether young or old, with a crimson kerchief tied about
her hair.

His thirst leaping for appeasement, Kardo climbed down
the tree and made straight for the spot of green. The sun
was now fairly low and would soon set. A faint breeze had
started to rise.

And then, suddenly, on his way down to the valley he saw
his carabao. It was grazing among forty or fifty others in a
fertile hollow behind the row of trees he had seen from the
top of the *duhat* tree.

The carabao looked at Kardo with wide-eyed surprise. It
hung its head in shame, then began edging off toward the
green grove where he had seen the female figure at the well.
Kardo, knowing carabaos, sat down and relaxed. He reached
into the bag at his back and produced a handful of green grass,
sprucing up the blades to make them appear fresh. He had gathered this in an enclosure back in Nagtugawan and the dry
summer weather had curled up the tips of the leaves. He held
the grass aloft and in a familiar tone called out:

"Ngwaa...ah!"

The big bull, a long strand of grass dangling from between
its jaws, started to trot off. Kardo followed unhurried. Soon
he was whistling an old tune, and at the proper moment he
sang out the words:

Listen, my love, to this my call in the starlight;
Open your heart and hear my song in the night!

The carabao was just at the point of going into a full
gallop then, but at the familiar tune it stopped. Kardo proceeded with his song:

Come out, my love, to me in the cool of the night,
For the midnight bird is abroad in the starlight.

By this time Kardo, stroking the carabao gently, had
reached for the base of its tail. Now he was saying in a friendly
tone:

"You are no sight at all, are you, old rascal? So unwashed,
the mud caked on your back! But you have fattened up yourself, you rogue. Did you have a grand time staying loose so
long?"

And while he talked and stroked, his hand continued to
advance up the animal's broad rump...then along its massive back...now slowly down its neck and up again along

its shape...then atop its head, just between the butts of its
spread-out horns...on down its hairy muzzle—till in one
deft motion he had the nose of the carabao in his grasp. He
promptly fished out a piece of rope from his rattan bag and
strung it through a hole in the cartilage between the bull's nostrils.

It was sunset and his thirst burned anew as he looked in
the direction of the nearby banana trees. Kardo sprang to the
back of the carabao and urged it toward the house. From the
tops of the trees the bee birds sailed out into the cooling air
and sang to the setting sun. Swallow-shrikes flew round and
round, their silver breasts tinted with the gold of the sun. From
the deepening shadows under the thickets whistled two nightjars expecting darkness to be upon everything soon.

Kardo tied his carabao at the gate and hung his bag on a
fence paling. He straddled the gate and saw the same woman
dart from a plot of eggplants. He saw the curve of her back
and the lines of her arms and legs. Her dress was of home-
spun, as was the red scarf tied about her hair. While she ran
the scarf became loose and dropped to the ground. Her hair
streamed behind her as she shot up to the ladder; and when
she had fastened the door after her all was silent again except
for the hens clucking for their chicks to gather in the dusk.

Kardo stopped, suddenly conscious of his soiled pants. He
looked at his short-sleeved shirt that exposed his hairy arms,
and he remembered that his straw hat was weather-beaten.
He rubbed his feet together to remove the mud that had caked
up on them, and then he walked to the ladder and addressed
the closed door:

"May a stranger have a drink of your water?"

There was no reply.

"Please," he said, "for I have come from afar this dry
afternoon without a drink of water."

Still there was no reply.

"Just a mouthful of your water."

Only silence came from inside, and from outside the clucking of the mother hens. But he spoke again, thinking of water
to drink and of her hair and her back and the shapeliness of
her legs as she fled from him:

"If you will not give me water from your clay jar, may I go and drink from your well under the tree? Then after that, since my face seems so fearsome to you, I shall hurry away."

Then a voice, full of sweetness and pleading, came from behind the door: "It is not for you to speak so, stranger. There is just my little sister with me here, and it is not seemly that I talk with someone I have never met before. My parents will soon come home, and I should not be seen talking with you."

"It is not my wish to arouse your parents' wrath," he said. And he would have liked nothing so much as to continue speaking with her, but he was so thirsty that he got down the ladder and walked to the well beside a big *kakauati* tree gorgeous with bloom. The sunset burnished the pink petals on the tree, and Kardo took in the beauty of the scene even as he hurried to the well.

A large mother dog, its udders hanging heavy, sprang upon him without warning, the same instant that the girl's warning cry came from the house. Kardo dodged the fangs of the dog; and before it could turn to make another sally at him, he had executed a deft pass and caught it by the scruff of its neck. Its puppies whimpered hungrily in their burrow under a banana tree while Kardo bent smiling at their mother as it struggled to get loose for another attack.

And now he saw her coming down the path, the *kakauati* petals carpeting the ground for her feet. Her hair was tied into a knot now and her feet were small and shapely. She came running to him, asking if he had been badly bitten, but when she found him unhurt she brightened up and said:

"My poor dog!"

Her eyes were dark in the sunset, her cheeks reflecting the gold of the molten sky.

"I am not eager to get bitten," said Kardo with a wry smile. "Could you perhaps chain her while I hold her?"

"That I will not do," she said. "But I'll gladly tie a chain around your neck, and for a good reason—going where you should not go."

"As for that," said Kardo, "I should be none better pleased than to live in your house. And to keep me here you will have need of no chain whatever."

But she disappeared into the barn and soon they had roped the dog.

"Now," Kardo sighed, "I think I shall get that drink at last."

She ran ahead of him to the well and hauled up a bucketful of water. Kardo, pushing his head into the mossy wooden pail, drank deeply and noisily while she held the bucket for him.

When he drew his head out at last, he stood opening and closing his mouth, unable to speak, and she looked at the ground between them, her bantering mood gone.

Finally, after much hesitation, he came near her and placed his fingers on her hand. She looked up with a toss of her head, her eyes meeting his with defiance. Awkwardly he slid his fingers up her arm and down to her waist, quivering quite as nervously as she did. Then they sat down on the grass and watched the sun politely hide its face from them in a flood of glory.

Kardo and Luisa agreed that he should return to ask her parents the following Sunday, when he could change into more presentable clothes. The old people must now be on their way home from the mango grove at Bal-lag.

The carabao stood up now, too. The nightjars had begun to flutter more boldly over the shrubs, and tiny bats flitted overhead on translucent leathern wings. The moon came up gingerly over the hills as Kardo rose, clasped Luisa's hand in his, and walked to his waiting carabao.

It was well past midnight when he arrived home. He built a fire in the clay stove to cook a late supper, and as he sat before the fire he thought: "Soon she will be doing this work while I just sit watching her."

On the following Sunday bright and early, Kardo was seen hitching his carabao to his cart. Uncle Edrong and Aunt Canuta, in company with other old people, climbed into the cart. It was unknown at the time what they were up to; but it was noted that they had with them a flask of white rice-wine, a box of enormous cigars which Aunt Canuta had rolled, and a tray of betel-pepper leaves and lime—things that oldsters had to have when they intended to talk of serious things, such as the transfer of land and large cattle.

And the morning after, the party having returned, Kardo started asking his friends to be available for a trip to Lomilog during the last full moon before the rains of June set in.

Philippines Free Press
September 27, 1947

MAY DAY EVE

Nick Joaquin

The old people had ordered that the dancing should stop at ten o'clock but it was almost midnight before the carriages came filing up to the front door, the servants running to and fro with torches to light the departing guests, while the girls who were staying were promptly herded upstairs to the bedrooms, the young men gathering around to wish them a good night and lamenting their ascent with sighs and moanings, proclaiming themselves disconsolate but straightway going off to finish the punch and the brandy though they were quite drunk already and simply bursting with wild spirits, merriment, arrogance and audacity, for they were young bucks newly arrived from Europe; the ball had been in their honor; and they had waltzed and polka-ed and bragged and swaggered and flirted all night and were in no mood to sleep yet—no, caramba, not on this moist tropic eve! not on this mystic May eve!— with the night still young and so seductive that it was madness not to go out, not to go forth—and serenade the neighbors! cried one; and swim in the Pasig! cried another; and gather fireflies! cried a third—whereupon there arose a great clamor for coats and capes, for hats and canes, and they were presently stumbling out among the medieval shadows of the foul street where a couple of street-lamps flickered and a last carriage rattled away upon the cobbles while the blind black houses muttered hush-hush, their tiled roofs looming like sinister chessboards against a wild sky murky with clouds, save where an evil young moon prowled about in a corner or where a murderous wind whirled, whistling and whining, smelling now of the sea and now of the summer orchards and wafting unbearable childhood fragrances of ripe guavas to the young men trooping so uproariously down the street that the girls who were disrobing upstairs in the bedrooms scattered screaming

to the windows, crowded giggling at the windows, but were
soon sighing amorously over those young men bawling below;
over those wicked young men and their handsome apparel, their
proud flashing eyes, and their elegant mustaches so black and
vivid in the moonlight that the girls were quite ravished with
love, and began crying to one another how carefree were men
but how awful to be a girl and what a horrid, horrid world it
was, till old Anastasia plucked them off by the ear or the pig-
tail and chased them off to bed—while from up the street came
the clackety-clackety-clack of the watchman's boots on the
cobbles, and the clang-clang of the lantern against his knee,
and the mighty roll of his great voice booming through the
night: *"Guardia sereno-o-o! A las doce han dado-o-o!"*

And it was May again, said the old Anastasia. It was the
first day of May and witches were abroad in the night, she
said—for it was a night of divination, a night of lovers, and
those who cared might peer in the mirror and would there behold the face of whoever it was they were fated to marry,
said the old Anastasia as she hobbled about picking up the
piled crinolines and folding up shawls and raking slippers
to a corner while the girls climbing into the four great poster-
beds that overwhelmed the room began shrieking with terror,
scrambling over each other and imploring the old woman not
to frighten them.

"Enough, enough, Anastasia! We want to sleep!"

"Go scare the boys instead, you old witch!"

"She is not a witch, she is a maga. She was born on Christmas Eve!"

"St. Anastasia, virgin and martyr."

"Huh? Impossible! She has conquered seven husbands!
Are you a virgin, Anastasia?"

"No, but I am seven times martyr because of you girls!"

"Let her prophesy, let her prophesy! Whom will I marry,
old gypsy? Come, tell me."

"You may learn in a mirror if you are not afraid."

"I am not afraid! I will go!" cried the young cousin Agueda, jumping up in bed.

"Girls, girls—we are making too much noise! My mother
will hear you and will come and pinch us all. Agueda, lie down!
And you, Anastasia, I command you to shut your mouth and
go away!"

"Your mother told me to stay here all night, my grand lady!"

"And I will not lie down!" cried the rebellious Agueda, leaping to the floor. "Stay, old woman. Tell me what I have to do."

"Tell her! Tell her!" chimed the other girls.

The old woman dropped the clothes she had gathered and approached and fixed her eyes on the girl. "You must take a candle," she instructed, "and go into a room that is dark and has a mirror in it and you must be alone in the room. Go up to the mirror and close your eyes and say:

> *Mirror, mirror*
> *show to me*
> *him whose woman*
> *I shall be.*

If all goes right, just above your left shoulder will appear the face of the man you will marry."

A silence. Then: "And if all does not go right?" asked Agueda.

"Ah, then the Lord have mercy on you!"

"Why?"

"Because you may see the devil!"

The girls screamed and clutched each other, shivering.

"But what nonsense!" cried Agueda. "This is the year 1847. There are no devils anymore!" Nevertheless she had turned pale. "But where could I go, huh? Yes, I know! Down to the sala. It has that big mirror and no one is there now."

"No, Agueda, no! It is a mortal sin! You will see the devil!"

"I do not care! I am not afraid! I will go!"

"If you do not come to bed, Agueda, I will call mother."

"And if you do, I will tell her who came to visit you at the convent last March. Come, old woman—give me that candle. I go."

"Oh, girls—come and stop her! Take hold of her! Block the door!"

But Agueda had already slipped outside; was already tiptoeing across the hall; her feet bare and her dark hair falling down her shoulders and streaming in the wind as she fled down the stairs, the lighted candle sputtering in one hand

while with the other she pulled up her white gown from her
ankles.

She paused breathless in the doorway to the sala and
her heart failed her. She tried to imagine the room filled again
with lights, laughter, whirling couples, and the jolly, jerky
music of the fiddlers. But, oh, it was a dark den, a weird ca-
vern, for the windows had been closed and the furniture stacked
up against the walls. She crossed herself and stepped inside.

The mirror hung on the wall before her; a big antique
mirror with a gold frame carved into leaves and flowers and
mysterious curlicues. She saw herself approaching fearfully
in it; a small white ghost that the darkness bodied forth—but
not willingly, not completely, for her eyes and hair were so
dark that the face approaching in the mirror seemed only a
mask that floated forward; a bright mask with two holes
gaping in it, blown forward by the white cloud of her gown.
But when she stood before the mirror, she lifted the candle
level with her chin and the dead mask bloomed into her living
face.

She closed her eyes and whispered the incantation. When
she had finished such a terror took hold of her that she felt
unable to move, unable to open her eyes, and thought that she
would stand there forever, enchanted. But she heard a step
behind her, and a smothered giggle, and instantly opened her
eyes.

"And what did you see, Mama? Oh, what was it?"

But Doña Agueda had forgotten the little girl on her lap;
she was staring past the curly head nestling at her breast and
seeing herself in the big mirror hanging in the room. It was
the same room and the same mirror but the face she now saw
in it was an old face—a hard, bitter vengeful face, framed in
greying hair, and so sadly altered, so sadly different from that
other face like a white mask, that fresh young face like a pure
mask that she had brought before this mirror one wild May
Day midnight years and years ago. . . .

"But what was it, Mama? Oh, please go on! What did
you see?"

Doña Agueda looked down at her daughter but her face
did not soften though her eyes filled with tears. "I saw the
devil!" she said bitterly.

The child blanched. "The devil, Mama? Oh...Oh!"

"Yes, my love. I opened my eyes and there in the mirror, smiling at me over my left shoulder, was the face of the devil."

"Oh, my poor little Mama! And were you frightened?"

"You can imagine. And that is why good little girls do not look into mirrors except when their mothers tell them. You must stop this naughty habit, darling, of admiring yourself in every mirror you pass—or you may see something frightful someday."

"But the devil, Mama—what did he look like?"

"Well, let me see....He had curly hair and a scar on his cheek."

"Like the scar of Papa?"

"Well, yes. But this of the devil is a scar of sin, while that of your Papa is scar of honor. Or so he says."

"Go on about the devil."

"Well, he had mustaches."

"Like those of Papa?"

"Oh, no. Those of your Papa are dirty and greying and smell horribly of tobacco, while those of the devil were black and elegant—oh, how elegant!"

"And did he have horns and a tail?"

The mother's lips curled. "Yes, he did! But, alas, I could not see them at that time. All I could see were his fine clothes, his flashing eyes, his curly hair and mustaches."

"And did he speak to you, Mama?"

"Yes, yes, he spoke to me," said Doña Agueda. And bowing her greying head, she wept.

"Charms like yours have no need for a candle, fair one," he had said, smiling at her in the mirror and stepping back to give her a mocking bow. She had whirled around and glared at him and he had burst into laughter.

"But I remember you!" he cried. "You are Agueda, whom I left a mere infant and came home to find a tremendous beauty, and I danced the waltz with you but you would not give me the polka."

"Let me pass," she muttered fiercely, for he was barring her way.

"But I want to dance the polka with you, fair one," he said.

So they stood before the mirror; their panting breath the only sound in the dark room; the candle shining between them and flinging their shadows to the walls. And young Badoy Montiya (who had crept home very drunk to pass out quietly in bed) suddenly found himself cold sober and very much awake and ready for anything. His eyes sparkled and the scar on his face gleamed scarlet.

"Let me pass!" she cried angrily, in a voice of fury, but he grasped her by the wrist.

"No," he smiled. "Not until we have danced."

"Go to the devil!"

"What a temper has my serrana!"

"I am not your serrana!"

"Whose, then? Someone I know? Someone I have offended grievously? Because you treat me, treat all my friends like mortal enemies."

"And why not?" she demanded, jerking her wrist away and flashing her teeth in his face. "Oh, how I detest you, you pompous young men! You go to Europe and you come back elegant lords and we poor girls are too tame to please you. We have no grace like the Parisiennes, we have no fire like the Sevillians, and we have no salt, no salt, no salt! Aie, how you weary me, how you bore me, you fastidious young men!"

"Come, come—how do you know about us?"

"I have heard you talking, I have heard you talking among yourselves, and I despise the pack of you!"

"But clearly you do not despise yourself, señorita. You come to admire your charms in the mirror even in the middle of the night!"

She turned livid and he had a moment of malicious satisfaction.

"I was not admiring myself, sir!"

"You were admiring the moon perhaps?"

"Oh!" she gasped, and burst into tears. The candle dropped from her hand and she covered her face and sobbed piteously. The candle had gone out and they stood in the darkness, and young Badoy was conscience stricken.

"Oh, do not cry, little one! Oh, please forgive me! Please do not cry! But what a brute I am! I was drunk, little one, I was drunk and knew not what I said."

He groped and found her hand and touched it to his lips. She shuddered in her white gown.

"Let me go," she moaned, and tugged feebly.

"No. Say you forgive me first, Agueda. Say you forgive me."

But instead she pulled his hand to her mouth and bit it—bit so sharply into the knuckles that he cried with pain and lashed out with his other hand—lashed out and hit the air, for she was gone, she had fled, and he heard the rustling of her skirts up the stairs as he furiously sucked his bleeding fingers.

Cruel thoughts raced through his head; he would go and tell his mother and make her turn the savage girl out of the house—or he would go himself to the girl's room and drag her out of bed and slap, slap, slap her silly face! But at the same time he was thinking that they were all going up to Antipolo in the morning and was already planning how he would maneuver himself into the same boat with her.

Oh, he would have his revenge, he would make her pay, that little harlot! She should suffer for this, he thought greedily, licking his bleeding knuckles. But—Judas—what eyes she had! And what a pretty color she turned when angry! He remembered her bare shoulders: gold in the candlelight and delicately furred. He saw the mobile insolence of her neck, and her taut breasts steady in the fluid gown. Son of a Turk, but she was quite enchanting! How could she think she had no fire or grace? And no salt? An arroba she had of it!

"... *No lack of salt in the chrism*
At the moment of thy baptism!"

he sang aloud in the dark room and suddenly realized that he had fallen madly in love with her. He ached intensely to see her again—at once—to touch her hand and her hair; to hear her harsh voice. He ran to the window and flung open the casements and the beauty of the night struck him back like a blow. It was May, it was summer, and he was young—young!—and deliriously in love. Such a happiness welled up within him the tears spurted from his eyes.

But he did not forgive her—no! He would still make her pay; he would still have his revenge, he thought viciously, and kissed his wounded fingers. But what a night it had been! "I will never forget this night!" he thought aloud in an awed voice, standing by the window in the dark room, the tears in his eyes and the wind in his hair and his bleeding knuckles pressed to his mouth.

But, alas, the heart forgets; the heart is distracted; and Maytime passes; summer ends: the storms break over the rot-ripe orchards and the heart grows old; while the hours, the days, the months and the years pile up and pile up, till the mind becomes too crowded, too confused; dust gathers in it; cobwebs multiply; the walls darken and fall into ruin and decay; the memory perishes...and there came a time when Don Badoy Montiya walked home through a May Day midnight without remembering, without even caring to remember; being merely concerned in feeling his way across the street with his cane; his eyes having grown quite dim and his legs uncertain—for he was old; he was over sixty; he was a very stooped and shriveled old man with white hair and mustaches, coming from a secret meeting of conspirators; his mind still resounding with the speeches and his patriot heart still exultant as he picked his way up the steps to the front door and inside into the slumbering darkness of the house; wholly unconscious of the May night, till on his way down the hall, chancing to glance into the sala, he shuddered, he stopped, his blood ran cold—for he had seen a face in the mirror there—a ghostly candlelit face with the eyes closed and the lips moving, a face that he suddenly felt he had seen there before though it was a full minute before the lost memory came flowering, came tiding back, so overflooding the actual moment and so swiftly washing away the piled hours and days and months and years that he was left suddenly young again: he was a gay young buck again, lately come from Europe: he had been dancing all night: he was very drunk: he stopped in the doorway: he saw a face in the dark: he cried out... and the lad standing before the mirror (for it was a lad in a nightgown) jumped with fright and almost dropped his candle, but looking around and seeing the old man, laughed out with relief and came running.

"Oh, Grandpa, how you frightened me!"

Don Badoy had turned very pale. "So it was you, you young bandit! And what is all this, hey? What are you doing down here at this hour?"

"Nothing, Grandpa. I was only...I am only...."

"Yes, you are the great Señor Only and how delighted I
am to make your acquaintance, Señor Only! But if I break
this cane on your head you may wish you were someone else,
sir!"

"It was just foolishness, Grandpa. They told me I would
see my wife."

"Wife? What wife?"

"Mine. The boys at school said I would see her if I looked
in a mirror tonight and said:

> *Mirror, mirror*
> *show to me*
> *her whose lover*
> *I will be.*"

Don Badoy cackled ruefully. He took the boy by the hair,
pulled him along into the room, sat down on a chair, and drew
the boy between his knees. "Now put your candle on the floor,
son, and let us talk this over. So you want your wife already,
hey? You want to see her in advance, hey? But do you know
that these are wicked games and that wicked boys who play
them are in danger of seeing horrors?"

"Well, the boys did warn me I might see a witch instead."

"Exactly! A witch so horrible you may die of fright. And
she will bewitch you, she will torture you, she will eat your
heart and drink your blood!"

"Oh, come now, Grandpa. This is 1890. There are no witches
anymore."

"Oh—ho, my young Voltaire! And what if I tell you that
I myself have seen a witch?"

"You? Where?"

"Right in this room and right in that mirror," said the
old man, and his playful voice had turned savage.

"When, Grandpa?"

"Not so long ago. When I was a bit older than you. Oh,
I was a vain fellow and though I was feeling very sick that
night and merely wanted to lie down somewhere and die I
could not pass that doorway without stopping to see in the
mirror what I looked like when dying. But when I poked my
head in, what should I see in the mirror but...but...."

"The witch?"

"Exactly!"

"And did she bewitch you, Grandpa?"

"She bewitched me and she tortured me. She ate my heart and drank my blood," said the old man bitterly.

"Oh, my poor Grandpa! Why have you never told me! And was she horrible?"

"Horrible? God, no—she was beautiful! She was the most beautiful creature I have ever seen! Her eyes were somewhat like yours but her hair was like black waters and her golden shoulders were bare. My God! she was enchanting! But I should have known—I should have known even then—the dark and fatal creature she was!"

A silence. Then: "What a horrid mirror this is, Grandpa," whispered the boy.

"What makes you say that, hey?"

"Well, you saw the witch in it. And Mama once told me that Grandma once told her that Grandma once saw the devil in this mirror. Was it of the scare that Grandma died?"

Don Badoy started. For a moment he had forgotten that she was dead, that she had perished—the poor Agueda; that they were at peace at last from the brutal pranks of the earth—from the trap of a May Day night; from the snare of summer; from the terrible silver nets of the moon. She had been a mere heap of white hair and bones in the end; a whimpering withered consumptive, lashing out with her cruel tongue; her eyes like live coals; her face like ashes...Now, nothing—nothing save a name on a stone; save a stone in a graveyard—nothing! nothing at all! was left of the young girl who had flamed so vividly in a mirror one wild May Day midnight, long long ago.

And remembering how she had sobbed so piteously; remembering how she had bitten his hand and fled and how he had sung aloud in the dark room and surprised his heart in the instant of falling in love: such a grief tore up his throat and eyes that he felt ashamed before the boy; pushed the boy away; stood up and fumbled his way to the window; threw open the casements and looked out upon the medieval shadows of the foul street where a couple of street lamps flickered and a last carriage was rattling away upon the cobbles, while the blind black houses muttered hush-hush, their tiled roofs looming like sinister chessboards against a wild sky murky with clouds, save where an old evil moon prowled about in a corner or where a murderous wind whirled, whistling and whining, smelling now of the sea and now of the summer orchards and wafting unbearable Maytime memories of an old, old love to the old man shaking with sobs by the window; the tears streaming down his cheeks and the wind in his hair and one hand pressed to his mouth—while from up the street came the clackety-clack of the watchman's boots on the cobbles, and the clang-clang of his lantern against his knee, and the mighty roll of his great voice booming through the night: *Guardia sereno-o-o! A las doce han dado-o-o!*"

Philippines Free Press
December 13, 1947

TWO IN A CLEARING

ROMEO C. VELASCO

It was very late in the afternoon. Into a dark haze of green, lofty Mt. Apo had cast its shadow upon the Guianga valley. Diosdado, with the lassitude of a farmboy heading for home, came up the beaten path that skirted the abaca groves. Once he turned to look where his uncle's corn clearing gently sloped down the dry gully. His tiredness showed on his deeply tanned young face. Heavy with young ears, the stalks of corn leaned imperceptibly in the early evening wind. In a month more, his uncle had calculated, they would be ready for picking. Diosdado could almost see where the swarm of locusts would appear—perhaps tonight forcing a way through the rows of green stalks. A bit farther down the shoulder of the gully, hedged and separated from the corn clearing by a sparse growth of abaca, was the palay patch—what was left of it. Diosdado sank down on a fallen trunk of abaca and waited for his uncle, *Mang* Sitoy, to come up the slope.

"Do you think they will reach the corn tomorrow, *Tiong?*" Diosdado asked, as *Mang* Sitoy halted on the path and gazed at the corn.

Mang Sitoy was silent, as though all the more wearied by the boy's question.

Diosdado said nothing more, remembering too well that his uncle was also tired. It had been a hard day for the two of them in the clearing.

Since early morning, while the grass was still wet under their feet, Diosdado and *Mang* Sitoy had already been up, and busied themselves with preparations to protect the small clearing of palay. Days before they had already been warned of the approach of the swarm of locusts—young black hoppers, wingless still and much more destructive than the full-grown ones, so his uncle had feared.

The people from down the valley had come in the evenings telling of the destruction wrought in their clearings by the swarm. Everyone of the valley folk felt with dread the coming months, what with the last drought which had already effected its share of devastation in this luckless year ("...and not a handful left of the last harvest, nor could one even spare a grain for a badly stricken neighbor!").

There were no signs of the swarm as yet when they arrived at the *palay* clearing. The young palay, still hardly a half-foot high, stood in neat green rows, their bedewed stalks not yet touched by the morning sun. Diosdado and his uncle groped into the abaca grove which bordered the palay patch, on the east side. It was from here where his uncle had reckoned the swarm might come. Drops from the abaca leaves wetted Diosdado's face and sprinkled his back, as they brushed their way, peering into the soggy abaca growths. But before they had penetrated farther into the groves, Diosdado saw, first, stray hoppers here and there, then the main body of the swarm, farther still inside the cool shade.

"There they are, *Tiong*," Diosdado cried, amazed at the sight.

"Don't disturb them, son!"

The black hoppers fairly carpeted the ground: they spread thickly on the dry abaca leaves and fallen stalks rotting on the ground, on the bits of grass, ferns and shrubs about; and farther still, where the eyes could penetrate through the trunks, on vines and saplings which crowded the much-neglected abaca plantation. Every bit of space was so thick with locust, Diosdado could see, that the whole dim area in the shade looked as though it were evenly covered with birds' droppings. As yet, the swarm showed no signs of movement.

Diosdado and *Mang* Sitoy emerged from the abaca groves presently, the look in the uncle's face full of foreboding. His eyes strayed sadly at the rows of young palay.

Mang Sitoy turned down along the side of the clearing, examining the ground. "We must dig the pit now, before they feel the warmth of the sun," he said. "You start from the other end. Hurry, son."

Diosdado watched what his uncle was doing. Then without saying a word, he started digging into the still damp soil. The pit, a foot deep and stretched out along the edge of the clearing, would serve as a trap where they could drive the swarm into, and later destroy those caught or cover them with earth. "Dig deep, son," *Mang* Sitoy said. The two of them were anxious to finish the pit and only once in a while *Mang* Sitoy would glance along the fringe of the abaca groves.

But before they were half-through digging the pit, as the early morning sun filtered in through the haze of the cool shade, the head of the swarm already emerged from the abaca groves and brush, trickling in testily, little by little, to the rows of young palay.

"Quick, gather those dry abaca leaves!" Mang Sitoy shouted.

"What about the pit, *Tiong?*"

"There's no time for that now, son. They have started to move!"

Hurriedly they gathered armfuls of dry abaca leaves. *Mang* Sitoy piled them along the side of the clearing where it was fringed by the abaca groves. This *Mang* Sitoy set on fire. Silently Diosdado and his uncle worked piling more of the dry leaves into a line, then going back for more, and for what kindlings were on hand.

Once, in his excitement, Diosdado paused to watch the behavior of the swarm. The swarm was eddying out through the abaca trunks, creeping, like a threatening black flow, feeling, seeking for an outlet, and nearer and nearer towards the open it came—towards the patch of young palay, already innocently casting streaks of long shadows under the morning sunshine. As the hoppers neared the wall of fire, they turned back, scattering their flowing lines of movement disrupted, hopping about in confusion. Diosdado watched with a slight feeling of childish amusement. He lingered for a moment, his young mind fascinated by the sight. "They are turning back, *Tiong!* They are going back—!"

But where the fire had not yet fully caught the wall of leaves, the swarm pressed in, taking advantage of the opening and pouring thickly into the palay patch.

Mang Sitoy hurriedly cut a bunch of abaca leaves, and with this, he began to beat the ground. Diosdado reached for a bunch of abaca leaves, and holding a bunch in each hand, he, too, began to flay the swarm. He sidled up to *Mang* Sitoy's side, and shooed lustily. With grim patience *Mang* Sitoy swept away the hoppers which weighed down the stalks of palay and had attacked the young leaves. By the time they were through with one row, they advanced to the next, meeting the swarm and driving them back towards the abaca groves. Diosdado jumped and stumped upon those which crawled up his feet, vexation now mixed with a playfulness growing inside him.

In a while, a portion of the palay patch, no, almost a third of it, was darkened hopelessly by the swarm.

For hours, they went on with their flaying, shooing and driving. Once reaching the edge of the clearing, they went back to the rows of palay and resumed their work. Dust rose around them under the heat of the sun; this time, their shouts becoming louder in the stillness about the clearing, drifting echoes up the valley.

Once *Mang* Sitoy paused to catch his breath, and looked up studying the behavior of the wind—or maybe, rain. But the clouds drifted on indifferently, skimming only the valley with a smudge of black.

By noon, the barricade of fire which *Mang* Sitoy had so carefully tended, sagged to the ground. And out in the sunshine, the swarm spread and enlarged, for now no fire blazed to block their advance. In a sudden fit of anger, Diosdado picked up a piece of clod and threw it at the thick swarm. But in a moment the piece of clod was lost in the black mass.

Now they started from the middle rows of the palay, for the swarm had already reached that far. And as the afternoon wore on more of the swarm spread about in the clearing.

Side by side, *Mang* Sitoy and Diosdado continued their work under the blistering heat of the sun. Diosdado sweated profusely. He wondered whether they would ever go home; he felt tired and hungry.

Diosdado watched his uncle straighten up to gather his breath, noting the sudden aged look in the old man's face as he gazed round at the rows of young palay—already half of the patch was gone. What remained of the young stalks were the bare midribs standing stiffly in the lowering sun.

Mang Sitoy wiped his face with the sleeve of his shirt, now mottled with dust and drying sweat, then walked to the shade, and sat on the grass. Diosdado threw the swish of abaca leaves and joined his uncle in the shade. Perhaps his uncle would want to go home now, he thought.

Silently, *Mang* Sitoy and Diosdado sat on the grass, watching the swarm of hoppers. The whole area of the palay was now shrouded by the black swarm, the ground in between the rows matted darkly. The dust was settling down, and what remained of the mound of abaca leaves down along the side of the clearing sagged to the ground, the ashes blackened still by the swarm.

"There's nothing more we can do, son," *Mang* Sitoy said tiredly after a while, as though to himself. "By sundown, the palay will all be gone."

For the first time, Diosdado felt fully the tiredness in his arms and limbs and the gnawing hunger inside him. The sun was now gradually slipping behind Mt. Apo; the enormous gradation of falling light cast by the mountain range slowly widening down along the valley, and dimming still the palay clearing.

Silently they got up and started up the path. Eagerly, Diosdado headed for the gentle slope, then onto the corn clearing, glad that they were going home at last.

"What about the corn, *Tiong?*" he asked again.

Mang Sitoy was silent, still looking tiredly at the rows of corn.

Then *Mang* Sitoy turned from the path toward the corn clearing, as though there was a sudden resolve in his strides. As he came onto the clearing, he grabbed an ear and wrenched it off. Then he turned again to the next one.

Diosdado looked with alarm at his uncle. But *Mang* Sitoy, still not uttering a single word, moved up the rows of corn, pulling the ears off the stalks roughly, as if he had suddenly lost control of himself.

"But they are still too young, *Tiong!*" Diosdado cried, unable to understand what his uncle was up to. Diosdado picked up an ear and examined it under the green husk. The ears came under his nails.

The next moment Diosdado looked up, he saw his uncle slashing wildly with his bolo. The stalks of corn were cut clean with each wide sweep of his arm.

"Gather them up." *Mang* Sitoy stopped to catch his breath.

Hurriedly, as though fearing the wrathful pose of his uncle as he stood in the middle of the clearing, the bolo glistening in the dusk, Diosdado gathered up the fallen stalks in his arms.

What remained of the patch after Mang Sitoy sat on the grass exhausted, were the bare, cut up stalks of corn, standing mutely in the dusk. Soon they would wither in the sun.

The Evening News Saturday Magazine
January 10, 1948

THE NATIVE VENDOR

ROMAN A. DE LA CRUZ

A woman appeared at the doorway of our cogon quarters one morning.

"Do you buy camote roots and pepper leaves here?" she asked.

At the mention of things for sale, all of us jumped happily to our feet and flocked around her. These meant delicious viands, and a break from the monotony of dried fish, dried shrimps and dried meat.

In those hills, where food had to be preserved with salt, and the farms in the vicinity were not so prolific with root crops and vegetables, products like these brought to us by the natives were always welcomed like rain in summer.

The woman had a long round basket slung to her shoulder with a strap made of tree bark. The mouth of the basket was covered with fresh banana leaves. She came inside at our behest and placed her basket on the floor. She took off the banana leaves from the mouth of the basket and displayed the contents. There was a bundle of newly-gathered pepper leaves atop the pile. This she took out next. Inside the deep basket, red and yellow camote roots lay, fresh from the fields.

"How much?" one of us snapped.

"The camote—eighty centavos," the woman coyly said.

"Too dear," everybody said, turning away.

The woman licked her pale thin lips with her tongue and blinked her small round eyes almost pleadingly at us. She sat down deliberately on a half-consumed sack of palay by the doorway and did not speak further. She was pale and bony and her clothes were patched up. The neck opening of her gray dress was sagging before her, revealing the upper part of a flat sunken chest, with an ugly varicose vein curling blue at the center.

"If you give that camote for thirty, we'll get it," our cook said.

"Oh, not at that price," the woman said. "I bartered these with bananas in barrio Talon, and I would not have accepted thirty centavos for those bananas."

"Yes, thirty," somebody insisted. "We don't believe you bartered them. You raised them yourself."

"We do not have any camotes of our own. I got these camotes from the hill over there where they are having a harvest." The woman was pointing with a thin white finger to the south, where the mountain ranges rose into the mist. It was the boundary between Altavas and Jamindan. When she spoke, the veins around her slender neck and the varicose vein on her sunken chest were charged with blood and bulged to bluish prominence.

Nobody wanted to evaluate the efforts the woman exerted to bring the vegetables to us. Everybody pretended to be unwilling to buy at her price.

"Look," I said to my comrades in English so the woman would not understand, "why do we have to haggle with her? Those camotes are cheap even for eighty centavos. Besides, she has to make a profit, hasn't she?"

"We will get that for sixty centavos," I said to the woman, still feeling like a heel.

"All right," the woman said coyly, placing her hands between her bony thighs and clapping them together self-consciously.

"How about the pepper leaves?" I said.

"Fifteen centavos," the woman said.

"Ten," someone haggled.

"All right," she agreed again.

Someone put back the pepper leaves into the basket and brought the basket to the kitchen where he poured its contents into our winnower. Another went to our officer-in-charge inside the room and came back with the money. He handed it to the woman, saying:

"This is all the change we have, sixty centavos. If you can change our fifty-peso bill you can get your seventy centavos." This was said in mockery, on top of a short payment.

She received the money with eagerness in spite of the shortage. It was in Japanese emergency notes. Six ten-centavo paper notes. The circulation of the Japanese money among the civilian population was then allowed by the guerilla army for the convenience of our intelligence agents in the enemy-occupied territory. The woman counted carefully the notes, secret delight playing in her eyes.

"You bring us some more next time: fruits, root crops, vegetables," our cook said. "Just any foodstuff you can secure, we will buy from you."

The woman smiled wryly. "I am afraid I cannot promise. This is the only chance I have of selling you something."

As no sale could be had from her in the future, nobody minded her anymore. She sat there quietly against the cogon wall by the doorway, watching us with her deep-set eyes as we moved about the office.

"Do you have children?" I asked casually. I was working on a table not far from the doorway.

"Nine," she said. "But five of them died of sickness during childhood. All my four are sick now."

"What are they sick of?"

"*Takig*," she said, meaning malaria.

"What medicine do you give them?"

"Water boiled from bark of *bita* tree. I was told the army has better medicine. I wonder if you would mind changing my money with medicine."

"Don't you need the money?"

"I do, but I need the medicine more, for my family."

"And your husband?" I asked.

"He has also *takig*, like me. We are all sick."

For the first time I realized how yellow her skin was, symptomatic of malaria. I got up and looked for our medical aid man. I found him in the kitchen and from him I got six tablets of atabrine. He was grumbling that we did not have enough for ourselves even as he gave me. When I went back to the woman to give the tablets, she extended back to me her money, the six ten-centavo notes we paid her previously.

"You keep your money," I said as I dropped the tablets on her open palm which was as yellowish as the atabrine tablets. She looked up in silent gratitude. I went back to my work.

After some time, the woman rose from her seat, took her empty basket from the floor and slung its strap over her thin shoulder. She then took her leave, expressed her thanks and got out of the door.

From our quarters, she walked downhill, painfully it seemed, with her thin yellow legs, toward the rivulet. She stood precariously upon a boulder and held her thin white hand over her eyes to protect them from the rays of the morning sun as she gazed at her home somewhere among the misty forested hills.

Evening News Saturday Magazine
February 14, 1948

SOMETIMES IT'S NOT FUNNY

CARLOS BULOSAN

That winter I was living with Bill and Leo in a little apartment house. There were two bedrooms upstairs, and a living room and a kitchen downstairs. We took turns sleeping in the bedroom; but since I worked at night and came home late, I usually slept on the couch in the living room. It was a very pleasant arrangement, because when I came home early sometimes, Leo slept on the couch. Bill worked during the day, so he always had a room upstairs.

The neighborhood was surrounded with small bars where juke boxes played all night long. I would stop at one of the bars sometimes and drink a glass of beer. But one night when I was feeling a little low, I sat at a corner table in my favorite bar and drank several glasses of beer. I was giddy when I stumbled into the apartment.

I lay on the couch without taking off my clothes and went to sleep almost immediately. When I woke up an hour later, I felt cold and hungry. I looked out the window and saw snowflakes falling, making soft little noises on the tall grass in the yard. I stood there in the darkness for a long time, listening to the lovely sound and contemplating the whiteness of the night.

Then I walked into the kitchen, hoping to find something to eat. I found a few pieces of bread and a glass of milk in the frigidaire. I sat at the table and started eating, and listening to the quiet sound outside in the night. I was about ready to lie down on the couch when I heard a slight knock on the front door. I did not expect any visitor because it was quite late, so I opened the door with some reluctance.

And there she was, a small strange woman, shivering and looking at me with pleading eyes.

"The night is cold," she said. "May I come in for a moment?"

I did not know why, but I opened the door and led her into the kitchen, helping her with the wet overcoat before she sat down. Then I made some coffee and filled a cup for her. I filled another cup for myself and sat with her, drinking silently and waiting for her to speak.

After a while she said, "My name is Margaret."

I put out my hand and touched hers, and there was something promising yet tragic about it. I got up and poured more coffee into our cups, wondering what to say. It was my first time to be alone with a girl. I was in that half-tragic mood when it started to rain. I could hear the water falling on the roof.

I went upstairs to see the windows. I closed them and returned downstairs. But when I entered the kitchen, I saw that the girl had slumped down in her chair. She was sound asleep. For a moment I did not know what to do. Should I carry her upstairs to one of the empty bedrooms? She looked so tired and helpless.

I went upstairs and fixed a bed for her. Then I returned to the kitchen again and lifted her carefully and carried her to the bed. I took off her shoes and stockings and loosened her clothes around the neck. And when I felt satisfied that she was comfortable, I put out the lights and watched her breathing silently in the dark. Then I went downstairs again and lay on the couch, my hands folded under my head, thinking deep thoughts far into the night.

It was the first time that a girl had entered our apartment. Bill and Leo and I had been living together off and on for six years, and we had never thought of breaking up the company unless, of course, one of us got married and wanted to live in another place. I was thinking of all these things when I went to sleep quietly. When I woke up it was already morning and I could hear the snowflakes falling in the yard, making a similar noise that leaves make in the autumn when they fall to the ground.

Quickly, I rushed upstairs to see if Margaret was still asleep. She was. But she had turned her back toward the door and I could not see her face, so that her unusually long hair was twisted about her and made a cute little nest in the bed. I wrote a simple note saying that when she woke up her breakfast was ready on the table. I tacked the note on one of her shoes so that she would not miss it.

Then I went to the other room and saw that Bill and Leo were sleeping together, their back to each other. The blanket was falling away from Leo, so I lifted it up and covered him. I went downstairs then and started to prepare breakfast, thinking of Margaret, wondering what kind of toast she wanted with her coffee.

I was already eating when Bill came down hurriedly, drank a cup of coffee and rushed out to work. He did not say a single word. I was washing the dishes when Leo came down. He ate his breakfast slowly and seemed secretly happy. Then he went to work. I could hear his heavy shoes crunching in the thick snow down the pathway.

After a while Margaret came down, too. She was lovely. She was young and lovely. She was happy and lovely.

"Good morning," she said.

"Good morning, Margaret," I said.

She sat at the table then, and it was like a song. I leaped from my chair and set the plates in front of her. I rushed to the stove and fried some eggs. I glanced back at her. She was quiet and lovely. I put the food before her and sat down, watching her, absorbing her, feeling something sinking deeper and deeper inside me. She was lovely.

Then she said, "Leo proposed to me last night."

I was stunned. I found her in the night. I took her out of the snow. I was angry. I was mad with Leo. I was mad, mad, like that time when I was a little boy and my cousin stole my precious toy.

"I promised to marry him," she said.

I was stupefied. I carried her upstairs. I put her safely in bed. I tucked her inside like a good little girl. I prepared her breakfast. I waited for her to come down. And now she had promised to marry Leo? I did not even see him last night. How long did it take them to get acquainted with each other?

"We will get married as soon as possible," she said.

Then I knew that my little dream was broken, and the pieces were rolling away from me. I could hear a man walking down the pathway. He was kicking the snow. Was he angry too? Was something he had been building up for years stolen away from him?

But I could only say, "Congratulations."

"Thanks," Margaret said. "You were very nice last night."

"You were nice, too," I said.

"Always," I said. But something soft died inside me. But I said, "We will be friends always."

I left her then. I was absent-minded in the shop that day. My thoughts were at home, with Margaret. I had just met her that evening. But I felt that all the years I had hidden inside me were coming out into the open, drying in the bright summer sun. And the sun was not too friendly, but not too cruel also. And when I came home from work that evening, I rushed upstairs to see if Margaret was already sleeping. But I found Leo and Bill sleeping together in Leo's bed. I could not understand it.

I went to the other room and found Margaret sleeping in the bed where Bill would have been that evening. I was puzzled. I went downstairs and prepared the couch, thinking of Margaret. Once before dawn, I heard the soft sound of moving feet in Bill's room, and afterward the noise of splashing water in the bathroom. Toward morning it began to rain, and I could hear the monotonous sound it made on the roof. Peacefully, I was lulled to sleep.

When I woke up Leo and Bill had already left for work. I went upstairs to see if Margaret was still sleeping, and she was alone. I went to the kitchen and prepared breakfast. I had already set the table when I heard her coming down the stairs, pausing at the window in the living room to watch the rain falling. And then she came to the kitchen and sat at the table.

I said, "Did you hear the rain last night?"

"I did not," she said. "I didn't even hear you come in, although I tried hard to wait."

I felt comforted. Just a little sentiment like that—and I felt vast and large. Perhaps the long years of living alone budded at last, and bloomed in Margaret's presence.

"I have wonderful news for you," she said.

I looked into her face. I looked into her eyes.

"Bill proposed to me last night," she said. "And I promised to marry him."

"I thought Leo had proposed to you," I said. "And I thought you had promised to marry him."

"That was the other night," she said softly.

And then there was nothing I could say to push away the darkness that came to terrorize my life. I stopped eating. I sat looking into her eyes, but there was no light there to show me the way out. I looked, hoping to stand on some huge promontory of thought and reach out my hand into the darkness and push it away so that the broad light of day could come again.

I went to work, but it was like a dream. I did not remember anything, I went through the motions of working, but everything seemed mechanical. Once I found myself staring blankly into space. I also heard myself groaning, but I could not understand it. And I was afraid I would start talking to myself.

I came home late that evening because there was some extra work for me at the shop. I found Bill sleeping soundly in his own bed. Leo was also sleeping in his. I went downstairs and lay on the couch, wondering what had happened to Margaret. It began to rain at dawn. But I fell asleep when it started, making it seem like the noise of rustling leaves on some far-away mountainside.

The next day was Sunday. It was our day off. When I woke up, I found Leo and Bill eating breakfast. I joined them at the table.

"Where is Margaret?" I asked.

"She is gone," Bill said, laughing suddenly. "She came, and she went."

"I thought you were going to marry her." I said.

"I was not the only one who was going to marry her," Bill said sarcastically. "Leo is another man. The first night."

"That is the only way with some women," Leo said cynically. "Propose left and right. The racket started with a cute little man in legendary garden and a delicious apple tree."

Bill started to laugh loudly. Then Leo joined him. Then I knew that they were chiding me; that Margaret was another page in the history of their lives.

Then Bill stopped laughing. "Why didn't you propose, too?" he asked me. There was genuine feeling in his voice, sympathy in his face. "You could have done it. But now she is gone."

"Yes; but now she is gone," Leo said with finality.

Bill started laughing again. He was almost choking. He slapped the table with his palms, stamped on the floor with his feet, so great was the mirth that Margaret's two proposals had evoked in him.

"But sometimes it is not funny!" I screamed above his laughter.

Leo was startled. Bill stopped laughing suddenly. They looked at me. But they could not understand the tears in my eyes.

It was like the end of a long prayer. I jumped from the table and rushed outside and ran madly across the snow. I raced down the street, not knowing where to go that cold morning.

I kept saying, "Margaret. Margaret. Margaret."

This Week
February 15, 1948

ANOTHER COUNTRY

EDILBERTO K. TIEMPO

Between him and the girl was an empty chair. The book she was reading was in German. An unusual girl, he thought, taking a book to a concert. From the stage came cacophonous sounds of violins and cellos being tuned up; the tympanist, his ear cocked, testing his drums; a cadaverous oboist doing a few bars. Moreshwar Nadkarni and his Egyptian friend passed by and paused nine or ten rows to the front, looked around and sidled to two vacant seats. A few months back Moreshwar had spoken to him in Hindustani, breaking off into English when he appeared surprised. "You are not from India?" "I am from the Philippines," he had said. They were both amused at the mistake. They had talked for a while, Moreshwar telling him, among other things, about the eight other Indians in the University, and he saying he was the only one from the Philippines. Moreshwar and the Egyptian were both Moslems and were taking graduate work in hydraulics.

Another time he had met a Hawaiian who asked him if he was from Hawaii. In his first week in the University his barber was rubbing off the shaving cream behind his ears when he finally surrendered to his curiosity. "Are you from Pakistan?" "Try again," he said. "Ceylon?—you know, around that area." "No." "I give up." A little later the barber said, "In my kind of work you've a lot of time to study all shapes of heads and all kinds of faces. And it's hard to tell what head comes from what country. There was one time I was sure about a fellow's head. He had a turban around a long coil of hair. Now I told myself this man is an Arab. I got a lot of hair from him, including hair from his face. 'You're from Arabia?' I says when I was almost through with him. 'No,' he says, 'I'm from India.' I was sure he was an Arab. Now I tell myself, 'No, you can't be sure about your geography.' He chuckled. "Took me three times longer to clean him up, and I didn't charge him no extra for it."

This guessing game about his nationality was a source of amusement for him. As they stood in line for lunch, an American at his dormitory asked him where he came from. "Can you make a guess?" he had asked in turn. "From Mexico perhaps. Or some South American country. Your accent, you know." "Yes, that's true. We also speak Spanish in the Philippines." He didn't want to be thought of as Mexican after George McKearney, his roommate from Sioux Falls, had told him a Mexican was capable of sticking a knife in your back. But of course that was absurd. Stabbing in the back could happen anywhere.

He looked at the girl again. Her hat was like a skillet perched nonchalantly on her auburn hair. Most of the young girls around didn't wear hats. She was still reading the German textbook. A girl who would succeed, he thought. The man at his right, bulging in his chair and looking like a football tackle, was absorbed in whispered conversation with a voluptuous girl with him.

He felt alone. His eyes wandered over the heads in front of him. Happy people, healthy people, with the air of casualness, yet possessed of the joy of living. His gaze rested on two young Chinese, to his left, seven rows ahead. He had met a number of Chinese on the campus, and they had greeted him cordially perhaps because they had fought a common enemy during the war.

A loud applause greeted Dimitri Mitropoulos as he walked over to the podium. His immediate impression of the conductor was of a rawboned, agile Mephistopheles looming darkly before the orchestra, poised for flight, his coat tails like restive wings.

The girl put down the book on her lap, a finger between the pages. When the first number started she inserted the program as a marker and her hands became quiet on the book. The orchestra was playing Harty's suite arrangement from Handel's *Water Music*. His mind was still on the girl and the empty chair between them. He wanted to talk to her but he had no legitimate reason for moving over to her side. At the conclusion of the piece and while the audience was still applauding, more people came in. A man stood at the end of his row and asked if the empty seat between him and the girl was reserved. This was his chance to occupy it so that the man would have one pair of knees fewer to cram past. He sat down casually beside the girl.

The next two numbers were from *Le Bal Martiniquaise* by Milhaud. There was a part of *Creole Song*, the first piece, that sounded like rice being winnowed in flat rattan baskets. At home during harvest time girls squatting on pandanus mats jerked the winnowers in slanted little twists with adroit flecks of the wrist to gather the unhusked grains to the bottom. If the girl beside him were Clarita, hearing the passage they would have looked at each other knowingly. He wanted to tell the girl beside him about the sound of the winnowing, but perhaps she would not understand. *Beguine* came next, and then Gould's *Minstrel Show*.

At the intermission many stood up to go out to the foyer; the girl turned to her book again.

He spoke to her, "*Sie studieren Deutsch sehr fleissig.*"

She looked up from her book. "I beg your pardon?"

"Sie studieren Deutsch sehr fleissig."

"*I—ja—I—ich müsse meine Aufgabe—morgen—für morgen fruh studieren.* Don't say anymore," she broke off laughing. "As you see, I'm just a beginner."

"I'd have been embarrassed if you spoke it well. I have only a smattering myself." He went on, "You'll come out with a Phi Beta Kappa the way you study."

"Oh, I'm not that ambitious. How come you know German?"

"It's a requirement for graduate work in the Philippines."

"So you are from the Philippines!" She regarded him with casual speculation. "We didn't know much about the Philippines until the war. We're pitifully provincial in some ways, really. You were there during the war?"

"Yes. I came here only last fall."

He wanted to tell her many things about the Philippines; how it was the only occupied country in the Far East that resisted the Japanese to the end, about the Americans losing relatively few men because of the guerillas, of his people's special feeling for the United States.

"I'm proud of my country," was all he could say.

"You have good reason to be."

"Are you from Illinois?"

"From Iowa. I come from a very small town called Red Oak. You may not see it on the map at all."

She had a clean, honest face, not pretty, nor plain, nor striking but it became warm and vibrant when she smiled.

"What's your major?"

"Bacteriology, believe it or not."

"What do you do with bacteriology with a town that's not on the map?"

"I don't have to go back to Red Oak, do I?" More quietly she said, "Dad is a country doctor, and I suppose I got it from him. What are you taking?"

"Architecture."

"That's a man's job, too, like bacteriology. You must need it in your country, after what happened."

The people who had gone out were returning to their seats. A large pigeon-breasted woman had a difficult time squeezing her way through to her chair three rows in front.

"A major operation, parking herself," the girl observed in a low voice but with laughter in her eyes. "I don't want to be in her path."

On the stage the orchestra members were going back to their places. There was applause again as Mitropoulos walked to the podium. Mitropoulos bowing, bowing acknowledgment, then facing the orchestra, his bald head shining, the musicians tense as he raised his baton. Symphony No. 2, in E minor... Rachmaninoff. *Largo-allegretto moderato.*

Her name. He'd ask her name. He could, casually, the way he had started conversation. He might even walk her to her dormitory after the concert. Call her up some time, ask her to a movie.

It was different talking to a girl. He had several American men friends. George, his roommate, tall and ponderous and iconoclastic. He was in the fight in Cherbourg and was now in his last year in law school. George never hesitated to point out the things he thought were wrong in America; the way he talked, the U.S. needed a violent revolution. "Look at our smugness. Have you seen anything like it?" "But your people aren't smug, George. Look at what they did during the war." "Oh, yeah? Can't you see them settling back to the same old complacent pattern?" There was Clifford Meyer from New York; his grandfather was a Jewish rabbi. A very sensitive young man, Cliff; afternoons in the fall they used to take walks when the leaves were turning. You always felt comfortable with Cliff. You didn't have to talk if you didn't want to. But there were times with Cliff idly watching the deer in the park or the ducks in the nearby pond, or sitting in a movie with George when he could not help feeling a kind of abnormality. They were fine fellows; still it didn't seem normal not having anyone to talk to but men.

Being the only boy in the family and having a girl like Clarita, he couldn't help missing a girl to talk to and go around with. Like talking to this girl beside him. He knew this was how that American soldier felt in his country. He was thinking of Lt. Rexford, who had come in a submarine from the American base in Morotai a year before the Leyte landing. Rexford had come to the guerilla headquarters with a group of other G.I.'s to put up a signal station and make reports on the tides and weather conditions. Rexford and his companions had been away from home for over two years. Sitting out a dance given in their honor at a guerilla bivouac, Rexford, a reticent young man, opened his billfold, got out two tiny socks, and showed them to Clarita. "My son's." He also showed his wife's picture with the baby. "He was born three months after I left home." Rexford, he knew, would have felt silly showing the little socks to a man.

He recalled another time shortly before the liberation of Manila, when a young G.I. stopped Clarita and his sister on a sidewalk. "Look," the young man told them, "I've just received a letter from home after six months!" To the astonished girls he displayed an old snapshot from his wallet. "My mother. And the gangly girl is my sister Carol. That fellow there—he's grown up a bit, hasn't he?" Seeing the girls somewhat disconcerted by the suddenness of his approach, he said apologetically, "I know it's rather unusual, coming up and talking to you this way. But we were in the Solomons for so long, and we couldn't talk to the people there. You—you're like us."

Clarita and his sister were touched by the boy—for indeed he was still a boy. They took him home.

The music had stopped, but in a moment the orchestra went on to the *allegro molto.*

There was another time, one evening when his sisters and Clarita were in the hammock on the dark porch. Lourdes and Clarita were singing old songs with Pacita accompanying them on the harmonica. A group of G.I.'s came up the stairs. One of them said, "May we come up? We were listening outside." They gave their names, and after a while joined in the singing. One of them borrowed the harmonica to play hillbilly music while the rest clapped and stamped their feet to the rhythm. Later, a soldier noticed a piano in the living room and asked the girls if any one of them knew "Deep Purple." Lourdes played the opening bars, and then turned to the man. "I don't know it very well and I don't have the score. Why don't you sing it and I play along?" He sang and the others also sang and hummed. "Now," said Lourdes, when the song was over, "I'll play it." And she gave a swing version, complete with flourishes.

"Don't play it that way," protested the man who had requested the piece.

"Desecrating a memory, no?" said Lourdes, laughing, and played the rest of the piece with exaggerated sentiment.

When they were leaving one of the men asked, "May we come again?"

"Yes, do," said Clarita. "But don't forget chocolate bars, please?"

With a girl like that, and a sister like Lourdes. . . .

He looked at the girl beside him. She, too, seemed to have the warmth and friendliness of his sisters and Clarita. He could ask her name, walk with her after the concert, take her to a movie some evening. . . .

The orchestra was starting the third movement now, *Adagio.*

He wondered. . . .

There was a girl from Missouri, a student in fine arts. They sat side by side in Contemporary Art. The first day in class he saw her drawing the face of the professor. In the following days her facile hand caught the profiles and heads of the others in the room. Or it was the twisted figure of a ballet dancer one day, a triple-headed monstrosity of a man another day. All the while she was only half-listening to the lecture and the discussion. A talented girl. Sometimes he walked with her to the fine arts building not far off; there she showed him some of her work. She was a quiet girl, and when she talked it was to give vent to her distaste for the traditional, and to her almost psychic adulation of contemporary abstractionism beyond which, she said, the visual arts could not go any higher.

One day he said to her, "Is it alright for me to take you to a movie tonight? Maybe you'd like to see *Humoresque*."

He would not have spoken like that to Clarita or any other girl in the Philippines. He would sound like a country lout.

But a moment before inviting the girl he recalled that the white barbers downtown refused to cut the hair of Negroes, that a colored football hero cheered by thousands on a Sunday afternoon as he dragged himself with the ball to the goal line had to go to a neighbor city forty-five streetcar minutes away for a haircut Monday morning. He also remembered that during the liberation of the Philippines the Negro soldiers detailed as stevedores in his town associated only among themselves, lolling under acacia trees along the sidewalks or sitting on ammunition boxes at the wharf while the white Americans wheezed by in jeeps and acted as though they didn't belong in the same army. To him it was difficult to understand why the Americans, who had gone all over the world to fight, among other things, for equality, considered the "Niggers" not their equals.

His mind returned to the barber shops. Aliens like himself—Chinese, Iranians, Indonesians, Pakistanis, Egyptians, Thais, Afghans, Burmese, Malays, Marshallese—were not discriminated against. Perhaps the barbers served the foreigners only because they have to. Perhaps this was also the feeling of the American girls from the various local church organizations who took the men from foreign countries (American young men escorted the foreign girls) to the International Tea. White and black and half-black and red and brown and yellow were there. Fifty-three countries were represented. Their flags arranged fanwise at the entrance to the hall hung from staffs bound together at the base. A miniature United Nations. Everybody affable. He could not believe that the affability of the young hosts was only superficial, that there was condescension, or that they were asked to this tea only out of a sense of duty.

Is it alright for me to take you to a movie tonight?

"I'm sorry," the girl from Missouri had replied. "I can't. I have much studying to do tonight."

Now he looked at the girl beside him. Her face was softly outlined in the half-light. Her hands were relaxed on the book. Perhaps the girl from Missouri really had much studying to do that night. But might not she have said, as seemed typically American, "Please ask me again?" His friend Cliff had hinted about racism, for him to be prepared for any unpleasantness; he himself would not consider marrying anybody but a Jewish girl.

There was a hush at the conclusion of the *Adagio*. Mitropoulos lifted his baton for the final movement. *Allegro vivace*.

Clarita. Even compared to attractive American girls, Clarita would still look beautiful. She was not white. She was bronze-golden. That was the main difference between her and the girl from Missouri. Clarita's nose was not so thin nor so high-bridged, yet it was not flat; it was the right kind of nose for him.

(After God had created the fishes of the sea, and the fowls of the air, and the beasts of the field he scooped up clay, spat into it, kneaded it, and formed a woman. This he placed in his oven and waited. After some time he drew the woman out. Lo, she was charcoal black; God had baked her too long. In the same manner he formed another; it came out pale, for he had taken it out too soon. God formed another woman and waited. This time he wanted to be sure she was neither black nor pale. When she came out of the oven, she was golden brown).

He wondered what Clarita was doing at the moment. Curled up in bed, likely, reading a book. When he got back, they'd again do the things they had done together; tramp in the woods or along moss-banked brooks, take their bicycles to the country with a lunch basket, ride tandem on a carabao probably, sit on the beach watching the homing sailboats in the gathering dusk. . . .

The hall vibrated with a mighty applause. The girl turned to him. "Clap," she told him. "Clap. Don't you want an encore?"

He saw Mitropoulos bowing, bowing, bowing. He turned to his musicians, signaling them to rise. The clapping stopped when Mitropoulos finally relented. "I'll play Berlioz' *Dance of the Sylphs.*"

As the orchestra played again he looked around. Happy, happy people, healthy people, possessed of the joy of living. In the semi-darkness he couldn't see the two Chinese students, nor Moreshwar and the Egyptian.

"I'm sorry," said the girl from Missouri.

But there were many besides George and Cliff, many who had accepted him, at least made him feel race didn't matter. The Cranners, for instance. Mrs. Snyder, his dormitory matron. His classmate Hugh and his charming wife; the boys at the dormitory. There was Jim Nitchell who had asked him to spend a week or two in the summer with his family in Laramie, Wyoming. Jim had seen him one Sunday evening in the dormitory cafeteria and gone to his table. "You are from the Philippines, aren't you?" Jim had been in the Philippines for eighteen months as a lieutenant in the division that fought the Japs in the streets of Manila. He was going back to the Philippines, Jim said, after his graduate work in organic chemistry to teach in one of the Manila universities. When he told him he had left the Philippines September of 1946, he noted a sudden eagerness in his voice. "Which did you take, the *Meigs* or the *Gordon?* I knew there were only two boats that left Manila last September." "The *Meigs*," he answered. "Then," Jim said, his lean, intense face breaking into a large grin, "you must have met Pilar del Rosario on board." He replied he had seen two del Rosario girls but couldn't remember which was Pilar. Pilar, Jim said, was the younger, the prettier one. She was now at Bryn Mawr. "She's the girl I'm going to marry."

Since that Sunday evening, possibly because he had happened to travel on the same boat with a girl named Pilar, Jim and he had become good friends. It was strange the way things turned out.

Another encore. *Iberia* by Debussy.

The girl beside him. He could ask her name casually. Maybe the girl from Missouri did have plenty of studying to do that night. He couldn't bring himself to ask her to see the *Humoresque* another night.

When the ovation finally died down and people started getting up, the girl turned to him. "I could stay another hour," she said. "Lovely evening, wasn't it?"

"It was."

"Weren't you," she said as they stood up, "bothered by Mitropoulos' bald head?"

He turned to the serious face under the skillet hat. "No, not at all. Were you?"

"No, not really. He did so well I couldn't see it. But during the times it obtruded—you know it does obtrude—I even wanted—don't laugh now—I felt like running my hand on it."

He wanted to laugh because for a moment it seemed it was Clarita who was talking; it was an American girl he was now following through the crowded aisle. Without her name, without her skillet hat, she would be one of the anonymous faces he saw on the campus every day. Near the door to the foyer a couple at his left edged in between him and the girl. He could have joined her again but he didn't.

He might meet her again, he thought, as he stepped out into the chilly air outside. She might even smile in recognition, but he would not know it was she—warm and friendly, a girl who in another country had taken a lonely American soldier home.

Evening News Saturday Magazine
March 6, 1948

RECEDING DARKNESS

MANUEL A. VIRAY

Len was slowly mounting the last steps of the Overhead Pass spanning Miranda Square and Quadalkiver Street, when he saw the unmistakable round head with the shining hair, carefully brushed back and flowering over the delicate ear. Before he could call out her name, he saw her vanish amidst the crowd descending the stairway towards the opposite side.

Hurriedly Len turned back. Driven by an irrevocable necessity, he snaked his way downwards, until he reached the bottom step. Momentarily he stood there and it seemed as if the morning sunlight briefly glowed on a crest of brilliance.

He saw the dark curly hair. She had freed herself from the teeming throng. As she came nearer, he noted a furrow on her forehead, the first hint of a line weaving its way from the side of the high nose to the corner of the full mouth. In the plaza itself, there were very few people, sunbaked peddlers, urchins in underwear, wandering peddlers, and somnolent shopkeepers in the crowded, dark, and endless rows of stalls. He heard the familiar firm click of her footsteps again and softly he called out her name.

She turned around as he reached her in clear, strong strides, a look of disbelief, surprise, and gladness in her large, dark-brown eyes.

The same glittering smile that he knew unfolded slowly. "Marita," he said.

"Len," she answered. It was a reply compounded of a suddenly remembered disorder and sorrow, and edged with pity. "Where did you come from?"

The interrogation was casual. "You are not glad to see me?" he asked her.

"But I'm. Whatever gave you that idea?" She laughed in that peculiar throaty way of hers.

"Where are you going?" He took her by the elbow and steered her skillfully through the hustling crowd.

"Home," she said: "Excuse me a minute. I have to buy some oranges."

He saw the look of the fat vendor shift from Marita to him as she dropped the oranges into a paper bag. "Let me pay for them," he offered but she stopped him with a "Don't be silly." He asked her where "they" were staying. She told him.

"You are not in a hurry, are you?"

"Well. . . ."

"How about some refreshment? Something cold. Ice cream?"

She looked undecided.

"After all we have not seen each other for seven years." He looked at her intently.

"All right." She smiled briefly and he piloted her to The Focus, one of those comparatively clean, well-lighted places, bravely squeezed in the sordid area bisected by Madiera Street.

They sat opposite each other. There was a gleaming white vase with artificial flowers atop the circular table.

"You have not changed much. Where have you been?" he said.

The waitress stood by and patiently waited for their orders. Len looked up and then gazed at Marita: "Caramel, walnut, pineapple?"

"Vanilla," Marita said, laughing softly remembering how seven years ago she used to play the same trick on him at the Legaspi Garden.

"Fruit cake or apple pie?" he asked taking up the cue of remembrance.

"Chocolate cake," she said.

Len repeated the order and said, "Make it two."

"Where have you been?" he asked again.

"From church," she explained. "We ran out of fresh butter. That's why I came from the other side of the Overhead Pass."

He nodded and lighted a cigarette. The waitress set down their orders.

"How has it been?" There was a look of seriousness on his lean face, a dulling of his brilliant, extremely mobile eyes.
"It's rather late raking up the ashes,'" she said. "Don't you think?"

He smiled slightly and his mind wandered back across the long receding darkness of the years. The same phrases kept coming back to him, scenes kept bobbing up and down his mind. "That's the same line I used to bandy about, remember?"

She nodded her beautiful head as she pressed the solid scoops of ice-cream with her spoon.

"Have you been happy?" he asked, his spoon in mid-air. "I mean, truly happy?"

"Yes, of course. Perfectly happy. I mean...." But the words refused to come. "But let's not talk about me. Let's talk about you. Where have you been all these years? You never wrote me, you know."

She kept her head down as if to minimize the silent reproach, as if to still the agony. He wondered if she was angry at him and he put down his spoon, tried to retrieve his burning cigarette, changed his mind, and put it down again.

"Don't be discomfited. After all, it has been a long time." She looked up at him. "We are normal people, we did what we thought was right." She smiled.

"That's right. It has been a long time. I completely lost track of you all the time I was down south."

"South?"

"Legaspi, Tacloban. Later I moved to La Carlota. Vic invited me. I did a spot of work for him. He had his hands full with his plantation. I used to wonder, when the nights were quiet and starry, where you were, what you were doing. I imagined all sorts of things. Yet I could not help myself. I could not come back to the city. All the time I could feel the hostile look, the smarting blow on your face that evening. The high pitch and the shrieks of your mother."

"Father and mother are dead," she said.

"I'm sorry, I'm really sorry." He looked at her and shifted his gaze. "Your Father never liked me. It must have been the memory of that evening that kept me away all the time."

She did not say anything. She cut a slice from the cake slowly.

"I was restless all the time. I could not stay in one place long enough. I left Vic. He understood. Then I went to Iloilo. The war caught me there."

"You never joined the underground? Or are you a Major or a Colonel of some kind?"

"No. How could I? You see how it was. I was disgusted by the petty jealousies and internal disputes in the organization there. I never liked the self-styled heroes who sported guns of patriotism but were not above coercing a poor farmer into giving them his only carabao or harvest of corn. I was never cut out to be a hero. I got here only last week. Were you here in the city all the time that the conquerors were here?"

"Oh yes. We left Ermita when the Americans were in Bulacan. My mother-in-law wanted us to be with her."

"I'm glad."

"Where did liberation catch you?" she inquired.

"In the hills."

"Alone?"

"Of course. I never married." He cut himself a piece of the cake and nibbled at it. "Tell me, how is he? I read about your marriage in the papers. It seemed ages and ages ago."

She contemplated the cake and the ice-cream. "He's nice. Much nicer than I expected. He is much older than I am. Five years, in fact." She stopped the question on his lips. "You don't have to explain anything. I understand. I don't blame you in the least. I loved you passionately then. Only the young can love in such a manner. But all that is past. One loves perhaps, first with shaking violence. Later, one loves in an entirely different manner, not the agitating passion of youth. Something like—"

"I know what you mean."

"We'll never be able to define how one love dies and another is born. I suppose I deceived myself into believing in the first year that you would come back. I kept saying to myself you would. You have but after seven years." She was speaking in a matter-of-fact tone.

He winced perceptibly but Marita was not looking at him. Her eyes went beyond him and she talked with a certain objective fluidity, past the disorders and the early sorrow, past the shaking vibrations of the heart, as if she were reciting Browning's *My Last Duchess.*

As she spoke, Len thought how strangely she rambled. There was a certain coldness, he thought, well, not a coldness but a surgical purity which was scarcely human.

"Tony started coming to the house. For a time I disregarded him. But you see how this sort of thing develops. He was nice and very decent. I told him about you. He understood. I thought for a time that perhaps it would diminish his affection for me. You understand, don't you?"

He played idly with the tall glass of water, turning it around and around.

"That's why I said we were perfectly happy. We have had our share of misfortunes, a burned house in Ermita, the nights of shelling, terror and suspense. But we have been happy."

"I know. All of us suffered."

Suddenly she said: "Shall we go?"

He stood up and asked for the chit. "Let's. Can I walk you home?"

They went out of the restaurant into the garish and clattering day. He was about to ask a question when she said: "Are you staying here permanently?"

"I suppose so," he replied, piloting her across the street. They turned at the curb and walked on, his strides matching hers. "Can I see you again?"

"It would be better if you did not. It's not that Tony will not understand. He does. But I feel it would be better for all concerned."

They stopped at the next street intersection, where the cabs were jostling each other for positions of advantage.

"There was a child, Marita," he suddenly said.

"Yes. When I told you I was hurrying, it was because she is sick."

"She?"

"She bears my name." She got into the moving cab, while the conductor vociferously shouted their destination.

"But can't I see her?" he said, tailing the moving vehicle. "After all she is my child."

"Don't worry. She has passed the crisis. She is all right now. Besides, she does not know you." She patted him quickly on the arm. "Tony understands."

Her last words were lost in the gust of wind raised by the lurching cab.

Evening News Saturday Magazine
March 27, 1948

BROKEN GLASS

MANUEL A. VIRAY

Tonio helplessly reiterated to himself that this was 1943; that this was a conquered city: battered, formless, caught in a nightmare, the men and women moving about their daily tasks, hugging their fears closely to their hearts, barely conscious of physiological functions, sharply aware of the struggle for life, and talking automatically, gesturing pitiably like somnambulists in a whispering darkness. The bar of heavy sunlight falling athwart the street and splashing on the edges of the tall uneasy canyons of the miraculously-intact and towering buildings was a sickly feverish orange reflecting the secret subtle change of an invaded city, a defeated people.

Part of the sidewalk was a raucous "parallel" market where the hawkers of priceless *Pirate* cigarettes, small gay birds chattering inside bamboo cages, shoestrings, cheap soap cakes, and shiny shirts, shouted their wares in a persistent, hoarse lexicon. His countrymen hurried through the street, while the conquerors moved about with heavy, arrogant tread, their hobnailed boots resounding on the loose plank of the wooden bridge or stopped and talked to each other in their hissing tones and with guttural syllables.

The expensive haberdashery store he used to frequent before the outbreak of war was now a noisy, blaring restaurant and as Tonio entered it, the loud strange song emitted by the scraping loudspeaker, the steady whir of the revolving electric fan, the conversation inside expanded in volume, screened on the fine membranes of his mind.

As he took his seat by the glass window overlooking the turgid Pasig, he saw a profusion of sweating, unkempt soldiers deeply engrossed in their cups and shouting uncontrollably and vociferously around the circular table near the cashier's raised platform. At a near-by table two officers were talking to a

waitress who, time and again with a forced laugh, adroitly
disengaged a hand from her bare brown arm. There was something familiar in the shapely back turned to him, something
odd in the presence of such an attractive figure in this boister-
ous restaurant. The curly, brownish ends of the hair, the sloping
curve of neck, the tapering leanness of the torso ending at
the young hips—all these, somehow were caught in a vortex
of helplessness, in the tepid, languorous air entangled with
delicate spirals of curling smoke, irritating noise, movement;
smelling somehow of the sweat of battle, cruelty, ferment, and
rot.

From where he sat Tonio saw the slow flexible smile of
the taller officer, his gesticulations of cocksureness. There were
bottles of beer on the table.

Moodily, Tonio ordered a cup of coffee and a piece of cake,
which he knew would taste vapid and stale for flour was scarce
that year and the little that was rationed to the eating places
was now slightly moldy. The waitress who took his order
kept a straight face, which all of a sudden seemed harsh. The
plucked eyebrows, the shining nose, the red lips, the sagging
breasts, the large hips, and the tight belt looked garish and
cheap. He was about to ask her as she turned away who the
girl with the two officers was but thought discretion was the
better part of curiosity. Who knows—in these days you never
knew your comrade or enemy, friend or foe? Even on the sidewalk a short snatched conversation could be misinterpreted.
He wished the waitress would return soon.

A huge shadow fell on the table cover. "Tonio, you found my
place soon enough. I'm glad to see you're here." It was Joding,
his waist fairly bursting under the tight belt, his sharkskin shirt
damp with perspiration, his small pig eyes appearing smaller
because of the fat jowls, the hair evenly parted and slicked
with pomade—Stacomb, no doubt, Tonio thought, pre-war
stock. Joding was speaking in the vernacular. He was patting
Tonio on the back. He had a fat cigar in his hand. But he
did not sit down and Tonio felt a sudden disinclination to stand
up, but he was about to open his lips when Joding said: "You
were wondering at a particular back."

Tonio pulled out a Pirate from his pocket and lighted it,
trying to hide the momentary flicker of his eyelids. Then he

laughed uneasily, "That's true. I thought perhaps the girl with the two officers was Marta."

"It is Marta," Joding said, flicking his cigar, his enormous ring with the solitary emerald embedded in it, glinting in the failing afternoon. The almost omniscient absorption in details was the secret of Joding's material success. "But be careful. Don't let the two officers catch you looking at her."

The waitress set down his order and Joding moved away with a studied ostentation towards the next table, smiling lightly and nodding his head.

Tonio busied himself with his coffee and covertly glanced once more at the two-officer table. It was really Marta. The fine forehead, the clear eyebrows, the slightly-tilted nose, the full lips appearing a little beaten by weather and worry, the surprising body, soberly draped by the regulation uniform of the Asaki Cafe.

Jaime had asked him to see the Asaki. "Who knows," he said, "we will have better news from there. The progress at Morotai. Installations in the Bay area, perhaps. Look for someone who is adept at interpreting the mumblings of returning soldiers, outpourings in a drunken stupor." And here he was, surprised by Joding whom he had slightly known in college and who appeared sharp and unpredictable although his last words were accompanied by the significant flicker of the ash on the green table cover, a gesture which was obviously a warning, and surprised by Marta, too. He had never seen the two officers before.

Tonio squeezed his cigarette on the wooden ashtray and sipped his coffee. Weak but scalding.

There was a brassy laugh. Tonio knew that laughter, ringing, deep. He did not turn around, very much afraid to see the familiar blue veins of her lovely throat as she laughed, head tilted backwards, the thick curly hair falling on her shoulders. It's strange that I still run away from the fragility of beautiful things. The sensibilities of the mind are helplessly trapped, the sensitivity to beauty has a price tag. O, yes, he and Marta had gone out together. They were good friends. He remembered other things besides and unconsciously he touched his nostrils, feeling for drops of blood because all of a sudden he felt a powerful onrush of blood rising up in his head.

He picked up his fork to slice the cake, desisted, and put it down again. He sipped his coffee and lighted another cigarette. This time he glanced boldly at Marta. Her face was turned to him now. The two officers were drunkenly nodding. The empty beer bottles had increased. Marta was staring at him. Tonio thought of Joding and recklessly told himself, "Let him look, let Joding look. I don't care." He looked at Marta straight in the eyes, but she only looked at him uncomprehendingly, her beautiful face perfectly composed. They looked at each other without recognition. The thought of a smile formed in Tonio's mind remained a mere thought. This time he sliced a piece of cake.

He saw Marta and himself again. Three years ago. 1941. They were coming out of the sunlight and shadow of Escolta, leaving behind them the clean, sunlit purity of the wide space above the street and between the buildings.

They had just come from the glittering haberdashery store, Marta matching his long strides, firmly and clickingly, her footsteps resounding on the pavement. Before that she had always upbraided him for turning his eyes at the tall, laughing girls walking rapidly past them, their hips rhythmically swaying, their dresses whipped by the wind.

She said: "No more thoughts of laughing women with wind-whipped dresses."

"I know," Tonio said," we are in the midst of war." He knew what thoughts were running in her mind. Everyone was caught in the last flurry of shopping, buying prime commodities, and badly needed supplies. He himself had bought two pairs of shoes. He was at the haberdashery store when Marta saw him. They had laughed recklessly as they made their purchases for the enemy was strangely silent that day. No bright formations of menacing planes with their cargos of death, no anti-aircraft fire. Everyone moved hurriedly, though, intent on the particulars of survival. Marta had made her own purchases, too. Now she was hanging on his arm as they mounted the circular stairway leading to the mezzanine floor where the soda fountain was. There was a semblance of bustling activity inside. But as they sat down, the hovering tautness which they knew on December 8 made itself evident there. The voices of the customers were muted as if in the transient moment of refreshing themselves they were deathly afraid. Even the waiters balanced their trays on their palms and delicately skirted the narrow spaces between the tables with flowing but precarious movements. Almost all the people inside ate jerkily, unconsciously gripping their fragile glasses, minimizing their gestures. It seemed as if they all wanted to enjoy this transient moment—a moment, which they thought, would be like the others in the past when there was a long peace and it was possible to engage in easy talk, in a felicitous appreciation of the bounties of life, in graceful living. But the semblance of relaxation was harsh and strangely quivered in the dully lighted soda fountain. An oppressive element hung in the air, reducing the regularity of mortal breath. Everything appeared tentative, terribly naked. The men were silent; their tight lips revealing the hidden panic even as they curled their hands around the chilled drinks and assumed an air of indifference to death and danger. The women, wearing their dresses in a cruelly exquisite manner, smoked continuously, their bright eyes glittering, the forced gaiety in their voices sounding hollow and flat. The cowl of assurance was slowly, irrevocably slipping. Everyone lived on borrowed time.

Through the smoky haze in the mezzanine, Tonio and Marta saw a group of young Americans in new khaki uniforms, their insignias shining even in the dull light. There was a red-head with a deeply-lined face; a tall well-built, blonde-haired young man with a fine classic profile; three dark-haired fellows. At another table there was a Filipino girl observing, obviously waiting for somebody. She kept opening her red handbag, the long strap of which hung on her thin shoulders, looked at a slip of paper as if to verify that she was not mistaken, then peered at her watch which was pinned above her small, young breast. At a table in the corner, a solitary American sat morosely, his massive bulk and noble head almost indistinct because of the smoky haze.

He looked as if he was drinking and thinking on borrowed time, too. Both his arms were on the table, the right hand hugging a mug of beer.

Tonio did not know what happened but suddenly Marta said: "Let's go and join Robinson Crusoe. He looks bored."

Always Marta acted on impulse. He would not have dared, if he were alone, invite himself to the lonely American's table. He had noticed a group of their countrymen talking to the blond and the redhead and as they talked Tonio noted the snatches of temporary gaiety and sober, earnest exposition. But it appeared as if Marta's impulse was not tempered by anything but a generous wish to talk to the lonely American, tell him he was among friends and that he need not bury himself in his drink, talking to no one.

"Let's go then," and as they picked up their bundles and moved towards the lonely man, Tonio noticed that Robinson Crusoe was still staring at his glass with a sober contemplation, heedless of the sounds and movements around him.

"May we join you?" Tonio said.

The lonely man looked up, glanced at the vacant table they had left and smiled, getting up halfway from his chair. "Sure, sit down."

"We saw you and we thought perhaps you would not mind having company," Marta spoke with subdued verve.

"Of course not. I'm glad you decided to. Drink?" He came to life and motioned the waitress as Tonio pulled a vacant chair on which to put his purchases.

"This round is on me," Tonio said and ordered two beers and a creme de menthe for Marta. "It's her favorite drink."

Tonio introduced himself and Marta.

"Reeves—Tom," the lieutenant said, extending his hand, noting the disparity in their family names, "You know I thought for a moment as you sat down that you were married, newly married."

"O, no!" cried Tonio and Marta. "We're just friends."

Tom smiled mischievously, his blue eyes twinkling.

"Been here long, Lieutenant?" Marta asked.

"I just pulled in a month ago. Air corps." He fingered his mug of beer again, abruptly gulped down the remainder. Both Tonio and Marta had read of the disaster in Parañaque. Every plane destroyed, not a single wing left, pilots grounded. The waiter set down their order.

"Parañaque is a mess," Tonio said.

"I'm sorry," Marta said quickly, looking at the lieutenant.

"That's alright, Ma'am." He looked so young and earnest as he said Ma'am that Tonio knew that something had clutched at Marta's throat. He, too, was thinking of the brutality of history, the sending of young men to fight wars in countries not their own. He can't be more than twenty, Tonio thought, looking at the clear skin, the bright young eyes, the smooth lips. Here he is among strangers. They could not say anything heroic, or encouraging, or reassuring to him, lest they fall into the bathos and mistrust of suspect words like democracy, libertarian tradition, brotherhood of men, etc. Marta delicately sipped her drink. Tonio drank his beer.

As if divining what they were thinking, the lieutenant said: "I understand how you feel. This is my last day of leave. I'm going back this morning."

"I see," said Tonio, wiping the beery foam from his lips.

"This thing is stronger than any man. We go to war because we have to even if we know the consequences. They say it is our duty. We do not attempt to explain why lest we become unprepared for the immediate task at hand."

"That's true," Tonio looked at Lieutenant Reeves.

The lieutenant looked at Marta. "You know for a moment when you came in I thought you were my girlfriend." He turned his head towards Tonio and smiled as if to ask him if he minded. "The same eyes, the same hands, hair, throat; it's uncanny. My girl . . . she is of Italian extraction. She is taller though."

Marta smiled.

The lieutenant glanced at his watch. "Goodness gracious. I'll be late. My convoy leaves in half an hour. Well . . .," he extended his hand to both of them, "I'll shove along. Thanks for your company. I'll see you again."

As he walked away from the table, picking his way through the crowded soda fountain, Marta said: "Keep them flying, lieutenant."

"Right," the lieutenant said and motioned the group of five, including the blond and redhead, that it was time for them to leave.

Tonio looked at Marta to tell her she was foolish encouraging the young lieutenant with such words, since he did not have any plane to fly any more.

I wonder what happened to Tom, Tonio thought. He was jerked by that first and last meeting and imagined that either he was killed in Bataan, concentrated in Capas, or perhaps interned in Cabanatuan. He took another sip of the coffee and looked again at the next table. The shorter of the two officers was talking and laughing drunkenly, trying to paw Marta. Marta tried to remove his restless hand from her arm when suddenly he lurched sidewise and would have fallen from the chair had not the other one caught him. Marta's right arm which had shot out knocked off an empty glass from the table. It fell with a crash and a sharp tinkle on the floor, broken into fine fragments. The tall one tried to talk in a sober manner to his far-gone companion but was repulsed. Tonio thought, "How have the mighty fallen," as he saw the broken glass on the floor, which looked as if it were a globe someone had knocked off in a fourth grade class, ages and ages ago, and symbolizing the brittle quality of life, easily fragmentized because of man's greed and lust for dominance.

Does she remember that incident at the soda fountain? Tonio the Optimist. Now she works at a cheap cafeteria, trying to be nonchalant in the midst of brazen laughter, drunken pawing, but unable to free herself.

Tonio saw her on her knees, picking up the broken pieces of glass. She glanced up and suddenly she smiled at him with radiant recognition. Tonio slightly nodded his head as she stood up to help the tall officer straighten the drunken one. They are going to leave now, Tonio held himself and suddenly his spine stiffened while a quivering singing sound rang in his ears. He asked for his chit and after paying it, stood up. He glanced at the two vanishing officers at the door.

It was already late and the last suspiring brilliance of the waning day splashed in the sky. Suddenly he was filled with such an unaccountable elation and vibrating happiness, the reason for which he could not find because he was thinking of Jaime's words, that if there was anyone who could find a girl or a man who could play a double agent, it was he, Tonio. Tonio of Intelligence. He seemed to hear his name being shouted senselessly and silently in a rapturous note in the shaking air as he followed the lurching drunks. Tonio of Intelligence. Tonio the Cool Killer. Tonio.

Sunday Times Magazine
May 2, 1948

ALL OVER THE WORLD

VICENTE RIVERA, JR.

One evening in August 1941, I came out of a late movie to a silent and cold night that made me shiver a little as I stood for a moment in the narrow street. I did not have to hurry home for I lived across the street, in an old apartment house that seemed to be already crumbling. It had been warm in the theater and I was sure it would also be warm in my room. So I stood in the street, letting the night wind seep through me. The houses on the street were dim, with the kind of tired dimness that seems to hang over sleeping houses. But above me, above the houses, the sky was bright and alive, quick with stars.

After a while, after the last of the movie-goers had straggled down the street, I turned to our building. There was a small hall just inside the front door, and beyond it was an open courtyard. My room, like all the other rooms on the ground-floor, opened on this court. Three other boys, my cousins, shared the room with me. As I crossed the open space to my room, I noticed that the light over our study table, which stood on the corridor that skirted the rim of the courtyard, was still burning. Earlier in the evening, after supper, I had taken out my books to study, but I had gone to a movie instead. The boys must have forgotten to turn the light off.

I went around the low, makeshift screen that sheltered our "study" and there was a girl bent over the table, reading. We discovered each other with a start. I had never seen her before. She was about eleven years old, with long straight hair that fell to her shoulders and which framed a thin, oval face with great big eyes. Her skin was unexpectedly fine and smooth, a pale olive that glowed richly in the yellow light. She was dressed in a faded blue dress, and my book of Greek myths was open before her, still clutched in her hands. She looked at me with a sort of muted alarm, an apprehension that was held in leash, that just waited.

"I know," I said. "I like stories, too. I read anything good I find lying around. Have you been reading long?"

"Yes," she said, not looking at me now. She got up slowly, closing the book. "I'm sorry. . . ."

"Don't you want to read anymore?" I smiled, trying to make her feel that nothing wrong had been done.

"No," she said.

"Oh, yes," I said, still trying, "it's rather late. Time for sleeping. But you can take along the book."

She stopped, turned to me again, looking to see if I were sincere. Then she reached out and picked up .the book. She did not move away yet, but stood looking down at her feet.

"You live here?" I asked.

"Yes."

"What room?"

She turned around, faced across the courtyard and nodded towards the far corner, to a little room near the communal kitchen. It was the room occupied by the janitor, a small square room with no windows to it, except for the opening where the front wall of the room was unfinished.

"You live with Mang Lucio?"

"He's my uncle."

"I've never seen you around. How long have you been here?"

"About a month."

"Where did you live before?"

"With my mother."

"Why did you leave her?"

"She's dead."

"Oh," I said, feeling somehow that I've transgressed. "What's your name?"

"Maria."

"Well—goodnight, Maria."

She turned quickly and ran across the courtyard, straight to her room. She went in and closed the door, not looking back.

I went into my own room, undressed and lay in bed smoking a cigarette. It was warm in the room and I was suddenly wakeful. Far-off the rumble of the city could still be heard. But in the room itself, it was quiet. In the house, the noise of living had died down. People were safe in bed, and those who dreamed, with no grievous things on their minds, could dream of better times. And those who were wakeful could look back and ahead, and if they had not lived too long in the world, they could still find that life was gentle. Thus, I lay in bed. And even afterwards, when the night had grown colder, and you felt suddenly alone in the world, caught in the mystery that came in the hour between sleep and waking, the blurred and vaguely frightening loneliness only made you feel closer to everything, to the walls of your room, to the other sleeping people in the room, and in all the other rooms in all the other houses in the world, to everything within and beyond this house, this street, this city, everywhere.

I met Maria again one early evening, a week later, as I was walking home from the office. I saw her walking ahead of me, slowly, as if she could not be too careful about her steps, and with a kind of grown-up poise that was somehow touching. But I did not know it was Maria until she stopped and I overtook her.

She was wearing a white dress that had been old many months ago. She had on a pair of brown sneakers that must have been white once. She had stopped to look at the posters of pictures advertised as "Coming" to our neighborhood theater.

"Hello," I said, too casually maybe.

She turned to me, but looked away quickly. She did not say anything, but she did not go away either. I felt her shyness, but there was no self-consciousness, none of the tenseness and restraint of the night we first met. I stood beside her, and moved with her from board to board showing stills from the different "coming" movies.

At last when there was nothing more to look at, she turned to me. It struck me then, the curious depth in her eyes, as if she had lived forever in this world and had known all the happiness there was, and all the sorrows too. Only the happiness had long dwindled away and now only the sorrows remained. And there was something else. Something lonely? Something lost?

"I'll return your book now," she said.

"You've finished it?"

"Yes."

We walked down the twilight street. Magallanes street in Intramuros, like all the other streets there, was not wide enough. It was dirty and cluttered, hemmed in by old, mostly unpainted houses, unwieldy and sagging, tired and dead in the darkness of the fading day.

We went into the apartment house and I followed her across the court. I stood outside the door which she closed carefully after her. She came out almost immediately and put in my hands the book of Greek myths.

"My name is Felix," I said.

She smiled suddenly. It was a little smile, almost an un-finished smile. But it was a beginning.

"I've got another book for you," I said.

She started to say something, but no words came out. She was shy again. She looked away from me.

"I'll bring it around later. Or you could come over and get it from me," I said. "It's a nice book. You'll like it."

I walked away. At the door of my room, I stopped and looked back. Maria was not in sight. Her door was firmly closed.

Though summer was over, the hangover of the warm months still seared the August afternoons. Specially in Intra-muros. But, like some of the days of later summer, there were afternoons when the weather was soft and clear, the sky a watery green, with a shell-like quality to the light that almost made you see beyond and through infinity. So that, looking up the sky made you lightheaded.

One day, I walked out of a newspaper office where I worked, straight into just such an afternoon. I was tired. I walked slowly, towards the far side of the old city where there were trees and where traffic was light. The people who lived along the street had surrendered to the heat, and now sat by wide-open windows, or in doorways, in undershirts and kimonos, unmindful of passers-by, waiting and watching, as if poised to snare every stray breeze. When I came to the university, where I went to the night classes of the law school, I just couldn't turn away from the afternoon. So, instead, I went on through the gate of the city wall, to the treelined drive.

On the shell-sprinkled path under the trees there were then other leisurely strollers, office-workers and students, la-borers and children, all apparently with no destination. It gave me a strange lift of freedom. I went up the sloping drive that curved away from the gate, and on the first bench that I came to, at the end of the drive, I saw Maria, primly seated. When she saw me, she smiled, that same unfinished little smile.

"Hello," I said. "It's a small world."

"What?"

"I said, it's nice running into you. What are you doing here?"

"I always come here."

"Doesn't your uncle miss you?"

"No. I go everywhere."

"Where?"

"Oh. Places. Up the wall. The boulevard. The seaside."

"What do you do in those places?"

"Nothing. I just sit."

She fell silent. She looked as if she thought she had talked too much. Her lips were pursed. She looked down the drive, away from me.

"Maria," I said, "do you have any brothers and sisters?"

"No," she said.

"Uh—your—uh, *Mang* Lucio," I asked. "He's your only relative?"

"Yes."

"Where did you live before?"

"On the other side of the town."

"What did your mother do?"

"She sold things."

"Did you—are you—in school?"

"Yes?"

"What grade?"

"Four," she said, rather reluctantly.

"Well, that's good."

"No, it's not," she said, suddenly vehement. Then she paused. And added quietly. "I'm too old for that grade. I—I'm too big."

"You don't like to go to school?"

"I do," she said, as if appealing for reason. "But—I stop too often. If I have to drop out again, I. . . ."

"Yes."

"I'd rather stop going."

"It's not so bad as that."

"I'd rather stop going right now. They laugh at me."

"If you stop, how can you ever catch up?"

"They're just children. I know much more."

She said it simply, a simple truth. She knew much more than what the schoolbooks had to offer. She looked as if she knew much more, and I believed her.

"I know you like reading," I said.

"Yes."

She was suddenly far away. The afternoon had waned. A strong breeze from the sea had risen. The last thinning warmth of the sun was now edged with cold. The trees and buildings in the distance now seemed to flounder in a violet haze. It was a time of day that infused stillness into everything. Even the movements of people and machines seem to tone down, to untense and work limp. Maria and I sat together, held in some spell, a clutch of unity that made the silence between us right, that made our being together on a bench in the boulevard, man and girl, stranger and stranger, a thing so true and natural, like the growing shadows in the wake of the setting sun.

In September, the weather changed. The season of rains had come. The city grew dim and gray, like an old beggar, and there were no more walks in the sun. But Maria and I had grown better friends. I continued to give her books, and our conversations became longer. She smiled a lot easier too, wider smiles, and sometimes I could make her laugh. She had acquired other friends in the apartment house, one of whom was my cousin Rita. There were times, when coming home, I would find her in the room next door, where my aunt lived, doing something with Rita's hair.

Meanwhile, I had got a raise in salary and was no longer a cub on the newsdesk. My work in school was more than fair. Even the seemingly eternal rain could not do anything to dampen my growing ambitions, my belief that life was good, and will be better.

Except when I was around Maria. And then, I could see how foolish and awkward I sounded. For she seemed to know better, and what she had known was not a happy and gentle thing. And in her eyes the future as an undetermined, hidden thing, that no one could really know. But what really silenced me was the faith that shone through the things she knew, the times that she listened to me as I talked about the great and fine things in store for me, for every one. It was a faith in me, and a faith in herself, in the great and good things that could happen, and to her too.

And I did not know that those things could happen to her.

In November, the sun broke through the now ever present clouds, and for three or four days we had long, clear weather. Then, my concentration on my work wavered, and my mind began flitting once more to the sky outside, the sunshine and the gardens on the old walls, to the benches under the trees in the boulevards. Once, while working on a particularly bad copy, my mind splintered, the way it sometimes does, and coming together again, I suddenly thought of Maria. The thought became remembrance, going all the way back, and it was even clearer now, the outlines sharper, in fuller focus. The electric light, the shadows around us, the book opened to page 37, the something lost in her eyes. . . .

Late in November, I caught a cold, which developed into an uncomfortable little fever. The office gave me two weeks sick leave. After four days, I was back on my feet. I didn't have to go back to the office however. So, when my aunt went to the province on business, and also to visit the folks, I tagged along. I felt restless, unmoored. It was as if I had strayed away from myself. I suppose you got that way from being sick.

We stayed a week in the province. It was too long. I wanted to go back to Manila after our first three days there. The town seemed overflowing with soldiers, trainees and reservists, who were billeted in the barracks in the town. The place had the air of a boomtown, which depressed me. The people looked too healthy and well-fed and it did not somehow seem right. My mind kept going back to our cramped room in the crumbling apartment house, to the narrow, hemmed-in streets of Intramuros, to the shrill voices of children perhaps in the courtyard, to the captive people of the city. To Maria. What was she doing? Was she thinking of Christmas? Like my young nephews and nieces and cousins? Whom was she asking for a gift? I could hardly wait to go back.

A pouring rain stayed with our train all the way back to Manila. The moving landscape was a series of dissolved hills and fields. What is it in the click of train wheels moving through rain that makes you feel so gray inside? What is it in having been sick, in going away and coming back, that makes you feel as if you are an occurrence in the patchwork accidents of night and day, in the sorrowing quests of people?

In December, we had our first air-raid practice.

I came home one night through darkened streets, peopled by shadows. There was a ragged look to everything, as if no one and nothing cared anymore for appearances.

I reached my room just as the siren shrilled. The lights went off. I sat down in a chair in the corridor. All around me were movements, laughter and talk—anonymous, disembodied sounds. The dark was darker than the moment after moonset. There was a rustle close to me.

"Is that you, Felix?"

"Yes, Maria."

I could feel her standing beside me, breathing softly. I did not move in my chair, my hands cold. The blackout had become too long.

"I don't like darkness," Maria said.

"Oh, come now," I said. "When you sleep you turn the lights off, don't you?"

"It's not like this," she said. "This—this seems all over. Everywhere."

We did not speak again until the all clear sounded and the lights went on. We blinked in the sudden brightness, a little surprised to see everything as it was before, a little uncomfortable at the sight of each other's faces, as if we knew the faces but could not remember the names.

The war happened not long after.

The first few hours, it did not seem real. It was like living on a motion picture screen, with yourself the spectator at the same time. But, the sounds of exploding bombs were real enough, thudding sickeningly against the unready ear.

In Intramuros, the people left their homes on the first night of the war. The rumors told of a great raid, scheduled that night, and directed against the old city. So, most of the people living there packed off for the walls, to sleep in the niches there. When I arrived at the apartment house, I found it empty except for the janitor. Our rooms were locked. Mang Lucio told me that my cousin, who worked in the army, was coming back later. He will sleep in the house, to guard our property. But I was to go to the walls (he gave me directions) where supper was waiting.

"How about Maria?" I asked him.

"She's with your aunt," Mang Lucio told me.

On the way to the Aurora Gardens where the people had evacuated, I met my cousin. He told me we were both to sleep in the house, if I did not mind. I didn't. He had some food with him. So I turned back.

We ate canned pork and beans with the rice. We slept on the floor so that we could read by the hooded light, which we rigged up to hang as low as possible, so no beam could escape outside. The empty building creaked in the night and sent off hollow echoes. We slept uneasily.

I woke up early. It was funny to wake up to stillness in that house which rang with children's voices the whole day everyday. In the kitchen, there were sounds and smells of cooking.

It was Maria, frying rice.

"Hello," I said.

She turned from the stove and looked at me for a long time. I waited. Then she turned back to her cooking. After a while, she said, "Good morning."

"Are the folks coming back?" I asked.

"Yes. When I left, they were preparing to go."

"How did you sleep last night?"

"Fine."

"Where you not scared?"

"At first."

"Then?"

She was silent for a while. Then she said, "I thought, there was nothing more we could do. Besides, the walls were pretty thick."

"Nothing happened last night?"

She didn't answer.

"Are you and your uncle going away?"

"I don't know."

"Didn't he say anything about it?"

"No."

"We're moving away."

"Yes, I know. To Singalong, your aunt said."

"Oh. Well, that's not very far away."

"Isn't it?"

"No," I said.

"Perhaps," she said, "perhaps—if we go away, we might live near—near you."

"I hope so," I said. "Maria."

She turned to me.

"Don't be afraid."

"Of what?"

"Of—of anything. The war. Oh, everything."

She did not say anything. I went to the row of sinks that faced the row of stoves and washed my face. After I had toweled my face dry, I found Maria, through with her cooking, still standing there, watching me.

"We'll probably leave this afternoon," I said. "So, we'll all be around till after lunchtime. We won't have to say good-bye till then."

"No," she said. Then she scooped up the food she had cooked and went out of the kitchen. I went to my room, dressed and went out. I did not see Maria on my way out.

I did not go home for lunch after all. The war had stepped up tempo, and we all had to stick to the city desk. We had food sent in and we worked while we ate. Already the novelty of the war had rubbed off. Air-raid alerts were frequent and the strain of waiting for the planes to come over and drop bombs was just as hard to take as the reports that came in. It hurt to look at the faces of people.

We knocked off about six in the evening, with the understanding that we come in again about eight. I went down the now unfamiliar street. Few people were about. The shops were all closed. Restaurants had only one door open. Before I reached the apartment house, complete darkness had shrouded the old city, as if the day had hastily evacuated too.

The building was unlighted. Nothing moved in it. I went a few steps inside and called. Nobody answered. I went back to the street and stood for a long time in front of the house. Somehow I could not go away just yet. I had our new address in my pocket, but something did not want me to go away. A girl's face, a look in her eyes, a voice. . . .

I was about to go back in when a flashlight burst in my face. It was a civilian volunteer police.

"Do you live here?" he asked me.

"I used to. I'm looking for the janitor."

"Why, did you leave something behind?"

"That's right," I said.

"Well, you better move along, son. This place, the whole area has been ordered evacuated. Nobody lives here anymore. I've been in there. It's empty. Whatever you left behind is lost now."

"Yes, I know," I said. "Lost."

Evening News Saturday Magazine
June 5, 1948

THE BODY OF LOVE

Teodoro M. Locsin

The town of Sandoval is bounded on the north by the church, on the south by the great haciendas, on the east by the country club, where one relieved life's tedium, and on the west by the home for illegitimate children.

It is a town of some twenty thousand people, ruled by five families of which the Zaragosas are the richest and most powerful.

The founder of this family was Don Julio—who began with only the clothes on his back. Before he died, he was the owner of seven haciendas strung out from one end of the province to the other. He was rich not only in display—not one of those prodigals always skirting the edge of bankruptcy— he was a true millionaire, which was as rare, and therefore to be respected, to be held in reverence as a saint that had been canonized. One passed him in the street and made a mental genuflection as before an altar. Such a man moved, commanded the world one lived in. His intercession could make all things possible.

His children, to whom he was as sternly just as to a laborer on one of his haciendas, held him in awe. So did the rest of the town. He had made so much out of nothing, nothing he did could be wrong. Had he lost his senses and attacked a woman—that would have been, somehow, justified. His little jokes were repeated and repeated and became folklore, his least advice, it was generally held, if heeded, would make any man's fortune. He was cautious, patient, clever. He had property and he had cunning. The people of the town thought of him a little as they thought of God.

But this is not the story of Don Julio, it is that of his daughter Margarita. And it is not really her story, but of what happened long after she was dead.

Margarita was the youngest child—death followed the delivery. She was, of all Don Julio's children, the one he loved the most, and when it was the age for her to marry, everyone wondered what man would find favor, not in her eyes, but his. Surely, no man could.

She was a frail-looking girl—the sheltered daughter of the rich, whom life had not hardened, who would fall at the first stroke, perish from the first blow. She went to a convent school and saw her father only two months of the year, between terms, but she wrote to him diligently, every week, informing him in all particulars of her life in the school.

The nuns were very nice, and there was one who was nicest of all, she once wrote to her father. It would be wonderful to be one of them.

To this Don Julio made no answer, but when the school term was up, told Margarita that he was growing old, very old, and needed her at his side. To her, now that she was out of school and, if not in years, in responsibilities a person of maturity, he turned over in lease the largest of his haciendas.

She went once, to see the tremendous place, then did what Don Julio expected her to do—turned over the administration to one of his most trusted men, Pedro. Pedro had grown old in his service, had children for whose education Don Julio paid, was mentioned in his will. He would not risk losing Don Julio's favor by cheating the daughter except with the utmost moderation.

Margarita was the one most favored in her father's will. She would get the hacienda now under lease to her, and another. She was rich in reality and richer in expectation. Who could marry her?

There were many who aspired to her hand in their thoughts, but the thought of Don Julio frightened them. How could they escape the accusation that there was calculation in their mind, how could they prove otherwise, show that they loved her for own sake alone? The will of Don Julio, leaving her so much, would stand forever between her and the man, like a sword. Besides, Margarita, without her money, would not be Margarita but a different person — if one faced the truth.

How Margarita, who was determined to marry for love, came to choose the man she would marry came about thus:

At a dance beyond her father's legal control, she drew up a list of all those who had hinted, since they could not speak openly, that they wanted her. She put the richest at the head of the list, the poorest at the bottom.

The poorest of all was a young lawyer, the son of a widow, a clerk with a salary of eighty pesos in one of the law firms in the capital of the province. He was the one, Margarita said to herself, she would marry. The others were after her to improve their fortune, but this poor lawyer had nothing and his love must be an honest one. And if it was not, well, there was the greater act of charity in marrying him, for whereas she would merely make the others richer, this one she would make rich beyond his dreams. Her money would come to him as comes to a blind man the gift of light.

She danced with him all evening and hope entered his breast. She gave him every encouragement. Finally, she asked him if he loved her—which he said he did. She was a woman who, having everything, had nothing to gain and could not be moved merely by material considerations. She consorted freely, shamelessly, with the poor.

It was happiness, and—such is the nature, I suppose, of that condition—it could not last. If her father had not intervened, something else would have spoiled it for her. We are not in this world to be happy, this life is a trial and a preparation for—I know not what. At any rate we must give up the pursuit of happiness as we must give up everything else, it is an application we must withdraw.

Don Julio caused the dismissal of the young man his daughter loved from the law office. His daughter he threatened with disinheritance.

"I am going to be frank with you, and brief. If you love me, give up this young man, or I will leave you poor."

There was nothing for the young man to do but accept Don Julio's offer—a position in Manila in the office of one of Don Julio's friends. If Margarita should go and join him, he would lose that work. If she stayed away, he would prosper.

It was an arrangement one must admit eminently just.

Margarita became sick. In a year, Margarita was dead. Of love, it was clear. Of the deliberate frustration of her love, there was no doubt. She was dead of it as though she had been burnt at the stake.

And now the story really begins. Sixteen years after his daughter's death, Don Julio joined her. His properties were distributed among the surviving heirs. He was only a legend now. As for Margarita, she had been buried in her family plot in the cemetery just outside the town. She should be, by now, white gleaming bones.

Over the graves of the propertied ones rose marble monuments—of angels, the Crucified Christ, the Virgin, some Christian saint. Some token of future resurrection. Over Margarita's grave was only a plain slab of stone. For she had died in the displeasure of her father, and it sufficed that she was decently interred, that the dates of her birth and death were written under her name, with this hope: "Rest in peace." She had been no duteous child.

She had not been embalmed when she was married to death. Don Julio had absented himself from the funeral and it was a thin crowd that followed the body to the cemetery and saw it lowered, in its coffin of hardwood, into the waiting grave.

This, I must warn in advance, is a true story. You will not believe it....Sixteen years after Margarita's death, her brothers decided that it was time to bring daughter and father together. The two bodies would be laid at rest in a common sepulchre—one as big as a house, as splendid as a palace, with marble steps leading to the single tomb of Margarita and Don Julio. It would be like something out of a book.

The body of Don Julio, when his grave was opened, was in a bad state. There were expressions, among those present, irrepressible, of disgust. A heavy cloth was immediately thrown over the body by one of the sons.

The body of Margarita, not embalmed, had lain in the earth in its coffin of wood with no protection. Now it lay before them, blooming as in life, in a state of miraculous preservation. Not even in life had she been so beautiful in the sight of men.

In voiceless wonder her brothers and only sister, her aunts and uncles, her nephews and nieces, her cousins and friends looked at her. Then a heavy sigh—from someone—was heard.

"A miracle. A great miracle."

Her brothers and sister said nothing but their faces showed agreement. It was a miracle and their sister was a saint.

There is natural explanation, of course, but why should one favor it against the supernatural, the miraculous? Life is dull enough, bad enough, God knows we have need of a little poetry. How can we look truth in the face all the time? We must be thankful for such mercies.

The story spread like wildfire. The newspapers took it up. From the neighboring islands people came to the town to look, to wonder, to pray—to be confirmed in their belief that there was something greater than themselves. And to make a little money.

The body was taken to the church where it was placed before the high altar. A plate of glass was placed over the coffin, so that all might see Margarita plain, from her fair head to shining toe. Margarita became a holy, a magical object. Women began to rub their handkerchiefs on the glass which covered the coffin. With the handkerchiefs they could henceforth ward off sickness and death.

The report was circulated that objects and articles which had touched or been near the body were good medicine for whatever ailed man. Soon people were entering the open grave, the young ones jumping into it, the old slowly lowering their fragile frame, and taking stones, earth, debris. These were sold in the town.

Also taken were leaves, bark and roots from trees growing nearby, even the grass that had grown around Margarita's grave. These were mementos which commanded a price. Pictures of her body, taken in the church, were sold for fifty centavos. Thousands were sold. Tickets for the national sweepstakes were hawked as blessed by the vendors and found quick buyers. Candles, to be lighted in front of the altar, were in great demand, and the candle-makers had a wonderful boom. The prosperity spread. The restaurants were filled, the hotels—there were three of them—whose rooms were usually empty, now lamented their lack of accommodation. Even the places of entertainment—the movie-houses—were beneficiaries of the miracle. One, after all, could not pray in church all the time.

The town authorities consulted with the brothers and sister of the dead about the permanent disposition of the body. Immune against time as it had shown itself, it should not be kept in some dark tomb but displayed where all could see it, under glass, till the end of time. The body of such a saint belonged to the town, to the country, to the world.

Thus exhibited, immortal fame would come to her family— and prosperity to the town. Meanwhile, the natural processes of decay, suspended by a rare combination of lack of humidity and other circumstances, into which it is needless to enter here, had been at work, resuming operation. The body of Margarita was again open to attack. The face blackened. The health authorities issued a warning.

One man said it was the work of the devil, another agreed with him. No one could stop it. The people read helplessly the notice posted on the door of the church, telling them that an examination of the records had revealed that Margarita had died of consumption. The body, declared the health authorities, was unsafe, the people must keep away from it on pain of sickness and death.

Quickly the body was taken to the cemetery and laid beside that of Don Julio and sealed up. It had been out of its grave for thirty days. It had been again in the light, among living men and women. It had brought much money to the town, now it must be buried again. It was—in the words of the health authorities—no longer safe.

Thus the miraculously preserved, the pure and immaculate, one might say, the uncorrupted body of love, exposed to the will and designs of men, had blackened, in the end had poisoned the very air one breathed.

Philippines Free Press
June 12, 1948

PORTRAIT OF A PATRIOT

J. CAPIENDO TUVERA

I don't know why you should be surprised like that. You are married yourself, and sending kids to the world. And you are only twenty-one. Twenty-two? Well, I am twenty-four, if I am a day. I don't know about your wife: you have not shown her to me yet. But you know Mameng. Well, she is not very well just now, but wait until she shall have delivered. It will be her second. For the past week she had been having trouble, so last Thursday I brought her to the hospital. The doctors say she will be all right. Of course she will. As if I hadn't prayed enough for her.

Which? Oh, so they wrote to you about that. Well, I don't blame you for what you say. Mother and everyone else back home have said the same, a hundred, a thousand times. I don't go home but that there are people laughing in groups and talking in guarded whispers as I walk by. They are a bunch of simpletons. Just think, even *Tio* Manuel has upbraided me to my bones. I am sick of it. That's one reason I seldom go home to San Roque. They often send letters to me, telling me I was a fool if ever there was one. They don't send the letters to the house, maybe because they are sure Mameng is another fool herself and would resent what they have to say. I get them at the office. Well, I don't really mind any more. There are a lot of other things to do than eat your heart away on maudlin things like that.

The last time I went there was in November. The streets were strewn with dead leaves. There was a chill everywhere. You saunter to one of the bars where you used to go (you think, oh, it was not so long ago), trying to guess who might be there now tossing the plates or laughing with the girls. You don't find anyone of those you had expected to see. There is only a little child sweeping eternal dust from the walls and then looking up sheepishly to tell you there is no wine. San Roque is dead.

But, of course, Fidel, you must go there too, if only once. You would like to see *Ca* Bito, in the first place. I have not told you, have I? He lost a leg. The Japs swooped down on us once. He was the sentinel, and all of a sudden, before he could say whoa! a bullet had pierced his right thigh. Ericson had it sawn off somehow, and now *Ca* Bito walks around on a pair of crutches.

Say, I believe in this thing luck, old man. Look at me. I was del Pilar to everyone. The Japs themselves came to know it was I. Numberless times this fellow del Pilar ambushed squads of them, with a few men of his, in the hills. The Japs felt outraged and fought back like wounded catamounts, swearing to get me if it was the last thing they did. But everytime I had a lucky break. Once, I went too far between two boulders, my pistol had fallen to the ground, and a Jap had all of me at the end of his gun. But I am here, no? Somehow one of my men saw him, and gave him the works, as Ericson taught us to say. If that is not luck, then I don't know anything about it.

Do you really intend to live there all your life? They tell me Koronadal is a piece of heaven: cheap lands, the green earth everywhere, contentment, and all that. So it's true? Maybe, but I don't see how you could live there happily with all those strangers. You ought to have a good reason, and I am ready to believe it. For all you know, I might join you there yet, what with everybody making a mess of what I have done.

There is really no madness about it. Do you know what I think? I think I could never have been as happy as I am now if I had gone instead to all the corners of the world and lived like a king. Right now I won't give Croesus a thought. Or ever, Mameng is one thing you can really be happy living for.

Of course, it was not quite easy in the beginning. The family came to the wedding, all right, but you could see it was a mere gesture of politeness. Everyone was cold to it. They had wanted me to marry Salud. They had put the idea into their heads that marriage was something you did for the sake of honor and riches, and not for happiness. Well, I told them to leave me alone. Thank God that's what they have finally done, except that they write those letters to spite me. I am sure one of these days they will stop doing that too, like the way they have stopped seeing me, and then I shall feel a lot better still.

The day before the marriage they called me home. I was in Paniqui, having decided to stay there until after it was over because of their continued hostility. I went, thinking they had changed their minds after all. But all I got were reproaches and heapfuls of humiliation. *Tio* Manuel was there. He had taken a leave from the airport just to be home.

The moment I got into the house I knew what awaited me. *Tio* Manuel was blaspheming in that famous grandiloquent manner of his. From the porch I could hear his voice booming inside the house as if his audience were a pack of recruits to whom he was demonstrating a military blunder.

"Here he is, the stupid fool!" he was saying, throwing his fists into the air. "Wait until I get my hands on him." A swift murmur of encouragement and approval came from the others. Mother was there, her hands clasped on her lap, and she stared icily at me as I walked lightly into the room.

"All right, I give you one more chance," *Tio* Manuel barked, pulling his hand which I took to kiss. "This time, I won't hear any of your smart philosophies." I walked over to Mother's seat and bent down to kiss her. She just sat there straight and sphinx-like, and her eyes avoided mine.

"Whoever thought you would be a fool to think of marrying her! *Tio* Manuel said, standing menacingly before me as soon as I had taken a seat. "Why, son-of-a-lightning, you could have wanted to marry this chair and expected more from it! This chair, do you see?" I looked down at my nose. You know *Tio* Manuel. He is a soldier, and maybe would want you to look him straight in the eye, but I was afraid to do that. You could never tell but that he would think you were an insolent, good-for-nothing nephew trying to be smart, and would let you have the boniest side of his fists.

"Well?" he egged, savagely. "Well?"

"I'll marry Mameng," I said. Hmmm, it's funny now, remembering that. I was afraid at first—I think, from force of habit, then suddenly I felt something leave me. Where it was there came a sudden hard and angry welling. I did not resent the hostility with which I was received. I think it was natural, but I was mad at their unwillingness to listen and believe. I had tried to explain before. I had started to reason. I cajoled. I remonstrated. I humbled myself. I don't know what I hadn't done. And all I got were sharp reproofs that fell on me like a thousand bricks.

Well, something died out, as I said. It must have been the fear, for suddenly I felt I could do anything. I faced *Tio* Manuel and told him what I did. He raised his hand, as if to strike, and then let it fall with a futile slump on his side.

"*Tio*," I said, measuredly. "I used to come here. You did not know it, but I did. Nights."

"Fool!" he cursed, and walked to a chair in an angry stride. "What a story! Del Pilar coming to town. I wonder why I never saw you hanging from the flagpole?"

"But I came, and you must believe it," I insisted.

"All right, let's believe it," *Tio* Manuel said, mockingly, turning to Mother and *Tia* Sabel and *Ate* Loring, inviting them to sarcasm. "But do we matter?"

"Everybody else will keep on laughing," Mother said.

"I don't care for everybody," I shrieked.

"You are saying that to justify your folly." *Tio* Manuel shouted, and spat at the window.

They tried to assault emotions after a while. Mother and *Tia* Sabel cried. How women cry! They sobbed and howled and blew their noses. I had a mind to bolt away: I was afraid they might triumph yet, what with those hot torrents of tears. But I stayed, hoping I could let them listen.

"You have lost your mind," Mother said. "You have no feeling. Did I send you to school to have myself suffer like this?"

"Mother," I began. "It's like this—" but here she broke into renewed hysterics, and would not listen. That's what. They would hear nothing.

A month after, you had left for Davao. I joined Ericson's. At the time, Ericson had his headquarters in Sapang Maragul —that range of mountains rising over a narrow pass. All the time we never went to town; only once in a while would I get word from Mother through the farmers who sold their camotes in the market. I can't say how long we stayed there: that's the trouble, you never seem to know that time exists when you have yourself all cramped up in a tight place and scared, but not admitting it, at everything that moved. Anyway, oh yes, that was a lie. I did go to town. Of course it was not safe for me. The Japs were crazy hunting for me and Ericson; Mother was insistent that I should not try to go to town, nor near it. There was a handsome prize on my head. But I went. Once—twice a week. I would slip out of our area at twilight and be at the edge of *Ca* Baldo's sugarcane field before nine. That was the farthest I could go. There was a small hut—I think it is still there—which one of his tenants used in the daytime. It was safe in that place, and I am sure no one, not even the tenant, ever knew I went there.

Sometimes Mameng would be there ahead of me, but most of the time I arrived earlier. I would sit at the doorstep looking sharply into the dark forest of sugarcane and listening to the sounds that their leaves made. There is a trail along the fence leading from the group of houses at the opposite edge—remember?—and a hundred times I thought I saw figures walking on it towards the hut. Once a crash of moving feet came from the middle of the field. I could hear the sound of a body brushing against the leaves and breaking small shoots of sugar cane. I jumped down to the side of the hut, waiting tensely for whoever it was to come. After a while I saw something move towards the clearing where the hut stood. In a moment I found myself laughing: it was only a pig that must have gone loose somehow.

Mameng always came in a pair of pants that I had given to her to use. You could never tell that someone would not see her walking in the dark, and it was not safe finding out that she was a woman. There could have been a lot to talk about—the things I hadn't seen so long in town, the things we did in the mountains. But usually it was better to shut them up somewhere in the mind and just stay there inside the hut staring wordlessly at each other and forgetting the tall canes and the night between them.

Mother never knew about this: I never told her. That was a mistake, I admit, and I should have done better not to fall into it. When I told them afterwards, that time they called me home from Paniqui, they would not hear of it.

But you, of course, are different. Do you remember when we were kids? We used to escape from home on Saturdays and go to that hill across the river. Remember Tibag? And those forest of guavas around the hill?

The boys used to scare Mameng away because they said little girls had no business climbing guavas with us. They had no patience with girls, and hated tomboys. Mitic used to make obscene remarks. The others made fun of her when she got up to one of the branches and shook off the fruits. She was thin and strong and agile, and they laughed at that, thinking what a huge joke it was. Sometimes she cried, and then I would hate all of them and you and I would take her home.

I shall not soon forget those times. I may not know a pin's size of psychology, but I am sure my life took its first and final shape from them.

To think that Mother could remember all that and employ it for her purposes.

"I have always known it," she cried. "As a child she played with boys. What good would come from a girl like that?"

I said, "But, Mother, I was...." She gave a snort, and I swear she could have heard nothing but the sound of my words.

"Did she not climb guavas? Did she not run in races and tumble with boys in wrestling matches? Nothing! Nothing!"

"We were children," I said. *Tio* Manuel jumped up, as if a rat had gone up inside the leg of his pants, and banged a heavy fist on the window sill. Gouts of anger marked his face.

"Nonsense!" he yelled. "Are you going to deny what happened to her?" He walked furiously across the room, puffing with rage. "Could you love a woman like that?"

God knows I have always loved her. In high school—oh, hell, stop smiling like a fool. Of course you know, you know, you meddling wolf! You used to break upon us like a bolt of lightning while we talked under the acacias and then threatened to tell Mother if I would not do your lessons for you. If you were not Mother's baby I could have wrung your neck with a finger.

Well, we should have married in forty-three, but Ericson moved his headquarters away, and he took me along. It was necessary. The Japs had found out where we were, and but for a lucky break they would have dug graves and dumped us in with a toast. That's when *Ca* Bito lost his leg.

Mameng would not let me go, but of course that was impossible. We had arranged to meet at the hill. I could not risk going to town after what had happened. Tibag was hardly ever visited by Japs, and because it was near town, so that Mameng would not have to walk far, I had agreed that we should meet there.

"No, you can't go," she pleaded. "You must not. I am not well." I stared at her face and saw that her lips were pale. There was scarcely any color on her cheeks. She looked tired. Her eyes, when she looked at me, were red and heavy.

"What is it?" I asked. "Fever?" I fumbled in my pockets for the pills that Ericson used to give me. I guess I must have suddenly got fever too, hearing what she had said. With quivering hands I found the pills wrapped in soiled paper, and I gave them to her.

"No," she said. Suddenly she clasped my hands and I felt that hers were cold and trembling. It seemed to me I saw terror in her eyes.

"I shall have a baby," she murmured.

They say fatherhood always comes as a thrill. Well, I believe it. I felt my heart leap. What is it they say about that— a fluttering of tiny wings in the breast? It was like that. But, of course, only for a time. Afterwards, I was frightened. What of her? Was it not possible that I might get killed? And then what? We were not married.

But I tried to soothe her. It was the only thing you could do. Blast it, go on drinking. You don't have to stare at me as if I were a pair of women's legs.

"It'll be all right," I stammered. "I'll be back. It won't be long." I don't know what else I should have said.

I wish men had no memory at all. It's terrible thing. I don't ever want to be able to remember again her stooped and sobbing figure as she walked back slowly to town, the fleet and slender beauty of it growing fainter as the mist gathered in my eyes.

I wish you had been there when I left. Those Japs were a lot of trouble. If they hadn't brought you to the south to work on those Davao airfields, everything would have gone well. You would have known, and knowing, would have told the folks about it before they had any chance to form opinions. Now it's hard for them to believe. Perhaps they never will.

We stayed for six months in Surong, where we went. More than once, while there, I had wanted to escape and go back home. Go ahead and say I wasn't a patriot after all. I know no one who ever was. If there were any, I would have liked to know. The men with me, hiding away and quarrelling shamelessly over stolen pork and chickens, could not have been patriots. I could not see what we were hiding there for, when, if that was all we could do anyway, we should have been leading peaceful lives instead where our women needed us.

When we finally returned, everything had changed in San Roque. The high school building was burned down. The market place was a mass of rubbles. The poblacion, from Asiong's Bar to Co Chica's Lumber Yard, was razed, as they say, to the ground. San Roque was ugly to behold.

I hurried off to Mameng's house. On my way there I had learned that her father had been killed. When I reached her place, all that I found were two-three posts that had remained to taunt at the ruins around them. I went home to Mother. I had been away for long, and you should have seen how happy she was.

But a cloud came to her face when I asked her about Mameng. I understood. From that moment I knew what I had to contend with.

"Just tell me where she is, Mother," I said. "That's all I want to know."

"What for?" she asked, in a hoarse, angry voice. "Would you suddenly take a fancy for her after what happened?"

"I want to see her," I begged.

"She lives with her sister in Paniqui," she said trying to be kind because I had been away for long. "But are you going? And have yourself laughed at?"

I am starting from scratch, Fidel, as the saying goes. But I don't mind. People will go on talking, I suppose, thinking what a lame and flamboyant pretext I am making.

"Perhaps you have told the truth," Mother said. "Yes, perhaps. Even then, are you sure you were alone?"

"Perhaps you were alone," *Tio* Manuel said, with his pugnacious sneer. "Are people fools to believe?"

So, you see, everything boils down to that — laughed at! They see it as a big joke. Right now, in San Roque, I know they are laughing at a man who killed Japs, scores of them, and who finally got fooled by a woman—a jellyfish after all that vaunted courage. It's the price of patriotism. But I enjoy it. If you ask me, I am ready to do the fighting and the killing all over again. But I cannot kill faith. I cannot kill love. Those are things we cannot kill. Otherwise, what did we fight for?

Evening News Saturday Magazine
July 3, 1948

PROBLEM IN LIVING

CORNELIO S. REYES

Benito, thirteen, led his little brothers and sisters out of the massacre south of the Pasig. A big bundle of clothes hung from his right arm, and on his shoulder, slept one-year-old Juanito.

Ana, nine, followed, carrying a basket and pulling by the other hand Mercedes, a whimpering little tot of three.

Five-year-old little Tonio, his two small hands clutching to his breast a young pig, brought up the rear. The pig was a runaway from the fire that little Tonio found lost and cowering in the slum.

They started at midnight with their mother. But a Japanese bullet killed her before they were well on their way.

The day before, the Japanese had come to their district and started burning and killing. In the night there was a lull, and at midnight they set out from their slum, the thick cluster of dirty houses and muddy, tortuous alleys which the Japanese had not cared to enter.

In the morning they found themselves north of the city and in the midst of people already busy cleaning the rubbles and ruin left by a recent battle. A few of the dead still lay sprawled across the pavement or in the gutter.

Some people were building makeshift huts even now from scraps of burned sheet-iron roofings, half-burned woods and boards and all sorts of flattened tin sheets from all kinds of cans.

Benito was tired and little Tonio had begun to grumble saying he was hungry and tired and sleepy. Ana said, "Let's sit down and rest a while."

Benito thought there were a lot of burned sheet-iron roofings here, perhaps he could gather some and build themselves a hut like those the people were putting up. He approached a man nailing a sheet of roofing to the wooden frame of a wall.

"Where are your parents?" said the man looking at him and at his brothers and sisters.

"My mother was killed by the Japanese," Benito answered. "My sick father died before we left."

The man felt sorry. But orphaned children were not new. He himself had lost his wife and two sons. He told himself he had enough troubles of his own without taking up the troubles of others.

"You can build over there," said the man. "Nobody will bother you. Build a shade first. I will help you later. Help yourself with some of those wooden boards and sheets, then do some gathering later." The man pointed to his pile of burned roofings and half-burned wooden boards.

Benito asked little Tonio to help dig holes for the posts of their shade. Little Tonio tied his young pig to a big stone and began to dig with the pointed end of an iron bar. He scooped out the dirt with his hands and threw it on one side. The young pig began to cry for food.

"Oh shut up!" said little Tonio.

Benito put the baby on a mat on the ground beside little Mercedes who had also fallen asleep still whimpering for her mother. Ana took the pot and the can with uncooked rice from the basket and prepared to cook their food on an improvised stove of three big stones. She made sure there was enough water for the baby's broth when the rice began to boil.

When the baby woke up and cried, Ana put a little salt in the broth and fed the baby from a bottle. Mercedes woke up, too, and began to cry and call for her mother.

Little Tonio came very dirty with soot and grime from dragging wood and small roofings for Benito.

"I am very hungry," he said. "Let's eat now."

"Look at your dirty clothes," Ana scolded, assuming the position of mother as she had done many times in play. She seemed to enjoy it now. "Better be careful. You have only two changes of clothing and I cannot wash clothes yet. I have a lot of things to do." She had heard her mother say those same words many times.

Benito came and picked up whimpering little Mercedes.

"Stop crying now. Mother is coming soon," he quieted the child holding her gently close to him. "The shade is almost finished," he told Ana. *"Mang* Lucio is helping me. Take the baby there."

"I am hungry," grumbled little Tonio. "Let's eat now."

"Take the things to the shade," Benito told him. "We shall take our food there."

They sat down on the board floor before two plates of steaming boiled rice and a little plate of salt. Little Mercedes sat on Benito's lap. Benito would put some salt on a small heap of rice, take it with his fingers and feed little Mercedes; and then he would take another mouthful and feed himself. Ana and little Tonio shared the other plate. The baby lay on one side sucking broth from a bottle.

"Mang Lucio is taking me with him to work in the midnight shift at the depot," Benito said. *"Mang* Lucio said labor is scarce and they are taking even small boys."

"There is very little rice left," Ana told her big brother. "I don't think there will be enough left for tomorrow. And I think we should have milk for the baby."

"The baby is a year old now," said Benito. "Try to make some rice porridge for him? I will try to get some milk for him if I can."

"I want some more rice," said little Tonio picking up and putting into his mouth some grains that remained on the empty plate.

"Take some of mine," said Benito.

"Don't let him," said Ana. "He had eaten from my share, too. He is very greedy."

But little Tonio had already taken what Benito offered him. He ate it quickly. Then he stood up and went to the young pig which had been crying all this time.

"I am going to take him to some grass," he told Benito untying the pig. "He eats grass," he said proudly.

Half an hour before midnight, *Mang* Lucio came for Benito. They trudged the cold dark night to the depot.

The work was not hard. Benito, with a lot of others, pushed boxes of canned food over elevated rollers. Checkers sorted them out as they passed and other laborers piled them up.

At four in the morning there was half an hour rest for snack. They were given each a plate of rice and two sardines. Benito kept his in a can to take home.

A lot of the boxes they pushed broke. Now and then, as laborers picked them up, boxes flew open and cans scattered on the ground. There were plenty of broken boxes of canned milk, too.

Benito thought if he could ask any of the American officers, they might let him take a can home. He told *Mang* Lucio about his plan. *Mang* Lucio helped him to see the American officer. Benito was proud of his broken English. The officer smiled and then wrote something on a sheet of stationery. The officer told him he could take home a can of milk for his baby brother every day.

At eight in the morning the night laborers went home. Benito felt very happy thinking of how glad Ana, Mercedes and little Tonio would be to see the food he took home for them.

Benito heard the baby crying as he approached their hut. Ana had him on her little shoulder, dancing him around, trying to quiet him.

"He has been crying since early morning," she said. "I have made some porridge for him but he would not eat."

"I brought milk for him," Benito said, taking the baby from Ana. "Boil some water and I will prepare a bottle for him. Have you eaten your breakfast?" he asked.

"Yes," said Ana taking the pot. "I cooked what little rice was left. Your share is in the box."

"I am still hungry," said little Tonio.

"Don't believe him," said Ana. "He is very greedy. He wants to eat all the time."

"What is it you have in the big can," said little Tonio, his eyes rivetted on the can since Benito came.

"It's boiled rice and sardines, Tonio," he said. "We shall all eat after I have fed the baby."

The baby stopped crying after Benito had fed him milk. But he noticed he was hot with a fever.

Benito borrowed enough rice from *Mang* Lucio for their lunch and supper.

In the afternoon the baby would not stop crying. And he would not take the milk they offered him. His fever had risen very high. Ana was exhausted trying to dance him to sleep. Benito told Ana he would get a doctor.

Little Mercedes, bothered by the noise, could not sleep. She began to cry for her mother.

Benito called little Tonio who was playing with the pig outside the house.

"Stop playing with that dirty pig," he scolded. "Play with Mercedes and make her stop crying."

"Oh, stop bawling," said little Tonio, pulling Mercedes by the hand. But Mercedes would not budge.

"Stop crying," said little Tonio, "and I will let you play with my pig."

Mercedes stood up and followed him still crying.

"Scratch his belly," little Tonio told Mercedes. "Scratch his belly and you will see him lie down."

Mercedes scratched the pig's belly. It lay down on its side and put up two of its legs exposing more of its belly.

Mercedes laughed in glee.

After the doctor had seen the baby, he gave Benito a piece of paper and told him to get the medicine from a drug store.

Ana looked at little Tonio who had come in when the doctor arrived.

"Perhaps we can sell the pig," she told Benito, "Then we can buy the medicine."

Little Tonio, hearing this, gave a start.

"No," he said. "You must not sell my pig."

He rushed out to the young pig and hugged it, afraid of losing it. He untied it from the pole and called to Mercedes to follow.

"We will take him to grass," he said.

Benito had to see *Mang* Lucio about some money, promising to pay him on his wages.

Late in the afternoon the baby went into convulsions and rolled his eyes as if he were going to die. He quieted down in the evening but his fever remained high. Benito and Ana, afraid, kept watch. Even little Tonio could not sleep. They looked at the baby as he slept uneasily, breathing hard.

"Better sleep a while," Benito told Ana. "You can stay watch again after I have gone."

But Ana refused. "I could not sleep," she said.

Little Tonio approached Benito.

"*Kuya*," he said. "You can sell my pig tomorrow and get some more medicine for the baby."

"All right," said Benito. "Go to sleep now."

But little Tonio refused to asleep.

When *Mang* Lucio came for Benito, however, little Tonio was asleep. His little head fell on his chest, his little back at rest on the wall of their hut.

Benito picked him up gently and put him in his place on the mat.

In the dark, on their way to the depot, Benito cried. His mind kept busy all the time he worked.

During the snack hour he collected as much of the left-over boiled rice and sardines he could carry. He hurried home in the morning.

There was a smile on Ana's tired little face when he arrived. He looked at the baby quickly. He was sleeping quietly, breathing peacefully now. And the fever was gone when Benito touched his face.

"You did not sleep," he chided Ana seeing her tired hollow eyes.

"I could not sleep," Ana said.

Outside, back of the hut, little Tonio and Mercedes were playing with the young pig. Mercedes would scratch the pig's belly and when the pig thrust up its legs she would laugh with delight. Little Tonio, seeing how happy his younger sister was, joined her laughter.

Sunday Times Magazine
July 4, 1948

SO STILL THE NIGHT

Silvestre L. Tagarao

The door folded back on creaking hinges at the first impact of my knuckles upon it. All at once the doorspace was flooded with the orange glow of the lamp within and I stood there blinking and trying hard to adjust my eyes to the sudden light. I could vaguely see two figures, seated and with their backs toward me, and as the figures became clearer my fear vanished. A while ago, as I groped up the stairway quietly, I had a gnawing fear of some sort—the place being altogether new and strange, and the forest towering about like black, forbidding omens. I was afraid I would encounter some wild and hostile people, but seeing that those were women seated there with their backs toward me, and still unaware of my presence, I emitted an almost inaudible cough and then a little loudly said, "Good evening...."

One of the seated figures, and certainly the younger one, almost jumped up, and when she saw me standing there on the doorway, she made a loud gasp and blurted out some word, a name perhaps, and then stood still, wide-eyed, unable to recover from her surprise. Attracted somehow by the unusual behavior of the younger one, I did not notice the other one turn around also and was now regarding me with the more composed indifference of old age. But when I did turn my eyes on her, so brief a time it was, there was a quick flash, a sound, a rustle—for within that span of time the younger one had recovered and very swiftly cut across the floor, and before I could comprehend the quickness of that movement, I felt her body trembling against mine and I stood still, not knowing what it was all about, not knowing also what to do.

I thought the situation funny. But to her it was not; it was real. She had tightened her arms around my neck some more, her body shaking convulsively, her voice coming in broken tones, muttering a name, which in my confusion I could not make out, and she was crying, I knew. The old woman had disengaged herself from her seat and was now trying to break her away from me.

"Delia...," the old woman murmured, patting her at the same time, "Delia...please let him go...."

No avail. She clung to me more tenaciously, shaking me with the voluptuous movement of her trembling body. She kept on muttering the name, just that name but until now I could not make out because she had buried her face into my chest and she was crying like a child.

The old woman stood patiently by, still patting her gently. "Let him go, Delia..." she kept on saying, "let him go...."

And then she stopped crying. She also stopped muttering the name; her body stopped quivering and the arms around my neck weakened. As she began to slump down, I caught her and instinctively carried her to where she was sitting when I first saw her. She was unconscious.

The old woman had disappeared into a room and I was left there staring at her pale, lovely face. To me, the situation was increasingly disconcerting. I could not even understand the half of it. Somehow I blamed myself for having entered the house. But if I did not, could I possibly pass the night in the deep, dark forest teeming with uncanny sounds?

The old woman came shuffling back, holding a small bottle with a colored liquid. I began to move away, in the direction of the door, though still contemplatively, hoping that she would call me back should I be seen walking out. She did. She bade me sit down. Rather stiffly, I did.

I wanted to help. I thought it would take a long time more to bring her back. She passed the small bottle just below Delia's nostrils many times and I stood by, watching intently. Then she began to stir, move her hand and face, her body twisting slowly like one rousing from slumber. The old woman turned to me and said, "Please help me take her to her room."

After we had laid her down we returned to the chairs. "What is your name?" the old woman asked, as I sank into my seat. I gave her my name. And she did not say anything more. I let my gaze wander around. I noted how neatly the house was kept, saw some magazine pictures pasted on the

walls, a few snapshots and the almost wilted flower on a table
in one corner. The silence made the house so big at once. The
black forest around, with its growing sounds, became frightening again.

I began to speak. "I lost my way in the forest," I said,
"We were tracking a wounded doe which I had shot late this
afternoon. As the search stretched farther and farther, I felt
the weight of the rifle on my shoulder, so I handed it to my
companion. Somewhere, the trail of blooddrips stopped and we
did not know which direction to take. My companion wanted
to give up the search, but I succeeded in convincing him that
we try to separate and follow two paths and then meet at the
base of a tall, dead tree that stood like a giant skeleton in the
distance. We continued the search, and then, perhaps, I became so absorbed in it that I did not notice the approach of
night and became aware of it only when it was irrefutably
dark before me. I shouted to my companion but my voice was
lost in the strong heave of the leaves above me. I shouted
again and then again and then I decided that all I could do
was to grope my way through and hope for the best. When
I saw the light here...."

She had been watching me carefully. For a while, I thought
she would not believe me. But there were scratches and cuts
on my face and arms. She leaned forward. "You will have
to forgive Delia for her behavior," she said.

"Is Delia your daughter?" I asked.

She shook her head. The wind blew in and our shadows
danced on the walls like gnomes. Out of the deep silence, she
pulled out a sigh. She turned to the window, out into the darkness with its eerie sounds.

"Nestor was my son."

She stopped.

I could not understand but I could not ask.

"Delia is the wife of my only son Nestor," she said, turning to me again. "They were married some five or six years
ago—less than a year before the war, to be exact. I bought
this land here and gave it to them. They built this house and
asked me to live with them. Then the war came. Nestor was
called...."

I thought she was just trying to keep my curiosity. I waited
for the words that would follow; none came, she was looking

past my shoulders in the direction of the room we had been.
Then she half-rose and beckoned to somebody back there: Delia's
lovely figure was framed by the narrow door, the orange light
coloring her skin with a waxen polish. I stood up and she
approached. But she did not sit in my chair; instead, she bade
me sit down and sat on the arm of my chair; leaning her supple body against my shoulder.

For a time, I could not understand the expression on the
old woman's face. It seemed vexed. When Delia laid her hand
on my head, the old woman's lips twitched and I thought she
would scream. But she did not; instead, she stood up and offered
her seat to Delia. "You should take your seat here, Delia," she
said and left.

Once more, I was alone with her, looking awkwardly at
her, and she looking at me with the eagerness of a child. No
longer wan was her face, the light seemed to have suffused it
with pastel pink. Her eyes regarded me with a kind of tenderness, and then pulling her chair closer, so she could hold my
hand, the lips began to move, and her voice, clear and full,
now, pushed my confusion away and I listened attentively.

"I thought it was some kind of a dream, Nestor," she said.
"But I knew it would not be, because I have always waited and
I knew you would be back....I had prayed so hard that I
almost felt that my prayers alone were bringing you back to
me....But what I could not understand was why you just
stood there, not saying anything, not even moving, as if you
were not happy to see me, as if you do not want we now....
And five years...is too long a period of time to wait, Nestor...so very long, Nestor...."

Remembering what the old woman had told me, I did not
find it possible to say anything. I knew she would not believe
me if I told her that I was not really Nestor.

"You will find the house as when you left," she went on.
"That was all I did all these years. I knew that out there you
would be thinking of me and the place you left behind, and
knowing that your mind would always conjure a picture of us
the time you left, I made time stand still on that."

And then she was standing, holding both of my hands,
and pulling me up. "You must see our garden now! . . ." She
was a child a while ago, she was acting one now. "Oh, I can't
wait till morning to show you all things you left behind!"

"But it is dark outside, Delia," I protested, not wanting to get up. "It is so dark without, we could not possibly see a thing."

She laughed and her laughter was good, alive. Rumpling my hair, she pouted. "Is five years too quick to make you forget? Have you forgotten that beautiful little shaded lamp which you bought just after our marriage?...And I remember you saying, 'This is our lamp and therefore our light, Delia. The light within shall be very bright, no wind, however strong, can put it out. In the hour of darkness, we shall light it, and it will shine very brightly....'" She smiled, and after telling me to wait, she disappeared into her room. Just as quickly, she emerged holding a well-shaded little lamp, already lighted.

"Come, Nestor, let us go," she said, and I did not know how else I could resist.

She led the way, happily, holding the light in one hand and pulling me along with the other. Behind, I felt the old woman following.

"I want to show you the flowers which I have tended carefully," she chirped. "I will take you to the little well beside which is that beautiful bench you had fashioned out of some stray timber. You used to say that we would sit there of afternoons, watch the sun die behind the tall trees, and then when daylight begins to grey, we would look at the well and make a joint wish—remember?"

As we walked down a cleaned path, I looked briefly back and I saw the old woman standing by the half-opened door. I thought she would go down, too, and keep on following us, but when I looked back again she was still there, vaguely visible in the darkness that was left behind.

The light she was carrying pushed the darkness away. She took me all over the lot, still pulling me along, and there did not seem to be any ominous forest around. The lot was flat and cleared, no more tree-stumps, no more hollows. There was not a single blade of grass I saw, very painstakingly cleared it was. But where the flowers were and the little well, I could not know. Sometimes, she would go on a run, dragging me along, and then would stop and lean against me, panting heavily. Then again she would begin to run and I would run along, too, and then, after we had almost gone over the whole lot, she stopped and began laughing loud and deep, but for all that her voice was nice to hear. She was breathing heavily, too.

Then she raised the light against my face. "The flowers? the little well?" she asked, still laughing like a child. "Of course, you will not see those flowers and the little well. But they are here, right here—only they have not materialized yet. You told me there would be flowers here and a little well over there, with the beautiful bench, the sunset, the joint wish.... And then when you were about ready to buckle down to work, they called you away...for country, you had said...and then five years...."

I wondered why I could not say anything. She had stopped laughing; the hand that was holding the light fell to her side. "This is the very spot where we parted," she said. "I know because I have marked it with two white stones, the stone beside you was where you stood five years ago and the stone beside me was where I stood, also five years ago. That is why I brought you here. Standing here again, I want you to think and remember what had passed....It is not easy, I know. But, please, try to remember...."

But remembering on my part, was useless; speech, also. "When you left," she picked up, "everything became just like a dream. I began to live in a dream, and the dream was always that you would come back. So I waited. I prayed and waited. There were times when, while praying, I would seem to hear footsteps approaching, sometimes a voice familiarly yours, sometimes the touch of tender hands on my back. So I would keep on praying, harder than ever, wanting to hear footsteps again, or the familiar voice, or the tender touch of hands, no longer looking back, afraid that reality would blast the dream.... Oh, but sometimes I seemed to feel that it was really you by my side...something like you trying to reach out to me...."

I tugged at her hands so we could go back to the house but she did not yield. "I kept all your plans in my mind," she continued. "I did not want to forget them, not even the minutest of details. The flower beds. The meandering walk-paths. The bench by the little well. Not even a single blade of grass to mar our garden. Everyday I was here pulling out stray blades of grass. Everyday I kept tucking in place the white stones around the flower beds picking the worms out of those dainty flowers, watering them mornings and afternoons. Then

I would sit on the bench by the little well beside you and together we gaze at the sinking sun and when night has come we rose and looking at the well, made a joint wish....Five years of that, Nestor...only that...it is so hard to sit...so hard to be alone...."

I felt good when I saw the old woman entering the circle of light that engulfed us. "It's rather late now, Delia—don't you think?" she said. "And he might want to rest now." For a while, she looked at me and the night stood still. I nodded and we followed the old woman back to the house.

She had prepared a bed for me outside the room, but Delia insisted that I should sleep inside the room. The more persuasive of the two, I had to follow the latter; after all, no amount of resistance on my part would do. And then when I was about to lie down, Delia came in, with a loud burst: "Supper! Have you had supper already, Nestor? Oh, my...."

"I have," I said. It was a lie but it was good to hear my voice again in a long, long time.

I was tired, very tired, and I could not quell the disturbance in my thoughts.

The old woman called Delia and she left the room. I laid myself down. A stranger in the place, I let my eyes wander freely around the small room. It was bare except for a makeshift altar at the corner opposite my bed. An oil lamp burned weakly, faintly lighting an old image of the Virgin Mother. The altar faced the door, but even then the wind coming in from the window at the head of my bed swayed the oil light playfully. Outside it was very quiet. It was dark still, the line of the forest hardly visible against the dark sky.

I wanted to sleep, but the voices of Delia and the old woman whirred across my mind like bees in a swarm. At first it was a hum, rising and falling; words reached me indistinctly: later the tones were raised some more, became words and voices. I discarded sleep....The old woman sounded desperately pleading:

"It is not him, Delia...not Nestor...only a dream... You were asleep a while ago...rousing, you saw him...but it is only the vision that you saw...By morning, all these would vanish...it is only a dream, my child, believe me...."

Then Delia:

"But he is there, Mother....If I go in there, he will surely be there....In fact, he is there...I have touched him and he is real...a dream is different...only a feeling seen with the eye....This is him, Mother...real...seen with the eye and touched with the hand....I even felt his pulse beat...he is alive...."

Silence. Strange, deep, long. Sleep that was descending on me was arrested by the slow apparition-like appearance of Delia at the door. She leaned weakly against it and for a time I had the feeling that she was looking at me. Softly, she was soon moving toward the altar. Her eyes glistened against the pale light. Weakly, she went down on her knees and clasped her hands before her. The voice was very tired too:

"...dream...vision...morning...please...stay...Mother ...Mother...."

Then her pale, lovely face dwindled; even her voice. The interval seemed long; it should have been endless....

The oil lamp was still burning when I opened my eyes. The light of the lamp, however, was no longer felt, for the room was goldenly illuminated by the moonbeams flooding in through the open window. The image stood alone; at the door was the old woman leaning; by my side was Delia, peacefully asleep. I rose slowly and carefully, not wanting to rouse her. The old woman gave a start when I approached her. We left the room noiselessly.

"The moon is already out," I said somehow feeling the chilling air.

"It is almost morning," the old woman said.

"I want to start now," I said, "I think I can find my way."

"There is a path at the right side of this clearing," she said. "It will lead you to the road."

"Goodbye," I said, "and thank you so much."

"Goodbye," she said, "and thank you, too."

I found the road. The big round moon was riding proudly high. The road was bright as daylight. But everything was still yet. Everything was voiceless yet.

This Week
July 4, 1948

THE BOARDING HOUSE

D. PAULO DIZON

It was she who proposed the idea that they run a boarding house, but though at first he had half a mind to raise his
voice against it his better judgment told him to refrain from
voicing out his objection; for he knew she was as sensitive as
he was afraid of hurting her feelings. It was too soon for the
two of them to have a row; they had been married only five
or six weeks, and it had taken him more than a year of persistent wooing to win her.

So, all he could do about this proposition of hers regarding this business of running a boarding house was keep his
own counsel. It both surprised and hurt him that she, this
charming woman who was now his own wife, had a business
mind. In the first place, he, being a businessman, did not believe that women should double in business, unless it was the
business of the home. And as for the boarding house proposition, it did not strike him as pleasant, especially as it came
from her. She sounded as though she meant business, too.

Must we go to that extent? he said, trying as best as he
could to sound gentle and not against her. It takes a good
deal of trouble, you know, to run a boarding house.

I know I can manage it, she assured him. I grew up in a
boarding house. My mother used to run one herself. Not to
mention the fact that I am a Home Economics graduate.

Now, how could he bring himself at all to tell her that
he was much against it without hurting her? She was pretty
determined to have her own way in the matter of the boarding
house. That's why it hurt him. If I give in now, he thought,
I'd be giving in to her own ways later. And if I oppose her,
it'd hurt her. He had vowed to make her happy, very happy.

You seem to doubt my ability to run a boarding house, she said. It isn't that, he said. I just don't want you to do anything.

The very thought of it is horrible, she said. You have no idea, I suppose, how it bores me doing nothing all the time. You don't want me to grow plump and dull, do you?

I didn't know you were bored, he said sullenly. Everytime I asked you if you were happy you told me yes you were happy. Now you tell me you are bored.

I told you, she expostulated, a hint of irritation in her voice, that I am bored doing nothing. That's why I want to do something. After all, I only want to help you earn our livelihood.

Thank you, he said. That's very thoughtful of you, and at the same time it's very inconsiderate of you.

Inconsiderate? She lifted her pretty face up to him, and an angry look lurked in her eyes. Now he saw the beginning of their first row.

You didn't consider how much you hurt me by saying you want to help me earn our livelihood, he said. Do you honestly believe that what I earn is not enough? You have always known it is more than enough, isn't it so?

I am sorry if I hurt you, darling, she said. I didn't mean to, really. What I meant was that I want us to have some savings in the bank. We can never tell what may happen.

You know very well we have money in the bank, he said. Only it is in my name. But you are entitled to it just the same. And in the event of my death, it's all yours.

Let's not talk about death, she said.

I'm sorry, he said, if I mentioned something unpleasant. But I want you to know that you need not worry about anything at all. I want you to be my happy wife, don't you see?

I am not worried, she said.

As for anything that may happen, he continued, you need not worry about that, either. I am insured for fifteen thousand. The money in the bank, which will be in your name in the event of my untimely....

Before he could finish what he was going to say she stood up and walked out of the room. She walked out on him in a huff, leaving him bewildered, pained. This was the first time since she became his wife that this sort of thing had happened in their household.

When after their honeymoon in Baguio he brought her to his house, he remembered, he had said it was too big for just the two of them, and she was silent for a long while, and he knew she was thinking of the possibilities of making it look like new and very much of a home. It was a two-story building, very spacious, very cool-looking, and at the time he first brought her home to this house it did not look as if it had been lived in by a woman. His mother had long been dead, and she was the last woman to live in it.

She did a miracle of a job in making the house not only look beautiful inside but also very pleasant to live in, the first week she had taken over as mistress of it. While she was engaged in the housewifely task of putting the house to rights, as she put it, she was very happy, but when she found nothing else to do or to add to this or that, she began to feel the weight of aloneness, for she was alone all day long but for the presence of a reticent maid who was so efficient she didn't have to be told what was to be done in the house.

In the evening when he came home he was tired he had to relax his nerves, as was his wont even long before, by lying down, and there wasn't much to talk about except things that they had always been talking about since they started living under the same roof. And it was only very considerate of her not to remind him of his promise in the morning that they were going out that night to the movies or for just a stroll. He always brought home some American magazines for her.

And so it was that the pair, Mr. and Mrs. Meliton, set up a boarding house. They started with six male boarders, four of whom were working for the same firm where Mr. Meliton was chief accountant, and the other two were relatives of some of the boarders. All six of them lived downstairs, while the upper story was exclusively the Melitons.' There was room yet for four more boarders.

They got another maid to help Mrs. Meliton with the kitchen chores, and although Mr. Meliton had wanted to hire the services of a cook, Mrs. Meliton thought it unnecessary because, she had told him, she could do the cooking herself, and she enjoyed cooking anyway. They hung up a We Admit Boarders sign at the front gate, and in another week, they had nine boarders in all.

Mrs. Meliton, the young and lovely landlady, had interviewed each of the boarders before admitting them. She had made it understood that the boarding house was to be regarded as a decent place, which it was, she told them, and that the boarders, who were all males, were not to bring women in for the night, things like that, although of course, they could be visited.

The first month of the boarding house proved promising. It had kept the young housewife busy and happy, and they figured out that they could buy a refrigerator in three or four months out of the proceeds of the boarding house alone. Already they had bought a good radio.

The boarder last to be admitted was a strange young man who was in very bad need of a haircut. He was tall and had very broad shoulders, notwithstanding his lankiness. He had on a pair of almost faded denim trousers, tennis shoes, and a printed polo shirt, when he saw Mrs. Meliton about the last vacant space in the boarding house.

At first Mrs. Meliton entertained a kind of fear of the young man, for he did look different from all the rest. He looked more like a stevedore than her idea of a "professional." His face bore the marks of one who had lived a hard and bitter life, she thought; but it was gentle, and he spoke like a cultured man. His voice was low and soft and clear and the words he spoke were simple and sincere. At least that's how he impressed her.

We admit only professionals, Mrs. Meliton told him, but not without politeness. She tried as best as she could not to sound rude to him.

I see, the young man said.

May I ask you what your profession is? she said.

If what you mean by profession is how one earns his bread, he said, I am a violinist. A third-rate violinist. I play the violin in a night club, and I don't like it. I am required to play the kind of music I do not wish to play, and that's how I earn my bread.

So you're a musician, she said. That's nice.

A third-rate musician, he repeated. I have to play the wrong kind of music and I don't like it. You see, I am a poet.

Oh, a poet, Mrs. Meliton said as though surprised. I have heard so much about poets, but this is the first time I've met one.

You are not disappointed, I hope, he said.

Of course not. If you will excuse my asking you, do you earn much for writing poems?

I understand, he said, ignoring the landlady's question, you require your boarders to pay in advance. I am willing to pay you a month's advance. How much would you charge me, please?

For a while Mrs. Meliton was nonplussed. No, she said. That's not what I meant. I am sorry if you took it that way. You see, I am just curious about people who write poetry.

They never earn much for their wares, he said. They never earn at all. One writes poetry not for the money. It would take many volumes of books to write about why poets write not for money.

Oh, the landlady said.

I like this room very much, the young man said. They had been talking in the vacant room which she had shown him. The room used to be a storeroom, and it was located near the kitchen in the rear of the building. There was a low staircase leading to the narrow corridor to which the former storeroom opened.

I like it, the young man continued, because it is far from the others. I usually work at night, and in this room I shall be far from disturbing the others and from being disturbed by them.

They won't mind it, I am sure, the landlady said.

I am sure they would, he said.

He had paid for his month's board in advance, thanked her, and before she could say anything to him, if she wanted to say anything to him at all, he was gone.

When Mr. Meliton came home in the evening he was as usual very tired. His officemates were beginning to notice how very seriously and very conscientiously he was taking his work. With business picking up very fast, and with the firm making a good deal of profit, it was probable that he would become a member of the board of directors before long. On his wedding day the president of the firm and the other officials had given him and his wife a gift of expensive chinaware and a raise in salary, as signs of their appreciation for his services to the firm; and how he not only had lived up to their expectation, but actually drove himself.

He walked up the stairs almost dragging himself but happy to be home and in the company of his wife. She met him at the top of the stairs and greeted him with a kiss on the cheek, and leaning against each other, they entered their room. He slumped himself upon the softness of the bed, heaving a long, deep sigh of relief as he did so. She lifted up his head and pillowed it upon her lap and caressed his tired brow with her own tired fingers, for she too was tired from supervising the preparation of food, the setting of the table, and so forth. Really, it was no joke to run a boarding house, but it kept her busy and she enjoyed it.

It was while the boarders were having supper that the young man moved in. They had been eating with the landlady at one end of the table and the landlord at the other end and all the boarders laughing appreciatively at the landlord's corny jokes. He wasn't a good one at cracking jokes but the boarders laughed just the same to please him.

He had been knocking at the door for quite a while before the maid noticed it. Everybody stopped laughing when he came in lugging his personal effects in the manner of a stevedore, and with his faded denim trousers he actually looked like one. He carried a big bundle on his shoulder and a portable typewriter he carried in his free hand.

Good evening, he said. I hope I did not disturb you.

Not at all, Mrs. Meliton said. And she gave instructions to the maid to help him with his things. He disappeared into his room and emerged again empty handed, walked past the table where they were eating, and came back followed by the maid, both of them with their hands full. He carried a violin in its case in one hand and in the other he carried a bundle of books. The maid had her arms full of books and magazines.

He claims to be a third-rate musician and a poet, Mrs. Meliton told the others, as he disappeared into the room the second time.

That explains the long hair, Mr. Meliton, the landlord remarked. And the others laughed.

How can he write poetry with so much hair weighing down upon his bean? One of the boarders said; he was the new book-keeper in the firm where his landlord was chief accountant.

Mrs. Meliton instructed the maid who had helped the young man with his things to ask him if he wanted his food brought to him in his room. And turning to the other boarders, she said scarcely above a whisper: He might be too shy to eat with us, considering it is his first night here.

Are you sure he's not an impostor? Mr. Meliton said, attempting to make the others laugh. But they only chuckled.

She chided her husband wordlessly, with a look and a smile. He grinned sheepishly.

The maid came back in the dining room to announce that the newcomer only wanted hot coffee, black and gently sugared.

Gently sugared? Another of the boarders, a senior student in Education majoring in English, repeated. The fellow's trying to impress us with his poetry already.

Sometimes at night the young man who said he was a poet played his violin in his room. His fellow boarders seldom saw him, for he never came to the table to eat with them; besides, they all left for their offices or schools a little after breakfast everyday (except Sundays, of course). He always played in the quiet of the night. He played a sad wailing tune that seemed to tell of the lonely life he was living, and for all they thought of him, it never failed to touch them.

In their own private room the landlady and the landlord, he with his head on her lap, she gently caressing his face with her soft fingers, listened silently to the young man's music.

But on other nights the young man produced a lot of noise with his typewriter. There were nights, too, when he would leave the house with a loud bang of his door and come home with his violin dangling in its case from his tired hand in the morning.

They would be having their breakfast, the landlady at her end of the table and the landlord at his, laughing and talking as they ate, and he would walk past their table. He would greet them good morning without even bothering to throw a glance at them and would disappear into his room before they had a chance to greet him in turn. They wondered what sort of a fellow he really was, but after a few weeks they got used to his ways.

He was in terrible mood every time he had played at the night club. He would lock the door of his room and nobody outside it ever knew what he did the whole day. They could hear him stirring inside, and they couldn't imagine him reading or writing because they could feel the restlessness within. He didn't even bother to answer the maid who tried to bring him food.

At other times his closed room would be violently alive with the rattle of his typewriter. He would pound the machine for hours on end, sometimes through the night, and in the morning at breakfast those whose rooms were nearest him would complain to the landlady.

But sometimes he regales you with sweet music, she would say. He doesn't write every night.

Ask the maid to tell him to use a pencil instead of that scandalous machine if he wants to write the whole night through, the landlord said. We won't let him keep the whole household awake everytime he works, will we?

I'll tell him myself, she said. The maid might put it rudely and he might feel hurt. He seems to be very sensitive, too.

If he feels hurt, the landlord said, the door's wide open. We don't owe it to the world to tolerate a madman, do we?

For all we know he is writing a masterpiece, she said. Ten years from now, who knows, a memorial tablet might be nailed on the door of that room saying: In this room such and such a masterpiece was written on such and such a date by such and such....come to think of it, I still do not know the fellow's name.

He's probably a monk, the bookkeeper said. If he's not, he should be. I've never seen a fellow too lazy to have his hair cut, like that fellow.

Sometimes that fellow gives me the creeps, you know, Mr. Meliton said. We might wake up some night to find ourselves burning.

What terrible imagination, Mrs. Meliton said, giving him that gentle but chiding look, which in a way made her all the more beautiful. The fellow looks as harmless as a saint.

He must be St. Paul rewriting the Bible, Mr. Meliton said, a tinge of jealously in his voice. He chuckled at his own statement, but there was pain in it, and the others didn't think it a joke, so they didn't laugh the way they used to do.

Well, she said, if you really don't want him in this house, I will go tell him to move out. But at least we could be polite to other people.

You need not pull a long face, Clara, the husband said. You sound as though you were taking a fancy on him.

It was all quiet at the breakfast table. This was the first time since they got married that they spoke in that tone.

She stood up from the table and went upstairs. They didn't say anything to each other even when he came up to their room to dress for the office, and he didn't even say goodbye when he left. Instead he banged the door behind him.

For the first time since he moved in, the young man played his violin in the morning. It was the same tune he always loved to play that he played that day. Mrs. Meliton was in the bathroom when she heard him playing. Listening to his music made it difficult for her to decide whether to tell him to go or not. A man who could play that kind of music, she thought, is not capable of burning a house. Or maybe I don't know anything about anything.

She had put on her satin negligee and before she knew it she was going down the stairs. Was it the music of the violin, she asked herself, or my subconscious obedience to my husband's wishes? But how tell him in such a polite manner that he won't get hurt? He is a very sensitive creature, it seems. You can't just tell a fellow to move out, especially if he pays in advance. She could be polite in the telling, could she not?

She had been standing in front of his open door—strange that his door was not locked from the inside now—for a long time before he raised his eyes. The music died all of a sudden.

Good morning, he said. He smiled. He had on a fresh shirt the sleeves of which were buttoned at the wrists, a fresh pair of pants, and he looked younger and nicer with his new haircut. He must have had his hair cut the night before.

I was attracted by your playing, she said. You play very nicely.

Thank you, he said. Will you come in?

She had forgotten she was in her negligee; she wasn't supposed to appear before her boarders in such attire. It would have scandalized the landlord.

She noticed that his things were all packed, and the bed was undraped, for his beddings had been rolled neatly and tied with a piece of rope. He must have overheard us, she thought. She couldn't help feeling somewhat embarrassed. Then she felt his gaze on her. She tried to avoid his eyes.

I know what you came to tell me, he said. There is no need for you to tell me what it is you have to tell me. I also know how hard it is for you to tell me what you came to tell me.

I am sorry, she said. And when she raised her eyes she saw that he was staring at her neck. It was then that she realized she was in her negligee. It alarmed her.

She suddenly made a move for the door, but he was quick to hold her by the arm. He closed the door and locked it.

I have written a story about you, he told her. It is the best that I have ever done.

Oh, she said. She felt less afraid of him now; his voice, gentle and low, seemed to have reassured her. What about me?

There is in the story a scene exactly like this, he said. You coming into my room, one of the many rooms of your husband's house, fresh from your morning bath, and I, holding you a prisoner. I am going away, Mrs. Meliton.

She stared at him blankly, not knowing what to say or what to do under the circumstances. Then she didn't have to speak at all. He had gathered her in his arms—they were strong arms—and kissed her violently on the mouth. She might have resisted but afterward she could not remember having done so.

In the evening Mr. Meliton came home tired as usual. He brought her some American magazines, as usual. He greeted her with a kiss on the cheek when she met him on the top of the stairs, as usual.

He has gone, she told him, smiling sweetly, a little proudly.

He has, has he? Mr. Meliton said. Poor fellow, I didn't mean what I said about him at breakfast this morning. After all, he must be just one of those harmless fools who are crazy about the Arts. So he's gone, eh. You didn't have to be rude to him, did you?

He slumped his tired body upon the softness of the bed, his head pillowed in her lap. I shall miss his lonely music, he sighed.

Sunday Times Magazine
July 11, 1948

LOW WALL

ESTRELLA D. ALFON

I was taking a bath, standing under the cool clean water from the bathroom shower, soaping myself when I felt a small missile hit my back, and I saw a pellet of paper, such as little boys use to load rubber slingshot, drop to the bathroom floor. Looking around me, and looking up, I was just in time to see a pate lower itself, a man's head quickly disappear out of view behind the bathroom wall.

We had built our *barong-barong* in the days immediately after the liberation. It had not mattered to us then, as it had not to so many others by the fire left bereft what the *barong-barong* would be like. Enough to us that there would be a roof over our heads, and walls to hide the wretched bareness of lives pulled down to the veriest essentials by the liberation's conflagration.

It had quickly come out however, after a while when other houses sprang up beside ours, some of them meaner, some of them better than our own shack, than the shelter we now called home, and was in some ways inadequate and wanting.

We had pulled the charred wood from the ashes, their surface embers we had quickly hacked off to save the unburned core of wood underneath and had made these serve for posts. The twisted tin too, the blackened galvanized iron sheets; these too we had salvaged, and of these fashioned roofs and walls.

When the rains came, the water leaked in through the roof and wind drove the rain in through the flimsy, nail-hole-pocked walls. A storm would rattle the whole structure, shake it like a truckful of empty cans: and when the dusts arose from the seared upheaved streets, dust settled on food, and beds, and clothing inadequately protected by low, jerry-built walls.

For we had only salvaged the walls standing of adobe stone, and on these posed slats of wood, for wood was dear, and labor dearer and in those days, as you remember, money was not immediately to be found—and so our *barong-barong* had low walls.

Even the bathrooms. And so long as there had been no structure erected behind us, it had seemed the low bathroom walls were security enough from prying, peeking eyes.

But an auto repair machinery shop began to form in the back-lot. An enterprising Chinese had seen all the burned trucks and engines that were left of what had once been a Japanese army garage—and from scavenging around for spare parts he could shine to a usefulness the Chinese had progressed in business so that he now had a shop—one of the first repair shops in the city.

We had already dust and rain and heat to complain about. We had to add now the noise of machines grinding, and people scraping away the paint from vehicles, and other people spraying new paint on scraped auto bodies the spray machine making dolorous whining sounds.

Men worked in the shop, and we therefore quickly had peeping toms. They would hear the bathroom shower going, and they quickly found out that that meant someone was taking a bath. My sister-in-law was the first victim. She said she had seen someone peeking through a crack in the adobe while she took a bath.

We cemented all the cracks in the adobe.

Then one of my brothers, home from camp, caught sight of a hand one day clamped over the bathroom-wall, its owner probably readying himself for a lift. My brother rapped the hand smartly with a piece of firewood lying by; we heard a pained yelp, and the scamper of feet.

We had to raise the bathroom wall. But my father insisted on leaving an opening at top, for filing the wall up to the roof would darken the bathroom too much.

We were of course, by all these, admitting ourselves the defeated in this battle between peeping toms and our own outraged modesties.

We're fairly modern in our family. We go about in shorts, and sometimes in bathing suits. Bare thighs and bare shoulders and bare midriffs do not send any of us into hysterical oohs and aahs. And the young of the family have always been allowed to watch their elders dressing and undressing so that they could look upon the human body, ask what questions they wished, and feel no abnormal curiosity.

But there is something indecent in the fact of being spied upon while you're doing your ablutions that outrages the very sensibilities. I know it made me fighting mad.

I stood up on the toilet seat, looked out over the bathroom wall and surveyed the machine-shop yard. Before I could prevent myself, I had shouted a few invectives at a boy I spied sitting down on a dismantled automobile chassis.

I had seen the head of hair that had lowered itself from peeking at me and it had been just the shock hair he had. I strung together all the Tagalog words I had in the back of my mind for just such emergencies as this, and flung them at him.

Everybody in the yard let their work drop while they stared at my mixture of English, Tagalog, and Visayan swear words, but the shock-headed lad sat there and made no show that he had heard.

Then a Chinese boy also standing by nodded his head at me, rolled his eyes at the lad and thus indicated himself as witness that I had indeed placed my finger on the correct man.

All the people in the house had gotten wind of what was up. My mother gave me my clothes and had to literally take me off the toilet seat and tell me which article of clothing to put on my by now dried body.

We ranged ourselves like a tribunal at the iron-grilled window of the house as we waited for Papa to bring us the culprit.

My palms actually itched with the desire to slap his boob's face. My ears tingled with the desire for violence and my face felt flaming hot.

When the lad came he was sandwiched between my father whose nostrils seemed to flare with his anger, and a meek-looking man in a dirty suit of *maong*, who kept wiping at his eyes with the back of his hand. The lad himself was a sullen-looking creature. His face looked stony, and his hang-dog air was not repentant so much as sneering.

As always, in cases like this, you get keyed up to a moment, telling yourself what you'll do when the moment comes.

And yet when the actual minute arrives, all of a sudden, you feel a change of heart. That is what happened in this case.

All of a sudden, I seemed to be removed from this spot, this moment, this role. I watched as from a distance the spectacle of myself, my brothers, and my mother ranged before the iron grills of the window, looking with eyes of hate on the lad approaching. And I saw the lad, his head unshorn, uncombed, on his bare feet, the dust of the city; and on his frame the careless dirty clothes of the unloved. And all of a sudden, the itch went from my fingers, the tingle from my ears, and my face resumed normal temperature again.

The Chinese who owned the shop and yard came also, and it was to him my father directed his tirade. Papa said, "These are your men, you could at least tell them how to behave...." And the Chinese kept shaking his head, saying he would tell them next time, and that he does tell them but... and he would shake his head and chuck his tongue, and otherwise act the very sage of regret.

Then the man behind the boy, the dumpy little man with the dirty *maong* suit came forward to me. He was actually crying! And he flung his pudgy shortfingered palms out from him and said, I am his father!

He looked at me, at my brothers, and at my mother, and the tears kept streaming from his eyes, and he would sniff his nose once in a while, and then swipe at his streaming eyes with his *maong* sleeved arm.

Putting a hand on the shoulder of the young man, he pulled him; pushed him forward at us. The boy's father said, his face working with emotion: "Slap him! Curse him and kick him! Do anything you wish."

"I am tired of trying to make him learn. I am a widower, my wife, his mother, was killed, and I have to look for a living for him and four other brothers and sisters."

"How can I be a mother at the same time too? Yet I have tried...."

The man sobbed, actually! and mother and I looked at each other in amusement, consternation, and skepticism.

"I have tried—" the man continued. "And look what happens. He shames me, he disgraces me, he makes me cry here before you with the reality of how I have failed."

My brothers left the window, disgust making them go away. And my father was forced into quiet by the fellow's theatrics. The lad stood there, rubbing one dusty foot at the other, twisting his shirt, running his dirty fingers through his dusty dirty hair.

The father faced me, recognizing me as the party most offended, and kneeling down, tugged at my *bakya,* so suddenly I was surprised into surrendering it to him. He straightened up, gave me my own *bakya,* and holding his son near me, much as you would hold a dressed chicken to a singeing flame, he said, "Strike him, make him bleed, maybe it will knock some sense into him."

I took the *bakya,* replaced it on my foot, and said, "It is not our habit to strike people, and it is not necessary."

The man let his son go, and the lad stood aside.

Mother also left us. Father and the Chinese were talking earnestly off to one side and then conversation had turned to used cars and current prices.

I was left alone to deal with this tearful man and his dullard son. I felt robbed of my own revenge, the joy of the punishment I had thought of meting stolen from me. Yet there was no way to stop the father's profuse tears, and although I had longed for apology, this apology he was making was not making me feel mighty but miserable.

He was saying, "In school, the teachers tell me he won't study. I put him to work here, and what does he do—go peeking in bathrooms at ladies whom he should respect, the way I have tried to teach him ladies should be respected."

The man's speech was a curious mixture of Tagalog and English. He must have been a man with ambition once. I looked at the lad, his son, and in mind pictured the others, the brothers and sisters back at their home.

What happens to a man's heart when all his dreams for himself and his sons are realized not in glory but in the sight of a lad of fourteen, his hair unshorn, his feet bare, his eyes sullen, downcast but rebellious.

I rejected the thoughts in my head as sentimental, saying to myself, the man is just putting on an act, those tears are mere show.

And yet I know the man was not acting. And there would be other days, other people. And he would cry, but—I looked again at his son—it would not improve that lad.

I felt guilty in my heart of some fault, some vague shortcoming I had, that was responsible for that lad's being what he was, and what, I knew, he would surely be.

I turned away from the father and the son. I walked away. Looking back, I saw his face, his tears just drying, his eyes looking as though he would call me back.

But they turned, traced their way back to the shop yard. As they walked, the man kept pushing his son, and the son sometimes stumbled. The Chinese called out to the father: Finish your job! The man wiped his eyes and nodded, then prodded his son again with a push.

Sunday Times Magazine
September 19, 1948

THE CORRAL

EDITH L. TIEMPO

Pilar fed the fire on the open stove with more wood. The stewed pork must be hot or her father would refuse it again. She'd get the contained look, then the snort, then "Who wants cold stew?" Her father's own endearing way of saying no. She frowned and screwed up her thin pointed nose and chin until her whole face looked all chucked backward and upward. But the frown did her face good; her cheeks and forehead were stirred out of a wrinkled apathy and a nice flush started throughout her face. She didn't want to be irritated at her father because there had already been too much politeness between them lately, and it was a strain. For her, anyway, it was. The one taking it out on the other about little things, unimportant things that became so stubbornly important. Like cold meat stew. She picked up the tongs and jabbed at the fire until a hollow of red heat leaped under the pan.

Charita might be at the beach, too; Manuel said his wife might help them today with mending the nets. Pilar unslung a basket from the wall. She slid into it the pot of rice and the bowl of *camote* tops and squeezed into the remaining space three flasks of drinking water. She lifted the basket, testing its weight. It was all she could carry. That boy Elmo would have to go with her today. She eased the basket on the table and flung open the side door of the kitchen. The open door let in the salt wind from the sea. The wind was warm and smelled of moist dead rockweeds and algae. She stepped into the yard, pushing the door creakily shut behind her. Elmo was not in the yard. She shaded her eyes from the sun's glare while surveying the trail that led to the coconut grove and up the wooded hillock beside it. That boy wouldn't be getting firewood, he knew she was going to the beach.

A cart jerked forth heavily from the bend as she looked.
The carabao that drew it plodded forward, taking its case with
a heavy load. The cart was stacked to the top with wood fuel.
The driver sat up in front. He was a dark big-shouldered fellow
in his shirtsleeves. He clucked encouragement to the beast. The
man was big but his size was not obtrusive; what called attention to it was the suggestion of strength in the way he held
himself. Very quiet and assured. His legs were hitched up in
front of him, his hands held the reins loosely, his elbows resting
on his knees. He smiled at Pilar and his teeth were even and
white in his face that was dark like burnt clay. She did not
smile back. He was a stranger.

"I get off here, Gregorio!" From the rear of the cart a
small figure swung to the ground. Elmo. The rascal had gone
off to the woods the minute her back was turned. The driver
reached in back of him for a bundle of wood which he tossed
to the side of the road. The servant boy picked it up.

"Thanks, Gregorio!"

"No thanks. It's your share."

"A big share. When are you coming back?"

"Tomorrow." The dark man looked at Pilar. This time he
did not smile. He tipped his *buri* hat to her and turned his
face to the road. He clucked softly to the animal and the cart
bumped forward again.

Pilar caught at the boy's sleeve as he was about to run.
"Who told you to go after firewood? Who is that man?"

Elmo dug dirty fists into his eyes and she snatched them
away, saying wearily, "You're coming with me to the beach."

"Yes ma'am. Exactly." Elmo shifted the wood to his
shoulder and started whistling softly as they walked back to
the house. She knew what he was thinking now, the monkey.
She couldn't help it, it was exasperating the way he got around
her so easily. Well, she'd have to let him sneak off for a swim
when they got to the beach. He would sneak off, in any case.

"That man Gregorio, where is he taking all that firewood?"

"To the city, ma'am. He gets a good price."

When she said nothing he added, "I got a good bundle for
myself. Look."

They entered the kitchen and he slid the wood into the box
under the stove. She picked up the tongs and handed them to

him, and he stepped up to the fire and began stirring and shoving the brand ends into the blaze.

She leaned on the door panel watching him and thinking how after a month she still felt strange not to be sitting behind a desk watching a roomful of children at that time of the morning. Sometimes, like now, it didn't seem possible she had really left school. Yet it was true, it would be this kitchen from now on. No more walls hung with brightly-colored drawings of houses and people and flowers and weird-looking animals. It would be this room with the streaked smoky layer on the unpainted wood, and the lizards crawling in the black eaves and tapping their bloated bodies, and the bundles of unshucked corn seed dangling from the beams. The table-top criss-crossed by knife scars. Soot. Soap and water. The open stove, her one big responsibility.

Elmo was slightly bent toward the stove; he was looking deeply into the flames. The boy had grown as quiet as she.

Pilar straightened.

"Watch it now. I'm going upstairs." She added firmly, "and don't go running off again."

On the landing the cat was washing its face. She pushed it aside with her foot but it could not move. She was halfway up the stairs when the cat stirred and mewed at her. She wondered; and then she heard someone below in the living room. She stopped with one quiet hand on the banister. The cat was right. Slowly she leaned over the side of the stairway to look. Yes, as she had thought, it was Mr. Perfecto. He stood up. His great bulk seemed to rise out of the four walls and jar her by his presence. His look met hers uncertainly, however — as though they had had a misunderstanding. As though, she thought wryly, their main concern all these years had not been to keep up with a convincing good fellowship between them. What could he want? She had made it very clear she wasn't going back. He shouldn't have come. She turned and walked down slowly. She would be very calm with him, she would let nothing bother her, not her annoyance, certainly not the things she knew she was going to hear from this man. But already she felt muscles drawing tight across her face; and her mouth was stiff as two clam shell valves when she loosened them to speak.

"I didn't hear you come in."

"I forgot to knock. Is your father home?"

"He's at the beach with Manuel."

"How's the work going?"

"The corral may be up this week. Did you want to speak to Father?"

Mr. Perfecto settled back in his chair laughing, not loud but with laughter in his red face, in his big shaking frame.

"Speak to your father? No, not for a while. He's still too angry with me."

She looked at him thinking, I wish he didn't come. But she had thought the same thing—for how long now?—and always he had come.

"Why does he come here, Pilar?"

Even from the first she had felt it was meddling on her father's part.

"He is the school principal." Because she could not help it, she had smiled grimly and added, "Also, I am not unattractive, Father."

"Nor exactly young."

"He wants me to marry him."

"You have picked yourself a good one," he had sneered. "Don't be a fool."

Why the man had continued to come she didn't know, for outside of school they had nothing to say to each other, nothing *true*, nothing even perishable. She had told herself she should do something about him finally. And she shouldn't be so weak and let him turn her into an occasion for mockery from her father. But what had happened instead wasn't altogether her fault because to her bewilderment her father began to speak to the man. Even to take him in a rough, offhand fashion. The two of them gradually began to seek out each other like old friends, to smoke each other's cigars. Only once in a while, for the period of a few days, their mutual politeness made her feel indefinably safe; most of the time she was uneasy at the way they showed off like silly boys, through two or three hours arguing about politics, cockfighting, fishtraps, women. Often they got coarse in their talk as between men who understood each other well.

She sat now against the wall in front of him and as it often happened she found herself losing some of her tenseness in his laughter. She even laughed a little with him.

"Father hates for anyone to beat him, you know that. He's so proud of his chess game, and is such a poor sport. Manuel loses, for the sake of peace."

"I've managed to let him win, myself." Mr. Perfecto heaved his body straight in the chair. "But I can't go on doing that," he said significantly. "Besides, the old fellow is getting too smug."

"Yes," said Pilar, "isn't he?"

Mr. Perfecto smiled on her. "It's you I've come to see this morning. It's about your work, of course."

"Well?"

"You're well now, Pilar. Your substitute has asked to know how long she'll stay."

"I told you I'm not going back."

"I know you did, but that was when you were sick. I never really considered that letter of resignation."

"I'm not sick now and I still mean it."

He was quiet. And then he said, "This is strange." He leaned his fat face forward. "Perhaps we have to talk some more about this, you and I. I believe," he said, "you know what? — I believe you are running away from me."

"Please. I told you before, and I tell you again, you have nothing to do with it. Ten years I taught in your school and I'm tired. That's all."

"I don't believe it."

She shrugged. "You may believe what you like, then."

He leaned back. He asked in a flat voice, "Now that you've quit, what do you plan to do?"

"I have enough to do, don't concern yourself," she said coldly. "I'm taking care of Father. He's an old man now."

He laughed aloud. "He needs no woman. A man like that." He stopped laughing but it seemed to her his laughter went on and on in the fatty smile that lifted his cheeks and eyelids and agitated his face like the actual sound of laughter. As she watched him, a small thought whirred inside her head, a glinting spinning thought, that hardened into a pinpoint.

"The school doesn't need me, either. Look," she said rigidly, "you might as well make up your mind, I am not marrying you." She looked straight into his face and said, "It is best if you stop coming."

"What should I do? You are such a selfish inhibited person, Pilar."

She thought, he is ugly, fat and ugly and daring to say such things.

"Look at me," he went on, "I'm a normal man. But you think there's something excessive about me. Oh, don't bother to deny it. The funny part of it is that all these years you have held away, in spite of yourself. It's monstrous."

"You know it all, don't you? Naturally, I have nothing to say."

He rose heavily, looked down at her. "You don't want to be a drudge. You can't be. I want you to marry me, Pilar."

When she said nothing he said regretfully, "I wish you could be your own self some day. You've been thrashing around. Do you have to be so suspicious?"

Her reply was a cold stare.

"If you weren't such a hypocrite!" His whispered words were venomous. "You won't admit you have some feelings."

"That's enough."

He reached for his hat on the table. "You will change your mind." He stood clutching the hat in his fat tensed hands. "You can't send me away, you do not want to."

"I will — I am."

"But you don't want to. That's right, isn't it?"

She sat unmoving.

"Isn't it?" he asked, then threw up his hands.

When he had gone Pilar stood up as though she had awakened from a numbed and dreadful sleep. She went into the kitchen still slightly dazed. The servant boy was pouring the steaming stew into a clean casserole.

The boy looked up. "We can go now, if you're ready."

She tied a scarf about her head. No, she wasn't going back to the school, the man must have no more reason to come. She picked up the basket and the boy followed her out of the yard to the trail through the coconut grove.

The sun was hot now. It was almost noon. Their shadows striped the path slantwise before them. In a little while they approached the low hillslope to one side of the path. Fallen trunks of trees and withered stems of coconut fronds strew the slope. That fellow Gregorio must have dragged them out there to dry before splitting them.

She thought of the afternoon ahead, and hoped Charita had decided to come to the beach. The two of them could work on the nets, and the men could go ahead with the corral. It was almost finished, it needed about three dozen splits more. As soon as the men had strung together the bamboo splits, her father would hire the divers to set up the finished trap in the sea. Maybe in two or three days the corral would be up.

The path went straight through the grove and the sea was visible ahead through the gaps between the coconut trunks. She saw Charita and Manuel on the sand beside the shed, mending a net spread out between them.

"You were gone a long time," the old man complained. He sat at the door of the shed and his large frame almost filled it.

Pilar smiled, shook a reproachful finger at him. "*You* talk. Elmo and I are hungry, too."

Charita got up from the sand to help her. On the floor of the shed they spread out the rolls of banana fronds the boy had cut on the way. Charita ladled out the stew.

Pilar said, "Mr. Perfecto was at the house."

Manuel and Charita said nothing. The old man looked up from his food.

"What did he want?"

"He asked me to go back to work."

"I thought you told him you were giving it up."

"Why, yes, Father, I did."

"Hmm," the old man grunted. "He shouldn't insist."

Charita told Pilar, "You refused to go back, of course."

"Of course," said Pilar, with a sidewise look at her father.

The old man was enjoying his rice and meat. "What did you tell Perfecto?" Before she could answer he said, "You should have left your teaching long ago. You've been very foolish, all along. I hope you see that now. I hope you remembered that when you talked to him this morning."

She kept her eyes on her plate. "There's nothing I told him that I hadn't already told him before. I said I was tired of the school." She raised her head suddenly, her eyes glinting. "Yes, I did tell him something else." She looked up at her father, at his barrel chest, his heavy arms and shoulders, his unruly grey hair. "I also told him that as you are now old you needed someone to look after you."

He snorted. "You told him that." He was mocking. That he should be made her flimsy excuse! "What did he say, then?"

She smiled, to his surprise, she could see that. "You rather enjoy being my reason, Father, don't you? You rather like it." She lowered her plate and leaned toward him. "Dutiful daughter! But Mr. Perfecto didn't seem convinced, Father. He asked me to think it over — to think *him* over, that is. And maybe," she said, "maybe, I will."

At noon the following day she and Elmo went out a little earlier. They were still some distance away when they saw the cart on the outskirts of the grove, and the carabao unhitched and grazing at the foot of the low slope. As they approached they saw Gregorio himself seated on a log on the grassy incline, eating his lunch. The man saw them coming but said no word to greet them or to show he had even seen them.

Elmo called, "You need help today?"

He did look up as they came near. He brushed his mouth with his hand on his trouser leg. "Tomorrow you come," he said finally. "I didn't do much today."

Pilar lowered the basket. "Let's stop here a little in the shade, Elmo. My arm's tired."

She turned to Gregorio. "Go on with your lunch."

"I'm through." He balled up the scrap of cloth where he had taken his meal and crammed it into a basket.

Pilar untied the scarf from her head and let it slip down around her shoulders. She sat on a log, rubbing her arm.

Gregorio stood up and stretched his body and his arms and threw out his chest. She thought it indelicate the way he stretched and yawned in front of her but she showed no sign. The man's great fists closed, his shoulders hunched as he drew deep breaths, and with his movements the muscles on his arms stirred and bulged under the dark skin. He had removed his shirt and had on a thin undershirt wet with his perspiration. He stopped stretching. And it came to her that the man did not care what she thought — he cared no more for her little sensibilities than would his carabao.

"Hot day," he said. "Hot, hot day." He stooped and reached for the bottle of water in his basket. "Oh, oh," he said, looking anxiously at the little water left. He put the flask to his mouth

and tilted his head back and his throat showed itself moving
up and down as he guzzled the water.

Elmo higher up the slope had picked up Gregorio's ax. He
swung clumsily and brought it down on the log between his
feet.

"Let that alone," she called.

Gregorio said, "He's just playing." He turned from Elmo
and smiled at her. His teeth were strong and startlingly even,
his eyes were black and friendly and alive in his brown face.
He said, "I wondered if perhaps you were angry when I kept
the boy. He helps a little."

She smiled back and felt good, seeing him quickly flush
with pleasure. "No, I wasn't angry."

"He ties up the bundles. I don't make him split the wood."

"Not with your ax, he can't," she laughed.

"Yes, it's a big ax." He looked straight at her face, his
dark glance struck boldly into her eyes. He looked at her arms
and her hands, but longest at her face. "*You* can't lift it," he
said. "You're so little yourself. So little."

She sat up. His eyes carefully avoided her body, but she
was angry, as though the man had actually reached out and
explored her littleness. She stood up from the log and in a
thick silence raised the scarf about her shoulders to her head.
Elmo saw her tying the scarf and ran toward them. The boy
looked at her and she nodded without a word. Elmo picked up
the basket and walked down to the path.

Gregorio said nothing. Before she could leave he turned his
back abruptly and strode to the fallen logs. He reached for his
ax. He braced himself, swung it high and brought it down
with vindictive force on the log in front of him. Again and
again the ax swung blows upon the log. He had his back to
her, and she could not stir for looking at the skin that moved
underneath its surface like smooth rounded mangoes on his
arms and back and underarms. Muscles moving, bulging, disappearing as he braced himself and swung the ax. He was angry
with an inarticulate anger. Turning away, she picked up the
basket. She stood there, but he seemed unconscious of her presence. The splinters flew about him with each blow. In a quick
movement she set down the basket and took out a flask of
water

"Gregorio," she called.

He lowered his arms in the act of swinging down the ax. Slowly he turned his head and located her where she stood on the low incline.

She held up the bottle. "You'll be wanting this by and by."

The man threw down the ax. He did not move. Sweat rolled down his face and glistened on his arms. He wiped the drops from his temples with the back of his hand.

She said, "I'll leave it here on the log."

He came toward her. He reached out but she ignored his outstretched hand with care, and bent and leaned the flask on the log. He stood before her as though waiting for her to speak again. She had nothing more to say. She picked up her basket and walked quickly down the slope.

Gregorio got the flask. "Thanks."

She did not answer. She did not look back but walked away quickly through the grove to the beach.

After lunch she lay on the floor of the shed and watched the divers roll up the fish corral and push it down the beach to the boat at the edge of the water. The corral, finished at last, was beautiful; the splits were strung evenly and close together and sharpened points at both ends. The men, eight of them, had stripped themselves almost naked, leaving only a width of cloth about the loins. She felt their excitement. She liked their casual roughness, the way they moved and talked to each other. They were going to dive into the sea five or six fathoms to the sandy bottom to plant the rest of the piles needed to hold the corral in place. Out in the sea was a semi-circle of coconut trunks planted a few days before; the men were going to finish the circle and have the corral attached to it, if they could, before nightfall.

Manuel and her father pushed the boat into the water and the men scrambled into their places and took up their paddles. They cut into the water with clean strokes, bending down their hard backs and thick brown necks with each thrust. Their deep voices floated over the water and were drowned out intermittently by the loud wash of the waves hitting the shore.

Manuel and the old man left the water's edge. They dragged the net near the shed to a place where the two of them sat in the shadow cast by the roof. Pilar was sleepy. It was the warm sea wind and the regular beat of the waves. Even without opening her eyes she could sense the movement of the water

as though it swayed away from under her, as though she drifted
on it. Once she opened her eyes and looked far out on the sea
and she saw the boat with the men in it. They had stopped
paddling. She could hear their distant voices. They were now
at the unfinished circle of stakes.

She shifted on her other side. The wind blew on her back,
through her clothes cooling her skin until the heat lay just
under it, inside the pores, and she felt washed and cleaned all
over. She remembered what had happened that morning on the
slope. And then she thought of Mr. Perfecto. But thinking of
him at this moment did not annoy her. She smiled to herself.
No, in this place, in the blowing wind and with sleep misting
her thoughts, he was only an amorphous image. A neutral
image. She was free of him.

Manuel and her father were talking in low voices and she
was so drowsy all she could hear was mumbled drone of their
words. Thin tails of smoke from fishermen's huts floated over
the palms to one side of the coconut grove. Hens scratched
around on the swampy ground at the distant edge of the grove.
She heard the far-away barking of a dog. She placed an arm
across her eyes to hide the glare of the sun....

For some time before she woke up she had been hearing
the far shouts of the divers. She half-dreamed. She was with
them as they lifted the net from the bottom of the corral, and
she saw the great fish thrashing around in the meshes; their
mouths opened and closed in dumb shouts and their eyes were
indignant blobs of white in their flat heads. She woke up,
trying to grasp at the fading bits of the dream, trying to continue it in the far shouts of the men. It was gone and she had
not understood its strange outlines, its disturbing rage. She
turned over to look at the divers and she sat up, a little surprised at what she saw. She must have been asleep for some
time, maybe a couple of hours. The corral was set up in the
water. The men were still diving by turns to attach it more
firmly to the stakes, their brown bodies sparkled as they splashed
around in the water. It was late sunshine that fell on the sea,
and it gleamed on the naked bodies and made them shine like
great burnished clay jars. One diver stood alone in the boat.
He had one foot on the edge of the boat, his hands on his hips.
He looked like that fellow Gregorio, big and dark and shining.

His companions called out to him and beckoned, and the man stretched his arms and plunged.

Manuel spoke quietly to her, "Charita told me your dress is finished. Said you could go over and try it on."

She rose from the floor. She rubbed her side which was numb; she had lain on it too long without moving.

The old man looked at her with eyes that were darkly commiserating.

"You can take it easy now. The corral is up."

"The corral is up," she repeated. "I'm glad, Father." She tightened up the scarf about her head. "I'm going on home ahead. I think I'll stop at your house, Manuel."

Her brother looked up from the net and smiled at her. "It's pretty. I know you'll think so."

The dress was pretty. It was past sundown when Charita finished the little alteration on the neck. It was so pretty she wore it going home, and all the while she was suppressing a smile as she hurried between the tall coconut trees bordering the dark trail. When she was a hopeless old maid, and that wasn't too far off, either, she knew she would still be fussy about a new dress. More so; she would have to be.

She turned around the outskirts of the grove and came to the joining of the trail and the footpath that went past her house. As she stepped into the path she saw a cart heading toward her. A lighted lantern swung near the carabao's rump and the lantern jogged up and down with every bump in the path. She stepped back under some guava trees and watched for the cart to come near.

It was Gregorio. He clucked softly to the carabao. He did not see her because she kept well in the shadows of the guavas. She stood there startled at this sudden secret sight of him. Breathlessness like pain gripped her all over and she stood waiting in expectation for she didn't quite know what, puzzled at herself, but inside herself a bright core glowing. The cart jerked forward and passed by, so close she could hear the animal's heaving; she could have touched its flank if she dared move. Carabao and wheel and driver lurched by. Then it was past her, and she wanted to cry out but the cry had no voice.

When a woman had seen Gregorio she would know him anywhere, on a boat, diving into the sea, on a slope cutting wood, on the sand mending nets and building traps. Behind a desk in a schoolhouse. She would know him even in the dark. Having seen Gregorio she would keep seeing him in all men.

But Gregorio had not seen her. No man had ever really seen her, except Mr. Perfecto, and how could they know what she was like? She might wear the prettiest, newest dress and Gregorio might pass by her and not see her at all. And that was as it should be. With Gregorio the wood cutter it would have been very improper otherwise.

She stood under the guava tree looking after the cart, at his straight back. She thought, Oh how I hate you — you who are so right, so hatefully right, Mr. Perfecto.

This Week
September 26, October 3, 1948

THE GI AND THE LAUNDRYWOMAN

STEVAN JAVELLANA

From the window of her hut that was set among the sparse bamboos at the edge of the soft road with its deep hollows of oozy mud she peered intently at the multitude of dull-green tents that had mushroomed like a magic city in three days. She hung there at the window, her long bony hands clutching the window sill, her thick brows knitted in an ugly scowl over the almost non-existent bridge of her flat nose, her little, red-rimmed eyes gradually filling with water as she stared defiantly through the heat waves that trembled over the motionless long stalks of the palay in the ricefields.

Then to her sharp ears came the sound of harsh and loud voices and fresh outbursts of laughter and the sound of feet thrashing the thick mire of the road. Her frown deepened in disapproval as she leaned over the window to see the better who were coming by.

They were young girls from the village who were carrying back to the camp the clean clothes of the American soldiers. There was Maring, a pert young lass of sixteen, quite pretty, who was in fact a cousin of hers. With her were Eced, a fair girl whose pimples stood out angrily on her perspiring face and Sara, a stout, dark, ugly girl whose face was mottled with powder because she sweated too much. With them walked Vito, the village ne'er-do-well who, because he was the son of a rather prosperous farmer, affected the airs of a dandy. He was a slim youth with thickly pomaded hair.

She did not like him at all, this Vito, because it was he who began all the nasty stories about her that amused the people of the barrio, about why she was still not married at her age, and other insulting remarks that she would rather not remember. She could not understand why the girls listened open-mouthed to every word that he said since he was an affected dandy. Anyway, those silly girls in the barrio did not have the brains of a lazy turtle.

She spat loudly and scornfully out of the window and the four young people turned to look at her. She saw that a miraculous grin was already forming in the corners of Vito's weak slack mouth and he said distinctly: "There she is, the old maid!"

The others smiled knowingly and the ugly black girl actually giggled and this maddened her. In her fury she slammed shut the window and heard the young man break into loud guffaws while Maring tried to hush him without success. Then they went on their way, the mud sucking at their heels.

She stood motionless inside her lonely house. In the throbbing quiet that was almost alive, keeping her breath soft, her sharp eyes roving gauntly about the room, she could almost feel the loneliness steal upon her from the corners. Her heart was thumping wildly as if it would burst. She felt that she could not breathe.

She opened the window again and saw that there were more people coming up the road, bringing clean clothes, bringing bananas and melons in baskets and eggs and some native trinkets and native-made abaca slippers and women's purses made of *buri* decorated with figures in black *nito*. They would go home carrying dirty clothes and all kinds of canned goods and American money.

Her eyes glittered, her mouth twitched convulsively and a half-smile broke her mouth as a daring resolution formed in her mind. Quickly she went down from the house and looked into the three nests. In the first nest she got five eggs, and in the second there were eight. Her white hen was still laying in the third nest and as she came near, the fowl suddenly opened its drowsy eyes while its fluffy throat contracted and expanded in spasmodic breathing. The hen spluttered in protest and ruffled indignation as she reached down beneath it and brought a prize of seven eggs, big and reddish and warm.

She washed her face with cold water from the jar and slipped on a white dress that had been neatly folded and had lain unused inside her trunk for a long time. She also got a large handkerchief that had belonged to her brother Ramon which he had left behind when he was sent to Mindanao with the other soldiers before the Japanese came to Panay.

She tied the corners of the handkerchief together and carefully laid the eggs inside. Then she left the house and followed the muddy road leading to Tiring landing field. Many people were going the same way. Many groups were coming down the paths from the other villages, walking one by one on the dikes that separated the rice fields, the bright-colored dresses of the girls occasionally blowing about in sudden gusts of wind in the open fields making bright splashes of color against the green growing palay. All the groups were converging toward the strange little city of the tall white men.

Her heart fluttered a little in excitement. She held the handkerchief more firmly in her fingers as she came near the magic forest of tents. Civilians were milling about everywhere at the entrance to the camp and the guards were letting everybody in. She was carried inside by the crowd and while the laundrywomen and the peddlers were drifting into various tents she stood undecided, not knowing what to do next.

So she walked along slowly, glancing once in a while at the endless rows of tents that flanked both sides of the airstrip, olive-green tents in clean and neat precision. She saw many Americans inside the tents, reading, talking, singing and joking.

Then she heard the voice. "Hey, you!" it said. She stopped and turned about. A big young giant was coming from the nearest tent, walking toward her with a lazy slouch, his strides long and his hands swinging out and they were big hands. Perhaps he had the biggest boots she had ever seen. She thought for a moment that perhaps it was not she who had been called and she turned to go but the giant put out an imperious hand and growled, "Yes, you. Do you understand English?"

"Yes," she stammered uncertainly.

The American stopped before her and put his hands on his hips. "What do you have there?" he said, pointing at her handkerchief.

"Eggs," she said.

"Are you going to sell them?"

"Yes," she said.

"Come," he said, stretching out his hand, "let's see them."

She extended the handkerchief and he took out an egg, inspected it closely holding it to the sunlight. She looked at his face and saw that he was very young. Perspiration stood on his nose and forehead and rolled down the sides of his face to his thick neck and down his breast. And he had deep blue eyes like the color of the sea beneath his thick brown eyebrows.

"Are these fresh?" he asked.

"Yes," she answered.

"How many do you have?"

"Twenty," she said.

"How much will you take for them?"

"I don't know," she said.

"I will give you three dollars for the lot," he offered.

"Yes, sir," she said.

"Come with me, then," he said.

Inside the tent he undid the handkerchief and put the eggs inside a cardboard box. Then he gave her the money. She was about to leave when he said, as an after-thought, "Do you wash?"

"I...I don't know," she said.

He smiled, thinking that she had not understood, and when he smiled it was a big, friendly smile, his mouth quirking up at the ends to reveal a dimple in his left cheek, his red lips curled in, and his large white teeth showing.

"Dirty...clothes," he said slowly, indicating the fatigue jacket he had on. "Do...you...wash?"

"Yes," she said.

"All right, then," he said. He shouted over his shoulder to another soldier who was dozing on the next cot. "Hey, Bill," he shouted, "We've got a washer woman now."

Bill swung his feet over the side of the cot and eyed her sleepily. He pulled his laundry bag from under the cot and counted the dirty clothes. Then he made out a list.

"All right, here you are," the tall young giant said amiably. "These are my dirty clothes and my name is Peter Fitch as you can see on this list. Now, let's see," Peter went on, meditatively putting a broad forefinger on the tip of his nose. "Oh, yes, do you have soap?" He reached down and flipped two cakes of sweet-smelling toilet soap on the top of the pile of dirty clothes. "There you are," he said. "Do you think that will be enough?"

Her eyes brightened with surprise. "Shall I use this to wash the laundry with?" she whispered tremulously, fondling the wrapper of the soap with her fingers. She had not used such sweetsmelling soap on her own body for three years.

"Well," he said," you may use any kind of soap for the clothes and you can have that soap for your own use. By the way, do I have to pay you now?"

"No, no," she said, tying up the clothes in a bundle.

"Can we have them three days from now, say, Saturday?"

She paused and counted the days and said "Yes, Saturday." She rose and said, "I shall go now."

"Wait a minute," he said, and he knelt and fumbled for something under his cot and as his hands moved, eyeing him shyly she saw how golden was his hair and how the muscles of his shoulders moved. At last he brought out a little packet which he handed to her.

"For you," he said and as she opened the brown cloth packet she found that it contained three shining needles of varying sizes and threads of different shades of green and brown and many buttons. As he rose he placed a tin can of sausages on top of the laundry. "I also give that to you."

"Thank you so much, sir," she said, inserting the cake of soap, the can and the sewing kit into a side of the bundle.

He did not say anything; he just smiled as he got a cigarette and lighted it. And when she was at the door of the tent he called her. "Hey!" he shouted. "Where do you live?"

She paused and looked around and shifted the heavy bundle to her other arm.

"You take the road from this gate of the camp," she said, pointing with her hand. "You walk on and on and the first house on the right, among the bamboos is my house." She looked down and added: "It has been a lonely house."

She smiled weakly and walked out.

It was a lonely house. The brittle nipa roof leaked because there was no man to cut the cogon from the fields with which to patch it. The greedy brick-red *mayas* with sharp black beaks no longer made their nests in the eaves and she missed the way they used to fill the air with their twitterings in the early mornings. Only shadows remained in that house which had not known the laughter of children and the patter of little bare feet on the floor.

It was a lonely house. The man who had raised it—her betrothed—had run away with another woman just after it had been built and had never been heard of again. That was many years ago. Her father, her only surviving parent, had died soon after. And just before the invasion her only brother had been sent to Mindanao with the other soldiers.

It was a lonely house. Its walls had never been witness to love and complete happiness, its roof had never hidden the ecstacy of two lovers from the skies. It was a house chaste and inviolate and aging; it was not unlike her.

But tonight, as she sat cross-legged on her mat on the floor with the oil lamp beside her and counted the contents of the bundles, turning out the pockets of the trousers and the shirts that were muddy and sweat-stained, the house did not seem lonely. The clothing of Bill, the black-haired youth, she put aside but she inspected Peter's very closely until she discovered a big tear in the elbow of one of his khaki shirts. Forthwith she threaded one of the shining needles and began to darn the tear with loving care until the oil in the lamp ran low and she had to replenish it. But the tear was mended and she leaned back and viewed her handiwork in the lamplight with a satisfied smile on her lips.

Every morning, from eight o'clock until noontime she would hear the sound of shooting from the camp at the Golf Club. And she could also hear the shooting from the Dawis side of Tiring landing field, carried faintly in the wind. There would be single shots and the heavy and continuous volleys and the barrage of bigger guns. Sometimes, as she washed at the well way back of the house, she would pause and look up and wonder what the shooting was about. After all, the Japanese had been defeated. She could not understand why the Americans were wasting so many bullets. And she wondered if Peter was among those who were shooting and how tired and thirsty he must be coming from that sweltering heat and she imagined him, sweaty and red, as she first saw him. And smiling at the remembrance she applied more soap to the collar of his shirt and the cuffs and rubbed the cloth until the dirt was washed away.

At midday, as she was at her window watching the clothes that were hung out to dry on the line she waited for the coming of the vaqueros who pastured their carabaos near the landing field where there was tall luscious grass because no one dared to come near before the Japanese had been driven away. The sun splashed brilliant sun-glints on the leaves of the scraggly hedge that bordered the road.

It was Paeng, the twelve-year old brother of Maring, mounted erect and proud on the back of his carabao, who came first.

"Hoy, Paeng," she called, "Why do the *Kano* shoot every morning?"

The boy looked at her and said, "Because they are practising."

"For what?" she wanted to know.

He attempted to wither her with a look for being so ignorant but she would not flinch under his gaze. The boy spat on the ground before answering in a superior way.

"For the invasion of Japan, of course," he said.

"Of course," she echoed dully. "Thank you, Paeng." But the boy had already dug his heels into the sides of his toro and the animal was running down the road, its hooves clicking on the earth.

She closed her eyes because the glaring sunlight seemed to hurt them and she wanted to shut out the sight of the clothes of Peter that had filled with wind and were billowing like live things on the clothesline. Her heart became taut and thick inside her breast and that old feeling of being unable to breathe overcame her again. Yes, of course, there was still a war to be fought and won—perhaps the bloodiest of all the wars yet. That was why these big, white young soldiers were here, drilling, marching, shooting, hardening their bodies for the fight. There was still a war to be fought and he would be in it.

Her mind remembered a picture in a magazine that Peter had given her. It was a picture of three dead American soldiers on the beach.

"No! No!" she groaned.

And looking out of the window she saw his clothes dancing in the wind.

More than ever before she looked forward eagerly to the afternoon when she would take the clothes to camp and see Peter still whole, still big and smiling.

One afternoon as she was taking down the dry wash from the clothesline in front of the house she heard footsteps behind her. Looking around she saw six people, a man and three women and two boys who were carrying suitcases and mats.

It was the man who spoke. "Good afternoon," he said. He was a thin man of around forty, with large protruding eyes and very thick, very black lips.

"We have come from a long trip," said the man in a high-pitched voice, "and we are wondering if you could give us a night's lodging."

The women nodded in assent. She glanced at them and saw that they had short curled hair and their cheeks were pink and their lips were painted red. Their hands, which were soft and slim, must never have known labor because they were soft and the fingers tapered to long, blood red nails. They had on thin silk dresses and their feet were shod in abaca sandals dyed in many colors.

"Please let us rest awhile," the tallest one said. "We are very tired."

Adela clasped the clothes to her breast and said, "I'm sorry. But my house is rotting. The floor has given away in many places and the roof leaks. There will not be enough room for us."

"Well, that is the hospitality of these barrio folk," complained one of the women bitterly to the bug-eyed man. "This is the fifth time that we have been refused. We shall sleep in the open tonight, I'm sure."

She was a kind-hearted woman but she did not want the villagers to point at her, saying, "Look at the women that Adela has lodged in her house. Perhaps she has become one of them."

Her house, although listing, would remain respectable. "No," she said, distinctly. "But I know a house where you can stay for the night." And instantly she could have bitten off her tongue for talking.

The faces of the strangers brightened and the man said eagerly, "Where is it?"

"The next house," she said reluctantly, looking down at the grass as she spoke. "If you don't mind, the owners of that house were killed by the Japanese in it and traces of blood still show on the floor."

But the strangers were already walking toward the next house without thinking to thank her. She watched and saw them push in the door and go inside. She ran up into her house as though the air in the yard had suddenly become stifling and she shut the door after her.

She peeped through a crack in the wall and saw the two boys who had been carrying the belongings of the strangers leave. Not very long afterwards the bug-eyed man also went to the camp.

She sat behind the closed window and watched the road through a slit. The sun finally set behind the mountains and dusk enveloped the trees and the grass with a shower of shadows that lengthened and deepened. There she sat upright, her heart beating loudly in her breast as she heard the sound of boots on the hard road and an American voice asking, "Is it a long way off yet?"

It was already dark but she could make out four figures and she heard the voice of the bug-eye reply, "We are here. That is the house."

After that she always kept her door shut and bolted because several times some American soldiers had knocked at her door, yelling, "Hey, open up!" But, huddled in a corner, she would keep quiet and they would finally cease calling and find the way to the house.

She had not stopped watching those who came to visit the three women in the next house, however, and she recognized two or three men who stayed in the same tent with Peter and once she saw Bill.

The firing every morning did not cease and it still held the same terrors for her while she was at the well washing the soiled clothes. There were mornings when the three women in the other house would come down and bathe in the well, clad only in their silk, perfumed chemises in which they were as good as naked because the chemises, when wet, showed their bodies. And sometimes, keeping her eyes on the wash, she envied those women, their beautiful bodies and their pretty faces. Looking up at them she would catch them watching her with arched eyebrows and they would smile knowingly at each other as though they knew the secret wish in her heart. Always blushing, she would pick up her wash and leave the three women at the well.

Then one evening it happened.

It had begun to grow dark but she had not yet lighted the oil lamp. She heard quick heavy footsteps on the stairs and, turning, beheld Peter standing there, clad only in his trousers because it was warm. The bulk of his huge body against the doorway was immense. He was looking piercingly at her and there was a strange glitter in his eyes.

"Peter!" she whispered.

"It is you, Adela!" he said. He caught her hands in a grip that was not gentle. Firm hard lips pressed against her ear, "Why did you not tell me?" He began to touch her.

"Peter!" she gasped. "Peter, you are mistaken!"

"Hey, Pete," called a voice from below in the road, "that's not the house."

As if by magic his muscles relaxed and he dropped his hands to his sides lifelessly. His voice was again soft and respectful, the voice of the Peter that she knew. "I am sorry, Adela. I made a mistake."

He turned and went down the stairs and the smell of him was lost in the wind that came in from the open door. She stood there listening and she heard the stairs of the next house creak and the door open and shut.

She heard laughter in the next house, laughter that was shortly followed by a silence like the awful silence of death. She sank weakly to the floor and crouched against the wall and shivered. At the back of her mind was the consciousness that her body and her house were still inviolate, were still pure, but there was not much pride in that any more. She felt old and weak and tired and robbed of something that was sweet and precious and which was lost to her forever.

From somewhere near the fringe of banana plants that girdled the house, and beyond in the rustling leaves of the palay in the paddies, the crickets began their sharp clicking chant and a few big Hawaiian bullfrogs, lazily paddling about with their short fat legs in the cold water of the rice fields, rumbled a few tentative croaks in their soft bulbous throats.

She bowed her head and wept brokenly as though for someone dead.

Philippines Free Press
October 9, 1948

THE FIFTH MAN

STEVAN JAVELLANA

It so happened that when the ship sank, leaving a wide circle of bubbly foam and burnishing the rough sea with a film of glossy black oil, a mass of wooden planks that had been ripped away by the terrific blast was left bobbing up and down with the rise and fall of the waves.

To the four men who had survived the shipwreck and who were struggling desperately to keep their heads above water, that floating bit of wreckage meant at least temporary safety. With one thought in mind they began to swim toward it.

The first man to reach the float, strangely enough, was the weakest of the four, physically. All the bodily exercise that he had ever taken was tapping his fingertips on the keys of his old portable typewriter. He had always scouted the need of exercise and defended the opinion that all a man needed in order to get ahead in the world was a keen perceptive mind and a fertile imagination. He was a great dreamer, this first man, and a writer.

A flock of frisky waves had sent the raft dancing toward him. The movement of the raft reminded him of the stylistic posturings and the rather affected gestures of a dancer of the *rigodon,* a dancer who was now advancing with dignity and hauteur, curtsying, bowing, now stepping back gravely to the precise time and the measured steps of the dance.

As the raft swept by him, he clutched at it with his long, thin fingers and held on tenaciously even as a wave buffeted his frail body against the rough boards. Slowly, and rather painfully, he pulled himself up over the side of the raft and stretched out his long body on it in extreme exhaustion. He closed his eyes and imagined that he was dozing on a gently swinging hammock.

The raft dipped a little to one side as the second man boarded it. The first man opened his stinging, bloodshot eyes apathetically to stare at the newcomer who had invited himself onto the raft. The second man was short and swarthy; he had a small body and thin black arms. He had a shifty, sly way of looking out of the corners of his eyes which the first man found rather disconcerting.

The first man looked away, telling himself that he did not like the second man who had taken possession of the opposite end of the raft. Being a creative artist, the first man prided himself in the belief that he had an intuitive mind; that is, he liked or disliked a person at first sight. He was not the type who enjoyed company and, while he was not actually averse to meeting very close acquaintances on an occasional afternoon, he avoided meeting strangers. Actually he was a lonely soul. In his heart he craved companionship, the understanding friendship of one or two to whom he might speak his dream and bare his inmost thought without reserve or hesitation. But he was a sensitive soul, and ever fearful of having his feelings bruised, he preferred to walk alone on his lonely way.

"Step down from your ivory tower," his few friends sometimes counseled him, "and talk with the crowd. You might, if you tried, find people very human and, sometimes, gentle, too." But he never did because he felt conscious that within him were many beautiful things waiting to be sung and he did not want bitterness or hurt to tarnish and dim their glow.

Fortunately, the second man did not offer to start a conversation. He brooded at his own end of the raft and looked darkly at the sea. By this time the third man had almost reached the safety of the raft. He must have been very tired because he swam with weak, choppy strokes. As the waves threw him back again and again, he would float on his back for a while to regain his breath and his strength and then try for the raft once more.

"He certainly has grit," thought the first man with grudging admiration. "He must be used to taking big risks and taking them in his stride."

A wave thrust the raft forward; the swimmer clutched at its side and hauled himself over with shaking arms. He was a middle-aged man, big-bodied and hawk-nosed, and in his face the first man, who rated himself a good judge of character, found the courage of one who would indeed gamble for big stakes.

For a while the third man sat there crouching and shivering a little, his legs dangling in the water. He shook his big head slowly from side to side, his eyes closed, as if to get rid of a dizziness, and then he opened his eyes and looked at the two men.

"Disagreeable business," he murmured curtly, addressing neither of the two others in particular. He looked away sternly at the horizon, and did not favor them with another glance after that.

"We would do well to balance ourselves," said the second man to the first, "or else we shall capsize if we are tossed by a wave." Indeed the raft was listing badly to one side, which was almost submerged in water. The first man nodded wordlessly and slid his rump across the boards, his hands firmly grasping the sides of the raft so that he would not be washed away by the next big wave that hit it. So did the second man. But the third man just grunted and hardly stirred in his place.

"Another man will surely sink us," said the first man, as a huge wave threw them dizzily into the air and then sucked them into a deep trough. And, like a fish out of the water, the fourth man flopped onto the raft. He was a big, well-fed man too, like the third man, but his body was all flesh and his belly lay like a slack, half-filled sack under his weight. His face was black with oil, and water trickled from his sharp nose and from his mouth as he lay gasping for breath. The second man glanced at him with ill-concealed disgust and turned his face away.

The planks that formed the raft were barely above water by this time. The first man thought, rather maliciously, "Why should there be so many survivors of the shipwreck? It would have been better if they had gone down with the ship." He was naturally a generous soul and kind, but the danger of the raft being swamped made him selfish. "I hope that he dies," he thought. "Then we can just push him off and lessen the burden of the raft."

The prone man began to stir at last. Slowly he turned over on his side and they saw his face. It was a face that no doubt had been tended to with great care. Now its fatty folds looked soggy as if saturated with much water. His lips were blackish-white like leeches pickled in formaldehyde. His grey eyelids fluttered and parted, exposing eyes red like sunripened tomatoes. With great effort he propped himself on his elbows, raised his fat body, and sat up. He looked at the others with a frank stare of appraisal.

By this time, however, the three were not interested in him any more because they were looking at something out in the water. He followed their gaze and saw still another man struggling against the waves and making some headway toward the raft. He, the fourth man, the newcomer whom the others had silently begrudged a place on the raft, muttered angrily, "But surely another man will swamp this raft. There is no place for one more." This was the truth, too, for the raft was already half-submerged by the weight of the four of them.

"I wish I had a pistol," said the third man softly, but with a menacing undertone in his voice. "I'd shoot him if I could." "But that would be murder," blurted out the first man involuntarily, shocked at the idea.

"Would you give up your place on the raft for him?" asked the third man quietly. "Because if you would, that would be quite all right with us, you know."

"No, of course not," said the first man quickly, abashed, and he cursed himself silently for having raised his voice at all, having no desire to draw attention to himself.

"And of course it would not be murder," added the third man, smiling just a little. "It would clearly be self-defense. This raft will not hold five people. His coming is a danger to our lives. If I shot him to ward off that danger to my life, that would be an act of self-defense."

The fourth man was about to say something, perhaps to protest against this reasoning, but remembering himself, he shut his mouth. And, from the very silence of the rest, the third man knew that they had willingly or unwillingly agreed with him.

Seeing the fifth man coming nearer the raft, the fourth man turned to his companions in alarm. "What shall we do?" he quavered. "He means to board us."

"I'll tell you what we will do," said the second man. "We will repel his attempts to board us."

"How can we possibly do that?" asked the fourth man. "We don't have any weapon."

"That is easy," said the second man with an air of cunning. "If he tries to hold on to the raft, we shall stamp on his hands with our feet. If his head comes anywhere within our reach, we can use our fists, or our belt buckles. Let us each guard a corner and one-half of the two sides of the raft."

Not a voice was raised to agree or to protest, but as if by common unspoken assent, each of the four men on the raft edged self-consciously to his allotted portion of the raft to guard it against the swimmer in the water. Because of this menace to their common safety, the four, who had hardly spoken to, or even looked at each other save in pointed dislike, now seemed to have struck at least a temporary alliance against the fifth man.

The big waves began to settle down and the hollows to fill out, and the sea became comparatively calm. Now they could see that the fifth man was making faster headway toward them. They could see his sunburnt arms and shoulders, massive with hard muscles and shiny with oil, work like efficient brown pistons, automatic and powerful, dipping and churning, dipping and churning....

As he watched the fifth man swim closer, the first man began to have misgivings. How could they ever hope to keep the fifth man from boarding the raft? With one blow of those tremendous arms he could fell any of them; he could sweep them all from the raft and appropriate it for himself. It was not a pleasant thought. He looked at his co-possessors and saw from the expression on their faces that they were having the same fearful doubts.

At that moment the fifth man reached the raft. He held fast to the edge with wide, muscle-sheathed hands. They were calloused hands, the hands of one who had been used to manual labor; the fingernails were broken and there was dirt under them. The back of his thick, strong neck, just below the fringe of long, tangled hair, as well as his bulging shoulders and arms, had been toasted a deep brown. He had laid his face on the crook of an arm and he allowed his body to float limply in the water.

It was as if the four men had forgotten about their agreement. Not one of them dared lift a hand against the newcomer;

not one voice was raised in protest. Instead they all watched him with a curious apathy as he held on to the raft with his eyes closed, breathing deeply. Huddled to one side, they watched him with the giddy helplessness of cornered animals waiting for the spring of a deadly beast which, being winded, had momentarily lost some of its strength.

The tiny raft was now listing badly toward the end where the fifth man was hanging on to it, and the four men on the raft crawled to the opposite end to keep it from overturning. Even so, the planks of the raft were exactly on a level with the water.

Very slowly the fifth man raised his head. The four men on the raft saw the face of a strong man. Jaws and mouth were firm and tight, the cheekbones rather prominent, and the eyes had a disquietingly penetrating look, as if they could stare for a long time without blinking.

Yet, in spite of its strength, it was a face that one could meet and forget the next moment. No individuality reposed in its strength. The impression one had was that one had seen the face before, or perhaps thought he had. There were so many other faces like it. The fifth man could be twenty-five or thirty-five.

The fifth man gave them all a swift passing glance that was not exactly hostile, yet was not friendly. He shook his wet, shaggy head and, placing his palms flat on the surface of the raft, raised his big body half out of the water and began to ease it over the side onto the raft. That portion of the raft sank in the water, and the four men scrambled to maintain their balance on it.

"Wait!" a low, imperious voice boomed out. "Do not board this raft!"

The fifth man, who apparently had been used to obeying orders, hesitated for a moment and slid back into the water. But he held on to the raft.

It was the fourth man who had spoken. His flabby face still had the color of flood-streaked clay, but somehow he seemed to have captured an air of authority.

"Don't you see that this raft will not hold another person?" he asked crossly. "Can't you see that even by just holding on to the raft you are able to pull it under? Why don't you swim away?"

"I have swum a long way to get to the safety of this raft," answered the fifth man. "If I should swim away now I will surely drown."

"Where did you come from?" asked the first man softly. "We didn't see you."

"I have been around all the time," answered the fifth man. "I was on the steerage deck of the ship. I have traveled in steerage and in third class compartments all my life, where I was so lucky as to get a ride. But I supposed there is no steerage deck on this raft, so I shall have to ride in your company, if you don't mind."

"But we do mind," protested the third man. "That is, you can't get on now. If you do you will surely drown us all."

"That would be a sad thing," said the fifth man regretfully. "But I don't propose to sink alone."

"You might try to keep afloat in the water," suggested the fourth man in a kindlier voice. "You can hold on very lightly to the raft and perhaps it won't sink."

"I have been in the water long enough," said the fifth man. "I mean to rest on the raft."

The second man, who had all this time been watchfully silent, took the opportunity to shout heartily, "Welcome to the raft, brother!" He smiled expansively, baring his big yellow teeth, as he extended a hand toward the man in the water. "Here, let me help you," he continued. "We can push off some of these men."

His former allies moved away, looking at him in fear. But the man in the water just stared at the proffered hand and did not take it.

"When I decide to get onto the raft," said the fifth man distinctly, "I won't need help from anybody."

The second man withdrew his hand as if he had touched fire and, reddening, turned to frown at the sea.

"One of you has to get off the raft and into the water," said the fifth man, "because I'm getting on."

"But we were here first," spluttered the fourth man. "Priority of possession has given us a certain title to this wreckage which no subsequent claimant without a better title can defeat. That is the law."

"The law of the shipwrecked is the law of the strong," said the fifth man ominously, pulling a wicked-looking dagger from his belt. He struck the blade into the raft where it stood quivering. "And that is good law anywhere. If I were to kill any of you, or all of you, for the raft in order to preserve my own life, no court in the land would convict me of any felony. The law of survival is superior to all other laws."

The four men regarded the fifth with a new respect. They had not expected to hear such words from this uncouth, coarse-looking fellow. The first man fell to thinking about the historical case of that sailor who, tried for the murder of several persons whom he had forced to jump out of a life-boat, was subsequently acquitted of any criminal liability.

"One of you has to get off the raft," repeated the fifth man, grasping the handle of the dagger with his hand.

"I'll tell you what we will do," cried the third man in desperation. "Allow us to fight this out among the four of us. The loser gets thrown into the sea."

The others stirred uneasily and started to protest, but the fifth man cut them short.

"This is what we will do," he said. "Each of you will tell me his usefulness. The least useful will give me his place on the raft."

"And who will be the judge of our usefulness?" asked the second man.

"I will be the judge of that," said the fifth man, stroking the keen blade of his dagger.

"But that is unconstitutional!" roared the fourth man in rage. "What right have you? What jurisdiction have you? I refuse to consent to being tried by you or to be bound by your decision."

"Hitherto many things have been decided for me without my consent," said the fifth man. "Now I will judge you. And I have the power to enforce my decision, as you can see. Let us get this over with. I am freezing, you know."

The man in the water looked at each of the four men on the raft. The first man seemed dazed, the second man looked surly, the third man was grave, and the fourth man defiant.

"You," said the fifth man to the first man, "suppose you start."

"I?" whispered the first man as though he had been abruptly roused from a reverie, as in truth he had been. It had always been like that with him; the threat of approaching danger always numbed his limbs and dulled his brain. "I? Well...I...I admit, I am not very useful," he began, wetting his lips, but as he felt the stiffening attention of the others, he hastily amended, rather lamely: "That is, others would not see that I have done anything useful. Words are the tools of my craft—honest words, truthful words, simple words, beautiful words, words that touch and soothe, words that prick and sting, words that give solace and comfort, that give contagion and unrest. If successful, I make it possible for others to see the beauty of morning through my eyes, to feel the pulse of passion through my heart, to hear the hum of life through my ears. But perhaps I am selfish, too, because I aim to give satisfaction to myself first of all: the satisfaction that I give others is incidental. Am I useful? . . ."

The second man said: "To different people I am a different man. I am called Visionary, Fanatic, Firebrand, Agitator. But in truth I am the Sower, and fertile is the earth of piers, factories, and fields. I roam city streets and mingle with the crowds. I seek out the dispossessed in their hovels, in the slums where filth and ugliness are a familiar pattern and where disease is brother to poverty. I disappear among the scattered hamlets of the countryside to talk with the serf-clan. I bring enlightenment to the multitudes from whom knowledge has so long been withheld. I may sow discontent, but I bring the truth. I may cause bloodshed, but I bring equality, true equality." His eyes were shining, and his voice was hoarse with emotion. "I am the new Missionary, the Preacher of the new Religion, the new Credo that teaches that one who does not work has no right to live."

"I give no beauty, I preach no religion," said the third man in a flat, unemotional voice. "But I believe in tolerance, in the theory of live and let live. I believe that the freedom of the individual to possess property and amass wealth is the best inducement for a man to work. I believe that free, private enterprise and competition do much for the progress of the nation and the elevation of the living standards of all the people. I possess wealth and property acquired through my natural acumen and effort. This wealth I invest to produce greater wealth, and in the process I give employment and sustenance to many who are willing to work. I give up a good portion of my wealth in taxes. I, too, believe in work, not as an end in itself but so that it may give rest and comfort afterward. You may judge if I am useful."

The fifth man looked at the fourth man and the latter said, "I believe you expect me to say something for myself too. Well, I am a politician. I suppose that name sounds detestable to you; perhaps it has unwholesome associations. But I have devoted all my life to the interest and welfare of the masses. Their advancement and prosperity and happiness is uppermost in my mind and directs all my actions. It is true that I wield much power, but I hold that as a sacred trust for those who gave it to me. I am a servant of the people."

The first man said to the fifth man, "And who are you, if I may ask?"

"Just call me the man in the water, the fifth man. And now, I am getting on the raft."

The fifth man vaulted easily over the side of the raft. The dagger was clutched firmly in his hand.

Evening News Saturday Magazine
October 30, 1948

WE FILIPINOS ARE MILD DRINKERS

ALEJANDRO R. ROCES

We Filipinos are mild drinkers. We drink for only three good reasons. We drink when we are very happy. We drink when we are very sad. And we drink for any other reason.

When the Americans recaptured the Philippines, they built an air base a few miles from our barrio. Yankee soldiers became a very common sight. I met a lot of GI's and made many friends. I could not pronounce their names. I could not tell them apart. All Americans looked alike to me. They all looked white.

One afternoon I was plowing our rice field with our carabao named Datu. I was barefooted and stripped to the waist. My pants, that were made from abaca fibers and woven on homemade looms, were rolled up to my knees. My bolo was at my side.

An American soldier was walking on the highway. When he saw me, he headed towards me. I stopped plowing and waited for him. I noticed he was carrying a half-pint bottle of whiskey. Whiskey bottles seemed part of the American uniform.

"Hello, my little brown brother," he said patting me on the head.

"Hello, Joe," I answered.

All Americans are called Joe in the Philippines.

"Any bars in this town?" he asked.

That was usually the first question American soldiers asked when they visited our barrio.

"I am sorry, Joe," I replied. "There are no bars in this barrio."

"Oh, hell! You know where I could buy more whiskey?"

"No, Joe. I am sorry. We do not drink whiskey."

"Here, have a swig. You have been working too hard," he said, offering me his half-filled bottle.

"No, thank you, Joe," I said. "We Filipinos are mild drinkers."

"Well, don't you drink at all?"

"Yes, Joe, I drink, but not whiskey."

"What the hell do you drink?"

"I drink *lambanog.*"

"Jungle juice, eh?"

"I guess that is what the GI's call it."

"You know where I could buy some?"

"I have some you can have, but I do not think you will like it."

"I'll like it all right. Don't worry about that. I have drunk everything—whiskey, rum, brandy, tequila, gin, champagne, saki, vodka...." He mentioned many more that I can not spell.

"Say, you sure drink a lot, don't you?"

"I not only drink at lot, but I drink anything. I drank Chanel Number 5 when I was in France. In New Guinea I got soused on Williams' Shaving Lotion. When I was laid up in the hospital I got pie-eyed with medical alcohol. On my way here in a transport I got stoned on torpedo juice. You ain't kidding when you say I drink a lot. So let's have some of that jungle juice, eh?"

"All right," I said. "I will just take this carabao to the mudhole, then we can go home and drink."

"You sure love that animal, don't you?"

"I should," I replied. "It does half of my work."

"Why don't you get two of them?"

I did not answer.

I unhitched Datu from the plow and led him to the mudhole. Joe was following me. Datu lay in the mud and was going: "Whooooosh! Whooooosh!"

Flies and other insects flew from his back and hovered in the air. A strange warm odor rose out of the muddle. A carabao does not have any sweat glands except on its nose. It has to wallow in the mud or bathe in a river about every three hours. Otherwise it runs amok.

Datu shook his head and his wide-spread horns scooped the muddy water on his back. He rolled over and was soon covered with slimy mud. An expression of perfect contentment came into his eyes. Then he swished his tail and Joe and I had to move back from the mudhole to keep from getting splashed. I left Datu in the mudhole. Then, turning to Joe, I said: "Let us go."

And we proceeded towards my house. Joe was curiously looking around.

"This place is full of coconut trees," he said.

"Don't you have any coconut trees in America?" I asked.

"No," he replied. "Back home we have the pine tree."

"What is it like?"

"Oh, it is tall and stately. It goes straight up to the sky like a skyscraper. It symbolizes America."

"Well," I said, "the coconut tree symbolizes the Philippines. It starts up to the sky, but then its leaves sway down to earth, as if remembering the land that gave it birth. It does not forget the soil that gave it life."

In a short while, we arrived in my nipa house. I took a bamboo ladder and leaned it against a tree. Then I climbed the ladder and picked some *calamansi*.

"What's that?" Joe asked.

"Philippine lemon," I answered. "We will need this for our drinks."

"Oh, chasers."

"That is right, Joe. That is what the soldiers call it."

I filled my pockets and then went down. I went to the garden well and washed the mud from my legs. Then we went up a bamboo ladder to my hut.

It was getting dark, so I filled a coconut shell with coconut oil, dipped a wick in the oil and lighted the wick. It produced a flickering light. I unstrapped my bolo and hung it on the wall.

"Please sit down, Joe," I said.

"Where?" he asked, looking around.

"Right there," I said, pointing to the floor.

Joe sat down on the floor. I sliced the *calamansi* in halves, took some rough salt and laid it on the foot-high table. I went to the kitchen and took the bamboo tube where I kept my *lambanog*.

Lambanog is a drink extracted from the coconut tree with pulverized mangrove bark thrown in to prevent spontaneous combustion. It has many uses. We use it as a remedy for snakebites, as counteractive for malaria chills, as an insecticide and for tanning carabao hide.

I poured some *lambanog* on two polished coconut shells
and gave one of the shells to Joe. I diluted my drink with some
of Joe's whiskey. It became milky. We were both seated on the
floor. I poured some of my drink on the bamboo floor; it went
through the slits to the ground below.

"Hey, what are you doing," said Joe, "throwing good liquor
away?"

"No, Joe," I said. "It is the custom here always to give
back to the earth a little of what we have taken from the earth."

"Well!" he said, raising his shell. "Here's to the end of the
war!"

"Here's to the end of the war!" I said, also lifting my drink.

I gulped my drink down. I followed it with a slice of
calamansi dipped in rough salt. Joe took his drink, but reacted
in a peculiar way. His eyes popped out like a frog's and his
hand clutched his throat. He looked as if he had swallowed a
centipede.

"Quick, a chaser!" he said.

I gave him a slice of *calamansi* dipped in unrefined salt.
He squirted it in his mouth. But it was too late. Nothing could
chase her. The *calamansi* did not help him. I don't think even
a coconut would have helped him.

"What is wrong, Joe?" I asked.

"Nothing," he said. "The first drink always affects me this
way."

He was panting hard and tears were rolling down his
cheeks.

"Well, the first drink always acts like a mine sweeper," I
said, "but this second one will be smooth."

I filled his shell for the second time. Again I diluted my
drink with Joe's whiskey. I gave Joe his shell. I noticed that
he was beaded with perspiration. He had unbuttoned his collar
and loosened his tie. Joe took his shell but did not seem very
anxious. I lifted my shell and said: "Here is to America!"

I was trying very hard to be a good host.

"Here's to America!" Joe said.

We both killed our drinks. Joe again reacted in a funny
way. His neck stretched out like a turtle's. And now he was
panting like a carabao gone amok. He was grasping his tie
with one hand. Then he looked down on his tie, threw it to

one side, and said: "Oh, Christ, for a while I thought it was my tongue."

After this he started to tinker with his teeth.

"What's wrong, Joe?" I asked, still trying to be a perfect host.

"Plenty, this damned stuff had loosened my bridgework."

As Joe exhaled, a moth flying around the flickering flame fell dead.

He stared at the dead moth and said: "And they talk of DDT."

"Well, how about another drink?" I asked. "It is what we came here for."

"No, thanks," he said, "I'm through."

"Surely you will not refuse my hospitality?"

"O.K. Just once more."

I poured the juice in the shells and again diluted mine with whiskey. I handed Joe his drink.

"Here's to the Philippines," he said.

"Here's to the Philippines," I said.

Joe took some of his drink. I could not see very clearly in the flickering light, but I could have sworn I saw smoke out of his tears.

"This stuff must be radioactive," he said.

He threw the remains of his drink on the nipa wall and yielded:

"Blaze, goddamn you, blaze!"

Just as I was getting in the mood to drink, Joe passed out. He lay on the floor flat as a starfish. He was in a class all by himself.

I knew that the soldiers had to be back in their barracks at a certain time. So I decided to take Joe back. I tried to lift him. It was like lifting a carabao. I had to call four of my neighbors to help me carry Joe. We slung him on top of my carabao. I took my bolo from the house and strapped it on my waist. Then I proceeded to take him back. The whole barrio was wondering what had happened to the big Amerikano.

After two hours I arrived at the air field. I found out which barracks he belonged to and took him there. His friends helped me take him to his cot. They were glad to see him back. Everybody thanked me for taking him home. As I was leaving the barracks to go home, one of his buddies called me and said:

"Hey, you! How about a can of beer before you go?"
"No, thanks," I said. "We Filipinos are mild drinkers."

Evening News Saturday Magazine
November 6, 1948

SCENT OF APPLES

BIENVENIDO N. SANTOS

When I arrived in Kalamazoo it was October and the war was still on. Gold and silver stars hung on pennants above silent windows of white and brick-red cottages. In a backyard, an old man burned leaves and twigs while a greyhaired woman sat on the porch, her red hands quiet on her lap, watching the smoke rising above the elms, both of them thinking of the same thought perhaps about a tall, grinning boy with blue eyes and flying hair, who went out to war, where could he be now this month when leaves were turning into gold and the fragrance of gathered apples was in the wind?

It was a cold night when I left my room at the hotel for a usual speaking engagement. I walked but a little way. A heavy wind coming up from Lake Michigan was icy on the face. It felt like winter straying early in the northern woodlands. Under the lamp posts the leaves shone like bronze. And they rolled on the pavements like the ghost feet of a thousand autumns long dead, long before the boys left for faraway lands without great icy winds and promise of winter early in the air, lands without apple trees, *the singing and the gold*!

It was the same night I met Celestino Fabia, "just a Filipino farmer" as he called himself, who had a farm about thirty miles east of Kalamazoo.

"You came all that way on a night like this just to hear me talk?" I asked.

I've seen no Filipino for so many years now," he answered quickly. "So when I saw your name in the papers where it says you come from the Islands and that you're going to talk, I came right away."

Earlier that night I had addressed a college crowd, mostly women. It appeared that they wanted me to talk about my country; they wanted me to tell them things about it because my country had become a lost country. Everywhere in the land the enemy stalked. Over it a great silence hung; and their boys were there, unheard from, or they were on their way to some little known island on the Pacific, young boys all, hardly men, thinking of harvest moons and smell of forest fire.

It was not hard talking about our own people. I know them well and I loved them. And they seemed so far away during those terrible years that I must have spoken of them with a little fervor, a little nostalgia.

In the open forum that followed, the audience wanted to know whether there was much difference between our women and the American women. I tried to answer the question as best as I could, saying, among other things, that I did not know much about American women, except that they looked friendly, but differences or similarities in inner qualities such as naturally belonged to the heart or to the mind I could only speak about with vagueness.

While I was trying to explain away the fact that it was not easy to make comparisons, a man rose from the rear of the hall, wanting to say something. In the distance, he looked slight and old and very brown. Even before he spoke, I knew that he was, like me, a Filipino.

"I'm a Filipino," he began, loud and clear, in a voice that seemed used to wide open spaces. "I'm just a Filipino farmer out in the country." He waved his hand towards the door. "I left the Philippines more than twenty years ago and have never been back. Never will perhaps. I want to find out, sir, are our Filipino women the same like they were twenty years ago?"

As he sat down, the hall filled with voices, hushed and intrigued. I weighed my answer carefully. I did not want to tell a lie yet I did not want to say anything that would seem platitudinous, insincere. But more important than these considerations, it seemed to me that moment as I looked towards my countryman, I must give him an answer that would not make him so unhappy. Surely, all these years, he must have held on to certain ideals, certain beliefs, even illusions peculiar to the exile.

"First," I said as the voices gradually died down and every eye seemed upon me, "First, tell me what our women were like twenty years ago."

The man stood to answer. "Yes," he said, "you're too young.... Twenty years ago our women were nice, they were modest, they wore their hair long, they dressed proper and went for no monkey business. They were natural, they went to church regular, and they were faithful." He had spoken slowly, and now in what seemed like an afterthought, added, "It's the men who ain't."

Now I knew what I was going to say.

"Well," I began, "it will interest you to know that our women have changed — but definitely! The change, however, has been on the outside only. Inside, here," pointing to the heart, "they are the same as they were twenty years ago, God-fearing, faithful, modest, and *nice.*"

The man was visibly moved. "I'm very happy, sir," he said, in the manner of one who, having stakes on the land, had found no cause to regret one's sentimental investment.

After this, everything that was said and done in that hall that night seemed like an anti-climax; and later, as we walked outside, he gave me his name and told me of his farm thirty miles east of the city.

We had stopped at the main entrance to the hotel lobby. We had not talked very much on the way. As a matter of fact, we were never alone. Kindly American friends talked to us, asked us questions, said goodnight. So now I asked him whether he cared to step into the lobby with me and talk shop.

"No, thank you," he said, "you are tired. And I don't want to stay out too late."

"Yes, you live very far."

"I got a car," he said, "besides...."

Now he smiled, he truly smiled. All night I had been watching his face and I wondered when he was going to smile.

"Will you do me a favor, please?" he continued smiling almost sweetly. "I want you to have dinner with my family out in the country. I'd call for you tomorrow afternoon, then drive you back. Will that be all right?"

"Of course," I said. "I'd love to meet your family." I was leaving Kalamazoo for Muncie, Indiana, in two days. There was plenty of time.

"You will make my wife very happy," he said.

"You flatter me."

"Honest. She'll be very happy. Ruth is a country girl and hasn't met many Filipinos. I mean Filipinos younger than I, cleaner looking. We're just poor farmer folk, you know, and we don't get to town very often. Roger, that's my boy, he goes to school in town. A bus takes him early in the morning and he's back in the afternoon. He's nice boy."

"I bet he is," I agreed. "I've seen the children of some of the boys by their American wives and the boys are tall, taller than the father, and very good looking."

"Roger, he'd be tall. You'll like him."

Then he said goodbye and I waved to him as he disappeared in the darkness.

The next day he came, at about three in the afternoon. There was a mild, ineffectual sun shining; and it was not too cold. He was wearing an old brown tweed jacket and worsted trousers to match. His shoes were polished, and although the green of his tie seemed faded, a colored shirt hardly accentuated it. He looked younger than he did the night before now that he was clean shaven and seemed ready to go to a party. He was grinning as we met.

"Oh, Ruth can't believe it. She can't believe it," he kept repeating as he led me to his car—a nondescript thing in faded black that had known better days and many hands. "I says to her, I'm bringing you a first class Filipino, and she says, aw, go away, quit kidding, there's no such thing as first class Filipino. But Roger, that's my boy, he believed me immediately. What's he like, daddy, he asks. Oh, you will see, I says, he's first class. Like you, daddy? No, no, I laugh at him, your daddy ain't first class. Aw, but you are, daddy, he says. So you can see what a nice boy he is, so innocent. Then Ruth starts griping about the house, but the house is a mess, she says. True it's a mess, it's always a mess, but you don't mind, do you? We're poor folks, you know."

The trip seemed interminable. We passed through narrow lanes and disappeared into thickets, and came out on barren land overgrown with weeds in places. All around were dead leaves and dry earth. In the distance were apple trees.

"Aren't those apple trees?" I asked wanting to be sure.

"Yes, those are apple trees," he replied. "Do you like apples? I got lots of 'em. I got an apple orchard. I'll show you."

All the beauty of the afternoon seemed in the distance, on the hills, in the dull soft sky.

"Those trees are beautiful on the hills," I said.

"Autumn's a lovely season. The trees are getting ready to die, and they show their colors, proud-like."

"No such thing in our own country," I said.

That remark seemed unkind, I realized later. It touched him off on a long deserted tangent, but ever there perhaps. How many times did the lonely mind take unpleasant detours away from the familiar winding lanes towards home for fear of this, the remembered hurt, the long lost youths, the grim shadows of the years; how many times indeed, only the exile knows.

It was a rugged road we were travelling and the car made so much noise that I could not hear everything he said, but I understood him. He was telling his story for the first time in many years. He was remembering his own youth. He was thinking of home. In these odd moments there seemed no cause for fear, no cause at all, no pain. That would come later. In the night perhaps. Or lonely on the farm under the apple trees.

In this old Visayan town, the streets are narrow and dirty and strewn with corral shells. You have been there? You could not have missed our house, it was the biggest in town, one of the oldest, ours was a big family. The house stood right on the edge of the street. A door opened heavily and you enter a dark hall leading to the stairs. There is the smell of chickens roosting on the low-topped walls, there is the familiar sound they make and you grope your way up a massive staircase, the bannisters smooth upon the trembling hand. Such nights, they are no better than the days, windows are closed against the sun; they close heavily.

Mother sits in her corner looking very white and sick. This was her world, her domain. In all these years I cannot remember the sound of her voice. Father was different. He moved about. He shouted. He ranted. He lived in the past and talked of honor as though it were the only thing.

I was born in that house. I grew up there into a pampered brat. I was mean. One day I broke their hearts. I saw mother cry wordlessly as father heaped his curses upon me and drove me out of the house, the gate closing heavily after me. And my brothers and sisters took up my father's hate for me and mul-

*tiplied it numberless times in their own broken hearts. I was
no good.*

*But sometimes, you know, I miss that house, the roosting
chickens on the low-topped walls. I miss my brothers and sisters.
Mother sitting in her chair, looking like a pale ghost in a corner
of the room. I would remember the great live posts, massive
tree trunks from the forests. Leafy plants grew on the sides,
buds pointing downwards, wilted and died before they could
become flowers. As they fell on the floor, father bent to pick
them and throw them out into the corral streets. His hands were
strong. I have kissed those hands. . . many times, many times.*

Finally we rounded a deep curve and suddenly came upon
a shanty, all but ready to crumble in a heap on the ground,
its plastered walls were rotting away, the floor was hardly a
foot from the ground. I thought of the cottages of the poor
colored folk in the south, the hovels of the poor everywhere in
the land. This one stood all by itself as though by common
consent all the folk that used to live here had decided to stay
away, despising it, ashamed of it. Even the lovely season could
not color it with beauty.

A dog barked loudly as we approached. A fat blonde woman
stood at the door with a little boy by her side. Roger seemed
newly scrubbed. He hardly took his eyes off me. Ruth had a
clean apron around her shapeless waist. Now as she shook my
hands in sincere delight, I noticed shamefacedly (that I should
notice) how rough her hands, how coarse and red with labor,
how ugly! She was no longer young and her smile was pathetic.

As we stepped inside and the door closed behind us, immediately I was aware of the familiar scent of apples. The
room was bare except for a few ancient pieces of second-hand
furniture. In the middle of the room stood a stove to keep the
family warm in winter. The walls were bare. Over the dining
table hung a lamp yet unlighted.

Ruth got busy with the drinks. She kept coming in and
out of a rear room that must have been the kitchen and soon
the table was heavy with food, fried chicken legs and rice, and
green peas and corn on the ear. Even as we ate, Ruth kept
standing, and going to the kitchen for more food. Roger ate
like a little gentleman.

"Isn't he nice looking?" his father asked.

"You are a handsome boy, Roger," I said.

The boy smiled at me. "You look like Daddy," he said.

Afterwards I noticed an old picture leaning on the top of a dresser and stood to pick it up. It was yellow and soiled with many fingerings. The faded figure of a woman in Philippine dress could yet be distinguished although the face had become a blur.

"Your...," I began.

"I don't know who she is," Fabia hastened to say. "I picked that picture many years ago in a room on La Salle street in Chicago. I have often wondered who she is."

"The face wasn't a blur in the beginning?"

"Oh, no. It was a young face and good."

Ruth came with a plate full of apples.

"Ah," I cried, picking out a ripe one, "I've been thinking where all the scent of apples came from. The room is full of it."

"I'll show you," said Fabia.

He showed me a backroom, not very big. It was half-full of apples.

"Every day," he exclaimed, "I take some of them to town to sell to the groceries. Prices have been low. I've been losing on the trips."

"These apples will spoil," I said.

"We'll feed them to the pigs."

Then he showed me around the farm. It was twilight now and the apple trees stood bare against a glowing western sky. In apple blossom time it must be lovely here, I thought. But what about wintertime?

One day, according to Fabia, a few years ago, before Roger was born, he had an attack of acute appendicitis. It was deep winter. The snow lay heavy everywhere. Ruth was pregnant and none too well herself. At first she did not know what to do. She bundled him in warm clothing and put him on a cot near the stove. She shoveled the snow on their front floor and practically carried the suffering man on her shoulders, dragging him through the newly made path towards the road where they waited for the U.S. Mail car to pass. Meanwhile snowflakes poured all over them and she kept rubbing the man's arms and legs as she herself nearly froze to death.

But she clung to him wordlessly. Even as she scrubbed her arms and legs, her tears rolled down her cheeks. "I won't leave you, I won't leave you," she repeated.

Finally the U.S. Mail car arrived. The mailman, who knew them well, helped them board the car, and, without stopping on his usual route, took the sick man and his wife direct to the nearest hospital.

Ruth stayed in the hospital with Fabia. She slept in a corridor outside the patients' ward and in the daytime helped in scrubbing the floor and washing the dishes and cleaning the men's things. They didn't have enough money and Ruth was willing to work like a slave.

"Ruth's a nice girl," said Fabia. "Like our own Filipino women."

Before nightfall, he took me back to the hotel. Ruth and Roger stood at the door holding hands and smiling at me. From inside the room of the shanty, a low light flickered. I had a last glimpse of the apple trees in the orchard under the darkened sky as Fabia backed up the car. And soon we were on our way back to town. The dog had started barking. We could hear it for some time, until finally, we could not hear it anymore, and all was darkness around us, except where the head lamps revealed a stretch of road leading somewhere.

Fabia did not talk this time. I didn't seem to have anything to say myself. But when finally we came to the hotel and I got down, Fabia said, "Well, I guess I won't be seeing you again."

It was dimly lighted in front of the hotel and I could hardly see Fabia's face. He had not come down the car, but he had moved to my side, and I saw his hand, extended. I gripped it.

"Tell Ruth and Roger," I said, "I love them."

He dropped my hand quickly. "They'll be waiting for me now," he said.

"Look," I said, not knowing why I said it, "one of these days, very soon, I hope, I'll be going home. I could go to your town."

"No," he said softly, sounding very much defeated but brave. "Thanks a lot. But, you see, nobody would remember me now."

Then he started the car, and as it moved away, he waved his hand.

"Goodbye," I said, waving back into the darkness. And suddenly the night was cold like winter straying early in these northern woodlands.

I hurried inside. There was a train the next morning that left for Muncie, Indiana, at a quarter after eight.

This Week
November 14, 1948

FLOOD

J. Capiendo Tuvera

The rain was falling heavily upon the muddied canvas roofing of the cart. Through a tiny slit across its side Tino could see the carabao that had been unhitched an hour ago, grazing by the side of the thin sluice of country road at a crop of stunted grass in the shade of a thick-leaved *banaba* tree. The strained heaving of its haggard rumps was gone now. Almost violently Tino nudged Mon who lay curled up in a corner of the cart still warming himself with the last few puffs at a cigarette.

"Are we not leaving?"

At the sound of Tino's prodding voice he picked up his crumpled straw hat, yawned, and crawled slowly on his knees to the opening at the head of the cart.

Tino heard the sucking sound of Mon's bare feet in the mud. He placed his face once more against the slit in the canvas roof and saw him dragging the carabao back to the cart. All around, as far as he could see, except in the grassy humps of little hillocks, brown puddles had quickly gathered, their ragged edges flowing out to meet neighboring puddles. Now and then sharp blades of lightning, like scimitars of a hidden god, slashed viciously at the curtains of heavy clouds that draped the sky.

"Must be five now," Tino said.

"What?"

"I said we didn't have to rest at all," Tino screamed above the rain; "it's almost night now." He went back to the center of the hay matting and sat holding his knees up. Mon pottered about under the rain, fixing the yoke on the carabao and slapping its dripping hide to please himself.

"I should have allowed Risio to come instead," Mon said. "There's more chill in my bones than you think." When he finally got up onto the front rail of the cart, Tino shoved the whip into his hand and grumbled.

"Here," he said gruffly, "let it fly."

"You haven't changed," Mon said. "Always running, breaking your neck in foolish hurry."

"It's not foolish," Tino said. "Suppose she is dead?"

The whip rose and whistled through the cold wet air as it fell on the rump of the carabao. The animal jerked forward as if it were going to break into a gallop, and then fell into a sluggish gait as the gluey road mud clamped tightly at its legs. Tino allowed himself to fall back with the sudden jolt of the cart and cushioned his head with his palms. Under the bamboo floor of the cart the wheels creaked plaintively.

"Last month, when I came, she was well enough," Tino said.

"Her health fell very fast," Mon said. "Every day you could almost see it disappear in shreds, bit by bit. But a new doctor is treating her now."

"They shouldn't have brought her out of the hospital," Tino said. "She was already getting well there. And I used to see her every day."

"Mother couldn't afford it any more. Three hundred a month. You know what that means."

While he lay inside the cart, Tino looked up at the curve of the canvas roof above his face. His eyes followed the tiny bluish lines that stretched promiscuously across the surface of the canvas where the raindrops rolled down to its frayed and flapping edges. Feeling cold, he lighted a cigarette and blew curls of smoke above his face.

"She isn't dead, Mon, is she?" he asked.

"No," Mon answered. Tino rose from where he lay and moved up to the head of the cart, resting his hands on the single bamboo rail on which Mon sat. The cart turned around a bend in the road where rocks jutted out precariously from a tall ledge of earth. From there the ground dipped into a slow, gradual decline that ended in a profusion of stunted trees. Beyond that the ricefields of San Roque began: a wide expanse of wilted yellowness trembling beneath the torrent of August rain.

"I am going to marry her, you know," Tino said. Mon threw his leg out against the base of the animal's tail, then leaned back upon the canvas roofing.

"I know," he said.

"You know?"

"She told me."

"Risio knows, too?"

"No."

Tino looked around at the familiar, homely sight before them. It had been more than a month ago that he had passed here. That time it was also with his cousin Mon, who had been sent to bring him to San Roque. He remembered very well; farther down this road there was the Patling river, only two miles before reaching San Roque, and there they had stripped themselves of their clothes to bathe. Tino barely knew how to swim, only the "dogcrawl," as they called his stroke, and Mon had laughed at him. He was usually sensitive about his lack of knowledge of anything, but that time he did not really mind. After all it was only swimming. He liked the feeling the country gave. There was Ngili, to the west; you could stretch an arm and take it in your palm. Tall and slim and alone in the distance, the mountain seemed to stand like a woman in a tiered dress, with the Patling at its foot moving smoothly like an attendant procession of pious white-robed girls. And the air! The air was born in the upland hills, great and big and secret, and all of a sudden it would come down from there in sleds of wind to muss the pliant heads of *ledda* that fringed the fields. "No тв," Mon had said. "No ventilators. No rubber wheels to stir the dust. The air here is easy and full and unselfish."

Tino tried to remember what she used to say to him about San Roque. He had gone to see her every afternoon while she was in the hospital, and after the first few weeks there had been nothing much to talk about any more except themselves. He would push her around in her wheelchair for a while, then she would ask him to stop by the main door, and together they would walk to the shade of the tamarind tree reaching up with its branches to the eaves. "Maybe what I need is only some clean country air," she would say. "Like what we have in San Roque, remember?" "We can always go there," he would say. "Yes! Even when, even after." "Go ahead," he coaxed. There was something appealing and forever young in the way she would laugh afterwards, unwilling to say what she had in mind, what both of them desired and prayed for like a wordless, necessary exordium to living. "Of course," he said, throwing a loop at the floating end of her wish. "We can even play throw-the-can again, and hide under women's skirts." "You remember, too?" "You got whipped," he laughed.

The cart gave a violent jolt as the carabao responded instinctively to a roll of thunder that sped across the sky. A little way off, some houses appeared—small, cogon-roofed boxes crowded up in certain places and leaving wide, bare patches of earth between. These patches were not really bare now, because they had been filled by pools of water ruffled by the bouncing drops of falling rain.

"Does the city get flooded like this, too?" Mon wanted to know.

"Why, yes, every year," Tino said. "Last year the water rose to my thighs."

"Nieves was there, too," Mon remembered.

"Yes."

That was true, and he had almost forgotten. For four days he had gone to the hospital where Nieves was, fearing that the doctors would send him away because he lined the corridors with the profuse drip of his shoes. Because it was cold they didn't go out to the corridor as they usually did. His aunt would be coming later, and while they waited for her he trimmed her fingernails with his small penknife. "You know," he said, placing the knife down and holding her hands up, "even if you were not my cousin I would still love to do this for you." She looked up innocently and told him to go on trimming. "Why?" she said. "I like your fingers," he said. For a moment his cheeks and his fingers and his temples burned, while love swelled like a terrible pain. In the swift rush of self-consciousness he wanted to withdraw his hands, but they remained there, as though they must, his fingers searing hers, until abruptly she drew away and buried her face in the pillow. "Go away," she sobbed. She was crying when the nurse came in with her tray of food. "Let me do it," he said, taking the tray, and the nurse stood dumbly for a while and then walked away trying to hide the smile on her face. The soup spilled from the spoon when she shook her head out of its way, and he could have screamed with helplessness if his aunt did not suddenly throw the door open and walk into the room. Nieves dried her eyes hastily when she saw her mother. He took up the spoon again and let her have the soup, while his face glowed with taunting laughter.

"Do you hear that?" Mon said. Tino started. The palms of his hands, he realized, were limp and bloodless. He had been holding on to the rail for a long time, more than an hour, he was sure, his weight unconsciously laid on his hand. He lifted them and slapped them vigorously against his sides.

"What?"

And he had said that to her, too, "I thought Luz was everything to you," she had said, two days later when she wasn't hurt any more. "What?" he cried, and while they sat together on the edge of her bed, her hair beating little rhythms across his face, he felt suddenly big and strong and complete.

"That sound," Mon said. "Can you recognize it?" Tino strained his ears against the almost deafening rain. Slowly his face darkened, and his eyes shot up with anger.

"No!" he cried unreasonably.

"I expected it," Mon said. "When I saw those pools gathering in the fields, I knew the river must be big and terrible."

Patling was now in sight. Across the clump of bamboos on its bank, they saw the rising waves galloping swiftly to the east. The furious sound of their brown, flitting passage was nearer, unmistakable.

"We can't cross," Mon said.

"We can try," Tino said, limply.

"You?" Mon laughed, and reined the carabao in. The sucking sound of the animal's hoofs in the mud stopped and Tino sat up to watch the brown water in the river broken by white-fringed scallops of foamy waves.

"We can't cross," Mon said.

"This time?" Mon mocked. Above and around them, the silent, stealthy darkening of country dusk was spreading through the silver maze of raindrops. If this were not now, and he was not going home in a hurry, Tino would have found in the approaching dark the same thing he used to find in it, a sense of deep, grateful aliveness. They would lean out of the window and stand together to watch the other patients walk back to their wards. "You should have taken up medicine instead," she would say. "I thought you were going to." "That would have meant five more years of waiting for us," he said. "As it is, we have only four." "Four years," she would say; "will I be well then?" "Why not?" he said. "You are, already." She would touch her cheeks, as if she couldn't believe she wasn't thin and pale anymore, and then spread her fingers on the window sill. "I'll stand like this by the window," she said. "And make sure that you come home just as you must."

Mon clucked his tongue noisily at the carabao and kicked its rump.

"Come on, horns," he said. They turned back on the road and Mon started to guide the cart towards the houses they had passed some time before.

"It's useless," Mon said. "But tomorrow we will cross at any cost." Tino remained silent, sitting back against the railing of the cart. He knew if he spoke now he would turn cramped and light and childish within, to be torn away by the harsh rasping in his throat. For a moment he seemed to hear the noise of the rain outside vanish away to meet the twilight and in its place a hundred streaming waters pounded upon a nameless bulging within him.

"I know how you feel," Mon said, as if divining his thoughts. "But after all she is also my sister. You can't feel worse than I."

Tino wondered if that was right. When you had a sister— oh, well, that was foolish, trying to imagine how a brother would feel, since he had no sister anyway. But no, it can't be worse than this, this wide, edgeless loving, this secret, indefinite unmaleness. Once he told her he was going to a dance. "They are my friends," he said. "I can't refuse, you know." "No," she said, "you are not going." "Yes," he said, "I am going." He walked out of the room into the street below. There was something pleasant in his hurried leaving, a sense of winning that he relished. He wondered what she would do about it. He swung himself lightly into a bus by the gate, and through the window he looked back at the hospital behind him. The bus moved on, and soon the hospital was not in sight any more. Then suddenly the crimson sense of winning paled within him and he realized he had done wrong. When someone alighted from the bus, he followed without thinking, and in a moment

he was hailing another bus that would take him back to the
hospital.

"Maybe I won't go back to the city for some time," Tino
said.

"Why?" Mon said.

"Until she gets well enough, anyway. Was she very weak
when you came?"

"Couldn't move a hand," Mon said. "Only her lips."

Mon halted the animal abruptly and turned his face around
the front edge of the canvas roofing.

"Someone is calling," he said.

Tino joined him at the front railing of the cart. Someone
was walking out from behind a mango trunk and waving at
them. He broke into a lithe trot over the brambles at the bank
and called out to them.

"It's Risio," Mon said.

Tino grabbed his raincoat and jumped down from the cart
to meet him.

"Well," he said. "Well?"

"There's a raft here," Risio said. "I have been waiting for
you since noon. They had to send me because of this damned
flood."

They walked together to the edge of the water. A bamboo
raft was tied to the trunk of the mango, tossing restlessly with
the swirling undertow. Above them the rain fell noisily among
the leaves of the tree. Tino looked across the river and his eyes
searched through the drooping shrubs for the familiar trail that
led away from the opposite bank, but he saw only the white-
brown tongues of the flood licking hungrily at the green stalks.

"I'll leave the cart and the carabao with some of those
people there," Mon shouted from behind them. Risio leaned
back, the buri palms on his shoulders rustling noisily against
the trunk, and watched Mon disappear in a hundred flying
pellets of mud.

"I thought we would have to stay here for the night,"
Tino said.

"Mother sent me," Risio said, "because of the burial tomorrow. I don't know how it can be done, in this rain."

The waves of the river tossed and spun and beat mercilessly
against some boulders on the bank from which Tino watched
the water. His legs stood against the lash of the waves for a

while, and he felt as if the waves would rise higher yet and drench him and wash him away like the fallen leaves of the tree.

"She is—dead?" he murmured.

"Yes," Risio said. "This morning."

Tino walked farther away from the bank, but the water under his feet crawled out coldly before him, and while a wind from the hills swept past in a tiny gale, the water leaped up in sprays and beat against him to meet the heaviness in his chest and the darkness in his face and his eyes.

Risio turned his face quickly away.

"Mon shouldn't stay too long," he said.

Evening News Saturday Magazine
December 4, 1948

THE CHIEFTEST MOURNER

Aida L. Rivera

He was my uncle because he married my aunt (even if he had not come home to her these past ten years), so when the papers brought the news of his death, I felt that some part of me had died too.

I was boarding then at a big girls' college in Manila and I remember quite vividly that a few other girls were gathered about the lobby of our school, looking very straight and proper since it was seven in the morning and the starch in our long-sleeved uniform had not yet given way. I tried to be brave while I read that my uncle had actually been "the last of a distinct school of Philippine poets." I was still being brave all the way down the lengthy eulogies, until I got to the line which said that he was "the sweetest lyre that ever throbbed with Malayan chords." Something caught at my throat and I let out one sob—the rest merely followed. When the girls hurried over to me to see what had happened, I could only point to the item in the front page with my uncle's picture taken when he was still handsome. Everybody suddenly spoke in a low voice and Ning who worshipped me said that I shouldn't be so unhappy because my uncle was now with the other great poets in heaven—at which I really howled in earnest because my uncle had not only deserted poor Aunt Sophia but had also been living with another woman these many years and, most horrible of all, he had probably died in her embrace!

Perhaps I received an undue amount of commiseration for the death of the delinquent husband of my aunt, but it wasn't my fault because I never really lied about many things; only, nobody thought to ask me just how close an uncle he was. It wasn't my doing either when, some months after his demise, my poem entitled "The Rose Was Not So Fair O Alma Mater" was captioned "by the niece of the late beloved Filipino poet."

And that having been printed, I couldn't possibly refuse when I was asked to write on "My Uncle—The Poetry of His Life." The article, as printed, covered only his boyhood and early manhood because our adviser cut out everything that happened after he was married. She said that the last half of his life was not exactly poetic, although I still maintain that in his vices, as in his poetry, he followed closely the pattern of the great poets he admired.

My aunt used to relate that he was an extremely considerate man—when he was sober, and on those occasions he always tried to make up for his past sins. He said that he had never meant to marry, knowing the kind of husband he would make, but that her beauty drove him out of his right mind. My aunt always forgave him but one day she had more than she could bear, and when he was really drunk, she tied him to a chair with a strong rope to teach him a lesson. She never saw him drunk again, for as soon as he was able to, he walked out of the door and never came back.

I was very little at that time, but I remember that shortly after he went away, my aunt put me in a car and sent me to his hotel with a letter from her. Uncle ushered me into his room very formally and while I looked all around the place, he prepared a special kind of lemonade for the two of us. I was sorry that he poured it out into wee glasses because it was unlike any lemonade I had ever tasted. While I sipped solemnly at my glass, he inquired after my aunt. To my surprise, I found myself answering with alacrity. I was happy to report all the details of my aunt's health, including the number of crabs she ate for her lunch and the amazing fact that she was getting fatter and fatter without benefit of Scott's Emulsion or Ovaltine at all. Uncle smiled his beautiful somber smile and drew some poems from his desk. He scribbled a dedication on them and instructed me to give them to my aunt. I made much show of putting the empty glass down but Uncle was dense to the hint. At the door, however, he told me that I could have some lemonade everytime I came to visit him. Aunt Sophia was so pleased with the poems that she kissed me. And then all of a sudden she looked at me queerly and made a most peculiar request of me. She asked me to say ha-ha, and when I said ha-ha, she took me to the sink and began to wash the inside of my mouth with soap and water, the while calling upon at least a dozen of the saints to witness the act. I never got another taste of Uncle's lemonade.

It began to be a habit with Aunt Sophia to drop in for a periodical recital of woe to which Mama was a sympthetic audience. The topic of the conversation was always the latest low on Uncle's state of misery. It gave Aunt Sophia profound satisfaction to relay the report of friends on the number of creases on Uncle's shirt or the appalling decrease in his weight. To her, the fact that Uncle was getting thinner proved conclusively that he was suffering as a result of the separation. It looked as if Uncle would not be able to hold out much longer, the way he was reported to be thinner each time, because Uncle didn't have much weight to start with. The paradox of the situation, however, was that Aunt Sophia was now crowding Mama off the sofa and yet she wasn't looking very happy either.

When I was about eleven, there began to be a difference. Everytime I came into the room when Mama and Aunt Sophia were holding conference, the talk would suddenly be switched to Spanish. It was about this time that I took an interest in the Spanish taught in school. It was also at this time that Aunt Sophia exclaimed over my industry at the piano—which stood a short distance from the sofa. At first I couldn't gather much except that Uncle was not any more the main topic. It was a woman by the name of Esa—or so I thought she was called. Later, I began to appreciate the subtlety of the Spanish *la mujer esa.*

And so I learned about the woman. She was young, accomplished, a woman of means. (A surprising number of connotations were attached to these terms.) Aunt Sophia, being a loyal wife, grieved that Uncle should have been ensnared by such a woman, thinking not so much of herself as of his career. Knowing him so well, she was positive that he was unhappier than ever, for that horrid woman never allowed him to have his own way; she even denied him those little drinks which he took merely to aid him into poetic composition. Because the woman brazenly followed Uncle everywhere, calling herself his wife, a confusing situation ensued. When people mentioned Uncle's wife, there was no way of knowing whether they referred to my aunt or to the woman. After a while a system was worked out by the mutual friends of the different parties: No. 1 came to stand for Aunt Sophia and No. 2 for the woman.

I hadn't seen Uncle since the episode of the lemonade, but one day in school all the girls were asked to come down to the lecture room—Uncle was to read some of his poems! Up in my room, I stopped to fasten a pink ribbon to my hair thinking the while how I would play my role to perfection—for the dear niece was to be presented to the uncle she hadn't seen for so long. My musings were interrupted, however, when a girl came up and excitedly bubbled that she had seen my uncle —and my aunt, who was surprisingly young and so very modern!

I couldn't go down after all; I was "indisposed."

Complicated as the situation was when Uncle was alive, it became more when he died. I was puzzling over who was to be the official widow at his funeral when word came that I was to keep Aunt Sophia company at the little chapel where the service would be held. I concluded with relief that No. 2 had decamped.

The morning wasn't far gone when I arrived at the chapel and there were only a few people present. Aunt Sophia was sitting in one of the front pews at the right section of the chapel. She had on a black and white print which managed to display its full yardage over the seat. Across the aisle from her was a very slight woman in her early thirties who was dressed in a dramatic black outfit with a heavy veil coming up to her forehead. Something about her made me suddenly aware that Aunt Sophia's bag looked paunchy and worn at the corners. I wanted to ask my aunt who she was but after embracing me when I arrived, she kept her eyes stolidly fixed before her. I directed my gaze in the same direction. At the front was the President's immense wreath leaning heavily backward, like that personage himself; and a pace behind, as though in deference to it, were other wreaths arranged according to the rank and prominence of the people who had sent them. I suppose protocol had something to do with it.

I tiptoed over to muse before Uncle as he lay in the dignity of death, the faintest trace of his somber smile still on his face. My eyes fell upon a cluster of white flowers placed at the foot of the casket. It was ingeniously fashioned in the shape of a dove and it bore the inscription "From the Loyal One." I looked at Aunt Sophia and didn't see anything dove-like about her. I looked at the slight woman in black and knew all of a sudden

that she was *the* woman. A young man, obviously a brother
or a nephew, was bending over her solicitously. I took no notice
of him even though he had elegant manners, a mischievous
cowlick, wistful eyes, a Dennis Morgan chin, and a pin which
testified that he belonged to what we girls called our "brother
college." I showed him that he absolutely did not exist for me,
especially when I caught him looking in our direction.

I always feel guilty of sacrilege everytime I think of it,
but there was something grimly ludicrous about my uncle's
funeral; there were the two women, each taking possession of
her portion of the chapel just as though stakes had been laid,
seemingly unmindful of each other, yet revealing by this studied
disregard that each was very much aware of the other. As
though to give balance to the scene, the young man stood his
full height near the women to offset the collective bulk of Aunt
Sophia and myself, although I was merely a disproportionate
shadow behind her.

The friends of the poet began to come. They paused a
long time at the door, surveying the scene before they marched
self-consciously towards the casket. Another pause there, and
then they wrenched themselves from the spot and moved—no,
slithered—either towards my aunt or towards the woman. The
choice must have been difficult when they knew both. The women
almost invariably came to talk to my aunt whereas most of
the men turned to the woman at the left. I recognized some
important Malacañang men and some writers from seeing
their pictures in the papers. Later in the morning, a herd of
black-clad women, the sisters and cousins of the poet, swept into
the chapel and came directly to where my aunt sat. They had
the same deep eye-sockets and hollow cheek-bones which had
lent a sensitive expression to the poet's face but which on them
suggested TB. The air became dense with the sickly-sweet
smell of many flowers clashing and I went to get a breath
of air. As I glanced back, I had a crazy surrealist impression
of mouths opening and closing into Aunt Sophia's ear, and eyes
darting toward the woman at the left. Uncle's clan certainly
made short work on my aunt for when I returned, she was
sobbing. As though to comfort her, one of the women said,
in a whisper which I heard from the door, that the President
himself was expected to come in the afternoon.

Towards lunchtime, it became obvious that neither my aunt nor the woman wished to leave ahead of the other. I could appreciate my aunt's *delicadeza* in this matter but then I got hungry and therefore grew resourceful: I called a taxi and told her it was at the door with the meter on. Aunt Sophia's unwillingness lasted as long as forty centavos.

We made up for leaving ahead of the woman by getting back to the chapel early. For a long time she did not come and when Uncle's kinswomen arrived, I thought their faces showed some disappointment at finding the left side of the chapel empty. Aunt Sophia, on the other hand, looked relieved. But at about three, the woman arrived and I perceived at once that there was a difference in her appearance. She wore the same black dress but her thick hair was now carefully swept into a regal coil; her skin was glowing; her eyes, which had been striking enough, looked even larger. The eyebrows of the women around me started working and finally, the scrawniest of the poet's relations whispered to the others and slowly, together, they closed in on the woman.

I went over to sit with my aunt who was gazing not so steadily at nothing in particular.

At first the women spoke in whispers, and then the voices rose a trifle. Still, everybody was polite. There was more talking back and forth, and suddenly the conversation wasn't polite anymore. The only good thing about it was that now I could hear everything distinctly.

"So you want to put me in a corner, do you? You think perhaps you can bully me out of here!" the woman said.

"Shh! Please don't create a scene," the poet's sisters said, going one pitch higher.

"It's you who are creating a scene. Didn't you come here purposely to start one?"

"We're only trying to make you see reason.... If you think of the dead at all...."

"Let's see who has the reason. I understand that you want me to leave, isn't that it? Now that he is dead and can not speak for me you think I should quietly hide in a corner?" The woman's voice was now pitched up for the benefit of the whole chapel. "Let me ask you. During the war when the poet was hard up do you suppose I deserted him? Whose jewels do you think were sold when he did not make money....When he was

ill, who was it who stayed at his side....Who took care of
him during all those months...and who peddled his books
and poems to the publishers so that he could pay for the hospital and doctor's bills? Did any of you come to him then?
Let me ask you that! Now that he is dead you want me to leave
his side so that you and that *vieja* can have the honors and have
your picture taken with the President. That's what you want,
isn't it...to pose with the President...!"

"*Por Dios!* Make her stop it—somebody stop her mouth!"
cried Aunt Sophia, her eyes going up to heaven.

"Now *you* listen, you scandalous woman," one of the clan
said, taking it up for Aunt Sophia. "We don't care for the
honors—we don't want it for ourselves. But we want the poet
to be honored in death...to have a decent and respectable
funeral without scandal...and the least you can do is to leave
him in peace as he lies there..."

"Yes," the scrawny one said. "You've created enough
scandal for him in life—that's why we couldn't go to him when
he was sick...because you were there, you—you shameless
bitch—"

The woman's face went livid with shock and rage. She
stood wordless while her young protector, his eyes blazing,
came between her and the poet's kinswomen. Her face began
to twitch. And then the sobs came. Big noisy sobs that shook
her body and spilled the tears down her carefully made-up face.
Fitfully, desperately, she tugged at her eyes and nose with her
widow's veil. The young man took hold of her shoulders gently
to lead her away, but she shook free; and in a few quick steps
she was there before the casket, looking down upon that infinitely sad smile on Uncle's face. It may have been a second
that she stood there, but it seemed like a long time.

"All right," she blurted, turning about. "All right. You can
have him—*all that's left of him!*"

At that moment before she fled, I saw what I had waited
to see. The mascara had indeed run down her cheeks. But somehow it wasn't funny at all.

Sands and Coral
March 1949

TENDERNESS

T. D. AGCAOILI

Your son is guerriria, you know *ka?* Your son is bad man, so you are bad man also, no?

I am a good man, said the old man. I have never harmed anyone in my life.

Yes, but your son is guerriria; therefore you are bad man, the Jap insisted.

I...

The Jap slapped his pale wrinkled face. The old man wept suddenly like a child. He wept in convulsive sobs. He clutched at his bony breast and beat his head with his knuckles.

Crazy, said the Jap. Let him beat his head. He is crazy.

Then he began to roar with laughter. Crazy old man, he roared. The old man looked at his torturer with tears in his eyes.

I don't know where my son is, he said. I don't know where he went. This is God's truth!

Sinungareng!

He was thrown back into the cell. Later the Japanese caught the boy and threw him in with his father. He was a lad of about fifteen. His eyes were young and bewildered but dark with impotent fury. He was tall and bony like his father. His hair was long and disheveled.

When the door was thrown open, a sharp blade of light from the lone bulb in the main office cut into the dark interior of the cell, but for a moment the old man stood trembling over the crouched figure of the boy. Only when the Jap sentry kicked the boy farther into the cell did the old man recognize him.

My son, he cried.

The boy looked up, and when he saw it was his father, he stood up and put his long arms about the old man wordlessly. The father remained trembling in the arms of the boy.

Yes, son, he said. They threw me into this dark room when they could not make me talk. They wanted to find out about you.

The first night was a night of terror for the boy. The old man could not sleep. The mosquitoes were hungry and the boy paced back and forth inside the cell, beating his fist against the darkness and cursing lustily to himself. Once he stood before his father's huddled form and listened to find out if he was asleep.

You must try to sleep, son, the old man said. You lie down beside me and try to sleep.

The boy obeyed. Do you think they will kill us, father?

Call the name of God, the old man said.

The boy was silent for a moment calling the name of God in his heart. Then suddenly he sprang up and walked back and forth in the darkness again. Back and forth, back and forth into the deepening night. And then it was morning. The two prisoners heard the roosters crowing in the nearby yard and the Jap sentry clearing his throat.

About midnight the following day the door flew open and the sentry pushed somebody into the cell. It was dark, and the old man and his son, who were sleeping in a corner, woke up with a start but they could not see who it was. Then, suddenly, the darkness was shattered like a thin sheet of glass by the shrill cursing of a woman's voice.

The sentry was chattering in unprintable Nippongo with another soldier outside the cell. Then they laughed idiotically. The woman rattled the iron bars and kicked the wooden door.

Stop that noise, the Jap sentry shouted, or I shoot you.

The woman spat at his face and cursed him mightily.

What you say? the sentry addressed the aperture.

Why did you put me inside this dark cell? the woman cried.

Donto-to know, said the sentry. Maybe you also guerriria.

The woman began to curse anew. She was still cursing when the old man approached from behind. The woman shrieked in fright at the touch of the man's cold and bony hands.

Who are you? she challenged.

I am an old man, said the voice. I have been here more than a week now. There is another one—he is my son. Son, he called, come here.

For a few days the three prisoners were left to themselves unmolested. Twice or sometimes three times a day they were fed with limited rations which consisted of rice gruel and dried fish. They were given a jar of water which they were told to use sparingly. A Japanese fetched the water from a water-pump two blocks away. Neither the boy nor the old man was allowed to go out and do any work except to empty the slop-pail. This was done by the old man under heavy guard. The boy was considered dangerous, and he was never allowed to leave the cell.

The woman told them that she was the wife of an underground leader who had been beheaded by the Japs at the river near the Campo Santo. Her name was Marcela. In the darkness of the cell they never saw completely what the woman looked like. They saw her long dark hair and the general outline of her body. It was never bright inside the cell. Whatever faint light that came from the little, aperture in the wall merely served to accentuate the darkness.

And you? asked the woman of the boy. Why are you here? You seem to be very young.

First, the boy said, it was my father. They arrested him because he would not tell them where I was. I am a guerrilla, he whispered. I killed two Japanese.

You killed two Japanese? the woman said.

Yes, said the boy. With a knife. They raped my sister. I was hiding under the house when they came. I knifed them when they were coming down the house. I knifed them in the dark and then I fled. My sister was later killed by the Japs when she refused to tell them where I went. They spared my father because he is old. I guess they are going to kill me.

You are young, said the woman.

I am almost sixteen now, said the boy. Then suddenly he was weeping.

Don't mind me, he said. I am tough, but whenever I think of my fate I cry. I can't understand this war. Why did they ever come here? We don't like them!

Hush, said the woman. How do you know they are going to kill you?

I know. I feel it. I killed two of their men, didn't I?

Yes, but maybe they will spare you.

The bastards will surely kill me, said the boy. I don't want to die so young. I never did anything wrong in my life. Is it wrong to kill the beasts who—I loved my sister!

The old man, who was dozing in a corner, heard the boy weeping and he stood up to console him. His bony back bumped against the wobbly stand and the jar of water broke with a crash on the tiled flooring of the vault.

That was the end of their water supply. For many days the three prisoners were given food to eat but not a drop of water to drink. The old man was delirious after the second day. On the third day he died. The woman informed the sentry.

Patay-do! he exclaimed. And then he began to laugh his loud idiotic laughter. Aha-hah-hah, shaking his head. Okay-*ka*, he added, there is nothing more to do but bury him.

The old man was buried that night in the backyard. The boy was not allowed to attend the burial.

And now the two were left alone in the darkness with the mosquitoes and the silence. The woman slept in one corner and the boy in another. Most of the time they would sit silently in the cell thinking their own dark thoughts. Then one day the boy came to where the woman was seated and touched her in the dark.

I am going to die, he said. I know I am going to die.

Don't say that, the woman said. It makes me want to weep.

But I know I am going to die, he insisted. I...I have been thinking of many things. But this thing I am going to tell you came to me just now. It was...it was like a—how shall I say it?—like a light in this darkness. I don't know how to say it but I feel it deeply.

What is it? the woman said.

You know...I have been thinking...before I die, I wonder if you would let me...touch...you?

What do you mean? the woman said.

I want to feel your body, said the boy.

You don't know what you are talking about, said the woman.

But I know, said the boy. I want to touch you. I want to know how it is to feel a woman's body.

You are crazy, said the woman.

I am not, said the boy. I know I am not. This thing came to me just now, as I said. I am not crazy. May I touch you now, Marcela?

But what good will that do to you? asked the woman.

I don't know, said the boy. I just want to feel you with my hands. I just want to be assured that I am not alone. I am afraid in this darkness. No, no, it is not that! I am not afraid. It is just that I want to feel you, that's all. And...and... I have never in my life, he said, suddenly lowering his voice shyly. I have never, Marcela!

This boy, said the woman.

It came to me like a light, the boy continued. Suddenly I felt that if I could touch you I would become a man. I want to be a man before they kill me. Don't you see? I feel that if I touch you.... So Marcela, please?

Marcela began to weep. The boy put his arms around her shaking shoulders and his hands began to feel her body. And Marcela wept silently in the darkness. She wept and then she felt limp.

The woman did not respond. She lay down quietly. The boy touched her again and this time the woman's body felt soft and warm. And she was not weeping any more. She put out her arms in the darkness and pulled the boy tenderly to her side.

Then the door flew open and the sentry dragged him out of the cell.

They will kill me now, the boy said.

But they did not kill him. They questioned him. They tortured him. But they did not kill him. They threw him back into the cell with the woman. For a long time he lay moaning in the darkness. The woman ran her fingers through his hair and touched the welts all over his body with tender hands.

Don't say anything more about dying, the woman said one day.

But they are going to kill me, the boy said. I know they are only waiting for me to talk. They can't make me talk.

They are not going to kill you, said the woman with vehemence. But she did not feel any conviction.

They can kill me now, the boy said. I don't care. It was not like this before. But now they can kill me.

In the silence the boy felt that the woman was weeping. You are weeping, he said. Why are you weeping?

I have made you happy, said the woman. I know I have, and now I am weeping for you.

The boy was silent, thinking. And then he said: Do you think that when I die it will mean the end of me?

Don't feel that way, said the woman. She touched the boy tenderly in the darkness. And don't forget, if they kill you, you can't die completely. There will be that which you have given me. Do you understand? I was married, the woman continued. I had one child. He died when the war broke out. Now I will have this again which is yours and you will not die even if they kill you.

You mean, said the boy...you mean that you...and I....

Then the door flew open and the sentry dragged the woman out of the cell.

Towards midnight they returned the woman to the cell. The boy was waiting for her.

What happened? he asked. You were a long time away. Did they feed you?

Yes, said the woman.

I can smell that, the boy said. But he was not angry. And then, after a while, he asked, with sudden brusqueness: Did they—?

No, said the woman. But her body tensed against his angry grip. No!

The boy put his arms about her. Then he drew back. They did, he cried. They did! I smell it!

Yes, said the woman sobbing. Three of them. They took turns.

God, the boy cried. God!

He hit his fists against the walls.

The woman came to the boy in the darkness and she put her arms tenderly around his sobbing body.

This Week
February 6, 1949

GATE

KERIMA POLOTAN

At the corner where she had alighted, she looked at the house to see her cousins by the window smiling as they watched her. Then when she reached the door, she stood there and said, I am going to a dance tonight. Her cousins smiled again and she knew this time what it was they thought: that she had never gone to a party in her life. What had happened now?

She sailed lightly into the house, into her room, into the corner of her room where her bed stood. She looked at the bed—the spread which lay awry with the sleeping gown she had forgotten to fold neatly in the usual hurry of morning. She sat on the edge of the bed while her feet explored the floor for her slippers. She started to undress. The warm slightly nauseating smell of other people's sweat mingling with her own, the suffocating odor of cigarettes, the dust of city streets—thick as a palpable film—all these the fabric of her dress had caught and as she wriggled out of it, she inhaled the smell full in the nose and swiftly, like a sudden blow, her stomach contracted and threatened to misbehave.

They chatted gaily through supper, her three cousins and she. Every once in a while, she would feel Ester's look alight on her and stay there for sometime. When this happened, she would turn full towards Ester, a smile hovering on her lips for she knew what it was Ester wished to ask and she—she would not say, she would not tell them. Let them guess, she said, let them guess.

At seven, she was dressed. Discreetly, they had left her alone towards the end of her preparation and they were somewhere in the house. Where she sat inside the room, their laughter came clearly to her interspersed with brief silences that were not really silences for, in her mind's eye, she could see the girls, wherever it was in the house they were gathered, sitting back and thinking their thoughts about her and then leaning forward to look at each other and compare those thoughts.

She had gone through a similar waiting once, fifteen years ago when she was nine—not for an escort to take her to a dance but for an aging teacher who sold hen's eggs in his house that stood on the fringes of a high school campus. It was a lonely distance to the place and since she went there only on Sundays when school was closed and people were in church, she usually arrived to find hardly any life stirring. At first, the wide unmoving silence had frightened her but she came to look forward to those mornings—it was some rare sort of joy for her to be there at last, alone in all that green space, walking over the newly wet grass. Once in a while something would tell her to look down—when she did, it was to cry out happily at sight of a dew sitting wholly and perfectly on the nail of her big toe. Then came the fun of trying to bear the drop still unhurt all the way to the hut. Sometimes, it slipped off heartbreakingly a few feet away from her destination. But whether or not it did, she sat on fascinated by the toe which had almost borne a perfect dewdrop from the campus to the hut.

The town market was farther away and prices there were high but this campus where the eggs were sold at two for five was but five minutes from their own house. When the old man was feeling generous, he let her have two free and she kept the extra nickel.

Often she had to wait long for the teacher in a makeshift classroom just beyond the fruit trellises that rose in the earth to the back of the house. When there were high school boys cleaning their plots, then she employed her wait watching their hoes rise in the air and then cut into the earth with a muffled thud. She enjoyed that; the hoes rose and fell, clods flew about the sharp glint of steel in the sunlight. It was like a game, following the steel and the short-lived journey of the clods. Finally, the old man came, there would be the eggs wrapped in soft cloth, the money given over, a final look at the hoes and Sunday morning was ended for her.

One day, she had waited as usual and there had been only the teacher's eighteen-year-old son busy among the plots. She had watched and watched till the sun hurt her eyes and she had lain her tired head on the arm of her seat and gone quickly

to sleep. She had not long lost consciousness when from nowhere, two arms roused her, held her tightly by the shoulders
and turned her fiercely around. There was a face and a mouth
that kissed and kissed and kissed and a pair of arms that went
around her body, encircling it and drawing it violently to his.
Blindly, she fought back, baring her teeth and seeking to sink
it somewhere. When they caught the feel of flesh she was sure
was not hers, she sunk her teeth, so like the hoe into the
ground, and bit down with all her terrified strength, crying
tearlessly all the while. Briefly, it was as though she drowned
—then sudden freedom: the arms were gone, the trembling
male body, too, was gone. And unseeing she had stumbled from
the place to a footpath that led to a river beside the school.
There the tears had come, profuse at first and with much
sobbing, but in the end she was lying on the sand, sleeping
fitfully....

   She had left the river when the sun was high in the sky.
There were questions to answer afterwards at home: the eggs
she had not brought with her, the money she had lost, her
swollen eyes, her dress dirty with river water and river sand
and the many morning hours she had stayed away.

   Account, account, her mother had screamed at her, striking
her palm impatiently, with her own hand. Where, Why?

   But no voice had come—nor tears, for once more she
stood alone in the hut near the grooves and the plots, fighting
desperately those arms that held her tightly and the smell,
the engulfing urgency of a male body so near, so very chokingly
near her....

   He's here, Ester said coming upon her in the room.

   She walked to the living room and saw Tony standing in
the porch, the living room light barely reaching him. She put
her head out of the door and said, Come in now and sit down.
I shan't be long.

   There was the scuffing of shoes on doormat, the sound of
steps on the floor. Tony took the seat by the door and said to
her, Don't hurry, please.

   During those last minutes, in hurried search for bag and
handkerchief, she recalled how Tony had come to the office
that afternoon. They had talked for a few minutes when he
said casually—as though the thought had come to him only

then—Would you care to go to a dance with me tonight?
Would you?

Would she? She had smiled then, a crooked ridiculous smile
to hide her embarrassment. In one of those illogical workings
of her mind, she remembered having once been witness to a
scene such as this. There was another boy, another girl, and
she for audience. Would you care to go to a dance with me?
the boy had asked the girl. Why, yes, the girl had replied
with a saucy toss of her head and the answer had carried a
particular promise of gaiety and fun. She had stood by watching
the play, noting the tilt to the girl's head, the naughty look
in her eyes that meant many things, the studied helpless
gesture: I have nothing to wear but I shall go anyway, flutter
of lashes, because you ask. Seven, the boy, fairly jumping out
of his shoes, had asked again. Ooooh, seven, or eight p'r'aps?
And when the boy left, her friend looked at her, smirking in
triumph. That, she said with a smart snap of her fingers, is
how one does it!

How had Tony gone about it now? He had leaned slightly
forward across her desk, a very earnest, a very young man,
asking her that question: Would you, would you? She had
uttered nothing but had nodded her head instead and then
said good-bye with bewildering suddenness.

There had been other boys before, other dances, of course,
but to all of them she had always said no with strange unusual
abruptness for it seemed to her that when they asked her that
question they leered secretly and their hands fumbled for the
knob to the door she kept shut firmly inside her. It became
some joke in school to see who could take her to a dance.
Angered and frightened, she had struck back first with words,
then with silence, finally with hauteur. Later on, when those
years in school saw her graduated into the working world
where she now moved among men who were brash and quiet,
dignified and vulgar, intelligent and stupid, but who shed all
these differences when they began talking about women in
words finely edged with indelicacy, she had acquired a bantering attitude to hide the panic within her. The men said, smacking loudly: she was easy, two cocktails afterwards I had her
and brother, can she love! The women, coiffed, well-polished,

fragrant-bodied: last night was something even the devil can't make him forget—he'll crawl back for more, watch my smoke, huh!

Hearing all these a few steps away where she had pretended to bury her head in work, her panic grew—for suddenly in that world she had come upon, where the bright whipping quip was held at a premium, it seemed as though they were forever at ugly war, these men and women she knew, forever stalking each other. When they came together in what they called was the climax of the hunt, it was in unsaid derision for the other and to gloss over the experience with not a little touch of mockery during lunch hours, between sandwich bites. The tale grew more racy as the amused laughter mounted and the air conditioning unit in the corner whirred and came to life. No one ever noticed her groping her way from the group to the busy intersection downstairs where she had taken a jeep straight for home. And in the dampness of her little room, she had fallen onto her bed, reached for her pillow and beat it in inexplicable fury. So very like that time by the beach after those arms had gone around her body, so very like that morning in the fear, the terrible fear, the shock, the feeling of lostness and end and death.

You're taking too long, Ester said through the door.

Was I too long? she asked Tony who had shifted at the sound of her approach.

He smiled, unanswering of her query.

They had not reached the landing when Ester called, It is cold and you will need this.

In the shadow of the porch she saw her cousin holding out her wrap. She climbed slowly back for it—and there in the dark, the old terrifying dismay swept over her again and she trembled quietly.

I—I don't think I can go, she whispered lamely to Ester.

Silence. Then: Put this on, now. Then: Why?

You know, oh you know, and with these words, she entered the house again, half-running into the sanctuary of her room.

When she had rested a while she tiptoed to a window. Tony still waited by the gate—and to his waiting was such patience as could outlast even eternity.

How now, how?

You must go this time, Ester said softly. You must go now.

Oh, Ester, she moaned.

I went down for you, Ester continued. He said you mustn't hurry. He said you don't even have to go—if you wish you can stay and you two talk.

Somewhere in the neighborhood, a radio was flicked open and a record ground out a forever ever song.

Ester said, but I want you to go this time. Now, with Tony.

She looked out again. He hadn't moved at all, he hadn't moved from the gate, not towards the house nor away from it.

Low and grieving, she said, I cannot go, Ester. I can not go.

She heard Ester walk through the living room down the steps into the garden. Through the window, she saw Tony hesitate, then move slowly to go.

Tony, oh Tony, she called in her heart. Then she closed the window and turned into the friendly safety of her unlighted room.

Literary Apprentice
March 1949

PATTERN

Carmen Guerrero Nakpil

It had all happened before.

"And this is Miss Sarte, Mr. Bruno." Then, as she turned, she met that pleasantly startled, frankly admiring look that a minute later would become probing and speculative; that swift interested smile; finally the conventional How-do-you-do in a voice deliberately caressing.

And she, how many times had she played this part before; the side glance that was supposed to be intriguing; the head tilted ironically; the long soft hand with its glittering rings stretched in warm, indifferent friendliness; the careless hello tossed casually but confidently like a depth charge at a doomed submarine.

She wondered if this one would straighten his tie to ease his Adam's apple, or offer her a cigaret instead. Um, she thought, a bit of poise and a little maturity, for he was holding out a thin silver cigaret case. Now, as she raised her head and blew out the smoke and said, "Thank you, sir"—Now, what do you suppose he will say?

"May I get you another drink?" was what he said. Her highball did look stale, but men always said that anyway at cocktail parties. And what could a girl do but humor the poor clumsy dears. "Yes, please. A very small one with lots of ice." There, that would take care of Bruno for the next few minutes.

She turned to Molo who had introduced Bruno and he was still watching her. "I never fail to enjoy the impact you make on them, Esmeralda. It's amazing. Even with a blind man you wouldn't fail."

She smiled indulgently at him. "You were one of the worst ones yourself, remember? So, don't laugh now."

He tapped his upper lip with a mocking finger. "Oh, I don't know. I got over you rather indecently soon. But I was just thinking, if they wore asbestos suits, perhaps they wouldn't catch fire so easily. Of course, it would help a lot more if you wore the suit, or even, a nice bulky Mother Hubbard."

She laughed and said with exaggerated innocence, "Do you suppose it could be my large, brown eyes, Molo? They always tell me I have nice eyes."

While he was choking over his drink, Bruno came back with two new highballs. She chose the more harmless-looking of the two and smiled her thanks. Molo walked away, still spluttering and coughing.

"Would you care to try that tango?" Bruno said as if he didn't much mind whether she did or not. Hmm—the familiar escape into perfunctoriness. Or perhaps, it only meant that he was a better dancer than he was a talker. Anyway, she didn't like the idea of dancing at cocktail parties.

"It seems so silly to get so nicely settled with fresh cigarets and drinks and then to go and leave them all for a dance. Don't you think?" she said.

"All right, we won't dance then." They were always very tractable and willing to please in the beginning. "Let's find some corner where we can sit and talk. Cocktail parties are so impersonal and I," he smiled the required amount of flippancy, "I am anxious to get personal."

"What about the bar out there? It's so small and so crowded it couldn't help bringing us together." I'm getting so I can say this sort of thing in my sleep, she thought.

His hand under her elbow was neither too tense nor too relaxed, nor too warm nor too unimpressed. Just coming along nicely. They crossed the large smoke-filled noisy room and emerged into the garden where a circular bar had been built around a rubber tree. But people were deep around it. She was ready to sail in regardless, knowing that there would always be a stool for her, and a lot of handshakes and a lot of friends. But Bruno held her back.

"Look, let's take that garden seat instead. Less competition there."

"What's the matter? Don't you like free enterprise?" she asked.

"I'm a totalitarian, where my women are concerned. All or nothing." For one who had wanted to tango so badly a few moments ago, he was really unreasonably articulate. She told him so, and he found it very funny.

They sat and she noticed that his arm was resting nonchalantly on the top of the bench, without, however, so much as touching her bare shoulders. Smooth and unobstrusive. His tone when he spoke was as blank and non-committal as a reporter's.

"Who are you?" he said, looking into her eyes.

"I am a Lost Cause," she said, relishing the effect on him.

"Good. I will be the Effect That Is Very Much Here. A lost cause, huh. I'm a crusader myself, you know, I like to fight against great odds."

"That won't be necessary."

"Tell me something else. How do you manage to look like that?" Ah, he was going to try his hand at compliments.

"It's really a tough job, but I'll tell you if you promise not to tell anyone," she said with a comic air of secrecy. "I spend my mornings soaking in a mudhole, just like every female buffalo who is careful of her looks."

He laughed disproportionately. Like all the others.

"Do you always feel as bored as you look?"

"Say, I don't remember telling you I was giving a press conference this evening?" feigning indignation at his question. "But if you want to know. Yes, I am bored."

"Whose fault?" he asked pointedly.

"Mine, I guess. No initiative at all," she said.

I wouldn't be if people, especially men had some originality left. They all follow the same dreary pattern in their drearily identical advances and then expect a girl to find them each so refreshingly irresistible. Really, it is one thing to offer a girl a compliment or a proposal and leave it to her to pass judgment on it, and another thing to expect her to take it on its full face value everytime. For example, I could tell you now, Bruno, that in a few minutes you will start telling me how different you are from other men, that women do not interest you as women but as human beings, how you don't like to go to Jimmy's and pay a girl to be nice to you, how you'd rather win (sometimes the word is woo or subdue) a girl who is fine and spirited, someone like, say, me. Then you will start a long and involved pseudo-intelligent discussion of sex. Oh, nothing coarse or vulgar, of course. Only the sort of dispassionate, academic exchange of views we "moderns" have learned to indulge in. Of course. I shall act dumb about your motives. I will be as clinical as you. But, why do men think that talking about it entitles them to monkeying with it? Then you will say, ever so negligently, or ever so ardently, or ever so amorously, "May I take you home?" And you wonder why I am bored.

The bantering half-serious talk went on.

"What do you do?"

"For a living or for fun?"

"Both."

"For a living I design and decorate homes. I'm a lady architect, or hadn't you heard? For fun, judging from what some people say, I wreck homes. And you?"

They probed each other playfully.

"What do you think of happiness?"

"I think it's overestimated. It's really not that important, you know." And, "Do you like men who like you?"

"Only if they like me as I am."

"Meaning...."

They told each other great untruths and little truths about each other.

"You know, I've never really been in love."

"Lack of inclination?"

"Merely lack of opportunity, I think."

Or again, "I really should have been a writer. I am quite a liar."

"Don't say liar. Say prevaricator. Because you lie in your heart but not with your tongue."

It went on and on.

"Did you come with anyone in particular?" Bruno asked at last. Well, here it comes, she thought. "Forgive me for asking, but one never knows at cocktail parties. I don't want to tread on anyone's toes."

"Always the gentleman. I came with a girl friend. So that makes me public domain, doesnt it?"

"Thank God for that."

"I'm afraid it's all my doing, though. I like to go stag."

"What about having dinner with me? We'll bring your friend of course, although I haven't met her yet."

"She's somewhere around, drinking creme de menthe. Someone told her it was an aphrodisiac and she's drunk nothing else since." They laughed again.

"I'll ask Arturo for her. We could go somewhere later to dance."

"Oh, I don't think so. This party won't be over for hours yet, and besides I never have any dinner, anyway."

"How about just going for a drive, then, we'll see what turns up. It's still early." Instead of looking at his watch, he moistened with his tongue the tip of his forefinger and held it up in a characteristic gesture of a hick weatherman. It was rather cute but she had the feeling that he'd done it a thousand times before, and under similar circumstances. She was also uncomfortably aware that she had gone all over this with other men. It was like a play that had been rehearsed too long and played too often.

But Molo was walking towards them. He was followed by a very tall, very young, young man with a mustache.

"Oh, there you are. Rodolfo here says life has become impossible for him ever since he saw you dancing at the Riviera the other evening. What was she wearing?" he turned to the young man. "Oh, yes, you were wearing one of these floor-length bathing suits you affect. Do make life possible for him again, will you?" Molo was bending over her hand with a wicked grin.

The young man just stood there fingering his tie. Oh, God, the tie-tugger type.

But Bruno was saying urgently at her side. "Where can I call you? Will you see me sometime this week?"

Even as she extended the scarlet-tipped hand to the young man with a mustache, she told Bruno, "You can give me a ring. I'm in the book."

Half an hour later, the young man, after three drinks and twenty tugs at his tie, was saying, "May I take you home, Miss Sarte?"

Two hours later she was turning the key in her door and thinking:

Tomorrow, unless she was mistaken, there would be flowers. Long-stemmed cut flowers from Bruno. Large engraved card. Studiedly careless hand. "To the lost cause I found last night" or "I simply had to do this." Sweet pink roses from the mustache. She could bet to a word what the card on that would say, "To Miss Sarte, who deserves flowers like no woman ever did."

In the afternoon, her phone would ring. "There's a new restaurant opening at the Boulevard tomorrow night. If you are free, we might give it a try..."

The first date. A second or third. Then whoever it was would try to hold her hand, perhaps kiss her on the cheek. The inevitable three words (they would be four if he said, darling) would be proffered as legal tender for a longer kiss. Then a false proposal or a genuine proposition. And so it would go. Even love had become standardized, mass-produced, de-personalized. And there was never anyone real. Never anyone one could cling to and be comforted. Only the eternal hedging and parrying and distrusting.

Suddenly, Esmeralda felt a hundred years old.

Sunday Times Magazine
April 24, 1949

BROWN GIRL

DELFIN FRESNOSA

The whole countryside lay prostrate in the heat of summer. Dust lay thick on the road and the slightest disturbance, even the merest breath of wind, was enough to raise it, creating something like a fog in the middle of the day. The ditches alongside the road were dried up and cracked. But it was not merely the heat of the sun and the dust that seemed to make all the countryside so abhorrent. There was something besides, and more terrifying because it chose to strike primarily at the spirit. This was the utter desolation of the landscape.

Usually at that time of the year there would be laughter and gaiety especially among the younger folk because it was the season of harvest. There would be many people out in the fields harvesting the ripe grain. And in the villages along the way there would be much noise and activity because once more they were assured of ample food for the months ahead.

But the villages had been emptied of their people. Nor could a single animal be seen, never a cat or a dog or even a chick. The houses looked abandoned and many were already partly rotted. Also some had been burned to the ground. And out in the fields only sere and stubby grasses grew. It seemed that even the birds had left to seek more congenial haunts.

But the place was not merely desolate. Danger lurked everywhere, the danger of sudden death, of a mysterious and complete disappearance. That was why people had come to shun the place, avoiding it as it were the abode of devils.

Thus it was exceedingly strange when one afternoon a woman could be seen trudging along the lonely stretches of the road. She was alone. She moved very slowly, her feet almost dragging in the dust of the road, as if she were very, very tired. She had a small branch which she had plucked from a tree to protect her from the sun, but the leaves were already

wilted. At best it was a useless shield against the rays of the
sun for the sun still roasted her bare arms and legs and face.

In another hand she carried a small bundle wrapped in a
piece of dirty flour sack. This contained her clothes, some
canned food, a few small toys and various odds and ends. Thus
she looked like a beggar or a refugee with all her worldly
belongings contained in a small bundle.

From all appearances she had come a long, long way. Her
unshod feet were caked with dust and blistered. Her clothes
were tattered and dusty and stained with sweat.

She was with child. This, together with the ache and
tiredness of her whole body, was what made her progress so
slow and laborious. She looked like an ant, a mere speck
crawling along the road in the vast expanse of the countryside.

Indeed she had been traveling steadily a good many weeks
already. There were times when she had been able to beg a
free ride in some trucks, but the greater part of the way she
had to cover on foot. She had passed through many towns
that teemed with people and through some villages that were
still populated, but mostly her way had lain in vast expanses
of desolate and unpopulated countryside.

Sometimes perhaps she wondered where all the people had
gone. Could they all have gone to live in the towns? Or had
they all died in some mysterious sort of way?

The fact itself of her being there, trudging alone and in
the intense heat of the day was enough for one to doubt her
sanity. For there had been no lack of well-meaning people to
tell her that it was sure death to go out there. They pointed
out that no one dared go out there alone any more, that even
the most stout-hearted would venture to make the sally only
with many others and heavily armed. But she had dared to go
alone and apparently unmindful of any danger that might be
lurking behind the tall grasses and clumps of trees and bushes.

Whenever she came to a place which was inhabited she
readily became quite an object of interest. In most cases the
first ones to notice her were the children. Sometimes they
merely stared and gaped at her or played some harmless pranks
on her. But there were also some cruel ones who made her
passing through the place exceedingly miserable. The same
was true also of the grown-ups. There were those who were
cruel and suspicious and sadistic. On the other hand, there were

those who merely asked her who she was, where she came
from and where was she going.

She said that just then she was going home, to a certain
place called Puting Sapa. That was where her father and
mother lived. She had also a number of brothers and sisters.
Then she said also that she had come a long, long way. Since
the time she had left home she had stayed for quite a long
time in a place that was very big and which had many large
and tall houses.

And usually those who had never heard of Puting Sapa
told her that perhaps she ought not to try to go there, especially
at that time. They said that it was very dangerous to try to
travel from one place to another.

Then there were those who knew about Puting Sapa and
they said for her not to attempt to go there because the place
had become now a sort of no man's land. They told her that
she might be taken away, perhaps never to be heard from
afterwards.

Then in the last town she passed, there were some people
who came from Puting Sapa itself, but she could not wholly
remember who they were. They told her that no one was living
there anymore. They said that the people of Puting Sapa had
either been killed or had emigrated to safer places. She would
not be able to find there those for whom she was looking: her
parents, brothers and sisters.

But even this could not dissuade her. She had come a long
way and that town was the last before Puting Sapa. She might
as well go on. Perhaps what they said about her parents and
brothers and sisters was not all true. It could not possibly be.
She had been thinking about meeting them again, not only
for weeks and months, but for years. Now Puting Sapa was
only a matter of a few kilometers and she wished that there
were not so many questions asked of her. But those from Puting
Sapa would not let go of her so quickly.

They were greatly surprised to see her. It had been a
number of years since she had been taken away and most
people had come to think that she was already dead. But there
she was, hardly changed at all except that now she was with
child. And maybe the main reason why she wanted to be with
her old folks again was because her time was drawing near.

It was a most understandable wish and especially so considering what kind of creature she was.

There were those who knew her quite well and they said that she was an idiot. They remembered that she had been carried away by Japanese soldiers. But the Japanese had long since been driven away from the country, so the father of her child could not be one of them. They asked her if she had any husband and who was he. But they could not learn anything from her. She would only look at them blankly, her thoughts at home already in Puting Sapa.

She was finally able to slip away from the town. She had long learned how to slip in and out of towns and populated villages without getting picked up and jailed. In most cases the approaches as well as all the exits to a populated place were heavily guarded. But she had come to learn how best to elude them.

And so it was that finally she was on her way to Puting Sapa. She did not care very much how hot the afternoon sun was and how the rough stones of the road hurt her blistered feet. She was barely conscious too of the desolation that extended all around her and as far as the eye could see. Once in a while she would remember what many had told her about how dangerous it was to be out there, but there was no telling from the way she appeared whether she was afraid or not.

Later she had to leave the road for a trail, and it was greatly overgrown with weeds and grass so that it was barely discernible. But instinctively she could still follow it even though it was so many years since she had passed there. She quickened her steps, for then it was but a matter of a few more hours and once again she would be home. The afternoon was not far gone. Maybe she would be able to make Puting Sapa just after nightfall. A glimmer of brightness showed in her eyes.

Then finally she came to where she had known the village to be, but there was none there any more. There were no houses standing there any more. The place was overgrown with grass and clumps of bushes. On closer scrutiny one might see the charred and rotting remains of posts, but even these were largely hidden by rank vegetation. So that had it not been for her being a native of the place, she might have thought that there never had been any habitation there.

She did not tarry long at the site of the former village. Twilight had already fallen, but there was a promise of a moon. Insects hidden in the bushes made lonely music, but except for that, the silence was profound.

In time she reached the place and she was gratified somewhat to see that it had not been razed to the ground, but the house had fallen of its own accord, the skeleton of the roof on the ground, the walls flattened and fairly rotted. There were still some of the posts standing, but they were tilted in various directions. Grass had overrun the yard and extending to the sides and to the back of what used to be their house where once they had cultivated and planted bananas, corn, camotes, and various other vegetables, there was now only a thicket. The brook itself, whence the place took its name, was hidden by thick grass growing along its banks. One could only tell that there was a brook nearby because of its murmur.

Before she went to sleep that night, she cried a bit at first. She thought about her folks and tried to imagine what manner of fate had overtaken them. It would have been very comforting to find her mother especially now that her time was fast approaching. Her mother would have been kind and thoughtful and she would have helped her not to be afraid when the time came. But because she was very tired and also because she always found it hard to burden her mind with many thoughts, she was soon able to fall asleep. She slept on the ground, on a bed of dry leaves.

In the morning she found that it was not only the darkness of the night that had so accentuated the sinister atmosphere of the place. The light of day further revealed the starkness of the tragedy that had apparently overtaken it. But despite all the things that she saw and also those that she had heard about the place, she decided to stay there indefinitely.

And having thus made up her mind, she immediately went about to try to make something habitable. She covered a part of the skeleton of the roof with leaves, and under it she cleared the ground of weeds and grass and she placed some wood and leaves on the cleared ground to improvise à bed.

For her food, she was able to find some wild fruit in the nearby thicket and she also chanced upon some camote plants in what used to be their garden. There still were in her bundle some bits of food which she had begged in the town. And she knew that there were many plants whose roots were edible and she was prepared to subsist on them if need be.

For a little later she did not want to leave the place at all. It did not matter that there was no one there besides herself. She did not feel lonely. Sometimes to please herself, she tried to recall the days when she was still very young, when there were still her parents and her other brothers and sisters. If she tried hard enough, it seemed to her she could see them, some in the house, others in the fields, all doing their various chores. Meanwhile, she worked at clearing the surroundings with the purpose of planting some corn or camotes there. She trampled down and in some instances uprooted the thick growth that hid the brook and soon she was able to see again its clear running water.

She was home at last.

Then, one morning, a number of men who were passing by happened to catch sight of her. They stopped to investigate. They questioned her, peered into her place of refuge and even examined the contents of her bundle. They were men she had never seen before, but they spoke her dialect. They all looked emaciated and sickly and their clothes were quite ragged. All of them were armed.

One of them said, "Come along with us. Your child will be born in freedom."

"I do not understand," she said.

"There's freedom now only in the mountains."

And so she had to leave Puting Sapa once more, the home she had found again. She did not know if ever she would be able to see it again. She followed the men because they were armed and she was alone and her time was near, but where they were leading her to, she did not know.

Philippines Free Press
May 7, 1949

THE REFUGEES

DELFIN FRESNOSA

When they arrived in the town it was already night. They were among the very last to get into the town. They were very tired, listless and hungry. It seemed they could hardly drag their feet any more and perhaps would have gladly flung themselves on the side of the road and taken a long, long rest. But the girl in-charge of the two other children had an idea that they might be able to find some place where they could ask permission to cook their supper. At least she wanted to be with people coming from their own barrio. She had been to town only a very few times before, never alone by herself, but usually in the company of grown-ups. Now she was on her own and moreover with two small children in her charge. The town appeared rather terrifying and in her tiredness and distress, she could very well have cried. But the plight of her charges was even greater, although perhaps they were unaware of it and thus, instead of giving way completely to her terror and anxiety, she took a little strength and courage.

There were so many people in the town. The street they were on seemed to be one of the busiest thoroughfares of the whole town. There were shops on both sides and they were full of people. People were also on the sidewalks and even in the middle of the street when there were no cars passing by. She was quite bewildered and also terrified by so many people. There were now even more, she thought, than during the fiesta she had attended once. It was not the time of the fiesta nor was it any holiday, but the crowds seemed much bigger. This time also almost all the people she saw were dressed very poorly, some even only in underwear, many others only in dirty and ragged working clothes.

At the next branching, they left the busy thoroughfare and struck off along a quiet sidestreet. She was more than glad they had left the crowds and was now in a less-frequented small street. But now it seemed they could hardly walk another step, especially the small boy who was her companion. He had come to whimper continually and perhaps only the fear of being left behind urged him to stumble along. She herself was none too steady on her feet and many times she had to stand still for a moment because she felt a dizziness assail her.

"Please, Teria, let's stop for a while," said the boy, and without waiting for what the big girl had to say, he plumped down the bundle he was carrying and sat down on the pavement. He let out a long drawn-out sigh as his buttocks settled on the hard cement.

"Oh, all right," Teria said. She put down the little girl she had been carrying and who, for the past hour or two, had been dozing off and on. It happened that the little girl was placed near the bundle and she used it to prop her back. She settled herself without another whimper. Teria next put down a small bundle she had slung over an arm. She placed it on the cement gingerly because it contained a number of plates. Once unburdened, she felt a delicious emptiness in her arms. But her back still ached and she was footsore.

It had been a long journey from the barrio to the town, a matter of some fifteen kilometers. The worst part of it was that they had only to rely on their feet to negotiate the distance. The more fortunate had been able to ride on carts and carretelas and even if they were old and decrepit, they were thrown together with other people and household effects. Almost the whole population of the barrio was evacuating to the town. Whole families from other barrios and from the hinterlands were moving into the town. There had been an order for all people of that place to move to the town where there was comparative safety.

Teria and the two other children had packed up only the things they could carry and which they considered very necessary. These included some clothes, a few plates and some rice. The rest of their belongings, they left behind. There was much that they had left, a sow with young, chickens, a little more than a half-sack of palay, and all because there was no one to carry them. Teria was not hopeful she would still find any of them upon their return.

She had no idea how long they would have to stay in the town. There were some who said that it would just be for a couple of days, but there were others who were not very optimistic and said that their forced stay would last for a number of months. They were not entirely uninformed of the hardships and the uncertainties of evacuating to the town, for they knew what had happened to some acquaintances from other places. Most of them prepared as if they were going to stay away from their homes for a long spell. And so, it was they felt they could not be overly concerned beyond their immediate families. Teria and her two charges had mainly to shift for themselves. They found out that whatever their plight, they could not hope for much assistance, and thus on the road to town hardly any one bothered to relieve them of their burden, nor would they even wait if anybody lagged behind.

Her companions were still too young for the long trip to town. The boy who was going on eight was able to manage it and even was gallant enough to carry a small bundle which contained their clothes. But just the same he had to call for many stops along the way. The other child was a girl of three. Teria had to carry her in her arms from time to time because it was more than her heart could bear to see the child limping and stumbling along. Teria herself was only about fourteen, but the responsibilities of taking care of the two children caused her to appear like a prematurely grown-up person. She was even long before that occasion and by force of circumstances a sober-minded girl and could be largely depended upon.

She had been orphaned at an early age. Her father had never been heard from since he went to Bataan and her mother had died about the second year of the Japanese occupation. Fortunately her mother's sister took her in. The aunt needed someone in the house to help her in the lighter household chores because at the time she was going to have a baby. From then on she lived with her and although it was quite a hard life, because her aunt was poor, still it was preferable to having to live with others not of her blood.

Her aunt had borne six children, but there were only two left. Like her, they too were now orphans. Perhaps the little girl Lucia was still too young to comprehend the significance of the tragedy that had overtaken their family. But it was

quite different with the boy. He was old enough to realize
what had happened, but now there was hardly a moment for
reflection. The news that the bullet-ridden bodies of the man
and his wife had been found was soon followed by the order
that the whole village be evacuated.

On the way to town she had ample time to wonder how
it would be from now on because she was certainly going to be
both father and mother to the two children. It would be comparatively an easy matter tending them because they were well-
behaved children in the first place and they were used to the
impoverished life in the farm. But the real trouble was how
she would be able to feed them. Even if they were allowed to
return to the barrio after a couple of days, there was nothing
she could do to eke out their livelihood. Beyond this point,
however, her mind refused to go any further. And she could
only draw a little solace by saying that perhaps the future
would take care of itself.

There was the little hope also that perhaps they might
get some help from a woman in the town who happened to be
a distant relative. It was always in her house where they put
up whenever they were in town, as on fiestas, Christmas or
Lent. She thought perhaps they would be able to stay there
during the time they were in town. Or more perhaps, she might
be kind enough to help her solve the problem of what to do
with the two children. Thus it was she wanted to get there
as soon as possible and it was this thought that sustained them
and urged them on even when their feet could hardly bear them
up any more.

But after they had sat awhile on the pavement, she found
that the two children were already fast asleep. She herself
could hardly keep her eyes open. Her body ached all over and
her arms and feet seemed to have turned to lead. She thought
hazily that there was nothing else in the whole world she
wanted but just to lie down and go to sleep. But it would not do.
She prepared to go on, but first she would wake the boy up.
Of course it would be impossible to carry him too, and she
could not leave him behind either.

"Pio, Pio, wake up," she said. "Let's get going. After all
it's not so far any more." But even after she had shaken his
body vigorously a number of times, all that she could get from
him were grunts and mumbled replies. "That's the trouble with

letting you rest even for a minute. Pio, wake up. We cannot spend the whole night here."

There was nothing however she could do to wake him and finally she decided that there was no other course left but to find something in which to spend the rest of the night. She was in luck because she did not have to seek far for such a place. Just a very short distance away from where they had stopped she came upon the remains of a building. Only its concrete walls remained standing. In the enclosure formed by the walls many makeshift sheds had been put up and were occupied by refugee families. But on the outside there were none because the area gave immediately onto the pavement. This was where Teria considered spending the night. It reeked somewhat of urine and rotting garbage, but she did not care to seek for another place. She took each child by turns and deposited them by the wall. Their bundles came next. Finally, when everything was done, she too made ready to go to sleep. It did not matter at all if they did not have any supper. After all, it was not the first time any of them had to forego a meal. In the farm there were a number of times they did not have anything to eat.

The next day, after breakfasting on some bread, they started once more for the house of their relative. If the night before one could barely estimate how crowded the town was, in the daytime one saw how almost every available place was tenanted. The school buildings, the school grounds, the churchyard, the town plaza, were all occupied by refugees. There were many more who had been able to put up some sort of makeshift shelter in the vacant lots; still others, who perhaps had just newly come, made use of any available cover and even the mere shade of a tree was worth taking.

Teria again tried to see whether she could locate any one from their barrio, but she was altogether disappointed. There were so many people, men and women, young and old. They could make but very slow progress through the crowded streets.

Finally they came to the house of their distant relative. It was small and aged. Its roof and walls badly needed repairs, but more than that, it appeared dangerously near collapse. It was a wonder then that it had not fallen down, because at the time they arrived, there were many other people besides their relatives' immediate family. There were two other families at least with their full complement of children and a couple of unattached grown-ups who had just happened to stray in. Teria wondered whether they might still be able to squeeze in, but she hoped fervently that they might be allowed to stay, for really, she did not know of any other place to go to. She felt uneasy though when she noted that their coming seemed to arouse general displeasure among the many people of the house.

The woman who was their relative could not turn them away especially after she was told of what had happened to the parents of the two children. She was a kindly-disposed woman, a mother of some eight children herself, but at the time she was overburdened with worries so that the attention she could extend to the newcomers was only the most perfunctory. As days passed, it came to be given more and more begrudgingly.

In a sense it was understandable. She had two grown-up sons who had taken to the field. They were army veterans and she had at least hoped they would never again shoulder guns. She was greatly worried too about the two families that had made their house their homes, at least temporarily. One family especially gave her much to worry about for it made her feel as if she and her own children were the interlopers and they were there only on sufferance. The head of this family was said to be her husband's uncle, a well-to-do merchant of a barrio that had also been evacuated. He was a testy old man and vastly domineering. The affair had reached such a pass that she had even gotten to be somewhat ashamed of her husband's very meager earnings as a baggage carrier in the town.

For the first few days Teria was still too unsettled to take much stock of the strained relationship that existed among the people of the house. Evidently living together had frayed their nerves and had set them up against one another, but in their ill-concealed dislike for the three newcomers they were more or less united. The well-to-do merchant was the more outspoken. From the start he disliked having to sacrifice space and freedom of movement with three more comers. Then also the small boy and the little girl were so dirty most of the time and because they were always hungry, they hang about the kitchen when his own family was eating. Perhaps in his efforts to try to stifle his pity he wished they were some place else.

The children's relative could foresee what was coming, but she had grown utterly powerless in her own house. Thus it was she did not even raise her voice when her well-to-do kinsman got into a tantrum and ordered the three of them away. The small girl's constant snivelling had finally goaded him beyond endurance. It did not matter that the child whimpered because she was always hungry. He ordered Teria to betake herself and the two other children away. They left. But they did not try to seek for another house where they might be permitted to stay. Teria knew that it would be fruitless. But it did not pose a very grave problem for them any more. At least by that time they had come to know how most refugees provided shelter over their heads. That very same day she and the boy started work on a kind of shelter so that by nightfall they could sleep in it. They used sticks, discarded tin cans, cardboard, even leaves and pieces of cloth.

For Teria and her companions, the next problem was food. They went about it in a haphazard way. It was the same thing with many of the other refugees. Sometimes they were lucky enough to get something from the relief agency branch in the town or a handout from some well-to-do inhabitant. There were also times when she or the boy was lucky enough to earn a few centavos for a bit of work and they could thus buy something for their stomachs. But there were days when the only food they could get came from the refuse cans, and when the worst happened, Teria and the boy went for hours on empty bellies. For the little girl at least they always managed to have even a handful of soft-boiled rice. It was only natural that they were greatly tempted to steal sometimes.

Then finally the boy Pio was able to get some form of work which assured him at least food and some place to sleep in. There was a man who owned some carretelas and Pio was taken in as a common drudge and his work included cutting fodder for the horses, clearing the stable and helping in the house. He was given a corner in the stable to sleep in, and soon he came to smell something of the barn.

He was able to bring Teria, Lucia, his sister, some money at times, although he was not paid any salary. But he said that sometimes his boss let him have a few centavos. He also brought them scraps of food. Teria thought that he was quite doing well.

But one day the little girl got sick and died. It was a short illness of about three days and after that she just seemed to cease to struggle. She had grown so pitiably thin that somehow it seemed a wonder that she could ever stand up at all. She had become nothing but skin and bones. They felt infinitely saddened of course when she died, but in their innermost thoughts they felt somehow thankful and glad that she should be relieved so soon of all her miseries.

Teria felt quite lost for a long time after the death of the girl. When she was still alive, she had to get some food by any means because she could never bear to let the little one go hungry for a whole day. But when there was no one anymore to hustle for except herself, sometimes she just let her stomach grumble and go empty.

Then one night, a bunch of young rowdies assaulted her in her toy house. The terror and hurt she experienced was a little too much for her mind, and for several days afterwards, her dread was such that she could even have willingly embraced death. And so one morning she fled from the town. There was only one place where she thought she would find refuge and that was the farmhouse they had abandoned. It did not matter she had no idea how things would be there since they left it months ago. She was like a mortally wounded beast that seeks its home to die. She never came back.

And in the town, their toy house was quickly taken over by another refugee family. The next time that the boy Pio visited it, he found only strangers living there. He asked about Teria, but they did not know. They also denied any knowledge about whatever things Teria might have left behind.

Sunday Times Magazine
May 29, 1949

THE FIGHT

T. D. AGCAOILI

The heat of summer simmered over the flat sands as the sun rose to its zenith, dazzling and white like a mirror, and, like a mirror breaking, its pieces fell shining and brilliant on the river.

The source of the river was high up in the blue Cordilleras and never at any time of the year was the river bed dry. When the rains came in July the river would rise, noisy at its mouth like the sea, filling the whole breadth of its bed, overflowing the banks, and sweeping away the bamboo bridges. In an earlier summer such bridges were built to span the narrow but deep strip of water between the town-side of the river bank and the sandy island where the summer houses stood in which the townsmen stored their belongings against the threat of rampant summer fires.

It was still May and the heat was white. It clung to the leaves of the trees, seeped into the fine dry sand, and lay like colorless fire on the surface of the inert stones and pebbles. It clung to the bodies of the women washing clothes at the river's edge, making darker their dark hair and browner their brown bodies.

Only Nena Judalena, distinct in her red swimming suit as she sat by the river edge soaping her arms, her feet dipped in the water, was white. Young Pepe Dalloran, idling in the water nearby, his body laved shoulder-high, followed with his eyes the tractile swelling and contractions of Nena's bosom under the glistening fabric of her arms with virgin grace. She was fair, and her heavy hair, like fine skeins of spun copper, was a light brown, as was the hair of her Spanish mother, the fabulous Doña Elena, who lived in the town's biggest house and who seldom went out except to church on Sundays, riding in the only Cadillac in the province.

Pepe had seen Doña Elena on several occasions, and although he was always awed at the sight or thought of her, he hoped that Nena would never grow up to be like her mother, cold and distant. He hoped that she would have something of her father's warmth and amiability. Don Andres, whose admonitions against being called a Don by his drivers and conductors, did not keep them from addressing him deferentially as such just the same, was liked by everybody in town. His prosperity did not seem to affect his attitude toward the people among whom he had grown up from childhood as a traveling salesman's son. . . .

Nena, now through soaping her arms, threw her perfumed soap into the *batya* of Sela, her family's laundry-woman, and straightening up, eased herself into the shallow water. The sight of her white limbs as she stood erect a moment in the knee-deep water constricted Pepe's throat.

Nena was feeling the bottom of the river gingerly with her feet as she waded in his direction. When the water reached her waist, she paused and looked for the first time at him.

A smile formed on her lips.

"Hello," she said. "Is it very deep over there?"

"Not really," he said, getting up from his kneeling position.

Seeing that the water barely reached up to his chest, she continued moving toward him. When she was near enough, she extended her hand to him. It was something he had not expected and he felt deliciously thrilled as he hastily reached out with his own hand and felt the petal softness of her fingers.

"Your name is Pepe, is it not?" she said.

"Yes," he said. "Our house is next to yours."

"I know," she said. "I saw you yesterday shooting at a bird in your yard."

"I hit the bird, I saw it fall," he said. "But I could not climb over the wall into your yard to retrieve it."

"I know, those pieces of broken glass on top of the wall are sharp," she said. Suddenly, she dipped her head into the river. When she emerged, her hair clung all over her face. She combed the strands of hair away from her face with her free hand and then turned to him again. "I picked up the bird and buried it."

"You could have roasted it on a spit and eaten it. Bird meat is nice, all tender and sweet," he said, remembering how fat the bird had looked in the sights of his air rifle.

"Mama would have scolded me if I had," she said. "Besides, the idea of eating bird meat!"

He kept still, silent; but she did not seem to notice that she had hurt him. She was laughing gaily, her body slightly buoyed up by the current, but holding on to him firmly with both hands while she kicked in the water, creating a white foam around her feet.

"Teach me to swim, please teach me how to swim," she was saying. Accidentally swallowing, she frantically sprang to her feet, gasping.

He laughed at her while he gently patted her back to help her regain her breath. "There now," he said, his own hurt gone.

She laughed again. "How do you breathe while swimming?" she asked.

"I'll show you," he said, and kicked the bottom of the river while he dipped his head under the surface. For a moment, before he rose for air, he saw her young clean limbs, white through the clear water.

He came to the surface and with easy strokes struck out for a deeper part of the river where he knew there was an eddy. He had never been more conscious of his swimming, knowing he was being watched; and as he reached the fringe of the eddy he cleaved it with powerful strokes, fighting the current that swirled around his shoulders, and noting by the shoreline that he was progressing quite well. Another boy of his own age jumped into the swirling water, and a contest was tacitly on between them as they swam side by side toward the upper end of the eddy. He hoped that Nena would understand that though he was swimming against a fresher adversary, he was still winning. He was tired and his chest aching when he reached the slower water. He tried to touch bottom, but could not, and swam on easily, with his legs moving under the surface, buoying him up. His adversary, whom he now recognized as a boy who lived in the block next to his and who was called Bastian, was coming up.

"I will race you again, going downstream under water," Bastian said.

"Some other time," Pepe said, not looking at him.

Bastian followed Pepe's glance and smiled sneeringly. "Oh, you don't want the mestiza to see you beaten," he said.

"I can beat you any time," Pepe said, moving downstream to rejoin Nena.

Bastian quickly grabbed his arm and said. "Try it now."

"Let go off me," Pepe said.

"Try and get away," Bastian said.

"I don't want any trouble," Pepe said, still swimming downstream toward Nena.

"You're afraid," Bastian shouted.

And perhaps he was really afraid. Bastian had never been in his circle of neighborhood playmates or school acquaintances. The fellow played with a rougher group of boys—boys who hung around the lobby of the lone movie-house in the town, or worked sporadically as pinboys in the bowling alley near the the market, or lingered on the street corner adjacent to the Modern Hotel that offered a bold and inviting front before the garage where the buses from other provinces and from Manila stopped.... Pepe was vaguely aware of Bastian's reputation as a bully and fighter. And he was afraid.

He reached Nena's side.

"He's coming after you," she said.

He looked back but saw no sign of Bastian.

"He's swimming under water," Nena said. "I saw you beat him. He did not like it. He will make trouble. Let us go away."

Pepe quailed at the thought of fighting. Five years before, when he was only seven, he had fought another boy who had with one kick destroyed the house of sticks that he was building in his front yard. The boy was taller than he by a head; and when he complained, the boy's companion, a boy of high school age, goaded them into fighting, and before he knew it, Pepe was exchanging blows. The fight had been brief. The wind was knocked out of him, and he was soon crying in anger and helplessness as more blows landed on him and the leering face of his enemy was everywhere, taunting, elusive, hateful. He was grateful when the high-school boy finally ended the fight by telling his companion to stop. "He's beaten," the fellow had said, "his nose is bleeding."

Since then Pepe had always been afraid of getting into a fight, and he had gone far to avoid getting into one.... But now, with Nena, he was not sure of what he feared more: to flee and show his cowardice, or to fight and risk being beaten up again.

They both saw the figure of Bastian approach under water.

"Let us get out of the water," Nena said, reaching for his hand.

"No," Pepe said, pulling back his hand.

He saw Bastian circle around them, his half-naked body graceful and golden under the water.

Then Bastian came up and faced Pepe.

"You are afraid," he said, laughing. He looked at Nena, leering. Then he suddenly dipped his head into the water. Pepe could feel the heat of the sun on his own skin, and scooping up water with both his hands, he laved his sunburned neck and shoulders. His eyes followed Bastian under the water and suddenly understood, before the action was accomplished, that Bastian intended to touch Nena's legs. He promptly plunged into the water and pulled Bastian up by the hair.

They both came to the surface holding their breaths, measuring each other quietly awhile.

Then Bastian laughed. "You're afraid," he said.

"I'm not afraid," Pepe said.

Before Pepe expected it, Bastian's fist descended on his head, glancing from his ear. For a moment he was gripped with terror. Then he remembered Nena, and the initial feeling was replaced by a maddening anger. The blow was foul. All right, he would show him. From his previous swimming contest, he had seen that Bastian was not as good in the water as he. He would use this knowledge, this advantage. He feinted for Bastian's face, taking a deep breath, but dived under and, reaching with both hands for Bastian's ankles, dragged him down. Then, releasing his hold on the ankles, he put an arm around Bastian's waist. He tried to deliver a blow on the dark flat belly, but felt his fist held back by the resistant current, and even when it landed he knew the blow was without power. He rose to the surface for air and then dived under again just as Bastian, gasping, also rose for air. From behind he caught Bastian's head in the crook of his arm, his forearm pressing hard and tight against the other's chin. It was a hold he had seen in a movie. He was aware of many voices, now, including Nena's cries, mixing with the gurgling noise that Bastian made, and a wild throbbing in his own head. Pepe was no longer afraid. In fact he felt new power surge in him, tensing and coiling as he wished it in the arm that held Bastian as helpless as in a vise.

"Give up?" he asked, but when he saw the dark scowl of defiance on Bastian's brow, he became insensate, wanting more than anything else at this moment to have his power recognized. He leaned back, then abruptly leaned to one side, forcing Bastian's face into the water, holding it down, pressing the chin harder with his forearm. Bastian's legs were beating wildly. For a moment Pepe thought that he was drowning him. He lifted the face from the water, turning it toward him. He saw the blinking, bloodshot eyes, and a discharge streaming like a pale thread from his nose.

"Give up?" Pepe said. Seeing Bastian nod, he relaxed his hold and let him go. Bastian closed his eyes gratefully and then suddenly went limp and fell face down into the water. Pepe leaned forward to reach him, but other hands were ahead of him; and for the first time Pepe was aware that people had gathered around to watch the fight. He even recognized a couple of Bastian's friends, and he stared at them coldly, looking for a sign of belligerence; but he noticed none. He wondered why they had not ganged up on him, but when he saw his uncle Fred in the water with all his clothes on, he understood why. Realizing how hastily his uncle must have stepped into the river when he saw it was he who was fighting, he wanted to laugh with relief.

But all he did was say: "He started it," addressing his Uncle Fred but wanting everybody to hear.

Nena was still there, and now he turned to look at her as she said: "Yes. That fellow tried to annoy me."

Sela, the laundrywoman of Nena's family, was also there and in turn she spoke, addressing Nena: "You finish your bath now and go home. If the Señora should hear about this, oh!"

Nena laughed at her and shook her coppery hair. She reached for Pepe's hand, and in front of everybody asked him to stay with her. Pepe was embarrassed and would have walked away, but he caught his Uncle Fred's eyes which were smiling at him good-naturedly and advising him to go ahead and keep Nena company. Turning their backs on the crowd, they moved away in the water, Nena pulling him after her. Then she dipped her head under once, and in the summer sun he saw, as he, wading, planted his feet firmly in the bottom of the river so that the two would not be dragged downstream, her hair shining like burnished gold.

Pepe was in the middle of his supper, relishing the tasty warm broth of *marungay* leaves boiled with slices of roasted dried meat, when somebody called at the foot of the stairs. Rita, Pepe's younger sister, left the table to see who it was. His mother paused from eating, her eyes turned toward the door. Pepe continued eating as he listened to Rita talking with a woman whose voice he could not place.

Rita returned to the table, her eyes filled with wonder, and Pepe could not help but stop from eating in order to listen.

"Come on. Who is it?" their mother asked.

"It's...." Rita looked over her shoulder.

And Pepe, following her glance, saw who it was. His mother stood up from the table and went to meet the woman who had halted at the threshhold.

It was Doña Elena, Nena's mother.

Seeing the way she looked around the room, briefly and coldly, and then toward their repast laid out on the table, Pepe felt suddenly ashamed, as if he were being scrutinized in his nakedness. For the first time he wished that they were not living in this small old house of nipa walls and bamboo flooring; he wished....

In defiance he went back to his food, scooping up a handful of rice and stuffing it into his mouth. He picked up the bowl of *marungay* broth, and raising it to his lips, drank. He could sense the eyes of Doña Elena watching him.

He brought down the bowl resoundingly on the table. Then he cocked his ear to listen, for Doña Elena had stepped into the room and started talking.

"It's about your son."

"Pepe? Has he done anything wrong? Broken a window, perhaps? I always warn him against shooting that air-rifle his father sent him from Hawaii."

"It's not about his air rifle at all."

"Ho," Pepe heard his mother high with relief. She was now becoming more composed, Pepe knew. Very soon she would be asking Doña Elena to supper. Unless she was stopped in time, she would be telling the Spanish lady about Pepe's father who was in Hawaii, working on a sugar plantation and sending money to them monthly, without fail, for his children's schooling, especially for Pepe, who would some day become a doctor. To his mother, being a doctor was the highest profession for any man, certainly the most honorable, for was it not a doctor who had snatched him from the jaws of death at the time he was sick with pneumonia when he was only three?

Pepe stood up and faced the room.

His mother was speaking. "I always tell Pepe to play his violin while he's on summer vacation. But he prefers his rifle. I understand it's your daughter Nena who plays the piano that I hear every afternoon. She plays beautifully. When is she going back to Manila to study?"

"That's what I came here for," Doña Elena said, her words queerly accented. "I don't want to send her back to Manila until her classes open in June. But if she continues...." She hesitated a moment, looking in Pepe's direction. Then she proceeded, her voice firmer: "If your son Pepe persists in going around with her, I'll have to send her back to college as quickly as possible."

Pepe looked at his mother, trying to read her mind because he suddenly realized that it was her reaction which was important. But his mother's face did not give away whatever she might be feeling. She was almost as cool and, it seemed, as tall as Doña Elena.

"Pepe, come here," his mother said. She had forgotten even to offer a chair to Doña Elena, and anyway the latter perhaps preferred to stand. Rita was leaning against the old study table in the center of the room, listening but holding herself apart.

Pepe approached his mother fighting down a desperate urge to run out of the house. He could not yet fully understand the purpose of Doña Elena's visit, but he could sense it; and he knew it was no good, that it was an insult, and that he did not want to have any part in it.

But at the same time he knew that running off was impossible because this thing concerned him more than anybody else, more than even his mother, who was facing the situation when it should be he instead.

"Here is Pepe," his mother said, turning to him. "What have you been doing with Nena? Tell me."

"We met at the river this morning, *Nanang*. And this afternoon, when the sand became cool, we played hide-and-seek in the summer huts with the other kids."

And he smiled inwardly, remembering how ingenious Nena had been in hiding. She was also so agile that the others had had a hard time catching her and making her "it." She had enjoyed playing with them so much that on the way home, when it was getting late, she had asked him if she could not join in some of their evening games, too. And he had told her she could because he found it very difficult to deny her. She was as friendly and unassuming as her father, Don Andres.

"You did nothing else? You did not hurt her?"

"No, *Nanang*. Why should I? In fact, this morning I fought another boy who annoyed her."

"It seems that you should be grateful to my son," Pepe's mother said.

"Because your son played with my daughter, the other boy annoyed her," Doña Elena said.

Feeling betrayed, Pepe looked at the Spanish lady, searching for some expression in her face that might belie her words. But he saw only her belief in her own words.

I hate you, I hate you...he found himself thinking.

Turning to his mother, he was surprised to see a weary look come into her eyes. "So what do you want done now, Señora?" his mother asked.

"Tell your son not to play with my daughter again."

"Pepe. You hear the Señora?"

He nodded.

"He promises. You can be sure he will keep his word, Señora. And now, please go."

Pepe saw Doña Elena take a step forward, her hand raised in a conciliatory gesture toward his mother; but he did not wait to see how his mother would take it. For suddenly he could feel a hard lump choking him, and he knew that at any moment now he would either cry out in anger or burst into tears. He rushed for the door, brushing past Doña Elena's billowing lace skirt.

Coming down the stairs, he met Don Andres, who tried to hold him back smiling.

"Hey, where're you rushing to, *hijo?*"

Pepe stared at the face of Don Andres for a moment before he pulled away his hand.

"Have you seen my wife?" Don Andres asked.

Not trusting his voice, Pepe nodded toward the house. He went out into the yard, the summer night heavy with heat and trembling with stars. He walked between the rows of lime trees and *macopa,* and the fireflies darted away to let him pass. He reached the high wall separating his house from Nena's, and looking up, saw that the lights in her room were already on. He waited for some sign of her moving in the room; then the lights blurred as tears, stinging, finally came.

Sunday Times Magazine
June 5, 1949

UNSEASONABLE SUN

VICENTE RIVERA, JR.

In the near dark Lino awoke slowly without opening his
eyes. He lay luxuriously in his blankets, feeling the cold morning wind seep through to his bones. When he sat up he saw
that the stars were still in the sky, bigger somehow, closer. To
his ears came the soft whisper of surf. From where he sat he
could not see the sea, but he did not have to see it. It was in
the room with him now, just as it had been there in the night,
as it had always been with him since he came to the town.
It was his friend now, a companion in loneliness.

He had come to the town because suddenly there was nothing for him any more in the city. After the war it seemed
to him as if all at once he walked alone. Walking the streets
of the city, with the hideous hulks of wrecked buildings bending
over him, it was as if he walked among shadows, among the
ghosts of a dead time. And when he read the ad in the paper
about the need for a teacher in this town that he had never
seen, he came at once.

And the first thing that he liked was the sea. That was
why he decided to board in this house, although it was nearly
a kilometer from the schoolhouse. It was the first friend he
made, and if it did not completely protect him against loneliness, at least it shared some of itself with him. There was
little enough that he had, and he found this good; in the meantime it was something to live on.

As Lino sat by the window, the stars disappeared one by
one, almost as if a curtain were being drawn against them.
Everywhere light began to creep in, changing the face of the
world. He thrust away his blankets and bounded out of bed.
Almost as if in alarm, he snatched up a towel and rushed out
of the house. With a peculiar gait he ran down to the sea's

edge. He went straight into the surf, flinging his towel away at the last moment.

He swam, painfully it seemed, a few yards out, and then back again. In three minutes he was back on the shore, rubbing himself briskly. As he stood on the beach, alone under the whitening sky, he felt small and big at the same time. In this silent world of sea and sky it seemed as if he were the only man alive. It was like being master of everything. So he stood, looking off to the east where the horizon was now aglow, almost feeling a oneness with it, almost happy.

And then he saw that he was not alone. Two men, with oars on their shoulders, were coming down to the beach. Again he seemed gripped by alarm and with his towel wrapped about him he hurried away. He did not run now. He walked, but, like his swimming, painfully. He tried to swerve away from the oncoming men, but he was not as fast as they were. They had cut towards him, and as they came near, both said good morning. He returned their greeting and walked on.

"That's the teacher, isn't it?" one of the men remarked.

"Yes," the other said. "He's always up early."

"He's lame; isn't he?"

"Yes, but it doesn't keep him from swimming. Or trying to."

And so Lino gained the path that led to the house, and their laughter came back to him, not hard, not jeering, just the healthy laughter of whole men.

Later, as he walked to the schoolhouse, he could not help marveling again at the look of freshness about everything. The whole town was awake now, and on the streets, in the houses, in stores, people were up and doing something. Some of them were just walking like him, but they had an air of going somewhere, of arriving and falling to on a piece of work. As he walked he had a sense of the town rebuilding, growing.

He had found the marks of war here, too, the shells of broken homes. But there was this difference: in the city the waste of war stood against the backdrop of an imminent wasting away. As if those things which had remained standing were just waiting for a signal and they, too, would crumble. Here, against the mountains and the sky, what had been lost seemed temporary and not too important.

And here he had a sense of himself building, too. Here he had no loss. Here he had only a beginning.

Lino now turned into the school gate, and the felicitous feeling of the walk through the town left him. It was like having been free, only to fall into the same old trap again. He could not just walk through the schoolhouse as through the streets, impersonally ignoring people, passing them by. Here he was caught among people again, caught in their glances, looked at, measured, judged. And there was nothing he could do, nothing that he could offer so that they might put out a hand and say "Friend."

He had gone to his first class hopefully, remembering that he had come here for a beginning. The week before school opened, just wandering around the town, getting acquainted with the other teachers, he had been sure that he had done the right thing. He had turned off blindly from one path, wary and hopeful, not caring very much, on to a new, tentative road. And that first week he knew he had struck out in the right direction. And then school had opened and he had gone to his first class.

It had not been bad, that first day. He had just been a little scared. It was not bad the first two weeks, the first month. The class listened to him, laughed with him sometimes, believed a lot of things he told them. He had been delighted, and that was when he first had the sense of building.

It was almost as if he were whole again, and nothing of the tragic things had ever happened. It was like the world and the time before the war, when he belonged to every day and was one with all people. It was as if he had never known hate, or pain or despair or loss.

And then, little by little, he had begun to find the chipped festering pieces of himself that he thought he had lost on that other road, lying everywhere on this new road, too. People kept turning them up for him to see and feel again. The youngsters that he thought trusted him, believed in him, in their young unfeelingness, thrust these broken pieces of himself at him. And it was then that he felt out again, once more a thing apart.

It was nothing at first. Just smiles, surreptitious laughter, a glance that fell uneasily on his mind. And then it

came out in words, bold, well-defined. *He's funny. He's old.
He's lame. How would you like to dance with him?* They were
just youngsters. They did not know anything. They were cruel
only because they did not know anything. He told himself that.
But, already he was alone again. Already he was a thing apart.
A thing apart.

Lino entered his classroom. It was a cheerless room. The
floor was hard-packed earth. The walls were old galvanized
iron roofing salvaged from the old schoolhouse. The school
building, like most of the other public buildings, was temporary, makeshift, awaiting the hand of the builder. But it had
seemed like a haven in the beginning.

Now that he was in the room, Lino felt the tiredness of
the walk to the school come on him. He let himself slip heavily
down to the chair. He put his books and notebooks carefully
on the table. It was like this everyday now. There was no
excitement, no aliveness, no reaching toward the day's work.
It was just that now: work. A waiting, an enduring of time
until he could walk away again, down the road to the freedom
of his own room and the companionship of the lonely sea.

"Mr. Casas," the voice said, as if in reiteration.

Lino looked up.

"Good morning." It was Miss Patricio. "May I come in?"

"Oh, yes," Lino got up hastily, scraping his chair. "I
guess my mind must've been wandering. I didn't hear you the
first time, I'm afraid."

"I'll only be a moment. It's nearly time, I think." The
girl looked at her watch. "It's just that I want to know if
you're going to join our little party."

"Party?"

"My home economics class is planning to bake some cakes
and cook up a few special dishes in honor of the new school
stove. Some of the teachers thought it would be a good idea
if we—the teachers—contributed a little something to buy the
materials needed. You know, flour and baking powder and
such."

"Oh, yes. I think—yes, I'm in. How much do I give?"

"How much can you give?"

"A peso?"

"That'll be all right."

Lino had only a peso on him, in his shift pocket. He fumbled for it now, making of it a very intense business. It was always so with him whenever Miss Patricio was around, or any other pretty girl in fact. It made him acutely aware of his own limitations, of his baggy khaki clothes which could never look neat, of his rough chin which he could not shave closely enough. But most of all it made him aware of his game leg, made him see in his mind's eye its deformity, its withered, dead look.

"I hope this is all right," he said, handing her the money. "If it's not enough...."

"Oh, this is all right. Thank you kindly." She said it lightly, smilingly, looking at him with dancing lights in her eyes.

Miss Patricio always treated Lino like that, as if she wanted him to crinkle his eyes, too, like her, and skip and jump maybe. But it only made him remember a time better forgotten, made him feel inadequate and quite old. She probably meant well. She had made the first move to be friends. And of all the teachers she was the most companionable, talking easily to him. The others were friendly, too, but somehow they seemed ill at ease, just a little strained. It was his fault, perhaps, because he did not open to them easily. But it was different with Miss Patricio, and from the start he had found her gracefully fitting into his moods, until after a time there were no moods when he was with her.

The bell rang. Lino almost jumped up. He saw that Miss Patricio was still standing by the door and that he had been looking at her without seeing her. She was still smiling.

"Well," she said, "back to work. See you at the party. Oh, I forgot. It's tomorrow afternoon, after classes. Bye."

Lino went out to the courtyard, where the students were now converging. He watched them coming, in groups or singly, talking, laughing, shouting, restless, young. Especially young. And somehow this thought seemed to strike at him so that it hurt. He looked at their faces, and it was as if they had never known grief. The war had done nothing to them. They were ignorant and happy. They were strong and brave in their innocence. For a moment he felt a tenderness for all of them. And then the second bell rang. The classes began to file into their respective rooms. Lino stood aside to let his class pass.

At ten o'clock Lino had a vacant period. At this time he was assigned to the library with a couple of other teachers to supervise the study period of students who also had no classes. The library was built like a barn, made of the same salvaged materials as the classrooms except that it was bigger, with a higher ceiling. Inside there were chairs and a couple of bookcases. Lino did not like it there. There were too many people, for one thing. And he did not care for the conversation he had to carry on with the teachers. Usually he just slipped in and sat with the students, reading a book he always carried with him.

He had been reading for some time, ignoring the hum that the students made in low-conversation, when a girl gave a little shriek. He would have ignored it if the girl had not addressed him. "Sir!"

He turned slowly around. He first glanced at the other teachers, at the far end of the room, toward the rear. He saw that they were looking in his direction, too. Miss Patricio was among them. It surprised him a little because Miss Patricio was not usually assigned there at this hour. The girl student was now in spirited and high-voiced argument with a boy.

Lino stood up, his mind not having quite grasped yet what it was all about. And the girl was addressing him again, appealing to him, her eyes angry and near tears. Then he saw the boy hold up a notebook and fling it at the girl. The notebook hit her in the face and she burst into tears.

It was like a pantomime and Lino did not attach any significance to it. He was trying to recall the name of the girl. She was in one of his classes, a pretty, slant-eyed girl who seemed always to carry an arch look about her. He remembered how it irked him to see the smile that seemed like malicious laughter. And then suddenly Lino realized that the girl was addressing him directly, shouting at him.

"What kind of a teacher are you—," she was saying now, "you weak, foolish man. You—you cripple! You can't even control your students!"

Even then nothing seemed to penetrate into his brain, and he stood on one foot, not knowing yet what to do, a little surprised.

And then he saw that Miss Patricio was there now. He saw her jerk the girl around by the shoulder. He heard her tell the girl to go to "Mr. Casas' room. You stay there and wait. I'll find that boy and we'll investigate this matter. Mr. Casas will talk to you."

With the eyes of all those in the library on them, they had walked out of the library toward his empty room. On the way, the things that the girl had said finally made sense in Lino's mind. And when they did, he wanted to laugh suddenly. Everything was suddenly funny, but most of all he was funny. They had sat down solemnly facing each other, Miss Patricio's eyes, anxious and troubled, gravely regarding him. And then, after a while, the boy came in, chastened and frightened.

Almost immediately Lino started talking to them ("Mr. Casas will talk to you.") and he told them how people suffer very much, and hope very much, and how there is a lot of sorrow and pain in the world. He was talking to himself. And after a while the bell rang and his class filed in, but he kept on talking. And Miss Patricio still sat there. And everybody listened.

School was over for the day. The soft shadows of the afternoon were turning blue-black, lengthening on the grass. Lino stood quietly at the gate of the schoolhouse watching the students go home. And now they seemed sad to him. The games were over, the hopes and expectancies of the day left behind, the strife forgotten. It was late afternoon, and evening was on the hills.

The wind no longer belonged to day; it was colder. But inside, Lino felt warm, as if the day that had gone was now within him, carried by an unseasonable sun. For the first time he did not feel hidden now, nor was there reason to hide now. Everything had come out now, the shadow gone, and the brightness there was the brightness of day.

The girl came up to him and stepped forward.

"Miss Patricio," Lino said, "do you mind if I walk home with you?"

Philippines Free Press
June 11, 1949

HOUSE FOR SALE

LAZARO M. ESPINOSA

Mr. Danilo slowed down the car and stared at the house which they were approaching. When they came in front of it, he brought the car to a stop and read the number on the gate.

"Yes, this is the house," he told his wife.

He pushed the car's door open and stepped out. His wife followed him and placed her hand on his arm. Both stood still and studied the house closely. Satisfied, they walked towards the gate. Mr. Danilo picked up a piece of stick and with this tapped on the gate several times, calling out good day as he did so. A thin woman, around forty years old, looked out of the window and, on seeing them, asked them to please wait. The woman then went out to meet them.

"What is it, please?" the woman said as she opened the gate.

Mr. Danilo introduced himself.

"Arturo, one of my subordinates at the Atomic Export and Import Company, informed me yesterday that you were selling your house," Mr. Danilo explained. "Arturo said he is a cousin of yours."

"Oh, yes," the woman said. "Please, come in."

"Yes, we are selling it," she said afterwards when she and her guests were already seated in the receiving room. She was thin and pale. Excited over the interview that had just been opened, she looked paler yet. Mr. Danilo noticed that she felt uneasy. She impressed him as one who was not used to meeting people, strangers specially.

"How old is it now?" Mr. Danilo inquired as he coolly swept the room with his eyes.

"Two years," the woman said. "It was completed on May fifteen, nineteen forty-seven."

Mr. Danilo nodded solemnly. He continued to study the room and what other parts of the house that could be seen from where he was. The receiving room impressed him as spacious enough and cozy and the sky-blue paint was to his liking. However, he took care not to betray his feelings. He remained grave and solemn, even critical.

"It's made of second class wood," Mr. Danilo observed.

"The posts are of ipil," the woman said.

"And the roof. Is it of galvanized sheets or aluminum?"

"Galvanized sheets," the woman said.

Mr. Danilo remained quiet for some time, as if he was taking time to arrange in his mind the information he had just received.

"Well, how much do you ask for it?" he asked.

The woman did not reply at once. She had long fixed in her mind the price she wanted, but now she found it quite difficult to tell. She had the feeling it might be considered rather high; honestly, however, she thought it was reasonable enough. When she spoke, her voice faltered.

"Four thousand."

Mr. Danilo nodded again. He looked up at the ceiling while his fingers drummed at the top of the table standing between him and his wife.

"I understood from Arturo that the lot is not yours yet," Mr. Danilo said.

"It still belongs to the subdivision," the woman said. "But we have already paid two years installment on it. Should you buy the house, we will transfer the contract papers in your name. All we ask is that you refund us what we have already paid."

"And how much have you paid?" Mr. Danilo asked.

"Four hundred pesos," the woman said. "You will have to pay the subdivision six hundred more."

A brief but heavy silence followed. Mr. Danilo shifted his attention to the woman. He watched her with scrutinizing eyes, wishing to find out more about her. Being a businessman, it had become customary with him to study people. He concluded that this woman was, aside from being meek, naive. In the very active world he moved in, they would consider her "very easy." He quickly saw that this fact would prove valuable, and that it could be taken advantage of.

"This type of house could be constructed for only a little over five thousand now," Mr. Danilo said.

"It cost us seven thousand," the woman said.

"But two years ago, the cost of building materials was very high."

The woman said nothing. She was a complete stranger to the subject, and she had no courage to question the accuracy of Mr. Danilo's statement. Still, she felt convinced that her price was fair enough. She sat stiffly erect, knotting her fingers on her lap.

After a while, Mr. Danilo asked that they be shown the other rooms of the house and the woman willingly obliged. She showed the couple the two bedrooms, the dining room, the kitchen, the toilet and bath. All the time, Mr. Danilo remained composed and solemn. He examined each room lengthily: the sidings, the floor, the ceiling. He even felt the paint, watching out for cracks. He observed, incidentally, that there was very little furniture.

What Mr. Danilo saw of the house satisfied him, but he kept quiet. He remained quiet even when they had returned to the receiving room. Once again, he swept his eyes about the room. Mrs. Danilo, who was getting fat, began to feel warm and she started to fan herself with her handkerchief. The woman noticed her and she sheepishly apologized for her inability to provide refreshment for her guests.

"Were my boys at home," she said, "I could have sent them to the store for soft drinks and cakes. But they are in school."

"Oh, don't bother," Mrs. Danilo said. "So you have children?"

"Two," the woman said. "Both boys."

"And I suppose your husband is in his office working?" Mrs. Danilo said again.

The woman looked down at her lap. A shadow fell on her quietly sad face. It heightened her rather tragic appearance.

"He is in the province," the woman said.

"I see," Mrs. Danilo said. "Vacationing?"

The woman raised her eyes and gazed at Mrs. Danilo. Meeting Mrs. Danilo's eyes, she lowered hers again on her lap. She seemed to be debating with herself.

"I might as well tell you," the woman broke. "My husband is sick."

Mrs. Danilo's mouth fell open. She was mildly shocked.

"He has tuberculosis," the woman went on. "Early last year, he became very sick and when he had himself examined by a doctor, it was found out he had TB. The finding upset him and made him worse. But the tragic thing about it all is that a month later, he was thrown out of his job."

Mrs. Danilo, her mouth still hanging open, nodded. She was quick to be touched and already she was feeling sorry for the woman.

"They gave him a gratuity equivalent to his salary for two months," the woman continued. "It was on that that we tried to live. But it's all gone now. Why, we have already even sold some of our furniture."

Mr. Danilo's interest had been aroused too. He bent forward and listened attentively as the woman told her tale. But unlike his wife, he reacted differently. He found in it certain ideas.

"Do you see, then, why we have decided to sell our house?" the woman said in conclusion.

Mrs. Danilo had forgotten about the heat. But now she started to fan herself with her handkerchief again.

"And after you have sold the house," she asked, "where will you live?"

"My sons and I will join my husband in the province," the woman said. "With the money we get, I will put up a small store there."

"That is a good idea," Mrs. Danilo said, wishing to encourage.

There ensued another pause. The woman gazed at Mrs. Danilo, gratified at the sympathy she saw in her. Then she remembered that so far neither of the couple had spoken about the house yet. She returned the conversation to the original subject.

"I hope the house satisfies you," the woman said.

Mrs. Danilo took the change of atmosphere in the conversation with a deep breath. She straightened up.

"Yes," she said. "It's nice. I . . ." but her husband's hand, rudely falling on her arm cut her short. She turned to her husband and in time saw him throw at her a sharp glance.

"It's nice enough," Mr. Danilo said, "but we feel four thousand is too high for it. As I have already said, this type of house will cost only a little more than five thousand to build now. If we will have to pay four thousand for it, we might as well have a new house built."

His words upset the woman. Mr. Danilo saw it clearly, because the woman was incapable of hiding her feelings. She wanted to make a reply, but she felt confused, arrested. She was not sure if Mr. Danilo's assertions could be refuted. On the other hand, she knew she was totally ignorant about the construction business. She made an embarrassed movement with her hands.

"You cannot get it then for four thousand?" she said, limply.

Mr. Danilo's face turned graver. He shook his head, slightly thrusting his lower lip out to better drive home his point.

"I am afraid we cannot," he said.

The woman felt disconcerted. She began to knot her fingers together again.

"Reduce the price then if you must, but please, only a little," she said.

Mr. Danilo continued to shake his head. Things were shaping up the way he wanted them to. Meanwhile, his wife turned her face to him, eager to know what was in his mind. For herself, she thought four thousand reasonable enough. Moreover, she had come to like the house. She was eager to own it.

"How much do you bid?" the woman asked, seeing Mr. Danilo reluctant to speak.

Mr. Danilo felt his chin and pretended to be thinking deeply.

"Three thousand," he said.

The woman's lips faintly quivered. She looked down at her fingers which she was nervously twitching.

"But that is too low," she protested.

Mr. Danilo showed indifference. He tried to indicate that he had begun to lose interest in the matter. He even frowned.

"Heaven knows," the woman said, "we will not be selling it were it not for the tragedy that has befallen us."

Mr. Danilo smiled for the first time. But it was a smile devoid of sympathy, faintly derisive.

"But of course," he said. "For what other reason would you want to sell it?"

"I mean," the woman said, "it has become so precious to us. It is almost a part of us now."

The grin on Mr. Danilo's lips widened.

"Frankly," he said, "I understand your situation. But sentiment has no place in business dealings. I understand why you should place more worth in your house. It has sheltered you. You have learned to love it. But you should not expect others to rate it as high as you do. To others, it costs only as much as it actually does."

The woman sat speechless. She wanted to offer a defense, to say that in appraising her house, all that she had considered was its own physical value. But she could find no words. Mr. Danilo noticed the struggle in herself and he felt secretly pleased. In business dealings, it paid to confuse the other party. Heaving a sigh, he stood up. He wanted the woman to understand that he had considered the interview over and he motioned to his wife to stand up herself.

Mrs. Danilo felt confused herself. She found her husband's action abrupt and unexpected. It affected her rudely, the way a song sung out of tune would. She had hoped he would increase his price. She wanted the house. She stood up reluctantly.

"Well, we are leaving," Mr. Danilo said.

The woman looked up at him. She remained seated because she could not gather sufficient strength with which to stand up.

"You...you are no longer interested in buying it?" she inquired.

"I shall be business-like," Mr. Danilo said. "I will pay you three thousand two hundred. Think it over and let me know your decision tomorrow. Here is my card."

The woman took the card. She grasped the arms of her chair and pushed herself up. Then she accompanied the couple downstairs.

Mr. Danilo bade her goodbye. Mrs. Danilo did likewise. The woman smiled her faint, sad smile and opened the gate. She held it open until the couple had passed.

"Goodbye," she said.

Mr. and Mrs. Danilo entered the car.

Mr. Danilo started it and soon they were driving away. Mr. Danilo drove slowly. He seemed in no hurry. Seeing the shadow of a smile on his lips, Mrs. Danilo found courage to say her fears aloud.

"You should have raised it to three and a half at least," she said.

"Why should I?" Mr. Danilo said.

"The house is worth more than that. Don't tell me you did not like it?"

"I liked it."

"Then why didn't you offer more? It would still be cheap for three and a half."

"But why offer more when she will accept my price?" Mr. Danilo said. "Three hundred pesos is a lot of money."

"How do you know she will?"

Mr. Danilo eyed his wife coldly.

"Sometimes you can be very stupid," he said. "When it comes to business matters, leave everything to me. I am by far a better businessman than you are."

Mrs. Danilo felt hurt and she looked at her husband acidly. Mr. Danilo saw her displeasure and he explained himself.

"You saw and you heard," he said. "Her husband is sick. They have no more money left. They have no means of income. She has already sold most of their furniture. Already she looks starved. They are not in a position to wait for a better price. Didn't you see how eager she was to have the house sold?"

Mrs. Danilo thought her husband's words.

"Do you understand now?" Mr. Danilo asked.

Mrs. Danilo nodded. She said no more.

Sunday Times Magazine
July 3, 1949

THE FOREST

F. SIONIL JOSE

Dr. Goddard was one who, I believe, should have been endowed with an extra lease on life as a matter of privilege and not of right. When we entered the mountain country he knew that death lurked in every crevice, behind every shrub and stand of grass, unlike in the plain which we had left, where one could sense death even when it was far away. The plain receded and the wilderness closed upon us. We felt the stifling humidity of the lowlands wane, and gone was the sonorous rattle of machines that crowded the battered roads, the dust that rose in clouds and hid the faces of people and houses. Now the pleasant coolness of the forest was all around us.

Dr. Goddard, who had been quite uncommunicative and glum when we were in the lowlands, took on a blitheness of spirit. Even his conversation became chummy when we pitched tents in the shadow of a hill after the long, rigorous march.

"Peace at last," he remarked as he eyed the densely wooded hillsides hunched before us. Farther, beyond the sky's ponderous blue, straddled the mountain ranges. It was a beautiful day, with the tall grass glinting, although farther away from us, out in the remoter hills, many were still dying.

There was no road to our area except that which we left a quarter mile down the trail, shaved by bulldozers from the tough rocky breast of the mountain. The doctor was arranging the surgical instruments. He paused and laughed softly, as if to scorn the tangled growth that hid the enemy: "I remember when, as a boy, I loved the wilderness with a zeal that was almost fanatical. The forest gave me a sense of being nearer myself."

It was good to listen to the doctor speak. What he said had an unmistakable truth. What boy would not relish the open, the barefoot freedom of the creek and the wild, green throbbing of a field?

Soon I was busy sledge-hammering the pikes that would hold the tents of our receiving station. The corpsmen would fill it with what they would bring from the deeper wilds. The receiving station would also be a miniature recreation center. There would be the coffee and the gum we often distribute. Around us would be those who could not share these—the dead and the wounded in litters.

Dr. Goddard said, "When it finally comes, this that brings you nearer God, it would come over you like a blissful sleep."

I had seen the unspeaking lips of the dying droop and the eyes grow glassy. I had heard the final, punctuated gasping and I had seen life flowing out of the fatigued, pain-wracked body and I knew what he meant. But how was I to know then that this doctor, skilled with the scalpel, who was nearest death, would ask for no second chance? How was I to know why one woman they brought from the hills, one enemy who was dedicated to death, and one woman shattered by the lust of men desired the continuance of the flow when for them the meaning of life had already been lost?

Death came to the enemy in the morning, in the afternoon, throughout the fearful stretch of day. Out in the distant ridges we could see the planes jettison their gasoline on the forest. I heard the litterbearers speak of bodies burned and bloated. We exchanged furious shots with the enemy, who were later rolled back and forced out of hiding by flames or out of their holes by bombs and rockets. Staggering and defeated, the enemy retreated. We knew then that, like us, they had their own maimed and dead.

The mountain people would trek in after sick call: children ragged and dirty with tropical sores, who gazed with awe at the impressive array of medicine bottles; highland women in bedraggled, brightly colored garments, undernourished but strong, who helped us carry our supplies up the precipitous mountain trails, and the highland, scantily-clad guerillas. They were a shy people, who talked among themselves in subdued tones and yet, in their timid way, they remembered to bring orchids from the forest for the doctor, who accepted the flowers gratefully.

The privates came one afternoon. We had just finished cleaning the surgical instruments. The sick bay was not full.

Those we could not handle had been moved to the evacuation hospital in the lowlands, where they could be given more specialized treatment.

From the expression on their faces I could tell that the two were shaken up as if by a hideous experience. After I had called the doctor, one of them explained: "We were on our way to the regimental headquarters when we approached their village and saw these natives dancing and beating brass drums. We thought it to be one of those tribal feasts. When we approached they all scampered away. Our first thought was that we had trespassed on a sacred native ceremony, in which our presence was not welcome. . . .

"Then we saw what they had left behind."

The other continued breathlessly. "There were eleven of them, but the other ten were dead. As for the last one, we hope you can do something for him. He is out there in that bundle carried by those who. . . ."

Outside under a moss-covered pine tree, in the golden flood of afternoon, two highlanders were waiting uncomfortably. We hurried to them. The man they had brought—the enemy—lay in a ghastly heap, his eyes closed. A closer scrutiny of his bloody face revealed that both his ears were shorn, his mouth was slit and some of his teeth pulled out. When the two soldiers spread the blanket with which they had wrapped him we saw that all his fingers had been mutilated. Dried blood was thick all over him and it was a surprise to see him alive after so much loss of blood.

"We kill," one of the soldiers said, "but then we do it swiftly like this," and he flourished a thrust at an imaginary chest.

The enemy's eyes opened and when he saw us he covered his face and turned it away.

"You wash his wounds," the doctor said.

The enemy was hastily brought into the receiving tent and laid on a stretcher. I brought to him compressed bandages soaked in alcohol, but the moment I touched him he started to jabber, so that the wounds in his arms and face started to bleed again.

"How can I make him know I am trying to help him?" I asked. I made empty gestures about cleaning his wounds and even showed the red cross that I had on my sleeve.

"There are interpreters in headquarters," one of the soldiers suggested when he realized our dilemma.

In half an hour one came to help us out. He was a short fellow. He talked slowly to the wounded soldier, who kept casting furtive glances at us while we watched. The interpreter explained that the man had been abandoned by his companions along with the other ten who had already been killed by avenging highlanders.

After a while the enemy ceased jabbering. A resigned silence possessed him. In his small eyes, where fear and contempt were articulate only a few moments ago, it seemed as if a new hope was flickering. He winced bravely when I swabbed his wounds and took off the clots.

But as I ripped off with scissors his torn and bloody uniform to change it with the cleaner standard garb of the station we saw the nauseating wound on his chest, swollen and yellow with sickening pus. And when he saw us staring at the wound he quivered and started to cry.

The interpreter spat on the soft earth and, without looking at us, shook his head. "If this is the kind of sojer we are fighting, Doc," he said, "then there ain't no hard sailing for the boys out front. He wants to know, Doc, if he has a chance. Look at da insignia on his shoulders and that one on his chest. He belongs to the suicide corps of da Jap Navy."

We did everything we could for him, gave him transfusion and stuck a couple of morphine syrettes into his arms to assuage the pain, but at dusk, after having begged us for more attention, he joined his ancestors.

Our supply from the medical depot came one morning. When the sergeant who went to take the supplies returned he was accompanied by guerillas composed mostly of highlanders and their lowlander lieutenant. They were a healthy-looking group, who had had more than a month of steady fighting in the hills on a K-ration diet. The guerilla officer, a tall, thin man with a pinched handsome face, had been raising havoc in the hills with the enemy long before the liberating forces augmented his handful of guns and men. Now his ranks had been swelled and he took justifiable pride in his company.

After the penicillin had been safely stocked in the iceboxes, I attended to the men's ailments and distributed foot powder, multi-vitamin pills and atabrine. Some of the men could talk fluent English, having had their schooling in some of the scattered grade schools in the region before the enemy came.

When I was through with his men the officer, who had all the while been watching, approached me nervously and asked if I could spare him a bottle of quinine tablets. I said I could spare him some but not a whole bottle. He wanted no less and I asked him if it was for malaria. If it was I could spare him a whole bottle of atabrine, which was just as effective as quinine. The doctor's permission was necessary, however, before I could give away a bottle of quinine.

He was soon inquiring about the doctor's personality, if he wasn't a grouch of a man. The doctor a grouchy man? Give the fellow limitations to his moods. The doctor was a first-class surgeon. "He wouldn't be with the outfit to handle emergency cases if he weren't that good," I said. "But in spite of his importance he is sociable. You can walk right in."

He hesitated before he entered the doctor's tent and when the gray canvas flapped down on him I forgot him completely until the following day.

It was a fine, polished morning. The mist hung low and above was an untarnished sky. The stillness all around us was interrupted by the sleepy drone of planes winging above the sonorous blam-blam-blam of their bombs far beyond the hills. It seemed so peaceful, as if there were no war and death in our midst. Even the doctor, in the company of the two other doctors in the receiving station, was filled with bright banter.

Sick call had not started yet and the receiving station was empty except for a helper tidying up the place. Then a band of highlanders arrived, carrying an improvised stretcher. In it was undoubtedly the most beautiful woman of the highlands I had ever seen. She had finely-chiseled features and on her pallid face were the traces of such rustic beauty as only those who welcome sun, wind and rain can possess.

I chanced to look at one of the highlanders who had brought her in and recognized him as one of the guerillas I had treated the other day.

I asked what had happened to her, but he would not tell me. Seeing that he was unreasonable to the question, I called the doctor.

He took a practiced look at the moaning woman. Already the blanket that wrapped her up was soaked with blood. The doctor's face was stolid when we placed the patient in the emergency tent. She gave the doctor one lingering look and then, in a shaky voice, she asked if she would live.

The doctor smiled encouragement. "Yes, you will," he said.

All through her anguish afterwards as we swabbed at the abrasions on her young, wholesome body she kept entreating incoherently that she be allowed one more chance at life. Then the anesthesia took effect and her pain and moaning ceased.

At dusk, when mess was over, the doctor and I sat alone in the receiving tent. Some of the boys in the station and those in the supply dump below us had gone to see a movie in the camp of the technical intelligence boys a hill away. It was a quiet evening marked by the whir of the generator, an intermittent guffaw, the restless moving of a patient in the sick bay and the measured scrape of the sentry's marching.

We had a radio and we were comfortable. I slouched on a cot and the doctor sank into a sofa he had scrounged from the house in the last town we left. He recalled the lieutenant who called the day before.

I said, "He asked me for a whole bottle of quinine."

"Do you think he has a conscience?" the doctor asked.

I had not expected the question. "I don't know," I said. "That is a question only he can answer, I guess."

"He told me he has," the doctor said. "That was why he wanted the quinine. He had stayed in the hills long enough to get himself a woman."

The woman we treated that day came quickly to my mind. I was starting to ask a question when the doctor took his pipe from his mouth and nodded. "As you know," he went on, "the woman jumped off a cliff."

"But what has it got to do with him?" I asked.

"The lieutenant left for the lowlands today," the doctor went on. "No civilian is allowed in army trucks. He didn't want her along...."

Everything became clear. "He could have at least married her," I said, "and then left."

But I knew why he did not marry the girl. If he had, their marriage would have been an obstruction to his social position and career, particularly back where he came from.

In the lowlands people would always look upon his wife from the hills with haughty condescension.

"He said he had a conscience," the doctor observed. "That was what he wanted the quinine for."

I was silent.

"He offered me a very handsome price if I did the abortion," the doctor continued thoughtfully. But the doctor did not do that. The woman jumped off the cliff and lived but only for a few hours more. She died the same day and it was the same sullen-faced mountaineers who took her body the next morning. Not even the doctor's unquestionable skill could save her from death's hungry embrace.

The days in the wilderness were boring. The boys did not have much or even enough of relaxation except movies in the evenings. The last town, with its hole-in-the-wall shanties, its honky-tonk dance hall and its adulterated liquor, was more than thirty miles away. Anyone on leave and bent on having a good time would be exhausted by the time he reached the town.

"Of course we are far from civilization, but we may just as well make the most of it," the doctor said when we set up the prophylaxis station later. It was not really a tedious job. The station was just a small tent, with the liquids propped on one side, the urinal on the other, some literature on venereal disease-prevention on a table and posters on the posts.

For the most part of our time in the wilderness the pro station was seldom used. Then one afternoon a squad of PFC's on leave from the front came and asked for several pro kits.

"You don't look prepared for a long trip," the medical technician bantered as he handed them two pro kits each. "Come on, boys, pass the information and don't fail to come for beauty treatment when you are through."

They laughed when I asked, "Shall I list you down now, so that all I have to do afterwards is jot down the time of the exposure?"

It was cold—like late autumn, so the doctor said the following morning, when he was practically dragged out of his cot to do a slicing job. A crisp, morning wind sprang up from the hills and swept down the camp. I was shivering when I readied the instruments in the emergency tent.

Three badly shaken men were there waiting. They had toiled more than a mile from the last road accessible by truck to reach the station. One of them, who said he was from the quartermaster, was not badly hurt. Neither were the other two. They had nothing but scratches and scalp wounds that needed a stitch or two. Their truck went off the road, they explained, and they had managed to jump off before it plunged down the grade. One of the passengers, however, was not so fortunate.

In the pale glow of morning they unwrapped the poncho. A woman was there, moaning, and one discerning look at her twitching face and I knew it was she, perhaps, who entertained the squad who got the pro kits that afternoon. Her arms and other parts of her body were lacerated, but she was still alive and when she was aware that she was already in the station she turned to us as if we were gods and begged us to save her. She must live, she cried softly.

I was not able to eat a good breakfast that morning. I had long grown impassive at the sight of blood and raw flesh, but my thoughts persistently groped back to the lacerated breasts and the pubis that was smashed.

"The best plastic surgeon," the doctor said wryly, "couldn't have helped her if she had lived. Those who came yesterday afternoon for pro kits, I pity them if they went to her. Those sores on her back, they couldn't be anything but venereal disease."

The woman died on the same day and neither the men who brought her nor the fellow with a truck from the quartermaster service showed up again. So she was taken by the grave detail and buried, her identity unknown.

We had been in the heart of the wilderness for almost a month when one night the crafty enemy, who had been pocketed behind and cut off from the main retreating force, struggled to our area in small groups. They used the lush cover of mountain growth and slithered noiselessly through the grass, like swarms of silent ghosts, past the defense perimeter. Then they hurled grenades at our tents and at the wounded there. It was a gallant but futile attempt and they were caught and bayoneted and shot.

We did not sleep the whole night, not even when reinforcements from the rear and the front had rushed to our succor. We were busy with the casualties and I missed the

doctor when more emergency cases poured in at the receiving
tent. When I asked one of the doctors where he was he replied
that the doctor was among the casualties and was dying in
the emergency tent.

I learned afterwards that he had been in the middle of
the sick bay, where the wounded lay, and that he had tossed
back one grenade to the fleeing enemy, one other grenade
exploding before he could throw it away. It was a touching
display of valor, but in war courage and sacrifice are cheap
commodities that cannot be appraised at their fullest value.
And the doctor's right hand, the steady, potent hand that
wielded the scalpel with dexterity, was no more than a bloody
pulp.

I walked to the stretcher where he lay. His eyes were half-
open as if he wanted etched in his mind the last clear vestiges
of living, and his eyes turned to me weakly when I entered.
Noticing the loose tourniquet on his battered arm, I stopped
and tightened it.

But I saw scorn in his eyes and he cursed softly: "Damn
it, I am going to die. Can't you let me alone?"

He uttered it so heartlessly, so clearly—he who said once
that life was purposeful. He said it as if dying was insignifi-
cant, as if it meant but the trivial application of anesthesia.

Then I saw them all again, the face of the enemy, his
mouth slit, his ears gone, the highland woman, broken but
beautiful in her own disgrace, having jumped off the cliff and
regretted it, and the woman of the world, her breasts lacerated,
her pubis smashed. All of them were transfixed in an attitude
of supplication, of begging for one more moment on this earth.
And here was this doctor, this man who saved lives, surrendering without misgiving to the dark foreboding spirit of the
forest.

It did not make sense at all. I was walking among my
bottles, my records and my instruments, with tears still smarting in my eyes, when one of the medical technicians bobbed
out of the emergency tent and told me that Dr. Goddard was
dead—and may I please fill up the necessary blanks?

Sunday Times Magazine
July 10, 1949

THE MONEYMAKER

Karia, our maid, had told me the story. She said the men who carried the big jute sacks slung on their backs and who walked by the yard at sunset were moneymakers. Children were inside those sacks. The men carried them to a bridge made of bones and there cut off their heads, then squeezed the blood out of their bodies. That was what they made money out of, children's blood. Karia had shown me a bright new coin, and I had been greatly impressed by its reddish gold color. I asked her why they did not take older people, too, and she said that was because when you get old you were no longer innocent and your blood would not make good shiny coins.

I still clearly remember that before she told me the story, I had spent my afternoons waiting for the sun to set. There were guava trees growing in our yard, and I'd sit on the top branch of one of them and enjoy myself watching the orange sun take back all the light it had been giving away to the farm all day. It started about five o'clock every afternoon, when all over the fields the yellow heat changed to the cool colors of honeysuckle. Then the gray dusk would come in, and all the happy pink and orange and lavender tints gathered away from the earth to the sky, on the borders of clouds and behind mountains, till finally they all melted into the sun. When all was gray except for a few gold-hemmed clouds that were close to it, the sun, like the bright coin, would slip away into a slot at the slope of a green mountain.

But after Karia told me about the moneymakers, I was too scared to stay outside at that hour. I kept to my room all afternoon and waited for them to pass by. At least one of them always did, with his sack and his long curved knife, his face always hidden by a wide floppy hat. As soon as he was in sight, I'd run to the door and lock it. If I was all alone in the room I'd crawl to the corner where the crack was, and pressing myself as tightly to the wall as I could, I'd watch.

I never asked Grandma about it because Grandma did not like questions. Papa answered my questions but when he was around I forgot most of the things I wanted to ask, for there were so many other things I had to say. He came every Sunday and stayed only a few hours and then went back to his work in the city.

There had been only Karia to ask about things and it was from her that I tried to find out what the moneymakers did with all the money they made.

"Why, they buy food and clothes and they have many other wives and houses."

"Karia, do they kill their own children?"

"Sometimes they do, but not often. There are many other children they can kill instead."

One afternoon I saw at a distance two of the moneymakers walking together but one of them did not have a hat on. That meant I would see his face. He would have red eyes, for sure, and I knew what his mouth and nose and his whole face would be like. I once heard the preacher talk about "gaping caverns of hell," and I knew that was what the moneymakers would look like.

With him walking a distance away from our house, there was such fear in me that I could hardly move and breathe, but when he turned away from the road, and jumping over a small ditch, took the path that passed right by the walls of our house, I actually started to tremble and sweat and feel cold.

But still I waited for the face. I was disappointed. It should not be, but there it was, his face, looking just like other people's. Black hair, dark eyes, just enough nose, just enough mouth, just enough ears. Of course moneymakers could probably change their appearance the way witches could, but still his eyes should have been red, because the color of the eyes, I knew, could never change.

I was so absorbed with staring at his young ordinary face that I did not see Karia at once. But there she was in her red silk dress with the silver buttons going all the way down back, which meant that there was something big happening, because she never wore that dress except when she went to town with us. She was standing on one side of the house, also watching the hatless moneymaker.

I tried to get a good look at her face to see if she was afraid. I was not too surprised when I saw her smiling, because anyway she was too old for him to kill. He came and stood beside her and I could see their lips moving, though hard as I tried, I could not hear them. Once he looked up in the direction of my room and I trembled until he looked away. He and Karia talked some more and then he left.

She remained standing there, just staring at his back, while I had to bend over and hold my stomach to keep back the effect of my excited impatience. I could not stand it any longer and through the crack called out to her in a low whisper. She did not hear me so I opened the window a tiny bit and called again. When she looked up I stretched out one arm and waved for her to come up.

I pulled her with me to the bathroom.

"Did he have children? Did he?"

"Children?"

"Yes, to make money out of."

"Oh, that," she smiled. "No, he is not a moneymaker. He is Tino."

"What did he have in his sack then, if he is not a moneymaker?"

"He's been out harvesting rice." She was still smiling.

"That's why he has no hat on, like the others?"

"Yes, that's right."

"Karia, do you think moneymakers have red eyes?"

She looked at me as if she were not listening very well. "Why should they?" she said.

"I don't know...because they kill people. Karia, why do you have your red dress on? Are you going anywhere?"

"No, where should I be going?"

"Then it is for Tino."

"Of course not," but she was smiling. "I have to go and get supper ready."

Tino stopped by the house every afternoon about the same time the moneymakers passed. But one day he came earlier than usual. Although I was not very sure that I was not afraid of him, even if Karia did say he was not a moneymaker, yet I would never find out what he really was unless I joined them in the yard. My curiosity overcame my fear and I joined them —after I made Karia swear to me by all the elves in the mounds that nothing would happen to me.

Most of the time he and Karia were just laughing, and I was too busy looking at him and trying to make out what was inside the sack he had with him to care whether they talked to me or not. He must have noticed me, though, because before he left he said:

"Do you want to see what is inside this sack?"

I shook my head, though I really wanted to.

"Oh, come now," he smiled. "You don't really think I am a moneymaker, do you?" And when I looked at Karia he added, "She's told me what you thought. But look inside this sack and you'll see."

Karia nodded and I remembered her oath that nothing would happen to me, so I looked in. It really was rice.

"Is it yours?" I asked him. Karia gave him a funny look at my question and all of a sudden neither of them was smiling anymore.

"Yes," he answered as if he were angry, so I asked him, "Are you mad at her or at me?"

They laughed at that and he said he was not mad at all.

Grandma always woke up earlier than I did. She'd read in her room or walk out to the fields, but I cannot remember any time in which she did not wait for me to have breakfast with, unless she was sick. Except that one morning I came down and found her almost through with eating. She said she had to go to the granary, to give to the harvesters their share of the season's crop. I had never been to the granary before, and because I'd heard so much from my friends in town of all the money that we had in there, I asked Grandma if I could go with her. She said she had to hurry away, but added that I could ask Karia to take me there after she was through washing the dishes.

I could see Grandma through the window as she walked away. She had with her Grandpa's cane which Karia said he never used when he was alive but kept hidden in his closet instead. It was the dried tail of a *pagi*, a creature of the sea, though now it looked like an old brown piece of wood with knobs and knots throughout its length. Karia said that anyone hit by that cane, even playfully, would wither and dry up and get thinner and thinner and die. That was why Grandpa never used it. But Grandma was so frail and small that she needed some kind of protection when she went out by herself, so it was right for her to take it along. Of course everyone was afraid of Grandma really, even Karia, though when I once asked her if she was, she said, "No, of course not."

As soon as Karia was through with the dishes, we went. We walked through the rice paddies because that way was shorter. The granary stood a few hundred meters away from the rice fields under the coconut trees. Karia knew the way, so I walked behind her on the narrow trail. There were a lot of young coconuts, just about the size of an egg, that the wind had blown down to the ground, and I stopped to pick them up. On one end they had hard, petal-like growths which I played with as I did with rose petals. Only, this was more fun because the growths broke off with a crack, and when they were all removed there was uncovered the white smooth surface of the fruit with a faint pink ring crowning it.

Karia asked me rather impatiently to hurry, so I caught up with her and walked by her side. I had thought of some more questions I wanted to ask her but she looked so serious that I thought I'd better tease her first into good humor. I began on another nut and sang out as I tore each hard petal away. "You love him, you love him not, you love him...."

She glanced down at me but no comment.

"You love Tino, you love him not, you love Tino...." That time she smiled. "Aha, you love Tino, you love Tino, you love Tino...." It was the last petal. I threw the nut away, then turned to her.

"Karia, why do they become moneymakers?"

"Who?"

"The moneymakers."

"Oh, you're still thinking of them?" She was smiling.

"Of course. I still watch them every afternoon from my room."

We had reached the granary.

There was dust billowing around the mounds of gold, and on one mound Tino stood. Of course it was only rice that he was knee-deep in, but it did look like gold from afar. Karia caught his eye as soon as she entered, but he did not even smile. Once in a while he passed his hand over his brow and then fiercely shook the sweat from his fingers. I wanted to come closer to him so I could touch the rice. It looked so rich and plentiful, but Grandma saw me and motioned me away. "The dust will get into your lungs," she said.

There were three men measuring the rice with big cans. Grandma hardly took her eyes away from them except in moments when she would hurriedly write down some numbers in her notebook. I soon tired of watching and Grandma would not let me touch anything. Grandma was like that, always forbidding me to do the things she forced other people to do.

I walked out of the granary and played under the trees. When they finally got through, it was past midday and the shadows of the coconut trees had bent away from the left to the right, and my own shadow had come up from behind and now walked directly in front of me.

As we crossed the rice fields, Tino came hurrying behind us. I thought he wanted to talk to Karia but I was mistaken. It was Grandma. He walked beside her, but as I was a few paces ahead of them, I could hear only bits of their conversation.

Once Grandma said, "I can not help it. It's all your fault. You should not have borrowed money from me last year. Besides, you should learn to live on your own share of the harvest and not spend so much." She said it loudly and angrily.

Tino answered in about the same tone. I looked back. His face was red and he was saying, "You can't say that. You have never tried to live on that amount yourself."

I could not hear Grandma's answer to that, but after we had gone some more yards, their voices grew louder. Grandma said, "Well, you're not getting any money or rice from me with which to marry her. And if you think I will condone her parents' debts to me and let her go wihout serving her time, you are mistaken." She said this in a very decided and angry voice. Karia paused awhile and I thought she was going to turn around but she did not.

I looked back again and saw Tino walking from Grandma. He took a short cut across the paddy, his bare feet sinking into the thick piles of dried rice stalks. His face scared me, it had a very angry look as he kept it turned in Grandma's direction, and shouted, "You old leech, you've killed others this way, but you'll see. You'll see. You thieving old usurer."

I shook all over. I waited for Grandma to say that she had never killed any one, but all she screamed at him was, "You imbecile, get off my land," and she brandished her cane in the air threateningly.

She looked very proud and very brave standing there, her small white hands holding Grandpa's cane high. Though she was so tiny, she appeared taller than Tino who stood at the center of the sunken paddy, his dark face shining sweatily in the noonday sun.

That night it did not take much persuasion from Karia to make me go to bed early. I was so tired from the day's walk I did not even note when she blew out the candle and left my room.

Next morning I woke up before dawn. The day had started just like all the other days on the farm. The cocks were just beginning to crow. From my bed I could see the mountain, with the giant cotton clouds about its peak, still a solid dark-green. I reversed my position and with my chin in a pillow waited for the yellow-pink light of morning to wake up the mountain and wash its face so that its purple and pale yellow and fresh green hues would come out.

From downstairs there came the quiet hum of voices. But since every morning the farm hands dropped in at the house and stayed a few minutes before they went on their way to work, I did not pay much attention to the steady sound of talk. Nor did I particularly notice then the hush that followed. These voices and silences had always been part of the morning stillness.

Lavender was spreading on one side on the mountain and I had been following its progress when a new but familiar voice came from downstairs. I jumped out of bed. It was not a Sunday yet I was sure it was Papa. I ran to the window. His car was there.

I almost tripped on my long flannel gown as I ran down the stairs and out into the hall. Quite a few of our laborers were there, some sitting on benches, some squatting on the floor. They were all strangely quiet, unlike other mornings. Only the overseer and Berto talked in the corner, but so softly that I could not have heard them even if I had been interested.

"Good morning," I beamed at everyone happily although only a few took notice of me to smile.

"Where's Papa?" I asked, turning around, hoping that now someone would say something nice. Berto pointed to Grandma's room. It was all so strange, the way everyone was acting.

"Papa," I called out even before I entered the room. He was at the door instantly. "Shhh-shh..." he put a finger to his mouth. Grandma could not be asleep at that hour, but I was too glad to see him to ask at once what the matter was. Instead I jumped so he would pick me up and kiss me. With my arms around him I looked into Grandma's room....

A nurse was in the room, bending over the bed so that I could not see anything of Grandma except her face, which was very white and wrinkled. When she slept, everything about her face was small, now it had shrunk even more. Here, her eyes were closed into tight slits, her nose was so tiny, and though she had a mouth there were no lips on it.

But it was not Grandma...it was my tub which Papa had given me long ago and which I used to fill with water and float celluloid ducks and chickens and men and women in. It was my tub, and it was filled with blood, red and thick and messy with soaked cotton and gauze, and there were brown tricklings on its sides, and there were stains on the floor. I shivered and felt I should hold my stomach in and my head straight.

"He'll be all right soon." The voice came from behind me and I jumped around. Our family doctor had just entered the room. "The blows she gave him were surprisingly strong, but they're nothing serious."

I wondered whom he could be talking about. Grandma was the one who looked sick, but he was not referring to her.

"Did he say why he did it?" Papa asked.

"No. He seems more disturbed by the fact that he has received blows from the cane. I don't think the state of your mother-in-law worries him as much as that."

Papa had nothing to say. "Are you sending him off to prison?" the doctor asked.

I thought of Tino and how Grandma had waved her cane at him and of all the things he said. He must have come while we were all sleeping and must have tried to kill Grandma. Of course he did not know what a light sleeper Grandma was. Also, Tino did not know that Grandma slept with Grandpa's cane beside her.

Papa had now answered the doctor's question. I pulled at his coat. "Papa, it's Tino, isn't it? I know it is, because he called her names yesterday, he called her a usurer. What does that mean, Papa?"

He looked down at me, though I could not tell whether he was listening or not. "He also called her a leech and said she had killed other people. That's not true, is it?" He still said nothing. "You should have seen Grandma. She shouted at him so loudly and waved her cane and told him to get out." My voice rose a little and Papa put his fingers to my lips. He glanced at the doctor, who had walked to the window, his back turned to us.

"Papa, did Grandma ever kill people?" I whispered.

"No, of course not."

I was going to ask him something else, but Grandma groaned and looked as if she were trying to open her eyes. Papa went near her bed but motioned to me to stay away, so I just stood there by the door. It was so confusing and yet it was not. Tino had wanted money, I knew. And Grandma had not wanted to give it to him. Tino had tried to kill Grandma. I looked at my white tub again. And then it all came to me, all of it, so very clearly, and I knew.

"Papa," I called softly but he waved me away.

I had to tell someone.

When I went out into the hall, some of the laborers were still there. I looked around to see if there was anyone to whom I could tell what I knew, but all their faces were so closed.

Then I thought of Karia! Why had I not thought of her earlier, when she was the one? I bunched my white nightgown at the waist so it would not gather dirt at the hem, and ran out to the kitchen. I'd tell her I knew. She had lied to me. They had fooled me, both she and Tino had.

There were some women in the kitchen, all busy rolling cigarettes and weaving sacks. Only Karia was idle. She was sitting by the door, blowing her nose on the hem of her skirt. I stood in front of her, letting go of my nightgown because the air coming in from the slits of the bamboo floor was cold.

"Karia, you're a big liar."

She looked up at me and then away, staring out of the window into nothing but a square of morning blue sky.

"You and Tino are both big liars. You said he was not a moneymaker, and you said moneymakers made money only out of children. But he was going to make money out of Grandma. He was, I know." Her face twitched as if she were going to cry. I went on. "Tino is a moneymaker, but he won't be able to make money out of Grandma now."

"Stop that!" It was Papa's voice and when I turned around I saw he was addressing me. But of course he did not know what I knew. Karia's shoulders had started to shake, but her head was bent so low we could not see her face.

Papa touched her head and said, "He'll get well, Karia, and then we'll see what we can do for him."

But her shoulders shook even more though she tried to stop. "The cane, she beat him with it. The cane...." She went on, bending down lower to blow her nose.

Tino would get thinner and thinner and die, and it was very hard to choose between being made money out of and withering away.

Philippines Free Press
July 23, 1949

AND BEYOND, THE HILLS ARE GREEN

Antonio S. Gabila

After he had left Mr. Coleman's office, he forced a door in his mind shut and mentally locked it. He had a feeling that he was not walking straight or steadily, this thin, grey-haired man who had worked for others 20 years of his life, 16 for Mr. Coleman: for it is never easy to cut yourself adrift from the things you have grown used to. And this was exactly what he had done, this timid-looking, unassuming man of 52: he had exiled himself forever from his husky ledgers and tall columns of figures, from his adding machine and his sharp-pointed pens and pencils.

Back at his old, ink-stained desk, he dumped personal papers, old letters, pictures, magazine clippings, and a paper-covered detective novel into three huge manila envelopes and managed to keep a straight face. But when he saw the dark, ragged notch on the right-hand edge of the desk, it took all his self-control to keep his mouth from quivering.

He had been nervous that first day in the office and when he heaved the heavy adding machine onto his desk, he had sliced off a piece of wood from the edge, exposing the white wood underneath the paint. The wood was now dark brown with age and dirt and because every morning when he came in he would touch it—for luck. Now, he bent over and touched it for the last time—and that was when his courage almost broke.

He leaned back in his chair and the rusty spring squeaked. He looked around at the eight people in that dark, cabinet-lined room, people he had often drunk a cup of coffee with or invited over to his house to help him celebrate a birthday or a christening. They were over their books and columns, their fingers busy pecking at the black-and-white keys of their machines, adding up innumerable figures, balancing accounts, checking invoices and vouchers, entering debits and credits in the books. Until the round clock on the wall struck twelve. Then they would put a light pencil mark on the figures, take out their lunch boxes and sit around in groups of two's or three's, talking while they ate, about their flower gardens, their babies, the movies they had seen, the people they knew—but never about the dreary figures they worked on, as if lunch time was sacred only to food and private small talk.

Mr. Coleman had told him he could get his check from the cashier right away, so he stood up and went down to the second floor, to the cashier's grilled window. The man smiled at him and pushed a slip of paper and a packet of bills towards him: the whole office knew that he had resigned, but few knew why.

He smiled back while he signed the slip, but he bent his head more than he should because there was a lump in his throat and he did not want to be seen swallowing it. He did not speak because he was afraid his voice would prove traitor to the steeled heart, but when the man said, "Good luck, Ped," he had to mumble something in reply; and then he left without having counted his money which he never did before—and he had been a cashier himself once and the habit of checking and rechecking cash received or disbursed was strongly ingrained in him. But not now, not now when something stronger than habit had thrown the old familiar things out of kilter.

Mr. Coleman had not looked surprised when he had broken the news two weeks ago that he had bought a piece of green hills and that he was resigning at the end of the month. And when he went in to say goodbye this morning, Mr. Coleman had been very kind.

"Pete," Mr. Coleman had said. "I'll be dammed sorry to let a good worker like you go. But I know how much you want to, and I admire you for it. By golly, but I do. And if ever you want to come back, there's always a place for you here. Good luck, Pete."

And impulsively, he had answered, "Thank you, sir, but I don't think I'm coming back, although I appreciate your kindness very much." He had intended only to thank Mr. Coleman, but there it was, he had said more than he intended to, because his heart was filled to overflowing with the dream and the courage that went with it.

He went upstairs to his desk, but he did not sit down because he saw by the clock that it was already a quarter to twelve and he wanted to be home by noon. So he went up to his officemates, and they gathered around him, the chief accountant being the first to grab his hand and shake it. They said many words of encouragement, but he could see that they didn't believe he was doing a wise thing, resigning and giving up a good, steady job at his age. However, he managed to let out a laugh or two, shaky laughter, it was true, because their skepticism was fast eating away his inner courage. And he was glad when he stepped outside of the building into the sun and the dust of the city.

Standing at the curb where he usually waited for his bus, he refused to think any more of the things he had left behind, and instead stared at the people around him, men and women going home for lunch, and he wondered how many of them were like him who had no job to go back to at two o'clock... but here he checked himself mentally because this was something he was trying to avoid, thinking backward instead of forward, opening doors behind him instead of locking them.

Before he reached his house, he knew what he would do: he would knock, not open the door himself, and before anyone could say a word, he would ask, "Does Mr. Pedro Valdez live here?" in a low, foreign voice that would set them laughing. But when he found the door open and his three children playing on the cement walk, he became frantic. They ran towards him, shouting, and all he could think of doing was hug them close and pray that everything would turn out right, dear God.

"You're home early, Papa," said Nanette. She was twelve and old enough to understand that when Papa came home early, something had gone wrong, like that time he was sick for over a week—he had come home in the middle of the morning then. "Are you sick, Papa?"

"No, Nanette."

"Then—"

"Shssh. Let's go in. Come, Papa is hungry."

"I'm hungry, too," piped up the youngest. So he swung him up and carried him into the house.

In the open doorway, his wife stood, still slim and still pretty in a tired sort of way after fifteen years of married life.

He summoned up a smile and said bravely and unnecessarily. "Well, I've done it."

"You old fool," she said. But she said it fondly. And he stood there, uncertain, unbelieving, with the little boy in his arms, until she relieved him of his load.

"Table's ready," she said. "I was waiting for you."

"But I thought—" he said.

"We'll talk later," she interrupted. "The children are hungry."

And all through the meal, he looked at his wife, wondering, and each time she saw him looking at her, she smiled as if she were enjoying it all.

For many days and many nights they had argued: he was not very articulate, words were slippery and unreliable on his tongue and they did not quite express what he had wanted to say. He had tried figures, writing them down and using them to persuade, but she had always been impatient with figures and she had stuck, stubbornly, to her one enduring argument: We're too old to start all over again, don't you see? It isn't as if we were 20 or 30. It was an argument he heard over and over again from well-meaning friends; and he had to admit that they were young no longer, that it wasn't practical to change to a new way of life in the middle fifties. It wasn't what one in a hundred would do. But he had not given way.

I have looked into my heart, he had said, and saying it, he had felt as though he were repeating some old, over-used line. And I know what I want. I know that I want to do this more than anything else in the world. Now.

And that was how it was. She had cried, she had worried. At night, they would lie awake, side by side, each chewing away at his own thoughts, knowing they were thinking of the same thing but pulling in different directions.

Two weeks ago he had told her he was filing his resignation effective at the end of the month. He had said it quietly, almost timidly, but she knew there was no dissuading him, there was no way of making him change now. So she did not say anything then.

That morning, two weeks earlier, she had been rummaging among the things in her chest, looking for a set of table linen. She found the treasure chest she had not looked into since her marriage, and, curiosity overwhelmed her. When she opened it, she found the brown rose petals and the clippings tied with a pink ribbon. They were poems she had written when she was in college, and there they were, in small black print with her by-line on each one. There they were, the secret part of her he had not known. She had sat down on the floor and read and re-read them and it was for her like going down the stairway of the years to a time and a world she had almost forgotten with her preoccupation over day-to-day existence.

Many times, during the early years of her married life, she had cried alone because she felt like she was caught in a tight trap: she had railed at the inflexible bonds that had tied her down to kitchen, church and children. But the years had softened the harshness of the unyielding routine....The small prints blurred and she knew she was crying. She wiped her eyes on her dress and peered down to read the lines she had written so many years ago:

> And beyond, the hills are green.
> The old man from the city peered:
> He had not seen such greenness in years.
> Now, he can only look, and cry.

When, after lunch, she showed him the clippings, he stared at them, not understanding. He read her name above the lines of print, and looked at her, surprised, quick words on the tip of his tongue. But she laughed, happily, like a young girl.

"Read," she said, insistent, half-defiant. "Read them."

And so he read them, one after the other; they were rather good, for a college student. When he came to *And beyond, the hills are green,* his mind lingered on the lines, softly his lips savored the sound of the words.

When he raised his eyes, they were misty. He put an arm around her and kissed her greying hair gently, something he had not done in years. Then she pushed him away, shyly.

"I don't know what's gotten into us," she said. "And at our age."

But I know, he told himself, I know what has gotten into us. I knew it the moment we hit that stretch of highway with the wide, rolling hills around us—so cool and green and laden with peace. I had wanted to stop the bus then and there and get down and never come back to the city again.

And he had gone back, the Sunday after, because all through the week the hills and the meadows kept haunting him, the memory of unbelievable greenness would not leave him. He had made mistakes, obvious mistakes in the books he could not find any excuse for to the head accountant. So he had told her he was going back to the office to finish some work that had to be done before Monday. Instead, he had walked up and down those low, sprawling hills and tested the spring of grass underfoot. He had even laid himself down to feel the coolness of the short-bladed grass in the shade of a mango tree....

And then he had talked with the farmer, the incredibly tanned, sunburned farmer who was as old as he but who looked as if he could live another fifty years more. And they had talked and talked: the man had wanted to live in the city all his life; he had gone to school and stopped because there was no more money to buy books; so he had gone back to the farm and married a farm girl and been unhappy all his life. Perhaps, he would care to buy the farm? There were a hundred coconut trees, an avocado orchard, a creek on the north side....

When he went back the third time, the farm was his, the green hills were his to have and to keep, to walk on for as long as he wished, to die on and be buried in. It was worth a lifetime's savings....

Yes, he said in his mind, I know what I want. And he looked at his wife, at the fine wrinkles on her face, the hands that once were fair and smooth and beautiful to look at. He was glad she understood.

"You old fool," she said fondly. "Only you would think of doing this."

It sounded like an accolade to him, banishing lingering fears. He knew, too, that only she would understand a thing like this, only a girl who wrote poetry in her school days would appreciate a secret dream and make it come true. Only his wife.

Philippines Free Press
August 6, 1949

GRANDFATHER

AMANTE E. BIGORNIA

The things I remember most vividly about Grandfather were his terrible temper and his great big voice that perfectly matched his massive figure. When he spoke in anger, it was like thunder and it did not take much to make him angry. No matter what caused his ire, he would boom out, *"Anak ti diablo!"* with his eyes fiercely burning beneath his bushy brows, the veins on his temple throbbing, the blood suffusing his dark face till it became the color of ripe *lomboy*. Grandfather was an awe-inspiring sight to behold when he got mad. Even after he had become a hero, a dead hero, I could see him only in his outbursts of temper, his eyes flashing, his voice like thunderclaps.

The years did not seem to affect Grandfather at all. At the time I speak of he was still strong and husky, his superb figure in a taste of perfect preservation in spite of his host of grandchildren. He was a giant of a man, Grandfather was, and his thick, jet-black hair stood up from his scalp, making him appear taller than any man for miles and miles around.

My earliest recollection of Grandfather is of one of his rampaging outbursts of fury. It was during the burial of one of his sisters. Grandfather misunderstood something his sister's husband said regarding the manner of disposing the conjugal property. With a mighty roar, Grandfather lunged at his brother-in-law, his bolo glinting dangerously in the afternoon sun.

"Son of the devil!" Grandfather bellowed like a wounded bull, crossing in a single bound the circle of men who were drinking from a demijohn of *basi*. It took five strong men to stop Grandfather from hacking *Lelong* Andres to bits, and only after some of them had received ugly wounds.

For all his dreadful temper, though, Grandfather had his good points. One was his extraordinary tender regard for Grandmother. No one could escape noticing his warm affection for the pale frail woman who was his wife. Grandmother had but to lift one bony finger and Grandfather was a changed man. People said it was because she once almost scratched the daylights out of Grandfather when she caught him making a play for the widow, *Nana* Sipa. But of course that was not true; Grandfather did not have any fear of physical pain.

When the war broke out, Grandfather took us to the hills east of the town. Foreseeing that we might have to stay in our "vacuasion" for a long time, he built a long crude shack in a thickly wooded gully which opened into a little valley. As soon as the shack was finished, he gathered the menfolk and they cleared a part of the valley so it could be planted when the rains started.

Not long after, Grandmother died. We buried her on a knoll overlooking the home village. "She must lie where she can always see her village," Grandfather explained. He dispensed with the nine-day novena.

Other families moved into our gully and soon it was as if it were our old village back in the lowlands. *Tata* Kulas the *pensionado, Lacay* Selmo, Igme *Botete, Tata* Andro, *Lelong* Inciong, *Baket* Juana, Cardo *Mais*—they all came and built their huts close to ours, bringing with them their big broods and scanty, dilapidated belongings. In the evenings they would gather in the clearing before our shack, the men talking about the war, the women about their chores, while the children played. The gully had become a village.

The Japanese never reached our place and life went on peacefully in the gully. Children were born and old people died. The chickens and pigs were allowed to roam and the carabaos were pastured on the grassy hillsides.

Sometimes the menfolk would venture back into the village to retrieve whatever belongings they had left in the mad scramble to leave before the Japanese swept through the town, or to gather in the harvest which had been abandoned in the fields. And they would come back to the new village, their back straining under heavy loads, and even before they could unburden themselves they would be talking excitedly about their near-brushes with roving hands of the enemy and of the devastation which the invaders had wrought on the town.

Then the first rains came and the little valley below our gulch was planted with corn and beans. Little patches of earth beside the huts of the industrious wives became vegetable gardens.

It was at this time that we learned of Father's death. He had been bayoneted to death during the march from Bataan to Capas. Mother almost succumbed from grief and for some days our house was full of wailing and sniffling. The neighbors came to sit with our bereaved womenfolk speaking in low, almost conspiratorial voices, not so much to sympathize with us as to find some relief from their own individual sorrows in the presence of our great grief.

Grandfather took the death of his son as calmly as he had taken the passing of Grandmother. "Do not grieve too much," he said stoically. "This is war, and can we ask of God to be spared while others are not?"

It was also about this time that Grandfather decided to visit the old village. "I must see the house and fix it up," he said quietly. "The roof needs mending and I must brace the north side. Otherwise it will collapse when the strong rains come."

That was not his real reason for wanting to go back to the village, I now know. He could have sent two or three of his sons to repair the house. He must have just wanted to see the old house again, to draw strength from the home which he had built himself almost half a century earlier. There, in the nearness of things which held the memories of a lifetime, he had hoped to fill a little the void within him which was ever widening with each loss of someone he loved.

In that trip to the old village, Grandfather took me along. He also took my cousins, Juanito, his namesake and favorite among his grandchildren, and Alejo, who though somewhat doltish, was big for his age and strong as a horse. We made a curious crew.

The old village was deserted when we reached it. In the morning sun, from a distance, the cluster of houses under the trees looked unchanged, placid, pinched but warm-hearted. Not even an old dog greeted our return.

We approached the old house warily. It was as if within those walls which had sheltered us all our lives there now lurked a nameless terror ready to spring at us; the half-closed windows were like malignant eyes furtively watching our every step.

As we were going up the stairs, Grandfather stopped abruptly. His body stiffened and he clutched at the railings for support. "Stop talking," he commanded us softly, straining his ears for sounds that escaped us. Then he turned around and looked up the main street. We followed his eyes.

From a side street stepped out a patrol of seven Japanese soldiers. They were coming towards us at a dogtrot. It was my first sight of the enemy and I bolted upstairs in unreasoning fear, but Grandfather caught me by the waist and held me back. "They have seen us," he said almost in a whisper.

We all stood transfixed there on the stairs staring at the Japanese who advanced toward us with their funny gait, their rifles pointed. They stopped in front of the house and formed a semi-circle. They were panting a little.

A more fierce-looking group I had never seen. They looked at us with evil grins on their faces, their ill-fitting uniforms making them look all the more fearful-looking. One of them, apparently their leader, stepped forward. He was without a rifle but he had a pistol and a long sabre strapped loosely to his hips. He was bull-necked and had long powerful arms. He motioned my Grandfather to come down.

"*Guerrira-ka?*" the Jap growled at Grandfather.

Grandfather glowered at him and shook his head.

"*Firipino* friend, Nippon *frenka*. Shake *hans*, huh?"

Grandfather extended his right hand to grasp the proffered paw of the enemy. Before we knew what had happened, Grandfather was flat on his back behind the Japanese. He lay there for a moment, too stunned with surprise to say anything, and then picked himself up. The Japanese broke into loud guttural guffaws, clawing the air with their hands and rifles.

Grandfather turned purple with rage; his hands trembled with suppressed violence. In a moment, I thought, he would give out a thunderous roar and lunge madly at the enemy. But he made no move to retaliate. The Jap officer, seeing the smoldering hatred in Grandfather's eyes, slapped him on both cheeks, then flung him to the ground again.

When Grandfather picked himself up the second time, there were tears in his eyes and his jaws were corded with tightly locked muscles. The Japanese seemed to be enjoying the spectacle and they grunted to each other, their faces breaking into big-toothed grins.

The officer asked Grandfather a lot of questions in Japanese. Grandfather simply could not understand. The Japanese ranted and slapped and kicked Grandfather in the shins and in the groin and Grandfather took the punishment, standing there before them, bewildered, ashamed and lost. Never once did he cringe, though. He tried his best to keep his face away from us.

Then the officer drew his sabre and I thought it was the end of us. Juanito began to cry and Alejo started to jabber incoherently. I stared at the gleaming blade, too scared to do anything else.

"Danso!" the Jap commanded. Grandfather stared at him, perplexed. The Japanese grinned. "You, big man, *danso*," he said in a less gruff tone and began dancing himself.

Grandfather looked about him in utter bewilderment. The other Japanese began to sing a funny, crazy tune, clapping their hands to keep time. *"Danso!"* they echoed their leader, who swung his sabre flat on Grandfather's back as if to punctuate their command.

Grandfather danced. It was a weird dance. It could have been funny—and it was to the Japs, who kept laughing and soon forgot to sing. Grandfather gyrated awkwardly, painfully, like a child frightened into showing his precocity, and suddenly he looked very, very old to me.

The Japs finally got tired of their fun and after a few gibberish cries at Grandfather they left. They walked down the street in their funny swagger, laughing and grunting at each other.

When they had gone, Grandfather said that we had better go home. He sounded very weary. He didn't even go into the house. All the way back he walked ahead of us, setting a fast pace, his head held high. Not once did he look back to see if we were keeping up with him.

Without being asked by the people who had come around to meet us, Grandfather narrated the whole episode with the Japanese. It would come out, anyway, he knew; we had come back with empty hands.

In a slow, toneless voice, Grandfather told the story of our little adventure in town, simply, directly, without omitting anything or glossing over any detail. When he came to the part where he was made to dance, his voice faltered but he got over that and even let out a mirthless laugh. It was as if the thing had happened to someone else and not to him and he had neither commiseration nor contempt for the poor fellow.

When he was through, it was as if he had said, "Now I have told you. That is the whole story. I will have none of you talking about it again."

Out of fear or respect for the old man, but more likely because they appreciated the trouble he had gone through, no one made mention of the incident. And after he had left and become a hero in his first raid on the Jap garrison in Baugen, no one spoke of it out of deference. Only a few of us knew of the one time that he was reminded to his face of the episode. And we were all children.

It was two weeks or so after the incident in town when this happened. We were playing before the house and as usual were making quite a racket. Suddenly a window shutter was rudely flung open and there was Grandfather's irate face glowering at us.

"*Anak ti diablo!*" Grandfather roared at us. "Don't you have enough respect for your elders to allow them some sleep?"

We all started to go, but Alejo, the doltish cousin who had been with us in town refused to budge. Instead he struck a swaggering pose, his arms akimbo. "*Danso!*" Alejo shouted at the furious old man, mimicking the Japanese officer who had made Grandfather dance, "*Danso!*" the dolt cried again, giggling in his idiotic manner, and fled.

For a moment Grandfather stood there framed by the window glaring at us wrathfully, the veins on his temple threatening to explode. His lips moved jerkily but nothing coherent issued from them.

Grandfather did not leave the hut the whole afternoon. He closeted himself in the *silid* and refused to come out to eat.

No one could say what he was sick of. No one dared go in and ask him.

It was after supper the next evening that Grandfather finally came out. In the harsh light from the kerosene lamp he looked pale and haggard. He had called together all the members of his family who were now seated on the floor and on crude benches lining the walls.

As soon as he emerged from his *silid*, Grandfather began talking, without the usual preliminaries. "I am going to the mountains," he announced. "I am joining the guerrillas. A runner who passed here not long ago said they need men. I am going to join them.

"In my absence, I want Tomas to head the family." *Tata* Tomas was his eldest son. "I want you all," Grandfather continued, sweeping the whole assemblage with his eyes, "to follow him. Now listen carefully to these instructions."

In slow, even tone at first, Grandfather defined the duties of each of his sons and daughters. He must have thought over these duties at some length, so detailed and comprehensive were his instructions. Except for his voice, the house was in deep silence.

Before Grandfather was half-way through, his voice broke and then tears were streaming down his face. It startled all of us. It was the first time I saw Grandfather cry. Our elders started to cry too, softly, silently, careful to stifle any moan. The children stared in shocked disbelief at the massive figure of Grandfather now looking strangely weak and helpless.

Long before cockcrow I woke up and heard Grandfather moving about. All the others had gone to sleep. Once he bent down to light his cigar from the lamp and I had a glimpse of his eyes. They were bloodshot and swollen. He had been crying the whole night.

I was very much puzzled. I saw much profound grief only when someone died. In the eerie half-light the hut suddenly became a house of death.

As the old man moved silently around the dimly-lighted room, stopping now and then to look long at a son or a grandchild lying on the floor, his eyes thrown in impenetrable black shadow, I saw for the first time that he was an old man, a weary old man. For the first time also I felt pity and a great love for him—he was my grandfather. An urge to tell him that welled in my breast. But I was too sleepy to pay much attention to my emotions. I curled myself into a ball and went back to sleep. In the morning Grandfather was gone.

Philippines Free Press
October 8, 1949

PAYING A DEBT

Lazaro M. Espinosa

Aling Simang held Ana at arm's length and examined her from head to foot. Properly groomed, she looks pretty, *Aling* Simang told herself. Aloud, she said: "You are ready. Go and bid your father goodbye."

She then took Ana's clothes and placed them inside a small *tampipi*. She cut the picture of the Virgin Mary and the Infant Jesus from a calendar on the wall and pasted it inside the cover of the *tampipi*. Then she tied the *tampipi* with a small abaca rope, placed it on her head and went to the stairs. After making the sign of the cross she went down.

Ana met her at the foot of the stairs and told her that she could not find her father.

"He was here a while ago," *Aling* Simang said.

"I can't find him," Ana said. "I have already gone around the house."

Aling Simang was irked. She felt angry over her husband's leaving and depriving his daughter of the chance to bid him goodbye. Then she understood.

"The sentimental fool," she whispered to herself. She took Ana's hand in hers. "Let's go," she said.

The sandy cart path in front of their house led to the provincial road, but as this was circuitous, *Aling* Simang decided to take the footpath across the fields. Besides, she did not want to be seen by her acquaintances and friends in the barrio who would likely ask her where they were going and why.

Some twenty minutes later, they came to the road. To the north, *Aling* Simang saw a cart coming towards them and she paused.

"Somebody is going to town," she told Ana. "Let's wait. It might turn out to be someone I know and we can ask a ride."

They went to an acacia tree nearby. *Aling* Simang placed the *tampipi* on the ground and watched the oncoming cart. As the cart drew near, she recognized the occupant.

"It is *Aling* Dira," she said. "She will give us a ride."

Aling Dira, a fat woman past middle age, looked out when the cart had drawn to within a few yards of the waiting two.

"Oh, it's you, Simang," *Aling* Dira said. She told the driver, who was her nephew, to stop the cart.

"Where are you going?" *Aling* Dira asked. "Is that your daughter Ana?"

"Yes," *Aling* Simang answered. "We are going to town. When we saw you, we decided to wait, hoping there is room for us in your cart."

"There is," *Aling* Dira said. "It's only four cavans of palay I have here. I am taking them to the *kiskisan*. Of course, that is still a kilometer away from town, but that isn't too far."

Aling Simang picked up the *tampipi* and placed it inside the cart. She helped Ana get in and then climbed in herself. She sat in front of *Aling* Dira who had become all smiles on seeing them. Noting the *tampipi*, *Aling* Dira remarked:

"It looks as if you are going farther than town."

"No," *Aling* Simang said. "We are going to Doña Luisa's house." She stopped abruptly on realizing what she had said. She had wanted to keep where they were going a secret.

"Doña Luisa?" *Aling* Dira repeated. "But why the *tampipi*?"

Aling Simang took some time to answer. She hated to tell the story behind their going to Doña Luisa's place. However, since she had mentioned Doña Luisa's name, and also because *Aling* Dira was one who could be trusted with confidential matters, she finally decided to tell everything.

"You see," she said, "I am giving Ana to Doña Luisa for a year."

Aling Dira, affected by the news, opened her mouth in surprise.

"You see," *Aling* Simang went on, "we owe her a large sum of money. One hundred pesos. Do you remember when Desto was hospitalized early last year?"

"Yes, I heard of it," *Aling* Dira said.

"He was operated on," *Aling* Simang continued. "His hospitalization and operation cost us two hundred pesos. As we had only one hundred then, we borrowed the rest from Doña Luisa. We promised to pay her after the harvest."

Aling Simang paused for a moment as her mind returned to the time of her story. She began to pick it up piece by piece.

"Now you know what the typhoon did to the crop last year. It destroyed more than half of it. Ours, particularly, suffered very much. When we harvested, we were able to gather only around twelve cavans. That was just enough to pay the interest on the money we borrowed."

Aling Simang paused again, wondering whether she should go on and unburden on *Aling* Dira the rest of her story. If there was one thing she loathed, it was telling other people about her troubles. She felt that they had already more than their share of troubles as it was. But *Aling* Dira seemed eager to be told.

"Considering what had happened, you should have asked her to wait until this next harvest." *Aling* Dira said. "After all, it was not your fault that the typhoon ruined your crop."

"That we did," *Aling* Simang said. "She said she was willing to wait, but the trouble was that her husband, Don Felipe, knew of the money she lent us. And you know Don Felipe."

"That miser!" *Aling* Dira said, quickly getting indignant at the mention of Don Felipe's name. "Does he think he can carry his money to the grave?"

"Don Felipe would not agree to wait another year," *Aling* Simang went on. "He said that it was he who lost heavily in the typhoon; that the individual losses of his tenants were his collective loss; that in spite of the typhoon, the government would not condone his real estate tax. At our begging, however, he agreed to wait until June. Well, Desto decided to go to the city to work as a *peon* for his compadre, Ambo, who is a carpenter. But the whole summer, they were able to work only a total of eight weeks. When Desto returned two weeks ago to prepare our field for planting, he was able to bring home only thirty pesos."

"Then, why didn't you give the amount to Doña Luisa?" *Aling* Dira asked. "At least it would have shown your willingness to pay your debt."

"But another problem came up," *Aling* Simang said. "I went to Doña Luisa with the money. I said that if we would give it to her, we would have nothing left with which to meet the planting expenses. Now, I said, suppose I gave the money to her, would she lend it back to us in order to enable us to plant? She said that Don Felipe would not allow that."

Aling Simang sighed. She swept her hair back, feeling all over again the agony and the headache that she had felt at the time. *Aling* Dira, deeply touched, sighed too.

"*Ay*, such is life sometimes," *Aling* Dira philosophized. Taking advantage of the break in *Aling* Simang's narration, she took a small box which was lying by her side. She opened it and *Aling* Simang saw it contained a few pieces of betel nut meat, a small jar half-filled with lime, several *ikmo* leaves, a package of native cigarettes, and a box of matches.

"Do you chew, Simang?" *Aling* Dira asked as she put a piece of betel nut meat in her mouth. *Aling* Simang shook her head.

"I don't," *Aling* Simang said.

"But certainly you smoke," *Aling* Dira said, extending the package of cigarettes to *Aling* Simang even before the latter could say yes. *Aling* Simang took one and lighted it. *Aling* Dira placed a little lime on an *ikmo* leaf and put this too in her mouth.

"Now, what happened?" *Aling* Dira asked, returning to the story of *Aling* Simang. *Aling* Simang took the cigarette from her lips.

"Well, I told her how helpless I felt," *Aling* Simang said. "I asked her to please ask Don Felipe to wait longer. She said she would do her best but that she was afraid Don Felipe would not agree. Then, five days later, she called for me. She said one of her girl servants had eloped and she was now short of help. That since Don Felipe would not agree to wait any more, why not pay our debt by letting her have Ana for a year. Seeing me silent, she assured me she would not give Ana hard chores. That she would merely have Ana sweep the house, polish the floor and furniture, and keep her four-year-old daughter company.

"Well, Desto and I talked it over," *Aling* Simang continued. "He was very much against it. He said if they were really in need of a servant, why don't they take him."

"But that would be worse," *Aling* Dira said. "For who would then farm your field?"

"I told him so," *Aling* Simang said. "I said, for that matter I could take the place of Ana. However, who would look after him and our small son? Now, yesterday, he finally agreed to let Doña Luisa have Ana. He realized that if we would not be able to plant our field this year, Don Felipe might take it away from us and give it to somebody else."

Her story now over, *Aling* Simang heaved a sigh again, feeling very much relieved. The telling of her story had left her short of breath. To be sure it would not be brought up again, she quickly turned to another subject.

"I have heard your youngest son is now studying in Manila," she said.

The new subject instantly interested *Aling* Dira, being one close to her heart. "Yes," she said and proceeded to tell about her son, how she had observed that he was studious, how she had decided to send him on to college with the help of her elder children, hoping he would succeed and become a professional. She was still telling about him when the cart stopped. Looking out, she saw that they had arrived at the *kiskisan*. *Aling* Simang stood up and thanked her.

"Don't mention it," *Aling* Dira said. "I am sorry we could take you only this far."

Aling Simang said it was all right, that the ride had saved her and Ana a lot of walking. She got off and told Ana to do likewise. She took the *tampipi* and placed it on her head. Then she told Ana to thank *Aling* Dira and bid her goodbye.

Aling Dira gazed at Ana and smiled as the latter sheepishly said thank you and goodbye. Feeling pity for her, *Aling* Dira counselled: "Be a good girl, Ana. Bear in mind that it would hurt your mother deeply should you ever displease Doña Luisa."

Ana bowed her head meekly. *Aling* Simang smiled at *Aling* Dira's show of sympathy. *Aling* Dira's words of admonition suddenly reminded her of what she had been wanting to tell Ana since they left home. While they continued on their way, she addressed Ana.

"Listen carefully to me, Ana," she said.

Ana looked up at her mother, her eyes intent. The stones in the road showed, and they felt sharp under her bare feet.

"You'll feel lonely at first," *Aling* Simang said. "But do not cry. Doña Luisa would not like that. Besides, after three or four days, the loneliness will leave you. I will also try to visit you regularly, every Sunday perhaps."

"Please do, *Inay*," Ana said, feeling soothed by the thought.

"I want you to act like a grown-up from now on," *Aling* Simang went on. "You are one now anyway."

Aling Simang paused, feeling that she had lied. Ana was only twelve years old.

"Anyway, it is time you should," she said. "Poor children have to. Rise up early and wash your face. As soon as Doña Luisa is up, go to her and ask her for your assignment. Maybe she would like you to sweep the floor, polish the furniture, and keep her small daughter company. Do your work well. Do not loaf and chat with the other servants. When you have finished your work, go to a corner and keep quiet. If you are keeping her small daughter company, be careful not to make her cry."

Ana listened with bowed head as her mother spoke. Now and then she stepped aside to avoid the sharper stones. Her young mind tried to understand what her mother was saying as best it could. She saw herself sweeping the floor, polishing the funiture and playing with Doña Luisa's daughter.

"Do not go around the rooms. Do not pry into the desks and drawers and shelves. Should you ever do something which would displease Doña Luisa and she would reprove you, do not answer back. Bow your head. The thing to do is avoid displeasing her. Remember that you are not at home where your father and I can forgive you your mistakes. You will be living in a different home where the people are no relations of yours."

Aling Simang raised her face to see how near to their destination they were. Doña Luisa's house was only about a hundred yards away now.

"And one more thing," she said, "you should not eat with them. Help wait on them. After they are through, help put away the dishes. Then you can eat with the other servants in the kitchen."

For the first time, Ana felt disturbed. She went over her mother's words and her young immature mind told her that it would mean she would have to wait around an hour before she could eat. Why, she would be very hungry by then!

"But why can't I eat with them, *Inay?*" she asked. "Why can't I eat with them the same way I eat with you?"

Aling Simang did not know whether to get angry or not with her daughter for what she considered an impertinence. Looking at Ana, she saw her brows wrinkled up in a confused frown. She felt her heart go soft.

"Servants are not supposed to eat with their masters," she simply said. "Besides, you can wait an hour, can't you?"

Ana nodded.

"Then wait."

Arriving at the gate of the adobe wall that surrounded Doña Luisa's house, *Aling* Simang asked Ana to pause. She looked her over and wiped the perspiration off her forehead.

"Will you remember all the things I have told you?" she asked.

Ana swallowed and nodded. Her throat felt dry and suddenly she wanted to cry. Suddenly she felt nervous and scared.

Aling Simang stared silently at her daughter. She saw how her daughter felt and she opened her mouth to console her, to tell her not to feel nervous or she would get angry with her. But no words came out of her lips. Pushing the gate open, she held Ana's arm and they walked in.

Philippines Free Press
October 29, 1949

TEMPEST

A. OLIVER FLORES

He sat opposite her, eyeing her sulkily as though there was something in her that he could not understand. In the coolness of the mid-afternoon made even brighter by the flowers in the garden just freshened by a young rain, the pair sat at the porch of their luxurious house: she looking very young and pretty in a well-fitting printed house dress, and he a contrastingly poor sight in a blue lounge robe, his face tightly drawn and his thinning hair badly tousled, indicative of an exhausting struggle against some treacherous affliction. His enormous weight sank deeper into the thick cushions of his chair as he crossed and uncrossed his fat legs in a deliberate effort to distract her attention from the magazine that she was reading. She did not notice his act, however.

While he fumed secretly at her seemingly unsolicitous attitude, back of his mind he was thinking of his doctor. The years that the doctor had attended to him, he (the physician) had time and again assured him that "everything's going to be all right." Lie! that's what that fool of a doctor had done all the time, just lie! Damn him! Next time he comes to see him, he will tell him to go to hell.

He gripped the arms of his chair, his eyes still fixed on her. He wouldn't have minded it very much if she didn't look so very young and desirable; if those young scoundrels in town didn't turn to ogle at her whenever the two of them walked the streets on their way to church on Sunday. Damn them too! He knew what was in their minds. He knew that they were thinking that he was the most affluent *hacendero* in all San Diego while she was only a humble girl from a humble family that had once been harassed by a few mortgages. What if he happened to have the mortgage papers in his hands? What if he had often visited the family? Wasn't he an old friend of theirs? Besides, he was an unmarried man then, and like most unmarried men he was in need of a woman to keep him company and share with him the pleasures of his good fortune. Now, was anything the matter with that?

Yet San Diego talked, as they had never talked before, when their engagement was announced. They called him a very lucky man, and his bride a very dutiful daughter. When friends (those he had invited to the wedding, that is) congratulated him on his decision to settle down at last, he had remarked, on the jovial spirit of the occasion: "*Amigos,* life begins at fifty." Fifty plus four to be exact. A difference of about thirty four, the all-knowing town gossips had whispered.

That didn't bother him at first. There was something he could do about the difference. A strict diet would check the widening beltline, a regular bottle of imported dye would eliminate the white tell-tale streaks and, above all, the marital exuberance that had welled up in him would keep him feeling forever young. He was full of hope and out of that fullness he formed many plans, big plans that would melt any woman's heart. He was going to prove that it was not merely luck or circumstance that had won him a lovely mate, that it was mutual love, too. With all the good things he had to offer, he could not fail.

After five years there was the price of over-confidence to pay. No change had come to the wife; she was as quiet and indifferent as ever. The only times she showed some sign of life was when he took her to social gatherings where she met former friends, the young ones especially, with whom she chatted gaily as though she was still one of them. But back inside the house, alone with him, she would be the silent girl again; seldom smiling, seldom, if at all, evincing an interest in the many fine things around her.

With the frustration came the frightening attacks. The old malady had come back, and its latest stroke had so shaken him that he had thought his end had come. For seven days he had been limp with pain and fear and anxiety. He had lain in bed wheezing and tossing, asking the doctor over and over to do something even while the medical man was practically exhausting his knowledge of his profession on him. Somehow, the doctor, who was really a capable one in spite of what he was thinking of him now, helped him pull through. Now he was

strong enough to move about the house once more. But if the
pain had been eased, the fear and anxiety hadn't entirely left
him. Each time he sat down for a rest, that thing inside him
quickened abnormally in its beat, stirred this time by the bitterness that had sprung from his week of agony.

The serenity of her pose mocked him. There he was, feeling wretched all over, and she had to sit in front of him reading, looking very comfortable in her own peace that she didn't
even care to look up at him and say a word of concern. The
silence was becoming unbearable, and his grip on his chair
tightened still.

That must be a very interesting story you're reading, Divina, he managed to say at last.

She lowered the magazine a bit and looked at him.

Yes, it's a beautiful love story, she nodded with a fleeting smile.

Oh, you must be very fond of love stories, he pursued with
effort.

Every woman likes beautiful love stories, she said.

He snickered inwardly at her remark. He pursed his lips,
not wanting to continue with the subject he had (regrettably
now) brought up.

Mind if I go on reading? he heard her ask.

Of course not, dear. Go ahead, he murmured. But inside
him he was saying: Of course I do mind. Why don't you throw
that damn magazine away? You read of love and gush of its
beauty, but why can't you have a heart for it?

Why couldn't she come to his side and stroke his hair and
ask him if there was anything she could do for him? Why
couldn't she just talk about the two of them, about that cruise
to the South which he had suggested to her before his attack,
or about what she would want for their approaching wedding
anniversary? Why couldn't she supervise the decorating of the
house instead of letting the maids do the job alone? Why couldn't
she, with feminine enthusiasm, pick out the color scheme for
the curtains and draperies or attend to the arrangement of the
handsome mahogany set which he had recently ordered from
the best local furniture shop? Why couldn't she ask about the
price of that rare ornate flower vase in their bedroom so that

he could tell her proudly that he had spent a small fortune for the article in an exclusive curio store in Manila?

Perhaps if he had a son things wouldn't look so barren. But even Nature seemed to have a hand in his misery. Five years now and there wasn't any sign of her begetting him an offspring.

He felt very tired. And in his tiredness one alarming thought stood out of the swirling rest. What if the next stroke would be the finish? If in the last attack he had had a narrow escape, the next one could be worse. The thought infuriated him, but he did not try to discard it; instead, he allowed it to dwell in his mind with savage, fascinating relish.

He wondered what she would do after he was gone. He wondered how long she'd grieve—if she'd grieve at all. Probably she wouldn't care very much. Perhaps she'd even be glad.

Again he thought of those ill-mannered young men in town. They'd certainly be pleased to see her free. They'd sympathize with her for a while, and when the act was over, she'd be laughing with them again—happy in her freedom.

At last she was through with the story and she put down the magazine with a sigh of satisfaction. Then remembering something, she stood up and asked that he excuse her, saying that she had a relative to visit that day. He nodded with an inaudible grunt, and she stepped into the sala still blissfully unaware of the pair of hot eyes that stuck on her back. When she disappeared into one of the rooms, he slumped against the back of his chair and breathed heavily. He stayed there alone for a long time.

That night, after the usual tasteless supper, he went directly to their bedroom to rest his weary body. As for her, she elected to stay in the brightly-lit sala to continue with the magazine she had been reading that afternoon. The whole day few words had passed between them. To him, silence had become an enemy. For in the silence that hugged the spaciousness of his house, the thoughts came easily, taunting him of his condition, feeding on his feelings of self-pity. Now, while he waited for her to come to their room (cursing the infernal magazine in her hands), he felt the silence bearing down on him again. He sat up abruptly and propped his back with the pillows so that he could breathe with less difficulty.

It must have been an hour before she entered their sleeping chamber. She went inside a built-in closet, and after several minutes, came out in flimsy blue negligee. Then she sat in front of her dresser and proceeded to brush her hair. He watched her with that same intent look at the porch. He took in the shapeliness of her back, the silkiness of her hair, the smoothness of her arms, the gentle contour of the face in the mirror, the pinky whiteness of her ankles — everything that made up the fineness of this woman who was his wife. Mentally he was again saying that she was his, all his, but the telling sounded hollow.

With great effort he got out of the bed and wobbled slowly towards her. He placed his big hands on her shoulders, feeling their soft roundness. She had stopped brushing her hair, and in the mirror she saw him bend forward and place his lips on her head. He kissed her hair again and again, then let his quivering mouth run down her cheek, her neck, and finally he sat down beside her on the padded stool and took her in his arms and buried his face in the warmth of her breast. She did not say a word. Her arms hung unmoving at her sides, the right hand still holding the brush.

After a while, he raised his head when he could not wait for her to break her silence. He cupped her face in his big hands and looked deeply in her eyes like a hypnotist trying to work a patient into a trance.

Divina, about that cruise I once told you about, he whispered. What do you say? I can hire a boat just for the two of us.

I'm afraid I can't stand the sea, she said. I might get dizzy.

You'll be all right, dear. The weather is fine these days, he replied.

Let's invite friends then, she suggested. It would be livelier.

He drew himself up quickly, and his hands slipped from her cheeks and came to rest at the base of her neck.

But Divina, he said hoarsely, I want us to be alone.

Don't you think, she said, it would be drab with just the two of us?

He stared unbelievably at her while his fingers crawled caressingly around her lovely neck, which was soft and warm and small. When the tips met, he suddenly put on the pressure.

Realization was swift and panic swept over her when she saw the bloated veins in his temples and the strange glint in his dilated eyes. She tried to scream to attract the attention of the maids in the kitchen, but the vise-like grip thoroughly checked the attempt. She tried to beat him off with the brush but her head was spinning, her strength ebbing fast, and the horrible face before her was spreading like a mass of wax melting from intense heat.

Just as consciousness was about to leave her, the encircling fingers suddenly loosened with a jerk that sent her tumbling to the floor. He staggered away from the stool, clutching his chest with both hands. He gasped once, twice, staggered again, and crumpled in a heap beside her.

Painfully she rose on her knees and stared at the still body. As she came out of her giddiness, she noticed that her left hand was pinned under his left hand. Quickly she extricated her hand and stood up. His hand was bluish and cold.

The next moment she was flying from the room, crying out loudly in the night for help.

This Week
November 6, 1949